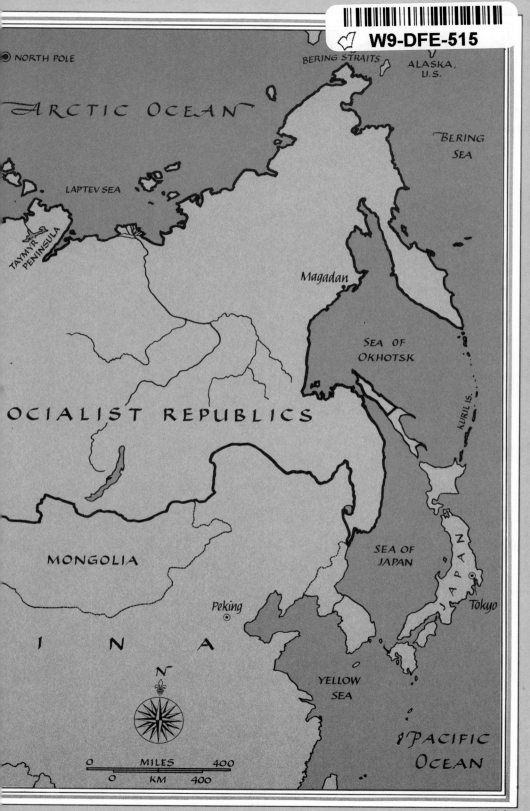

W9-DFE-515

NORTH POLE

BERING STRAITS

ALASKA, U.S.

ARCTIC OCEAN

BERING SEA

LAPTEV SEA

TAYMYR PENINSULA

Magadan

SEA OF OKHOTSK

KURIL IS.

OCIALIST REPUBLICS

MONGOLIA

SEA OF JAPAN

JAPAN

Peking

Tokyo

N A

YELLOW SEA

N

PACIFIC OCEAN

| 0 | MILES | 400 |
| 0 | KM | 400 |

palacios

THE MARCH

By W. S. Kuniczak

THE MARCH

MY NAME IS MILLION

THE SEMPINSKI AFFAIR

THE THOUSAND HOUR DAY

W. S. Kuniczak
THE MARCH

MIDDLEBURY COLLEGE LIBRARY

1979
Doubleday & Company, Inc., Garden City, New York

8/1979
gen'l

PS
3561
U5
M3

Library of Congress Cataloging in Publication Data

Kuniczak, W S 1930–
The march.

1. World War, 1941–1945—Fiction.   I. Title.
PZ4.K9648Mar   [PS3561.U5]   813'.5'4
ISBN: 0-385-00204-1
Library of Congress Catalog Card Number 78–22598

Copyright © 1979 by W. S. Kuniczak
All Rights Reserved
Printed in the United States of America
First Edition

For my Mother

THE MARCH

OCTOBER

The Road

THE DAY WAS PERHAPS THREE QUARTERS OF A MORNING OLD, it would soon be noon, and as he walked within the dust cloud, occasionally tripping over carcasses, broken wagon wheels, spilled bedding, brass-bound trunks, urns, canary cages, and more warlike matter, his eyes were shut against the sun's white glare and against the day.

Now and then they opened.

Then he saw the plain, flat and cruel as a butcher's table, the road cast in the dust like a warrior's spear, dead horses, carts, and artillery pieces spilled like discarded playthings in the fields and ditches, a scarecrow procession of dazed men. Off to the side was flat country, stubbled fields scorched as hard as concrete, the white splash of a cottage wall, the derisive finger of a steeple thrust above black trees, and then a mound of sabers glittering at the crossroads where some other men had been disarmed on another day. He felt more than saw the wayward swaying pinpoint lights of bayonets askew every which way in the huge glare that turned hot metal into lesser suns. These entered all his pores and pierced his eyelids with a scarlet glow.

I must have sunstroke, Abel told himself, and set about examining the quality of his pain, that settled upon the bridge of his nose like a carrion bird, stinking and replete, positioning itself with talons and huge flapping wings.

Certainly, the fields were strangely tilted and the forest hung askew at the foot of the sky, and the dust cloud behind him had acquired an odd solidity so that it lay like a soft yellow casing on the road, glittering with the fine particles of protruding metal. In open fields, tripping on burned corn stubble and baked clay, he had felt the white sun as if it were a hand pressing him into concrete. He couldn't understand why the sun was white. He had become accustomed to a scarlet sun, the bloodred glow that penetrated the curtains of dust and his inflamed eyelids.

He thought that he should remember something of these days in which life, as known to him and his kind, had come to an end but he remembered practically nothing. He thought he really ought to make an effort to remember. Only two days seemed to have any kind of meaning that made them different from all the other days, and one such day (which seemed to have been only yesterday) was a day on which he had found an old newspaper crumbling in a ditch, a stained and soiled copy of the *Continental Daily Mail*, possibly abandoned by a vanishing ambassador or Foreign Ministry official, and such was the incongruity of this find that he had sat down in a ditch and bowed over the torn and crumpled sheets as though they were a rare and precious relic. He had passed blind man's fingers over the tattered newsprint as if eyes alone wouldn't be enough. The ancient headline made its own triumphant announcement about *Peace in Our Time*, and another (smaller) whispered about Munich. It didn't matter what he was reading anyway; it could have been the Koran for all that he cared. What counted was the astonishing idea that a man could sit still by that roadside, under those murderous and indifferent skies, and read a newspaper. He had sat in the dry ditch with his English paper, totally absorbed, feeling an odd elation as though he were drunk. The newspaper, and whatever trappings of normality it could have represented, had acquired an extraordinary value. In war, he had learned, especially in disaster, men formed inexplicable, passionate attachments to the humblest objects; they would collect balls of thread, treasured lumps of wax, rubber bands, tinfoil, pencil stubs, picture postcards of places they had never seen or cared about; any possession, no matter how trivial, was a confirmation of their worth. And suddenly it had seemed essential to find out the date so that this wholly remarkable occasion could be properly remembered. He had gone back to the road to stop strangers and to insist that they immediately tell him what day it was. Immediately. Was it still September? No one seemed to know. No one seemed to find anything unusual about him, a ragged apparition with sunken red-rimmed eyes and the smile of fever. No one seemed offended, and everyone had tried to help him as best as they could. Abel stared into the flat attentive eyes of drugged men, buttonholing corporals and colonels, polite but insistent. In the meantime, the newspaper which he waved before them had disintegrated like an antique parchment. They listened to him with the grave courtesy of children, occasionally nodding as if everything he said bore a profound significance, but when he reached out to touch them they recoiled in horror, sought instant shelter in the mute, swaying crowd. Finally a wounded corporal of cavalry who still had his horse and saber despite the novel truths of a modern war, told him that it was the fourteenth of October, and a horseless captain of field artillery added, apologetically, that it was also the eighth day since the capitulation of the last remaining major segment of the Polish Army, the shattered army of which they, these wavering shadows on the pitiless hot road, had once been a part. Thank you, Abel cried, overjoyed; thank you very much. Not at all, said the corporal, really, it is nothing. Oh, but on the contrary, Abel said, it is a great service. No, sir, not at all, sir, the corporal said.

Thus yesterday had been identified.

The only other day that had acquired an identity had come a month earlier, when the war had been comparatively new, the army virginal and hopeful, when there had been regiments on the roads and not the shocked and incoherent formless mobs, and when Abel could still claim to have been some sort of a soldier. He had followed the scouts of his division into Sadowa Wisznia, a small town within siege-gun range of Lwów but empty of Germans, looking for Tarski, whose acting adjutant he was supposed to be. He couldn't find this old family friend anywhere and finally tracked him down at the general's staff conference. The regiments had left the road and moved under the canopy of the forests north of the town, to hide at least for one brief and merciful moment from the wheeling bombers, and the staff had sat down to work in a small cream-and-cinnamon-colored manor house, a timeless little structure that reminded Abel of his grandfather's home. This manor, like the other, squatted like a mushroom against the textured background of the trees, and Abel (watching, listening, feeling totally useless against a trembling wall) heard once again all the phrases with which he had become so terribly and contemptuously familiar even after only a few weeks of his war: *the situation hopeless, German circle tightening* . . . and the inevitable orders for attack. Outside, there was a hurricane of bombs; inside, the calm and patient murmuring of professional voices: *Item*: no ammunition, food, water, or medical supplies (and communications reduced to company runners). *Item*: effective combat strength down to one fifth of the Table of Organization and Order of Battle. *Item*: German activity confirms that the Polish strength, location, and possible attack plan are no secret to them.

(So, Abel had whispered with deadly lack of tact to Tarski, so what else is new?)

A leathery brigadier studded with wound stars like a firmament conducted the briefing and Abel, watching, wondered if twenty years earlier in another manor house or wayside peasant hut, in other woods and different circumstances, this same lean soldier, with remote yellow

eyes and the bearing of a Jesuit certain of paradise, had not been issuing orders to his father. It had seemed a distinct possibility. The
briefing revealed what everyone had been so painfully taught in their
weeks of marches and battles: the road to Lwów was closed by the Germans, whose wheels and tracks could traverse the miles faster than the
worn boots of the Polish soldiers. The Germans were once more behind
them and before them, entrenched in a forbidding complex of morass
and quicksand in the Janów Woods. But that had not been all, there
had been more, astonishing news that Russian armies had come into
the country shortly after dawn and had been pouring in all morning
like an ocean of mud-brown, ankle-long greatcoats and Asiatic faces,
rattling along the country trails in huge tanks and antique armored
cars, jogging on long-haired ponies. There were reports of small, pathetic fights on the undefended border, and summary executions of
officers which nobody could bring himself to believe. What does that
mean, eh? asked a nervous colonel. Another wished to know whether
these new invaders had come as friends or as new enemies. Well now,
look here, said a major with a monocle, they are brother Slavs. What
the hell would they want from us, now of all times? They may be
Bolsheviks and we all know what *that* means, or I *hope* we know, but
dammit, after all, they *are* brother Slavs! And where exactly are they,
sir? I mean on the map.

The general shrugged fastidious shoulders, made a peremptory gesture, an orderly brought tea. Abel had watched and listened and suddenly the window beside him left its masonry and sailed, majestically
intact, toward the conference table and splintered there with a resounding military crash, sheering off penciled regiments and routes of approach, cutting off areas of assembly, slicing infinitesimally the green
and brown topography of the land. Calm hands brushed the debris
aside and the work continued. *Attack at sixteen hundred hours, all regiments in line, we shall go this way and then that, north of the swamp
at Wereszyca, hammer a gap here below Brzuchowice and the woods at
Janów* . . . and so on, but Abel didn't listen. It was as if the sailing
window frame had removed his need for attention. He heard but he
didn't listen. He watched a small brown bird picking his martial way
among the debris on the windowsill, a sparrow treading with the resolute competence of a giant raptor, beak up and open, small eyes glittering, pinfeathers rising.

Little mock eagle, he thought with quick affection, so valiantly strutting.

Night had brought the battle, a bloody and unreal time of erupting
earth and whirling, disappearing trees, grenades and bayonets, field-
pieces firing shrapnel at six hundred paces. Immersed in the night

around him, yet feeling no part of it, he had gone forward across pastureland redolent of clover, climbed green mounds and ran through russet groves, his eyes fixed on the clean-shaven patch of whiteness that was the back of Major Tarski's neck, thinking of definitions. By definition, battle was a clash of armed men in violent mass conflict, a confrontation of armies, but, he thought (at such times as he was aware of thinking), it defied definitions, it seemed to be the ultimate expression of mankind's dissatisfaction with itself, less a historic event than bad fiction written in flashes of muzzle blast, explosions, the thin-drawn *hurrah*, men transformed into grotesque apparitions uniformed in darkness, men falling, leaping into trenches and out of them, impaled on barbed wire, men who were making sounds that no man was supposed to know how to make, the sandy soil turning into quicksand underfoot, boiling smoke, and then the meadows far beyond the trenches, and then the rubble of farms and villages and the toppled orchards where hunched hysterical beings who could have been men staggered among the fences and fell, with squeals and grunts, among the stabbing bayonets and flailing rifle butts. It was, he thought, remembering, as if a sack filled with impenetrable darkness had been maliciously ripped open with those bayonets, engulfing them all. He had gone on with the others splashed with blood, blind and deaf to everything around him and unable to utter a single human sound until (at last!) the night itself grew pale. No one had taken prisoners and no one had bothered to try to surrender. The mounds of corpses had grown waist-high in the village streets and all that he had been able to think about, to see, to consider as the central point of a definition, were the red stacks of the massacred dead and his own stained hands. His boots had finally slid in the sodden soil and he had fallen and, unaccountably, slept. Tarski had later told him that such inexplicable sleep was not at all unusual.

Eventually dawn had come and had brought brief rain. The shower cut with unexpected violence but after it was over it was impossible to believe that any rain had fallen. Only the steaming pools in the concave faces of the dead told that the month-long glare of the sun had been momentarily displaced, and he had felt as if his mind had fallen off a hillside, and stared about, comprehending nothing, and then how fitting (he had thought) that he should have got his wound in the first peasant cottage into which he stumbled after it was all over. How ironically simple it had been to become a wounded hero of his country, Abel thought. He wondered what had become of that Glory his father talked about, where had it gone and why hadn't it been there, on his first battlefield, when he needed it most. Was he the only man unable to appreciate the beauty of battle, the noble principles of slaughter for a cause? Something was wrong with him, he was sure, otherwise these and other absurd antiquities would have made perfect sense.

These, then, were his sole trustworthy memories of a war and he felt that he had been cheated out of something that generations had sung about, revered, built monuments to and praised. Now as he walked behind his major, content to be alive but not quite sure how he had managed it, he did his best not to think at all. The mass of wagons, animals, and men flowed in the dust cloud as if they themselves were particles of dust, each mote removed from every other by jealous molecules, distinct and locked within itself, kept separate by its own identity and purpose but joined by definition. Wrecked armies, he realized in perplexity, are bewildered people.

The war was over, as Abel understood it, only its runaway mechanisms continued to function. Autumn would soon be over. The icy gray captivity of winter was moving toward the shattered and exhausted land. The long column of defeated men had spread on the highway, on the road to Lwów, less as men than as fragments of an era. He was a part of it. From time to time these shuffling particles split and whirled aside as staff cars and limousines pushed among them, bleating, rich leather bags strapped aloft, the white faces of the passengers hostile in the windows and, all too often, a famous face among them.

(Cowards, cowards, Tarski muttered then, his eyes fixed rigidly ahead, his ears closed to the command of klaxons. What happened to the valiant speeches made before the war?)

But, Major, Abel wished to say, my Honarary Uncle, my Father's Dearest Friend and Mother's Former Lover, you're being absurd. In peacetime men buy and sell each other every day, so why not in war? Since when has war contained a higher moral sense than peace, why should it suddenly ennoble its participants? Everyone has a right to run for his life along with maiden aunts, cocker spaniels, and archives for a memoir.

Above the whirling dust cloud silvered airplanes rolled in the sky like porpoises at play.

He slanted his eyes upward, waiting for the moment when the aircraft would begin to form their familiar attack echelon, wondering why it took the flying machine gunners such a long time to start work that morning, thinking, since he was what he was and could not think in any other way, not of machine gunners and pilots but of the Angel of Death. The sun had been burning away the morning mist for hours.

The planes were of a kind he had not seen before: short, stubby, deafening at two thousand meters. He thought that with all the diving into ditches that he had done daily for thirty-seven days (such cruel days of falling facedown in the dust, constantly burrowing into shallow furrows of parched earth, seeking shelter; of frantic leaps into any crevice, any fold of land, that offered an illusion of protection from the ubiquitous bombs) he would be able to reach the roadside ditch in two bounds when the moment came. Beside him, Tarski muttered one of the mild obscenities that had become so frequent, his blue eyes wintry gray with loss as though reflecting ruins, and motioned toward the open fields and the black cliff face of the forest wall. Abel felt his knees jerk with the accustomed reflex, the first preparatory motion for jumping into ditches. But the throaty roars overhead didn't change in pitch, there was no whining announcement of the dive, so he stopped, confused.

—Well, he said through a dizzy headache. Are they coming down? Or not?

Then he was staring into Tarski's dust-encrusted eyes, the pupils shrunken to the size of coal chips.

—What was that, my boy?

—The planes, Abel said. Are they coming down?

—Oh, said the major sadly. (Sadly? Tragically, Abel thought; surely he was speaking less for himself than for a generation for whom a world had ended.) No. These are not Germans.

—Not Germans? Then why get off the road?

—But even if they were, said the major. Even so, ah, do you think anyone would think us a military objective?

—No, thank God, Abel said.

—Did you say *Thank God*?

—Did I? I don't know.

He heard a short mocking laugh, peered through dust, saw a pale young man in a leather coat sitting on a milestone, noted the dark liquid eyes, long wry mouth, white teeth. A young Jew, he thought, feeling his muscles twitch. Why is he derisive? Where did he steal a tanker's leather shortcoat? Why such savage pleasure?

—Not German?

The major's face had become as yellow as clay. His fists had clenched tightly. Then he said: I think we should get off this road as soon as we can.

It was impossible to believe that anyone but Germans could play in the sky. These had been the war's only certainties: that the Germans' brightly silvered planes rose in their hungry spirals along with the sun, as though without them the sun would remain crouched in the eastern marshes, while deep below their crystal airs Abel and his kind marched in the ringworm of caked dust for forty-five days and nights. He had become accustomed to moving in the thick protective carapace of dust and didn't want to leave it. His survival seemed to depend on particles of dust. Besides, he argued through the multicolored flashes in his head, weren't Tarski and he officers, and weren't their men somewhere on the road? Why was it all right to leave the road today when it had never been all right before? What had changed in their lives to bring that about?

He asked the question, heard the mocking laughter, saw the black eyes in the pale face as though in a mirror that reflected his own private history, thought of the contradictions of his own mixed blood and was convulsed by hatred all the more intense for being full of pleas for love and understanding. Tarski leaped as though touched by fire. He seized the pale young laughing Jew in the leather coat and dragged him off the milestone.

—You laugh, you bastard? Something pleases you?

—No, Abel cried, or thought he had cried, or perhaps merely thought that he was crying as Tarski struck the young man, knocked him down.

The major lives in a barren world of duty, he tried to explain, a haunted nervous place buttressed against conspiracies, guarded by righteousness, love of country, honor, and always under siege. Such men could die for their country with a smile, and kill for it too.

—You damned deserter, Tarski cried. Filthy swine. What's your regiment?

(He's not a soldier, Abel tried to say.)

—Damned . . . stinking . . . treacherous . . . disloyal . . . Tarski cried pale as death. He struck the young man again and stooped and picked up the scabbard of a discarded saber. —What's your name?

—Traurig, the young man muttered through a broken mouth, and covered his head.

—Laugh at us, would you?

—Major! Abel cried.

Tarski began to beat the young man with the dented scabbard in a kind of controlled epilepsy of fury that horrified Abel. Uncle, for God's sake, Uncle, he whispered, and thought that he was shouting, his hands were frozen to his chest, his legs had grown immobilizing roots deep into the soil. The young Jew shouted and the major cursed while tears ran down his face.

—Laugh at us, would you? Mock us, would you? Jeer at us, would you? Moscow looks good to you, you scum?

—Major! Abel cried.

He felt like weeping. He felt the cruel blows upon his own head and also felt the ribbed grip of the saber in his own clenched fists. Of course, of course, the major was right, or thought that he was right, Abel thought, appalled; he had his entire universe to maintain.

—Laugh at us, would you?

Now Abel moved and caught the major's shoulder, and Tarski threw down the scabbard and kicked it as far from himself as he could, and the pale young man in the leather coat (his face split and bloody and suddenly ballooning) fell backward into the ditch.

—For God's sake, Abel whispered.

—That damned disloyal swine, Tarski said, and made a helpless gesture. Thinks that his time is coming now . . . laughs . . . filthy traitor . . .

—Beating him won't help, Abel said.

—They've lived among us for six hundred years and *still* they do that? Will they never learn loyalty to their country? What is a man to do?

—You don't know why he laughed, Abel said, and felt his stomach heave and covered his mouth. He may have been laughing . . . oh, because . . . well, anything . . .

—Poland bleeds to death and this man is laughing?

Then he began to wring his hands as though he wished to crush them and Abel felt the pain in his own burned hands. —God, Tarski said. Oh God. What is happening to us?

He wouldn't look at Abel. He kept his eyes away from the young man who wept in the ditch. The young man sobbed and cursed in Yiddish (which Abel didn't understand) and in Hebrew (which Abel no longer remembered) and the major rubbed his eyes with both fists as though he wished to erase, as painfully as he could, the imprint of a crime. His face was drained of blood, with deep black circles stamped under the eyes, looking as it had looked while his battalion died at Koronowo, as it had been when he was told that Germans had marched into Warsaw and (later) that the Russians had taken the city in which he had been born. He would not know how to apologize unless this could be done horizontally; that is to say, unless he was saying *I apologize* to someone who was profuse in his own apologies to him. Bound by fierce inner disciplines, he expected similar restraints from everybody else. By no means a brutal, evil man (it would have been inconceivable for him to act dishonorably), he was bewildered by the pain that he could inflict and would be ready to offer up his life in reparation but he would expect to be understood as a reasonable, compassionate man who was a friend to horses and small children, and whose lapse from the civilized proprieties was surely justified by sacrilege.

Meanwhile, the young Jew was trying to climb out of the ditch, and suddenly the major's face had been suffused with blood and he was marching up the road with his eyes fixed rigidly ahead. Part of both these mutually inaccessible worlds, Abel understood each of their various agonies, blamed neither victim, pitied both. He pitied no one more than himself in that revealing moment and loathed himself for it, and caught up with the major at an accidental barricade fashioned of an overturned army ambulance, a taxi with flat tires, and a huge bomb crater. Exhausted, Tarski had got into the cab and massaged his knees.

—Ooof, he said. Phew. Ah.

Then he said: How much further is it to your granddad's house?

—We ought to be there by tomorrow morning, Abel said, and patted the roof of the cab. No chance to get this thing moving, I suppose?

The major fiddled with the gear lever. —Dead as coffin nails, he said, his large eyes gray and opaque with the distances he had crossed in the last thousand hours. Then he said: Six weeks, just six weeks, who could have believed it? No more than a summer holiday . . .

Then he sighed, shrugged his shoulders as though to shift the weight of an invisible knapsack, and nodded toward the stubbled fields and the black forest wall on the near horizon.

—Well, he said. Let's get off this damn road.

—Why? Abel said.

—Use your head, will you? Tarski said, irritated and picking at the dust caked at the corners of his mouth.

—I seem to be a little slow this morning, Abel said.

—It's been at least twenty minutes since those pilots found us and airplanes have radios. And that little swine in the leather coat wasn't sitting on a milestone to watch a parade . . . And, anyway, why do you people always argue so much?

—What people? Abel said.

Tarski's arm flew upward, jerked toward the ditch. He opened his mouth, closed it, and finally said: Young people.

He turned his head away.

—Young people? Abel said.

—Oh dammit, Abel, do what you are told!

—Yes, sir, Abel said.

Above them, the roar of motors deepened, and suddenly one of the planes dipped delicately as if performing a complicated aerial curtsy and a long stream of miniature postage stamps fanned out behind it, catching the pink of the sun.

—Look, Abel said. He's dropping leaflets.

—I've seen them before.

—Leaflets instead of bullets, now I know that the war is over.

—It's far from over, Tarski said at once.

—Who's left to fight it?

—England, France. They have everything.

—A lot of help they've been in the last few weeks.

—We were an outpost in a common battle, Tarski said. We bought them precious time. But never mind that now, we've no more time to waste. How long d'you think it'll take the Bolsheviks to set up their roadblocks? They'll be all over us in another quarter of an hour.

—A fortnight ago you would have talked about breaking through, Abel said softly, not wishing to hurt this normally lenient man whom he had often loved and whom, unaccountably, he could sometimes hate.

—Would I? Would I have? Well, perhaps I would. But have you seen anyone we know on the road this morning? Have you seen one of our men in at least twelve hours? You can look but you won't find one of them about, they've made themselves scarce. They don't want to wind up behind barbed wire any more than I do. They've scattered in the woods. It's all very well to say that they might be somewhere on the road but I know better. I trained them myself. And my own training tells me to get off this road.

The major got out of the useless taxicab and staggered a little and jumped across the ditch. Abel followed. He watched yellow tendrils of dust trailing off the major's gaunt and bowed shoulders, thought of smoke and fire and of the major as a burned-out meteor torn from the mass of an exploding planet, flung into the black infinity of space.

. . . Young people, he had said. He had not meant young people.

And suddenly Abel's beautiful handmade riding boots were covered with vomit.

And now a quick breeze came off the forest as the planes dipped and rolled in the brilliant sky, showing their scarlet stars. All sounds and smells were suddenly fresh and quite impossibly clear; all color was sharply etched in the deep monochrome of morning. The heady redolence of crushed hay, bursting pine, and enameled leaves made him a little drunk.

Soldiers who had long ceased to look anything like soldiers, and civilians whose eyes seemed glazed like the eyes of primates, lay among the trees, caught in the stupor of total exhaustion. Lost human cattle driven to the forest, mired in hopelessness and the uncertainties of a threatening future. If anyone awoke them they stared drunkenly about and could not get up. Gray shadows filled the no-man's-land between field and forest with undefined menace. Light deepened among trees, suddenly empurpled, and the secretive distances stepped out of the shadows.

He was alone in that intimate moment, temporarily separated from his meteoric major, and suddenly aware of the quick upsurge of his ancient love for this man whom he had known throughout his entire childhood. It was Tarski who had given Abel his first set of Sienkiewicz, the books on which every Polish child was supposed to be raised. He had given Abel his first air rifle and had taken him on a partridge hunt when Abel was seven, and then connived with the head gamekeeper to credit one plump bird to the boy's insufficient weapon. Tarski was probably his father's oldest friend, they had been students together in St. Petersburg. He was the only man who could bring Abel's bitter mother out of her self-imposed exile in her rooms. He had meant a degree of normalcy and stability to the growing Abel, his visits had always been a cause for celebration. Yet Abel supposed that in a deeply buried part of himself, hidden from consciousness and conscience, he had always hated Major Tarski for being so successfully and completely Polish, with never a doubt in his delineated mind about who he was, his nationality seemingly ordained rather than imposed by the accident of birth and as legible as the badges of rank he wore on his shoulders. Such effortless identity was an affront to Jews and to that part of himself which Abel could, conceivably, call Jewish. He did not think himself less Polish than Tarski himself, he had been born into a properly Polish and Catholic family, but that Catholicism was comparatively new to Abel's father, for all its awful intensity. Abel's father's father had never converted, nor would he, nor would anyone expect him to do so, and there was always the shadow of his uncle Avrum, who had not changed his name as Abel's father had done and who remained so completely and terrifyingly a Jew. Avrum Mendeltort's name was forbidden in the Abramowski household but the prohibition didn't erase the man. Whenever Abel felt that he hated Tarski, never knowing whom he really hated at such moments, it was because the major's effortless authenticity made Abel's father grotesque, and when he loved him, never entirely sure whom and what he loved, it was because in that assurance of authenticity he could confirm his own. Under the major's close-cropped shock of iron-gray hair, beneath the gnarled skin, hid a likeness to someone in a yellowing photograph that Abel carried about with him wherever he went, his foolish talisman against the loneliness and cruelty of time. There lay the seeds of his own character, he knew, and he waited for them to take root in the fertile soil of his imagination.

He looked for Tarski, then, feeling suddenly abandoned and resentful at being left alone with shock and with sunstroke. The major had staggered to a halt among a scattering of unkempt civilians at the head of a path. Someone was speaking softly to the major, a woman whose delicate fabrics had been torn and smeared beyond recognition but whose gestures had remained vivid. The major had inclined his head politely, his back slightly bowed and his heels together, while his hand traveled swiftly to his tunic pocket and returned with a gleam of silver. Abel knew that the major's cigarette case contained only one hoarded half-smoked Gold Flake cigarette (like Abel's father, Tarski had his tobacco shipped to him from London), and he began to choke with hysterical laughter, and crammed both his burned hands into his mouth. Even here, then, even among the debris of his destroyed life, he would observe the proprieties, and was this splendid or was this absurd, and did it matter that the "Blue Danube Waltz" was no longer playing, and Abel hurried forward groping for his lighter, as befits an adjutant (suppressing his laughter), but the major had found some matches of his own. The woman smiled her warm gratitude as though at any moment a bell might ring to end the intermission and she, and the major, and Abel, and the wrecked armies sprawling in the forests would return to their seats in the boxes of the opera, and held the butt between two twigs with thumb and forefinger and, in two quick puffs, the butt disappeared. She couldn't have done that any better if she had practiced for a week with her eyebrow tweezers, Abel thought, stumbling away from this passing gallantry, stiff-legged like a somnambulist and no longer laughing.

The major bowed, saluted, clicked his heels. The woman smiled and smiled. The smell of ruptured pine drifted among the tree trunks like incense around the columns of a roofless temple.

Then the sun was directly overhead. It was noon. Abel walked a step and a half behind the major down the chaotic corridors of forest paths and clearings, quite unaware now of the dead pine needles crushed under his boots, the whipping undergrowth and branches. Tarski seemed even less aware of time and of place. His eyes were once again remote and colorless with the distance between himself and some wintry moment far back in a calendar of his own, as if his presence on this path, in this forest, within the sound of their city's bells—church bells hung tinnily on the breeze—was accidental and irrelevant.

Abel spoke first and instantly regretted breaking the sheltering silence.

—The people are moving on the roads again.

—What was that? What people?

—The people. You know . . . the civilians.

He looked at the blurred figure marching with such blind resolution and purpose and be began to tremble. His own harsh voice stupefied him in the grumbling stillness of the forest. He desperately wished to apologize for breaking the silence as though it were an object of value that he had dropped and shattered accidentally.

—The people, he said again perversely, and made a vague irritated gesture toward the road which showed clearly among the trees at this point.

His other hand came up in its cocoon of reeking stale bandage, curving like the burned neck of a rapacious bird toward the left breast pocket of his coat and the yellowing photograph that he carried there. The photograph had had a permanent place on his father's desk among the litter of possessions, framed with curlicues in gold. It showed three rows of young men in antique military tunics, all but one with the solemn frozen faces of children kissed by strangers, the pose brought sharply into focus by their high tight collars. Their legs in glossy boots were crossed with precision, left over right. With one hand each of them supported a great crooked saber; the other hand was either slipped Napoleonically into the tunic or bent at the hip. These were the officers of one of Pilsudski's brigades of the Legion. There was a youthful Tarski grinning from ear to ear. A young and eager miniature of Abel's father sat at the extreme right edge of the photograph, staring into the camera with innocent eyes.

It didn't seem believable that this man had ever been young enough to pose with other junior officers in a photograph. Surely not that huge, complex man with his fears and hungers. Had he had hopes? Had he had illusions? The innocent eyes suggested that he had. The photograph was a challenge to credibility, its date a time machine, its flavor antique, its passing gallantry incomprehensible through the yellowing curtain of the years. Abel had often tried to read the expression in his young father's eyes. He remembered, although he had no wish to recall, his father's strangled voice exploding when he was enraged . . . So long ago. Years and continents. But it seemed like only yesterday.

He listened to the sound of bells which came, distilled and biting, through the creaks and mutterings of the nearby road. These were the church bells of his city, his home. He had left it once and the leaving had been permanent; he hadn't expected to see Lwów again. He could sense the nearness of its ancient streets, the dusty smell of classrooms, the dome of light above the Grand Theater, the lilting accents of its special drawl . . . Pain ripped through him with an intensity that robbed him of breath.

—They're going home, he said to himself.
—Home? Who's going home?
The word didn't seem to have any connection with the moment.
—All these people. My God, how the roads have changed.
—Changed? How changed? They are the same as always.
—This time the people are returning, don't you see the difference?
—Oh, that, the major said, and shrugged his narrow shoulders.
A soft, persistent murmur like that of a river came from the yellow

road and the people on it. Tarski's face dissolved in the shadows; all its hard lines, the new as well as those remembered from childhood, flowed into each other and robbed him of substance, so that, for a moment, the face acquired the quality of a twice-exposed negative, reminding Abel of his youthful father. Abel's curved hand came up once more to twist the silver button on his left breast pocket.

He didn't know why he had stolen the photograph and taken it with him to France, England, America . . . all those other places. It was a symbol of a kind but he didn't know what it represented. Perhaps he only wanted to remember what he was leaving behind: the feel of objects in the vast apartment so cluttered with objects, the empty life, his mother's bitter disappointed face, his father's unlimited illusions.

He couldn't properly understand how Tarski could feel so at home in this Polish forest, as he himself had felt once and would have continued to feel if the roads had not become sad rivers of hopeless, terrified humanity and fear-crazed cattle, if the illusions of his father's photograph had acquired a substance. The forest had escaped him despite the assurances of the grotesque saber that his father had clutched with such intensity.

Abel wished that he had not begun to talk about the roads. He feared what the refugees' sudden turnabout might mean. Something had changed in the larger arena around him. There had been a subtle shift of forces . . . a rearrangement which, he knew, would affect him deeply. The people on the road knew something that he ought to know, or perhaps they sensed it. Their intuitions had been purified and sharpened by the weeks on the roads while his had been dulled. He didn't want to talk about this half-glimpsed rearrangement that had taken place. But having started to talk, caught up in the unfolding compulsion of his thoughts, he couldn't stop himself.

—I remember the villages that we passed, he said. You know, those villages where the people came swarming around us asking how far we were going to let the Germans come.

—It seemed easier to die than answer that question, the major said quietly.

—Well, now the people are going home again, Abel said. I can't understand it.

—There's nothing like the power of a man's native soil, Tarski said. The irresistible desire of people forced to leave their homes to come back. It may take a catastrophe to bring that out but it's always there.

—But why have they all decided to go home today? They don't even wait until the shooting's over. The fires are still burning. They ought to wait at least until the rubble is cold.

—We haven't finished fighting yet, you know, the major said gently as if admonishing a misguided child.

—The war is over, Uncle.

—We may have been knocked out of it for the moment but that doesn't mean that the war is finished.

—Well, Abel said. At least you admit that we've been defeated. I want to be done with the whole bloody business.

—We'll find a way to keep it going, the major said. Don't worry about that.

—You really believe that, don't you? Abel said.

—Believe what? said the major.

—That there is such a thing as winning or losing, that it's going to make a difference in the long run.

—Of course it'll make a difference, that goes without saying.

—You said we were beaten, you've admitted that.

—You didn't hear me say that we had been defeated. We can be beaten over and over again but we can't be defeated as long as we refuse to accept defeat. It is a matter of consent, don't you see?

—I've been thinking about this matter of consent.

Then the major stopped, cocked his head. —Did you just hear something?

A sound, massed like dark leaves, had intruded briefly; it passed in the shadows. The woods were never entirely without sound but their speckled darkness had a quality of silence.

—Perhaps we're coming near the Soviet picket lines? Abel asked in turn.

—Could be, but I doubt it. How much farther is it to your manor? I could do with a bit of a rest before we go on.

—Rest?

—Rest and food. Ascent to paradise. A dream, an illusion.

—So many words no longer have a meaning, Abel said.

The low white-timbered structure leaning against the centuries, so typical of the essential Polishness of this land and all the ancient hopes that it had contained, had made its own indelible imprint on his childhood. There he was part of the immemorial continuity of Poland; he found no need to question roots or antecedents. He could lose himself completely in the certainty of permanence that lay in every corner of the manor house.

Seen from the edge of the woods, as they would see it soon, the manor had something of the look of a dismasted ship: a long-beached caravel with all her voyages ended. Abel had always thought of it as a caravel. The sagging beams which served as the ridgepole created an il-

lusion of a slanting deck that rose fore and aft, turning the chimneys
into twin truncated masts on which no one would ever bend a sail
again. Nevertheless, a small boy could send it sailing far in his imagination.

In truth, it was a country manor house no different from a hundred
others in that part of Poland, no older than the others, and distinguished only by its famous stables. It was a remnant of what might
have been a rich estate in another century, a remembrance, a memorial
to an immoderate past. But through attrition of wars, insurrections, lost
provinces, sequestrations, unwise investments, and the eroding processes
of the years, it had become little more than a small landholding.

To break the sudden spell of recalled childhood Abel said, more
loudly than he had intended: Did you know that Stalin was supposed
to have stayed in our manor, the last time the Bolsheviks were here?

The major laughed. —Do you have a bronze plaque up there to commemorate it?

—Hardly, Abel said. And anyway it probably isn't true. You know
how it is with us, we love to make up legends. The Bolsheviks did use it
as some kind of headquarters when they were trying to take Lwów in
1920 but I doubt if Stalin was anywhere near here.

—He could have been. This is the area where he was operating with
Yegorov's army and his pal Budyenny. Not that it did him a hell of a
lot of good.

—Well, anyway, I think it's just another of Grandfather's stories. He
loves to tell stories.

—If it's true, the Bolsheviks might turn your manor into a museum.

—Worse things than that have happened.

—I have a curious feeling about what will happen because of what
happened here in the Bolshevik War. Stalin has done his bloody best to
wipe out every memory of what a fool he made of himself around here.
If it hadn't been for his personal grab for glory near Lwów, the
Bolsheviks might have taken Warsaw. Instead they lost the war. I'm
afraid he'll make us pay for that.

—But that's ancient history. What difference could it make to anybody now?

—Stalin can never forgive a slight or a setback, that's not the Georgian way. Every Russian who could point to Stalin's military bungling
went to the wall a long time ago. Yegorov was the first to vanish in the
purges. I have a feeling that Lwów will be the target of special atten-
tions.

—We could stay at the manor, Abel said.

—We're just like all the people on the road, Tarski said. We have to go home. Well, how much farther is it? You never answered my question.

—About two more kilometers through the woods, Abel said. There ought to be a clay road soon, a cut from the highway.

—I haven't seen your grandfather in more than ten years, Tarski said.

—Which one? They're both at the manor.

—Oh, of course, Tarski said, and laughed. I meant Pan Zygmunt. Tell me, how could two such totally different men live in peace together for such a long time?

—They're not so different, Abel said.

—Not different? You're just about the only thing that they have in common.

—Have you ever met my . . . Jewish grandfather? Abel said.

—No. Of course I know his sons. At least, two of them. Still, as my own father used to say regretfully about me, one should never judge a man by his sons.

—Good God, Abel said, and laughed, grateful for the excuse. Were you an evil youth, then?

—Let's just say that I recall my youth with a great deal of pleasure.

Then they were walking single file on the narrow path. They bowed right and left, ceremoniously, to avoid the branches that reached down toward them, so that their progress through the forest acquired something of a courtly ritual. The path turned and twisted. From time to time they lost it altogether. It would have been easier had they stayed on the highway in the glare of the sun.

Tarski said, suddenly: Tell me what you began to say about the people on the road.

And Abel said: They no longer ask us any questions.

Tarski nodded.

—As late as yesterday somebody still asked me how far we were going to retreat, Abel said.

—And what did you say?

—Nothing. I've stopped answering questions. The point is that the people on the roads always know so much better than the soldiers what is going on.

—I know, Tarski said, averting his face.

—Well, what have they found out? Yesterday they were going southeast with us, today they've all turned right around and are going back . . .

—Except for the Jews, Tarski said. Yes, I've noticed that.

Abel could see that the major was suddenly afraid. You do not see another man's fear as much as you sense it when there is no visible cause and you are left to people your imagination with causes of your own. So it was then. This glimpse of fear in a man whom he had learned to regard as fearless, whom he had sometimes privately accused of lacking the imagination needed for emotion, acted as fuel to his own uneasiness.

He didn't know what there was to fear now that the war was over. And it *was* over, no matter what the major said. War is a simple matter of killing and survival. He had killed no one and he had survived. He had not been afraid of death: the idea had been too remote. We are protected by our inability to create the image of our own destruction. What he felt now went beyond killing or survival. His life had not become dearer to him but he had caught a glimpse of possibilities that he could not define. He wanted to protect them, like papyrus under glass.

What did the people know?

How had they found out?

(Perhaps I should ask them . . .)

It would be something more immediate than the possibilities he wanted to explore. Survival had suddenly become essential, not for its own sake but for whatever illumination time could bring. The people on the road wouldn't be concerned with illumination, but in their animal instinct for survival lay the promise of time.

Abel felt cold then.

The pain in his accidentally burned hands—his ennobling wound—kept cruel cadence with the ragged pulse and with the stumbling shuffle of his boots on the forest floor . . . the beautiful handmade English riding boots so useless for combat but so much part of the panache, the flavor and the texture of this incomprehensible war.

He heard the thin sound of bells in the heated and sensitized air and he could almost tell from which church it was coming.

. . . The bells of St. Elizabeth's and his first communion . . .

Trees made the pillars of a natural chapel. The acrid dust of pine fronds was a kind of incense.

Abel shuddered: afternoons were getting colder now and the thick entwined canopy of the forest roof kept out the probing sun.

The craters along the roads would soon be glazed before sunrise.

. . . Day before yesterday, or perhaps it was another day, I saw a dead man sitting at his ease with his thin hands clasped around the slim trunk of a birch. The hands were black against the delicate white bark.

What was this war about? Why did it have to happen? So that the fleeing politicians, formerly of Warsaw, could say that they had kept their word to French and English politicians who hadn't kept theirs? So that the Martyr Myth could be bloodily maintained?

Undoubtedly future memoirs would explain it all.

Grandfather Zygmunt had once said that maturity meant understanding inexorable tragedy. If that was so, then Abel was quite ready to admit that he was immature, because tragedy, and need for tragedy, made no sense to him.

Laughter had always been a cure for the symptom if not for the disease. He must have made some sound (laughter? It didn't seem likely), because the major stopped, turned, and looked at him closely.

—Are you all right, boy?

Whatever fear he might have felt earlier had been put aside. Abel nodded.

—We mustn't give way now, you know, Tarski said. Now is the time to hold ourselves together, we still have our duty. The war goes on in France. That's where we have to go.

—You mean this senseless slaughter is going to continue?

—Senseless? You still find it senseless? Your father would be very angry if he heard you now.

—My father is often angry, Abel said.

—You'll think better of it in a day or two.

They passed a tethered mare and a foal pressed close to her side, both animals startled by the men's cautious passage, only their gold-flecked green eyes moving restlessly. The mare had been staked out in the woods, she had not strayed there. This was a signal of some kind, Abel knew, but his weary mind failed to decode it. Then they came to a dry track, the clay ruts burned hard as concrete, and turned to the west.

The Manor

TIME EDGED ANOTHER FRACTION OF A MOMENT to the edge of his cup.
There had been a sudden, violent rainfall earlier in the day; it had
washed the air and cooled it and had given it a particularly crystalline
quality, and all his perceptions had sharpened accordingly.

Imminent execution, someone had once said, is a marvelous stimulant for the creative instinct. Pan Zygmunt brought his ledgers to the
porch, where each day he had made his entries, some short and some of
many pages, since he was twelve years old. He sent the stable lad to
fetch him a pen, then, fumbling absentmindedly in his pockets, found
another.

He was wearing what had become for him the outward expression of
his thoughts: a brown robe with a cowl across his back and shoulders,
although he had never made a fetish of religion. He wore the monk's
robe as if to underline his retirement from capricious vanities; his ultimate allegiance had never been celestial. The robe was a birthday gift
from Jakob, who had sensed his friend's spiritual need. The old tailor
had sewed it exactly to the specifications that Father Boguslawski, that
most extraordinary of priests, had obtained from old monastery records.

Pan Zygmunt was aware of time's slippery motion. It was by no
means a new sensation; indeed, how many years had it been since any
sensation could be described as new? For more years than he cared to
remember he had observed this steady drain of his vitality. The faculty
of existing, along with life itself, had been gradually subsiding, but
awareness of the loss did not imply regret. He had few regrets. He
didn't mourn his dead. The deaths of his son and older daughter—executed so near to the spot where he now set up his slanting draftsman's
table—brought only sorrow at the waste of human spirit; he knew the
price that life exacted for the privilege of living, the cost of dedication
which is life itself. The past and the future are always with us; our

childhood is today, as is the moment of our dying. One should not mourn the dead longer than that moment. They return to the soil which is the beginning of the mystery: the source of our being. They become particles of the past and so of the future.

He neither regretted nor resented this essential depletion of himself, the droplets of time which drained from him as mead might from the neck of a bottle. On the contrary, the measured process was in itself proof of continuing existence and his sense of living. He welcomed the sensation in the context of himself as part of the land, a permanent component of his ancestral soil.

At times he was astonished that his reservoirs still contained anything at all, that more could come from him after eighty-seven years of continuing seepage. He sensed the loss only when he questioned the use that he had made of his share of time, wondering whether he couldn't have arranged the minor details of his life differently so that the final emptying would have greater meaning. But that was vanity, he knew, the sin of his people, and so he dismissed it; with his immediate prospects vanity was more than ever an illusion. The ultimate meaning of his own existence would lie in his ledgers. They were a faithful record of his alternatives, an interpretation of the personalities, events, and reflections that he had begun in 1864, the day his father's letter, sent the preceding year, reached him from Siberia. The letter was a transfer of an impassioned dream, the passing on of an imperishable ideal; it was no longer properly legible but its revolutionary romanticism could still set Pan Zygmunt's tired heart beating violently.

. . . Only through suffering could Poland be redeemed; the road through Golgotha led to resurrection.

It was the second of two letters pasted in the first of the forty ledgers, notebooks, and portfolios that represented seventy-five years of his life and, by extension, the life of his country.

The first letter had been written by his grandfather in 1831 after the crushing of the 1830 November Uprising . . . sent from the Hôtel Lambert in Paris to convey to *his* son that messianic vision of an idealized and unreal Poland that sent the young man faithfully in 1863 in pursuit of the dream and so to Siberia.

The letters had faded but the dream remained. Even so, Pan Zygmunt reflected, couldn't one seek salvation without crucifixion?

Strangers would never know the reasons for his choices; if they suspected the true nature of his life they would most likely turn away from it. But it was to be hoped, and fervently prayed for to whatever Gods might be induced to listen, that his grandson, Abel, the product of his private vision of his country, would eventually join the long line of men who had gone from this manor to serve an idea. This would take time,

he knew; the young man would squander many years, stumbling blindly
by himself. The nature of Abel's idea didn't really matter provided that
it was something greater than himself. In this regard he could be
trusted to find his own way: sooner or later all the paths converge. And
then the ledgers would find their importance. They would point Abel
to his source, and once a man knew who he was and where he had
come from he could begin to turn his spirit outward.

No, he thought, his reservoirs had not been foolishly expended. At
this point it no longer mattered how his life force had been drained
away. He had made his covenant with his land and he was anxious to
keep his side of the bargain. In exchange for the privilege of being a
fragment of . . . how can one say it . . . eternity? . . . he would give
his Self.

He opened a ledger at random and read the entry for January 1,
1936.

*Thinking of Pilsudski I see the tragedy of greatness; the tragedy of an
increasing loneliness, of a growing impatience with those who could not
understand, irritability and explosions of frustrated anger, of a failure
which nevertheless bore greater fruit than most men's successes. In all
respects he must be considered a failure—as a man and, eventually, as a
human being. Yet in that failure lay the elements of his greatness.*

. . . Yet on the day of the May Coup of 1926, when Pilsudski
overthrew the government and destroyed the noisy, impoverished, and
inefficient but democratic parliamentary republic, he had written, in
sorrow and foreboding:

*A journey of the spirit is a lonely business. There is no room for pas-
sengers, no time for arguments and quarrels. A man who goes against
existing Gods carrying the weight of others in his baggage is like a soldier who prepares for war by having his arms amputated and his eyes
put out.*

His land lay flat before him in a crescent frame of darkly textured
woods. The meadows without horses, the fields without crops, and, in a
larger sense, all the land beyond the borders of his woods were equally
his. There had been no definition of territorial limits in the covenant.

Again time stirred within him as though the draining reservoirs were
being gently nudged, imperceptibly tilted so as to speed up that familiar,
irreversible process; he felt a mild tremor in his arms and legs and then
his whole body trembled for a moment.

No, no . . . it wouldn't happen yet; not like that.

It seemed to him that the sun had suddenly become very bright. It
was poised on the feathery tips of the topmost branches, an act of ex-
quisite balance such as a ballerina might make between entrechats.

Would a curtsy follow? The twin black shadows of the Doric columns were slanting toward him.

He realized that the stableboy had not left the porch but stood quietly and patiently beside him.

—What is it, lad? he said.

—Please, master, the . . . the . . . the . . . *They* . . . have come to the village.

As always at such times, he felt the need to touch the soil, not as it was now (hard-baked under russet stubble, stripped of its crop for winter) but as it was in spring after the snow had melted and the rich black loam began to push life upward. This too was part of his covenant with his land: the mystery of renewal, the pledge of continuity for the human serial which ran from the time before reckoning to the time beyond it.

Old men, he reflected, have certain privileges.

Eccentricity is one of them.

If he were to go down to the orchard, near the duck pond where the soil was moist, and if he were to kneel there and to place his palms on the springy soil, who would question him?

He need tell no one that he drew the current of life directly from his land, that the earth nourished him and replenished him as though he were a tree, that he could feel a tingling in his scalp as though shoots and branches were pushing forward from his skull while his buried fingers became roots.

Years could pass (as they had) and great events could shake the horizons and people could enter his life and his memory as hours visit a season but the land would renew him and sustain him as long as he didn't break the covenant.

To love your land.

To preserve it.

To return to it.

Why do human beings cling to life so frantically? Probably because they have no idea of what life is about. Well, I've lived long enough. I've become very old. Someone had said that getting old is a very democratic process. The only autocratic decision left to us is the manner in which we bring the process to an end.

. . . To contemplate the scythe's approaching sweep, to clean one's life of the great lie and the grand illusion, to move with purpose back to the beginnings which define all of one's possibilities, is to arrive at the final faith which is impervious to the complexities of living or the simplicity of dying.

Once more he turned to the ledger but he knew that he would not write in it again. He saw that Jakob had come from the house and now stood beside him. He wondered for a moment why he hadn't realized before how very frail and shrunken his diminutive old partner had become. Old, old . . . yes, we're old. Shortly we shall both be taking the Taenaran Road. And yet there had been some moments in this house which had given promise of defying time.

—We'll have to start burying your journal very soon, Jakob said. The Bolsheviks are on their way.

—Yes, the boy told me.

The boy had run off the porch when Jakob appeared but he had not gone far. He stood at the bottom of the wooden steps, working the toes of one foot into the parched soil, staring at Pan Zygmunt with enormous eyes like a two-legged fawn poised to bolt for his life.

—I saw them from the study windows, Jakob said. You know, at the back, where the track doubles past the orchard.

—How did they seem to you? Pan Zygmunt asked, and knew the question to have been both foolish and unnecessary, so he added quickly: Are there many of them?

—No, not many. They seem in no hurry. They have some of our people with them, carrying something. I couldn't make out what it was.

Jakob, of course, could be trusted to ignore unnecessary questions. But there were two questions which Pan Zygmunt wanted answered, so now he said:

—Where will you bury the ledgers? And how will you let Abel know what you've done with them?

—Oh, Zygmunt, Jakob said. You'll do it yourself!

—Come now, old friend, why should we start lying to each other after so many years? You know they will take me. But don't you think *you* had better leave before they get here? One never knows what such cattle might do.

—Where should I go? the small old man said quietly. (And after hesitating for a moment, because he didn't wish to scratch open an old wound, Pan Zygmunt said:) Well . . . I know how you feel about your Jozef . . . and my Magda . . . but perhaps to Lwów . . .

—No, Jakob said, that's not what I meant. I didn't mean *Where shall I take this old carcass so that it might keep kicking for another year or two?* I meant *Where should I be but here?* I have been here for twenty-four years. This is my home as much as it is yours. I promise I won't interfere with your passion . . . after all, how could I? We both have our own roles to play out to the end, though mine may not be very clear at the moment.

—Well, perhaps they won't take you. They might think that you're just the steward . . . harmless from their point of view, maybe even useful . . . after all, isn't that the role you've been playing for twenty-four years?

—No, Jakob said. I don't think they'll take me. They've always underestimated Jews and I don't think that a Russian can change. Besides, don't you know that I have all my traditional weapons?

—Listen, you old tiger, Pan Zygmunt said, smiling. Timidity just wouldn't suit you. It's too late in the day for you to play that game.

—Don't underestimate the nature of timidity. If you examine it closely you'll see that it's just another form of arrogance. Yes, it will do very well for the Bolsheviks, they'll expect it from me, and if you don't startle cattle by showing them that you are something more than they expect they'll always leave you alone.

—For twenty-four years you've insisted on masquerading as only my steward. Was that part of the same theory about cattle?

—In part, Jakob said, smiling. Why incur more than one's natural share of ill will?

—Such wisdom, Pan Zygmunt said, and both men laughed softly. If I had had you with me at the Versailles Conference we probably would have come away with Moscow as a province.

—If I had been there, Jakob said, they would have given Poland to the Jews.

They both laughed again. The boy, who had been watching them as if they were creatures from another planet, finally ran away.

—Now even children run away from us, Pan Zygmunt said. Tell me, old friend, would our own children understand what we had tried to do here?

—Ah, children, Jacob said with a sudden uncharacteristic bitterness, a quick anger shaded with contempt. Children, the comfort of old age . . . whoever said that never had children of his own.

—No, but seriously . . . do you think we've lived usefully? Do you think that any of our thoughts will remain after we are gone?

—Who can tell about thoughts? They live on the wind. But only a fool can expect his children to live by his thoughts.

—That sounds like more ancient Jewish wisdom.

—I wish it had been, Jakob said. It would have saved me from a lot of grief. No, it's not ancient Jewish wisdom, it's just the newfound wisdom of one very old Jew. And I'm not guaranteeing the quality of the wisdom. I am not even guaranteeing that it's more than knowledge.

—Did none of your children turn out to your liking?

—To my *liking?* Jakob said bitterly. To my *hating!* Why does a man want children? To continue the race? No, it is to serve his own foolish dream! And I had such a dream, you wouldn't believe it. My Sarah thought me insane, although that's why she came to me in the first place when we lived in Vilno. Were it not for the laws of nature I would have sired a son a month on her! In seven years we had seven children. I had such an unlimited appetite for children because I was a man with a dynastic dream! I plotted the careers of my sons while I still held them newborn in my arms! Oh, I can tell you, Yuval would be the man of commerce, a master of a clothing empire stitched with many needles. Aaron would enter the world of finance. Mordecai, who coughed from infancy and was nearly blind, would be the scholar, teacher, and interpreter of the law. A triumvirate, no less, which would combine Wisdom, Power, and Commerce. My fantasies were baroque, to say the least. I saw no limit to the possibilities if only I could have enough sons! But there were no more children after Avrum. And soon enough there were no more dreams.

—What did you plan for Avrum? Pan Zygmunt asked gently.

—There, you might say, is my greatest failure. As a moral, law-abiding man you would have to say so. But there is also whatever success I have had.

—I've never believed half the things that have been said about him, Pan Zygmunt said in a mild and measured tone which, he thought, might soothe his friend's distress. No one could be either as iniquitous or as ubiquitous as the tales make Avrum and remain believable . . . but you know how it is with our people, how we love to embroider a good story . . .

—Well, we Jews exaggerate as much as you do, but you can believe anything you hear about my youngest son. He *is* unbelievable, even I can hardly believe that I made such a man. . . . But I know everything that he has done.

—Then you *have* kept in touch with him? You *have* been watching over him, after all? How typical of you, Jakob!

—No, no, never, never, the old Jew cried fiercely. His blood is my blood, I feel what he feels . . . it is a fire that was lighted four thousand years ago . . . ! But do you know . . . no, of course you don't know, so can you *imagine* what it is like to have made a murderer? All that blood is on your hands, on your head, and blood cries for vengeance . . . ! Perhaps that's my punishment for stealing another man's young wife. And yet in my dreams he was to become something so far removed from what he *has* become that one would think we were talking about two different men . . .

—Your dream was a good dream.

—No dream is a good dream! Dreams are toys for amusement in the night! What do dreams have to do with things as they are?

But now Pan Zygmunt rose and eased the old man, who was so much older than himself and so much more fragile, into the chair behind the tilted table. He leaned against the carved weathered balustrade, smooth as polished metal, its intricate workmanship erased by the centuries.

—Calm yourself, old friend, Pan Zygmunt said. You know what Father Boguslawski says: *Don't get excited, it's only the end of the world.*

—What does that youngster know? He is only sixty! I was a father before he was born. But you are right as always, why should a man excite himself, it's bad for the heart . . . They will be hammering the nails into my coffin and I will tell myself *Don't get excited, Jakob, it's bad for your heart.* Ah, Zygmunt, I have dreamed a fool's dream and paid a fool's price, so what do I have to complain about?

—I've never heard you complaining about anything, Pan Zygmunt said. You're the least complaining man I have ever met . . . But don't you think your judgment of Avrum is too harsh? Say rather that Avrum is a soldier, fighting for his people. Wouldn't that be a more charitable judgment?

—Who wants your soldiers? the old Jew cried with the savage fierceness of a tormented child. Who needs more corpse makers? That's your Polish way, and much good has it done you. What do I want with your Christian charity? My God is a merciless God and we're a merciless people harried from land to land, not wanted anywhere, and that is as it *should* be because we are merciless to ourselves! And the people know this! They look at us and they ask themselves *Who are these strange men who stand above mercy? Would they be merciful to us if the tables were turned?*

His hands wrote their own violent paean in that quickened and sensitized air, so that Pan Zygmunt found himself responding to their signal as though he were a crystal in a receiving set.

—No, Jakob called from his promontory, the edge of his reason. No more crying out, no more anguish, we have filled the centuries with tears. No more books, no more legends, no more dreaming, we will take the way of the world. I understand the ways of the world. I burdened Avrum with a dream, but haven't all fathers always burdened their children with their own fantasies? At least my dream made no attempt to resurrect the dead! I dreamed of a future! Avrum was to be the diadem in my dynastic crown. He was to fill all the vacancies assigned to the unborn! He was to be the bringer of dynastic glory, the fountainhead of splendor!

His hands flew sideways, fluttering like dark wings. He leaned forward with the urgent swiftness of a descending hawk whose falling shadow is death's messenger. In the hunched concentration of his littleness he had become a feathery projectile hurtling toward prey.

—This word astonishes you . . . you who have lived your Stoic life of non-attachment to material objects . . . Why should I want splendor? Why do men need the sun?

—Illumination, Pan Zygmunt murmured, yes . . .

—What good are wealth and power without illumination? I wanted Avrum to enter the world of the spirit and to inherit his own mind . . . And what a mind it was! Do you know that he spoke five languages before he was twelve? Foreign languages. Hebrew and Yiddish and Polish as a matter of course . . . even I learned Polish . . . He read such books! I sent him to St. Petersburg to live with the family of a Russian prince . . . the prince needed money and I sent him a truly princely fortune . . . so that my future fountainhead of splendor would have the necessary advantages. Oh yes, I knew the ways of the world, I knew what was required. That prince would have set his dogs on me if I had come to his door but, thanks to him, Avrum wore the best-tied cravat at the Hermitage. He learned whist and bezique and chemin de fer. He wrote sonnets for his ballerinas and painted little portraits for his frivolous friends. He raced his thoroughbred on the Semenovsky grounds against young ensigns of the guard and mastered the illumination of a dueling pistol! One night he lost a thousand gold rubles on one throw of the dice *and staked his life to recover them on the second throw!* . . . In those days just before the Great War, St. Petersburg would have corrupted your pious St. Augustine . . . Think of that brilliant cosmopolitan aristocracy that revolved about the foreign embassies and the English Club . . . Karsavina was dancing *Swan Lake* at the Mariisky, and theaters were open seven nights a week . . . In some respects those were magic years, and I believed in magic. I wanted Avrum to absorb it, to master its beauty. But he became drunk on the fumes and scarcely touched the substance and became himself part of the panorama, that doomed and glittering procession of shadows without eyes, without heart, without mind . . . He Russianized his name, had himself ennobled, forgot who he was . . . I'm told he shuddered delicately at the thought of Jews . . . I had created a shadow, an illusion: yet another princeling . . . a *Russian* princeling, at that! Trust an old tailor to sew a fine coat!

—That whole world no longer exists, Pan Zygmunt said gently. And you're still carrying its burdens?

—To me it was like yesterday, Jakob said, remotely, then added as impersonally as though he were making his habitual entries in the manor's stud book: Why should men make dreams? You are right, as always, it is better not to think about it any more.

—We must learn to forgive ourselves, as Father Boguslawski says.

—It is too late for me to learn anything, Jakob said. How much longer do I have to live? One year, two? What is that beside my ninety-four years? I know everything about myself that I am ever going to know . . . I can no longer be awed or impressed by anything that anyone may do. Wonders confuse me. Life ended when innocence was lost.

His head fell forward. He shrank and diminished. It was possibly the final creation of his subsiding spirit: his weightless body descended through fathoms, measuring an infinity of night and no longer wondering what might lie beyond it: the strong and tested currents of an ebbing life. He was no longer the apocalyptic prophet, the plummeting hawk. He was again a slight and crumpled shape leaning against time.

—How can a young man comprehend the end of his world? he asked finally. It is no use saying to him *Don't get excited, it's bad for your heart.* A young man doesn't understand such an admonition, he thinks that his heart will beat forever . . . What went on in his mind in those later years, when he was forced to awake from *my* dream?

—At least he found his way back to his people.

Jakob had begun to nod mutely in his chair, a diminutive but exact affirmation of a pact that was both cruel and demonic, smiling without mirth into immeasurable distance.

—Without hope there is no God, he murmured to his visions, the processional that wound through the caverns of his mind, each figure stained and burning. Without God there is no man. But a man shouldn't dream. To be alive is all the accomplishment needed for a man.

—No, no! Pan Zygmunt cried quickly. That would negate our entire civilization, all our own efforts here, all of man's evolutionary progress!

It seemed to him that Jakob's silence cried scornfully and fiercely: What civilization? What progress? An evolution into what? But all the old man muttered deep into himself was: You speak from your experience, I speak from mine.

A flight of herons drove its stark wedge southward. Their precise formation was delicately tinted by the sun, so that, for an extravagant moment, they seemed like flamingos. The birds' descending wings, scooping air, traced subtle silvery patterns on the rim of the sun. A bar of shadow etched in scarlet imprisoned the sky, and the sun itself, as if brushed in passing by the wings of a magical bird, remained motionless, suspended over amaranthine leaves.

. . . A dog began to bark hysterically from the village, and another answered, and then another (Pan Zygmunt's own *Wilk*, tottering on the brink of its own abyss) joined the mindless chorus of challenge and counterchallenge, the promise of that unreasoning ultimate violence, the meeting of true faiths, which is a law of the universe beyond argument, like that of gravity. The warnings rolled unheeded over the barriers of time and the forest, but Pan Zygmunt thought that he had probably assessed them correctly. He had placed himself irrevocably athwart the path of events which now sped toward him on collision course.

Jakob slept heavily, completely.

. . . The evening clouds hung nervously electric, poised in the wings of the departing day like a troupe of passion-play actors awaiting their cue.

Pan Zygmunt also waited, armored in what Jakob had called Stoic indifference to joy, grief, and pain; but if it was Stoicism it was a Polish kind. Indifference had no place in it. On the contrary, it was rooted in absolute commitment, an unreasoning faith which went beyond the abstract. He felt more than ever part of the immemorial pageantry of the past. He supposed that his entire life had been a grand rehearsal for this moment. The letter-perfect actor would soon step forward, deliver his lines, and fade into the Chorus.

. . . We live like moths, he thought, circling ever closer to the flame until we enter it, as though this final ecstatic consummation were coincidental with attainment . . . Yet there is this to say about it, this to be remembered: the joy of living comes from making the attempt, not from success.

. . . A cloud of yellow dust puffed up from the track that led from the village. Pan Zygmunt smiled in appreciation of the peasants' subtle cruelty to the invaders whom they would be guiding.

The village lay just behind the first belt of trees, less than a kilometer away, but the track was devious. It was, Pan Zygmunt thought, a very peasant track, denying the obvious, as indirect as it was possible to make it, meandering through the woods and dodging obstacles and doubling back on itself; it followed the contours of the land, the dry bed of a stream, the secret run of the fox, and the people's fancy. The village was so close that on a clear evening he could hear the calls and the creak of the well beams, but the narrow track turned every trip into a tortuous expedition. None of the local people ever used the track. How like them to bring the Russians to the manor by the most natural-seeming but most roundabout and difficult route.

The dust cloud moved, extended.

Pan Zygmunt gathered up his ledgers. He thought for a moment that he might wake Jakob to take charge of them. The Russians would be beating on the doors in less than ten minutes. Why wake the man who looked so much at peace? It wouldn't last much longer. He would hide the ledgers in the study-office; Jakob could bury them later.

The house was cool, musty with undefined shadow in mysterious corners; whispering of ghosts, the minuet at midnight and the mazurka before dawn; redolent of all the ancient violences, the masked ball of conspiracy, lovers' quarrels, farewells, and the precipitous flight across the night on horseback into the unknown that lay so near to its placid surface. Its somnolent rusticity was a fraud, Pan Zygmunt knew. Yet even he sometimes liked to cherish the illusion that here he could be detached from the world.

In the high-ceilinged chamber that was the estate office, library, and study, Pan Zygmunt put his ledgers in three canvas feed bags and placed the feed bags in a wooden crate in which some books had come from Warsaw several weeks earlier. Everything seemed in order, Jakob would see to that. If there was anything remotely Polish about Jakob, whose family had come to Poland nearly a hundred years before Pan Zygmunt's own, it was the single-mindedness with which he drove himself in pursuit of duty. No obstacle was too great, no task impossible. Pan Zygmunt noted that the personal files had been considerably thinned out: his ancient political correspondence had entirely disappeared. Trust Jakob to prepare for the visitors; they would find nothing incriminating here, unless the room itself was evidence of a crime.

The walls were lined with books from floor to ceiling: the *Commentaries of St. Hyacinth*, the privately printed twelve-volume edition of Dlugosz's *Historia Polonica*, which Pan Zygmunt's great-grandfather had greatly admired, a recent photographic album of the Wit Stwosz carvings, portfolios by Matejko, Grottger, Gierymski, Dunikowski, and a dozen others; an illuminated reproduction of *De Revolutionibus Orbium Coelestium*, Modrzewski's *Reform of the Republic*, Mikolaj Rej on parchment with old wooden covers; Jan Kochanowski's first translation of the Psalms, the *Dismissal of the Greek Envoys*, and a loose-leaf portfolio of his sixteen thousand poems bound in morocco leather; the collected sermons of Piotr Skarga, Kochanski's treatise on the approximative construction of the rectification of the circle, *The Moral and Physical Order* of Hugo Kollontaj, the *Warnings* of Staszyc and his *The Human Race*; Sniadecki's *Theory of Organic Beings*, the private papers of Prince Adam Czartoryski (a partial collection); commentaries on Hoene-Wronski's *Messianism*, the collected writings of Joachim Lelewel, a volume of Lipinski's operatic fantasies and violin concertos; Alexander Fredro's *Maiden Vows*, *Life Annuity*, and *Vengeance*; a shelfful of the ballads, poetic and epic tales, and dramas of Mickiewicz; Slowacki's *Maria Stuart*, *Kordjan*, *Anhelli*, *Balladyna*, *Lilla-Weneda*, and the unfinished *King Spirit*; Chopin's collected compositions; well-thumbed old leatherbound editions of Krasinski (Pan Zygmunt's special favorite): *The Dawn*, *The Undivine Comedy*, and *Irydion*; the monumental collection of folklore of Oscar Kolberg; the scores and music of Moniuszko's *Halka*, *Haunted Manor*, *The Countess*, and *The Raftsman*; the collected poetry of Cyprian Kamil Norwid; a centenary

memorial edition of Wieniawski's concertos, études, and dance miniatures; *The Outpost, Chronicles, The Doll, The Emancipated Woman,*
and *The Pharaoh* of Boleslaw Prus; a long shelf filled with Sienkiewicz,
a shelf of Joseph Konrad-Korzeniowski; *The Homeless People* and
Ashes of Zeromski; the four volumes of Reymont's *The Peasants;* the
plays of Wyspianski and the symphonies of Mieczyslaw Karlowicz; the
Dreams of Power of Leopold Staff; some of Tuwim's work (although
Pan Zygmunt was not in sympathy with the young poets of the
Skamander group); and the *Ferdydurke* of Gombrowicz, which, he admitted, he couldn't understand.

Two walls were partially devoted to what Pan Zygmunt fondly called
"the foreigners"—from Lao-tze to Kafka—but he didn't stop there to
pass his hands lovingly over their stiff spines as he did with this fragment of his country's mind and imagination: the essence of what had
formed his own creative being. He was ashamed to bring his ledgers to
this company, yet, perhaps, he reflected, *They* wouldn't mind . . . *They*
would understand what he had tried to do: his small pathetic contribution to the endless dream. He wondered briefly whether the Bolsheviks would object to this manifestation of a spirit they had come to destroy, or whether they would dismiss it, as the world had dismissed it, as
something beyond easy comprehension and materially irrelevant, and
therefore of no value. Things beyond value have no value, he knew well
enough, the priceless is worthless; but each of these men had been
prepared to pay the necessary price.

He understood what Jakob meant by *splendor* because he lived in the
midst of it; he was surrounded by the indelible evidence of his people's
greatness, the power of their cumulative spirit. This could never diminish, it could only grow, expand, and seek new horizons. If a man is very
fortunate, he thought, if he has a national idea so powerful that it can
inspire, sustain, and nourish, but never impoverish, then he is close to
personal immortality. In the midst of Death we are in Life . . . Our
own end doesn't even bring a pause for grief or reflection, a momentary
halt in the continuous flow of which we had been an accidental fragment; there is no hiatus, no gap to be closed.

He went through the french windows into the back garden, which in
spring, summer, and early in the autumn was an asymmetrical jungle of
flowers and blooming shrubbery; this late in October the flowers were
dead. Everything seemed disordered here, there was some distortion.
He could not immediately orient himself between the conical beehives
and the orchard wall. Things lay about, abandoned, to no particular
purpose: a pair of rakes, a ladder with several rungs missing in the middle, an upended wheelbarrow, a mound of manure, and some yawning
baskets . . . Beyond the garden were the new brick stables. The old sta-

bles had burned to the ground in 1914 when Brusilov's army had brushed past the manor. The manor itself had been set on fire by Budyenny's Cossacks in 1921 but the peasants had beaten out the flames. They could not prevent those earlier Bolsheviks from murdering Leon and Maria but that, too, was part of the natural order, a part of the pageant, an act of passion in a play which could never be understood in another country. Pan Zygmunt had not been there when his children died; indeed, he knew, they had died in his place! He had been in Paris with Dmowski and Paderewski trying to convince Lloyd George that this Polish province, which Austrians called Galicia, was not in northern Spain! The willful, arrogant Welshman was hard to convince. He had fearful visions of French domination of the Continent and did all he could to weaken and diminish France's natural allies . . .

The stables had been rebuilt and restocked after the Great War, largely with what was left of Jakob's vanished fortune, his demolished dream . . . Pan Zygmunt walked toward the stables, which, he knew, were empty. The few horses which the Army had not requisitioned for that unreal, unbelievable, and incomprehensible thousand-hour day that had ended a few weeks ago, were hidden in the woods.

The horses, like the men and women of the manor (and of the village, the distant city, and the province, for these were indivisible in Pan Zygmunt's vision: all segments of one whole), had also played their role in the pageant. Pan Zygmunt bred white Polish-Arabs, that tall, deep-chested, extraordinarily graceful animal with a small nervous head and an abundance of creamy white mane. Their chief characteristics were sensitivity, beauty, and endurance; they were volatile, temperamental, and hard to control; they could be ridden only by a master horseman and he would never dare to use the whip or the spur. To take such animals to war was like brutalizing a Corps de Ballet, yet Pan Zygmunt, like his predecessors, always acquiesced to the requisitions. In giving their all they could not refuse what they treasured most. In 1683 the white herd had gone with Sobieski to save Europe from the Turks at the siege of Vienna . . . In 1794 they carried Kosciuszko's officers in his Insurrection . . . Pulaski took one to America in 1777 . . . Prince Jozef Poniatowski (and, for that matter, Napoleon himself) had ridden them into Moscow in 1812 . . . They went with Jozef Bem to the Hungarian Revolution of 1848. In 1916, the stables had been emptied for Pilsudski's Legion. Each time, the king stallion and the mares with foal had been left behind so that, after whatever human madness had abated, the stables could restock themselves. Now the remaining mares and their king were hidden in the woods, carefully attended by boys sworn to secrecy. The king was Rhetoric, out of Magnificent Obsession by Dream of Destiny: an animal of deep pride. When he had been foaled, Pan Zygmunt had worried that his head was perhaps a little too narrow but with maturity there were no visible defects. He was undoubtedly the greatest king stallion the stables had had, although his great-great-great-grandfather, Royal Prerogative (out of Unity by Reason), still remained a legend in the province.

Pan Zygmunt circled the house and came through the dead lilacs and rhododendrons to the front of the manor; the leaf-brown stench of withered flowers clung to the roof of his mouth. Jakob still slept on the broad veranda, made featureless by shadow. The stable lad who had run away had now come back; he sat on the lowest of the three steps, his chin buried in crossed arms, his huge eyes fixed on the disorderly mud-brown procession that had now erupted from the woods at the mouth of the track.

Pan Zygmunt had moved slowly and carefully, conserving his strength; at his age agility was dangerous if not impossible. Even so, his heart was fluttering, he could feel each minuscule expansion, and he was rather dizzy. Specks of white light revolved before his eyes like snowflakes seen through glass.

—Why did you run away before? Pan Zygmunt asked (speaking, he thought, to himself as much as to the boy).

—I don't know, sir. I was frightened, sir.

—What is there to fear?

The boy stared at him earnestly, troubled and afraid. His wide blue eyes were innocent, open to all experience; he would not be able to express what he had sensed or what his senses had begun to tell him. Too much had happened recently, there were too many questions which no one could answer. There had been a Great Fall again and the debris had created a certain confusion. Symbols had toppled and moved out of sight, truths reassembled their structural components; what had been the familiar beacons of the daily round no longer illuminated anything.

—I said, what is there to fear, lad? Pan Zygmunt asked gently.

The boy fixed his eyes again, like a small animal immobilized by the gaze of an adder, on the green-brown mass that trampled over the meadow toward the manor.

—*Them*, the boy said. They do such things . . . the people have told us.

—What things? Pan Zygmunt asked. What people?

—The people on the road, the boy said. They have told us . . . *Them* (and he nodded imperceptibly toward the spreading and advancing mass) . . . they've taken many people . . . they've killed many people . . . The people are now running away from them . . . Sir, what is going to happen to *us*?

—I don't know . . . *exactly* . . . what is going to happen, Pan Zygmunt said carefully.

This, he supposed, is true enough: I don't know the exact procedure,
the order of events. But he didn't want to lie to the boy or to himself;
he did not tell lies. He sat down beside the boy. He had to tell him
something, the boy expected it.

—Some things will happen here that you won't understand until
you're much older, he said. Perhaps it's something that no one will ever
properly understand. I don't know about that, I can't foretell the future, but I think you'll understand it when you're older.

That, he told himself, irritated with this typical evasion, is what the
old always tell the young. But it's the best that I can do at this moment.

—As old as you, sir? the boy asked. As old as Pan Jakob?

—Oh no, Pan Zygmunt said. You won't have to wait that long, that's
too long to wait. But until you're as big as Master Abel. Do you
remember him? Let's see . . . four years ago . . . you must have been
at least eight years old when he was here last, you might remember him
. . . I think he's old enough to understand this . . . at least I hope he
is.

—I remember Master Abel, sir, the boy said doubtfully. He is really
quite old . . .

—He's only about twelve years older than you. Twelve years . . . that
isn't much to wait. But perhaps you will grow up faster than Abel could
do. In times like these boys grow up quickly. Often they become men
when they are only twelve.

—But what should we *do*, sir? the boy said, insistent. What about
Them? Should we run away?

—Oh no, Pan Zygmunt said. Running away takes you away forever;
people who run away can never come back. You see, you start by running away from something . . . anything . . . and you end by running
from yourself. When that happens you can never stop running. As to
Them, as you call them, they're only . . . invaders. Invaders come and
go. Systems come and go. What never goes, what is always here, is the
people. The people always outlast the invaders. But you must have patience and you must never forget what you are.

—When *will* they go away? the boy asked. Will they be here a long
time?

—I can't tell you that. But I can tell you that *you* will be here a long
time after they are gone. I'd like to tell you a little story now. Would
you like to hear it?

The boy nodded but without enthusiasm. Pan Zygmunt could see that the boy didn't think this was a time for stories. But this story was one he thought the boy ought to hear.

—It's about a man known as Mahatma Gandhi, who lives in India, which is a very great country very far away.

—He is an Indian? the boy asked, interested.

—Well, not that kind of Indian, Pan Zygmunt said. Perhaps we had better call him a Hindu. He said that when people are invaded by their enemies there is a number of things that they can do. He called those things the Nine Tenets of Resistance, and this is what they are: We know nothing, we recognize nothing, we give nothing, we are capable of nothing, we understand nothing, we sell nothing, we help nothing, we reveal nothing, and we forget nothing . . . He is very wise and perhaps we should listen to him. Of course, *his* invaders are not like *our* invaders, and *his* way hasn't been *our* way, but perhaps it's time we found a new way to resist invaders.

But the boy was no longer listening; if, indeed, he had heard anything at all! The boy jumped up, tense and apprehensive, alert and poised for flight as he had been before. He skipped a few steps away from the manor. Pan Zygmunt also rose. He didn't think that the boy had understood him but what did that matter?

I didn't help him, he thought regretfully, but who can now help anyone? The ledgers, he thought suddenly, he should have the ledgers!

Behind him, he heard Jakob stir and take some steps along the veranda but he didn't turn. He faced the dark and shapeless mass which was suddenly acquiring definition, which had a certain texture, which was a pure unbridled force, a demented element of nature which now had faces, slack arms, slogging boots, fur hats and slanted caps, gray overcoats flapping at the ankles; which bristled with steel; which cursed and coughed and grumbled and spat in the dust; which exhaled a humid sourness, a sullen muttering dullness that was infinitely threatening.

Such faces, he thought in sudden anguish: such *primitive* faces . . . so . . . incomprehensible!

First came two horsemen who might have been officers; certainly the taller, leaner man who sat so easily in his saddle, who might have been a steeplechaser, who held himself at some distance from the other, had that undefined air of detachment that comes with authority. Men much like that had been frequent visitors at the manor between the last two wars, a time that now seemed an eternity ago. The other mounted man had never been a rider, he was merely an irritated man who sat on a horse. The horse was obviously exhausted. Each time the horse stumbled, the rider turned and shouted into the billowing peaks of dust where the amorphous mass herded the four peasants who carried the stretcher. Whoever was on the stretcher was hidden by dust. The peasants struggled with the stretcher, pulled and pushed by soldiers who were themselves weighed down by angular sacks, boxes, peasant bedding: the pitiful loot of an Eastern Malopolska village. Behind them other soldiers straggled in loose groups all the way back to the edge of the woods where the dust obscured them. Being invisible, still belonging to the realm of the imagination, they seemed more frightening than the others who now reached the manor.

The irritated rider shouted, waved his arms, and several bodies detached themselves from the larger mass and swept around the house into the back garden.

. . . A man tripped, a rifle went off with a definitive crack; the bullet rattled in the rhododendrons.

The irritated rider arched his arm overhead as though he were pronouncing maledictions, casting an everlasting curse at the manor, and half a dozen soldiers clattered heavily up the steps and across the veranda, shedding burdens.

. . . A cuckoo clock struck Pan Zygmunt on the shoulder; the wooden bird flew out with its metallic cry.

He had been tossed aside so lightly, brushed out of the way with such little effort, that his chest constricted; now when he needed all his dignity, all the fortitude the moment demanded, he was robbed of substance. He made an urgent effort to regain his feet, to be erect in this diminishing moment, to affirm his status as a human being. A coarse sleeve scraped his face. The stench of old sweat, urine, and raw spirits swept over him like an exhalation from the wells of the world . . . Inside the house doors slammed, boots pounded on parquet, objects fell and rolled; he heard shouts, questioning exclamations, the tympany of struck glass, the scream of the cook . . .

The flowing mass of men and horses slowed in a ragged crescent before the veranda. The heads turned curiously. The men's faces scowled and grinned. The bodies leaned on long rifles, squatted and milled about. The hands scratched, mopped the faces, showed dexterity with black tobacco and strips of newspaper. The boots scraped the ground. The four peasants put the stretcher on the grass as delicately as though it were a relic for processionals . . . they stood in a tight group of good black Sunday coats and white linen, vivid in the solidifying brown mass which had brought them. They would, of course, put on their Sunday coats to come to the manor . . . Their faces were mahogany red and wrinkled as walnuts; their hands, made suddenly useless, hung straight down beside them as though the men were ashamed of having no burden. One by one, the peasants hid their hands. Yet there was something special in the way they held themselves so separate from the soldiers: some small secret triumph they would share with no one. The man on the stretcher was uniformly yellow with thick dust but Pan Zygmunt caught the dull gleam of silver on one shoulder: a tarnished star and some braid. The man's feet were bare and his hands were clasped with curious intensity as though he were praying. Why is he wearing purple gloves? Pan Zygmunt thought, astonished.

And now the irritated officer started to dismount. His horse became nervous; he could smell the stables and would be wondering about his reception among strange animals. The horse began a tortuous pirouette, pivoting about his front legs, and the exasperated rider started to kick and pummel the horse. A soldier came out of the crowd to hold the horse's head. The rest of the soldiers paid no attention to the officer and his horse. A clear young voice, filled with sadness, gentleness, and compassion, rose out of the mud-brown crowd singing an old song.

The angry officer finally got off the horse; he shouted at Pan Zygmunt. Pan Zygmunt shook his head. This province of Poland had never been part of the Russian Empire, had never had the slightest connection with Russia, and few people here were fluent in Russian. Yet clearly the officer wanted instant answers. He drew his revolver as though this were a universal language and punctuated his demands with shots into the air. Each flat crack became an exclamation mark. Pan Zygmunt replied to each with a shake of the head. He waited for the final exclamation, the one that would explode in his chest.

But now the officer who had not dismounted, who soothed his mare with small pats and soft murmurs, whose finely formed dark Gypsy face stated clearly that *he* was not part of this provincial farce—an amateur performance of a tired classic—said in precise and unaccented Polish, in a voice which was disdainful and aloof: Where is the master of the manor?

This was the cue, the well-rehearsed moment. Pan Zygmunt stepped forward feeling a sudden rush of gratitude, an acknowledgment of all his certainties. Before he could open his mouth the boy who had been crowded from his memory cried in a high triumphant voice: He is not here! He has run away!

Their eyes met and exchanged a glance of swift complicity. There was a question and an affirmation and a pledge. It was a moment of rare understanding. Then the boy whirled and fled, pursued by the air of conspiracy that exists between men who have made a compact with God or the Devil.

The mounted officer nodded toward the peasants, repeated the question. And when Burda, the Wojt of the village, said We don't know, and Glowacki, the wheelwright, said I don't understand, and Klos, the blacksmith, said *Who knows where he is, the Devil take him,* and Mierzwa, the storyteller, gazed vacantly at the sky, the officer shrugged, said something to the irritated man who was rhythmically slapping the barrel of his revolver into the palm of his hand, and leaped from the saddle. He threw the reins to a soldier who came trotting up. His glance touched Pan Zygmunt without interest or curiosity, noting the brown habit. He walked to the stretcher and looked at the wounded man.

Pan Zygmunt stood rooted in sudden confusion, his purpose awry. The brief incurious glance had assessed and dismissed him, it rendered him soulless. Again he wanted to protest the degradation, to assert his right to human dignity: not to be judged and discarded by a glance! Then Mierzwa, who (Pan Zygmunt remembered) was a devious and complicated man, highly regarded as a storyteller for long winter evenings but not as much else, laughed affectedly and shouted: There he is!

So the cue had come, after all, though not as expected. Pan Zygmunt struggled to free himself of stupor, the weight that had settled on his shoulders with the boy's first cry. He took the necessary step toward the officer with the revolver. But the officer's eyes, suddenly enraged, had followed Mierzwa's pointing hand to the veranda, where Jakob stood trembling slightly in the chill of the advancing evening. The people had cried *Give us Barabbas,* he thought emptily, and Barabbas was given unto them.

—No, he cried. I am the owner here!

The angry officer shouted, waved his revolver, and two soldiers ran toward Jakob with pointed bayonets.

—Listen, Pan Zygmunt cried, hurrying toward the officer who spoke Polish, who wore no badges of rank but whose authority was unmistakable. Sir! *Panie Oficerze!* I am the owner, the man whom you want.

Lost in his contemplation of the wounded man, the officer said carelessly: How can that be? Aren't you people sworn to poverty?

—I'm not a monk, Pan Zygmunt explained, cursing his voice, which had betrayed him by trembling. This is my estate! That man is Jakob Mendeltort . . . the steward. He has been my steward for twenty-four years! Please, if you will only ask the peasants, they will tell you. They were confused before, afraid . . . please ask them!

—Mendeltort? said the officer.

—I beg you, Pan Zygmunt cried finally, feeling his spirit crumble.

—Mendeltort, the officer said quietly, and raised his eyes from the wounded man to look toward the manor. Now, wouldn't that be a coincidence?

—Yes, Mendeltort, Pan Zygmunt insisted. He's only the steward here.

But the officer had already left him, discarded him again; he spoke into a void. The officer moved swiftly and with purpose, as if his momentarily diffused energies had found new concentration. He caught Jakob's arm and pulled the old man close against his chest and began talking to him in a low urgent voice. Jakob's head moved in affirmation, then in denial. What have I done? Pan Zygmunt whispered to himself. What is happening now? The officer gave an order to the soldiers who were holding Jakob. The old man had suddenly become a bundle of black rags. The two soldiers turned him around and pulled him into the manor behind the officer. The cool dry shadows of the doorway swallowed them at once. The irritated officer stood staring dumbly at the empty doorway like a dog which had been anticipating the flavor of a bone and sees it snatched away. He played with his revolver. Then he loaded it. Then he began to shout and the brown mass was once again in motion: men stacked arms, discarded equipment; sentries tramped off to the corners of the manor; a soldier started marching up and down the veranda in front of the door. The peasants took off their oilskin caps and bowed to Pan Zygmunt.

—Why did you do that? Pan Zygmunt cried to Mierzwa, who stood back, astonished, because this master of the manor had never raised his voice to anyone.

—Do what, sir? Mierzwa said. What did I do?

—Why did you tell them that Jakob was the master here? What in God's name possessed you to do such a thing?

—I look ahead, that's what, Mierzwa said, stiff with sudden virtue. Some people—mind you, I'm not saying who—will say anything that comes to their heads. But I can look ahead.

—To what, you fool? What are you talking about?

—Well, Mierzwa said. It was either you or him, sir, wasn't it? Either these *Ruscy* would've taken him or they'd start sniffing around for somebody else, isn't that right? So isn't it better if they take him? That's what I mean by looking ahead.

—No! Pan Zygmunt cried from the depths of his pain, from the sudden knowledge of what he was about to hear, as if to deny the fear were to erase its cause. That's wrong! You shouldn't have done that!

But Burda said, suddenly enlightened: Well, sir, I didn't think of it, that's true, but there's a lot of truth in what Mierzwa says. Yes, sir, that's the truth all right!

Glowacki said: Old Mierzwa, who'd have thought it of him?

And Klos said: Yes, sir, if it's got to be either you or him it's better it's him. You're one of Ours, after all, and him, what is he?

—What do you mean *What is he?* cried Pan Zygmunt. Hasn't he been good to you? Hasn't he been fair?

—Oh, he's been good enough, Klos said. Never gave nobody no trouble 'sfar as I hear tell. Been fair enough on wages, easy on the rents . . . but, well, sir, good or no good, he's just a Jew, isn't that right? So what's the choice, eh?

—So it's better it's him than you, sir, Burda said.

—No, Pan Zygmunt said. That's not the way we've been thinking here. That's not what we were trying to do here, don't you understand?

—Well, Burda said. As to that, about what you was thinking here, and that, about what you was doing, you'd know best yourself sir, wouldn't you? We wouldn't know about things like that. We don't have time for thinking and that. That's for the gentlefolk, I always say. A peasant's got his hands full enough.

—But we were doing it for you, for all of us, Pan Zygmunt said. To give us a new unity, a new national spirit! Haven't you been listening to Father Boguslawski?

—We listen to him every Sunday, Glowacki said.

—But who can understand all these things? Mierzwa said. Maybe Chinamen. People say that he lived a long time among Chinamen.

—Don't take it so hard, sir, Burda said. Pan Jakob was . . . is . . . an old man, lots older'n you, and maybe his time would have come soon anyway. It's like they say, sir, it's the way of the world.

—Praised be the Lord Jesus Christ, Mierzwa said, bowing to Pan Zygmunt, who, rendered suddenly mindless, said mechanically: For a century of centuries . . .

The four peasants bowed with the dignity of their particular centuries, fortified by their own certainties. They began to walk across the meadow toward the nearest trees. The village lay just beyond the trees. Cutting straight through the woods they would be in the village in ten minutes; they would not use the devious track, which was reserved for strangers.

Pan Zygmunt found himself alone with the man on the stretcher: a long hard body fallen like a block of sandstone, a leathery gaunt face smeared by a week's growth of beard. The man's stillness only added to the violent distortions of the afternoon.

What have I done? Pan Zygmunt whispered to himself. What has happened here? I must have said something . . . done something . . . which endangered Jakob, but what could it be?

He sought immediate answers in a recapitulation of the day and, going beyond the day, he stumbled through his years, but answers eluded him. Yet there must be answers! Life could not pose the questions unless there were answers! Jakob had spoken of a God who was merciless but He was not sadistic! How could I have failed to read all the signs?

He knelt beside the stretcher but he didn't know whether he had knelt to help the wounded man or to pray. The act of prayer suddenly seemed like futility itself. His throat was dry; prayers would have died there like travelers confused in the desert. He felt no new life entering him from the soil, perhaps the land itself had no more life to give to him and his kind. What can I do to repent? As Jakob had once said, it is not enough to know that he who endures to the end shall survive.

Perhaps all this was merely a hallucination, the product of a mind unhinged by incomprehensible events. Perhaps I shall remain forever kneeling beside wounded men, at the feet of uncomprehending peasants, on land which has repudiated me.

Unsuspecting, he had broken the covenant with his land, or so the pulse of the soil told his kneeling body. He didn't know when this moment of betrayal had taken place, or how it had come about . . . perhaps this too was something merely imagined, a thought without foundations, an act lacking substance, but he knew that he must pay the price of broken covenants demanded by Jakob's merciless desert God.

. . . A cry, as of a small animal dismantled alive, came from the house. The sun still hesitated in the treetops. Then, as though this sound of pain had been the signal for which it had waited, the sun fell behind trees.

The chill was immediate.

Long shadows ran toward him from the forest, out of the deep past. They eveloped him with an icy whisper.

He thrust both hands into the sleeves of the habit and hugged himself against the knowledge of his infirmity, the perishable moment of his years, his spiritual extinction, and the impermanence of dreams. Had all his life, then, been nothing but a dream and he himself no more than an author of illusions? Part of the answer, he knew, lay in the weakening cries which came from the manor with dreadful regularity. This had been his only true inheritance.

He found that he was opening and closing his mouth, inhaling and exhaling to the accusatory rhythm of the cries, and echoing them in whisper.

Let it end soon, he prayed; his own life would be extinguished by Jakob's final silence.

His eyes fastened upon the gleam of a silver star, the tarnished braid of the man on the stretcher: a Polish cavalry brigadier general, to judge by his badges. His torn and soiled uniform was a catalogue of events, a form of testimony which, at another time, Pan Zygmunt might have found convincing. He wore a yellow-brown rag across his eyes, but whether this was a bandage or a blindfold it was impossible to say. He made no sound, no movement, prone on his back like a toppled idol, an overthrown monument to an impossible ideal, so that, for an impassioned moment of grief and regret Pan Zygmunt thought that the general was dead. But when he pressed his ear to the dusty tunic he heard the strong and measured beating of a heart. The general's wrists had been bound together with wire so tightly that the metal had disappeared in the flesh. His hands, grotesque in their swelling, had become empurpled like a cardinal's gloves.

Pan Zygmunt watched his own ineffectual hands probing for the wire. In his imagination the wire had become a link with the past, the present, and the future: a physical manifestation of the cries which filled his whole body. He didn't recognize the evidence of other connections. Whatever they may have been in a past which he no longer remembered, the span of centuries which had come so abruptly to an end this evening, their credibility had been destroyed by the reality of pain. Only new forms could arise from this reality; the past had disappeared.

But the general's lips were moving; he was trying to speak. Pan Zygmunt leaned over him the better to hear.

—Where am I?

The iron whisper had been cracked by thirst and fatigue.

—This is Duninowo . . . not far from the Lwów highway . . . I am Zygmunt Dunin . . .

He heard his own voice as if from a distance: the false creaky noise of an automaton, heartless and mindless, unfolding a recorded pattern of sounds without meaning.

The general's black lips split, drew into a smile.

—So . . . pleasant to be here again, he said.

—You have been here before, sir? We have met each other?

—Twice, I think. Once with the Englishman, de Wiart. Once, recently, to see your king stallion. My name is Anders. The Nowogrodzka Cavalry Brigade . . .

—Good God, forgive me, General, I wouldn't have known . . .

—I imagine not.

—Are you wounded, General? Where are you wounded? Is there anything I can do for you?

—I'd like to see . . .

Pan Zygmunt started tearing off the yellow-brown bandage. But the general was making his own rhythmic and metallic sounds: A little water . . . if you'd be so kind.

—I can find some brandy . . .

—They've given me no water in days . . . not much food either, but that doesn't matter . . . however, the water . . .

—I'll find some food, some milk! Pan Zygmunt said. And . . . shouldn't we do something about your hands?

—I no longer feel them.

Pan Zygmunt ran for water to the well, his heart leaped and hammered, his breath choked his throat. A thick pain pressed against his backbone, his arms became numb. Not yet, he begged. Please. No. The water splashed out of the wooden scoop. A glittering fog spread before his eyes.

—Here, sir, he said. If you could hold up your head . . . there . . . I'll help.

—Thank you, the general said.

—Why are they treating you like this? What do they want from us?

—Ask the Collector.

—Collector . . . ?

The general drank water, closed his eyes. —That handsome devil who looks as if he were born on horseback . . . the one who speaks Polish . . . His name is Szymanski, or something like that . . . he's here to collect the people they want.

—A Polish officer! Pan Zygmunt cried, astonished.

—No, the general said. He's theirs. A collector.

And then Pan Zygmunt knew the reason for the weakening screams which had now entered the beat of his pulse. The cries and his heart both fluttered uncertainly, hesitant as if unwilling to prolong the passion of the moment, yet persistent with their message of continuing life. Oh, Jakob, what have I done to you? Pan Zygmunt cried silently. But how could I have known? The irony of his attempt to preserve his own place in the passion, the immemorial pageant of the manor, which had unwittingly thrust the father of Avrum Mendeltort into torment, broke through the last barriers of his strength. Is there no ordered justice? he cried. No hope? Is there nothing in space and time but this great, overwhelming irony of events?

The answer, if it was an answer, came in a cry which was stronger than all the preceding messages of pain. It was an invocation, an appeal, and, possibly, a challenge. He took it as an order and an affirmation. It died on a half note.

. . . Only through suffering may we ascend to humanity; the passion on Golgotha had made not a God but a man.

The general said (patient, polite, and inflexible to the end): If you please . . . the water . . .

—At once! Pan Zygmunt said, held up the wooden scoop.

And at once the irritable officer appeared on the veranda. He no longer flourished his revolver.

He shouted.

Two soldiers came forward, lumbering out of the dusk like shaggy-headed bears. They picked up the stretcher and carried it into the house.

—To our next meeting, Panie Dunin, the general said.

—To our next meeting, sir, Pan Zygmunt replied.

He followed the stretcher to the manor, hardly knowing how he had got to his feet; the reservoirs had been finally emptied. The soldier at the door threatened him with a rifle, so he backed down the steps feeling a mild surprise that he was still capable of motion; the feeble cries had ceased on their last triumphant note, pierced in midflight like the legendary call of the Trumpeter of Kraków. Behind him, the soldiers had begun to light their bivouac fires. They brought hams and venison out of the back of the house, pulled dead geese and chickens out of their haversacks. White feathers, tinted a pale blue by the gathering darkness, floated through the air.

The irritable officer came to the head of the steps and stared at Pan Zygmunt gloomily, as though all that the old man represented—and the land, the country, and the distant city (still calling softly with its captive bells)—were a personal affront. He wore two tabs of dull metal on his collar and, as Pan Zygmunt watched, a gray louse crept out of his matted hair, lay parallel to the badges, and promoted him. He made a peremptory gesture to wave Pan Zygmunt away from the manor but when Pan Zygmunt remained where he was, unable to move, the officer turned and went back into the darkened house.

Pan Zygmunt stood like a penitent of another century at the foot of his steps. They were his as the house was his, and the land, the province, and the country, but they had suddenly become foreign to him. The blue-gray shadowed mass of the manor advanced and retreated before his fogged eyes. The old white-timbered walls appeared to be breathing. The winds of his imagination stirred invisible banners, chanted ancient cries which could no longer find an echo in his heart. The curved roof (which, Abel used to say, turned the house into a caravel) leaped toward the sky.

. . . Oh, let him learn to give uncharitably, he prayed to the vanished specters of his past. Let him abhor compassion . . .

He heard the manor, surely it was the manor, each weathered timber settling in the cool of its own autumn night, groan under the weight of men clustering in the doorway . . . Saw men erupting onto the porch carrying a little black-clad mannequin, noted the thin white wisp of hair awry in the moonlight, the yellow fingers of a parchment hand dragging across the steps . . .

The irritable officer was shouting and a bear-shaped man shambled into the orchard carrying a rope, and another followed, another grunted, picking up the ladder with the missing rungs. Pan Zygmunt also shouted, in protest, watched Jakob's body pulled toward the tree, stumbled behind the procession blinded by the fog . . . Felt his ineffectual old fists scraping against coarse cloth and watched a rifle butt swinging toward his head.

A sudden pain exploded in his face.

An animal was baying in the distance, and a drum was booming, and then the harsh coil of a hangman's noose hooked itself on the stubble of his chin.

He thought of Abel, who was so very different from himself and Jakob, the disappearing images of a canceled era, but who would surely join the immemorial march. Not even youth can plead innocence; there is no way to avert the terrible decree. It was the boy's nature to be careless, he argued as a lawyer at the Tribunal; he had spoiled himself into recklessness. Not because he was faithless, but because he was imaginative and always expected to keep the promises he made. I had not pointed him toward God, only toward a human ideal. In this respect, too, I have been a failure. Yet perhaps in that failure of omission rather than commission, the many things not done rather than anything accomplished, lay the seeds of success beyond the reach of most men's imaginations. It wouldn't occur to the boy, he pleaded, that his behavior was immoral as such things were reckoned, or that his modernistic thoughts were treason to his destiny and history; he didn't realize that all this was creating a reputation for him and that reputations kill as surely as the sacrificial blade. While we are so very young, he thought, we never realize that our actions have this terrible effect; it seems to us that people should judge us by what we feel and by what we think we are, rather than by what we show that we may be in the process of becoming something else. He hoped that Abel wouldn't make that necessary discovery after it was too late.

Must we always be too late? he thought, looking at Jakob's body turning on its rope, and asking the question for his dead friend as well as for Abel and himself. Words fell from him like stones, they made no sound in the fog below him. The ladder quivered gently under his feet as the branch bent under Jakob's turning weight. His eyes were blind with sudden disappointment.

. . . If they don't burn the house, and they have never done so, perhaps the ledgers will survive. And Abel . . .

Then, suddenly, the elegant officer had appeared on the porch, and he was shouting, spreading his arms, raising his hands palms out toward the hanging tree as if to will Pan Zygmunt to stand still, propped against the darkness . . . But Jakob was waiting. Pan Zygmunt stepped toward him through the missing rungs.

Time blew about him like a hurricane. Its roar filled his chest. The centuries which he had discarded were suddenly upon him with a savage cry. He was torn from his roots, sucked into the vortex, hurled into the dark infinity of space behind the stars, and vanished in the void.

The Forest

ABEL FELL TO HIS KNEES, and far on the horizon the burning sky went dark as if the forest and the near city, making public penance and act of contrition, had bowed before the shadow pressed upon them by night and new clouds.

The darkness danced before him, filled with moving shadows that sent him alternately into gloom and laughter. He knew that he and his military mentor were not the only men in the forest this night; the flare of a match, the pinpoint scarlet glow of an occasional cigarette, showed that there were others. No one spoke to them, no one else appeared on the track; it was as if each of the many invisible men had withdrawn into his own darkness deep inside himself and feared human contact.

Trees dwarfed them all, isolated them, reduced them to insignificant fractions. In this belt of woods, the last before the meadows of the manor, the trees were enormous. He felt their scorn, their soaring indifference to all the petty matters affecting mankind. He wanted to defy them, to send a challenge into their black crowns! But could he call up the necessary storms and invoke the lightnings? We need a little witchcraft here, a puff of sulphur and a touch of brimstone! Could we not possibly dispense, for a century or two, with all this solemnity, this melancholy worship of antiques? For all his efforts, he couldn't quite summon up the old laughing Gods, the Green Gods of the Forest in whom he fervently believed. They had sustained him through indifferent years and might be induced to do so again.

. . . No doubt the necessary levity will come back, he thought, when I need it most, when this damned weariness and confusion have had their honorable burial, when I can start to put together again all the fragments of the Essential Abel. When the Green Gods convened to plan the reconstruction they would undoubtedly employ the Essential Catherine, whose magic was proven. His weary mind tottered between images of childhood and recent experience and found no firm anchorages in his memory. Consideration of the immediate future would have to be deferred. Nameless threats leaped up before him, the two opposing currents of his blood collided and distorted vision. He peered through signs and portents that he couldn't read into a future where nothing was certain, out of a past where little was defined.

The forest closed about him in darkness and gloom and opened suddenly in surprising clearings of brilliant starlit sky. Tarski had gone to reconnoiter the edge of the woods and Abel was alone. He was conscious, then, of a special content, a sort of extraterritorial meaning that did not properly belong to the moment and that illuminated, in its own imperious glow, the cruel and unnecessary alliance that time and distance, both powerful enough to do their work alone, formed for their war against the brief and perishable human nearnesses.

In youth, in those expansive, ample, and unexacting moments when the coining of an epigram looked so convincingly like wisdom, he had thought that love should be pursued like glory for it's own sake. He had kept a diary in those experimental years, *The Journal of Abel Abramowski*, bound in imitation leather and locked with a key, in which he questioned and examined and rationalized and kept a wobbly watch over his conscience, stumbling like a child pursuing butterflies from one thought to another. None of these thoughts were properly his own. He stole them from the Dekabrists and Zola, Proust and Andreyev, Bergson, Flaubert, Nietzsche and Kazantzakis, Buber and Marx, St. Thomas Aquinas and Marcus Aurelius, whom he robbed with the hungry innocence of an explorer claiming an already populated continent for his distant sovereign. He read them in either Polish, German, French, or English along with Karl May's *Winnetou, the Red-skinned Gentleman* (a Christmas gift from his sardonic uncle whose name was never mentioned). And there had been, of course, the Polish literary fare from *Pan Twardowski*, the legendary gentleman who had sold his soul to the Devil, to *Pan Tadeusz*, who had tossed his boyhood imagination to the moon. He had been a pendulum in perpetual motion between hostile extremes, with no more logic to guide him than folklore, poetry, and epigrams provided.

When he began his wanderings, France offered her demonic logic, England provided the poise of anti-logic. America had offered the illuson of a firm, pragmatic direction.

In Poland, as he remembered it, time and the age in which a man lived seemed to change from city to city; in Lwów it was enough to enter a new street in order to move several centuries forward or back in history, so that the past was always present and always handy to ameliorate the effects of the present. But in America, where he squirmed for two years between cynical realities, there was no history earlier than the day before yesterday and no consciousness of history. And immigrants, from being people incessantly bombarded by and guided by discernible centuries, became lost souls cursed with no purpose beyond the needs of a mercenary moment. The common denominator, mark of merit, honors and prestige, as well as the sole accepted object of all aspirations, were openly commercial—something that Abel was unable to grasp or understand. Exposure to this savagely mechanistic culture was a shock comparable to landing naked and unarmed upon the rim of a hostile planet. In the small-town, ruthlessly pragmatic college where he taught Slavonic myths to five torpid students, among the intellectual mechanics so busy molding fresh cogs for the machinery which operated their gigantic country (and later, driven out by boredom into the New York literary and theatrical jungle), he fell completely in love with Catherine, needing her beauty to sustain him. By her own claims and definitions she was not beautiful but she conveyed an instant impression of beauty, so that everyone, men as well as women, grew momentarily silent when she entered any public place. The women gave, perhaps, one small sigh before acknowledging that there was no contest. Everything that he remembered about Catherine became flavorful and seasoned his longing. Her letters became a safe-conduct through mediocrity. He lived like a true exile only for her letters; without them he was fleshless, mindless in the wilderness. When she stopped writing in the middle of summer he lost all his bearings. As summer ended and the news from Europe acquired a certain frenzy, a touch of shrillness bordering on hysteria, he tried to break through the walls of American indifference as if some reassurance could be gained that way. But Americans, he found, had so much cold suspicion and contempt for anyone other than themselves that they couldn't care about what happened or might happen to anybody else. In late summer they said, as likely as not, that if Germany did go to war and invade the Poles (who, after all, were not French or English or anyone whom Americans had ever admired) it would be because the Poles deserved to be destroyed. What had they ever done to deserve compassion? What had they ever given to the world except a few pianists? It was an unknown land precariously pitched at the edge of Europe, a geographical equation like Darien or Antarctica, and furthermore: hadn't the Poles been cruel to the Jews? Such ignorance stupefied him and made him contemptuous.

In America, Abel had become a Pole as well as he could, unable to fit himself into that surreal *Lebensraum* that offered only groveling sycophancy or outright rebellion. He had come to the land of Jefferson and Paine and found them long gone. His little Polish label had suddenly acquired an immense importance. He yearned for Europe with her centuries of violence, her immemorial treasons, her history of monumental and bloody commitments, as he yearned for Catherine. I am behaving like a fool, he thought, there is no sense to dreaming. Shé is lost to me. I must destroy this intolerable yearning. Nothing except to see her will destroy this yearning. She is not as I have imagined her to be; simply by living she must make mistakes from which I shield her in my imagination.

He grew to hate America, to which he had come with such hopes that his eyes had filled with tears at the sight of the towering stone illusion rising from New York Harbor. Into his disappointment went all the bitterness of a disillusioned lover: America had betrayed him. He asked himself why he had come, from what had he been trying to escape? Was he an immigrant? He supposed that he might have been, although he hadn't consciously aimed at such a status. Had he left Lwów and Poland because he had begun to shake in old loyalties, because the fine prism of his true identity had become clouded by his father's inability to become a Pole? It was a possibility he had to consider.

Poland and Catherine . . . Catherine and Poland . . . they had become intertwined in his desire and hunger, so that he could no longer think of one without experiencing the loss of the other. One *was* the other, he thought—each lost when his letters from Catherine ceased.

Remembering brought pain. He didn't know if he would still be able to withstand its bright intensity. And yet Catherine, the forest, Lwów, and Poland were all he could think of. He longed for that eventual physical collapse when all thought would become impossible.

Luckily, he knew, he still had some of his defenses in good working order: the shield of the Jester had not been battered beyond recognition. He could still summon a sense of irony, laughter of a kind, a mild sort of cruelty with which to dissect gloomy profundities. Fatigue made him light-headed and careless with his thought and this also helped. (He could declaim. He could chant incantations.) He could be pitiless or loving. Words were his weapons. He could gather himself more or less together out of such pieces that lay close to hand and hold fast against all the assaults of his violated senses. Madness is by no means a cure-all, he knew, but it comes close to being an antidote for fear, and in the name of whatever it was that he was seeking he was quite willing to embrace a short personal insanity. One simply couldn't take anything very seriously when the Great Solemn Truth was wearing baggy pants and a conical hat! The thing to do was to get rid of this deadly seriousness as quickly as one could and to return to the joyful business of living, making love, seeking new experience, and resolutely turning one's back on what had proved to be, despite the frenzied efforts he had made in America, yet another illusion. To pit one frenzy against another is a loser's gambit. It is the nature of history and all things past that they have no future; thus, possibly, the Americans had been right, after all . . . One thing was certain: that nothing was certain; there wasn't a damn thing on which one could depend when one's moral backbone was up against the wall. To depend on moral forces other than one's own was utterly unrealistic, to adopt the credo of another man, simply because it offered *him* a reason for being, was not only folly but a form of treason to one's own possibilities. Whatever philosophy one is fortunate to stumble upon must be personal but all else must be kept at arm's length because, unlike pure thought, the objects and ideas of the relative world are all perishable and only a damn fool would lean on a cracked stick.

. . . A cold wind blew up suddenly from the depths of the forest, carrying with it the stench of the swamp, the sweet rot of fallen monoliths drowning in the mud pits.

. . . A fox barked, insistent, and the tree crowns stirred in a gathering wind. A small furry animal moved at the edge of his vision, hugging the forest floor where the air was warm. It had the coloring of an otter and some of an otter's joyful sense of mischief. But what would an otter be doing so far from a river?

Sharp creaks and cracklings, whispers, grunts, sighs, and weary rustlings drifted among the trees, but whether they were there only in his memory it was impossible to tell. This was a lovers' forest, and sighs and all the other sounds that crept across the screen of his imagination were not foreign to it. But this time, he thought, on this remarkable occasion, he sounds were far removed from love and from loving; death was around him in the mortal weariness of exhausted men and in their expectations.

Tarski returned then, and sat down on a boulder, his head between his hands. Abel could see that the major's hands were shaking. He's even more tired than I, Abel thought, astonished, how does he keep going?

—Well, he said, trying to be cheerful and sounding like a liar to himself. If it's all clear ahead we can be at the manor in a half hour or so. I can just hear Grandfather Zygmunt now: The prodigal has returned, we'd better kill something!

The major nodded, said nothing.

Abel said: Just think of sleeping in a bed again. Think of hot food, a tablecloth, eating off china plates . . . Who'd think one could forget civilization in only six weeks?

—They're there already, the major said quietly.

—Who? Abel said, and for a moment he really didn't know what the major was talking about.

—They have their bivouac fires all over the place.

And when Abel, refusing to believe what he had been told, asked how the major knew that these were bivouac fires, and said that, after all, seen from the head of the track the whole manor house was no bigger than a matchbox (that the fires could be something innocent, inconsequential), the major said wearily: Good God, boy, don't you think I know a bivouac when I see one?

—A fire is a fire, Abel said, insistent. There could be refugees camping in the meadow. This could be anything, anything at all. They even might be burning leaves.

—At this time of night?

—Bonfires, Abel said. Anything. Why bivouac fires?

—It would hardly be a jubilee celebration, the major said quietly. Take my word for it, I've seen enough night encampments to know what I saw.

Abel was appalled; his mind refused to consider any threatening possibility. The Soviets were there. He didn't understand why he had been surprised. It was inevitable that invaders would come to the manor; they had come to every other fragment of his country. Yet even in that moment which had thrust his private world, his childhood and progenitors, through the armor plate of his contrived indifference, his first shocked bitter thought was *No rest, no food,* and it was only second thought which focused on Pan Zygmunt and Jakob Mendeltort. The orderly progression of assumptions and expectations which he had already translated into certainties collapsed immediately. He was again a knot of contradictions inextricably tangled about his own self: a mass that would have defied the sword of Alexander. No evil plot could have bound him tighter about his invisible core, or better hidden the loose ends that might have been threaded through the eye of a definition. . . . The tethered mare and horses had been clues. He had ignored them. History was a clue.

—So they are there, he said finally. Well, that doesn't necessarily mean that anyone is hurt. Why should they bother with a couple of old men?

The major said quietly: There wouldn't be a reason.

—You're quite sure about that?

The major nodded. The knot of Gordius had no meaning for him. Tarski had been defined by action; he had no existence outside the manifest, Abel was convinced.

—You're not lying to me? You wouldn't lie to me, would you?

—Why should I lie?

—I don't know, said Abel.

—I never lie, said the major.

—I know that. That's why I believe you.

One must believe in something, the major muttered, and shrugged.

—I've always trusted you, Abel said. "You've never misled me. You wouldn't do it now. And, anyway, the war is over; you said yourself that we were no longer a military objective.

—Yes, said the major. That is what I said.

—So if nobody can be bothered to harm *us* . . .

—They shouldn't do any harm to two old men, the major finished Abel's uncompleted sentence, then explained wearily: I went about halfway across the meadow. I heard them singing. There's no point in talking about it any more.

—They were singing?

—They always sing.

—Well then, said Abel, looking up, relieved. It can't be so bad there . . . I mean, if they were singing, don't you think that's an encouraging sign? They couldn't very well harm anyone and then sit around singing, could they?

—I'm sure that everything's in good order, the major said precisely. Stop worrying about it.

—I can't do that very well, Abel said. Grandfather Jakob is a very old man. Grandfather Zygmunt isn't much younger, you know. He has a bad heart. There must be some way that we can make sure that nothing's happened to them.

—No, said the major. We still have our orders. We're not to expose ourselves to unnecessary danger. The Army needs us, it doesn't need old men. We go on to Lwów, and then to France. We're not to resist the Bolsheviks or provoke them but we are not allowed to let ourselves be captured or disarmed. The marshal's last order was quite clear about that.

—Right now the marshal is having his dinner in Rumania, Abel said.

—Stop this nonsense, the major said sharply. It doesn't become the uniform you're wearing. I'll say this just once more! There's no reason in the world why any civilized human being would want to hurt a couple of old men. So pick up your pack, Abel, we're going on.

He started walking down the track, back the way they had come. After a moment Abel followed him. Thoughts threatened him the way clouds menace the head of a mountain. Anger had been a bright illumination but its flash had been momentary, hardly a spark in the darkness of weariness and confusion. The man of action had not been confused: he had reconnoitered, assessed the situation, made his decision, and that was the end of it for him. The man of imagination couldn't even stumble upon a beginning. Abel no longer felt the various cadences of his pain. He was no longer walking on a clay track winding through a forest but on a curtained stage. He had followed Tarski for forty-five days through the ritualized leaps and bounds into ditches: a puppet in search of a puppeteer . . . through the red night of that memorable village where his immaculate boots had been spattered and his mind had tumbled off a hillside . . . the long road from defeat . . . largely because this was his role in the drama, but partly because Tarski had become, *in loco parentis*, the rock which would bear the foundations of his hopes. The war had been too short for comradeship and friendships, and there had been no one else whom he was willing to trust.

The trees crowded close about the track as if to erase it, as though this narrow man-made scar was an intolerable wrong. The trees stated clearly that man had no rights in the forest and was permitted there only on their sufferance.

The wind had died down.

The last of the day's warmth left the forest floor, and the animals had ceased calling to each other.

And now, more and more often, they were coming across large trees that had fallen; and Abel found an odd exhilarating satisfaction in the sight of these contemptuous giants toppled by the wind, as if their fall held out a promise of a new beginning. They were nothing like the giants of Bialowieza, where it took a dozen men to span the base of their trunks and where the trees had names given to them respectfully by men. The giants of Bialowieza could indeed be defiant of time, but here, in these woods, defiance died on the wind; nameless and rootless, rotting in the shadow, the trees were empty boasts, the remnants of ancient pretensions.

A sudden flash of silver gave life to the shadows, a nervous motion broke into the stillness, and a great white horse trotted out of the night. The narrow head was high, the delicate nostril flared, the mane was a watery turbulence. The horse stood at the edge of the track like a triumphant carving, sullen and imperious, one sharp slim hoof poised as if to test the consistency of the air which quivered around him with reflected moonlight. It had been years since Abel had seen him but he knew him at once.

—Rhetoric, Rhetoric, he called softly, holding out his hand.

The horse wouldn't come to him, he knew well enough, although once, when Abel was a child and the horse a foal, he had held the velvet muzzle in his hands and traced the contours of the golden eyes.

—Oh, King, he said. Your White Imperial Majesty.

His outstretched hand offered no temptations to the horse, which had never known a bridle or a saddle and which, in royal fashion, had never been bribed with a lump of sugar.

—Forgive the *lèse majesté*, Abel said, withdrawing his hand. One quite forgets one's place living among humans.

The great horse played with the moonlight as a pool might play with the torches of men who fish after sunset; he and the moon had secrets to confide, reflections to exchange: masterless brothers in a magic moment. Then the horse tossed his head in one imperative motion, the silvered mane flew; the horse crossed the track, picking his way delicately through the ruts and deadfall, and vanished in the shadows on the other side.

The light had come and gone, life had appeared and disappeared, and the dark forest, malevolent in contrast, darkened perceptibly.

Then Tarski halted, listening.

The forest was ending. They could no longer hear the refugees on the road. They were hearing trucks, horses, and the droning murmur of a sleepless town.

—We'll rest here for a bit, Tarski said quietly. Ready for a rest?

—Yes.

—The comrades ought to have some pickets or an outpost around here somewhere. Let's draw a good breath, get some bearings, then push on. From now on we had better be careful.

—Is that Lwów up ahead? Abel asked.

He realized immediately that it could not be Lwów. The lights were too few and too dim, the sounds were too timid.

—No, that's Malechow, Tarski said.

—Then we're almost home. If we pushed on we'd be in Lwów by morning.

—Do you feel like pushing on?

—I could try.

—We'll rest for a while, the major said. A tired man makes too many mistakes. A leaden head doesn't make inventions.

—Mine could be gilded for a Christmas tree, Abel said.

The major smiled, nodded. —There's nothing wrong with your head that a week at home won't cure. You've been away from us too long, that's all, I should think . . . How long have you been away?

—Almost four years. But it seems much longer.

Then they were quiet for a series of reflective moments, listening, because they heard the sounds of a large body passing nearby, breaking twigs and branches, and so they knew that it was not an animal but a man. Like all the other men in the forest, they avoided their own kind as much as possible. There seemed to be a universal wish not to be drawn into contact with anyone else. This was the first heritage of Poland's incomprehensible September, a retreat to the depths of each individual's being where he might come to terms, in safety, with his own shocked mind and violated spirit. When the darkness was relatively silent again, Abel said carefully:

—We *could* go down into Malechow. If we took off our coats nobody would know that we were officers.

—And what would we do there?

—Perhaps someone would give us something to eat.

—Are you that hungry?

—It must be near to ninety hours since we've had anything hot to eat. But no, since you ask, I don't feel very hungry. Still, I could use a bed.

—Once you lie down you'd never be able to get up again.

—That sounds like paradise.

—And it would end like paradise ended, Tarski said.

He laughed softly and began to whistle an old Russian drinking song, a student song from before the Revolution, that Abel recognized as one of his father's favorites.

—Do you think that they're in Malechow?

—Why not? They're everywhere else around here. If you don't mind I'd rather not walk into a bleary-eyed, trigger-happy Kalmuk with booze in his belly. So do your best on leaves for an hour, tomorrow night you'll sleep in your own bed.

—And then what?

—Then we'll see.

—Are you really going on with this?

—That goes without saying.

—Do you understand why I can't go with you?

—I wouldn't even try. That's a matter for your conscience, not for mine.

Then he added with a slyness that Abel would not have suspected: But I'll give you a few days in Lwów to change your mind.

Abel laughed, said: Why did you ever become a soldier, Uncle? You'd make a fine lawyer. You have that necessarily devious mind.

—Well, I set out to study law along with your father, but then the Great War broke out, and then the Russian Revolution, then there was their Civil War and our own war with the Bolsheviks . . . bullets tend to knock the law out of a man's head. Then, later, soldiering seemed like the most useful thing to do. I had got used to living like a soldier. It would have been too hard to go back to the law. And, anyway, we don't often get to decide our own fate.

—And now the Bolsheviks are here again, Abel said.

—For a while.

—You think it's only for a while?

—What else is there to think? In spring the French and English will start their offensive and drive all this scum to the Urals, along with its German friends.

—What do you think they're going to do here in the meantime?

Tarski went on whistling for a minute longer, then said carelessly: I don't know what they want from us this time, why they came here, but I don't want them to get their hands on me.

—That major, Abel said reflectively, before that last attack, the one with the monocle . . .

—Benedykt? What about him?

—He said they were our brother Slavs, remember?

—What else could you expect from a man who has two good eyes and wears a monocle? Old General Olszyna, the commandant of Grodno, thought that they came as friends. He drove out to meet them. They put the poor old man up against a barn door and shot him to pieces.

—Their leaflets tell us that they've come as friends . . .

—There are other leaflets that urge our men to shoot all officers. That's not very friendly. Now, why don't you get a little sleep?

Abel breathed the sweet stench of rotting leaves, the powdery smell of dryness made vivid by chill. He felt a deep hollow pounding start at the roof of his consciousness and ebb to his stomach. Beside him, Tarski sat astride a fallen beech as though still on horseback.

Abel asked sleepily, incurious: How do you know about that general at Grodno? We were never there.

Tarski closed his eyes, yawned, stretched, and said up to the stars: Oooo-hah!

Then he said, his voice cracked with exhaustion: Somebody told me on the road.

Then he said: But it's never that simple with the Russians, any Russians . . . White, Red, or whatever. They simply aren't like anybody else. You always know where you are with the Germans. You may not like where you are with them but you always know what you can expect. As to our brother Slavs . . . hmm . . . God himself doesn't know what to make of our brother Slavs.

—Well, Abel said, searching with care among the debris of his thoughts, weighing and considering, reaching instinctively for the traditional crutch, the alpha and the omega of his father's judgments: Throughout our history . . .

—Ah, history, history, the major said abruptly. I'm up to here with history . . . Besides, son, these are not the Russians that I used to know.

—You mean that you can't understand them any longer?

—I mean that I don't know what to expect from them! You simply can't make any assumptions about Russians. Listen, do you think that our Russian border is just another national frontier? It's the edge of the world! You step across and you are truly on another planet, and nothing that has ever had any meaning for you makes any sense at all. Everything over there is the opposite of what you've been taught to believe, everything is different . . . Their culture, the sources of their thought, your precious sense of history, my sense of morality . . . Their concept of man himself is incomprehensible to us . . . And it's not just the difference between European values and the outlook of Asia! That would be too simple, it would at least offer a rational explanation . . . I've known as many Russians as I've known Poles and I've always liked them and, let me tell you, that didn't make me popular in some quarters. But understand them? Follow their reasoning? Never, not even in the best days in St. Petersburg, when it was still called St. Petersburg, when I first knew that mad uncle of yours, oh, long before I even met your father . . . I didn't meet my Russians in a history book or in a newspaper.

—Then you should know what to expect from them.

—I know what to fear, Tarski said as though he were speaking to himself as much as to Abel. Yes, I think I know what to fear.

Then he was silent for a long moment, nodding to himself, so that Abel thought this man who had so many admirable qualities, and yet whom Abel could no longer admire, had fallen asleep. Abel pitied him because the man was only what he was and would never be able to cross his own narrow boundaries. He is like my father, he thought: a man complete in himself and yet only a fragment of what he could be.

But finally the major said in a voice which seemed as aloof and remote as the roof of the night: There's something that I have to tell you . . . Back there, when we were near the manor . . . you remember?

—Yes?

—When we were talking, after I came back . . .

—Yes? You suspected something wasn't right?

—I saw two bodies hanging on a tree, the major said wearily.

—Two bodies! Abel cried.

—One was a woman, I think . . . wore some kind of robe . . . they were on the other side of the fires. I couldn't see them very well.

—Two bodies! And you told me there was nothing to worry about!

—I still say so. Two bodies, one possibly a woman, doesn't mean that anything has happened to your grandfathers.

—But this shows violence! This is proof of violence! What else would you need? If they can murder two people, they can murder four . . . a hundred! Why didn't you tell me?

—It would have meant your death, the major said simply.

—My death! Abel cried.

—You would have done what all young fools do, rush headlong to disaster. I wouldn't have been able to control you.

—So, Abel said. To save me from myself or, more likely, so that you wouldn't have to see that you can no longer control anyone, you told me there was nothing to worry about!

—You wouldn't even have got near the manor . . .

—So you told me about the happy Russians singing around their fires, Abel said, contemptuous. You liar! Who are you to talk about human beings . . . senses of morality? You're a cold, calculating, self-righteous machine. All compromises justified! You're not a human being at all.

Tarski rose suddenly, his face gray with anger even in that insufficient light, but his voice was tight, quiet and controlled: Two dead men do not make a country, Abel. Our whole country is carpeted with corpses, hundreds of thousands of people have died in these last few weeks, and God only knows how many millions more are going to die. If you must be angry, fight to avenge all our dead, not for some private family reason of your own.

—You callous bloody-minded bastard, Abel said.

—Abel, cried Tarski. As long as you're wearing that uniform . . .

—It'll come off as soon as I can find something else to wear! You've just lost the right to tell me anything. I believed you. I might have followed you even to your precious new war . . . But you've lied to me, so what else have you lied about? I'm going back to the manor house! If there is any kind of war that can make sense to me that's where I shall find it.

—You are a soldier! Tarski cried. You have no right to make decisions on your own behalf.

—You and I don't even belong to the same species, Abel said, and rose.

—Wait, Tarski said. Listen. A man may appear brutal, often callous, He may sometimes seem unconcerned with the value of human life. But can't you also think of him as brave, resourceful and—in his profound understanding of the word—a patriot? An honorable man?

—I'll leave that to his profound understanding, Abel said.

Tarski said quietly: For the last time, I order you to stay. If you leave now you'll be a deserter.

But Abel didn't listen, knew that he would never again listen to

Major Tarski or any of his kind. He slung his haversack on his shoulders and headed back toward the forest path.

The night had acquired a solidity which seemed impermeable, elusive, and eternally mocking, as were all the definitions for which he was seeking. The moon had slid under a heavy cloud laden with thunderbolts, the promise of winter. Whole companies of congealing hours were yet to march past before the winter came, before the fires burned down and the last tendrils of smoke blew away from the ruins. Now, the hours which he paced through the indifferent forest were only an interlude before a cold captivity.

The moon fled through the clouds, the clouds seized the moon, and, for a moment that seemed like a lifetime, Abel felt an unreasoning fear that the moon would never reappear, that there would never be another sunrise, and that the night was permanent.

But gradually, as he walked, night gave way to the cold morning hours and then it was dawn, and tree crowns were suddenly clear and black against a pearl-gray sky, still and pale as water under ice, and then he was listening to the muted clatter of a military encampment in the near distance. He pictured the invaders in the meadows he knew as intimately as his own lost childhood, heard nearby calls, the drone of a song, the neighing of a horse driven out to pasture under the icy stars . . . Smelled burning chicken feathers and meat and the acrid reek of black tea in a metal cup and sour bread and pine and dry soil and the stench of unwashed male bodies under military greatcoats . . . Saw the huge bonfires taller than the house, and the grotesque shapes with heads made animal by fur. He heard the screams of a butchered sow and thought of a bestiary gone mad.

The windows of the manor house were full of lanterns and shadows that seemed to be on fire. The main door hung drunkenly open to the soft autumn morning and flights of moths splattered their dark bodies against broken glass. The tallow candles in the windows of the village huts gleamed among trees, went out one by one.

He was no woodsman but he knew this forest. The trees and clearings were his memories. The meadow was childhood. The curving roof of the old house had been the quarterdeck on which the child Abel had stood for hours, driving a mutinous crew . . . And never mind, my hearties, that shortly we'll fall off the edge of the world . . .

He saw the oak tree, darker than the others because of the great flower of flames unfolding behind it.

Strange fruit swung gently.

Grandfather Zygmunt had turned into a brown potato bag in his monkish robe, and Grandfather Jakob Mendeltort's wispy white hair was moving in the breeze. The two old men hardly bent the branch on which they were hanging. Grandfather Zygmunt's bare feet turned clockwise with a gentle grace; Jakob, perverse as ever, twisted anticlockwise. Dead dreamers, Abel thought, paying for the privilege of having been human. His eyes were dry. He thought that he was beyond such simplicities as sadness. The Russian soldiers' lazy laughter shocked his imagination and his hopes for mankind.

From where he lay in a tangle of roots, ferns, and brambles on the lip of the ravine behind the orchard, Abel looked toward the hanging men, saw them as his past. On the green mound that barely cleared the tops of the trees stood a gray stone tower, partially a ruin, which an ambitious ancestor had tried to call a castle. Each of his childhood friends (the trees, the stones, the absent horses) had something to say. Other friends lay in ranks, in companies and battalions as they had fought on every hillock, in each clump of trees, in streets which no longer had order or delineation, in mounds of immolating rubble, along village fences, driven into the soil as if to sanctify it and to stake the claim of future generations. And had they all known in their final moments that sacrifice without consent was only empty ritual which mocked the sacrament?

The two dead hanging men seemed suddenly nameless and unknown to him. They seemed to be weightless in the light morning wind.

And now three other men appeared on the porch between the Doric columns. One was the old village priest, Father Boguslawski, whom Abel knew as well as he had known the dead men, and who was also suddenly nameless, a part of his past. The two other men, who now came off the porch and into the orchard, were Russian officers. One of them shouted, scratched his shaven head, stamped in enormous concertina boots, and the soldiers began to get lazily to their feet. The other Russian officer adjusted the hang of an elegant tunic over theatrically flared breeches, corrected the angle of his blue military cap, and drew on his gloves. Firelight made them vivid in scarlet and white.

The elegant Russian officer turned his back on the oak tree and its dangling burdens, and looked across the overgrown autumn flower garden toward the ravine, and Abel was suddenly and unreasonably certain that the dark Gypsy eyes were fixed ironically on his. His right hand traveled to his side where the heavy Vis pistol had hung for six weeks, but his hands were shaking, and the Vis (he remembered, angry with himself) had been buried under a roadside chapel several days ago. The Russian, who stared unsmiling across the ravine, seemed to understand, his eyes were full of paradox and conflict in the uncertain light. He turned and touched Jakob Mendeltort's cracked shoes with his fingertips, gave them a thoughtful twist.

The dead man revolved.

The priest was saying something in a low, pleading tone, and Abel strained to hear him.

—A decent burial, the priest said. Is that too much to ask?

The unkempt Russian officer cursed terribly and kicked the priest, and the priest staggered backward, flapping his black-robed arms, and tripped over a rake. Then, on his knees, he said: What harm would it do?

—It isn't enough to kill a man, the elegant officer said in perfect, unaccented Polish. Corpses, you see, have a way of staying alive in people's memories, and memories make legends. Graves can become a sort of monument, you see. Legends must be destroyed before they are born.

The priest said: I don't understand you.

The elegant Russian said: Why not? You make your living from a legend made out of a corpse. Your name is Boguslawski, is that right?

—Yes, the priest said.

—He Who Praises God, the elegant officer translated for his sullen and unkempt subordinate, then turned his back on him, said to the priest, amused: Your name could get you ten years for religious propaganda. You've known this pair long?

—Yes, the priest said. They were decent men, they deserve decent burial.

—I know the kind, the Russian said abruptly. Graveyards are full of them. A generation raised on the classics, with an ideal of fidelity and steadfastness and faith in the impossible, and so full of their precious Poland that there's no room in them for any other love. Duty and Responsibility and Honor and Sacrifice: the simplest philosophy possible for a civilized man. They don't take into account the processes of change; they defy the realities of living, trying to reduce them to the simplicities of faith; they stand athwart the path of human evolution into a higher order. Life is a series of frantic responses to events beyond our control . . . and all such men can do is argue about it!

The priest bowed his head, waited silently.

The officer said: Have I surprised you, priest?

They were so close in the still air that even the old priest's labored breathing had become audible. Or perhaps (Abel thought) it was the old house which was breathing then, the trees which sighed and whispered. Abel could hear the soft creaking of the turning ropes.

—You seem to know us well, said the priest.

The officer glanced into the branches and again touched Jakob Mendeltort's cracked shoes. —My father was Polish. He also couldn't understand that all ideals must change as reality changes.

—God teaches differently, the priest said.

—The Gods of yesterday are the toppled idols of tomorrow and not worth one drop of blood spilled on their behalf.

—My two friends wanted change, the priest said.

The officer smiled, looked into the branches, said softly: I know, I remember . . . arguments, discussions . . . The enemies of freedom do not argue, priest; they shout and they shoot . . . And that's the end of all the arguments.

—How does it help you to hang two old men?

The officer shrugged politely, lit a cigarette. —Hanging these two was an accident, he said. It was unnecessary. My dour comrade misunderstood my order. He is a zealous man, trained in the new way. But in the long run it doesn't make much difference provided nobody makes saints out of them.

—God help you, my son, the priest whispered.

Indifferent, the darkly handsome officer said: I warned you about religious propaganda. Or are you trying to become a martyr?

—No, the priest said.

—I'm told that it's a sin for priests to seek martyrdom.

—Yes, said the priest. It is.

—Then your God and mine are in agreement, said the officer. The last thing we want is to create any Polish martyrs, we have enough of our own on our hands. Memorials to a dead past are inconvenient when you're setting up a new social order.

—Then hide our dead, the priest said. But let them be buried.

—I know my business, I assure you, at least as well as you know yours, the elegant officer said, and gave a brief order. Surely, you don't believe that this is something new?

—I don't suppose that anything could be new for you or for me, the priest said.

—You see? the officer said, laughing. We are in agreement.

Abel closed his eyes.

In his brief war, the short accelerated course in death and destruction, he had seen many horrors, dead men, women driven mad by loss, lives destroyed for no apparent reason . . . but had it really been a war, or was it rather a simple military execution of a way of life? No one had asked the dead if they had consented to their sacrifice. There could be no such thing as a mass ideal, he thought, looking at the dead men swinging on their ropes. Now, they could tell him nothing. Sooner or later, he knew, he would have to define himself completely or be forever at the mercy of others' ideals.

And, in the meantime, a grave had been dug.

Two soldiers had picked up the ladder with the missing rungs, the

ladder that Abel recognized as the one through which he had fallen
while stealing apples from a neighbor's orchard, and they leaned the
ladder against the oak, and one man climbed the ladder and swayed
above his laughing and joking companions as he sawed on the ropes
with a pocketknife. The ropes parted, one after the other. The corpses
fell with a dry rustling sound.

Father Boguslawski had remained on his knees and now bowed his
head above the dark flat bundles that lay at the foot of the oak tree,
and the unkempt officer shouted at him and kicked him again, and four
soldiers came up and seized the black bundles and tossed them into the
hole in the ground.

—I thought we had an agreement, you and I, the elegant officer said,
amused, to the priest. There *is* no grave here, remember? No martyrs,
no corpses, not even what is sometimes called an administrative error
on which to light a candle on All Souls' Day. And there is nothing for
you to pray for, or about, since there is no one to hear your prayers except me, and I'm not likely to react to them.

The soldiers had kicked the hole full of dry earth and now stamped it
flat, and then two others came staggering around the side of the house
carrying an uprooted rhododendron bush and planted it into the freshly
covered grave.

—You see? the elegant officer said. I do know my business. When
that bush has rooted, no one will ever know what had happened here.

Then Abel heard the whine and stutter of a truck climbing in low
gear through the woods. The sound had probably been there for some
time but he hadn't noticed it before. The elegant officer lit a cigarette
and looked toward the sound and, immediately, two soldiers carried a
stretcher from the house and set it on the ground.

The Russian officers walked away, and the soldiers began to gather
their packs and equipment, their looted bundles, their dead chickens,
the bedding they had carried from the house, and the contents of Pan
Zygmunt's cellars. The priest got up, went to the stretcher, and knelt
beside it, making the sign of the cross.

—Well, Father, said the man on the stretcher. It seems as though we
are going to be companions on a journey.

—It would seem so, General. Are you in great pain?

—No, said the dry clipped voice that Abel remembered as issuing
commands in a manor house no different from his own, on another day,
in other woods, before a night of battle. The general asked: Did they
kill Pan Dunin?

The priest nodded, sighed.

The truck wound its way out of the woods, wobbled across the
meadow.

—There is our transportation, I believe, the general said. But we'll be back one day, we always return.

—So God has always willed, the priest said.

Abel crawled backward from the lip of the ravine. He stepped into the deeper darkness of the woods, rose, and began to walk. Ahead, the bells of Lwów, his home, kept calling in captivity. There was in them, he thought, a certain Polish truth.

PART TWO

NOVEMBER

Catherine

WHEN SHE AWOKE DAY HAD ALREADY DAWNED, but it was still early and the house was quiet. She lay very still on her cot, with eyes half closed against the gray intrusion of a November day, experiencing the luxury of silence. It was a false silence that existed only in her mind. Her father's measured breathing came forcefully from the leather couch under the glass-bead curtain (a gift from Cousin Wlada, the family's world traveler, artiste, and exotic conversation piece, who now made popping teapot sounds on the ottoman); her mother's difficult breath and Emil's childish snoring came from the combination of armchairs that served as their bed.

She listened to her family's sleep, the mingling of their breath which, in pagan times, would have meant a joyful congress of spirits, now manifested by white cloudlets in an icy room. She thought herself remarkably alone, the only wakeful person high on a mountain peak above clouds; in the imaginary blue abyss below her the world lay locked under a witch's spell, never to awaken. But the dull sounds of a waking city began to force their way through the velvet portieres of her father's study; the glass top of his desk, that expensive mass of ornamented wood no longer heaped with papers and books, captured the half-light which she would have gladly kept outside for a little longer. The light broke whitely on plates, cups, and saucers, gilded the Primus stove into a magic lantern; all that she needed to turn back the light was an incantation.

This room was magic early in the morning, the repository of Cousin Wlada's foreign adventures, where the child Catherine had crept to find transition between her fairy-tale dreams and the realities of the breakfast table, schoolgirl sailor collars. And here was Cousin Wlada herself, always here in Vuillard's heavily framed "Yvonne Printemps" no matter what corner of an exotic world happened to be her home of the moment. Here the child Catherine, no longer a child, could always visit with her glamorous cousin (actress and rather careless wife of a stiff and proper minor diplomat), whose lightning visits to Lwów turned Father's academic household into chaos. Wlada didn't visit, rather she descended, scattered gifts and sweetmeats and glittering phrases, tales of Paris and Arabia, and whirled away again leaving a particularly stunned and desperate silence. Yvonne Printemps could have been her portrait: the careless sunburst of her flaming hair, huge scarlet mouth wide in enormous pleasure, elongated eyes like a pair of intelligent lozenges, oh, and the life! She had arrived from her country home the day before yesterday on a peasant cart loaded with potatoes; her gifts were always timely.

Daylight advanced, encroaching on her thoughts, the precious moment of privacy and silence; light blew apart the shadows on the gilded frames. Outside, the black expanse of asphalt, spotted like a leopard skin with dead leaves, red and yellow, appeared to breathe as the leaves shifted in a gusting wind.

She heard the first tentative mutterings of the five Porembas in her parents' bedroom, and the thin morning sobs of Jankele, youngest of the half dozen Rashevskys in the dining room (a gentle child who hid under tables when an airplane flew over and who relived each night the terror of the highways): seven adults, four children tossed into the city by war and its aftermath. No sound yet from her own virginal room of girlhood, where Jurek Bednarski and Janek Stypenko kept an uneasy truce between Nationalist Poland and Nationalist Ukraine; each slept under a separate wall on sacking and paper, their backs to each other, Catherine's white-curtained bed unused; a senseless quarrel in a senseless time. No sound from the storage room, where Red Militiaman Ferenc Karoly, the uninvited guest with rifle and armband, came to sleep in the daytime. No sound from Bronka in the kitchen. And this brought the question: which piece of furniture must be sacrificed today? And had there ever been a time when firewood could be bought? It didn't seem likely.

Dark shadows shift, dissolve. Objects reappear: twelve chairs with backs like lyres, antimacassars. Once as a child, hearing the word for the first time, she thought that these were counterrevolutionists. Behind glass, books; these must be made to disappear today.

Father himself hangs framed in his darkly paneled study, which has now become the family's entire apartment, in a magnificent copy of Gauguin's "Self Portrait: Near to Golgotha," or so she thought when she felt prophetic: he didn't like to put labels on people, thought of them all as humans, did not permit a separate bench for Jews in his lecture rooms, protested "Aryan paragraphs" in the bylaws of professional societies; a quaint point of view which, along with his love for French Impressionists, drove him from the university less than a year ago. Dr. Poremba could have sat for Toulouse-Lautrec's "Paul Viaud as an Admiral," minus the horse pistol. Ancient politics among Silesian miners had driven him and his family to Lwów (as far from the Germans as Polish roads could take him), along with the Rashevskys, wealthy Jews from Zywiec, who, in turn, brought Janek.

(A recent conversation between Jurek and herself: Jurek, intense and always dramatic, a quality that she had found momentarily arresting when they had first met: *I won't have that Ukrainian traitor sleeping in your bed; as your fiancé, I insist that he sleeps on the floor.* Herself, untouched by his archaic romanticism but not wishing to add to the young man's distress: *It's such a comfortable bed, someone should use it . . . It's not as if I were going to be in it . . .* Jurek, dark hair falling across a pale forehead with the little scar acquired in the siege: *That's not the point at all!* Herself, knowing his answer before she asked her question: *Well, what is the point?* Jurek, eyes full of the knowledge of defeat, the pain of lost pride: *It's the idea that we still have something undefiled! Don't you understand?*)

And now the last two of Father's evocative favorites advance out of shadow, Renoir and Manet, each a source of a particular disturbance in harsh morning light; the "Artist" looked at her with Abel Abramowski's brooding eyes, causing a sadness, a touch of guilt because she had hurt him by not answering letters; the naked fullness of "Bather with a Griffon" stirred Catherine's own awareness of her unused body. With that awareness came an unaccountable measure of regret, some anger, some impatience.

This was the last day that she would see the paintings. Today was to be Camouflage Day (as Dr. Poremba put it, rapidly blinking a conspiratorial eye) or Vulgarization Day (as Cousin Wlada put it). Everything of beauty was to be taken down, rolled up, and hidden in the attic under dust or debris; the household was to become immediately proletarian. *Reductio ad absurdum.* Nothing was to be left that might disturb the new Soviet masters. (*We will achieve drab poverty if it kills us,* Cousin Wlada said.) And poverty is an enemy of beauty.

Books had to be destroyed; books are dangerous since they are evidence of an intelligent mind. The children would smuggle the torn pages out of the apartment and scatter them in parks; the leather bindings would become shoe soles. The children would collect pine cones and multicolored stones to fill the empty shelves. There was to be no sweeping or dusting from now on. No more window washing. Down with the bourgeoisie and its velvet portieres.

She got up, shivering in the sudden cold, wrapped in her own white breath; dressed quickly, taking advantage of remaining shadow. Ribbed brown wool stockings (must mend them later in the day) snapped to a childish garter belt, a skiing sweater, a wool skirt, and Carpathian slippers of tooled leather, a memento of a mountain vacation. Emil watched, as always, wide-eyed in the shadow of the vast armchair. And, as always, she was angry and oddly ashamed. Angry because her brother's ten-year-old curiosity was a reminder of new times, ashamed because her body, which troubled her so, had been created for a man's admiration, not a child's.

—What are you staring at? she hissed at the child. Go back to sleep, you little monster.

—Hee-hee-hee, said Emil, then cried: Monster! Monster! Monster!

Mother's long white hand rose out of the shadow and pulled the boy's blond tousled head out of sight.

—Are you getting up, child?

—Yes, Mother.

—I'll be up in a moment.

—No need. Bronka has gone for the water. Esterka and I will make the breakfast, if you can call it breakfast. It will all take a little while yet, go back to sleep, Mother.

—There is a lot to do today, isn't there? This is the day, isn't it?

—Camouflage Day? Yes, it is. Isn't it all rather silly?

—Yes, I suppose it is, but there is no need to attract attention.

—Yes, I suppose that's right.

—It's an odd thing for a mother to say to her daughter, isn't it? Don't attract attention.

—I understand how you mean it. And anyway, I would much rather have a man admire me for . . . well, the way that Father admires you.

The lie had left her a little out of breath; she didn't think for a moment that she had fooled her mother.

—For my brilliant mind? Professors should never marry other professors, that leads to inbreeding.

—And idiot children?

—And more professors. Well, I'll be up in a moment, I'll take your cot down; go along now.

—And students shouldn't marry students, is that also right?

—I'll never interfere in your marriage plans. It's your life, let it be your marriage. You're old enough to know what you want.

—I know what I want, Catherine said quietly, then added, uncertainly: But I'm not sure that Jurek wants the same things.

—Sometimes I think that no one should marry anyone, her mother said.

Catherine laughed quietly. —I thought you liked me, Mother.
—Oh, I would have managed to have you and Emil somehow.

She paused for a moment outside the door of her former room, listening, but the young men still slept. Jurek and Janek, as different from each other as night is from day, as she herself was from Esterka Rashevsky: one dark and volatile and the other fair. She did not like to think of herself as placid but that is what life demanded from her and her kind, she supposed. Pleasing, intelligent, undemanding, quietly competent, virtuous as a tomb. Sailor collars at the Ursuline Academy, the murmur of prayer. Clothes that hid rather than revealed, that made no promises. She wanted to make promises and to keep them too, but a Young Lady of Good Family learned from nuns how to be a woman; thank God for her mother.

Her mother had been a university professor, head of the department of psychiatric medicine and the university clinic; her eyes were always gentle but amused. She had aged well, remaining beautiful with her austerely brushed white hair, and the black which she preferred to wear, adored by her husband, for whom she was herself a major miracle.

Aware of herself as a woman's body, but not sure of the mind and spirit the body enclosed, Catherine listened to silence at Jurek's door; he considered her something of an icon, a mildly sacred vessel to be filled in some sanctified and unspecified future with a new Polish child. She had no wish to be a vessel, sacred or profane; if there was any filling to be done, she wished it for herself.

To please and to be pleased, surely not much to ask for in the twentieth century. A woman is not a receptacle for the seeds of history.

A guilty thought, regretfully set aside.

A moment's pause outside the Rashevskys' door, a soft knock for Esterka, whose dark beauty brought to mind unnerving words like *voluptuous* and *sensuous*; the "Bather with a Griffon" wore Esterka's face and, Catherine suspected, her roundly fleshed body. Is it true that Jews are concupiscent?

—A moment, Esterka whispers through the door.

She was nineteen, Catherine's age, and quietly confident, as if aware of herself as a source of pleasure to be sought and dispensed. How? By what means? Nineteen virginal years seemed like long enough to wait for the blessings of giving and receiving. And not as the parchment-faced nuns would have it but in equal measure!

Esterka's sister, sour-faced Kamila, ugly and not confident at all, was a twenty-two-year-old pillar of piety and a variety of fears, most of which had to do with violence and men. She lived in fear of painful violation.

Their parents: small, inconsequential people (he a leather merchant; she a leather merchant's wife) who lived wholly and unenthusiastically in the present, rootless and futureless in this or any country, hopelessly enmeshed in trading portions of their spirit for daily survival.

Not so Pan Rashevsky, the patriarch of the family, whom only Jurek refers to as Old Jankel or simply That Old Jew. (A Jew of Jews, as Dr. Poremba puts it, raising sardonic eyebrows in salute; a biblical monarch, in Cousin Wlada's words, which mock only in part.) His son's black eyes had the lackluster polish of abacus beads; his contained desert lightnings, vision of rocks that split ands sea that could be parted.

Another soft, unnecessary knock; once, twice.

The front door opens, closes.

There is no electricity. The dark corridor is hung with framed photographs (the family on vacation at Jastarnia with the cold Baltic Sea piling waves on the gray-pebble beach behind them; Cousin Wlada in *Virtue Enmeshed* and in Lope de Vega's *El Ansuelo de Fenisa*; Father in Rome, Vienna, London, and Paris receiving degrees *honoris causa*; Father in Warsaw at an academic congress; Mother youthfully posed as Virgin with Child, Catherine as the Child).

She felt a blend of pity, sympathy, curiosity, and undefined fear, and stood close to the wall so that Ferenc Karoly could pass her without touching. Militiaman, Hungarian Communist, red idealist; he had fought in Spain, had been an executioner of priests; a quiet, gaunt man in middle age who coughed a lot. A pinched face, dark and raw with the night cold he brought in from outside.

A voice without tone or accent, or rather a blend of all the European accents:

—Good morning, Comrade Catherine.

Quietly: Good morning.

He wore a paper-thin raincoat, shabby at wrist and collar, a threadbare scarf, no gloves on cracked and swollen hands, an oilskin cap with a broken cardboard peak and shining red star. There had not been enough Polish police greatcoats to go around all the militiamen; a temporary shortage which (Ferenc Karoly constantly explained), like the shortages of food and fuel and all the other innumerable shortages, would be repaired in due time. The red armband with hammer and sickle was clean and pressed, the rifle was shining with oil drained from mother's sewing machine.

—There was a little trouble last night in Bernardynski Square. You were not alarmed?

He used the intimate *thou*, which irritated Catherine.

—We heard some shots . . .

—Don't let that disturb you. It is inevitable, always so at the start. But it will get better. Everything will be better in due time.

—We hope so . . .

—The start of a social revolution must always contain an element of . . . well . . . uncertainty. He spoke in a gently chiding tone as if to a child: There are malcontents, you see. But I am keeping you from your work? Yes, please excuse me. Excuse me, yes, he said, and stepped into the icy storage room that had been Bronka's room, then stuck his head out again. —Has Panna Bronka gone for the water?

With strange proletarian logic he addressed Bronka with Old World courtesy. Everyone else was citizen or comrade.

—I think so.

—She shouldn't walk that far with those heavy pails.

He coughed deeply, a dry rattling sound, and pressed his chest with both hands, and dropped his hands quickly as if the gesture had been an admission. Catherine said, feeling sorry for him: We'll make some tea today, there is still some left.

—Thank you, Ferenc said. But I can't take your tea. In due time I shall be issued everything that I'm supposed to have. It is simply a matter of patience and revolutionary discipline. Tea is not a necessity, you see.

—As you wish, she murmured.

—The cold does not bother me, you see. I am used to the cold. There is not that much difference between cold nights here and in Hungary, or, for that matter, Spain. The Pyrenees can be very cold.

She nodded and began to move toward the kitchen door, a gray rectangle edged with sharpening light; day could no longer be denied. At the far corner of the corridor, between the antlered hat rack and the umbrella stand (a brass shell casing, Austrian-made, Ukrainian-fired, dating from the 1918 struggle for the city which the Poles won and the Ukrainians lost, a fratricidal interlude which neither the Poles nor the Ukrainians could manage to forget), dust particles went through a momentary transformation into a golden aureole. It was a moment of glittering illusion which brought instant sadness. The new day had come despite all her wishes.

And this was a particularly dangerous moment, when the mind's laboriously constructed defenses had been reduced by sleep, and she was willing to believe that the time in which she was alive had been an evil dream.

She resented her need to be afraid of Ferenc Karoly. Nor did she want him to treat her with consideration, as if kindness from an enemy were the equivalent of treason.

She searched her mind for epithets, unkind thoughts: skin like an old newspaper, a beak of a nose enmeshed in old scars. She couldn't hate him for his Communism because she thought of it almost as an illness, an unfortunate condition like the tubercular explosions that rattled his ribs, possibly curable in dry mountain air.

He coughed, excused himself, wiped the red thread of blood from the corner of his mouth, and said carefully: There are two things, Comrade, or rather three. Three small matters. May I have a moment?

She nodded, waited.

—First, I am going away. We are sending brigades into the countryside to work with the peasants, a matter of resettlement and reorganization. Rural collectivism must be accomplished before winter.

—Winter is almost here, she said reflectively. She wished that he didn't find it necessary to explain.

—Yes, it is cold now, every night is colder. The days are still warm.

—Yes.

—I hope to return.

This time she didn't nod, merely waited, thinking that his austere, monkish face looked especially used and gray on this telling morning; his voice seemed to be equally difficult and gray.

—I think it likely that I shall be sent elsewhere from the country.

Despite herself she found herself asking: Where?

—It is not up to me to choose where I serve.

He spoke with pedantic precision, hesitating before every word, as if each had to be carefully selected and as carefully placed, like unsure footsteps in the dark, one after the other. Soft voice, deeply troubled eyes. An odd determination.

—I want to warn you, he said.

Fear made her weak, nauseous; she concentrated all attention on a patch of darkness just under the ceiling, a spot of dampness shaped like a bear's paw.

—Is something wrong? she asked.

What an astonishing shrillness, what a childish tremor! So much for morning illusions of normalcy. Reality was not like that. Reality was a Communist militiaman with a long, antiquated rifle, the iron clatter of hobnailed boots ascending the stairs. (When? Not why, but when?) Her voice had been reduced to a tremulous whisper:

—I said, is something wrong?

He looked with gloomy eyes at the framed photographs, opulent winter furs, Jurek's romantic military cape, as if each were a criminal offense for which punishment was due.

—Excuse me, comrade, but times are difficult, you see . . . Men are imperfect. Some mistake hysteria for revolutionary zeal. Later a minor deviation from the norm will be unimportant, but at the beginning . . .

—Yes, yes, yes! she said in that newly tremulous and uncharacteristic voice that sounded more like Kamila than herself. We are getting rid of everything today, all the books and paintings, everything! We will be just the same as everybody else!

He gently, no longer looking at her, stroking his rifle with casual affection: *And your fiancé?*

She was momentarily confused because her engagement, if one could call it that, was so very new.

—Jurek?

—Do you have another?

—No. No, of course, at least . . .

—He is a Polish officer who has not obeyed the registration order. If he is found here, as he must be found, it will go badly with you all.

—Oh, but, she said, suddenly relieved, he wasn't a real officer at all! He is a student, a journalism student. He was just an underensign in the war, and that is little more than an officer cadet . . .

—Nevertheless, that is a kind of officer, I think. It is only a matter of time before he is arrested.

—But how will the authorities know that he is here? Unless you . . .

—Well, obviously, quite obviously, he said, suddenly irritated, I haven't reported him. That's not to say that I shouldn't have reported him. But you will have to register all the inhabitants of this house with the militia. No one who is not registered may stay in this house. If you violate that order you will be arrested.

—But where can he go? He is from Warsaw, he doesn't know anyone else in Lwów.

—He has managed to meet you, he must manage to meet someone else.

She began: I don't think . . . And then stopped because the story of her meeting with Jurek and their unlikely engagement was too complicated; and anyway she wouldn't discuss it with this man at this time or, for that matter, at any other time. Instead, she said: But what has he done?

—It is not what he has done, it is what he might do. He is not in sympathy with the times.

She said, cried or thought she did, the volume of sound, accent, and inflection were quite immaterial: *But that is unjust!* And watched the gray face acquire the glossy hardness of an ornamental walnut, as if the sympathetic man who had ventured briefly outside his defenses had beaten a precipitous retreat.

—Please, he said, insistent: *Communism makes the elementary standards of morality and justice inviolable rules for relations between individuals and peoples.*

—But what does that mean?

—Communist morality encompasses the fundamental norms of morality evolved over centuries in the fight against social oppression. Communism is more than a transformation of political, economic, and social relations. It is the reeducation of man himself.

—But in the meantime? What happens in the meantime?

—You must believe in the future of mankind.

Thoughts went this way and that and finally hung askew. She glanced upward; that wet paw in the half-light . . . Yes, it was growing, it was visibly growing, the fingers had acquired mandarin nails gloved in mobile particles of gold. In a few minutes it will be possible to reach up to them and grasp them, and to replace one irrationality with another; incredible, isn't it, that there should be no other choice but the irrational? Ah, but a pipe has burst somewhere. That is because it is so cold in the apartment and outside. The weather was unseasonably cold, just as a few weeks earlier it had been unseasonably hot: a sure sign of a severe winter . . . Snow had already fallen in some parts of the country, according to Janek, who made frequent trips to the countryside for food and provisions . . .

A great bronze bell said something at considerable distance. Something glum. It didn't herald anything in particular. No solace nowadays in church bells. The bell had simply gone: gl-UMMM . . . glo-UMM . . . gl-OOOM . . . solemn and sullen like a retired sexton at a funeral, and that was that. Perhaps a drunken Russian swinging on a bell rope? And in the meantime Ferenc Karoly was lecturing on the imperatives of history.

She had to interrupt him; she *would* interrupt!

—When are you leaving? Will it be today? And will someone else be quartered here?

If only that pathetic tremor would leave her voice. Fear was degrading. Ferenc Karoly's absolute involvement with his own monologue was really a stupendous piece of luck.

. . . *Concern on the part of everyone for the preservation and growth of public wealth; a high sense of public duty; intolerance of actions harmful to the public interest . . .*

She had not consciously strived for information. Her attention seemed to be evenly divided between irrational alternatives and a sudden concentration of intolerable noise from, on the one hand, Ferenc Karoly, who was beginning to earn the mocking sobriquet that Dr. Poremba had bestowed upon him (St. Francis of the Kremlin); on the other hand, the street, where apparently an early-morning parade was in progress with drums and cymbals and military oompahs; and (on the *third* hand) the persistent shrillness of the telephone, which had begun to ring in Father's study. Three hands were evidently not enough. Wiesio Poremba, twelve, an enormous child, had begun a quarrel with her own little voyeur of a brother over their relative success in the morning breadlines. His mother, Pani Alicja, was loudly admonishing her daughters Luta and Ziuta, eighteen and sixteen respectively, on the need for sharing. On top of that Jurek and Janek started shouting at each other. (Traitor! Deserter! Jew's errand boy! Bourgeois pig! Reactionary!) Doors slammed like cannon, puncturing arguments.

. . . collectivism and comradely assistance; one for all and all for one; humane relations between individuals . . . mutual respect . . . man is to *man a friend, a comrade, and a brother . . .*

Esterka slipped between her and Ferenc Karoly, slipped into the kitchen, and closed the door.

But it was important to find out whether another Communist militiaman would replace Ferenc Karoly in the household. Another St. Francis wasn't very likely; it would probably prove to be a Savonarola. This was particularly important in view of Jurek, whose very existence had apparently become a crime, and the organization which he and Dr. Poremba were putting together. The city had become quite covered with a network of clandestine anti-Soviet conspiracies which bubbled just under the surface like life-carrying arteries. Father deplored all conspiracy but didn't oppose it. (*In spring, after the French and the English have finished off the Germans, they'll settle with the Bolsheviks as well. All that we have to do is wait!*) He had a forceful and authoritative ally in Patriarch Rashevsky, who preached and practiced a passive resistance, in Mother, who thought all armed resistance quixotic and suicidal, and in Janek Stypenko, who was all for resistance but didn't know whom he should resist. (*Poles, Russians . . . it's all the same devil for a Ukrainian.*) Pani Alicja stoutly backed her husband, who seemed to lose years off his age in the excitement of conspiracy; Pani Alicja did everything stoutly. Cousin Wlada was for simply ignoring the Communist vulgarity. (*They have no style, therefore they don't exist.*) Esterka's parents wanted to escape the proletarian paradise and to live under the Germans, who had *Kultur,* unlike the Red barbarians . . . They had no wish to resist anyone. Bronka's plebeian instincts were in an uproar over the conversion of churches into stables; she was the most violent and unforgiving militant of all, even though the Bolshevik Antichrist had already started converting some of the stables back into churches. The children played a new game called Breadwinner, competing for the biggest loaf and the shortest breadline every day, flying out of the house early in the morning, returning at noon, solemn as fledgling owls.

The household had become Lwów in miniature, with conflicts, differing opinions, ancient quarrels, and new aspirations; this one pulled this way, that one pulled the other, all hostile to the occupation, all convinced that only their philosophy promised universal salvation. Which was, in turn a reflection of the entire country.

Catherine? She was too busy running the microcosm to voice what she wanted, her wishes required passionate involvement, total commitment . . . to what? The aspirations of a nineteen-year-old girl are seldom conclusive, according to Mother. *Nevertheless* . . .

That left Esterka Rashevsky, who kept her own counsel. Catherine thought that she, Esterka, had a dream that reached beyond anything that *she* had ever known and wished that she herself, Catherine, could share the dream or have one of her own. But dreams, like poetry, are born in darkness, are they not? From the rubble of wrecked realities, tormenting questions, and nonexistent answers. Her life had included very little darkness.

Thinking of poetry and poets, she immediately thought of Abel Abramowski, whom she would probably see later in the day; she had not yet decided whether she would see him. Under all the possible varieties of circumstances, it was a difficult decision. She was rather inclined to think that she would not go to his parents' apartment, as he had asked her to in a little note of a few days ago, but perhaps she would. Thinking of Abel, she remembered a line of dialogue from an American film seen months or perhaps eternities ago: "You're trying to hang on to a world that doesn't exist"; a film which also contained the immortal words: "Five grand by five o'clock or I spill my guts . . ." rendered exactly and incomprehensibly in Polish subtitles.

What it all meant was beyond her at the moment, as was the Hungarian's monotonous droning:

. . . *honesty and truthfulness, moral purity, modesty and unpretentiousness in social and private life; mutual respect in the family and concern for the upbringing of children* . . .

Chaos brought salvation. She was obliged to shout to be heard and with her shouting the terror was gone.

—Will someone else be coming to live here?

. . . *devotion to the Communist cause, love of the socialist motherland* . . .

—I said . . . I asked . . . !

She didn't like to interrupt anybody's dreams but she had to know.

—Oh yes, of course, excuse me. When will I be leaving? It could be today, possibly tomorrow. You see, we must reorganize food production and the agrarian system before winter makes large-scale resettlement impossible. Otherwise there might be serious shortages next year.

—We have never had shortages before, she observed carefully.

—Well, Comrade Catherine, the war! The war! A certain disorganization is inevitable! But it will all get better.

She nodded and began to move toward the kitchen, a refuge from chaos.

—Of course, now that we no longer have to feed the soldiers, now that they are gone . . .

—Exactly! Ferenc said.

—Will someone else be quartered here now?

—I don't know. There is a shortage of accommodations.

He coughed for a long, painful moment, making obvious efforts not to touch his chest.

The telephone call had been for her. In the surrounding chaos, the summons began to acquire that totally unreal quality which telephones used to have for her in childhood, as if the instrument had a mind, will, personality, and intentions of its own. The voice was both melodic and metallic, drifting up and down, in and out of its own accompanying cacophony: loud music of an indeterminable kind, mysterious echoes, cracklings, the unraveled threads of half a dozen other conversations. But Catherine thought that she had heard it before. Right in midsentence it hit her:

. . . come today. Everybody in the entire house, not just us . . . Crackle-crackle. Then something about mousetraps. The incredibly familiar, half-remembered voice suddenly broke through with something about *circumstances.*

. . . Absolutely! Under no circumstances! As I said, the mousetrap . . . plonk-plonk-rattle-rattle . . . *Nitchevo . . . Da? Da? . . . Nyet!*

Nitchevo was that marvelously descriptive new Russian word which she, and the city and (she supposed) everyone living in the 77,000 square miles taken by the Soviets, had begun to learn and to use. The word lay somewhere between the French *Je m'en fous* and the Spanish *nada.* Everything was or could be *nitchevo* if you couldn't do anything about it. No luck today in the breadline? *Nitchevo.* No coal for the furnace in the cavernous cellars? *Nitchevo.* A winter of unparalleled severity lay just around the corner, but . . . *nitchevo;* we will manage somehow; providence will provide.

The crackling voice now pleaded rather weakly that she, Catherine, should not worry about it, or rather about him, whoever he was, and that she should come, instead, to the whine-rattle-plonk.

. . . one o' clock, if you can, under the billy goat.

With no supporting evidence she was suddenly quite sure that the voice was Abel's and that Abel wanted her to meet him at the old wineshop at 3 Dominikanska Street, which featured minuet-playing grandfather clocks, secretive couches designed for whispering at close quarters, gleaming mahogany of an antique era, and, above the entrance, a rampant he-goat with front hooves resting on bunched grapes. Why there rather than in his own home? But at this crucial point the telephone broke down altogether and all its sounds disappeared under an interminable whine.

Mother said: Who was that, dear? Could you tell?

Father said: Absolutely impossible these days to tell who is on the telephone. Last night I was calling Professor Karolewski about a possible reappointment to my old chair, if and when they ever decide to reopen the university, and I found myself speaking to and hearing from a lady of dubious virtue and doubtful antecedents who told me that she was far too busy these days to grant me an appointment. It was all rather unflattering.

Cousin Wlada said: Karolewski? Is that the impossible, musty little man who married Lala? What an abominably virtuous pillar of society *he* was!

—I think it was Abel Abramowski, Catherine said. He had sent me a note a few days ago asking me to see him. But now he talked about mousetraps. Quite ludicrous, really.

Mother said: You *have* been using that word rather a lot lately, haven't you? *Ludicrous.*

Father said: Abramowski is back from America? You must bring him here! He was my best student, a brilliant fellow, even though he did talk too much about the self-sufficiency of artists.

—He was quite mad, as I remember, Catherine said.

—I wonder what happened to Lala Karolewska, Cousin Wlada said. To me she was always the eternal female, a woman in her own right and independent of all social institutions. *Mon Dieu,* as if a woman could even hope to exist in a society as primitive as ours.

—Where are you meeting Abramowski? Mother asked.

—At Pan Koziol's on Dominikanska. At least that's what I think he said. I really couldn't understand very much of what he was saying.

—Be sure to bring him here! Father said.

—No, Mother said. I don't think you should. I am sure that Jurek would become completely confused.

—Ah, dammit, Father said. I had forgotten all about that engagement of yours. Of course you can't go about meeting other men in wineshops now that you are engaged.

—Queen Victoria has been dead a long time, Cousin Wlada said.

And I really can't imagine a girl losing her chastity at Koziol's. The place just isn't equipped for that sort of thing.

Mother said: Try to find out about Abel's father. He's been quite ill lately. Perhaps we could help.

Father said: I don't understand you women at all. You make it sound as if every decent woman was at least in part a demimondaine. Whatever happened to the traditional values?

—Dear Albert, Cousin Wlada said. Be as traditional as you like, it makes you quite endearing. A bit insufferable at times, a bit stuffy, but definitely endearing.

—Why do you call me Albert? I don't care for sarcasm.

—Go along now, child, and see to the breakfast, Mother said.

Father observed, giving up: This entire conversation is a bit insufferable. And Cousin Wlada said: You started it, Albert, with your confessions about amorous appointments. I'm not surprised the lady turned you down.

Father was really a dear, dear man. An endearing and enduring kind of man. And it had been Father who had said long ago: Be what you wish, but be different! It was hard to remember sometimes.

Now he said: I am afraid that I am quite as confused as Jurek is going to be when he finds out that the girl whom he is engaged to marry is meeting old suitors in wineshops. If that sounds archaic . . .

—Antediluvian, dear, Mother said. Now do be quiet and help Emil with all those scarves and sweaters. It's going to be awfully cold outside.

—And, anyway, Abel was not a suitor, Catherine said.

—What a time, Father said. When a ten-year-old boy is the family's breadwinner . . .

Emil announced: Today I'm going to get a whole loaf! Janek has given me a paper with a big Russian stamp on it. It lets me go to the head of the line!

—Where could Janek get such a paper? I think that he was just playing a little game with you.

—No, Mother, he swiped Jurek's pistol and turned it in at the militia and they gave him the paper with the stamp. Honest to God, Mother!

—You shouldn't say *honest to God*. You shouldn't say *swipe*.

—Bronka says it all the time, she also says . . .

—Run along now, child, and drink all your milk. Catherine, see to it that he doesn't leave a drop.

—What times, Father said. Honest to God, a man could despair. Did you say that Abel was talking about mousetraps?

The telephone had said a whole lot more than she had permitted her parents to know, a great deal more. It had bubbled love out of its black

depths and would have gone on bubbling, and babbling too, ludicrously, if it had not decided with the logic of all unmusical instruments to shut up. It had pleaded with infinite statesmanship for an appointment without giving one solid reason why she should grant its
wish; it had sounded exactly like Abel, who always *had* operated at the
outer limits of reason and logic, half in and half out of staggering lunacy, riddled with the dreamer's and the poet's sense of being, that secret and mysterious sense of all things that involved mankind. It was
just like him to talk about mousetraps.

She had been quite willing, certainly, to inform her parents about
Abel's mousetraps, but the rest was personally hers, what she could understand of the babbling, bubbling, creaking, twanging cacophony.
Nitchevo! And now she was going to meet a lunatic instrument! The
telephone hadn't helped her to make up her mind any more than
Abel's original note of two weeks ago had done; on the contrary, she
had immediately decided that she would *not* see him, then that she
would, and then that she would *not.* Now it was back to *would* and it
had a chance of staying there until it was too late; she was more or less
on her way to heal a dear madman, an utterly illogical instrument of
a man who swung like an insane pendulum from one idea to another,
staggering like a drunken child between personalities. Which was so utterly refreshing! He had used to make it his business, as a penniless student, to discover which of his affluent friends had unbreakable prior engagements and then invite them to mythical galas of his own, thus
gaining credit for being a frequent and open-handed host, who was inevitably invited in return and always accepted. *Ludicrous was* the word!
But a quite marvelous madman for all that.

It was just like him, wasn't it, to claim that the poet's singular state
of being, that completely abstract quality of mind and of feeling, had
been known to reverse the verdicts of history. And to claim it loudly
while, on the other hand, he denounced the abstract as a poetic aberra-
tion.

She had put down the telephone as delicately as if she were kissing
him on the lips. It was a symbol! In a society which operated exclusively on symbols, which had galloping chargers on the brain, this was a
blow struck for personal freedom. Yes, what she needed, what everyone
needed, were more blows, bigger and better ones. She was up to her ears
with sacred vessels! Change, that was the ticket, as the English said!
Well, she would start the process now and be damned to them all. Had
Abel changed? She hoped that he hadn't, at least not profoundly, even
though he did suffer occasional lapses into profundities. She hoped that
he hadn't changed at all, she was up to her Victorian flaring nostrils in

reason and in being reasonable and in logical thinking. It was high time for the madmen of this world to take over!

But logic wouldn't give up quite that easily; it hung on, pestering her with reason. Of course he would have changed! Four years in another world . . . *Ma fois*, as Cousin Wlada said, it only took a minute to become a woman. Less than that!

The trouble between Abel and herself had been a staggering, practically insurmountable age difference: five crucial years. She had still been pilloried at fifteen in damnable sailor collars, obliged to a pious binding of the chest. She had been quite unready for his violent, American declarations, frightened by his unhappiness. She simply was not used to being unhappy, she hadn't known anyone who was. That wasn't the Abel Abramowski she wanted to remember! His letters confused her at first, then annoyed her; he had assumed too much, expected more than she was able to give, it was presumptuous of him. A gentleman was never presumptuous. Later, having grown up a bit, she pitied him; and later still she had accused herself justly and logically of having drawn amusement from his unhappiness because, having grown up a bit more, she had been amused. She had stopped writing to him and now promised herself that she would make amends. He was a hard man to understand, that gloomy-eyed and frequently explosive Abel Abramowski, and harder to heal since he displayed a bewildering array of wounds; lots of wounds, mostly self-inflicted. At one moment he was the artist registering his protest by preaching the cult of uselessness in a utilitarian age, and in the next he would be off on wings of rhetoric and parable, equally confusing.

That was Abel, all over, just like that, insisting on self-annihilation so that he could emerge resurrected. And, of course, insisting on recrucifixion so that he could begin all over again. Completely mad, of course, but how beautifully mad, how desirably irrational! What could you do with an eighteenth-century madman other than love him?

The man of the imagination—the poet, the lover, and the lunatic—had always been an object of public amusement and so she had laughed a little, because in Abel's letters he had shown himself to be at least the first two and, in part, the third. Well, she would meet all his injuries head on, chest to unbound and quite admirable chest, and in the process strike a blow for personal freedom. Perhaps a couple of good blows, just to make sure.

And suddenly she was anxious to see him at once, immediately, right now! If he had changed very much it wouldn't be much good. But if he had not changed, as she hoped he hadn't, she would be able to lose the sense of herself, and to lose touch with the bewildering new times, in the parabolic flight of his imagination.

She tried the taps in the kitchen, as she did each morning, and heard the rattling gasp of trapped air, the groan and clatter of empty pipes; the filtration plant, or was it the waterworks, was still out of order. Well, perhaps today. In the meantime, there was the washtub and the laundry boiler, already filled by Bronka, whom Catherine now heard coming up the stairs with fresh water pails. The household's ration was six pails a day but Bronka always managed to get twice as much. She said it was all a matter of swinging your hips, just so, so that the *komandir* at the old public well had something to think about. *Honest to God, his eyes pop out of his head . . . ! You'd think he was a dog at a country fair!*

Breakfast was one slice of bread, either black or white, depending on what luck the children may have had the day before in the breadlines, and a cup of tea. The tea would soon be gone. The bottom was already showing in the tin box painted with mandarins and dragons. A cup of more or less fresh milk for each of the children. Later Catherine, Esterka, and Bronka would stand in lines to get milk from the peasant women in the marketplaces. The peasants brought what they could but it wasn't much. Still, one of the three was usually successful.

All stores were closed other than public bakeries and liquor stores where lines formed at daybreak, or the new State stores which sold nothing but bought everything from Meissen china to cameo miniatures to gold teeth by the pound to rubber galoshes. The Polish population had still to learn how to stand in lines (the rule of thumb was that you had to wait in line half a day for half a loaf of bread) so that there were innumerable rows, arguments and fights. It was a wonder that nobody got hurt.

Money was a problem; the Polish zloty were still legal tender but not for much longer. Nobody wanted to take Polish money and nobody had rubles. The Rashevskys spent their days in alleys peddling American dollars. Father mended shoes. There was, of course, no leather to be had, but Cousin Wlada had brought an elegant English pigskin dressing case and exotic calfskin suitcases. The attic yielded up an ancient buffalo-hide trunk. Persian and Turkish carpets provided excellent lining for old winter boots. Pani Alicja and Mother knit sweaters and scarves. One way or another, separately or jointly, the household earned enough each day to get through that day.

—Bronka, Bronka, Emil mumbled, his mouth full of black bread. What's life like in Russia?

—Oh, not that old story again, Catherine said. You go through this every morning.

—Well, Bronka? What's it like?

—You might as well play along with him, Catherine said.

—Don't I always? Well, child, it's like this, see? In Russia everyone is happy all the time. What d'you think of that?

—How so, how so! Emil cried, and clapped his hands. He jumped up and down. —How so!

—Well, Bronka said, it's like this. You will stand ten hours in line for a loaf of bread, and if you get it you'll be very happy. Then you will stand four hours in line for half a kilogram of sugar, and if you get it you'll be very happy.

—Ergo! Conclusion! Emil cried, triumphant. In Russia everyone leads a life of unending happiness!

—Where did you hear that word? Catherine asked.

—*Ergo?* Dr. Poremba says it all the time. Ergo! Ergo! Ergo!

—It sounds so silly coming from you. Quite ludicrous, in fact.

—Ludicrous! Ludicrous! Haven't you said that rather a lot lately? Ludicrous! Ludicrous!

Bronka laughed. Esterka smiled. Catherine said: Little brother, you are an insufferable little beast.

Emil gulped milk, one eye fixed carefully on his rival, fat Wiesio Poremba, who had announced that yesterday he had found the shortest breadline in town, absolutely *the* shortest, and that, consequently, he would be back in this very kitchen with a whole loaf of bread, perhaps even white bread, before Emil as much as managed to get out of the house. Well . . . perhaps not *that* soon, but anyway . . .

—No, you won't, Emil cried.

—Yes, I will, Wiesio cried.

—No, you won't! Because I have something that will let me go to the head of my line!

—You have a big mouth, Wiesio said, scrunching down his eyes, clearly intrigued but too sly to admit it. He held a runaway lead in the daily bread-finding competition, but that could change easily, and so he said with his friendliest smile: What have you got?

—Something, Emil said. Something.

—What is it?

—I won't tell you! But it will let me go to the head of the line. Today I'm going to be back before you. And I'll get two loaves! And, he cried, spoiling it all, losing his head completely: They will *both* be white!

They started scuffling on the stairs, going down, their boots loud on the stone steps.

Little Jankele Rashevsky had watched this morning ritual with envy and a mild resentment. He sipped his milk slowly as if to delay the moment of his own departure, his large brown liquid eyes totally unhappy. He said, not looking at anyone: If I could be allowed to go after bread . . .

—You must go to school, Esterka said quickly.

—Emil and Wiesio don't . . .

—There are no schools for Polish children, Esterka said. You know that, we've said all this before.

—I am a Polish child, Jankele said.

—Hush now, Esterka said, drink your milk.

—I don't like my school, Jankele said quietly. Everybody there is a Jew. I don't speak their language. They mock me. They call me names. They hate me because I am a refugee. I don't want to learn Yiddish. Why can't I go to St. Alicja's with the other children?

—St. Alicja's?

—That's what the other children call the classes that Pani Alicja gives here in the afternoon. I don't want to go to the Yiddish school. I want to go after bread like the other children. If you would only let me, you would see how well I could do. I would get lots and lots of bread, you'd see . . .

—It's better for you to go to school, Esterka said. Don't you want to learn? Don't you want to be wise when you grow up?

—My teachers tell lies about Poland, about us.

—It's a very good school, Esterka said. You should be grateful to have such a school.

—Everybody there is a Jew.

—You are a Jew, Esterka said quietly.

—I don't want to be a Jew, Jankele said. Jews are mean and ugly. I hate Jews.

—You mustn't say that, Esterka said gently. You mustn't think that.

—No! the child cried. No! But I don't want to . . . Why should I?

—Hush now, and drink your milk; you will be late for school.

The band had now begun to pass under the kitchen windows, blasting intolerable oompahs right into the thyme, rosemary, marjoram, and chives in the window box, an immense drum banging. *Arise, ye starv'lings from your slumber* (WHOOMPH!), *arise, ye prisoners of want!* An unnerving way to start anybody's day, as Cousin Wlada said. And did they have to remind you quite so noisily about all your hungers? And fears too, because there is an extraordinary amount of fear these days, every kind of fear. This is the thirty-ninth day of Soviet occupation, the fifteenth day since the incomprehensible arrests began.

Each day another friend disappears, vanishes without trace. Everyone is threatened. Arrests strike like capricious lightning at priests, peddlers, doctors, lawyers, teachers, farmers, grocerymen and milkmen, railroad workers, ditchdiggers, officers, policemen, merchants . . . everybody. The terror has no pattern, can't be understood, which makes it the essence of terror. It is as if a blinded, malevolent deity were insanely waving an accusatory finger, scattering thunderbolts in packages of monumental size. Men leave for work in the morning and never return. Or they come back to an empty house with their family magically erased. Whole families vanish overnight, from infant to octogenarian, as if mankind had finally learned the secret of dissolving human flesh into thin air. Each night when the household reassembles and finds itself complete, thanks can be given for a miracle. Indeed, thanks are given: the Catholic Porembas and Modelskis kneel in the dark-paneled study, the Rashevskys sit in the dining room. Thank you, Lord, for letting us get safely through another day. The fear is tangible.

The band said clearly, persuasively: *the in-te-ehr-naaa-tional unites the human ra-a-ace*. Well, Catherine thought: *That's* all very well, but does it have to do it to *us*? And do we have to be forever afraid? Catherine resented her fear, the need to be afraid. She did not want to be diminished at this of all times, to lie awake at night on her uncomfortable canvas cot, listening for the thunder of iron-shod boots booming in the stairwell, fists pounding on doors, doors splintering while flashlights poured their blinding beams into the eyes of victims struggling to awake. Yet it was impossible not to be moved to gaiety while thinking about Abel. Yes. She didn't want to be afraid, therefore she wouldn't be! Even though, just an hour ago, the streets had shaken to the coughing roars of black police vans, windowless specimen boxes hissing on rubber tires, the night-long all-pervading sound that didn't dissipate before early morning.

The trumpet said, joyously: *arise, arise* . . . and went on to explain that a new day and possibly even an entirely new era of human happiness had dawned, and that Catherine should immediately forget the five or six and sometimes even ten long trains, each of a hundred cars, doors bolted, windows boarded up or wreathed with barbed wire, that slid each day into the morning fog. It is unnecessary to remember, the trumpet assured her. The frightening time-without-joy in a city famous for gaiety is merely a temporary inconvenience due to the imperatives of history.

Arise, arise, the new day has come. The gloom is appalling. Men talk in whispers, fearing denunciation. Everyone is a potential informer. And there are rumors, rumors, everlasting rumors . . .

Bronka slices bread with a knife the size of a cutlass. She looks three-breasted, milkily abundant with the round black loaf clutched under her arm. —Have you heard? They took all the judges yesterday, every one of them, out of every courtroom at the same time, along with bailiffs, doormen, witnesses, the lawyers, everybody. Honest to God! Even the people who were watching.

—That's only a rumor, Catherine said.

—A rumor, is it? Day before yesterday it was all policemen. And the director of the electric works was shot. Ah, they'll be the end of us all, the Godless scum!

—No they won't. Just you wait till spring.

—Spring is far away.

She would *not* be afraid.

Nothing had happened yet to anyone she loved, nothing would. If she believed that nothing *would* happen, if she insisted on believing it, then nothing could!

Janek comes in then and stands black-bearded, somber-eyed, looking at Esterka, who does not look at him; he is a large young man who carries with him an air of suppressed violence, a deep-seated anger ready to explode; he is tormented by a variety of hatreds. Everyone is afraid of him except Esterka, who can make him do anything she wants. Are they lovers? Have they loved each other? Catherine doesn't know but thinks it possible. Janek had come upon the Rashevskys on the highway and led them to Lwów. The Russians kept him in the courtyard for a time, then let him go; they took away all the other soldiers. Janek says very little, he speaks only Russian. He will not speak Polish. He uses Polish only to insult Jurek. He gives small presents to Jankele and sometimes to Emil. Yesterday he gave Jankele a small red star to wear but the child threw the badge away. Esterka looks at Janek for a long communicative moment, then rises, wraps scarves around her brother's chest, clamps his dark round cap firmly on his head, and leads him to school. Janek follows.

Then Dr. Poremba marches out with shoes (father's manufacture) and the women's knitting. Dr. Poremba has discovered unsuspected talents as a sidewalk vendor; he grins, shrugs, nods, waves his arms, argues, laughs, tells deplorable jokes and sells absolutely everything. Then it is Mother's turn, she is a *lekpom*, a medical orderly, at a nearby clinic for prostitutes, a class of worker in very great demand. Next out of the apartment are Esterka's parents with their golden dollars, then Pan Rashevsky sets out on his mysterious daily rounds (he will return with ration books, work permits) and Cousin Wlada leaves for nowhere in particular. Her role is that of a newspaper; she gathers gossip, speculation, rumor, and occasionally a genuine piece of news all over the town; the cafés are still open and Wlada is an expert when it comes to cafés. It is through her that the household learns of a new Polish government formed in Angers, France, of a new Polish Army of 100,000, of the new Premier, General Sikorski, whom a great and picturesque English statesman has assured that England would never forget her Polish ally. (*Tell your army in France,* says Mr. Winston Churchill, *that we are their comrades in life as in death. We shall conquer together or die together.*) And a great American President, crippled of body but immense in heart, had called Poland the Inspiration of the Nations! This is reassurance which makes hope possible, this is no illusion; this is something in which to believe. The hope of a victorious spring provides the core of certainty around which mediocre days are able to revolve. The English are with us! In spring, the English and the French will move their great armies, crush Hitler and his ally Stalin, and put an end to the bewildering new times.

Finally it was quiet. The parade had taken itself farther down the street along with the banners that hailed Joseph Stalin, father of mankind, and signs that proclaimed undying loyalty to the Soviet Union on behalf of Polish Intellectual Workers. Rain fell, mixed with sleet; autumn had hung a dreary backdrop for the daily tragicomedy. The gray crowd shuffled off on wet asphalt; some dispirited men, among whom Catherine recognized several of her father's university associates, a famous humorist, a well-known poet, a professional cynic, a patriotic journalist, a beloved author of children's fairy tales, and a humanitarian playwright, pulled a large sodden float which depicted Something. Or rather, the Triumph of Something over Something Else. Whatever it was, Virtue Triumphant shivered with rattling teeth in a Grecian tunic pulled over winter underwear, while Evil lay comfortably prostrate in thick furs.

—There's Karolewski, Father said, astonished. Could you imagine him in a parade before the war? He would have thought it utterly beneath his dignity.

—Several of your friends seem to be there, Father, Catherine said.

—I wonder why they do it. So many of our people cooperate with the Soviets. I understand the Germans can't find anyone.

—We shall remember all these traitors, Jurek said.

Father said: I don't know if we can call all these people traitors. They have a point of view, a right to express it. If they believe in something we should at least give them the benefit of a doubt. Most of them, I should say, do it out of fear.

Jurek said: When the time comes, I'll have no doubt about my point of view. Traitors will be punished.

Catherine said quickly, ugently: Please let it go. Please don't talk about *when the times comes;* I don't want to hear it.

—Well, it *will* come.

—Yes, I know. But please don't put quotation marks around it. Please don't speak in italics.

—What do you mean, *in italics?*

—Please don't do that. I don't want to hear about *when the time* comes in quotation marks.

—I don't understand you, when the time comes . . .

—You will start shooting people, hanging them.

—Traitors must be punished. The organization is collecting quite an impressive list of names.

—Yes. To be shot or hanged when the times comes.

—Why should that astonish you, Catherine? Why should it anger you? I should have thought it was all perfectly obvious.

—That's why it angers me, because you think that it should be obvious.

—Sometimes I lose faith in you, Catherine. I wonder about your ideals. —I think you're simply trying to be difficult.

—I am not trying to be difficult. I am trying to say something I think is important.

—What is it?

—I don't know what it is but I know what it isn't. And it isn't hanging and shooting people.

—You can't shoot *and* hang people, Jurek said. That would be redundant.

She wondered why, for a rebellious fraction of a moment, she had wanted to strike that very handsome, dark romantic face, preferably with a glove. She wanted to do something resounding! While there was yet time! Someone should do it! It simply had to be done. Otherwise, she was absolutely sure, everything would have . . . *will* have . . . been for nothing! She wanted to hear those brilliantly white teeth rattling in that close-shaved, finely chiseled face, in that cropped and incorruptible military head . . . Of course she did nothing of the sort. It would have had to be a gauntlet, anyway, rather than a glove, and she didn't have one; besides, good manners, usage, the woman's duty to her consecrated oath . . . oh well, let it go. Still, she did have that near-irresistible impulse to inflict some kind of injury on his rectitude. He was saying all the right things and making them sound all wrong. He was desecrating graves before they had been filled. He was obviously so terribly afraid; *that's* why he spoke *in italics* about *shooting* people. Fear was to blame for everything; it *was* tangible, she hadn't merely imagined it. They were all so afraid that duly constituted Authority would never be regained. History had been dealt a sharp slap across the cheek, and all the sacred props immediately fell apart . . . Someone had said, she couldn't remember who had said it, that *sacred* was the traditional word of exiles to describe their fallen and insufficient systems . . . oh, everything was such a bloody, *bloody* mess!

Jurek said, with premature authority: You're being very difficult today. All I said was that, after the war, the traitors will be punished. There can be no excuse for treason, you know that.

. . . Of course, of course: My Country Right or Wrong! Long Live the Metric System . . . Immaculate Conception . . . the square of the hypotenuse. How could anyone still believe something so inexcusable, and how could she have thought otherwise? They were all wearing blinders, like carriage horses. They had learned nothing, none of them, from the short accelerated course of consecrated murder that had ended only seven or eight weeks ago. Did none of them know that the Authority of all sacred truths had been overthrown? The verities had gone into exile where they could be safe. Only people without props had been left to face captivity . . .

Jurek said: Traitors must be punished. Examples must be made. Order must be restored and maintained. After so much suffering, our nation must be great.

—Please, Catherine said.

—You shouldn't worry about matters of that kind. You shouldn't make things difficult for yourself.

—Everything will resolve itself correctly in time, Catherine said. Is that what you mean?

—That is *exactly* what I mean.

—Virtue will triumph . . . right triumphs over wrong . . .

—It always has. In our thousand years . . .

—And please don't talk about our thousand years.

—You must have faith in the ultimate victory.

—I thought it had to be belief in the future of mankind.

—It's the same thing.

—That's what I thought.

—Well then, you see how obvious it all is.

—Sleet thickened, whitened, turned to snow.

Abel

THE PARADE DISINTEGRATED as close to the opening of Dominikanska Street as the sodden intellectual workers could maneuver it. The Fire Department band, possessing greater revolutionary discipline, had resolutely continued to the Town Hall Square, where, in the twenty-one years of Polish independence, now officially known as the Years of Oppression, municipal parades normally fell apart, and serenaded Soviet sentries with the French national anthem. The firemen had made a poor showing with the "Internationale," and the "Marseillaise" was one of the few revolutionary airs in their repertoire. That and "The Volga Boatmen." They played these over and over, while sleet turned to snow, until a crowd of angry Soviet officers ran out of the Town Hall and scattered them with broomsticks.

The parading poets, journalists, and academicians had followed the beat of a different drummer, arriving as soon as they could in their familiar haunts: the café of the Journalists' Club, the opulent restaurant of the Hotel Georges, and the turn-of-the-century drawing rooms under the rampant he-goat. There, over glasses of gold-flecked Danzig vodka, fragrant Zubrowka with its little green blades of floating bison grass, and thimblefuls of Krupnik, their revolutionary fervor soared to new heights.

A truly clever man is never unfair, Abel told himself. I will be fair to these unlikely revolutionaries. Most of them parade with difficulty, their pants are so full. Some are opportunists. There may be a True Believer somewhere in this crowd but if there is I haven't met him yet. Fear is a great creator of belief in causes.

Abel! somebody cried. *How TOTALLY extraordinary! How magnificent!* And looking quickly over the tall back of the antique armchair, where he had thought himself invisible and safe, Abel saw Teodor Haussner advancing upon him. Teo the Terrible, former president of the Catholic Poets' League for Contemporary Morality. He loved superlatives and exclamation marks, had a superlative Ukrainian cook, loved the cook and everything Ukrainian, had once shaved his head in the traditional ancient Cossack manner, leaving only a Mohammedan pigtail at the top of his head, had been a frequent invitee to Abel's nonexistent celebrations. Not a bad sort, old Teo, but unreliable . . . and boring as hell. And far too noisy for this of all moments.

—Abel, my dearest, dearest young friend! When did you get back? How was *l'Amérique*, the land of Jefferson and Paine? Somebody told me you had been arrested!

—Not yet, Teo . . . but for God's sake stop yelling about it. (And to change the subject:) You're looking fashionably thin!

—Ah, Haussner said, yes . . . you *think* so? And Abel couldn't immediately determine whether the middle-aged, formerly epicurean poet spoke with regret or pride. But Teo had evidently decided to opt for revolutionary enthusiasms. Of course, my dearest fellow! The times demand hard lean men, a clear eye! Our eyes of stagnation at the pig trough are over!

—So I see, Abel said. Incidentally, Teo, where did you hear about my arrest?

—Somebody told me! Some fool! I needn't tell you how incredibly shocked I was, how immeasurably infuriated! What monumental slander! One of our best and most promising young poets! I asked myself over and over: Why? Why? Why? It was inconceivable that you should be arrested!

—Teo, be good, don't shout.

—I will tell everyone, of course, that the story of Abel Abramowski's arrest is a base canard! Without foundation! Now let me welcome you back among us once again!

—Teo, Abel said, giving up, waving Haussner into the dark armchair across the table: Sit down and be quiet. If you keep yelling I'll have to get out. Look, don't faint but the story about my arrest is true enough.

Haussner's small mouth hung open for a moment, his hands clutched his chest as if to comfort and reassure a dramatic heart, while his eyes darted rapid measuring glances to left and to right.

He whispered: How so, my dear Abel? How can that be? You are here . . . and I am compromised!

—I'm here, Abel said, because they missed me. I wasn't at home. But they arrested my father and mother, Tarski, and everybody in the whole house. I only just missed walking into the mousetrap.

—What mousetrap, for God's sake?

—They have a mousetrap operation set up in our apartment, the old Tsarist method. Everybody who walks in is immediately arrested.

—Abel, Teo whispered, visibly impressed, that is . . . terrible . . .
But . . . why aren't you *hiding?*

—I am hiding.

—Where?

—Here, of course.

—How can anyone hide in a public restaurant? That is ridiculous.

—I've someone to see here.

—But everybody can see *you* . . .

—They couldn't, till you started . . . Look, never mind all that, I'll
find a hideout later. My uncle Mendeltort is back in Lwów, and there
are some others . . . Maybe you can help me?

—*Mendeltort?* Haussner's excitement flew out of control before he
could do anything about it. Then he said, carefully: Mendeltort the
Jew? Oh my God . . .

Abel said, unable to resist the spiteful emphasis: That's my uncle
Avrum . . . I've no idea what he's doing here. He sent me word this
morning to see him, in secret of course. Otherwise my father would
have had a stroke . . . I'd rather not see him. Look, if you can find
room for me in that Babylonian apartment of yours I can forget about
my unmentionable relative.

—Me? Haussner whispered, eyes enormous. *Me?* Dear fellow . . . my
dear Abramowski, I couldn't do that! That is a perfectly unreasonable
request. Utterly presumptuous!

—And a gentleman is, of course, never presumptuous . . . All right,
don't get excited, I understand. Just do me the favor of forgetting that
you had seen me here.

—Of course, dear fellow, Teo said. You can depend on me.

—Oh, I do, dear Teo.

—And your dear father? Where did they take him?

Abel said, suddenly conscious of finality: Zamarstynow.

—Oh, Abel, I'm so sorry . . .

Teodor Haussner's suddenly brimming eyes, those eyes which the
poetess Wanda Walidomska had once called Pools of Brown Compassion, regarded Abel with immeasurable sadness, which, Abel thought,
he could measure with very little trouble. There was also the required
admixture of sympathy and regret.

. . . My dear fellow . . . dear, dear fellow . . . so terribly sorry.

—Thank you, Teo. I knew I could rely on your sympathy.

—Always, dear fellow, always. I do hope that you are not misunderstanding my position.

—Teo, Abel said. How could I? You've always had an admirable position.

—Thank you, I've always tried, I knew you'd understand. You were

always so sensitive to the beat of the moment . . . you were so percep-
tive . . .

—Teo, Abel said, why are you speaking of me in past tense?

—You were . . . extraordinary!

—The common imperfect?

—Which of us is perfect? But I have always tried to do my moral
duty as Man and as Poet.

—And it was always a superlative performance. Was it a nice parade?

—Terrible, dear fellow.

—It sounded impressive.

—Oh, dear man, so terribly cold for this time of the year! The slush
. . . Asiatic weather! But it was all somehow inspiring. How shall I say
it? The intellectuals and the masses marching together!

—Yes . . . tromp . . . slush . . . tromp . . .

—I felt a new faith! I sensed the regeneration of mankind! I am
thinking of doing an epic about it. I shall call it *Ascent from the
Abyss* . . .

—If I know you, dear Teo, it will be superlative.

—Thank you, dear Abel!

—But I never thought your previous views were so revolutionary, Teo.

And Haussner cried, wounded, eyes reproachful, hands suddenly mobile like frightened white mice: Oh, Abramowski! How could you say
THAT?

—Please, Teo, Abel said. Be less emphatic, Teo. I am not anxious to
attract attention.

—Please, Abel, I can't emphasize enough! You must realize my position!

He thought that Teodor Haussner, moral poet with admirable positions, Catholic convert like his own jailed father (. . . poor Father,
probably beaten to a valiant and unrepentant pulp by now in the old
Polish military jail at Zamarstynow, the jail from which no one came
out nowadays . . .), looked particularly convertible at this moment.
Poor Teo. Poor old Teodor the Apostate who had served such damn
good meals . . . such memorable repasts . . . with his superlative
Ukrainian cook whom he would mount from the rear as she bent over
the bubbling *pieroshki* on the stove . . . another admirable position,
which satisfied one appetite while inspiring another . . . Poor Teo
asked for his understanding. I grant it freely, Teo. Teo, go with God.
Or with the Devil. Whichever's winning at the moment.

—Good luck with the Abyss.

Teo bowed gravely, formally, and withdrew, making inconsequential
gestures in front of his chest which, at another time, might have been
religious. —Of course . . . excuse my indiscretion . . .

A great many people, making a tremendous amount of intelligent noise, pushed in and out of the three antique rooms under the rampant he-goat, looking for a table where they might preside. He couldn't have Catherine struggling with all that noise. The litterateurs were professionals in the noise department, they knew how to smash through anybody's sentence, how to hand each crystal syllable on cigarette smoke; he couldn't have her shouting to be heard.

Of course, he didn't even know if she was coming. He had half expected her to refuse because she was engaged. His father had told him immediately and emphatically about the engagement: some young officer. Well, damn it, if she had wanted an officer in the family, and wasn't it an honor to have one, why not pick *him*? *He* had been a bona fide officer, no question about that. Battalion adjutant. Had at one time hoped to be a poet, had in fact had a crack at it, had been known to declaim, but could be forgiven in view of his superlative military virtues clearly demonstrated by his Wound. Yes, he had been wounded, he had given tissue and a little meat. He had a sore hand. He had been wounded in the hand, which any litterateur worth a pinch of salt would be immediately able to identify as a Good Wound, none better. He had tripped over a sack of potatoes in a peasant cottage and had gone hand-first into a hot stove. The wound may not have been particularly honorable but it had hurt like hell, so it must count for something!

The brilliant noise was too much even for him. He had picked Koziol's because it was romantic, reminiscent of secure centuries, subtle and unobtrusive. A perfect place to whisper and make love. He had not taken processionals into account. With his ability to assume too much and hope for too much, and with his inability for logical progression from premise to conclusion, he would have made an excellent member of the General Staff. The war might have taken an entirely different course if poets had run it. At least, the declamations would have been professional. Even if rhyme and reason *had* been out of the question, there might have been rhyme! And the noise, because in war noise is half the battle, would have been . . . brilliant!

He would not expose Catherine to such a professional bombardment.

He hoped she wouldn't come yoked in sailor collars and straw hats with ribbons, the hats that had made her look like an incorruptible cabin boy aboard a battleship crewed by ravening pederasts, a nautical fantasy which used to rattle his teeth. Asiatic weather would probably take care of the straw, but what about that fat pigtail that used to fling itself about?

Imagine Catherine marrying a future general! Holy Mother of putative lieutenants! It was enough to start a revolution, mount the barricades waving multicolored banners, demand Bread for the Masses, All

Power to the Soviets; anything! Provided adolescent generals were immediately shot, old orders strewn about, and Catherine delivered at once to the Wounded Poet . . .

So it would probably be a fur hat instead of the straw, a soft black frame, in which her memorable face would taunt him like man's original temptation; and he would succumb at once, immediately if not sooner. Oh, take me to the Top of the Mountain and show me all the treasures of the earth . . . I'll take them! I'll take them! Just be damn quick about it!

Meanwhile, the noise, the brilliant boomings, Homeric harangues. There wasn't anything that he could do about it; he couldn't compete with the Literary Great no matter where wounded. These were Great Names with the power to stun by merely existing. They had been inspiring. They were the mind, voice, soul, and conscience of the Nation, and who could challenge someone who had that kind of a job? Not an impatient, slightly drunk, certainly uninspiring young man waiting for his girl friend who might not be coming anyway! Who was engaged, incomprehensibly pledged to marry a future field marshal, a whelp of a hero. How in hell had that fellow managed *that*? There must be something more to him than meets a prejudiced eye, because Catherine was not the standard porcelain-faced, watercolor-eyed, middle-class figurine who succumbed to heroes. She had a lot more in her head than patriotic sawdust. So how *had* he done it? And did he know what he had to cope with? Even Abel wasn't very sure.

Under those circumstances, the noise was a hands-down favorite over lovers' whispering. The Great Names would triumph, consider the names: Banda-Cyganowski, who had once had lunch with Gertrude Stein in Paris and had dined on the story for eleven years; Agnieszka Dlapanow, who sang lyrically, spiritually, of the many joys guaranteed by virtue; the delicate if somewhat wilting beauty of pastoral poetess Wanda Sierocka, a nunlike sweetness in publicly modest gray with just a touch of violet lace at the cuff and collar; the Nation's Social Conscience, Zygfryd Bunt; the brilliant critic, Sobiepan Bogomily, whose oracular pronouncements brought either instant immortality or death; the patriotic fervor of Jozef Gryszpan-Magdeburski, dramatist of the Napoleonic era; Professor Zbigniew Kukla, whose philosophy had inspired government after government no matter what its program might have been; the satirist and wit, enfant terrible of 1924, Mann-Bielecki, who always carried his head tilted to one side. (All the better to hear the Muses with, no doubt.) Too much for Abel to cope with. Even poor Teo had once been too much. Not a bad sort, old Teo, but so bloody boring!

Yes, he had changed. He had been unkind and a truly fair man is never unkind. He had allowed himself the luxury of contempt. It was like laughing at a one-legged man whose crutch had slipped on a banana peel. America did have her effect! Although, perhaps, the taint had been there before, because, God help us all, America's not to blame; these Poles with their late-Victorian advanced minds and convoluted thinking . . . they manufactured such magnificent pratfalls. One thousand years of flying lemon-meringue pies; my God, what a history! As bad as the Jews, who, at least, operated on some remote premise bordering on logic, and who did manage, once in a long while, to prove to themselves that a Tree was a Tree.

. . . Could anyone imagine two more unrealistic and irrational nations sharing one scrap of land for eight hundred years? God must have laughed himself to death when He put them there . . .

Oh, but, dear God, whichever of my Gods, bearded or clean-shaven, *please* let us not get into this business of the Poles and the Jews. The times are difficult enough without split loyalties. One felt one would go mad, anyway, with the whole bloody business, one drowning man kicking the other to death . . . and which had planted the first rotten seed? My family has been in this country seven hundred years but my father's father was the first of us even to bother to learn the damn language. And that's too late to start a dialogue. And if it's so immoral to be anti-semitic, why is it moral, right, and proper to be an anti-polonist? And vice versa. *Ad* nauseous *infinitum*. Perhaps I should have stayed in America, the land where even prejudice must be native-born!

One thing was certain from all this: Five vodkas had always been two too many for him . . . which also proved something. Because the Poles, as all the world would testify with pleasure, could drink their calvary horses right under the table.

Hopefully, Catherine would change all that again. He should have seduced her years ago, while he could still declaim; but he had been too busy seducing himself! He had been the Poet, not the lover, and he had forgotten the first of all his golden thoughts: that love was, contrary to Polish tradition, not the soft sighing of a violin but the exultant twang of bedsprings! Yet, surely, all was not lost. God being such a humorist, he'd surely get another crack at her. Now more than ever he needed revelation and nothing lifts the scales from the eyes like a good seduction, unless it's ammonia . . . One good sniff and your head is clear.

> *De temps que la nature en sa verve puissante*
> *Concevait chaque jour des enfants monstrueux*
> *J'eusse aimé vivre auprès d'une jeune géante*
> *Comme aux pieds d'une reine un chat volupteux . . .*

He could still declaim!

And he was in love! He was going at once to that crazed telephone to warn her not to come, because if she did arrive, innocent as a pigtail and a sailor collar, under the rampant he-goat, an ACT of PAGANISM would immediately take place. She should at least consult her mother, confess to her father, give herself a chance to be talked out of it, or there would be that Consequence! And he would never be the same again, whatever that was.

Five vodkas on an empty stomach, and now a golden Krupnik sent over by Teo, who had a troubled conscience, served as the deus ex machina which paralyzed Abel. He was effectively immobilized. He was deprived of means to reach the telephone. He was ecstatic at this providential intervention and sang *Te Deum ex Machina Laudamus*, blessed be thy name; he had made every intellectual effort to save Catherine, and now the matter was out of his hands, as is normally the case with intellectual efforts. It was beginning to look as if there would be some sort of consequence, after all.

The question was: where was this blessed event to take place? Like every tenth Pole in the city of Lwów, Abel was homeless at the moment. His apartment was full of bulky Russians in blue caps who flung themselves upon anyone who knocked on the door, the classic Russian manner of stocking Siberia, an indelible fragment of Polish racial memory. Father had had a lot to say about Tsarist methods, having been a student in St. Petersburg, as had Mendeltort, Major Tarski . . . everyone in that fantastic generation had been a bearded revolutionary . . . (Mendeltort used to say, and he ought to know: *In a society which is both repressive and frightened, students are always first to feel the club.*) It is impossible to imagine Father as a student, as a conspirator-plotting Polish independence, but that's what he had done. Someday I'll ask Mendeltort to tell me about him. Someday somebody ought to tell me about Mendeltort. If there is to be any truth for me, it ought to lie somewhere between those two violent extremes.

. . . Some day, somebody, somewhere, it was a hell of a way to reach a conclusion.

All this, however, wasn't going to get him a bed. Providence had already intervened once on his behalf; he didn't think he could count on any more divine generosity. As far as he knew, his *gimnazium* and university friends had been scattered all over the globe. The great names were, obviously, not to be counted on. Catherine's parents would be glad to have him, but that would knock his sensual imperatives into a cocked hat; one simply didn't, couldn't, repay hospitality by deflowering the daughter of the house under her parents' roof, so to speak, across the family hearth, as it were, mangling the Lares and Penates. It just wasn't done.

That left Mendeltort, at least for the moment, and Mendeltort . . . well. It was a problem to bugger the imagination.

(One could imagine, then, the friendly dark stranger saying: Pardon me, dear fellow, but what is it about your father's brother that boggles the mind or, as you put it, buggers the brain? Pardon me, the imagination . . . And Abel would reply: Nothing at all, dear fellow, unless you recall that he is a professional Jewish terrorist, a murderer several times over, described on police flyers in eleven languages, and that his very name has been *verboten* to me since earliest childhood. My uncle Avrum is a most peculiar man. How is it then, the stranger might continue, that you know so much about him? A murderer several times over, did you say? Why, my dear fellow, Abel would reply, I found out everything I could about him simply because I wasn't supposed to know anything! I have been studying Uncle Avrum for years. There is damn precious little I don't know about him. But, the stranger wonders, didn't you just say a moment ago that someone, sometime, somewhere, and all that . . . I seem to remember . . . My dear fellow, says Abel, those are just dates and places, names and dates. One should have more than that. One really should know more than that about peculiar uncles. Hmmm, yes, ahem, the dark stranger muses, might I not hear about Uncle Avrum? I am a collector of peculiar people, although I am a little overstocked these days. Still, your uncle sounds like someone to remember . . . and might we have another drink?)

We might. Waiter, another vodka here.

(Nevertheless, the dark stranger persisted, you do not think of your Uncle Avrum as a mere murderer . . .)

—My dear dark fellow, so much has happened to us all in eight hundred years, Poles and Jews, that it is now as though nothing had happened at all. Events decrease in substance as their cumulative quantity increases. There used to be a time, you might recall, when a man's murder made profound impressions . . . but that was all so many consciences ago . . . Now, leave me alone.

(You don't sound very friendly, said the friendly stranger.)

—My dear dark fellow, Abel said. There's an old Russian saying: When the wolf's at the door, make sounds like a bear. Or words to that effect.

Then he was smiling up at Catherine and she was smiling down.

—Who are you talking to?

—What? Who knows . . . myself, the Devil, God, it's all one anyway. I didn't think you'd come!

—Abel, you are immense! I had forgotten how immense you are!

—Immense? No, not immense. But gigantism runs in the family, we're all big-boned and weak-minded, idiots really, there must be a Prussian grenadier somewhere back along the line . . . Sit down!

—I *am* sitting down. *You* sit down. Abel, your nose is peeling. And you've hurt your hand!

—Those are my Wounds. I had two but one is all healed up. My God, I really didn't think you'd come.

—And you *have* had a drink or two, haven't you? Dear Abel, I'm so glad to see you.

—Catherine, Catherine, Catherine.

—You sound just like Emil!

—Impossible! His voice can't have broken yet.

—He shouts everything three times!

—The better to be heard, perhaps, intelligent child. Catherine, *how* are you? And why aren't you wearing a hat, that kerchief confused me.

—Women don't wear hats in Lwów any more, haven't you heard? We are all trying to look like the wives of railroad porters, or like those female locomotives the Russians brought with them, puffing along the streets in those silly white berets. I *was* going to wear a hat, a fur cap really . . .

—I knew it! Abel said. That's what I thought you'd wear.

—But Mother suggested camouflage. This is Camouflage Day.

—Your mother, yes, Abel said. How is she? And how's the professor? You told them that you were coming to see me?

—Of course I did.

—And nobody tried to stop you? Nobody warned you of Dire Consequence? What in God's name has happened to our better classes? The nation is lost.

Catherine said, laughing and talking through laughter: Abel, you make no more sense now than you've ever made, you're mad, you haven't changed at all! Of course nobody tried to stop me. Mother just smiled a little and looked pleased! My parents like me, they like me to be happy . . . though Father *was* a bit confused . . . he's such a dear old, well, you know . . .

And Abel said: Dinosaur. But a good one. A grand old dinosaur with a sense of humor. But a lovable dinosaur, Catherine said, the kind you'd keep at home. And Abel said: But they are not all like that, are they?

—No, they are not, Catherine said. Some of them are . . . unpleasant.

—Are you talking about anyone I know?

—No, I'm not, Catherine said.

—Is your fiancé a sort of dinosaur?

—Yes, he is.

—Then why are you going to marry him?

—I am not.

—You're not?

—No.

—Does he know it yet?

—No, not yet. I didn't know it myself until this morning.

—What happened this morning?

—You telephoned. It happened just like that! You telephoned, and it was all so silly . . . it was so mad, ludicrous! That mad telephone! After that there really wasn't any choice, was there? Does this make any sense?

—I can't think of anything that makes better sense. Poor little dinosaur . . . Catherine, I love you so much I'm ready to explode.

—I am ready to explode too, Catherine said. I want to go off like a gigantic bomb, the biggest bomb that was ever made! Just blow up everything! It's high time *something* happened. Abel, you dear madman, do you know what would have happened to me if you hadn't come back?

—No, Abel said. No. Tell me what would have happened.

—Nothing! Nothing at all! Isn't that terrible? Isn't that ludicrous? To be nineteen years old and alive and feeling like a bomb and have nothing happen? When so much is happening everywhere? Just to pass from nineteen to thirty with nothing in between? Abel, I'm so very glad you're back.

—I should have come back sooner. I should never have gone. America was . . . how do you say it? Ludicrous. Wasted time.

—If you had never gone anywhere, nothing *would* have happened! It couldn't! It's only because you were away and came back that everything else is so completely different! You *haven't* changed, have you? You *are* still a mad, eighteenth-century, loving lunatic? I don't think I could bear it if you had changed. Promise me that we'll never be tepid or cold or talk about hanging people, or talk in italics. I couldn't stand it if you started talking about hanging-people-when-the-time-came.

—I promise you that we'll never burn down, Abel said.

—Those people who talk about the Ashes of Old Loves, Catherine said. They really don't know what they're talking about, do they?

—They haven't the first idea of what they're talking about.

And Abel said, carefully threading words through the kaleidoscope of sound: Catherine, love, you haven't cut your hair, have you? Can you still sit on it?

—Yes, I can. It's all wrapped around under this silly kerchief. I'll take it down for you, if you like.

—No, don't, I'll take it down myself. I was afraid that you had cut it off. I want to hang myself on it at once. Immediately!

—There's so much noise here, I can hardly hear you, couldn't we go somewhere else?

—Yes, we shall, as soon as I can think of somewhere to go. Catherine, love, do you think you'd like to meet a dinosaur who has never burned down?

—A *burning* dinosaur?

—Like a perpetual flame, a candle of eternal dedication. The greatest human explosion I've heard of until now.

—Now that *is* something I would like to see. Who is he?

—My uncle.

—*That* uncle? The terrible one?

—That's the one.

—The one who murders people?

—He only murders nasty people, people who should be murdered.

—Are we going to be talking about murdering people?

—No, we're not. None of that has anything to do with us.

—You're quite sure that it does have nothing to do with us? That we won't ever be talking about things like that?

—Quite sure. We'll never even think about it.

—Then I'd like to meet him. What's he like?

—I don't know what he's going to be like. I only met him once, seven years ago, briefly, accidentally . . . Shall we give him a try?

—Your terrible uncle, Catherine said. Is that what you are going to be like when you are fifty-one? I don't mean that you'll be murdering people, but the rest of it.

—A perpetual flame? An ageless, deathless sort of dinosaur? I'll give it a try.

—Because, Catherine said, widely smiling, if it's at all possible that you'll be like that, like *him* . . . well, I really *should* see him, shouldn't I? It's an opportunity!

—Sly Catherine, Abel said. Catherine the Sly. The Great and the Sly. Beautiful Catherine who is sly, sly, sly!

—Lunatic, lunatic, lunatic!

The world after the flood must have felt like that.

The boomings and haranguing went on around them apropos of nothing; glittering phrases rained from somewhere under that archaic ceiling as if the world's biggest, costliest crystal chandelier had ruptured itself. Plink-plonk-PLINK! And again: *My dear, dear fellow, such terrible news! Let me be the first to offer my condolences! Heartfelt, deeply . . . Anything I can do, within limits . . . Of course.* Of course. Within limits. And why did they all have to talk like a book? Those late-Victorian emancipated minds. Gladstone liberals . . . trying to sound like a clean-shaven Karl Marx smelling of verbena, on his way to the British Museum, where the original Gutenberg Bible lies chained to the wall.

Someone was talking to him, bombarding Catherine, who must be protected. An irritating, critical little voice full of self-importance that begged to be stamped on: . . . *but you, as a published poet, that makes all the difference!*

He had to introduce him.

—Catherine, love, Pan Mann-Bielecki . . . Panna Modelska . . .

—Professor Modelski's daughter? Delighted, delighted. And how is your dear father? What is he doing now?

Catherine said: Now? At this very minute? I should think he is mending a shoe.

And he had thought that Catherine had to be protected! Still, the enfant terrible of 1924 was a formidable antagonist, who now said:

—What I like most about a revolutionary society is that sooner or later everyone is obliged to seek his true level.

The son of a bitch. Something would have to be done about the Mann-Bieleckis. Perhaps Uncle Avrum could be turned loose on them. Although the aging satirist wasn't tormenting Jews at the moment; he was trying to hurt a Polish girl, and perhaps himself. Why did they do it, what unbearable guilts were driving them to self-annihilation? And to think that I used to model myself upon Mann-Bielecki, longed for initiation into his mystic circles . . . Abel had a sweetly sick, fluttering pain in his stomach, as though he had swallowed a gigantic moth. He looked at his eight empty glasses and at Catherine's full one and at Mann-Bielecki's artificial boutonniere: a tulip made of yellow chicken feathers. He felt a curious, sickly horror at the sight of objects. Everything looked lifeless. His own dark face, reflected in the glass of an empty, dustless bric-a-brac cabinet, seemed inhuman. The aging satirist, head tilted, suddenly seemed to him a decapitated pig without the customary apple in his mouth. What in hell was happening to his head? When one is living, nothing happens. There are no real beginnings, the future is not already here. What he had wanted was the impossible: that the moments of his life should follow each other like those of a story told long after it had happened, or with the inevitability of a remembered tune. But he had failed to grasp even a shred of his past, so how could he hope to impose his will, like an author, upon the future?

And meanwhile someone, perhaps Teo, said loudly, ringingly: *I am, at heart, a liberal social democrat. I want to use the analytical tools of the Marxists, their urgency and passion, their relentless sense of time, without accepting a . . . theological view of the Dialectic . . .*

With a sense of sick finality Abel decided that he was going to be ill. This is not an existentialist nightmare. These people are real. And they are grotesque. They are not a cruel caricature, a deformed reflection trapped in a distorting mirror. They are righteous even in their rationalizations. They . . . we . . . are all mental pederasts buggering each other for a thousand years . . . surrounded by the sacred institutions of state and family . . . borne up by our consciousness of our own inestimable worth! It is future passions which, alone, can give color to events. None of this, based upon the past, makes any sense at all.

Teo said, crystally: *An anti-Cartesian attack upon the mind-body dualism . . .* And someone, possibly Gryszpan-Magdeburski, squeaked angrily: *Cartesian insistence . . . authority of consciousness in determining its own significance . . .*

And Abel knew that if he didn't immediately get hold of himself, by whatever part of him—past, present, or future—was conveniently protruding, he would gallop at once into total unreality: some damn Kierkegaardian lost soul without a Kierkegaardian God! All kinds of subterranean connections stood up and hit him on the head.

And, in the meantime, he had abandoned Catherine to the aging satirist. What had that headless pig done to her while he had been temporarily absent from the conversation? He had done nothing. She had not been shot down. On the contrary, she was giving it to Mann-Bielecki in a broadside of at least seventy-four cannon.

—Yes, I should think that's true, Catherine was saying. We can't really get away from what we are, can we, no matter what happens.

Mann-Bielecki jerked his head erect as if a cooing infant had suddenly reached up out of a frilly crib and smashed him with a club right between the eyes. He leaned forward, then back, then forward again, colorless pebble eyes rolling to left and to right, his yellow shoes creaking like a haunted staircase.

—What I really wanted to say, Abel, mademoiselle, was that I don't think, not for a moment, that you are in any danger of arrest. I had just heard about your father, Abel. The arrest. Obviously an error. You, as a published poet, member of the Society, have nothing to fear. A revolutionary society needs every intellectual it can get. We can, perhaps, get along without some of the toiling masses, but *they* can't make any meaningful progress without *us*. Intellect isn't manufactured like a shoe.

—I see, Abel said. That's very good to know.

—Yes. Well. I also wish to invite you to the banquet.

—What banquet?

—Oh, haven't you heard? The Society is giving a banquet tomorrow for representatives of the Poets' Union of Eastern Ukraine. The Town Hall, seven o'clock, dress optional, of course.

—I think I shall have a prior engagement, Abel muttered. And Mann-Bielecki added in that offhand manner that had made him a delight of drawing rooms for twenty-one years: You might find an opportunity to put in a good word for your father.

—Who with, for God's sake? Abel said. An Eastern Ukrainian poet?

—Commander Szymanski is going to be there.

—And who, may I ask, is Commander Szymanski?

—A Soviet officer, Mann-Bielecki said. A very interesting, cultured, civilized man. Descendant of one of those old Polish families from around Smolensk. Speaks excellent Polish.

—Another representative of the People's Culture?

—I think you'll find him interesting, persuasive, quite possibly helpful. He seems to be . . . a cut or two above the usual ragtag collection of our new masters . . . But the choice is yours. I would not *care* to insist.

Not care to insist!

—All right, Abel said. I'll come.

—It will be quite an impressive affair, I should think, the satirist went on, giving chapter and verse, smiling with confidence into distant memories of an indelible past. I am the chairman, naturally. Teo is secretary. Wanda Sierocka is going to recite again. Bunt is going to deliver his usual explosive exhortation, with the usual barricades and banners . . . you too can say something, if you like, as a representative of the younger poets. But don't speak for longer than five minutes, hmm? I don't think many of our guests will understand Polish. Well, dear boy. *Do svidania.*

—Goodbye, Abel said.

—Seven o'clock, Mann-Bielecki said, and moved into smoke. And was there, perhaps, a suggestion of sulphur and brimstone, was there a dark glow in the gray pebble eyes? This time, Abel's mind was definitely falling off a hillside.

—So that was . . . is . . . the famous Mann-Bielecki, Catherine said quietly. Could he really have had such an influence?

—There seems to be a great bell ringing somewhere, Abel said. Probably in my head.

—We'll take care of that too, Catherine said.

—They are so cunning, these latter-day Victorians, so bloody, bloody cunning. They talk like a book, they are so insidious with their bloody bookish authority. And now they are going to conquer the Soviets from within!

—We aren't going to even think about them, Catherine said.

—They are so delicate about the way they violate your mind, smile so distantly, politely, while they turn their bloody great screw. But it's all going to come to an end, even for them.

Catherine

THEY WALKED IN YELLOW LIGHT HALF FILTERED THROUGH SNOW, pressed close to each other. It was very cold. Icicles were beginning to snap off the crosspieces of square-cornered antiquated lampposts, off the occasional trees. Snap, snap. Like small dogs gnashing insufficient teeth; not unfriendly, but certainly, making themselves heard.

Catherine knew that she should be cold, she ought to be cold in her old cloth coat, not even hers but borrowed from Bronka for better camouflage. Her face, hands, and lower legs had become quite numb but the rest of her seemed to be on fire; she seemed to have become a container for molten metal and hot coals; there was a rare and delicious dessert that was made like that, baked something-or-other, cold on the outside, melting on the inside. Or perhaps it was the other way around . . . The child Catherine used to have it on her birthdays in another world . . .

Streetlights came on, one by one, here and there. Other lights filled an occasional window. Pale yellow rectangles, smeared by snow, a sickly and irregular illumination for a winter evening. Closer to afternoon than evening, but you wouldn't know it. She was aware of the hushed hurried pattern of her footsteps, Abel's lurching stride. Abel was lurching, no question about it. She hoped he wasn't going to be ill; he had turned white and red, flushed and livid in turn among the literati; the accidental symbolism of the national colors had not escaped her but she preferred not to think about it.

People appeared and disappeared in the gathering darkness like suddenly exorcised ghosts. They hurried, hunched over. There were long columns of black vans parked and unattended in each major street; she knew what they were and why they were there and fear made her breathless. So much for her morning resolution not to be afraid! But the snow helped. Snow turned the black vehicles into gently rounded mounds, accessible slopes . . . a memory of childhood skiing expeditions . . . a childhood of extraordinary happiness . . . why had it so suddenly left her without its comforting disguise?

She would not be afraid!

The avenues fell behind, gave way to narrow streets, one after another. The black vans, which people called *chornyi voron* in Russian (there being no equivalent in the Polish language, unless one wanted to talk about blackbirds, the birds of ill omen), disappeared. She was defenseless against sudden thought, the ominous clatter of an English nursery rhyme. The King was in the counting house . . . the Queen was eating honey . . . the Maid was . . . what was the Maid doing? She couldn't remember. But the blackbird had flown in and bit off a nose, just like that, for no apparent reason . . .

Then they were in a small square with an equestrian statue, the military hero wearing a powdery white hat. The horse and the hero had both turned a bright bilious green, as if suffering companionably through eternity with the same affliction. Here Abel stopped to read unfamiliar street signs.

She had never been in this part of the city, wouldn't think about it, a poor workmen's quarter, gloomy and ill-lighted. Sagging old houses leaned against each other rubbing cornices . . . It was impossible to imagine anyone being happy here. Ever. The houses said quite clearly that nobody was happy.

She shuddered (oh! she was so cold!) and, at once, Abel's arm tightened about her, a strong, protective, generous arm . . . She felt suddenly uplifted, gay, carefree, gloom forgotten; she felt she was smiling, the first woman who had ever smiled among those sagging homes; great lumps of warmth turned over and over inside her.

She had been right to come! There was nothing wrong with what she was doing. It was high time to stop being a gently unenlightened child and to become a woman, and if, in the process, one could also run away from the gathering gloom, fear, doubt, and the dreadful uncertainties of the times . . . well, what could be better?

There had been one or two quaking moments of uncertainty about what she was doing. She wouldn't have been Catherine if there had been no doubts. Centuries full of disapproving nuns had looked down upon her, yellowed traditions shook bony fingers, pursed ungenerous mouths . . . a convocation of lugubrious saints had marched up and down the corridors of her mind with bells, books, and candles, chanting exorcisms. But she had leaped across them like a liberated witch scattering showers of sparks. The moon was hers, if she could only reach it! Life was hers! Down with this worship of the moldering dead, who were they to teach the living anything? She insisted on her right to a grand and joyous life filled with great experience which would deny the deathly pall around her. If innocence, ignorance, and the rest of child-hood were the price of that sudden liberation, she would pay the price.

And what was that precious innocence, anyway? Like thought, it had become an intolerable burden. She was demanding immediate enlight-enment. She would telescope the disapproving centuries into instant knowledge so that she could and *would* be able to cope with the horri-ble new days.

And she loved Abel! Suddenly, immensely. She wanted to throw up a pyramid around him, anoint him with ointments, leap with him into hieroglyphics. She wanted to irrigate him and plant flowers in him. And not just because he was to be the dear instrument of her enlight-enment, the key which was about to free the woman locked within the child (although that seemed like a splendid reason to love anybody!), but as the owner of the long stride that matched itself to hers, and of the long arm that made her buoyant.

She had never felt such certainty. She was aware of herself as some-thing indestructible, practically eternal . . . the glowing core of some-thing timeless . . . She was electric, magic! On the threshold of conver-sion to something elemental! How could a bony admonition compete with that?

The dead eyes of the bilious hero no longer pursued her.

What a ridiculous impulse that had been, the whole Jurek business, but how inevitable in view of the centuries. The first time that she had seen him had been a brilliant morning in September, not yet hot, still redolent of night chill. He had been riding down the middle of an ave-nue that trembled to the beat of the dawn bombardment, the horrible rhythms that had followed her in and out of nightmares for a thousand hours. Great shells whirred overhead like runaway express trains. Homes, people, lives blew up. Masonry roared, collapsing. He had been calm, cool, towering, superb . . . patting the nervous neck of a beauti-ful horse, murmuring soothing words. He had called distinctly to her unquiet loneliness, investing her obscure and inglorious struggles with a kind of meaning. It was the kind of stunned illumination that one might experience if suddenly hit on the head with a tome of history . . . she had not thought about it.

Ziuta, or was it Luta, she could not remember (the two plump pack-ages of emotional pinkness being practically interchangeable), had run up to Jurek with a huge bouquet of freshly picked flowers. Catherine could not remember why she had picked the flowers; something to do with bolstering the household's morale under the terrors of the siege. Well, anyway, the admiring schoolgirl had handed the flowers to the beautiful young man on the gallant charger, and you could hear a hundred thousand romantic pages fluttering in that gesture, and you could hear all the gallant little songs . . . and picture frames released innumerable dashing heroes into the disappearing street . . . it was a denial of what was really happening! And he had scooped up the flowers in the way he would scoop up a lady's hand, touched them to his lips, grinning from ear to ear, touched the romantically askew visor of his lancer's cap, and rode off whistling a very old song. What could have been more touching, more reassuring? The sky-blue eyes that could never doubt the ultimate decisions of a remote God, laughing into roses . . . He brought a careless, unconcerned gaiety into the apartment. War, siege, hunger, fear, hopelessness . . . the new absolutes . . . suddenly disappeared beside this innocence. She hadn't had to believe anything that was happening until she realized, once the siege was over, that he had been untouched by war only because he loved it! He was the eternal lancer tilting for the honor of his ladylove! War was his mistress, her horrible voice had been sweet to him. And that song . . . *Wojenko, wojenko* . . . dear little war, beautiful lady war . . . had been his inspiration and his lullaby.

He had been such a beautiful young man, beautiful in the way that a forest fire may be thought beautiful if seen from great distance, so honorable, of such high principle . . . Bowing with infinite courtesy to his ladylove. *I kiss your hand, madame. For principle and tradition* . . .

(Father had said, not unkindly, being unable to be really unkind, of the distressed statesmen who had led Twentieth Century Europe with such dignity to the edge of the pit, and then politely stepped aside: *They were men of such high principle that, in the end, they had no principles whatsoever! I can only call them honorable purveyors of the irrational* . . .)

Ah, and she caught herself, laughing. There was that word again, *irrational*, it was beginning to put dents in her vocabulary like good old *ludicrous* . . .

(Bronka had said, bringing matters to the practical, possibly the essential: *Sniff, honest to God, this here princi-pal* . . . *it never kept a pair of feet warm on a winter night,* and Cousin Wlada, for once without laughter, seemed to have agreed. Mother had only said that Catherine should give herself lots of time before doing anything ah . . . conclusive . . . because some decisions were irrevocable. Not for the sake of God, who was probably far too wise and far too busy to attach much importance to human decisions, but for her own good.)

But, about Jurek. He had seemed to offer a love as spontaneous as it was irrational against the backdrop of a disappearing city, a quick, brave, impudent, and admiring gesture like that of the schoolgirl with her impermanent roses, and what could one do under the circumstances? Accept, of course. In the same spirit, in the same tradition that was blowing up the world; there was no other way to blot out *that* irrationality. So she had said yes, or had inclined her head, or perhaps she had only smiled, it didn't matter how consent was given; under the circumstances it was inevitable and . . . traditional.

Ah yes, tradition. The act of handing down statements, beliefs, legends, customs by word of mouth or practice; the handing over of something to another, a delivery or transfer; from the distant Latin of *trado*, a giving up, a surrender; through the Middle English of *tradicioun*, or betrayal . . . All of it had been an abysmal waste.

Then they were standing in the dank darkness of a gateway, surrounded by curved walls, and Abel was energetically sawing back and forth on a stunted bell rope. In the black depths of the tunnel gouged in the concrete, a bell was making shrill and violent announcements.

The house was like all the other houses in that quarter, a damp and chilly four-sided square box enclosing a dilapidated courtyard where a variety of sheds tumbled into each other. Five or six floors lined with narrow windows, like coffins stood on end, and a suicidal balcony running along the length of the façade about halfway between the sidewalk and the steep tiled roof that would enclose the usual clotheslines . . . Curiously gay, pink chimney pots. Window boxes. Cardboard in the windows. The gate was a huge semicircle split in half, then quartered, and further subdivided into concentric rectangles of gradually diminishing size like a Chinese puzzle box. The smallest of these now opened to reveal an eye; and a voice screamed in Yiddish. Surprisingly, Abel let fly with a comparable sound.

Then the concentric rectangles flew open, one after another, bang, bang, bang, bang (there were four of them), showing first a witch's nose and two furious eyes, then a forehead and fat cheeks studded with hairy warts, then adding chin, black shiny cloth, the shoulders of a wrestler, a mass of dark hair, and a rancid odor. The witch and Abel clattered at each other like runaway streetcars. Abel laughed. The windows banged shut, one by one, quartering the witch. The gate produced a narrow door the size of a big child. They went in through the door, Abel leading. Then there were five stone steps, a sort of hallway, and the staircase that rose in spidery spirals into an invisible roof. The witch screamed livid incantations behind them, banged a door, disappeared, but her voice pursued them.

Catherine followed Abel up the stairs, which seemed to sway and undulate in the unventilated darkness. She felt herself suspended above an abyss. The air seemed colder, but not fresher, the higher they climbed. The second floor, third . . . Smooth polished stone steps hollowed into troughs. The walls were slippery and damp when she touched them. She listened for the sound of the screws and the bolts which supported this perilous staircase working themselves out of the cement. She was quite certain that it was only the echoing imprecations of the black witch, and Abel's laughter, which kept her from hearing the rasp of the bolts.

And Abel was laughing.

—She didn't want to let us come up here, can you imagine? Mendeltort is away, she didn't think it proper for us to be there alone.

—When did you learn Yiddish?

—I haven't. There was a book in Yiddish that I once wanted to read, and there were some other reasons . . . Anyway, I tried to learn it but lost interest . . . It's not a hard language, just a German jargon, and besides the hands do half the work.

Now she could see a pale splash of light close under the ceiling. A dirty skylight blanketed by fog.

The streets had seemed more lifeless than ever. The fog had become sticky, like used surgical cotton. There had been many more black vans than usual waiting in the streets . . . all the way from the Politechnika to the Church of St. Mary Magdalene, in closely packed rows along Potocki Street as far as the post office . . . The church had been full of people praying, crying, lifting arms to the painted ceiling, demanding miracles. Were there to be no more miracles? The country seemed to live on them nowadays . . .

And Abel went on laughing, chuckling in the dark.

And suddenly she was shivering. And Abel was laughing. Great hoots and howls. Hoooo-ha-ha! Oh, my dear ever-living God, ha-ha. Omnipotent comedian. And she was shivering, suddenly afraid. Afraid? Well, not exactly, not exactly *afraid* . . . what then? Uncertain? No, *not* uncertain. Certainly *not* uncertain! She loved Abel and he loved her, and when you love someone . . . What was it that men did to you when you loved them? Oh, *that*, yes, well, she knew about that . . . there had been that long talk with Mother, long ago, that wonderful talk that made her feel beautiful . . . things Cousin Wlada laughed about occasionally, small implied things . . . Bronka saying things offhand, woman to woman, and you could laugh at them, they were so funny. But that's all very well! That was just talk, words, things heard and wondered about. Just a Someday thought. But you could always put the thought aside and turn to the picture of the lady with the parasol, the smiling gentleman, the doves and the cupids. And in waltz time, too! And there was never really going to be a Someday without cupids! He would . . . and she would what? And was she to take off her own clothes? She didn't think she'd be able to manage it, somebody had to do it. Oh, it's all very well to talk about it, think . . . but now . . . and

why was he *laughing?* And why was he no longer touching her, where
had his arm gone? He was gone in the damp, dark, malodorous shadows, groping along the wall, swearing mildly, then less mildly and
suddenly horribly. Her hip was frozen to the iron railing, her feet had
taken root in concrete . . .

—Ah-hhh! Goddammit all to hell!

And he was back, his dark face scowling, his thumb in his mouth.

—What, what . . . ?

—Goddam nail. Tore it on a nail. Looking for the key.

—A nail . . .

—Tore my thumb. Well, here's the key. Phew, it's damp out here.
Let's go in, love, and get a fire going, get out of these damp clothes.

Oh, he was being perfectly horrible about it! Luckily she was frozen
into utter immobility and so the moment could be indefinitely post-
poned. She really *should* give herself more time, just a little more, before making any irrevocable decisions. And this was an irrevocable one,
wasn't it? The end of one state and the beginning of another . . . and
what was so terrible about being a girl rather than a woman . . . what
was so terribly good about being a woman? Mother . . . Cousin Wlada
. . . And she was shivering, shivering in the arms of this man whom she
couldn't see, this stranger who had torn his thumb on a nail, her face
absolutely frozen to his chest. Was she, perhaps, going to be sick,
would she cry? Was it all going to be very messy? Or was she making
too much of it all, expecting too much out of something that should
be, and probably would be, beautifully simple? And she was walking
into a dark hall, a cold room, an empty apartment. She was alone with
this invisible dark man in this cold apartment and everything was happening far too quickly, and *now* was the time to say that she was sorry
but that, perhaps, under the circumstances, whatever the circumstances
would happen to be, they could just have a talk. Nice private gentle
loving talk, whereby loving things might be said, a confidence exchanged. Perhaps kiss gently, delicately. Romeo and Juliet, Tristan and
Isolde, Alcestis and . . . who did it with Alcestis? Perhaps something
like that, delicate and loving. To love is to do things which are gently
loving. Would he remember about being gentle?

She sought light, hating the dank darkness. Thank God for the windows. They were an icy pale blue and recently polished. The city's insufficient emergency lighting gave the windows a jeweled quality,
gleaming with pinpoint fires. Frost had begun to etch the panes with
wintry designs, making her think of Easter eggs, green fronds, delicate
tracings, cottage crafts, the paper cutouts of the Lowicz region . . .
None of these had ever been anything but lovely.

This brought back a measure of calmness. She could finally draw a

peaceful breath, stop shivering, bring her nervousness under comparative control. Her nerves were really in a deplorable condition. It was the
cold darkness that had made her shudder, the darkness of which everyone was so afraid these days, and with such good reason, but now the
darkness was no longer absolute; she saw a table, chairs; all kinds of
chairs, from the lumpy overstuffed variety that made her think,
curiously, of the literati, to the folding metal stools of an assembly hall.
A crimson armchair, like a throne. The room was large, a study or some
kind of meeting room, perhaps a clubroom, because of all those chairs.
She wondered who met here and why. Was this a terrorist headquarters, were murders plotted here, and what had happened to Abel's
terrible relative? He was probably out in the jeweled night, stalking victims. She felt like a victim. This was a murderer's temporary lair. And
she was alone in it with the nephew of a murderer, alone with a madman who, no matter how dear, how loved, now stalked into the room
behind the flickering glow of a thick wax candle, his face masked in
shadow, walking with extraordinary care as if afraid to spill one drop of
molten wax on the hardwood floor. And now she wanted to be left
alone, just as a moment ago she had wanted to have Abel here. Just for
a moment longer. So that she might become accustomed to the place.
Nothing was . . . is . . . really terrible if the surroundings were familiar. It was the unfamiliar which . . . well, which was frightening . . .
like this comfortable old city which had become foreign . . . all that
fear . . . the churches full of weeping desperate people . . . the roaring
black vans, the long trains, and the mute crowds massed outside the
prisons . . . thousands of people standing outside prisons with packages, letters, waiting . . . It was not a good time to make love.

Abel put the candle carefully on the table. He had found some kind
of a ritual candelabrum, an ornamented holder of many branches which
looked like an overturned brass spider. The flame flung itself about the
top of the sizzling candle as though anchored in wax and trying to escape. But, of course, it was trapped. Held by the smallest toe, so to
speak, in spluttering captivity. The struggling was futile, hopeless, and
(yes, she *would* use that word again, it was a splendid word under the
circumstances) ludicrous, because it was the nature of a flame to burn
as it was the nature of a young women to make love to young men and
damn the circumstances. And so all this jumping about the end of a
candle, and throwing frantic shadows about the empty walls, the shivering and the quaking, was . . . were . . . meaningless, useless, a sop to
convention, the conclusion having been assured at the moment the
flame had been struck. Everything was remarkably clear; it was all
going to be very pleasant. There was absolutely nothing to worry about.
Abel's face was moving in and out of shadow, and suddenly it was a

particularly dear, familiar, lost, loving, and pathetic face, somewhat clownish, with comic brown patches peeling off his sunburned warrior's nose, leaving it mottled pink. And he was sucking his thumb. Comic and endearing, young. His eyes were enormous, thanks to the somber shadows cast around them by the candle flame. They regarded her somberly, ludicrously across the fist he held to his mouth. How could she ever have felt afraid of him? He was no more ferocious than Emil. And really, when you've thought about it, at this moment she was so much older than he, so much more competent . . . Well! She picked up the hand which he held lumpily at his side in its white bandage cocoon, lifted it tenderly, pressing it to her chest so that she might, and did, feel his pulsebeat entering her own, and kissed it. He had wounds; she would heal them. That's why she had come.

And there really was going to be no trouble about it. Now as she stood with his hand pressed against her breast a great flash of desire went through her whole body. There could be no question of resistance; the demand was urgent and it was justified. His hand turned, cupping her and pressing . . . She felt that, surely, this insistent hand would leave a permanent imprint on her breast. No more imagination, no more searching among fantasies, no Perhaps or Someday. This strong and loving man who had become the root of her being put both his arms around her and brought her body hard against his own, and yes, suddenly it was there, that hardness pressed against her upper thighs through the thin cloth coat and the wool frock. If there were to be any retreat it would have to be now, but she was advancing! Her bones dissolved, and her legs suddenly had no strength. The will was there; the last thing that she wanted now was any kind of strength if strength meant resistance. She caught her breath in a half-laugh and a half-sob, wondering at the crystal clarity of the sound, the promise which it scattered through the room: so much like the innocent bugle of the morning. And Abel's mouth was on her own. The hard bruising lips tasted of sweet Krupnik, wine, and burned tobacco, sweet and bitter and equally appealing, so that she tasted them as if they were a confection made for her alone. She opened her mouth under his and sucked his probing tongue and, at that moment, his hand came up boldly inside her coat and under her dress as though this was the natural habitat for burned hands, a haven for torn thumbs; she felt the teasing rip of cotton giving way and then this large warm hand had closed upon her, stroking and caressing. How did he know her intricate design even before she was aware of it? No matter. He had remembered about being gentle, but the time for gentleness was apparently ebbing; she was impatient to get on with it, to be fierce with him. No more delays, no more preparations, nineteen virginal years were all the preparation that anyone could need, so let us, please, proceed to the milder forms of fierceness, whatever they were! She could not halt the sudden tremor that seized her whole body . . . the icy eruption . . . What ancient commands was she obeying now? Certainly nothing that had gone before resembled this moment. Her mind and body were suddenly one again, joined in the demand. She wrapped both arms around his neck and hung there, anchored in certainty. Then she was weightless, magically transformed into pure spirit, caught in midflight across the ceremonial fire . . . and, practiced as a ballerina, she gave a little skip in the air, wrapping her thighs around the hollows of his waist, which seemed fashioned expressly for this purpose. A swollen warmth now passed between her legs and she reached down between them and grasped the hardness that was so totally alien and yet so familiar and guided it into her own wet flesh. This man to whom she had become welded gave one spasmodic thrust, a heave of pure flesh, and in a moment of sharp pain and immediate pleasure she had received him, welcomed him; she was one with him and all the mysteries; she was exalted, she flowed like a river over a precipice. She cried out, filled with an immediate gratitude for the miracle of her body and its intricate design. Her body beat against his with increasing swiftness, its rhythm broken only by her cries, his shouts and his laughter. Yes, he was laughing! His eyes were full of tears! The tears in the joy or the joy in the tears . . . this was beyond her at the moment when the pleasure of these multiple thrusts seemed endless and she spiraled upward toward revolving planets and new moons, wholly given to this new experience which healed her and him, overflowing, beyond the gloom of admonitory centuries which had so bitterly and falsely maligned the holiest communion . . . which would have consecrated her miraculous body to sterility (patriotic vessels! stained-glass maternity! the desolation of the practical!) . . . Her legs crept upward along his straining body, and wasn't it miraculous that at each point of this ascent she found a firm mooring? Her knees locked underneath his arms; she spanned him with the spread of her encircling thighs, wishing them broader, wider, better able to enfold this magical male instrument and the man himself. She felt, seemed to feel . . . perhaps *imagined* his hardness break, flooding her in turn, the seeds drawn in, absorbed, and scattering within her seeking fertile soil. Their single body trembled with every muscle in the reflection of the dresser mirror illuminated by the sputtering candle. No gloomy-eyed nuns, then, in her consciousness.

Then who said what, and when? Abel had recited.

Et son bras et sa jambe, et sa cuisse et ses reins,
Polis comme de l'huile, onduleux comme un cygne,
Passaient devant mes yeux clairvoyants et sereins;
Et son ventre et ses seins, ces grappes de ma vigne . . .

. . . The chant created rhythms which made her beautiful, and she could finally read herself in Abel's suddenly fixed stare; she felt delight but also a certain sense of awe, at the power of her essential self which now began to flow again . . . a certain gratitude, a feeling of wonder, pride . . . And the sole fear now was *not* to be appreciated again! The lights of a far-off explosion invaded the room and seemed to invade her as well, a scarlet assault that mingled light and sound in one intricacy in that climactic moment.

. . . Sometime then, or shortly afterward, she had said: I have never been so happy in my entire life, and Abel, whose mind had understandably wandered far away, replied: Many women are like that, it's a question of time.

So much time had been wasted, but now she felt abundant, milkily replete, and she could look down at the suddenly understandable shapes and contours, the bulge of the breast, the swollen curve of her hip tapering off in shadow . . . everything had its function, nothing was accidental; she *had* been carefully and responsibly designed.

. . . And there had been cupids, after all. Stout grinning cherubs, just as bold as their brassiness could make them, molded in pairs into the four posts of the antique bed, which, in the amber light of the leaping candle flame, had acquired golden hues.

. . . And there had even been a real explosion, the booming rolling sound of a distant and unimportant disaster, which rattled the windows, dislodged the cardboard membranes, and filled the room with suddenly moving air. Abel had declaimed, or perhaps she had only imagined that he had, being lost in the parobolic compulsions of the moment:

Her eyes fixed as a tiger's in a tamer's trance
Absent, unthinking, she varied her poses
With an audacity of wild innocence
That gave strange meanings to each metamorphosis.

. . . Such sweeping changes, such discoveries. Her whole life seemed to have been pointed toward this singular moment. Curiosity was abundantly satisfied, but there was no sense of sin, no sense of anything other than pleasure, and even that seemed irrelevant to the moment.

Now she could finally appreciate herself, being so thoroughly appreciated.

It had all turned out so much better than she had expected. In her most secret mind she had expected to be brutally hurt, the legend of a painful deflowering having been a favorite topic of Sister Teresa, but there had been hardly any pain at all! So pain had also been a legend! Did that mean that the Authority of Pain had also been driven into exile? Would the wages of sin be henceforth, perhaps, less deadly?

God really couldn't be such an offensive, vengeful, unforgiving, bitter, and interfering old man as He had been painted.

Catherine said:

—I feel as if I had just broken with my entire past.

—Good, Abel said. That means that there is no past, you see, never has been . . . There's only the future, and that's how it should be.

She had been carefully taught, by nuns and by centuries, that pleasure was subject to the painful authority of shame and atonement. This now seemed blasphemous. God, surely, wouldn't demand compensation . . .

She kept this apparently suspended rule in mind as she said, happily, considering a future replete with pleasurable experience: What shall we do now?

And Abel chanted, mocking ecclesiastics: What everyone else does . . . Live!

—How shall we live? Where? When?

—Let's not talk about life, let's live it.

And she said, enfolding him again: By all means, isn't that what we had both decided to do? And as we increase in our knowledge of each other, and of pleasure . . . Still, I suppose there must be limits even in that.

—Why should there be? Man is a free animal, not a slave of instincts and of nature.

—But we can't go beyond the bounds of instinct and of nature.

—Why not? Man breaks the laws of nature all the time. This is his freedom. He develops science and conquers nature. He conquers instincts and develops culture. Pleasure is just one more enlargement of his freedom. The joy of living lies in the freedom to play with experience.

—Oh, Abel, she said. You are such a fool. There are some things that people *cannot* do.

—Name one, he said, grinning like a madman.

—I can't at the moment. But I'm sure that there are at least that many.

—A few minutes ago, my beautiful fallen woman, you would have added one more to your list. That's what comes of having lived so long among priests, peasants, and boiled potatoes. Only the Irish have managed to beat us at making the game of sin as dull and colorless as virtue itself . . . Ah, hell, one thinks of Petronius . . .

—One does not. Now what are you doing?

He had bitten open his thumb again and was painting hexagrams and other strange devices around and around her navel. She felt pleasantly corrupt.

—Witchcraft, the golden incantation to the lord of light, lust, and blood, he of the Persian pantheon. Your final liberation from the corruption of good manners. Ah me, which idiot saint was it who said that it was the eyes which were the smoke vents of the soul?

—Ah, Abel, she cried. I don't think . . .

He had apparently acquired magic powers. He had made her pliant. But she was not afraid. God would forgive them everything since there could be neither blasphemy nor sin without volition and she, for one, was beyond the exercise of will. And, besides, was he not the God of Love among other functions, and was not this an act of love, even if rather odd. And was it not his traditional métier to understand and forgive?

The blanket was thin, used, stamped with warlike hieroglyphics. Well, she had her hieroglyphics, no doubt about that, the irrigation and the planting might come a little later, and in the meantime the blanket was sandpapering her knees.

—Ah! Abel cried. Now we are liberated!

—Abel, she said. I don't think . . . this is painful!

He chanted, laughing: Pain is pu-u-urity, purity is pain . . . Thus we ascend into the lap of the Creee-ay-tor! And, ah, we purify the corrupt seed of centuries in the incorruptible. Now, sweetheart, over you go!

She hadn't bargained for anything like this. Her face was suddenly wet and she was desolate.

Later she smoked a cigarette, her first. Another infraction of the rules which had, apparently, not fled overseas. The room had become icy cold. The candle flame had blown out. The scarlet firelight had gone from the windows. Abel had fallen asleep with her hair wrapped like a bright, metallic scarf around his neck, and she was anchored to him. She wanted to get up and take her bewilderment off those cheap cotton sheets, but she didn't want to wake him, not just yet. His face was peaceful, thoughtless, sculptured as though he were dead, and the dead, of course, are always innocent . . .

That left her with the guilt, pain, and humiliation and she was damned if she'd bear the entire load. That *couldn't* be what being a woman was about!

Could he be dead? He didn't seem to breathe. Certainly there had been a moment when she thought that he might have been dying. But do the dead grin from ear to ear?

Well, he had fallen asleep like an innocent man, muttering something about being a shaded hamlet at a mountain's base . . . probably more Baudelaire . . . and she had immediately forgiven him everything. What else can one do? When the man kicks over all the regulations in the name of love, freedom, and other grand intangibles, states absolutes as if he had just invented them, shouts lines of Valéry, Juvenal, and furthermore . . . when he is the man who has just completed her metamorphosis . . . when he has driven *time* out of her mind . . . well, what else could she have done? But then it got cold.

That blanket had been cruelly abrasive. Her knees stung. She had been bewildered by the suddenly unpoetic turn of otherwise beautiful events. What had got into Abel, anyway, where had the poetry disappeared so swiftly? To be commanding, even cruel, was all very well; it could be just another way to claim her attention; but he had seemed to forget all about her at one point, it could have been almost anybody under him. It was most confusing. She rubbed her aching flanks. Twin globes of light, he had shouted, laughing, which had leaped at him out of darkness like automobile headlights! That hadn't sounded immediately flattering . . . Oh, that's what hurt! That he had taken her so lightly, in such excellent humor, as if she were no more than a well trained steeplechaser broken to the bit. Over you go, sweetheart, he had cried, and that had been that. All very well, perhaps, for an experienced woman of long standing, but this *had* been her maiden run . . . she had hoped for more poetry than hunting cries.

She started to cry again, then stopped. It was too cold for tears. They felt like liquid fire on her icy cheeks. How could one be so happy at one moment and sunk in such bottomless depression the next? Damn Abel, anyway.

She had to leave at once. She had to get home. She hadn't bothered to think about going home, foolishly assuming that such ideas as home, childhood, womanhood would have been illuminated by the great experience, so that, thereafter, she would be able to move back and forth in time, finding herself wherever she pleased: home, childhood, womanhood, Abel, innocence, or freedom . . . and in the practical sense she had forgotten time.

It was late, dark outside, darker than winter afternoons and evenings. The night meant curfews and the hissing of black vans. The friendly apartment was far away. They would be worrying about her. She had been inconsiderate.

And in the meantime, Abel was sleeping on her hair.

She tried pulling it loose but he started muttering. She would never get loose. She would be stuck here, held captive all night, until he awoke, and what would happen then? She didn't want to have anything more happen, not even poetry. And she would never be able to explain why she had not come home.

Mother would know, of course . . . and Father . . . and Jurek would . . . Damn Jurek anyway, triple-damn him! It was all his fault.

Except, of course, that the poor idiot, the eternal lancer, had had nothing to do with it; nothing! She was a grown woman now, exercising her own will, dispensing her body as she wished, and bearing conse-quences . . . Impulsive? Yes, she supposed that she had always been impulsive, generous, overwhelmed by the brightness of a singular idea . . . But no impulse moved her now when she needed one. Abel's face seemed gentle in the shadows; he would have no idea that anything was wrong, would not suspect how urgently she wished to get away from him. A stray beam of distant light had fallen on his wide marbled chest and the bright loops of hair coiled around his neck. He had wound her loosened braids around himself as if relishing captivity; both his hands were buried in her hair to the knuckles. She wanted to be long gone when he awoke. Tomorrow, well tomorrow perhaps they could talk. It might all seem easier to cope with, perhaps her depression would be gone, it had to be gone!

She would get up, softly so as not to waken him, sheltered by the darkness. She would not have to see her own body. She would erase his imprint off herself. She would remember only his appreciation and like herself again. And perhaps it seemed fitting, symbolically right to leave behind those golden loops that he relished . . . perhaps that would be enough of a sacrifice . . . an ancient ritual . . .

His trousers hung on a chair next to her, and from their pockets spilled the residue of his military past, the recently heroic experience: two rubber devices, a ball of string, a Swiss Army clasp knife with innu-merable blades (including, he had told her, an instrument for removing stones from the hooves of reindeer), a small metal compass, two silver buttons and a little pouch containing darning wool, a needle and black thread. She opened the clasp knife to an adequate blade but couldn't bring herself to slice away her hair. Perhaps if she would try pulling it loose once more . . .

And suddenly all the lights went on in the apartment; all over the city wherever there was an unsmashed bulb, a turned-on switch, an unuprooted lamppost, violent yellow light exploded and tore into the darkness. The effect of this immediate illumination was staggering.

Catherine cried out, made mindless by shock.

Why did this have to be done to her?

Someone had spliced a wire, replaced a connection, welded a piece of ruptured armature, pressed a lever, and destroyed the darkness. Simultaneously with the sudden glare, a great roar started up beyond the windows, one thousand cold engines turning over.

She was rendered sightless, terrified. It was like being struck by a gigantic fist. All at once, against all expectations, the darkness which had concealed utilitarian horrors, which had preserved fragments of fantasy and imagination, had been torn to shreds, and she saw the full ugliness of cracked and sagging plaster, the spattered gray sheets, a glistening brown wetness creeping down a wall . . . the tin cherubs were no longer golden, their simpering nakedness made her own nudity obscene.

She was coarse, yes, used, crumpled! Her legs, arms, breasts, hands, feet had lost harmony and form. They were dead slabs of bluish flesh, swollen bags streaked with sweat and Abel's insane markings . . . Abel's large body had lost firmness, it had the chalky whiteness of a corpse, he was limp, grotesque . . . they were both grotesque! And she was ugly! Everything was ugly! The last of those sublime enchanting fantasies that had floated like elusive music in the rarefied dark air, which had transformed the darkness into a love chamber, a magic room of beauty and pleasure, were immediately erased. She slashed at her trapped braids and watched yellow hair falling in thick showers around a man's dead face. And he still slept! He had not even moved! Her hair moved about his mouth as though it were alive. She felt despoiled, robbed. And now she started to cry in earnest, pushing both fists clumsily into her eyes as she used to do when she had been a child.

The lights went out as magically as they had come. Darkness fell on her, too late, no longer concealing. And now the windows shook to the coughing roars of the black vans.

She felt as if she had just been lifted out of the ruthless, impersonal hands of surgeons and now could not remember what had been cut out of her, the heart or the appendix . . . or perhaps the soul . . . the ingrown cyst of a love she had not hitherto offered to anyone. No, she would not become hysterical! She would simply go home.

She couldn't find her clothes. They, Abel and she, had taken everything off very neatly, having made a stylized ballet of garments and limbs, folded everything, and she had wondered at this unsuspected and illuminating facet of Abel's personality, whichever of his personalities this one happened to be, this orderly preoccupation with minu-

tiae as a preamble to shouting anarchy . . . but the chair on which they
had stacked her things had been kicked over later on (it had gone
sailing with a crash!) and now she couldn't find anything. White headlights splashed the windows as the columns of malevolent black vans
hurtled past the house, hissing like rubber-tired hearses toward the center of the city, and in these lightning flashes, measured as metronomes,
she tracked down as much as she had to have. Torn pants, wool vest,
skirt, sweater, boots lined with Persian weave, Bronka's coat; she pulled
these on, haphazardly, and abandoned the rest.

The stairs seemed endless. She felt that she was stepping into a bottomless pit that corkscrewed into the center of the earth . . . her hurried
footsteps rattled in the stairwell. She felt fragile. She knew that if she
happened to fall on those calamitous stairs she would snap in two like a
champagne glass. The third floor, the second. The hollow troughs
seemed to sink under her; it was like treading on the deck of an airship
falling through empty air. The house creaked and whispered. There
didn't seem to be another human being in the house . . . ah, well, people had begun to leave their homes at nightfall to hide in the parks . . .
crated their children in packing cases in the attic . . . they didn't return to their homes until dawn had signaled the end of the hunt . . .
But then she heard a scrap of conversation as she passed a door; someone was weeping, someone else was praying, a woman urged hysterical
children to get dressed in case . . . a man was cursing in a tearful voice.

Then she was at the bottom of the stairs, struggling with the gate.
There were bars, bolts, but no locks. She got the small door open and
stepped into the street.

The fog had become milky white, streaked with yellow tendrils. It
moved in thick, buttery swirls which clung to her face. The fog and the
snow muffled her footsteps, so that she ran almost without a sound
after an ever-retreating wall; if only she could reach it and enter beyond
it, she knew she'd be safe. The icy air formed a tight-fitting mask about
her mouth and nostrils and made breathing difficult. It didn't seem to
her that she was moving at all, and perhaps she wasn't; this could very
well have been some sort of a dream, and so she was perhaps motionless
and thoughtless on a whirling treadmill, while the blinded houses slid
past her with increasing swiftness on invisible rollers . . . Faster and
faster as if to catch the roaring trucks which burst through the fog . . .
each black truck packed with a dense upright mass of frosted-over people, lurching through dreamy tendrils, swallowed by the fog . . .

An arm came at her from the fog, followed by a dwarfed shape, and
she looked into the gray face of a one-eyed man, a bony fragment sud-

denly luminous in the pit of the socket. The black mouth opened, closed. She heard: . . . *for God's sake . . . the whole quarter, end of the world, or what? Twenty-two trains tonight* . . . and the man disappeared in the galloping mists.

This was no longer her Lwów, this was a foreign city, an Asiatic warren made hollow by fear, where people like herself were hunted in the streets. Street followed street and then she was on her own avenue, only a step from home.

She heard the thin screams, the cries, the shouts, and the curses. Glass showered tinnily from above and a white birdlike shape hurtled to the pavement. And now another figure loomed before her (yes, loomed, because he was a giant), a huge man made taller by the fog, which seemed to have decapitated him as well. She stepped aside, nimble as a ballerina, and a distant bell said something tremulous right into her ear. This small sound coming through the fog could no longer alarm her. It was no more alarming than the little bell swung by an acolyte while a priest hurried with the sacraments to a dying man.

And now it was the turn of a fleshless, bloodless-looking fellow in an unkempt military greatcoat to run out of the fog, one arm extended before him like the prow of a ship, one empty sleeve flapping behind him like the broken wing of a crippled brown bird. He shouted, hugely: Run for it, lady! They're taking us all!

Then two more men, a woman and a wailing child choking on hysteria, another woman and another man . . .

She fell against stone steps. It was the church of St. Mary Magdalene, the whore of Magdala who had become a saint, had been forgiven and elevated. Catherine's hand rose to inscribe the cross on her chest and forehead, but the words remained choked in her throat. The wailing hum of massed prayers fell upon her out of the open doors of the church, in yellow light . . .

Then she was in the middle of a mindless mob, terrified people in furs hurriedly drawn over nightclothes, some carrying nothing, others staggering under packing cases, all shouting, questioning, surrounded by rows upon rows of shaggy fur hats, oilcloth caps, and pointed bayonets.

. . . Two troglodytes in woolly Cossack hats lift a crushed girl off the cement, the same half-naked shape that had hurtled birdlike from a window a moment ago, and heave her into the back of a truck: she lands softly, *smack!* One expects sawdust to erupt . . .

The roaring trucks blew the fog apart.

. . . Two soldiers in blue caps curse the senile weight of old infirm Pani Lutycka, the recluse of the second floor, who now mouths imbecile prayers on a mattress while her fourteen cats shoot underfoot in every direction like furry torpedoes . . .

Cousin Wlada said clearly and distinctly: *Cela passe toute croyance!* She had remained graciously invisible in the mad mob of neighbors which quivers like a toothache, and Catherine was momentarily transfigured while her involuntary tears punched holes in the snow.

She cried out once, twice, fruitlessly, and began to search the vacant faces which slammed shut before her like chests carved in old wood.

. . . Kobza, the janitor, goes by, grunting and sighing under a wooden crate stuffed with straw, wood shavings, into which he had thrust four small children, not his, wrapped in old newspapers for warmth, neatly tied with string; their round solemn faces gleam like jars in the straw.

Something snapped within her. She heard a question asked in her new spiraling voice but it was ignored.

And now she began to run among the trucks, peering into the densely packed, scientifically arranged upright contents which seemed no more human than a load of fence posts.

. . . There is Kepi, who sold newspapers on the corner, slept in a crate in the cellar of No. 22, claimed to have spent five years in the Foreign Legion, waxed his pointed mustache, presented his newspapers with a Gallic flourish. An odd gnome of a man. Father had said that the Legion story wasn't very likely unless the French kept an outpost in St. Brigid's Prison . . . Kepi is walking arm in arm with young Father Zenek, the shy soft-spoken priest from the seminary, who is, perhaps, too young to be a full professor of philosophy and moral law, a gentle man and kind. He came each afternoon to the apartment to teach the now forbidden catechism to the children at St. Alicja's, must have been visiting someone on the street this evening. They confer, the fraudulent legionnaire and the true priest. Kepi says, solemnly, with the assurance common only to the *apache* of Paris and the *batiar* of Lwów: Wait till they hear in the Legion what's going on here! They'll chase these red louse catchers into a goat's horn! As I love God! And Father Zenek whispers: God may very well arrange something of the kind . . .

And someone urgently explained: This isn't an arrest, we've not been arrested. It's what they call a voluntary resettlement, common enough in Russia. And someone else said, bitterly: This is Lwów, not Russia. And an equally bitter voice said: Tfui! It's bloody Russia now.

An immense man, bearded like a lion, elbows a Ukrainian militiaman out of his way as he marches into a black van, vanishes inside. A monumentally fat woman slams another on the head with an umbrella as he tries to knee her into the back of a truck. (Save your hands for shoveling manure!) Another scolds a child for crying. (Don't let them see that you're afraid of them!) Another is openly afraid, proclaims it and wails.

The shouts soared, the cries and the weeping. She felt that she would shortly become unstrung and spin away into blessed idiocy.

Blessed be the idiots for they shall not have understanding, blessed be the insensitive for they shall not suffer, blessed be the cynical for they shall be amused.

. . . Sledge hammers rise and fall, inscribe great arcs on the dissipating fog, an ancient oaken door says DOO-OOM! and falls, and soldiers swarm into the tunnel with leveled bayonets . . . hoarse shouts, a clattering command . . . iron-shod boots strike ungentle sparks off the iron stairs . . .

People, in all their kinds and possible conditions, fell like statues into the soft glitter of the snow. Behind them, lost in the vacuum of fog, what? A disappearing world. Before them . . . the bleak caves of the imagination. Her shouts went unheard in the huge ululation of anger, blasphemy, prayer, and despair. She thought she saw the yellow moon face of Dr. Pormeba swept into the void but she could not be sure. She was numb, yes, but not afraid, her blood had become gelid, so does imagination bring about the longed-for punishment. And then a woeful and inadequate litany began among the living fence posts, the skirling of a thousand Jonahs, or perhaps ten thousand, vanishing at a gulp; they hanged their *Jezu, Jezu* like supplicants' silver crutches and burning brass hearts on the cracked firmament. Each upraised hand was a votive candle.

. . . One after the other, people are flung into the vans; they swarm across the tailgates of the trucks, which belch an oily soot; the tailgates are raised and chained, soldiers sprawl on the roofs of the cabs and point firearms and the odyssey begins. Tomorrow, and for days thereafter, relatives will beat upon sealed doors or wander through disembowled apartments looking for the lost, and the long trains will follow each other like abacus beads across an emptied countryside . . .

Why wouldn't anybody listen to the cries of anybody else? Here and everywhere. Ah, she thought, charged with an overwhelming weariness. Hush now, hush! We have fallen upon the fog like decapitated statues one and all, a cityful of people, a gaggle of geese, a whine of mendicants, a palaver of priests, an affluence of merchants, a torment of Jews, a snort of publicans, a matrix of matrons, a pride of lions, a legend of heroes, a scamper of cowards, a confluence of poets, and a gibe of critics. Eyeless and monumental in the bellowing trucks.

And then she could no longer focus her eyes. There were too many trucks, too many frozen faces. She did see Jurek, or someone who could have been Jurek (since the face was a bloody-black mask and unrecognizable), dragged by the feet through the snow like a slaughtered calf, his smashed head leaving a liquid black trail as broad as her hand . . . He had so wanted to die for his country!

Whole generations of us had been raised to die for our country, thus country more than others.

(Mother had said, *Why not teach children to live for their country? If only men could give birth once in a while* . . . That had been in the first days of the war while they stood on their balcony on a kaleidoscopic morning in September and watched the singing soldiers, garlanded with flowers, winding down from the Citadel on their way to trains. And Father said, distressed as he was seldom seen: *Going off to war with the good spirit of participation in a Saturday-afternoon theater performance* . . . *You'd think that, in our thousand years of Christianity, of civilization, we would have realized that the cannon of our misinterpreted history are pointed at us!* And Mother had said, gently: *It's an old savagery, much older than we.*)

She ran toward Jurek. She would make it up to him, whatever it was! She would make it up to everybody! Four soldiers, indifferent as the north wind and the velvet sky, lifted him and threw him with so little effort into a small black car, separate from the others, and the car snorted, coughed, belched, and rocked into the darkness before she could reach it. She wept. She was totally abandoned. Was she always to be too late, would her offering always miss its mark?

She saw the Patriarch, Pan Rashevsky, pace with the dignity of four thousand years toward the endless column of trucks which, for him, would also be an image torn out of innumerable memories, casually propelled by two young Jews with rifles and red armbands; his beard was windblown, made Christmassy by frost. She ran toward him, calling, then stopped and recoiled under the icy impact of his stare. He willed her back into the disguise of the billowing crowd, told her explicitly to be invisible and thus survive the night . . . And hands that might have been Esterka's reached down to him from a truck. Janek Stypenko jumped down to offer his back as a steppingstone.

She did not see her parents anywhere!

And for an unbelieving fragment of a moment, just as brief as the time it took her to form such an impossible idea, she buckled under hope. Perhaps they got away! Perhaps they had been warned! Perhaps . . . Oh, but hope was an unreasonable illusion, a word used by idiots.

Then both her arms were seized from behind, she was embraced, turned about, and found her face pressed against the cold rough surface of a cracked oilskin coat. Ferenc Karoly's inflamed eyes looked into her own.

—Comrade Catherine! What are you doing here? I thought you were away!

—I was, I was! she wept into his coat.

—You shouldn't have come back . . .

—How could I know that it would be tonight? How could anyone know? And what has happened to my family?

—They've been taken . . . Everyone, the whole family is gone . . . I am sorry, you must believe how sorry I am that you had to see it done this way. It is not normal, not as we would wish it. The times, you see, are uncertain. Certain measures seem more harsh than they really are . . .

—Oh, stop it, stop it, she wept, out of control. Don't tell me any more about the imperatives of history! I want to find my parents. Where are they? Take me to them. Please let me go to them, please help me find them.

—Please. Comrade Catherine. You must calm yourself. Please, you must be strong.

She cried: Oh, will you stop it? Will you let me go?

He said: We will leave this place. I will hold you so, by the arm, like this, and you must walk with me. It will look natural, yes? Nobody will stop us. Then I will take you to your friends and you will be safe.

She cried: Safe? How can anyone be safe? For how long? When will all this end?

—You must be calm, Comrade Catherine. We must all be patient. Times will become better. It is always difficult at first, there are so many hostile elements, you see.

—Stop telling me that times will be better! Take me to my family, please, I must find them.

—They were among the first to be taken, Ferenc Karoly said apologetically. They have already gone to the trains, you see, and it is no good going to the trains. Now walk beside me and look at the ground. You see? It is very natural. You look as if you were arrested.

Then he said: Very good, very good, it is *very* natural.

The sharp playful beam of a spotlight, lighthearted as a country clown, danced out of the shadows. It played among the windows of the house directly ahead and then slid down an ornamented piece of copper tubing, which suddenly took fire. The snowflakes were fiery and cheerful. The light fastened to them for a moment, swept on, found Catherine and Ferenc Karoly, inquired, and released them. The back of the militiaman's raincoat had cracked fore and aft and made him seem like a minor penitent who carried a thin cross.

. . . Harsh shouts, a supplicating protest, a high-pitched cry, a clattering command, the soft unhurried thud of rifle butts beating a man into submission, the roar of the motors.

Then there were desolate streets, gray walls with rows of blank black-papered windows hung like picture frames. Nothing in the windows, not even curiosity. Torn paper peeling back to show empty silence, the edge of a curtain, a fragment of fear.

Mendeltort

HE SENSED MORE THAN SAW THE BLACK LIMOUSINE sliding to a halt beside him, heard the clattering of hobnailed boots, the bark of command, and at once his body was in motion.

Into a side street, then an alley, then a narrow lane between houses, while an engine roared. Would they shoot? Never in the streets where anyone could see them, that wasn't the style. And wasn't it amazing, really: twenty million corpses to their credit and not a shot fired where anyone could hear it . . . except, of course, the target . . . But the dead make deplorable witnesses.

Another lane, too narrow for the limousine. But now doors slam metallically, the boots come up pounding. Not even a shout. Over a fence into a yard among clotheslines, another fence; and he was in the clear, running down a broad street among startled people.

His body had taken full command, it needed no direction from the mind, which, in that series of practiced and instinctive reactions, was left far behind. He could observe with detachment how the disciplined machinery of his flesh responded to the instant demands of a specific moment, so that the moment had become the event. Thought would come later. Later still, the questions would present themselves for analysis and answers. Namely: How had they got onto him so quickly, how had they known where he would be waiting for Meyer and his people (no light came into the doorway where he had crouched in shadow)? He knew when he was being followed, he knew how to spot even an eight-box; and no one, he could swear, had trailed him from the railway station. What nasty little bird had whispered in those Mongol ears? There could be only one, Meyer himself. But all that could come later. What mattered now was the machinery of motion. Knees rise and fall, the chest is suddenly constricted, then expands. The mind's first relevant signal comes like a radioed message: Get off the main street.

And a lane immediately appears, and beyond it is another and another, each lost and narrowly compressed between leaning houses, and they become a channel for his energy, as though he were an elemental force seeking a conductor.

. . . Only Meyer knew that he was in town and where he'd be waiting. Dear Meyer, he thought with quick affection: he'll live a long time.

. . . His ears were full of the drumming of his own pulse, the surge of his blood, and he no longer heard the hobnailed boots or the curving screech of tires; they, like his mind, had fallen far behind his undirected body. A shout behind him? Something like a shout. The iron-studded sandals were clattering once more on Judaean goat tracks among ravines, cliffs, and the whistle of the Cossack whip was shredding the night air; nothing is new, nothing is ever new, all there is ever to be found, ever to be experienced, is rediscovery of a forgotten past, the swift and terrible inheritance of the running man. The poetry of the running man has neither rhyme nor rhythm, it is the baying of the hound, the hiss of the arrow, the thunder of pursuing chariot wheels; nor can he ever count upon the seas to part before him and close upon the hosts of the Pharaohs . . . And he is once more in a broad avenue full of hurrying people and people who are momentarily struck dumb and motionless by his threatening appearance among them, and people whose mouths open and make no sound. The distant shout is long lost behind him. And suddenly everyone grasps the meaning of the running body, the suggestion of invisible pursuit, and there is instant motion other than his own as if a signal had passed from him to everyone else.

Which, indeed, it has.

All faces are immediately averted and everyone is running. Ancient wisdom; the lesson taught an imaginative people by their ruinous history.

(If you don't see it happening, you don't know about it; if you know nothing, you can't be made to tell; if you're not there to be questioned, who's going to question you? Authority is always a foreign imposition.)

He heard a shot, another, drew a breath. The circumspect NKVD didn't shoot in public. So it would be the others: the Ukrainian Militia or the KomBund Jews. An old wolf appreciates the good luck of having amateur hunters after him. No bullets came anywhere near him but, for all that, he was out of breath, sweating in the icy air and beginning to tire. Red seas were in his eyes, his ears were full of blood. He cursed Meyer for the amateur nature of the assignation, himself for agreeing to a meeting without proper cover, the fog for delay in identifying an obvious trap, the new Soviet street names for confusing him in a city he didn't know well, the strain of the last four weeks for making him careless enough to take chances. Life hadn't been so pleasant that death would make the saddest story he had ever heard, but only fools rushed blindly into anything.

. . . Then a safe narrow lane. Climbing upward. Yellow motes revolving. And silence behind him. The net had been thrown, had missed. Will be thrown again. The cobblestones were hurtling upward. But the body was no longer responding. No strength left anywhere in that huge perplexing bag of bones and ideas. He blinked back sudden tears of rage and exhaustion while brilliant globes exploded in his eyes. Heard his own whistling lungs. Heard the count beginning: one . . . two . . . three years ago I'd never have noticed the run . . . Nor would you have come on time to an appointment with a man only a fool would trust, in a city where you had few people of your own (and all of *them* diving, under cover), not with the feel of the net so close about you, idiot . . . Four weeks on the run . . . five . . . But, he laughed weakly (the cancerous croak an act of courage in itself), how does a terrorist retire? One is expected to die by the sword, one is not expected to become president of an insurance company, or to dig in a garden early in the morning. Geraniums in soldierly little rows; imperishable ideals, bright dreams lined up on the mantelpiece. Gathering dust and tarnish. Six . . . seven years ago he had looked upon Abel as his possible replacement. But would he have to put an announcement in the international press? ALL INTERESTED PARTIES REQUESTED TO NOTE (and there would be so many interested parties, their shirts of many colors), THE INFLATED LEGEND OF AVRUM MENDELTORT CAN NOW BE DEFLATED. Safely, safely. THE SYNONYM FOR TERROR HAS HUNG UP HIS BOMBS. Has been defused, rendered harmless as a firecracker. (HORTICULTURE "REAL LIFE'S AMBITION," SAYS NOTED ANARCHIST.) Pleasant dreams, at last, for the Hereditary Enemy, he need no longer peer under his bed. Nothing there from now on but another pisspot . . . And Avrum Mendeltort, a man of his people, who may have committed a few . . . shall we say . . . *indiscretions* here and there, promises discretion, humility, and that necessary meekness. The Jews are going to be saved with mimeograph machines. And he, who had been a terrifying myth and, perhaps, a single grain of hope, a symbol of power for a scattered nation for whom power has always been something that destroyed *their* lives, who has made of himself a rallying cry in a hostile wilderness, begs in the words of Marcus Aurelius that he may, if it please you, sir, cease to be whirled about . . .

Eight . . . by the clock, booming through the fog. Every clock in Lwów tells different time, only one is right: the one which hasn't worked for two hundred years. Twice in each twenty-four hours it tells the correct time. There is no way to turn around on the edge of a razor thrown across the clouds; no way to resign, pause, turn aside, or rest even for a moment. Abyss at each elbow, twists and turns, ascending and descending. *Tread at Thy Peril* is clearly written at the head of the path in every language ever known to man and all wise men know it, and that is why (other peoples' history and the Hereditary Enemy permitting) the wise men die peacefully in their beds, carried unknowing on the shoulders of the tottering madman in the cloud who walks to his inevitable end . . . The wall, the traditional dawn of execution morning hurtling toward him now disguised as cobblestones. DANGER! DANGER! COLLISION COURSE! COLLISION UNAVOIDABLE! And prayer, penitence, and charity will not avert the decree of the pockmarked bricks in the first rays of the final sunrise . . . Nine . . .

Ten.

He fell.

. . . *Yesli zavtra vayna*, a loudspeaker crackled in his ear.

Coming so suddenly into the silent square, still tuned to the reverberating frenzy of the violated city, he had the surrealistic notion of having stepped into a cavernous black crack.

Echoes were pale and insignificant in the shrouded square; the muffled cries of the raped and brutalized city had fallen far behind. *Polonia Capta, Polonia Devicta* was once again descending into her own Gehenna, among icicles and bayonets, and with her would go the remnants of the Jewish nation, those voluble, intractable millions who could only feel collectively or not at all. Rare lanterns cast a crepuscular glow among shuttered buildings where life itself seemed to be extinguished.

The square breathed out a hollow icy hush like a violated crypt. Mendeltort had a strong sensation of déjà vu, and with it one of dreamlike unreality. This was, at least in part, amusement at his own performance: a mildly contemptuous tolerance for his unvarying role. He supposed himself the only Jew in Europe, or the only Marginal Jew anywhere, who could never quite take himself with the deadly seriousness of tradition's martyr, or feed like a hyena on his national dead, or who could quite believe in his own existence.

His own legend had always stupefied him; it was the most fancifully embroidered of all the Jewish and Polish illusions, which made it intricate indeed. But useful, as all legends: in turn a nightmare or a dream. And in this city one could buy a Genuine Egyptian Dreambook almost anywhere.

So, he jeered quietly at himself, you moth-eaten prophet, another man's troubles don't keep you awake, and if you can't afford a carp be glad to eat herring, and don't be quite so ready to spit into a well until you have another.

But no man can straddle two horses at the same time.

(A respectful torturer in Allenstein, respectful because startled, said of another inexplicable moment of Mendeltort's amusement: You still feel like laughing? And he had replied: It's not what I feel, it's what I remember.)

He had been his own Judas of Galilee, his own Menahem Sicarius, his own Eleazar, son of Jair, holding the last spiritual fortress of the Jews: a legend wrapped around an idea. He had been more than all of these and less than either, whatever seemed needed at the time (but never satisfied that it was enough), and now he was tired. Fifty is no great age, but he had gone at least that far from the simple absolutes of youth and, in Meyer's words (well-meant, no doubt, if one dismissed the possibility of faith), he was beginning to look like a man who had attended too many funerals. He had packed more into his half century than most men could manage in a dozen lifetimes; too many old friends rotted in shallow graves. The art of survival had created its own academy, he had declined its honors. His own legend had made him inaccessible to love, yet surely that was the fuel which propelled his faith. Why did he do it? Why did people like himself do anything? *Er drait vi a fortz in rossel, er kert iber di velt*, was the simplest answer. Loyalty without faith had made Meyer absurd; the reverse had made a tragic clown out of Anatole Lopatsky, if the reports were true. Mendeltort stood between them, terrible in his own eyes. He felt a loving, almost proprietorial kinship with all those European prisons and inquisition cellars where he had left small portions of himself: a splash of blood here, part of a jaw there, a fingernail extracted somewhere else; and the dark places repaid him by placing their marks upon him with a respect that bordered on reverence. The scars were now innumerable, as were the memories: so many that he could seldom be bothered to recall them.

His legend rooted him in darkness, fixed and monumental, not unlike the mounted bronze hero busy galloping nowhere. People had lied about him in the best of faith, constructing a history to fill the morbid pit of their insignificance. The past and future were both beyond the reach of their imaginations; all they possessed was the bewildering moment of the present. The past was a comfort, offering ready justification for anything that might prolong the present; the future was only hope that the present might not get any worse. The people had become inco-

herent in their littleness, hence their need for legends and monumental
heroes, and only the Hereditary Enemy knew what it was all about.

And now it was properly dark and the wet, thickly falling snow had
subdued whatever remaining light there was, so that, in effect, he
loomed out of darkness.

Hunched-over people, shrunken in their terror, appeared suddenly
underfoot, threw startled glances, found him ominous. All this had the
dreamy quality of something experienced too often. The equestrian
statue wasn't one that he had seen before, and the cobbled passageway
between ancient houses led nowhere he knew, but this minor accident
of geography did nothing to repeal the sense of a repeat performance.
Cities like this one had witnessed his twilight arrivals for more than
twenty years. If one could think of a tumultuous parade of years as only
a moment, and lately, a matter of a year or so, it seemed to him that
his career had begun only yesterday, all these conspiratorial alleys
acquired a deadly sameness. The streets were always narrow in his part
of town, the houses were old, huddled against each other, the footsteps
on the stairs were always surreptitious. A hazy undefined yellow light
beckoned in the fog, the shuttered window of a little store incredibly
still open; it turned the grainy snow into golden spurs of sand and
billowing dunes. Ah, what damn nonsense, what poetic nonsense! Snow
is snow, is not sand. And I don't need a logical formula out of Idelsohn
to reach this conclusion. But the imaginary oasis promised temporary
human warmth, if not exactly the hot winds of a desert, a respite from
the agitated night that trembled around him. His dismal rooms could
wait; he had no wish to hurry his ascent of yet another gloomy staircase
to look at violent darkness through the windows of an accidental room,
the same room which he seemed to carry on his back from city to city
like a nomad's tent, to pitch on the perilous summits of an unventilated shaft.

He heard the sad hooting of a locomotive wobbling up toward him
from the southeast, beyond the Citadel and Kilinski Park and the football stadiums of Pogon and Czarni and (occasionally) the hopeless but
determined Hasmonea . . . out of the marshaling yard and sidings of
Persenkowka . . . and another answered mournfully from Podzamcze
in the north, the freight yards closest to Zamarstynow and its insatiable
prison, and three imperative howls, much louder because closer to him,
rolled down from the main terminal to the west, repeated by echoes.
He listened to this impersonal conversation of machines calling to each
other before they slipped into the fog with their human cargo, and felt
the loneliness of his kind, the sadness and futility of a lost mankind,

dwarfed by invisible stars and an absent moon, forever crying into a black and bewildering infinity.

A small black car with hooded headlights which cast two flattened, coldly probing beams through narrow horizontal slits, eerily foreign in the luminous dark, rolled slowly toward him; its miniature searchlight poked and rummaged in abandoned courtyards. It was high time to get off the streets.

A small man, cloaked in fog, hurried out of the sepulchral darkness of an alley, drove his blunt head into Mendeltort's midriff, opened his mouth to curse, saw Mendeltort's eyes so high above him, snapped his jaws shut, swerved aside and vanished. Mendeltort was remotely aware that the scurrying fellow had only one eye, the empty socket was ringed by angry flesh . . . And the other man who had galloped into him only minutes earlier, in that other street, had only one arm. This town, this country, and this continent were full of military cripples . . . war-crippled minds staggering under the burdens of a mutilating history. In Poland, generations followed each other into eternal trenches. They threw themselves upon operating tables like lovers upon couches. His nation had to be hauled out of the content of other people's history. Eretz Yisroel, which had now become a biological necessity, needed more than prayers, lamentations, and American money, nor would he settle for a plucked chicken of a state too weak to impose its will upon its enemies. He thought that quite soon, perhaps in a year or two, the Jews of Europe might be ready to wash their hands of Europe if there were any Jews left in Europe to do so. Four hundred thousand Poles were due for deportation before Christmas, according to Meyer; 100,000 from this city would go in the next week. And none of his people seemed to see their own danger, too many were euphoric about the Soviet occupation; it was enough to drive a man mad. But he was patient, a good conspirator; he knew how to wait. He had a Soviet passport, money, and a plan. He had no illusions. His seeds of violence needed prepared soil; the Soviets would fertilize it for him well enough. Let the euphoria run its course into disillusion; you can't save people who don't know that they have anything to fear.

He mourned Stern, Jabotinsky, the spiritual fathers of his own Hargan, that wholly dedicated group of modern zealots who carried war directly to the Hereditary Enemy. Stern died on a rope in Tel Aviv. Jabotinsky was selling life insurance there. But they had started something that would never die, that banished prayer, humility, wailing supplications. Bombs and bullets had become the universal language: The People would learn it in due time.

The small unpainted door which leaked yellow lamplight through a nervous network of knotholes and cracks resisted him only for a moment.

—*Sholem,* he said, coming in.

Four narrow faces, fringed in black, regarded him coldly. Eight liquid eyes reflected pale lantern glow, blinked the intrusion away. (A dybbuk, or what?) He smelled of danger, he knew; this had all happened many times before. He waited for the instinctive reaction of dread, sniffed for diffidence, the warm stench of garlic. Saw oilcloth and alpaca, shining gabardine. Heard the soft clicking of a tongue. Tsk-tsk. He felt fatigue settle like a boulder between his shoulder blades.

—Oof! he said, suddenly anxious for acceptance, and then went on apologetically: Can a man rest here? I'm cold and tired and I've lost my way.

—You are a stranger here?

—The new street names confuse me.

—So why shouldn't they? *Farfolen, farfroyren, farmatert,* that could be our story. Rest, have some tea, forget you are lost. What times these are, eh?

The smallest of the four men trotted toward Mendeltort from behind the counter with a glass of tea. The others bowed and whispered around the samovar so redolent of other Russian times: gendarmes with sabers and Cossacks with a whip, though Lwów had never belonged to Russians before. And deportations much more secretive than tonight's . . . little *kibitkas* whisking off the kidnapped and condemned to die in the taiga . . . Everything had become more efficient these days except the people themselves, they had remained *farfolen, farfroyren,* and . . . what was that other word? Lost, cold, and tired, anyway. Little black pink-rimmed eyes, mildly mocking. The capering small man made him welcome. The hot tea restored him.

—Is it good?

—It's good, Mendeltort said. How is it that you keep your shop open so late? The light shows outside.

The little man made exaggerated signs of fear, mouth round, hands fluttering, eyes full of mocking laughter.

—So because times are bad I must sit in the dark?

—Ey, Itzek, you had better not talk so much about the times, said one of the others.

He glanced up at Mendeltort and quickly away.

—Even the walls have ears and doors have a tongue, said another man.

The little man laughed, clapped his hands, shouted: *Vos macht es mir oys?* If they want to take me, they will come and take me. Why should I trip and fall down in the dark? If I say nothing they will take me, if I say something they will take me, so at least I'll feel better if I speak!

—Oy, such chutzpah, said the largest of them, and explained urgently to Mendeltort: All of a sudden he's so brave, a *shtarker karl*, but he doesn't have a family like the rest of us. Still, sir, you have to understand he doesn't mean everything he says.

—I mean everything! said the little man. The times are as they are and I say they stink! So if you want to send me to Siberia go ahead and do it but don't talk my head off.

—Right away it has to be Siberia, said one of the others. Who said anything about Siberia? What does all that have to do with us? If you make no trouble you will have no trouble.

—There is plenty of trouble here for anyone who wants it, said the little man.

—Itzek, hissed the fattest of the four men, none of whom was particularly fat. Don't talk so much in front of a stranger, *vos is mit dir*, man? (And to Mendeltort, anxiously explaining:) He hasn't been himself since he lost his family.

—It was a tragedy, said the largest of them.

—A bomb hit his house, the fattest of them said.

—No, it was a shell, said the man who had not yet spoken. His brains got scrambled in the fire.

—Nobody listens to him anyway, the larger man explained. You wouldn't know it to listen to him now but he's an *okuratner mensch*, always has been, never said anything dangerous before. Even the Endeks had left him alone.

—He can talk in front of me, Mendeltort said.

—I can talk in front of anybody I want, the little man said. I only speak the truth anyway, what everybody knows, so what can they do to me? They want to take me? All right, let them take me! And you won't hear a kvetsh out of me, either. I've lived a long time!

Mendeltort nodded, grinned, said to the little man: *Vi ruft men eich? My name is* Mendeltort.

—And mine is Fogel, said the little man, and went on, excited: Mendeltort? That Mendeltort? *Gottenyu!* (And then triumphantly to the others:) Ah, so I shouldn't talk in front of a stranger? So I should be afraid? Well, just see what kind of a stranger God sent us today!

—He's gone *meshuga ahf toit!* the fattest man exclaimed, winking at Mendeltort. Sir, you shouldn't ever listen to a crazy man.

—I hear that every day, Mendeltort said, smiling.

—Crazy, crazy, the little man said. But I'm a mensch for all that, and that's a lot more than just being a man or even a person. And if I want to speak, I speak!

—A man like you should guard himself, Mendeltort said gently. Your kind of man is needed by our people.

—Aha! the little man cried, looking at the others. So what did I tell you?

—We guard him, said the largest of his friends. We try to save him from his own *meshugaas*. But he has such a mouth!

—Such a mouth, said the little man scornfully. Such a mouth! God gave me such a mouth and I'm going to use it! A mouth is for more than eating with! A head is for more than wearing a hat! A heart is for more than a pain in the chest!

—There, sir, you see? said the fattest of them. What can you do with a man like that? You can't shut him up. He's going to talk himself right into a *chornyi voron!* (And to small Fogel, hopelessly:) *Me redt zich oys dos hartz!* Go on, talk your heart out! A man like you drives all his friends crazy!

Fogel laughed, capering and assuming poses, but Mendeltort didn't laugh at him, suddenly thinking of his own small angry and indefatigable father, seeing in his mind's eye the birdlike man who was a mensch in the true sense of the word (although in his glittering youth in St. Petersburg he had not understood it): a human being in the moral and ethical sense, not merely a person but a man with dignity and worth, the epitome of the old-fashioned European Jew who could be respected even if he was seldom understood, a man who carried within himself a whole philosophy of life, shouldering the immense burden until it finally destroyed him. He wished that these were other times so that he might have tried to visit the old man in his country manor even though he would not have been welcomed there. He had not understood or appreciated his single-minded progenitor, the old man whose dynastic dream had destroyed them both, but now, his corridors narrowing, he wanted to see him. No, not to make amends. To refuel his own resolution. Now, as then—the days of their difference— they would have little to say to each other. The old man didn't understand the concept of forgiveness, the son wouldn't ask for it. Such men as Jakob Mendeltort were rare nowadays. Soon they would be with Nineveh and Tyre, a new race was replacing both of them. It had emerged in Europe out of the debris of the nineteenth century, neither traditionally Jewish nor European in the cultural sense, a nation of unwealthy intellectual revolutionaries created (he sometimes thought, with pity and contempt) to be the laboratory for every socioeconomic experiment, and burning in the process; but yet another Jewish nation had begun to rise out of these newest ashes. He thought of Fogel, smiled, thought of young Berg, whom he had met in Warsaw before the war began . . . and again: his father. Now that the Damoclean sword, suspended for centuries above the Jews of Europe, had finally begun to fall on their heads, the Nation was exploding in every direction. It was finding its old vitality so rapidly in the face of imminent destruction that it seemed like a new discovery. One might say, Mendeltort thought wryly, if one was given to saying things like that: the battle cries of Simeon were hanging on the wind. One small man here making his irrevocable decision, and another there (such unlikely zealots) . . . an angry affirmation of a national existence . . . that is how every revolution is begun.

Mendeltort closed his eyes, willed away the image of his father. To go to him would be an indulgence, an unnecessary danger to them both. If there was one un-Jewish quality on which both men agreed it was the grim supremacy of duty over sentiment.

. . . What did the little store offer, anyway? Dusty strings of dried onions looking like the shrunken trophies of a headhunting chief; a box of cloves accounted for the heady aroma of not quite absolute, unaccepted poverty which makes up in spices what it lacks in soap . . . A bin of walnuts which had become black. Garlic, naturally. Ropes of dehydrated mushrooms. Blocks of yellow soap, putty, halvah, a barrel of pickles. Brown bunches of herbs on multicolored string. A sense of fatalistic merriment which denied hopelessness. Ruin without fear. An insane faith in a distant and disinterested God.

—What brings you to us, Mr. Mendeltort?

—Don't ask that, Fogel said. Why should you know too much? God brings him here, that's enough.

—To think I should see the day, said the fattest of them.

—See it, enjoy it, Fogel said. But don't talk about it.

—My grandson in America should see me now, said the fattest of them, and this too could be expected in that time and place.

—That is the place to be, said the grayest of them, a gaunt man with rheumy eyes and the ague of internal fever.

—Have some schnapps, Panie Mendeltort, said the larger man. As I love God, it's better even than the Atlasowka, it's the best in the city. Hey, Itzek, where's the Wisniak? How about a celebration? Where's your violin? Play us a little tune.

—A good Kazatzke! cried the fattest of them. Something to weep about! Oy, I remember . . .

A lunatic spasm passed across the narrow face of Fogel. He hopped like a tragic, lopsided crow among the crates and boxes, his caftan flapping behind him like an unclipped wing.

—We should all remember!

—We should all forget!

—We should live so long!

—We should hope so much!

—We should weep so hard!

—We should sing so loud! Has God forgotten us?

—Nifter-shmifter . . . What difference does it make so long as a man can still make a living?

—You think we are living?

. . . Desperate small men, Mendeltort thought, shaken by affection, clinging to their unappetizing lives. Old angers, never quite forgotten, lie tremulously hidden for the sake of safety . . . Well, what do you want at the roots of a reawakening nation? Nothing but bloody-handed heroes? It takes all kinds of insignificant people who become significant a hundred years later when legends become histories. And the anger will soon be taken out of storage.

But now little Fogel had produced a violin, and on his twisted and tormented face there appeared briefly the shadow of a momentary sadness.

—That's more like it! cried the largest of them.

—Play and you won't remember, cried the fattest of them.

The gaunt man had poured Wisniak all around. Was this indeed a time for celebration? The mournful merriment suggested a wake.

—Health and money! cried the largest of them, and the fattest of the undernourished trio cried: And time to enjoy them!

—May all our children have rich parents, said the gaunt man with the rheumy eyes.

Fogel bowed stiffly, his thin fingers curved around the neck of the fiddle like the talons of a bird of prey, and Mendeltort was suddenly aware of a pounding headache, the result of hunger, sleeplessness, and cold. Perhaps. But there was something else. He found it difficult to breathe in the overheated room. The music brought about some kind of mental and emotional paralysis. He desperately wished that he could escape the soaring lament, but he couldn't do it. He felt enclosed, alone, and Fogel was no longer little but towered above him. His head was heavy, it sank to his chest. Old memories flung themselves upon him: the icy glare of St. Petersburg . . . the madly logical faces of old revolutionaries around conspiratorial candles. And the inevitable cry for the lost glories of Jerusalem coming on frozen air from the half-tumbled synagogue in a provincial town. Oh, how that Fogel played! What a Jew he was! How he wept and pleaded on that wailing fiddle, sweeping in turn out of the depths of humiliation and despair to the heights of rage! How he craved vengeance! He burned with hatred like the legendary bush, vowing annihilation to all his tormentors. His whole being turned upon an inward flame, the sum and substance of his volatile people which had never known either love or hatred except as extremes . . . We are as alienated from each other as from the countries in which we are living, demanding turmoil in which to drown our lesser, personal disasters, our national unity is a myth, each man follows only the commands of his own conscience, guided by one or the other of our eternal hopes . . .

Fatigue had left him earlier but now it returned.

Ten minutes to curfew, late for his appointment, lost in a city he didn't know well, in a country which meant little to him, Mendeltort ground the sleep out of his eyes with huge hands.

He had been on the run for forty days and nights and he was beginning to make too many mistakes. He had no doubt that the NKVD in Lwów would be as anxious to get its claws on him as the Gestapo was in Warsaw. The Germans were turning their part of Poland upside down; the firing squads were working round the clock.

He had to go to ground until the loose remnants of his organization could be reassembled. The heart of the hurricane would be quieter, safer than its violent peripheries. There was no work for him in Lwów, Poland was doomed, let it be forgotten; Moscow . . . that was another matter.

Stray images clicked through his brain: names, addresses. Old friends and recent speculations. An improbable idea. Carry the war to the land of the enemy, anticipate events, prepare for what is sure to happen, pay homage to history. He didn't think that anything could surprise him in the twilight world of Russia to which he was returning. And almost anything could be useful if the preparation was meticulous . . .

Meyer would have some kind of an offer; he hadn't sent his emissaries to Warsaw for nothing. Something could come of it. Just bear in mind, Mendeltort told himself, that a toothless wolf still has his memories, that trust is for children.

He reached for the bottle, poured himself a drink. The vodka in the bottle was falling like a barometer; he was full of stormy optimism.

—*Mazel tov*, he said softly, getting up, adjusting his greatcoat, conscious of his eternal loneliness which offered some perspectives. The four men had quite forgotten him. They had closed their eyes, swaying hypnotically around their diminutive musician, entranced by the soothing luxury of suffering and sadness.

And beauty? Yes, there was an element of beauty. Mourning their past and present, they were unwittingly preparing for the future. And greatness, perhaps? A promise of greatness? Yes, that too, but not as evident.

Outside, the fog had begun to dissipate and the night grew colder. The snow had become desultory; it swirled about, uncertainly suspended on the fog, drifted more than fell . . . The city shook and quivered to the rhythmic roars of the nightly rape.

He walked along unfamiliar streets, at home in the shadows, and stopped from time to time to ask for directions between landmarks. There were few people in the streets; they huddled in doorways. His Russian accent was authoritative, redolent of whips, Poles listened to him with sullen attention; they were the long, long yesterday of his people sliding into night.

He concentrated on new Soviet street names: avenues newly dedicated to Comrades Molotov and Vyshinsky, Nikita Khrushchev (who had come storming into Lwów only eight weeks earlier as Marshal Timoshenko's political commissar), Leonid Brezhnev, and A. P. Kirilenko, all new men in the Ukraine, Stalin's creatures whom Mendeltort didn't know; they had all made their careers out of the Great Purge and the double famine. And there were the standard names from Ukrainian history: Krivoinos, the bloody-handed "Hooknose" who had invented those most amusing Jew trees (each branch of each tree bearing a hanging Jew), and Bogdan Chmelnitzky himself, that nemesis of Jews. Comrade Kirov, that martyred saint of Stalin's terror, had a street to himself, as did Dzierzynski, the Polish landed gentleman who had been the father of the Cheka, the OGPU, the GPU, and the NKVD. Mendeltort had known those enfabled heroes of the Revolution; the last-named made him feel that he was being haunted by his youth.

So much blood had been spilled for so little. So much more would flow. The form of oppression changed, its principle remained as it always had been. Both the Jews and the Poles whom Mendeltort knew said nowadays: But surely the Bolsheviks have changed . . . They can't have remained as they were . . . All movements mature . . . And, indeed, there had been a change in the Soviet Union, a monumental change, but of a far different kind than the naïve humanitarians could ever have imagined. The truth was that the great Russian Revolution to which the libertarians still addressed their prayers had now not even a nodding acquaintance with Stalin's private empire. The Revolution had fallen into the hands of ordinary gangsters who had made of it a profitable family enterprise. Only a criminal would place the fate of his nation in such hands.

He was alone, invisible in the striped convict shadows of an angled wall, his internal sentries were posted and alert, his eyes and ears reported directly to his instinct and left him undisturbed.

The state of being doesn't depend on the environment, he knew well enough, and yet the huge and complex mechanism of each cell is always asking *Shall I be?* And *How shall I be?* To continue an existence or to end it within defined time, a choice must be made, a certain set of actions must be put in motion so that there is no lack of life in time, otherwise life ceases to exist. But is there really an individual choice that can still be made? Or are we all passive victims of some external forces, divine or diabolic or whatever, the myth of our recollections driven by a racial memory of what might have been . . . Men and their nations live only in the moment of an action but this action is not real until long after it has taken place, and what lives then is not the action but only its memory.

Chance had made him as he was; he could have been Meyer. The People wouldn't know the difference for a hundred years. They were still talking, thinking, praying, being reasonable . . . It was no accident that Zionism was born in the West, where men could trade ideas. But talk made sense only where words were respected and worlds could be remade at will over coffee cups, and where the compromises had been made and justified and all the wolves were locked up in the city zoo. Men can be sentimental only about themselves, never about others; where blood is legal tender, the cost of legends is considerably higher.

Then he was listening to footsteps, drawing closer: one pair of hob-nailed military boots and one pair of galoshes . . . heard the high-pitched academic whine of Meyer's complaint, a muttered reply, searched for and catalogued other sounds (distant, impersonal), and stepped back deeper into shadow.

. . . A cat that wears gloves doesn't catch a mouse! Meyer was saying then.

Far away to the southwest, in the direction of the Town Hall Square, a loudspeaker boomed and dwindled. Mendeltort held his breath, feeling his heart beat up, and slowly released it. A very angry Meyer, looking like a boxer fresh from a bout that had gone against him, appeared under the streetlight on the corner. The light illuminated a scabrous patch of wall and Soviet soldiers on the attack on canvas and paper.

(. . . And if you lie down with the dogs, you get up with fleas, Mendeltort muttered to himself, remembering.)

Meyer was cursing quietly in Russian and shaking his head. His young companion, whose leather coat and accouterments creaked with each nervous step, looked sullen, angrily defensive. The pale yellow light made Meyer's face choleric; it splashed the broken white face of the young militiaman and inflamed his armband.

. . . Red armband, rifle, bandolier, police bayonet . . . The poor young fool looks as I used to, Mendeltort thought, amused: a fierce young Chekist twenty-two years late for the Revolution.

—So, Traurig, what went wrong? Meyer said. Is that the way you carry out orders? Or did they beat the brains out of your head along with your looks? And how am I going to explain this to Szymanski, will you tell me that?

The young man shrugged, looked at his boots. —Blame the fog, he said.

—Certainly, Meyer said with elaborate sarcasm. *That* will make me almost as intelligent as you, and *you've* just raised stupidity to the level of religion!

In his dark refuge, Mendeltort smiled despite his fatigue. Meyer was never as dangerous as when he played the fool; the young man searched for words, changed his mind and dropped the attempt.

—Nobody is going to make me look a fool, Meyer said. This is a critical time for us, there can be no mistakes. No cost is too great. The Russians must learn that they can depend on us, they can't be allowed a second's doubt. This is the greatest opportunity we have ever had.

—I do my part, the young man said.

—Then learn to think about what you're doing!

The young man touched the scar that had split his face, said softly: I think about it all the time.

—But not with hatred! Hatred is for fools!

Traurig laughed and Meyer halted as though he had been struck. He looked at his hands to see if they were trembling and pushed them both into his overcoat pockets. Like his clothes, his self-contempt seemed ready-made, handed down from a bigger man.

Mendeltort stepped from the shadows and waited on the edge of light. He wondered how long it had been since he had been able to hate anyone. The curious part about speaking his kind of truth was that nobody believed him.

—Why are you calling your young friend a fool?

Meyer saw him first, jumped, stared, spread his arms, searched for a smile, found it; it seemed to fit no better than his clothes. He had acquired gold teeth since Mendeltort had seen him last, the kind which go up in value each time that paper money loses worth. Mendeltort waited for him to recover from the shock of his reappearance; gratuitous cruelty had never been useful.

—My young friend, Comrade Traurig, Meyer said vaguely through a ghastly smile. A good young man but he has much to learn.

—And you're the man to teach him, Mendeltort said, nodding.

Meyer laughed uncertainly. —And who could do better? Haven't you and I learned long ago how to make an icy decision? Somebody has to teach him before it's too late, I do the best I can.

—But sometimes things go wrong, Mendeltort said.

—What do you expect if you depend on people?

—They get lost in the fog . . . They don't keep appointments . . .

Meyer laughed uneasily: Is that what happened to you? I *thought* you'd get lost. That fog . . . And anyway only a fool could depend on you to do anything expected.

—Perhaps that's why I'm still in the game, Mendeltort said.

—I don't know how you've lasted as long as you have.

—Neither do I, if you want to know, Mendeltort agreed. But do we have to talk about it in the cold?

Meyer caught his arm, squeezed it, smiled, said: What a man! All these years in the shadows, all that conspiracy, all those bombs, and he's still worried about the weather! Maybe it's time to try something new? Ah, did you have any trouble at the border crossing?

—No, not at the border.

—We *thought* you'd wait until the Germans and the Soviets opened up the demarcation line. We didn't think you'd try for an illegal crossing. You're too much of an old hand for amateur tricks.

—Is that how you knew when I was coming over?

Meyer laughed. —Well, what the devil, he said, his voice sly. You're not the only professional here. You never break a minor regulation, and neither do we. No point in risking an unnecessary bullet, eh?

Mendeltort smiled, shrugged. —We both seem to be doing the expected.

They moved away from the light. Snow muffled their footsteps. The pale young militiaman fell into step behind them.

—Maybe we are, Meyer said. Perhaps it *is* time to try something different. That is what we want to talk to you about.

—I'm willing to listen.

Meyer laughed again, nodded, turned, and shouted at the young militiaman: Well, what did I tell you? Didn't I tell you that this man's always ready to listen to reason?

—Reason, yes, Mendeltort said. But not to rationalizations.

—So who's rationalizing? You don't even know what we have in mind! If you'd come here a minute earlier you'd have heard me tell this young man how reasonable you are.

—Oh, Mendeltort said. Is that what you told him?

—You sound a bit chilly, Meyer said uneasily.

—This is the weather for it.

Meyer paused, cleared his throat, and said urgently: Ah, but this isn't winter, my friend. It's spring, a new era, the dawn of a proletarian Polish state, everything we've ever dreamed about.

—A lot of people have woken up from that particular dream.

—Then they're fools or traitors, Meyer said.

—You really believe that, don't you? Mendeltort said.

—Believe what? said Meyer. That only a proletarian state will wipe out anti-Semitism and give us a voice? Of course I believe it!

—I meant that Stalin would give you a free hand in Poland.

—It's in his interest to do so, Meyer said. We'll give him a Poland he can live with.

—What makes you think you have anything to give? Mendeltort said. Or that he needs you to get what he wants? And how long do you think you'll have anything after he gets what he wants?

Meyer laughed, contemptuous: Don't tell me you've become a Zionist pioneer in your old age. That wouldn't fit your legend.

Mendeltort shrugged, said: There are many legends.

—Somebody must really bring you down to earth, Meyer said. You must be made to realize that it's better for us to take control of a country we know and understand, a country we've lived in for centuries, where we already own thirty per cent of the commercial and manufacturing facilities and forty per cent of the retail trade, and run it to suit ourselves, than to go off into some desert wilderness, into conditions to which we're not suited, and build sand castles there.

—No one owns anything here now, Mendeltort said quietly.

—Yes, but we did own something, and our roots are here.

Mendeltort listened to the words, weighed inflections, added facts, impressions, sorted through events. He hadn't expected such an obvious trap. Knowing Meyer as well as he knew himself, David and Anatole Lopatsky, the shadow world of conspiracy in which they had lived, he thought he had considered every possibility, including treachery. But treachery was treason only if you betrayed an idea in which you believed. If Meyer had sold him to the NKVD, he had sold merely a man and not his own ideals; he couldn't blame Meyer. His own plan for Moscow was based on trickery: a trap for his hunters with himself as bait. What shocked him now was Meyer's crudity: a good conspirator should never be obvious.

Coming to Lwów, he knew now, had not been a fortunate idea after all. He had waited for one of those infrequent days when the invaders threw open the new border that partitioned Poland to exchange populations. Lost in the immense crowds which ran across the line—Jews galloping into the Soviet paradise, Poles in flight westward—he crossed the San River near Przemysl and caught a train to Lwów, only to stand for six tormenting hours in a mob of frantic countrymen. He had allowed hope to challenge experience and had thought that perhaps Meyer, once a trusted comrade, might have moved closer to his own point of view. Not many others had. So many others had moved in the opposite direction. And now it was clear that Meyer had made a *salto mortale* into the unknown. There was an inner chill confirming suspicion. His instinct, that faithful bellwether, was serving him well. But, in the meantime, this new enemy had to be disarmed.

Mendeltort's mind moved swiftly beyond the conversation.

Meyer said, angrily: What matters is for us to work with what we have, not go off on some crazy colonizing scheme.

Mendeltort said: So far you have nothing. You know the Poles won't let you govern them.

—Who's going to ask them? Meyer said, and laughed. They won't have a choice. And anyway, the Polish Communists will go along with us, they have no choice either.

—What Polish Communists? Mendeltort said, also laughing, watching the young militiaman, who had come close to their heels to listen. The leadership of the Polish Communist Party was tried and shot in Moscow in 1937, there isn't enough of it left to make a village council.

—That's why they have no choice but to rely on us, Meyer said, irritated. Why are you so blind? Why can't you see your own opportunity?

. . . The small black car, followed by an ancient charcoal-burning truck, was coming back. The whine of their engines filled the alley that flowed from the right. Mendeltort and Meyer stepped immediately into shadow but their young companion, feeling bulletproof in his revolutionary leather, stood perfectly still. Mendeltort reached out of darkness, caught the boy by the scruff of his neck, and lifted him, squirming and protesting, out of the sudden light.

—Put me down, the young man hissed. Don't touch me.

—Be quiet, son, Mendeltort said. Keep your mouth shut and open your ears. You won't learn anything otherwise.

. . . The white beam stiffened, then leaped once, searching the spangled darkness, there was another whine and roar, the vehicles drew away. The light diminished, vanished. Then there were only the distant and impersonal echoes of the manhunt in another quarter.

—Only one minute more and they would have got us, Meyer said, stepping from the doorway. That's your house, you see, over there; that is where we're going. They would have picked us up like carp out of a pool. (And then, with a lopsided grin at Mendeltort:) But then you've always had the Devil's own luck.

—Not always, Mendeltort observed. But most of the time.

Meyer laughed uneasily.

—Well . . . most of the time is as good as always.

The young militiaman was listening. Mendeltort wondered briefly who had smashed that pale face and why. It had been a blow to stunt a man's growth. It was suddenly important to tell all young men that their red armbands were only another desperate illusion.

Looking at the young man and speaking for his benefit, he said carefully to Meyer; Most of the time isn't good enough. It only takes one mistake and then it's all over.

—A matter of judgment, Meyer said. A matter of reason.

—Perhaps so, Mendeltort said.

Meyer peered upward, silent. Then he said, surprised: You're still willing to listen?

—What do you have to offer?

Meyer shrugged. —Power, an opportunity, he said, then went on rapidly: I'm talking about our emancipation in a proletarian state.

—It's never worked anywhere before, Mendeltort said. How do you imagine it's going to work here?

—The proletariat here has never been against us, Meyer said slowly, counting off on his fingers the points he was making. Our political roots are the same. The peasants have their hands full just staying alive, we are no threat to their bread and butter. So where was the trouble? You, Traurig, can you tell me where the trouble came from?

(Mendeltort suddenly remembered that Meyer had once been a teacher.)

—The bloody Endeks, said the militiaman, fingering his scars. Those bastard officers.

—The middle class, said Meyer. Envious merchants, greedy little bastards worried about profits. We owned too much to suit them, our capital moved faster then their own. They had the streets but we had the houses, that is our own saying. So they turned profit making into patriotism. Add a handful of nationalist students drunk on their bloody history, that damn Church, those strutting colonels, and you have the makings of a first-class economic war. Overthrow their system and you've gutted half the opposition! Destroy the middle class and all your enemies are gone! Well, we can't do that, we lack the physical power, but the Soviets will wipe the whole lot off the face of the earth, and they will also destroy the intelligentsia. They can't control this country unless they tear it down to bedrock, so who will be left to run it for the proletariat?

—The Russians will run it for the Russians as they always do, Mendeltort said quietly.

—No, you fool, Meyer cried. There will be a vacuum! Stalin knows he can't rule Poland from Moscow, he's the supreme realist. He must have local intermediaries. It'll take generations to breed and educate a new Polish ruling class who'd work with the Russians, their whole civilization stands in the way of that. But we think differently, we are flexible, we are naturally international-minded, we have no regional loyalties, we can fill the vacuum! Give the Soviets a year in this country and we'll be the only people with the intellectual and administrative ability left to govern it. The power is ours practically for the asking.

—That's treason, Mendeltort said simply.

—To what? cried Meyer.

—To us, Mendeltort said, and heard the younger man catch his breath. You have not only justified anti-semitism, you make it logical.

—You're a fool! cried Meyer.

—The future of our Nation can't be tied to Soviet bayonets.

—And what's *your* alternative? We've had enough messianic visions, dreams, and prophecies. You're as illogical as those Ben Gurion fanatics. Have you thought of what will happen to *you* in your Jewish sandbox? How will you play your little role then? Your Twentieth-Century Wandering Jew and Masked Avenger! Abraham in a sandpile! Mendeltort, are you looking forward to some sort of auxiliary deification? We need reality! Substance! Not imagination!

—Putting your money on Stalin doesn't say much for your hold on reality. Ask any Georgian Communist why they call him *kinto*, they understand his Caucasian mentality.

—What's this *kinto* business? Meyer said angrily. What are you talking about?

—It's the old Tiflis underworld word for a cutthroat thug, Mendeltort said.

Meyer threw up his arms and stared, incredulous. —The ruler of the most powerful and progressive country in the world and he calls him a common criminal! Mendeltort, you reason like a child! You and your obsession about Stalin!

—We are my obsession! Stalin's anti-semitism is policy, as opposed to dogma, in accord with his general exploitation of all prejudice, gullibility, and weakness. And you want to place the future of our people in his hands? Machiavelli might have been his mentor.

—I won't listen to this, Meyer shouted. Stalin a Machiavellian? He has never indicated anything of the kind!

—Because he never talks about his plans doesn't mean he has none. That's the mistake the garrulous old Bolshevik intellectuals made about the *kinto*, and they paid for it with their heads. Consider the Terror. Three million people starved to death in the Ukraine alone, three million more starved among the Uzbeks and the Turkomans, and do you know what Stalin said about that? *It took a famine to show them who is master here!* Three million people were shot in the execution cellars, twelve million more are buried in the Arctic. The home of your humanist revolution has been changed into a will-less mass of cattle who live in permanent fear, yet no one can ascribe authorship of the Terror to Stalin himself. His own victims pleaded with their last breath to speak to the *kinto*, convinced that what was being done to them was Yezhov's private vengeance . . .

—You've said nothing to convince me, Meyer cried, and tightened his grip on Mendeltort's arm. You've only branded yourself a counter-revolutionary!

—Perhaps we're talking about different revolutions, Mendeltort said gently. The one *you* want was murdered in the Terror.

—All I want is the final emancipation of our people!

—I don't really think that you care much about emancipating anybody, Mendeltort said, looking at the young militiaman. You and your friends are in this for what you can get.

—You think I'm that venal, that unscrupulous?

—Why else would you hand our people to a murderer?

—And what are you? cried Meyer.

A house is an object, objects have no life; but it seemed to him that in the sudden creaks and footfalls of another night the house itself was coming to life around him; the gray pile of earth-colored bricks, precariously pitched between skeletal trees and clotheslines competing for moonlight, heaved and groaned. The house was an old four-story building; if it had ever known prosperity, human warmth, a family affection, it showed no signs of it. Doors slammed an affirmation of an ancient ruin, as if the house had never been anything but the accidental home of fleeting shadows hiding from each other. He had never seen one of his fellow lodgers except the hirsute woman; he thought it likely that the shadowy procession was in constant motion, flowing like a gray stream through the caverns of the house and leaving stranded puddles for a day or two. He had learned to distinguish footsteps, the accidental voice. For some days there had been a deep tubercular cough. The light and heavy footsteps came and went on nocturnal errands, each hasty shadow wrapped in its anonymous shroud. And if one of them suddenly exploded into alcoholic humanity, and there were cries and curses and the clatter of thrown and falling objects, or the terrified wail of a child, it seemed no more than an exclamation mark buried in a page that is read in whispers. The twilight world takes vows of secrecy and silence.

They stood in the doorway.

It was cold.

They didn't look at each other.

Meyer looked old and gloomy. The young militiaman was muttering to himself. Mendeltort had already forgotten the taste and the warmth of the tea he had drunk in the little store. He thought about Fogel,

Langenfeld, Jozef Abramowski. He tried not to think about Meyer and the young militiaman.

The trouble with his people, he thought then, as always, was that they were the most difficult people in the world to lead. They often seemed to him like the legendary Russian nobleman who insisted on galloping madly in every possible direction at the same time. In Poland, some 100,000 had converted to Catholicism and ceased to be Jews. A million others remained Jews in the religious sense but thought of themselves as Poles. A large segment had abandoned religion altogether and didn't know who or what they were, yet another segment had hardly begun its social, economic, and philosophic climb out of the orthodoxy of the Middle Ages. There was no mass acceptance of emigration among the remainder of, perhaps, two million, they had no wish to pioneer a homeland, what most seemed to wish was to secure autonomy within the Polish state. Their strongest segment urged a so-cial revolution, a workers' take-over, followed by Jewish assumption of control. It was all quite simple if you read Theodor Herzl's *The Jewish Nation* or the *Razviet* articles of Abram Idelsohn, or listened to Erlich and Alter speaking at the sessions of the Second International on be-half of the Bund, or watched the activities of the American Joint Dis-tribution Committee in Poland and Russia. The vast majority of Poland's four and a half million Jews had no wish to go anywhere—unless it was America. Their Zionism was a Jewish-American legend, their unity a myth. Most of those who still thought themselves Jews, in either the religious or the national sense, were politically passive. Of the half million activists, 60 per cent belonged to the Bund of Erlich and Alter, an offshoot of the old Polish Social Democrats, who had done so much to overthrow decrepit old Europe and bring about a new civilization, but the Jewish nationalism of the Bund had proved too much for the Comintern to swallow. The Bund was in a permanent state of war with a splintered Zionist minority. It was backed by the KomBund, the Jewish Communist Workers' Union, and the Jewish National Socialists of the Ferajnigte. Only some unimaginable cat-aclysm could induce that huge majority of Jews to wash their hands of Europe, a solution sought by the minuscule Poale-Syon, who preached a reconstruction of a Palestinian state through class war and social revolu-tion, the Ceire-Syon, who wished the same result achieved by Fabian socialism, and the right-wing socialists of the Hitachduth, who fought all proletarian movements based on revolution. Their only link with the traditional concept of the Jew, Mendeltort thought, was the inability to recognize the existence of a fact; a tree is a tree, as Idelsohn had said, but only when a Jew decides that it is a tree, arriving at this conclusion after an involved progression of formulistic logic . . . Hence the inability to grasp a point of view other than their own, the lack of doubts as to the morality of their projects, an all-pervading sense of righteousness and self-justification . . .

Mendeltort didn't think that he was any different. And in the meantime, before Eretz Yisroel became a powerful reality, there was little point in worrying about varieties of confused humanism.

He looked at Meyer's angrily averted face; the young militiaman's eyes were intelligent, alert. Meyer would have caught on by this time how he had been tricked. It was important that this former comrade, now an enemy, not be stampeded into moving too soon. Mendeltort needed time, he didn't think young Traurig would shoot at him now but there were others within calling distance if he were to run. They would come for him in the night, and that was much better, and this time the Russians would lose patience with their amateur assistants and do the job themselves, and there'd be no need to injure the young man.

—It was a mistake to expect anything constructive from you, Meyer said then. I can see that now.

—Oh, there might be something, Mendeltort said carefully. It's possible that our paths are still parallel at some point. It all depends on what you want from me, and on what I can do.

—You're being reasonable? Meyer said coldly. It's a little late.

—Well, you know me. I have to be careful.

—Tell that to Traurig, Meyer said, contemptuous. He'll believe anything.

—It's good to be able to believe in something, Mendeltort said.

—Spare me your high-minded philosophies, said Meyer. It's all very well to theorize the morality of this and the other if you're not engaged. But on the level where people live and work and make their decisions . . . Well, it's a lot different.

—So tell me what you want from me, Mendeltort said quietly.

—We'll take that up at tomorrow's meeting, Meyer said, evasive. You'll be home tonight? It's important I know where to find you, in case we have to change arrangements . . .

—You can expect to find me at home, Mendeltort said, smiling. I need a quiet night.

Meyer laughed bitterly. —Who'd ever think the great leader of the people needed sleep? Does a monument get weary? But that's what you should do: sleep, rest, set your mind at ease . . . By the way, do you have many of your men in Lwów?

—No, Mendeltort said, relaxed then and sure of his next necessary movements. But you KomBund people wouldn't like them anyway.

They're mostly from the Ferajnigte, or from Begin's youth groups. Hardly your kind of material, wouldn't you agree?

Meyer laughed halfheartedly, made a chopping gesture. —We'll find a use for them. Incidentally, when you were in the Cheka, in the Civil War, did you ever come across a man named Szymanski?

It was Mendeltort's turn to laugh insincerely, as he said: You flatter me, Meyer. He must have been a boy during the Civil War . . . Is *he* behind your invitation, then?

—Wouldn't that make me a sort of Judas?

—Only if I were willing to be a sort of Christ . . .

—Which, of course, you're not, playing Abraham.

—Which, of course, I'm not.

—So, Mendeltort, Meyer said, holding out his hand. This is where we leave you, unless you want Traurig to stay with you to keep an eye on things?

And Mendeltort said cheerfully, not wishing Meyer to know that he understood the traditional gambit or knew Meyer's game, shaking his new enemy's hand with all appearance of sincerity, wondering if any part of an old friend was still there: I don't need anyone.

Meyer chuckled, grinned. —Of course, how could I have forgotten? You do everything alone. Mendeltort the *samotnik*, the lone destroyer of the iniquitous . . . Well, we'll talk tomorrow, expect me for breakfast. The meeting will open your eyes if anything can.

—Good night, Mendeltort said. Pleasant dreams.

The door opened. The stenches of the staircase were immediately familiar. Frau Katz told him, at once, about visitors, a man and a young girl, both Christian and not to be trusted, who had gone up to his room for no good and decent purpose, she was sure. She couldn't stop them, they had forced their way; can anybody stop the goyim from doing what they want? God visit all the ancient plagues upon them! Luckily they had not stayed long. She had heard someone running down the stairs as if all the devils were after them, and when she came out to lock the gate, which these senseless people had left open so that anyone might come in, she had seen the girl just before the fog had swallowed her up. They had probably stolen everything in the rooms, including the bed.

Was she sure that both the young people had gone? Yes, absolutely, she would take an oath. No oaths were necessary, Mendeltort assured her. And, as she watched him in perplexity, he climbed the morbidly insecure staircase.

So Abel had a girl. The boy had grown up. The image of the boy both as the careless, laughing, and irreverent student and as the serious, volatile, and passionately searching entity which he was sure to have become, assumed a new form. His own youthful history stood suddenly before him. To be a human being in the truest sense, a man or a woman must have an immense capacity for irrational commitment. His own life, which so often seemed to him one huge irrationality, an unbelievable abstract tragicomedy in which he played his own victim, judge, and executioner, had been so richly studded with lack of rejection. Even the paid contortions of a whore will open your brain, helping to form your dedication to the essential goodness of mankind. This is the dimension I inhabit, he told himself, ascending. That and the back-and-forth of history. It's neither reasonable nor acceptable but, nevertheless, true.

He rose step by step in the malodorous gloom among old cigar butts, powdery insects suspended forever in a dusty web, the groan of rusted bolts straining in cement. As he had fallen earlier through an imaginary abyss, descending to the roots of his being, so now he climbed the worn and crumbling steps of his imagination among the refuse, dust, and unswept litter of a vanishing reality on its way to join the moldering millennia.

He thought of Abel fondly and paternally. It was a pity that he wouldn't see him. Let him have all the girls he wants and more than he wants . . . let him steep himself in all available experience, so that when the time has come he will be able to give himself wholly to an irrational idea.

Outside his door he halted and listened to the stillness of the stairwell. Frau Katz had disappeared. He waited patiently until he could be sure that he would not be observed, and then began the cautious descent. He took his time. Each step was calculated in advance; none made a sound. When he was once again in the long narrow hallway that ran beside the staircase the length of the house, he moved as softly as a shadow to the doors, opened the smallest of the square windows with infinite care. The street was empty, abandoned to the night and the snow which had begun to fall heavily again. He scanned the empty gateways opposite the house, wondering if Traurig might have been left in one of them, but Meyer, of course, would know better than that. Satisfied, he made his way to the back of the hallway, to the rear door that led to the yard. The door was locked but it was only a matter of an absentminded moment to open it with one of the many small instruments that Mendeltort invariably found in his pockets, and to step out into the whirling snow. He thought with wry regret of the bed that he would not be using . . . He thought with neither regret nor surprise about Meyer.

The yard was narrow, ending in a fence in which large holes conveniently appeared. He squeezed his bulk through the largest opening, crossed the neighboring yard, entered and left the house beyond the yard, and turned down the street toward the railroad station. The snow kept falling. It was thick and moist. He knew that it would cover up his footprints in no time at all.

Catherine

IT SEEMED THAT SHE HAD BEEN SLEEPING FOR ONLY A MOMENT and the bed was still warm. She seemed to have forgotten where she had been, this transparent Catherine; the stars flashed bleak and difficult signals through the snow.

It is 11:42 in Lwów, a Thursday, and she the Thursday's child who has far to go, yes, it is 1939 and I search through the closet for a white chemise to take off later; at 2:15 I go to my appointment but stop on the way, the sun is gray through sleet, I would like to buy him a present but I see at 2:26 that the bookstore is closed. It would have been Verlaine, more to my taste than his, but why not? At 2:45 the drunken soldier says *Chasy!* and takes the watch, complains it is too small, not sufficiently *kulturny*, shows an alarm clock and six wristwatches on each arm, and that's the end of time; still I go on, perhaps a packet of Gauloises would do as well as Verlaine, but it is 1939 in Lwów, so I bring him nothing. I go with him and we are together and then we are not, yet it has happened and the transformation has torn out the roots of holiness in a gibbering city, the sky has hidden under snow clouds; the time ticks only for the drunken soldier but it doesn't matter, the trains run all night. Bleak barren mindless violated in the midst of an ascent, the city shifts about in the fog, the transparent Catherine absorbs snow which fits rather loosely; it is now (approximately) 24:30 in Lwów, a Friday, and I am still in fog, bleak and barren, and perhaps I should make penance for having presumed. The Stationmaster waves his flag and the locomotives heave into the night with their loads of fence posts, the marble Angel spreads her icy wings and practices smiling, the clock on the Town Hall strikes 24:45 All Souls' Day Lwów 1939. Where now, Comrade Catherine? That way . . . a little further on.

Verlaine or no Verlaine, I wanted something for him, so I stopped among the people crowding the steps of the Opera where the man they called *the Rosenkavalier* used to stand every night, winter and summer, with a fresh red rose in his hands, the bottoms of his trousers ragged, his cuffs fringed with ruin, and his paper collar glittering with ice during the Winter Season. When he died the city gave him a State Funeral, with the Mayor and the council, representatives of the rabbinate and the Christian episcopates, the Garrison Commander, three military bands, the three city regiments, and twenty thousand people walking behind the coffin, but nobody knew his name, so on the cross they carved *The Rosenkavalier* and each day, winter and summer, a bouquet of fresh red roses was placed on his grave at municipal expense.

At that time she had not yet become remote, an invisible observer cloaked in ill-fitting snow. She had still been a pulsing, sensing fragment of the city of *The Rosenkavalier* . . . She had felt the nervous gloom that like an insufficiently lidded powder barrel was always ready to explode into senseless panic, among hurrying people whose faces seemed gray to her and whose eyes were frightened, who stood in patient lines before shuttered stores and traded for foodstuffs, who surrounded Russian soldiers on every street corner to find out what their new lives were going to be like. Good, good, the Russians said; you'll have it good with us. With us everything is good, we have everything. (How about Amsterdam, says a grinning student, do you have much of that? There are five factories outside Leningrad that make it, the Russian assures him. How about *Londyn*, do you make that too? Yes, yes, the best in the world. With us everything is bigger and better.) She looked at the enormous portraits newly hung from the tallest buildings: the mustached man and the balding man in glasses smiled kindly upon her. She watched a group of pale young civilians who wore scarlet armbands and small red stars in their caps, and who had Polish rifles slung across their backs, putting up new posters like the one on the gate of her apartment house. The posters showed a cruel and rapacious white bird dying on the end of a Russian bayonet. The words under the pierced bird said that now the people had overthrown their masters, and that henceforth the region was to be called Western Ukraine, and that Poland was dead. Russian officers and civilian officials were everywhere carrying armfuls of silk dresses, radios, lingerie, furniture, elegant luggage, potted plants, an occasional crate of champagne and cognac, mounds of chocolate boxes . . . their wives were trying on the silk nightdresses they would wear that night to the theater. The shaggy-haired ponies were in the cemeteries nuzzling snow and birch bark while the black trucks were starting to line up in the side streets . . . a limousine hurtled through the crowd with an aspidistra in the back seat . . . klaxons blared . . . make way, make way for the Comrade Commander of the First Rank and his aspidistra, the freedom of the masses. She had found nothing to bring to Abel other than herself and hurried, not wishing to be late.

It is now . . . ah, but there is no way to tell the time after the encounter with the drunken soldier. She had become disembodied, a crystal madonna without worshippers. It was conceivable that eventually she would be able to reconnect her mind and her body, but not yet, not yet . . . She felt that if she were to look behind her now she would remain forever a pillar of salt tears. The locomotives bellowed at Podzamcze and that was connection enough. She would have to tread her way with great care through the impressions to the memories and so on, gradually, to whatever reality she would be forced to face . . . but would one lifetime of cautious remembering be enough, and how much of a lifetime could one reasonably expect?

. . . The black tunnel of a gateway is full of mottled shadows, hands in the pockets of gray-brown ankle-long overcoats hairy as horse blankets, smelling of sweat and onions and salt fish. The rifles with queer three-cornered bayonets are propped against gray stone. A mournful song meant for open steppes where echoes are unknown, quick bursts of roaring laughter. Horseplay. Crumbling mortar. Huge wooden doors hung on iron hinges, embossed with iron nails the size of a fist.

She looked at the old poster still pathetically clinging to one of the doors. Mud had been flung at it. Three months ago the poster had been a declaration. It showed a blackened hand with curved fingers burrowing greedily in earth while a Polish soldier struck at it with a bayonet. Under the hand and the soldier was the word *NIE!* in letters of fire. It was, she thought, such a soft, ineffectual word.

The other posters had gone up all over the city the day the Russians came riding in on great tanks splashed with marmalade from the factory on the edge of town through streets swept clean of people, unwatched and unwelcomed except for the band of Jews shivering in the cold light of the early morning, who met them at the city limits with bouquets of flowers. The great tanks made the city shake with their iron clatter. The roar was enormous. Gray dust, blue smoke, and black chips of asphalt flung high above stone valleys. A thick gray curtain hung below the Citadel. The flagpole was naked. The city didn't watch but it listened, heard the fall of streetlamps drunkenly bowled over . . . playfully flattened fences where unsuspecting maids had strung clotheslines . . . sidewalks crushed to dust. When the great roars ceased and resolved themselves into whispered echoes, the streets had filled with the remorseless scraping of sixty thousand iron-studded boots . . . iron-shod hooves grinding on cobblestones . . . Then later, buffeted by the crowds, jostled off the sidewalk by gaping Russian soldiers, she had found herself in Bernardynski Square, never fully conscious of how she had got there; she could not remember what streets she had taken or why she had come.

(A memory to enter with caution: She had stopped for breath in the cool doorway of the ancient church which gave the square its name. The damp darkness of the nave was heavy with old incense. The square was full of army officers, rank upon rank in tight military fours, but what struck her most forcibly about them was their utter silence, so that she had to rub her eyes to make sure that she was really seeing his assembly of men with cold eyes staring into nothing. Stiff necks above the neatly rolled collars of their greatcoats. The morning sun had gilded the bright brass buckles of their belts, whitened their silver eagles. Around them stood a double line of Russians with fixed bayonets. She had looked eagerly into the harsh faces of this human statuary but she recognized no one. The ten thousand faces had become one, withdrawn into an icy contemplation. She knew intuitively that even if she did find someone whom she recognized she wouldn't speak to him; they were no longer of the present, they were beyond the reach of human nearness. It was as if a crystalline wall, translucent but unbreakable, had been built around them; it made them seem no longer of this world.

(. . . In the square, a tall slim Russian officer wearing a round blue cap, a lean and handsome man with even white teeth shining in a Gypsy face, spoke to the senior Polish general, saluting politely, and a command was given in a tired old voice and all the many ranks stiffened to attention, as if this assembly of captives wished to affirm an oath, and cigarettes described blue smoking arcs in that sun-drenched air, and the column stepped off smartly, confidently, down the long Avenue of the Legions, the road of memories, that led from the city.)

She had been desolate, rendered mute by grief, trembling with premonition . . .

The snowfall dwindles, becomes desultory.

The locomotives cry farewell. No answer, no answer.

The moon begins to tear the ragged clouds, the clouds are quickly shredded. The fog presents her belly to the moon and swirls, ecstatic, but the moon is cold. The moon says: I am hollow. The clock says DOOM! emphatically and now the snow stops falling altogether. It is 1:00 Friday All Souls' Day, the ghosts will be propitiated with the light of candles. The manhunt is over.

. . . A small black beast rolled toward her, roaring. Fiery slitted eyes. Behind it came a cyclopean monster belching smoke. Into the shadows, Comrade Catherine! A white beam slashes through the darkness and splinters on snowflakes.

It was cold. How could Bronka have managed through the winters in this thin cloth coat? And did they have time to take blankets, furs, bedding, the ready suitcase, had there been time to collect their wits? At least, she cried, they need no longer wait for it to happen! They are gone. The locomotives stated clearly, crystally, that she was alone. The trains were rolling one after another through bleak snow-covered country, creeping stealthily in and out of sleeping towns, pounding in darkness, rattling over switch points, the track cleared all the way to the Ural Mountains . . . Yakutsk . . . Lake Baikal . . . doors sealed with lead, ventilating holes screened by metal plates bolted from the outside . . . to stop in wilderness.

. . . The apocalyptic beasts grind past whining and coughing and the light is gone. Night is finality, darkness is merciful. Later she hears *Stoy! Stoy!* and a rattle of shots but this is out of sight and she has been spared. And Ferenc Karoly says between his own tubercular explosions: How much further?

She pointed to the house across the street. One window near the roof was pale with candlelight and she remembered how the flame had danced and protested in the grip of wax and she began to cry. Her face was wet with snow, numb with cold, but she thought that the new tears were cutting acid grooves into her cheeks.

Then she was curled softly as a cat in the red velvet box of the upholstered armchair. The sly moon was fingering the rim of her glass. If anyone were to ask how she had got there, she wouldn't have been able to reply. A journey had taken place. Some other things had happened. Some things had been said. Abel had made camomile tea and there had been wine. The room was icy near the doors and windows but here, where she was enthroned in the center, she didn't feel the cold. Abel had taken her wet coat, boots, and stockings and wrapped her in blankets still warm from his body. He had dried her hair, her face, and her feet, he had rubbed her hands. The candle had melted down and the wick had drowned and Abel hadn't been able to find any other candles, but the moon had broken completely free of clouds, so there was light enough.

She was fragrant with camomile, buoyant with wine, yet she continued incuriously remote. She was alone in moonlight, plucking at memories, playing with strands of pale yellow hair that had remained trapped in the abrasive blankets, listening to the murmur of male voices in the kitchen, where Ferenc Karoly was telling Abel what had happened to her.

Her warmth was wholly centered in the belly; everywhere else she was cold as marble. She thought about the horse which had died in the well. The well stood in the middle of her courtyard, a low brick wall encircling a deep shaft, with a round wooden cover, but someone had knocked off this lid when the soldiers had been rounded up in the street and driven into the courtyard. Some horses had come in with the soldiers and they had smelled the water in the well and one of them, the biggest and the strongest, had pushed his way through all the other horses and got his forelegs up on the little round wall and slipped and fell inside. His hooves had scraped on stone all the way to the bottom. There couldn't have been much water in the well, there hadn't been much of a splash when the horse ceased sliding. The sound had been like that of a boulder falling into mud . . . some snapping twigs . . . a dry crack such as branches make when their sap is frozen . . . and then the groaning and the coughing started in the well. Deep and sorrowful. She closed her eyes and listened to the lost faraway groaning of the animal and immediately there was the memory of wild geese calling from behind the manor where Abel had taken her and Mother one spring day for a picnic . . . but this memory of spring fog over the marshes, the mournful call of the wild geese, and the melancholy birches could not compete with the memory of the dying horse. She had tried to close her ears to the deep sobs booming in the well but it had been hopeless. The soldiers in the courtyard questioned each other nervously and cursed the dying horse, and many of the soldiers were afraid, and the fear gradually spread to the people who lived in the house. This had been Catherine's first experience of fear. She had not been able to contain it, it spread to the city. Even the Russian soldiers who sat like mute choirs on the tiered steps of churches, and who held out their hands for watches and fountain pens, had seemed steeped in the miasma of fear, so that for some days it had been difficult to tell who was the conquered and who the conqueror. She had vowed then and later that she wouldn't be afraid and yes, there had been moments in each day when she was able to subdue this unnameable fear but it invariably returned. The soldiers were eventually taken from the courtyard and, in about a week, some men brought hooks and ropes and removed the horse, but no one had done anything about the fear. And she had been so sure only a few hours earlier that she could overcome it!

And here was Abel, made magical by moonlight, bringing the bottle.

—Dear love, how are you now?

She held out her glass and he filled it. The wine provided its own special fog that shrouded images, that opened inside her in unsuspected colors and exotic flowers.

—How about something to eat? Abel said. This place is stocked like a quartermaster store. Whoever makes arrangements for my uncle's hideouts does a fantastic job.

She shook her head. It was full of symbols but she was gradually
coming to terms with what they represented. Once you've reduced a situation to symbols and events into punctuation marks, you can cope
with them . . . it's only the faces, the memory of lost faces that had provided your circle of affection, that brings grief.

—There is, for example, Abel said, one hell of a good-looking turtle
soup. In a tin, of course. And there's a bottle of good sherry that'll go
beautifully with the turtles.

—It would probably be good a little later, she heard herself saying.

—Well, we have lots of time; years, I suppose. We have at least until
morning, anyway.

—What happens in the morning?

—Well, love, I've been thinking that we should leave the city.
What is happening here now is only the beginning.

She heard him and she had made replies but she had not been listening. There was a sudden chill. The child's face pointed, laughed, and
jumped out of view. The Father, the eternal exponent of love and of
reason, was dead among cinders. The Mother, wedged upright in a cattle car, was freezing to death. The Fastidious Cousin was gnawing a
bone.

Inside she was warm, immutable, but on the outside icy layers had
begun to form; like ice floes, she thought, piling up on top of each
other.

The sheet of cardboard which had played the part of a lower pane in
an inside window fell out with a sigh. Abel immediately went to push it
back in place but her icy tremor told her that this wouldn't help, that
the unseasonable snowstorm (and who had ever heard of snow on All
Souls' Day?) was not . . . *unreasonable*. It was nothing she could
verbalize. One of Father's lesser theories had been that if something lay
outside the vocabulary it was probably not worth looking into, but he
had never been adamant about that. A violent winter was pushing in
on the heels of an autumn which had been equally violent. Could she
begin to believe in divine malevolence? And yet it was all connected in
some unimaginable way.

She would give herself time, this transubstantiated Catherine made
of ice and crystal. Time definitely was the ticket, as Derek Belancourt
would say. And in the meantime there was something else. The Former
Soldier had emptied his pockets on the chair where they had hung their
clothes: the Swiss knife with which she had cut her hair, the cerulean
package which he hadn't used, the string, the old coins, and the little
compass. He was as lost in fog as she had been, this wholly loving, irrational madman who had covered her with ornaments and jewels. Now
she was being asked to help chart a course.

—Where can we go? she asked.

He was back before her but something had changed; she was no longer able to connect her mind to the images of the afternoon. It was as though she were standing outside herself, observing them both.

—My first thought was the manor, my grandfather's place. Do you remember, we had a picnic there.

—I remember the wild geese calling in the marshes.

—That's been a sort of refuge for me since I was a boy. The Bolsheviks have already been there. They've killed those two old men. Perhaps they've moved on.

—Then what you're looking for is a place of refuge?

—Yes, that's the idea. But perhaps you'd rather not talk about that just now?

—No, no, go on, she said. I'm really quite all right, you see.

—You're really kind of heroic, do you know it, love?

—No, just numb. How can anyone do anything heroic now?

—You're doing it. And you've infected me with a little of it. Did you know that heroism is contagious?

—Fear is contagious, she said. I know about that. And please keep on talking.

—If you're afraid for your family perhaps we can find out at least where they've been taken. If we go to that bloody banquet that Mann-Bielecki was talking about, speak to that *komandir* who impresses him so much . . .

—Let's please not talk about that, Catherine said.

—Sorry, love. I thought it might help.

—It doesn't. It can't. We mustn't talk about it, mustn't think about it.

—You're right, of course.

—That's the worst thing we could do, don't you see? I mean to think about it. We must never think about it again.

—Well, not now anyway, Abel said, and Catherine cried: No, not just now but never! We must never think about it, never, so will you please start talking about something else?

His boots stood at attention, heels together. The soft leather had come down in concertina folds. She focused her attention on the empty boots, waiting for them to make the first move. At any moment the lights will come on, the conductor will appear, the orchestra will strike up the last mazurka before dawn, the boots will clash their heels and the heels will make sparks. For shouldn't there be the Ball before the Battle, the kiss at the stirrup? *I kiss your hand, panienko, for honor and tradition.*

Abel was walking up and down, making emphatic gestures, saying:

Well, that was the first idea but it didn't last long, it's only a question of time before they start sweeping out the countryside the way they are emptying the towns, so how could it help us to go to the manor? There's no place of refuge left in Poland, we must leave the country. That isn't easy but it's not impossible, hundreds are doing it every day, there's a regular pipeline to get men to France. My uncle Avrum knows all about that, he's sure to come back here later in the morning, which, incidentally, shouldn't be far off. Do you have any idea of the time?

—No, she said. A soldier took my watch.

—Mine went the same way.

But the city made itself remembered. The spires and the towers began calling to each other with mechanical voices. The hands on the giant clocks twitched into place. It was three o'clock in the morning, two and a half hours before dawn.

—Well, love, what do you think?

—About leaving Poland?

—There is no other way for us even to love each other. Everything seems so infernally serious! When one is just hanging on and out of breath . . . Like bad weather! You are almost afraid to expect the sunlight.

—But what would we do in France? I mean in the practical way? Would you have to go back to the Army? I suppose you would.

Yes, she was finally beginning to feel warmth again. A new knowledge was stirring. The sallow nuns immediately reappeared but she waved them away. Tears might possibly melt the crystalline madonna . . . and wasn't there a legend about a statue coming to life through compassion? In any event, the legend was tearful, and the statue *did* become a woman, so perhaps she was on her way.

—Well, no, he said, troubled and suddenly peering into moments that she couldn't imagine (oh, but she could *feel* them!), past a length of flesh caught about a dead tree, past a swamp alive with hands that were still opening and closing, through a scarlet blindfold stitched with bullets, woven out of fire and smoke. His eyes reflected the fires, jumped to the explosions. The pendulum had swung and he was vulnerable again. The statement for the prosecution had been made in two words, the defense would be argumentative but helpless. The historical beasts were jumping up and down in the jury box and the ghosts consulted. He must have known . . . he *had* to know . . . that he didn't need to defend himself to her! In her new way, with all the blindfolds, expectations and antique exhortations vanished, she loved him, he was innocent, surely he knew that! But he was going on: No, I can't do that again. I can't believe in it, in killing people, and that's all there is to that whole thing.

—Yes, she said. We did agree we weren't going to talk about killing people.

—If there was anything more to it than that then there'd be no question . . . ! And there are all those beautiful words, aren't there? But the beautiful words have nothing to do with what they've been made to represent. There is no honor in bestiality, no duty in mindlessness, no sacrifice in murder, no service in cruelty. When you try to substitute the beautiful words for the ugly truth you only degrade them. No, love, I'm not going to do that again.

—You don't have to explain anything to me, Catherine said.

—I know it, he said. Perhaps I'm explaining it to myself again.

—Do you still have to do that sort of thing?

—Always. All the time. Did you think that I had doubts only as an excuse for idleness, cynicism, and indifference?

—I never thought that, never. I know what kind of doubt you have, that's why I said that you didn't have to explain anything, but it's true that nobody else will understand what you are trying to do.

—The dinosaurs who never had a doubt in their precise, delineated minds, Abel said. For them the very idea of any kind of doubt is a form of sacrilege!

—You know what they will do, of course? People like that . . . they always feel so desperately threatened by anything they're unable to understand, they'll feel they have to defend themselves against you.

—That's what your father used to say, Abel said, unthinking.

. . . And there were tears, after all. The crystal had shattered. The gloomy nuns advanced hopefully, the angel of death smiled in the doorway, and the mythical animals of childhood were capering about.

—Wasn't he really a wonderful man? Wasn't he really and truly wonderful? And wasn't Mother wonderful? Even Emil was wonderful in an intolerable sort of way.

—*Are*, love, not *were*, Abel said.

—No, love, *were*, Catherine said. They are gone, you see, and we must understand it, we have to accept it. If we should ever see them again that would be wonderful, but we mustn't expect it or hope for it or even think about it. It's all a part of something that I can't explain yet, I only thought of it a little while ago.

—You *are* heroic, love, Abel said.

—Oh . . . heroic. Do you remember Cousin Wlada?

—Not very well. Didn't she marry Professor Karolewski?

—No, that was a friend of hers. Cousin Wlada was particularly wonderful. She was so alive, so much a woman, do you understand? Do you see what I mean about people not being able to understand what you're going to do?

—I know what they'll call me, all those unbeautiful words.

—So you must know what they will do to you, or try to do to you.

—Yes, I suppose I do.

—So is there any point to going to France?

—No, Abel said. I suppose there isn't.

—I feel so hungry suddenly, Catherine said. It always happens after I've been crying. Do you suppose that we might have that soup?

—Coming right up.

—No, I'll get it ready. You open the sherry and the tins. Do you realize that I have never had tinned food in my life?

—This seems to be a day for many beginnings.

—Yes, hasn't it been that way?

Ferenc Karoly had found a whole box of scented white prewar candles, so that there was suddenly a great deal of light. They filled the ceremonial candelabrum. The shadows cavorted among Byzantine arches in a dark parody of gaiety which was, despite all the portents, occasionally convincing. The turtle soup proved too rich for their stomachs. They ate little of it. But there was some clear broth and several square plaques of unleavened bread and tins of Portuguese sardines and they made an adequate supper out of that.

Catherine was still conscious of a certain aura of unreality as though this were a meal set for puppets in a dollhouse. Thank God there was Abel; he provided a trustworthy connection between the hopeful simplicities of the morning and the still unknown Catherine whom she was now observing. I will place my trust only in the insubstantial, she assured herself. The impermanence of almost everything else had been demonstrated. And there was that other question that she had begun to ask . . . Yes, no doubt about it. Everything had become connected with everything else and reality was acquiring a totally different meaning.

She and Abel passed the wine bottle back and forth across the kitchen table, an act of communion, a pledge which was perhaps sacramental, a silent affirmation of her new awareness, but the militiaman refused to share it with them. He had not taken off his oilskin raincoat or his cap and the red star gleamed like a splash of blood. He had withdrawn into the austerities of his private visions. She broke a plaque of bread in two and passed one piece to Abel and he, in turn, filled her glass to the brim. She knew that he would always be there to fill it if she willed it so. I will not submit to the demands of terror, Catherine told herself; there still remains the quest for joyousness, for love, for a final affirmation of herself. She had gone so far from the simple wishes of the morning that there was no turning back. Dark torrents threatened to engulf her, but she would defy them! Perhaps what we all need is a new Faith if not a new God . . .

Meanwhile the supper was coming to an end. The bread had become crumbs, the wine was finished, the little Portuguese fish had turned to skeletons and tails. Ferenc Karoly looked at his watch and cocked his head as though he were listening. The windows had become blue like water under ice. The fog was returning. She offered the militiaman the last of the wine but he refused it.

His finger were drumming impatiently on the table, so she said: Is anything the matter?

—No, he said.

He explained elaborately that he neither smoked tobacco nor drank alcohol, that these were indulgences which he had renounced, that any indulgence deflected from purpose and that revolutionary discipline demanded total allegiance to the principle. He was, in fact, ill at ease in their company, making himself as inconspicuous as he could, and yet he didn't leave them. It was, she thought, as though he had committed a crime and couldn't bear to tear himself away from the scene of his moral degradation . . . a kind of spiritual martyrdom that made her think, in sudden revulsion, of flagellants . . . mortification of the flesh . . . St. Francis of the Kremlin, she thought immediately, and wondered how she could ever have thought of him as the enemy, the representative of fear. He had been courageous and kind, moved by a human impulse which transcended ideologies. It was ironic and yet so very human that he would now consider this impulse a mortal sin. Yet she could not, or would not, offer him affection or even sympathy; he no longer personified the terror of the times, he had become fragile and human in an act of compassion, she didn't regard him as a part of monstrous events, but he had placed himself beyond the reach of sympathy. Affection would have been yet another unforgivable indulgence. They were separated by no more than a kitchen table but it might as well have been the Mindanao Deep. If he had been moved to a quixotic human act it was only because all people had that capacity, she was sure. He was with her and Abel in the accident of the night, the momentary confluence of their separate courses, but he was not of them, never could be, and he made it clear.

Still, she had been well brought up. She knew her social duties. She asked the questions of the hostess, the lady of the house presiding over a convivial gathering. In the illusion of the dancing shadows, by candlelight after a late-night supper, this did seem to have a connection with reality. And it was so important that there should be talk!

So she said: Where are you from? And when he had told her she spoke about Budapest, the jewel of the Danube, where she had once gone with her father to an academic congress, the genius of Magyar poetry and music, the gaiety . . . this made him impatient.

Where else had he been? Where had he traveled? He must have seen so much . . . His words were measured and monotonous as a migraine headache. He said that in the Pyrenees it had been very cold, that in Berlin there had been some cases of cannibalism among starving workers, that the infant mortality rate among Welsh coal miners was 32 per cent, that when the Dollfuss people shelled the Karl Marx Haus in Vienna he had been slightly injured, that in the villages of Abruzzi and Catania there was no longer soil in which to plant seed, that there was not one rural school in all of Bessarabia, and that in Argentina 2 per cent of the population owned 60 per cent of the arable land.

But had he never known anything joyful? Had he never experienced a moment of peace?

He had been in the Red Square, he said, for the tenth anniversary celebration of the October Revolution. He had seen the March of the Nations. A Greek poet had wept in the arms of a Chinese general. A million people had embraced each other. A sight like that . . . that is peace, he said. This is hope. This is revolution. Yes, he had been joyful. Mankind was music and poetry enough for him.

Why had he come to Poland? He always came to where he could serve the Revolution. Where would he go from Poland? Wherever he was sent. Did he want nothing for himself? The dignity of all mankind, he said . . . the verdict of history would justify all necessary measures which, it might appear on the surface, suggested distress, a certain harshness . . . one must keep one's eyes fixed on the horizon . . . one must not become distracted by temporary inconvenience, minor restrictions . . . yes, the individual is sacred, certainly, but only as a part of the greater human whole . . . sometimes a lesser suffering is necessary for that greater happiness . . .

Somewhere along the line she had acquired a headache but kept her fixed smile. The headache was difficult to locate. She pressed her fingers to her throat as if to assure herself that it was still there. Ferenc Karoly recited his litanies, restated his faith, but she sought Abel's eyes. The monotonous droning had become contrapuntal to her private rhythms but Abel had averted his face. Why wouldn't he look at her at this moment when she needed him? She leaned over the averted face as though he were a child in the grip of fever, but it was *she* who had been pierced by microbes. Cruel and saintly, Abel looked away.

Perhaps he too lived only in her imagination and would dissolve with daylight. But she was committed to him and through him to herself. He was a force for irrational commitment, the dream of the poet, the

lunatic lover who leaped across continents in seven-league boots; they
had been One briefly in a silvered mirror; they had fixed time in place.
He had been an instrument in her initiation whose soul had been accidentally torn on a nail while searching for a key but she would heal
him, she was sure of that. There could be no remorse, not one backward glance. The past had been assembled in Bernardynski Square,
marched off, and demobilized. She was alone with Abel and that was
enough.

Ferenc Karoly got up and went to the window, where frost had
carved delicate ornaments on the glass.

It is now 4:00, a Friday, and the people are beginning to make their
cautious way back out of the parks where they had spent the night, carrying bundles of children wrapped in quilts, the sun will not begin to
rise for another hour but the streets are filling with mist, it is again a
morning. I will go back to the apartment to search among debris for
something to remember. I will stand in lines. Abel and I will make
plans, he will wait for his uncle who had not come, we will take some
candles to the cemetery because it is the Day of the Dead and they are
expecting candle flames, a flicker of memory.

Abel was replacing melted candles in the ritual branches of ornamental brass. Ferenc Karoly came back from the window and sat down.
Catherine collected plates. A truck roared somewhere near.

It is 4:05 All Souls' Day Lwów 1939 and I am blinded by a sudden
light which sweeps across the window.

She pressed her fingers to the arteries of her throat to locate the pain
which had left her head, traveling downward. The light was white and
sharp, it could not be the moon. The light of the moon was silver. Abel
was lighting a cigarette and the glow was red. She took his hand in hers
as though it were holy.

Light vanished quicker than the thought which held it. The clouds
had once more seized the moon and looted its silver. The night had
suddenly returned and stood between the candles and the door. The
pain had centered in her breast and the Mother Superior said clearly,
authoritatively: All may be forgiven. Repent! She was remote, icily suspended like a star in the night. What must I do? she cried. Make your
submission, child, the Mother Superior said, and opened parchment
robes to show the burning heart. Give up this man who is an illusion.
The Heavenly Father, who is never cruel, is the only Love. All man-
made things are impermanent.

Ah, but the night, cried the transparent Catherine. The terrible
night! Who made that, and is that permanent? Will we never know joy
again? And by Whose will is that?

(Joy and pain are alike an illusion said the parchment fragment of the night. Make your confession, it is not too late. We are waiting for you.)

. . . What does the happiness of one being matter if all may be happy? said Ferenc Karoly. What is one will in the collective will of all humanity? We submit to the collective will . . .

(Come, child, are you ready yet?)

Tell me about the night! she cried. Is that an illusion? Am I imagining the footsteps on the stairs? And that cry, that wail of terror in the stairwell, is that also a spiritual abstraction?

(Submit! Repent! Reject the insubstantial!)

Ferenc Karoly was on his feet, silent, head cocked at a crooked angle as though he had been hanged.

—Someone is at the door, Abel said. Must be Uncle Avrum . . .

The door burst inward, showering them with splinters, the flame of the candles ducked away from bayonets, the hallstand toppled, the room was full of huge men in blue caps. Blinding light. Boots pound the darkness on the other side.

—*Ruki vryh!*

(It is not yet too late!)

She is seized, lifted, thrown against the wall. Plates fall and shatter. Iron hooks have closed about her shoulders and the white point of a bayonet quivers before her eyes. The pain is white and sudden.

Had she cried out? Someone had. No, she had not been made mindless by shock. She was neither defiant nor afraid. She was ice-cold, trembling on the point of the light which pinned her to the wall. Once again she had been magically transformed.

Beyond the sharp boundaries of the light, gigantic shadows coiled and uncoiled, erupted with sound.

. . . Boots grind on broken glass. There are harsh cries of inquiry and command. A search is in progress. The bed groans. The armoire falls and for a moment the floor has an epileptic fit. There is a moment of expectant stillness, a question is poised and hangs unanswered, and then one futile crack of a fist descending on the kitchen table . . .

—*Nie ma go?*

—*Nie ma* . . . He's gone.

—He's a devil, then! And what have we here?

She stared into a violent red glow, the light of a flare which had replaced the white light that had imprisoned her. The sharp white light had been suddenly withdrawn. The bayonet had vanished. The powerful carbide battle lantern had been placed on the kitchen table. There were no more shadows. The red flare shrunk to a nervous pinpoint glow and floated out of the edge of her eyes. The kitchen was full of men in blue caps and bulky greatcoats.

She had detached herself from the marble Catherine, the icy madonna, and floated unconcerned through this gathering, holding her mind motionless as a reference point so that she might return whenever she chose. What was it that Abel had said about that sort of thing? That nothing really happens until it is a memory? Something like that. It seemed as reasonable now as anything else.

No fear. No concern. A wondering stillness. She flowed in melting solitude, the final peace of the moth in the flame.

But it was not to last. She became aware of Abel jammed against the wall by bayonets. His eyes were making declarations to her and she nodded mutely. It was all somehow familiar, even commonplace. The ruins of their supper lay strewn about their feet. The sacramental bottle had rolled against the sink.

What was this marvelously illogical instrument saying to her now? Because now was the time to say it, whatever it was. That man conquers the imagination and transforms nature? If he was saying anything it would be something like that.

She blessed him, wished him well. She placed a kiss delicately on the frozen air and willed it toward him but he had again averted his face.

Someone . . . a bulky Russian . . . was shouting at Ferenc Karoly, who swung his crooked head in uncomprehending circles, his eyes mute and empty. The Russian knocked the oilskin cap off his head, the red star rattled in the crockery. The top of the militiaman's naked scalp glowed an angry crimson. A fit of coughing doubled him up and the Russian drove a knee into his face . . . A round civilian with gloomy black eyes mopped sweat off his forehead with precise irritated gestures, muttering over and over: But where could he have gone? And a pale young man in a leather coat was staring at Abel out of a broken face.

Ferenc Karoly was marching on his knees toward the red star. He had cut both his hands on broken china and left twin thin trails of blood in the ruin of dishes. The Russian officer hooked the cap with the toe of a boot, flipped it out of reach, pirouetted gracefully as a ballet master, and kicked the Hungarian in the face.

—Where do I know you from? the young man said, puzzled, and Abel looked him up and down contemptuously and shrugged, and the young man said to the round civilian: I've seen this bird before somewhere . . . but where?

Ferenc Karoly had got to his feet again. His mouth bulged with blood and broken bone. His hands dripped blood. The Russian officer slapped his face once . . . twice . . . with an open palm . . . ripped off the scarlet armband, and threw him to the soldiers, who grasped him as impersonally as a bundle of discarded rags, hauled him beyond the light. Then their boots were clattering on the stairs.

. . . Hollow voices were booming in the stairwell, the perpendicular darkness clogged with threats. A blow . . . the soft scattered thuds of a rolling body . . . and finally the well-remembered groan.

All of this could have taken no more than ten minutes. The time was galloping at breakneck speed, hissing like snow through the cracks in the window; they had not been able to immobilize the clocks, Abel and she. The Russian officer was shouting and the soldiers were stuffing their pockets with tinned food. Her senses had become diffused, so that all sights and sounds had become one and she was hearing and seeing everything simultaneously. She was transfixed by the pain in her breast. Pain and humiliation are an inevitable part of terror, as death is of war, why then the overpowering sense of wrong? It was incongruous. She was watching Abel motionless in his ring of flushed animal faces, and the ruin of their assumptions, hopes, and suppositions lay about her like caryatids fallen beneath their load. The pain was immense, the sense of loss at the point of attainment made her reel with shock. She was uttering piercing soundless cries and listening to them as though from a height.

> . . . To see a world in a grain of sand
> And a heaven in a wild flower,
> Hold infinity in the palm of your hand
> And eternity in an hour.

No, no, she no longer knew what this meant, didn't understand it, but the poem came forth with feeling and beauty and the waves from her mouth made the flames of the candles sway hypnotically, and through the delicate tracery of frost on the glass she saw the dancing points of blue-gray light come once more to the magic carnival of the morning and soon red bands would streak the sky and granite shadows would begin to soften and the inquisitive early light, prancing among promises, would seep in among them, and would she then be able to remember the incongruous pain?

So it was all to be deferred again! She bowed before the suddenly granite Abel and the marble Catherine. The Russian officer spoke sharply and the round civilian spread his hands, murmured, shrugged, shook his head, began to explain. A flat dry popping sound came from outside, barely brushing against her consciousness, and when she looked through the window she saw the black bundle of rags pitched on snow, the soldier shooting into it again, a thin fluttery arm rising for a moment, falling, becoming motionless and curved on whiteness like a question mark, while other soldiers were methodically knocking down a tool shed and upending crates . . . The round civilian had become as pale as the boy in the leather coat. He sat down at the kitchen table. The Russian officer marched out of the room. The round civilian shouted: Well, why don't you do your job! I'm not a policeman! And the pale boy in leather was peering into Abel's immobile face and shaking his head. Would this night never end?

(I do know him from somewhere, the young man said. I do know him . . . And the other man said: So who is he? What's he doing here? [And suddenly, to Abel in a tone which was almost pleading:] Who are you? Who is this woman? What are you people doing here and where is Mendeltort?)

The young man reached inside Abel's jacket, took out a wallet, and threw it on the table. The round civilian started going through its contents. Hmmm, he said after a moment. Aha! And then: Well now, that's not so bad, considering . . .

She wanted the night to end immediately, now!

She longed for the morning so that the dark oppressive isolation of the night might be blown apart. Time creaked on frozen hinges. It was, perhaps, half past four in the morning, getting on for five, and yes, the snow outside was definitely white, the gap-toothed fence was sepia, brown, and yellow . . . But where was the sun?

(Well, said the round civilian with a curious smile, so the old fox got away but we've got the cub . . . Yes, perhaps that's just as well . . . just as well! And the young man was asking if this meant that everything was all right after all, if the commander would be satisfied, because he [the young man was emphatic about this] had done *every-thing* he had been told to do . . . The round man made vague gestures, shrugs, but his smile broadened and he said: As to *that*, hmmm, no, I don't believe he will be but it is always possible to explain this and that . . . one can always *reason* . . . As for the other, well, it could turn out quite *excellently* . . . ! Yes [said the round man], I think it'll turn out very well indeed.)

Morning was almost there. The cold November sun was about to rise.

Yes, the white glare of the carbide lantern had noticeably dimmed, its rim of shadow had disintegrated, the window was fluid with pearly gray light, and she listened to the flow of the morning as she might hear the sea in a shell.

She heard the round civilian talking to the Russian officer in the other room. Words coupled and uncoupled like cattle cars sealed with lead, wreathed with barbed wire, remote and alien as the night. At any moment now the night would be gone! The pale young man took a turn about the kitchen, up and down, up and down, frowning in concentration, and suddenly he was offering her a cigarette and she was taking it because, to be sure, it took time to smoke a cigarette and she had to speed the night along in any way she could! Surely, they would be safe with sunrise.

Any moment now!

And the two soldiers who had seized Abel by the elbows and were pulling him toward the door hadn't got the message! They were the residue of darkness and the night was over! —Goodbye, love, Abel said. The frosted windows had captured the red of the sun.

And what of Catherine? Catherine didn't know. There was a hand clamped about her elbow, the stairwell and a descent among creaking shadows, a motion which propelled her into a small black car, the swift hushed flow of houses with incurious windows, the fluttering posters which announced dead plays, invited to shuttered cabarets; there was the powdery swirl of snowflakes and the first morning flurry of children hurrying to the breadlines, none of them had a thought to spare for her and neither did she. Streets turned and narrowed. The red banners had been starched with frost, the ornamental arches had collapsed under the weight of the snow. The giant portraits smiled and nodded in the wind. The steeples pointed skyward. The booming of a drum announced the start of a parade.

The city spoke to her with bells, mute clocks; her cries were soundless.

A long gray brick wall topped with iron spikes kept her company for a considerable time and then there was an iron gate around which clustered gray frosted-over people with packages and bundles.

The gate opens, closes, and she is inside.

The tower clock strikes five.

INTERLUDE

A *Train in December*

WEEKS HAVE GONE BY. Icy black hours slant between horizons, spanning the continent. We see no sun in the gray days. There is no way to relate the present to our imagination. Our only connections with the past—memory and reason—are twin steel threads unraveling behind us. Each of us has begun to die our own particular death, alone in the mass of the dying. We are freezing, starving. We die of hunger and exposure. Our corpses are long thin tubes of rolled-up rags, pale blue at each stripped extremity. The train is our world: a hollow black starved planet rattling through a month of nights; yet it seems each day that the hurtling night flight is only imagined. A vast convulsed hand seizes us at nightfall and shakes the long string of ice globes, that snaking unclasped necklace of icy black boxes, throwing us about. It drops us shortly before dawn in the white wilderness we had marked the day before. The wilderness is always the same; it is then, perhaps, the same wilderness: vast space without horizons, whiteness without borders, where only snow whirls in ghostly flurries as we stand, once more thrust into the day, like parachutists in the whistling doorway . . . we fall into the snow, make the first footprint, mark our trail, and the dead and the dying are hauled off the train, and we squat over streams of our own spilling blood, the milestones of ordure, and so we chart our progress into the unknown in excrement and corpses.

Resist, yes, we should resist: but who or what is the opposition? We are numbed by cracked faith, mute in the bewilderment of our contradictions. Our own blood has turned against us; it is surely freezing. The ice is against us, and the whirling snow which imitates angels, and the wind. The vast landscape of our inner desolation . . . we are beyond mere sense of loss!

I cannot comprehend this, Professor Modelski whispered to himself.

—Do you want something, dear? Are you asking for something?

—History is against us.

—What is he saying, Jasiu? Something must be done . . . !

—I don't think he knows what he is saying now, Jan Poremba said.

—Have mercy on our brother, Lord, Father Zenek said.

. . . CA-therine, CA-therine, said the wheels; Ca-*Ca*-Ca-*Ca*therine, stammering on switch points. The wheels are spinning in an icy wasteland. Lost, said the whistle of the locomotive: Lo-o-o-o-ost!

. . . Drifting in memory, a flurry of snowflakes: white paper ornamental stars clipped with nail scissors from exercise books are fluttering in the corner of the skull, dim images growing distant while the boxcar sways and lurches, and the wheels rattle over desolation, and bodies, objects, the dead and the living spill from their shelves and fill the frozen air with horizontal screams. Lost, unforgettable but dissolving so swiftly. Beyond imagination now and falling further behind with each turn of the wheels . . . She has been pinned to the horizon while we hurtle eastward. Land of ice and shadow. The distances unfold like cards flipped carelessly upon a tablecloth, foretelling the future. She dances in the past, transfixed by distance like a moth under glass. Unreal now because of the distance, fluttering on the corkboard of my memory. Never to be seen again, to be touched; never to touch. Innocent, promising . . . the words of a father. Lost and dissolving, the words of stricken patriots. Never properly understood, often thought about in anxiety and wonder, never contemplated (for how can you contemplate the totality of another being: a complete person whom you distinctly remember as having been a fragment of yourself?); the object of vague hopes, qualms; running with small arms outstretched, gurgling, stammering a memorized greeting, burrowing a small head innocently between the thighs where she had begun, embracing a kneecap, somehow justifying the difficult day which has ended: a life sprung from your sense of living, a creature of your flesh invisibly connected to every cell and cartilage in your body, now slipping away. Each revolution of the clattering wheels cuts deeper into the connecting flesh. Ra-*ta*, ra-*ta* on bridges. CA-therine, CA-therine. Severed and lost. What are those things falling off the shelves, are they people? They have limbs that break and heads that crack open. But what does that prove? Do they know that Catherine is lost, and that we ourselves shall never be found? In the darkness which is falling on us with each spin of the wheels . . .

—What can we do for him, Jasiu?

—Nothing, my dear.

—Pray, said Father Zenek.

—Prayer without faith is a mockery, an insult to God. It changes nothing.

. . . The rhythm changes: Ca-the-*rine*, Ca-the-*rine*, the wheels are now saying. Ca . . . the . . . rine . . . Yes. Slowing down. The giant raptor circles the wilderness; the violent talons have grown weary of the game. Night is about to end. The swaying black walls have become thinly streaked with gray horizontal stripes. A spider web of cracks is suddenly revealed in the darkness to which he is frozen, blue dawn light seeps between the boards; the night is melting in the gaunt steppe wind . . .

Motionless between bodies, boards, boots, and heads, Professor Modelski struggled upward toward the morning triumph. Up from the icy depths of desolation, the interrupted certainty of his death, toward the sudden gray vertical grooves that had split the darkness around the hinges of the door. Light was the magnet drawing him out of hopelessness. It cracked the grip of darkness, hissing an impossible promise between imprisoning boards.

You have not died, said the light.

(The morning miracle.)

It was a moment of fierce primitive joy that made him light-headed. (Another night is over and I am still alive! So, perhaps, since I've accomplished *that* much . . . in view of this extraordinary achievement . . . perhaps tomorrow also . . .) One had to believe it.

For all its brevity and the breathless illusion of its promises, the morning euphoria made him drunk with hope.

II

Esterka moved her lips, feeling the ice crack in the corners of her mouth. She thought that her stiff parchment skin was rustling, whispering of frost. It would split at the folds and crumble if she touched it, she was sure. Jankele's narrow body fluttered against her back like a stricken heart. Her own numb flesh was wooden, unresponsive; its quivering was remote. She felt it as a tremor seeping upward from the planks, so that it seemed as if the shelf, the compressed bodies of her brother, sister, and grandfather, the solid shadows of the boxcar and the train itself (all part of one another, welded together for all time) had drawn a long shuddering breath after the night's long run. To move a frozen cramped limb was agony; she was putting it off as long as she could. To think was an effort. Her bones were cracked with an interior pain as though their marrow had frozen; they had acquired a protesting fluidity which made her think suddenly of a river moving sluggishly under a coat of ice. She was one with the molded sky: immobile in a moment wrested from time, sunless and undiscovered. Making promises. Then she was falling, brutally detached; alone, original, and unique

because she was alive: the sole survivor of a monumental shipwreck
clinging to an ice floe. Rising below the invisible horizon, still out of
sight and reach and beyond imagination but made real by her need for
life, assured by God's mandate and Grandfather's prayer and her own
probationary membership in the junior Hargan, a steamer pitched and
bucked through ice to come to her rescue. The legendary captain was
on the bridge, wrapped in storms and lightnings, commanding the paralyzed waters to part, his wintry beard torn by the wind. His eyes were
burning beacons through the darkness. The sky-blue banner waved,
nailed to a paper mast; the mystic star of harmony and hope mocked
the hurricane. Here, she cried, here I am. But would her secret comrades hear her above the shrill darkness, would the awaited lifelines fall
on her in time? Hurry, I'm sinking. (No, I shall not drown!) It is so
cold. (No, it is nothing . . . nothing!) The black waves are splintering
my temporary refuge, the small white platform is cracked in two, sinks;
we are engulfed . . . And the violent sea boomed incoherent threats
against cliffs of ice; cries, moans, complaints, supplications, oaths
smothered her with echoes, made her hollow.

—Hurry, she said mechanically, hearing her new voice as though it
were traveling with the gray light from an uncharitable star. The train
is stopping. We must be first to leave.

—It is too cold, he whispered.

—If we hurry . . . (so wearily now), the water will be hot. Do you
have the tea leaves?

Jankele touched the cloth pouch hung around his neck, nodded. His
pointed face was shuttered with a sudden fear. It was more than fear. It
was a dread and loathing, a mute supplication.

—But . . . it is always cold when we bring it here.

—By the time that we bring it here, she corrected. You can drink
yours right by the locomotive.

—It will be cold anyway by the time I drink it.

—You must drink your tea.

—Why?

—Because it is hot. You must have something hot every day.

—But what if it's not?

His sunken eyes gleamed with sluggish tears.

Jankele, Jankele, she said, stroked his matted hair.

He wept. —He will be there . . .

—Who will?

—He will. He is always there.

—Janek won't hurt you. He likes you. Didn't he give you a little red
star when we were in Lwów?

—I don't want his stars! What does he want with us?

She sighed, shook her head, patted his. —Come now, don't be silly. What will Grandfather think to see you act like this?

—He will think nothing of it. He will understand.

—What will I understand? the old man whispered softly.

—The . . . the smell!

—It is enough to kill you, Papa cried mournfully. Like a stable! That we should come to this!

—Animals, animals, Mama was moaning then. Such people. Where do they come from, such people? Why did they put us with such people? Papa is a man of substance, we had our own house, and we have here, even now . . .

—Quiet! Papa roared, turning pale. Do you want everyone to know?

And Grandfather said to the black planks seeping refuse into his beard, the underside of the upper shelf a hand's breath away from his face: What is it like, this smell?

—I don't know, Jankele wept.

—Weep, weep, my son, Mama cried. What is there for us now but weeping? What will become of us all?

—Violence, anger, bitterness, all have their special smell, Grandfather said to the planks above him. It's good to know them, recognize them . . . but fear isn't the only answer to them. Fear answers nothing.

—I don't know what you mean, Grandfather, Jankele said. He was no longer weeping.

—Well, I advise you to learn it. Don't put it off too long.

Jankele shrugged, defeated, sought familiar ground.

—Perhaps I shall see Emil near the locomotive, he suggested.

—Yes. Yes, you will. Now hurry.

—Can I give him some tea if he's there?

—No, she said. You must drink it all yourself.

—But if he gets none?

—No, she said.

—But if I don't want it all? If it's too much for me?

—It's not too much. It's hardly enough. Now hurry, hurry, see, everyone's getting up. The train will stop soon.

—But if Emil wants, Jankele began, and she said: No.

III

Dr. Poremba was suddenly aware that the press of bodies around him had relaxed. He thought that if he made an effort he could move an arm. The grunting dark shapes were rising, moving, sliding off the shelves; their boots and feet wrapped in frozen sacking clattered and thumped on the floor beside his head.

In the thugs' corner they were in no hurry. They were talking. Cracked harsh voices pitted against the wind: Surma, Sowinski, the Unknown Criminal . . . the Zoological Gardens, as he called them. The mad screams and mutterings of old dying lunatic Pani Lutycka, bereft of cats and reason; Wlada's commanding imperatives; Modelski's last murmurs; the cynicism of Mann-Bielecki mocking his own fulfillment; Zenek's priestly ritual of instruction; the endless arguments of Kobza and Kepi about whether the French would rescue them in spring.

Faces, images . . . And suddenly the memory of his lost life, that easy and untroubled sense of civilized European permanence, had become unbearable. He saw it as an impotent argumentative swarm of dentists, lawyers, pharmacists, and professors, each pushing his dung-beetle career with the mindless persistence of Sisyphus, lacking the cultivated senses of an aristocracy or the honesty of peasants, oblivious to all but manner and form. Self-perpetuating by parthenogenesis. He thought of cancer cells multiplying in dank wombs. It had been so easy for us to assume that all was right with God's world simply because the sky hadn't fallen.

We lie becalmed in the eye of the hurricane, blowing bubbles of fantasy and imagination, while the storm is tightening around us like a fist.

He thought of black skies, crashing waves, ripped sails . . . shuddered in the cold. It was all very well to keep up a façade; in one way or another he had always sailed under suspect colors: never entirely one thing or another, coward or hero, man of action or man of the imagination. What he showed to the world was no more than could be printed on a Bertillon index card and that is hardly ever the measure of the man. Both Langenfeld and Zenek Lenski had called him hideously complicated names and he had laughed in their faces. He didn't think himself at all complicated. He had wanted *this*, and fate, or whatever cynical divinity governed occupations, had given him *that*. He had never seen much point in protesting the gulf between aspirations and possibilities. As long as his private sense of being wasn't violated, and the people he loved were is no danger of being diminished, he was content to let things flow as they would. (Why shake fists at the clouds? There are pleasanter ways of getting aching muscles.) You made your peace with life as it was, not as you might want it, and did the best you could with what you were given, and if somewhere along the line you were also lucky (as he had been so unbelievably lucky with Alicja), and shrewd enough to recognize luck as it appeared in whatever form, and bold enough to reach for it as it scampered past, well . . . that was a bonus. There were no guarantees. Agonizing about life in the abstract disgusted him: life was to be lived! It was a gift . . . perhaps a talent requiring dedication . . . not a subject for analysis like a neurotic dowa-

ger or a small-town lawyer with inflammation of the aspiratory organs!
Let's leave the probes and scalpels to the cynics who dissect life and
then object to the smell of the corpse. I am I and I am here, God help
us all, he said, and that's all there's to it.

He had never before experienced a moment of capture and, even
now, knowing what he did and supposing more, he couldn't quite believe it. By which I mean, he explained editorially, that I am not
resigned. I'm only weary, exhausted. Wanting rest. We are all suffering
from this strange debility: weakness and dizziness and lack of energy.
Inability to concentrate, inattention to the needs of others. Our minds
wander. We are no longer able to relate fully to each other. A sense of
doom follows us about like our own daylight shadows. Our memories
of duty, gratitude, loyalty, and friendship have become impaired; they
seem to reach no further back than the last day of peace . . . if not the
first day of captivity. We can no longer separate the contents of our
dreams from the nightmare of reality: men quarrel bitterly over imagined slights, avenge insults suffered while asleep! Everyone is suspicious
of everyone else; we fear being cheated or robbed and never stop to ask
of what we could be cheated and what we could lose? Ah, well, it's all a
matter of nerves, perhaps . . . In this insane surreal world of shadows
and illusions only the illogical made sense. He would not think of
Alicja and the children; to think about them would destroy his mind. It
was enough for him to cope with the unspoken fear that wholly inhuman malevolent forces had seized control of his life.

He knew himself better than to believe his own artful camouflage
but he could see fragments of truth embedded in it, much as it annoyed
him. Making false faces expresses the creative urge of the middle class.
In his own case, he knew, he was covering up an infinity of doubts
under the glib surface of devil's advocate and gadfly, but sharp wits and
good humor were part of the fabric and these were genuine. He was,
he hoped, truly an easygoing man with few gnawing hungers. In fact he
tended to ridicule small men with large aspirations. Mann-Bielecki was
case in point: at one time said to have been a competent lawyer who
scribbled sophomoric verse but who insisted that he be accepted as
dramatist and poet! What can you make of a man like that? Dogs
should howl at him! The creative urge must surely be one of the most
consuming human wants; misapplied, without either the talent or the
dedication, it is pathetic in its lack of solace. What Mann-Bielecki
chose to pretend to himself about himself was his business, each of us
manufactures his own fanciful constructions; but these work only if we
don't expect anyone else to believe us! Once you have heaved your private visions into the public forum you can expect the standard treatment of Christians in arenas.

. . . What I, the public Jan Poremba, Man of Letters, Husband &
Father, Soldier of Fortune, Literary Editor (and critic? God help us,
yes, a Critic!) believe, is more important than what I've pretended.
Someday I might discover what that is. My world . . . the writers,
poets, and dramatists among whom I move like a benign moon . . .
sees me as what it needs to see: an amateur magician, a conspirator
manqué, part jester-juggler and part guardian angel who carefully hid
his own temporary varieties of grief.

The boxcar shuddered; the couplings clanged together.

One had to believe that there had been more to that lost existence
than pharmacists and lawyers. Certainly more than fretful editors who
had suddenly recalled the unfulfilled promises of an adventurous youth.
The new reality demands a cool head and cunning, some of my youthful dedication to conspiracy, adventure with a purpose; and who in this
collection of debris is up to it?

Modelski was dying; he had found a refuge. But death is too easy in
the new reality. Civilization wasn't the answer; literature offered no
clues. History was an interpretation of something that may have never
existed. The only choices left were magic or madness.

IV

Professor Modelski struggled to awake. The morning triumph had
been an illusion. Emil said: When you were young, were you happy,
Mother?

—Yes. Very happy.

—How can that be?

—Someday you'll be happy.

—I? Happy? When?

—When you are home again.

—Oh, his son said.

. . . They must not die before him!

If he believed that they would live, surely they would! It was all a
matter of faith, after all . . . a thousand years of history confirmed it!
One had to believe that cruelty and brutality were not a human constant, that they were aberrations, moments of maniacal deviation from
that normal gentleness which never failed to reassert itself in time.
That too is part of our heritage, he thought: faith in the ultimate
goodness of mankind, the glory of innocence, the rewards of virtue.

His wife was speaking to him. He tried to listen, his attention splintered on the certainty of her death.

. . . must try to eat today, was what she was saying.

—You must eat today, he said. She nodded but he knew that she
would feed her salt fish and black bread to Emil. —So must you, she

said. (Her gloveless fingers were on his pulse. Then she put on her gloves.) —How do you feel?

—Stronger. Much stronger.

And she was smiling and his heart constricted. Her face was luminous with hunger, insubstantial. He brought his eyes into focus on that difficult gray sheen, the silvery diffusion of his imagination.

—You always were a deplorable liar, she said gently.

—I don't think I've lied very much, he said.

—No, you haven't.

—And you never have.

—Oh, I have, sometimes.

—You have? You never lied to me.

—No, not to you.

—But you lied to others?

—Sometimes. To protect you or myself. The way you lied to me sometimes.

—I don't remember ever lying to you.

—It was the way you saw yourself and all of us.

—Was that a lie?

—You really believed that things were as you saw them.

—Was I so often wrong?

—As Wlada says, dear, it's one of your endearing qualities.

—Doctors, he said. Psychiatrists. Married for twenty years and she is still professionally evasive. What was I wrong about?

—I didn't say that you were wrong, dear. I only said that you sometimes saw things more charitably than you should have.

Then she was gone among shadows, telling Emil: Don't scratch your face, dear; you'll only spread the infection . . .

. . . And he was warm, smiling and replete in the gathering darkness; the morning was darkening: the march of the captive blue-gray interlude between night and day had reversed itself. One form of violent motion was coming to an end. A roaring filled his ears, and his eyes were cloudy.

. . . His wife's gaunt face, hollowed by anxiety. Above his, peering down in the insufficient space between shelves. Eyes deep and dark with hunger, ringed with intense concentration . . .

Hands met, closed on each other, holding: cracked leather against threadbare wool. Then everything was still, hushed and waiting.

V

Alicja said simply: Modelski has just died.

Emil said then, softly: Will it be time to eat soon, Mother? Hush, darling, yes, soon . . . And Bronka said fiercely: Honest to God, they'll be the death of us, that godless scum! Godless, Sowinski croaked from under the ceiling. Godless, are they? I don't see *them* hurting any on account of it. (Heh-heh-heh, said the Unknown Criminal. Hooo! Haaa! said Surma. You tell her, Sowinski!) Godless, eh? That's better'n shit-less! Get down on those goddam knobby knees you've been on all your life, scrubbing your lady's ap-part-ment, crawling after priests, confessing your fucking shitlessness! Let's see you pray for *food!* (Hee-hee-hooo-haha!)

. . . And Surma, grinning, satisfied, spat in a long accurate arc.

. . . And Father Zenek was talking earnestly, lecturing without notes: The human mind can't cope with change unless it is gradual and orderly. We are not conditioned to absorb an avalanche of concepts. Observe the Aristotelian principles of sequence: all things, thought in-cluded, must have a beginning, a middle, and an end. There is then a logical progression. We cannot reason without logic. We cannot orient ourselves in new reality without reasoning . . .

And Mann-Bielecki said, loftily: Well, what about transcending both reason and logic?

. . . How I despise that man, thought Dr. Poremba, and Father Zenek said: To go beyond reason and logic when nothing is logical or reasonable? An admirable idea, but at this point civilization cracks . . .

—Aargh! Ungh! Creee-eee! cried Pani Lutycka, thrashing in blood and vomit.

—Somebody sit on that fucking bitch, Surma said.

Alicja said: Did you hear me, dear? Modelski is dead.

—I heard you.

VI

. . . They were chopping the ice off the doors outside; inside, the seal of her silence was shattered again. Each stroke of the sledgehammer thundered through her body like the beat of a drum. I am a drum, Es-terka told herself behind closed eyelids. Summoning the people. I order the ice mountains to split and to flow with courage, hope, and power.

. . . Ice splintered off the walls, clattered in long shards on the fro-zen floorboards like swords and spears thrown down in surrender. Jankele looked at her with wounded eyes as she pulled him behind her to the doors. Everyone was in sudden motion, alerted by her drum; cries and obscenities, pleas and oaths . . . There's not a moment to lose, she assured the invisible captain below the horizon.

. . . A fist arced overhead, struck: a face vanished downward. A cowled black woman crept on hands and knees to the lip of the slippery brown crater of blood, vomit, excrement, and urine that rimmed the ragged hole chopped into the floor, gagged and bucked. That we should be together with them, Mama whispered, bitterly resentful. Such people, foulmouthed, evil-minded, coarse, poor and dirty, smelling of the lowest class . . . And what if they found out that I have dollars sewn into my corset? They'd skin me alive . . . Quiet, quiet! Papa whispered. Quiet! Must you tell everybody what is in your drawers? But we are not like them, Mama protested; they have nothing, we have something. We are something, they are less than nothing. They must know that we are not like them!

The wind swept upward through the brown-rimmed crater, lashed her with an invisible whip. She gasped, felt the false fire of tears freezing on her cheeks, and, for a moment, her heart seemed to stop. Hurry, she told her invisible distant rescuers. Yes, they would be young; patriarchal beards were unnecessary. Love me, lead me . . . give me a life that I needn't question . . . and I will care for you . . . Jankele's fragile shoulder turned under her hands.

—Oh well, all right then, I'm coming.

—And keep away from the Ukrainian, Mama said.

—No good could come of it, said Papa.

—He led us safely through the villages, Mama, she reminded them.

—Don't tell me what he did or didn't do! I'm thinking about what he might do! They don't do anything for nothing, you can be sure of that. Such a man, that you should even know such a man is too much. An animal like that!

—Such times, so terrible, Papa said. And how will it all end for us, will somebody tell me?

—Don't ask, just don't ask, Mama said. Somebody might tell you and I don't want to know.

The door began to rattle, sliding in its rusty gutter over crushed ice. Pale gray light flung itself inside. She felt invaded, overthrown: an occupying army was establishing garrisons in her secret country, executing laughter. The wind assaulted her; it tossed her skirt over her head . . .

—Well, Jankele said, resentful in defeat. Are we going or not?

She was poised in the door for only a moment, her thoughts blank and fluttering. Before her was the glare of snow, tumbled gray sky, torn wispy clouds trailing among snowflakes. Silence. Isolation. Sense of space and vastness; the sense of self shrunken, microscopic. Then she was flying outward. Dark bodies thudded into the snow around her, gasping in the suddenly fresh and unfamiliar air. She lay in snow watching the ragged black bundles flung out of the boxcars: saw them untangle themselves in midair, acquiring arms and legs before they vanished in the snowdrifts. She heard their rediscovered voices as they struggled upward. Ziuta Poremba, hauling her brother behind her, trod upon her hand. She got up, gathered Jankele, seized his bony hand, hurried toward the locomotives which lay steaming and hissing at the head of the track.

—Out of the way! she cried, or thought she did; her voice was picked up by the whistling wind and hurled away among the other voices. —Please!

Nobody listened. A sharp elbow smashed into her side, made her gasp for breath.

—Come on, Jankele! Get out of the . . . please . . .

. . . A gray fist fluttered in front of her face, inflamed eyes told her that she was hated; she dodged the blow, tripped over a body. To fall in that mob was certain death.

VII

The train lay in a crooked arc, a blunted question mark scratched into the unbroken white surface of snow without horizons; it was, thought Ziuta, as if the headlong run through the night had ended in disaster: the train had crashed into an invisible barrier. Each day the string of cattle cars would lie in a straight line, the distant ends diminished and dissolving, so that the train itself seemed endless. Like this journey, she thought. As the unchanging landscape. As the procession of nights and days which had become indivisible. The train had become a bridge, spanning time and distance. It seemed that she had always been a part of the train; the routines of survival had become familiar. But now the leading half of the train had been wrenched sideways; the locomotives lay darkly askew on the visible horizon as though both time and distance had come to an end.

She was suddenly afraid, thrown off stride by the unexpected. Whatever safety there was for anyone lay in the known and the familiar. Yes, there was still such a thing as home: the family cave, the narrow spaces between sleeping shelves in a boxcar. The train had become a country, the car was a city in a nameless province, and her identity depended on a stenciled white number on a boxcar door. I am this, she could tell herself; that is where I'm from. Lwów had been an interlude; she thought of it as war and the death of Luta. Death terrified her; she thought that she would do anything to live. She watched the corpse of Professor Modelski carried from the train. Her father, bowed against the wind, trudged like a cart horse between shafts; he carried the legs. Father Zenek carried one dead arm, Bronka carried another. Pani Modelska supported her husband's head. Emil trailed behind. She tugged her own whining brother forward, deep into the crowd; she would escape from death in all its forms: she didn't want to see any part of it. Luta had called to her before leaping from the window but she had been frozen. It seemed to her that Luta was still calling. And suddenly she knew that everyone in the train would die. Her father, mother, brother . . . today or tomorrow . . . everyone. There could be no escape for them. She hated them all for reminding her of death and her terror. She longed for reassurance. The twisted neck of the train confused her. She knew that it was a sign that she had to decipher immediately: in the world of the train everything new was a threat, the unexpected was surely catastrophic. Everything was a portent, nothing out of the ordinary could be ignored. Wiesio sulked, complained; she had never liked him, she realized without surprise. In another time this might have been a horrifying discovery.

—I want to eat! Wiesio shouted. When are you going to get some food for me?

—Here's something you can eat, Surma said. Hooo-ha-ha.

She turned her face away from the other eyes, numbed by their predatory calculation, ill with sudden knowledge. Their laughter crackled in her eyes.

—They have food, Wiesio whined. You can get it from them.

—I go first, Surma said. Anybody got something to say?

—Get your ass over here, little bitch, said Sowinski.

—Hooo-ha!

A hand curved toward her, fastened on her shoulder. She thought of Luta leaping from the window and suddenly breathing was impossible again. Luta was dead; she hated her sister for being so safe. Wiesio stared at her with little button eyes, his small fat mouth formed a hungry circle. Food, he was saying. Grotesque masks leaped in and out of her line of vision: the struggling mass of people who fell and were trampled. They pushed toward the locomotives, where, if they were lucky, the first four or five might get a cupful of hot water. She jerked her arm, couldn't free it, opened her mouth to plead. No help would come from anyone, she knew. She felt the beginning of a terrible white smile. Her eyes swept over vacant animal faces seeking explanations. Then they were hauling her along the semicircular wall of boxcars.

—Please, sir, said Wiesio. You'll give me some food?

VIII

Mann-Bielecki stepped on a hard round object which cracked under his weight. He felt his ankle turning, looked down, saw the empurpled face of Pani Lutycka. She was no longer crying out. Perhaps she had died. He was immediately seized with unreasoning envy, then felt his stomach lurch. There had to be some way to make sure of life for a little longer.

—Here, you, lop-ears! Surma said in passing.

Mann-Bielecki looked about for someone to help him. He said: Are you addressing me?

—I am ad-dress-ing you! Give me that fucking scarf you got on.

—Well, but . . .

—Quick!

—Certainly, certainly, Mann-Bielecki said. Anything I can do . . .

The Unknown Criminal had climbed into a boxcar. He started throwing people out of it: the old and the sick who didn't have the strength to leave their dark corners. They made no sound, no protest. They knew that words no longer held value. He tried to grin, to say something brilliant, to destroy with one word these certainties of position which he envied, to be engaging and disarming as befitted the perennial wit, the aging but enduring darling of café society . . . But his mouth had split into a frozen mockery of a smile, his teeth were clicking like abacus beads, and his tongue was wooden . . . Just what do I *know?* What is the sum total tangible result, the quintessence of my so-called learning . . . erudition . . . that civilization I had tried to swallow at a gulp? Hurry it up, you clumsy whoreson, Surma shouted. He tried to hurry but his fingers seemed to have no connection with his hands, the hands functioned independently of the arms, the arms had nothing to do with the rest of his body. He couldn't claw apart the knot of the scarf. Words were no longer legal tender. A fist, the new currency of the realm, swung toward him; he dodged and hopped with small cries that he thought were laughter. Wiesio Poremba was grinning up at him and Surma was cursing. Ah yes, ah yes, here it comes, he said, a tight knot, don't you know, only another moment. Get on with it, you son of a bitch, Surma said. Or I'll tear it off along with your head!

The Unknown Criminal motioned and Sowinski swept up the Poremba girl, lifted her, and threw her into the maw of the boxcar, and Mann-Bielecki caught a glimpse of her terrified white face, and heard the thin wail spiraling toward him, and felt a spasm of envy and hatred and helplessness and fear and thought: Yes, someone should interfere, she is just a child, and then he thought: No, it's none of my business and, anyway, what could anyone do? Power and its spoils belonged to those who could take it.

. . . And there was nothing . . . ah . . . *revolutionary* about the criminals' ascent. One thinks of tigers among rabbits. The first law of the social jungle (civilization, don't you know . . . *civilization?*) was

. . . *is* . . . that someone should always set the tone for everybody else. Why else would there be literary critics? Body lice? Or priests, for that matter? God himself can't be understood without interpreters . . .

Mann-Bielecki hurried to oblige.

Civilization is a personal matter! Survival is a matter of a flexible spine. A grass blade will survive a hurricane which topples an oak . . . The first law of survival is . . . that one should survive! My death, for any cause, he argued briefly as a matter of form, would only increase the total of irreparable loss . . .

And anyway, the violated child was no longer screaming. One can live with silence. The scarf was loose in his hands, the knot was untied.

He handed the fringed flowered length of silk and brocade to Surma, thinking of ermines and an act of graceful abdication, incongruous mantles, glad to be rid of it. The wind clutched at his throat; he tried a winning smile . . . listened to little rhythmic cries: plaintive, perhaps, tearful, but not unnatural under the circumstances . . .

And in the meantime he had an abscessed wisdom tooth and a splitting headache.

—*Prima*, Sowinski said invisibly.

Perhaps one couldn't live with silence after all.

Sowinski peered lazily around the side of the boxcar door where, in the cold darkness, the thuds and whimpers had been drummed into another temporary silence, where grunts had become a laughter of a kind . . . Stretched, scratched, grinned, said:

—*Prima*, I tell you (arms wide enough to crack bones). Tight as a drum, all that yelling. But look at 'er go now.

—Sonovabitch held me up, Surma said.

A large fist appeared, puzzling the poet's will, and he studied its fiery parabolic movement as, he supposed, an astronomer might contemplate a comet; coming from beyond the bounds of his experience, it would vanish in another academic question. It exploded in his head's Arctic region, cracked the polar cap of consciousness, and at once the glaciers were in motion. The small bones of his face were moving under his astonished fingers. Sowinski laughed. Surma spat at him. The frozen spittle burned his forehead like a brand.

In the next moment he didn't know where he was, who he was. A door was open and the ladies waited but he had forgotten the notes for his lecture. It was supposed to be something about Plato. *What is honored in the country is cultivated there . . . Two thousand and three hundred years ago, Plato said . . .*

Hooo-ha-ha!

. . . Hold 'er down, Sowinski, Jeee-zus-watch-her-go, that's (hooo-ha-ha) what I call a natural talent! Part of our heritage is genius for national survival, ah, but at what cost? Are we . . . are *you*, young ladies and gentlemen, satisfied with what is honored in our country? Are you at ease about the manner in which it is honored? I am talking to you about necrophilia . . .

—Get off it, Surma, it's my go again.

—Up your ass, Sowinski!

. . . *C'est le mot juste*, ladies and gentlemen. V*ox Populi*, don't you know, V*ox Dei*. Up your ass! Man begins at the moment when a two-legged erect creature assumes control of nature . . .

(Hooo! Ha-ha-ha! Heeeee!)

—Mister, have you any bread? said Wiesio Poremba. You too can have a go at her if you want.

Words were his currency and his camouflage. He could restore their worth if he could find something that someone else, whoever controlled destinies and prescribed the forms, would take in trade for . . . a proper definition of himself.

He peered around, anxiously: saw plastercasts of faces moulded in fear . . . Felt better about his possibilities. Sooner or later someone would do something that would provide him with an object to trade. Then words would once again be a negotiable commodity . . . and he, once more removed from the terror of his own insignificance, taken out of the context of general destruction, could . . . ah . . . arbitrate his own survival . . .

A sight (a group of mourners bowed above a mound of shale and ice, a muttering priest . . . Pani Modelska's granite grief and Poremba's insufferable optimism) brushed past the edge of his vision as he hurried toward the locomotives.

He was immediately electrified, the thought made him breathless. Salvation through prayer?

Ah, no, he thought, exulting in discovery and weak with hidden laughter, that *must* be too simple! But then, ha-ha, never underestimate the power of another man's prayer! Not in a country where religious propaganda is punished with hard labor. One word in the right quarter would suffice!

. . . Professor Modelski had ascended to a realm of mist, poetic furry clouds . . . silence. No, I don't envy him at all. I share his terrified regret. And the vanished vision of an insubstantial life which I am trying to imbue finally with meaning (and preserve!) has suddenly become as abstract as God. Neither this life nor God is willing to tell me anything. There are no more voices, great or small. There are snow and silence, the doors of extinction. And all the yesterdays, stripped of their tomorrows, are a frozen waste.

IX

Esterka thought she saw the troubled red moon face of Dr. Poremba, heard Bronka's *Honest to God!* then her vision was blocked. She saw the urgent face of the poet, Mann-Bielecki, suddenly hollow as he gestured spasmodically toward a dark, bleak group of mourners and tried new Russian phrases on a soldier stolid as a boulder . . . Janek Stypenko picked up Jankele with one arm, embraced her with the other, and butted the crowd.

The open boxcars yawned with familiar stenches. Others, still shuttered, were like a curving lane of barns filled with bellowing cattle. And those few whose doors were never opened when anyone could see them, the prison cars said to contain denounced officers, intellectuals, social undesirables, their loads increased at each halt surreptitiously (the silent cars past which she hurried with her head averted), threatened her with questions.

Where are we going? What are we going to do there? How are we going to live? (We can only live together if our purposes are the same, Grandfather had said.)

The struggling mob around her was like no people she had ever seen. Were they really people, and how had they managed to fool her before? Perhaps they had been hidden underground in cellars or locked up in vaults so that she would never suspect their existence. Or had they ceased to be people only on the train?

And how did the others see her, as what?

Did they know, as she pushed and kicked her way through them, shouting at them in their own cracked voices, trampling the ill and the weak (the old and the gentle and the helplessly polite), that she was *not* like them? That it was all a kind of masquerade and that her presence among them was as surprising to her as it must be to them?

. . . Because I'm not like that, she assured them mutely. For me survival is a matter of ideals, I have a cause to serve.

Janek Stypenko went ahead, carrying Jankele. She carried the metal cup. The little pouch of tea leaves had been used for four weeks but it might still be good enough to color the water. Jankele leaped about in Janek's arms, demanding that he be put down.

—What are you scared of, little one? I won't eat you.

—Let me go (fiercely).

—Put him down, she said, and added softly: Thank you.

—What's he scared of now?

—I am not scared of anything, Jankele cried.

—He is too big to carry, she said diplomatically. You know how boys are . . .

And Janek said, shrugging: Ah, you people, touchy as a bomb. Can't see what good I'm doing hanging around you anyway. Be better off with my own kind, ought to get some sense.

—Why don't you? (With a ferocity that astonished her.)

His eyes were wide with anger. —Yes, why don't I?

—It's not that we're not grateful, she said. I told you we were.

—But that's as far as it goes, right? Thanks very much and I'll be seeing you a week from never, right? That's a lot of grateful.

—If you give something to someone or do something for them, and expect something in return, then you're not giving anything. That's trading, not giving.

—Oh, so it's trading now, is it? That's you people all over. Take all you can, give nothing. The peasant's done his work, the peasant may go. That's the way of it, right?

—It doesn't have to be, but you're making it so.

—Oh, it's me that's making it so, is it? And just how far d'you think you'd have got on those roads back there, in them villages, if I hadn't been along? And how far d'you think you'd get here if I wasn't around to bust heads and kick asses for you? But you don't think about that.

. . . And when had she started to become unkind?

—If you expect to be paid!

—Paid! Stick with your own kind, she says! It'll be a sad day for you when I do!

She caught Jankele's thin hand, thought of a bird's cold talons, the beating of a small creature's heart, hurried toward the locomotives, heard Janek Stypenko crying after her, crying, not shouting, bitterly as though his birthright had been taken from him (and had he only just discovered who he was and where and how he had been robbed?): Why? Everybody's got to belong to somebody, to something!

. . . I do, she said mutely.

Saw sharply slanting mounds (which, her sensitized mind told her, were buried roofs of surprisingly huge sheds) and, beyond them, something that looked like the bridge, smokestack, and spidery upperworks of a steamer silvery in the haze. A mirage called up by longing and imagination? She blinked her eyes, saw the smoke dissolve. Beyond it a gray flat sheet of water washed from the horizon.

She knew then that the journey in the train was over; they had come to the end of the track, the end of the earth. Here the world ended. From now on . . . what? The steamer would take her into another world . . . that endless gray icy sheet vanishing in mist, falling snow

. . . And suddenly the thought of losing the familiar world of the cattle car made her rock with grief.

What would come next? And what ocean was this anyway? And why had she been brought to the end of the world?

X

—May this hard soil be soft for our brother, Father Zenek was saying then, bowed over the grave. May this cruel earth be kind.

Pani Modelska felt the violent wind in her face, stinging her eyes like needles, and saw through what seemed to be a watery mist. The world must have looked like this just after the Creation. Not a tree, not a shrub. Nothing but rock and scree under galloping waves of powdery snow in the half-light of a Siberian winter. The wind, she thought, had cauterized her brain.

Alicja said in awe: Where in the name of God have they brought us? and Jasio Poremba, troubled, muttered uneasily: Say rather in the name of the Devil . . .

The wind howled inland off the stormy water, drowned the priest's prayers. The snow didn't become compressed under her boots but slipped away, like fine flour, offering no footholds. Dunes of snow formed and re-formed, rose and melted, transforming the desolate land-scape from moment to moment, so that she thought, emptily: The earth isn't finished here, it's still being constructed, whole geological eras must pass before human beings can appear here, they've brought us here too soon . . .

—I hate them, Emil whispered to the wind.

She said, automatically, looking at the grave: You must not hate people.

—Why not?

—Because . . . oh, how can you even say such a thing? We are also people. Hatred is . . . wasteful. Your father said . . . *used* to say . . . that to hate anyone was a form of suicide.

—My father is dead.

—He never hated anyone.

—Why not?

—Because . . . that would make us unhuman, she said.

—I don't care.

She caught the priest's glance above the burial mound, looked away, reached for Emil's hand, saw a long line of bowed and burdened men moving laboriously across the frozen water, then tried to understand what she was seeing next. What she had thought to be other graves were suddenly revealed as dugouts in which people lived, and she saw men rising from the ground, carrying sacks and boxes.

She realized that some time had passed since Father Zenek had said anything. His prayer was finished. Again, she saw his questioning glance pass from the graveside to the train and back. She supposed that they should go back to the train before the funeral was noticed. Her husband was dead, nothing more could be done for him, but it was difficult to leave him after twenty years.

. . . Nothing extraordinary had ever happened to him, he had avoided events; his *engagements* had been mental, his involvements philosophical, his passions intellectual: the curse of the teacher. He had never expressed his beliefs in physical action, thinking that much would be lost in the process as with most translations.

But the others waited: Wlada, Bronka, Jan and Alicja Poremba, and the priest. Snow pilled up against the shallow grave, furred its harsh contours . . . She turned her back on it. She made a huge effort to unfreeze her thoughts; they were surely frozen. Some people had died recently because the cerebral fluid had frozen solid in their skulls . . . Must focus my attention on the immediate present . . .

Someone was shouting: an infuriated Russian who galloped toward them.

Jasio Poremba had begun to curse into his beard.

. . . But I'm confused, she whispered to herself. None of this is new, threatening, or confusing to the three impassive soldiers trudging through the snow, to the furred officer with the windproof leather mask across his face, the shouting civilian . . . It's all a part of their naturally ordered lives, like breathing. Just one of hundreds, thousands of transports rolling back and forth across their vast country.

. . . If I were to go up to them . . . which is unnecessary because they're hurrying here . . . and say to them suddenly: Listen, I don't understand this, what is it that you're doing, why have you brought us to this wilderness where even the icy air kills, what are we to do here? —they would be bewildered. What's so incomprehensible about forced migrations that scattered entire nations in uncharted wilderness? Be reasonable, comrade, they would say.

Then she was nodding to the others, nodding her permission for them all to return to the train, the funeral was over. The priest smiled briefly and shook his head and knelt in the snow to pray for all of them. They looked at the Russians advancing towards them.

—I hate them, Emil said.

—Your father wouldn't want you to say things like that.

He wrenched his hand out of hers, stuffed it in his pocket.

—My father is dead.

XI

And then they were there, at the grave: the plainclothes functionary, the troop commander, and the stolid *soldaty* with their bayonets, and they kicked the young priest to the ground yelling Mann-Bielecki's denunciation into the priest's face, and then they seized Poremba and drove him off toward the prison coach.

That had been an inspiration of the moment: Mann-Bielecki hadn't thought that one priest would be enough to buy his new identity; he had tossed in Poremba, supposedly a reservist officer, for good measure. Now he stood shivering in the wind, muttering to himself. Such ancient music. Such staggering confidence in their own virtue here: blind faith in the ultimate triumph of good over evil. He wanted to exorcise the centuries, put a stop to the macabre polonaise, and send all sad ghosts scampering.

Cloaked in the pomp of the ritual, the isolation of the betrayer, Mann-Bielecki didn't fear their hatred, only their blind judgment. There is a particular purity at absolute zero, he wanted to assure them . . . *There exist in the world around us sacraments for evil as well as for good, and our life and actions are played out in an undreamt-of world, full of caverns and shades and twilight beings* . . . The love of self is still a kind of love, and in that dark love such acts of sacrifice are possible as to make Christ himself a music-hall turn. The need to propitiate the unknown calls for transcending limits . . . exultation . . . and none of it is at all illogical in the context of this shadow world where nothing seems real . . . And hatred for the solitary who transcends the limits and, by his act of sacrifice, hoists the herd another notch upward, who functions perfectly outside the herd, must surely be at least in part envy of his invisible resources . . . !

And in the meantime the Russians had dispersed the mourners, drove away the women, surrounded the priest. The officer personally kicked Poremba into the prison coach. The spiritual leader of these new wandering tribes, the plainclothes resident NKVD interrogator, waved a fistful of gray envelopes, the dossiers scribbled on packing paper and the flyleaves of books, and he, Mann-Bielecki, confirmed in a surprisingly clear voice his denunciation of the priest and the editor, and watched their faces through the ventilation hole while the doors of the prison wagon were bolted behind them, and he could see, backing off, a gleam of curiosity in Poremba's eyes, then something else. Assessment and judgment. A stepping back from the glare of reality. He had been catalogued and labeled and filed for future reference. It had never occurred to him before to suppose that Jan Poremba was . . . could be . . . a dangerous man.

. . . You shouldn't burden me with your dreadful mission, he told the dancing shadows, the historical ghosts: I don't want any part of it. I have my own invulnerable loyalties, you have no right to question them! Who are the dead and the soon to be dead to reproach the living?

It was cold. He was hungry. He turned back toward the train, trudging through the shifting white mounds, the insubstantial geography of his isolation. The wilderness had become personally his.

. . . I have always tried to live in the present, a part of the present, he told the vanished shadows. And I have welcomed change, yes, certainly, but this . . . ah . . . don't you know . . . there must be something comprehensible in any reality, something to serve as a reference point . . . a point of orientation . . . otherwise we are all made insignificant. Nothing is believable here, nothing is conceivable. Life least of all.

A large young man brushed against him and said angrily into his ear: Paid, she says, paid! Stick with my own kind. Serve her right if I did!

A woman said: Honest to God, they'll be the death of us. And what is Pani Alicja going to do now? Imagine splitting up a family like that!

. . . Who are all these people? Who invited them? How can I get on with my work if I'm constantly being interrupted? Silence please, gentlemen, ladies, visions, conscience. Silence!

XII

Then they were through the worst of the mob. Worst or best, who could say? Those who resigned themselves to doing without the cupful of hot water, who lay in the snow or pressed together around their boxcar doors, who wandered out into the snowdrifts, or who no longer had the strength to leave their tiers of shelves, didn't hurt anyone. But, Esterka thought suddenly, if they had the strength, would they still be resigned?

Somewhere and sometime, in a time and country she could not imagine, she would live with purpose and with meaning in a way which was still unclear. Don't ask when or where. Love me and lead me, Esterka told her distant companions and begged them to hurry. They ought to grow wings. Her dream was undefined; she had done nothing to trim its natural profusion. It promised a life which went beyond survival. Per-

haps it was true that there was never any end to struggle. And death
. . . even death . . . merely transferred struggle to another plane . . .
Perhaps it was true that nothing could be done about that. But it was
up to her, she knew, to imbue her life with meaning, and as long as she
nourished her secret dream, and worked for its fulfillment, her life
would keep on growing.

The steamer hooted mournfully. It wasn't about to sail anywhere. It
was gripped in ice, far from the shore at the edge of the mist. The shrill
whistle of a locomotive called out in reply. And there was yet another
sound that she couldn't immediately identify: a persistent droning
growing stronger.

Jankele cried out suddenly, clutched at her skirt, and at once she was
transported to the Polish roads of September where aircraft meant fear.

The small white airplane flew toward the train low over the frozen
lake. A huge orange globe leaped into the sky behind it, stabbing the
clouds, the mist, and the swirling snow with spears of scarlet light.

Plane, steamer, locomotive . . . The end of one journey, the start of
another. It was too much to grasp in one icy instant. She watched a
procession of mourners driven toward the prison cars among bayonets . . . She knew who they were but she had suddenly forgotten their
names.

—Listen, I'm sorry, said Janek Stypenko. I didn't mean all that, you
know?

Jankele was tugging at her skirt.

—That thing's not going to hurt anybody, Janek said. You don't
have to hide from airplanes any more.

Jankele shook and whispered but his voice bore no sound in the
wind.

—Well, here we are, Janek said. Now let's get the water. That's what
we came here for.

—I don't want any, Jankele said.

She said: You must have your tea.

—No, I don't, he said. And anyway, look there, the soldiers aren't letting anyone near the locomotive. You've brought me here for nothing.

The locomotive was guarded by soldiers, motionless as statues. The
soldiers seemed untroubled by the wind. They were, she thought with
sudden clarity, less men than concrete posts marking a frontier. They
neither saw nor heard the crowd as people . . . Red frosted faces stared
indifferently through the surging mob as though none of it was there.
The engine driver leaned on crossed arms on the rail of his open platform. He wore a leather mask which robbed him of features; without
it, she supposed, equally indifferent, his cheeks would have frozen off
during the run through the night.

—Well, that's that, said Janek Stypenko. Might as well go back. Unless you want me to try talking to them?

She shook her head; it made no sense to plead with a fence post.

—As for that other, what I said, I'm sorry and that's the truth of it, Janek Stypenko said.

She shrugged, fought for balance against the force of the wind and Jankele's suddenly renewed frantic tugging.

. . . Don't know what comes over me sometimes, Janek was saying then. I don't mean half I say half the time anyway. You know how that is?

She nodded, watched the thin black threads of smoke making an eloquent but impossible promise at the rim of the steamer's funnel. She would have given anything to be near a stove. To be warm. To have a full stomach. To control this sudden seizure of hopelessness and fear.

. . . You must come soon or not at all, she told her vision of the Hargan's legendary leader. While there is still someone left who can follow you . . .

The airplane, gleaming with red struts, seemed to be on fire. It came toward her swiftly out of the sun, a part of the sun, scattering swords of light. It banked over the steamer and a small black cylinder fell from it, turning end over end.

—No, no, Janek was saying then to Jankele. That's not a bomb. That's for messages and that.

She closed her eyes. When she opened them again the airplane had disappeared. The cylinder was no longer in the air. There had been no explosion.

—See, little one, what did I tell you, eh? It wasn't a bomb.

Jankele said in a hard thin voice she had not heard from him before: Why don't you leave us alone?

—What did I ever do to you, little one? Janek said.

—He doesn't mean it, Esterka said.

—He means it.

—We are all confused, she said.

—I'm not confused! Jankele cried.

. . . And suddenly she was laughing. No, not outside; there tears had spilled over, flowed hot as acid. The scars, she was sure, would be permanent.

Janek Stypenko was talking. Urging and explaining. She didn't listen. Her back was turned to him. His disappointments were not of her making, each of us makes our own. Slowly in a breathless wonder she turned her head. The airplane was coming back, flying alongside her train, low down. And a face looked out of the rear cockpit: helmeted. with round goggles masking all expression, giving it a gargoyle appearance; what she could see of the face was as white and sudden as the morning sky. The goggles flashed hidden and reflected fires.

Here I am, she cried mutely.

In truth, I should reach for you; but can you reach for me?

And she was laughing, no longer questioning the rightness of her commitment.

Janet Stypenko stared at her, stupefied; her laughter would feed his bitterness, she knew. She shrugged, dismissed him. Like her invisible companions, she was a soldier of a cause greater than herself. She was no longer one but a multitude, a warrior tribe hurrying to the edge of a desert in answer to the summons of a messenger . . . Unthinking, she gave way to impulse: reached out her arms and waved. Jankele was staring. And as the airplane swept by in droning thunder the snowy flutter of a handkerchief broke out against its silver. It passed, rising slowly into the north, with the new day's sunlight striking it like an unfurling banner: the strange and monstrous contrast against the plumage of the metal bird.

PART THREE

NINETEEN FORTY

The Major

MORNNGS WERE BAD ENOUGH, he thought, waking to the same unbelieving sense of entrapment, but nights were disastrous. The night invariably seized upon the fears and suspicions of the day, and on the gnawing doubt that lay below suspicion, neither of which could be uprooted because they couldn't be identified. Night gave them a form.

There had been a nightmare. It was the usual nightmare: fantastic shapes had coupled and uncoupled in a steamy mist. A brass band had been playing. There had been an undulating serpent with no mouth. The worst horror in the world, he thought, the horror beyond all life's horrors, is surely the sense of being hopelessly trapped.

It is the time which breaks us down, Tarski muttered into a clenched fist. Not the place or the people. Men can defy men and overcome place but there is no defense against time.

His stomach rumbled. Cold, damp and hungry, covered with plaster dust, cobwebby with sleep, Major Tarski struggled with his greatcoat (careful not to disturb the others who lay piled around him like the aftermath of a gas attack: green and brown mounds without blood or crosses in an icy field), rolled to the edge of the communal bunk, groped for his boots while typhus lice crackled underfoot, found the boots, put them on, rose, stretched, cursed the new day under his breath. The cracked and peeling cherubs simpering on the ceiling of the half-ruined chapel sent down showers of Byzantine plaster, and now his bowels were painfully convulsed. He sucked his bleeding gums, took care not to scratch the infuriating rash that covered his face, fought a brief rearguard action against collapsing sphincter muscles, reached the yard just in time. He stared with hatred at the gloomy sky, the onion cupolas, the sloping massive walls of an abandoned and discredited faith. Shit on the sons of bitches, he muttered into hands clasped before his face while watery blood was splashing his boots. How can a man orient himself between possibilities if his position hasn't been exactly defined?

Again he cursed quietly, remembering the obtuse NKVD interrogators (the Ox, the Robot, the Gorilla, and the Gondolier), who insisted that the Soviets had not invaded Poland in September, that there had been no war in the proper sense (whatever *that* meant), that what was going on in Poland now was *protective occupation*, and that, therefore, no one in the monastery compound could call himself a prisoner of war.

(Then what in hell are we! he had shouted, momentarily out of control and cursing his nerves then as now. A man must know what to call himself! The Ox had starting talking about protective internment. What's that, he had cried, who needs to be protected and against whom are you protecting us, why did you take us out of Poland anyway, it's contrary to the articles of the capitulation . . . But the Ox lost his temper, punched him in the eye, and had him pitched bodily out of the interrogation room.)

The day had barely started. The sun was just beginning to nudge the lowest strand in the barbed-wire fence, the Russian birches were blue beyond the low monastery wall. A flight of crows was slow on crooked wings. Thin crusts of snow lay scattered about like paper between frosted pools of mud. Undelivered messages, he thought gloomily: handbills and advertisements for a bankrupt circus, orders for lost battles . . . And in the meantime, a real piece of paper would save much wear and tear on the tail of his coat.

He was suddenly seized with unreasoning fury, bitterly resenting the accident of his captivity, winter's unnecessary aftermath and cruel commentary on the lost campaign. No one could hear him, no one was listening to him; there is a loneliness in this striped dawn air, these bars of shadow are a communicable disease. The huddled sentry in the gaunt guard tower was an unnoticed exclamation against the steel-gray unresponsive sky.

His fists were clenched on air, they were empty, and soon he was also emptied and shuddering like a sick old dog, and he looked at his demobilized fingers and tried to imagine them as filled with the ribbed metal grip of a saber, or grasping the smooth warmth of a Parabellum, or fashioning an act of affirmation that would render all thought unnecessary and negate this unacceptable reality of . . . well, how can one say it . . . loss of self. An act of sudden, unpremeditated violence may say more powerfully than any assembly of words: I am. Think of me as a man complete in himself. No, not that pathological nonsense that Abel talks about: all that tedious, useless . . . bloody useless . . . business about the falseness of society and man's estrangement from God and from himself . . . No, but to send a ringing message to the clouds, a final declaration of the unchanging principles . . . The Oath! Our covenant with our country and ourselves . . .

He thought, once again gripped in a clonic spasm, of the deserter in the leather coat whom he had beaten with a saber scabbard on that disastrous road of defeat . . . a dreadful young man who had unwittingly held up an invisible mirror . . . a dusty and terrible moment in which the purity of hatred had offered a sudden illumination. He hadn't understood it then, had in fact been appalled by his own animal brutality; now he could see it as simply as a battle order. The pale young Jew's laughter need not have been an insult, it had merely focused his own shock and shame. Whether that miserable little creature had truly deserted had not been the issue. But how could anyone even think of doing such a thing? How could such thinking be allowed? Who was that laughing boy to defy tradition, to refuse his sacrifice, to tell me in his act of treason that my whole life had been a lie? . . . If you accept one question you must hear them all, he said to himself, and added: I refuse to hear any further questions.

Duty demands. Honor.

Self-sacrifice affirms a principle.

Tradition.

. . . I should have killed him, I suppose.

And then he realized that as he thought of killing and tradition, sacrifice, honor, and the demands of duty, he had not been thinking of the young Jew in the leather coat who may or may not have been a deserter, who may have laughed or not, who had merely drawn attention to himself in a declarative moment. He had thought with hatred about Abel. Thought vanished instantly, as though sabered.

He scrunched his eyes, peered blindly against the new sun. He pulled up his breeches. Several men had come out of what had been the monks' granary and someone else was hurrying toward him from the refectory hall, which was now the NKVD administration and interrogation building. Jozef Abramowski went by slowly, nodding to himself.

Tarski averted his face, then remembered that there had been something he had wanted to ask Jozef about, a rumor started in a careless moment by one of the Russians, a comment which had swept the camp like wildfire, and wondered for an amused moment why he had never thought of Jozef as an officer, why it seemed so unnatural for this limping lawyer to have rank and title other than academic or professional. He cursed his odd new inability to act without thinking, ordered his thoughts to dress from the right. —You're up early this morning. A little stroll?

—As with you, Adam. A call of nature, you might say, the tall man said quietly.

—Have you been having another little chat in the administration building?

Jozef nodded.

—Someone told me that you had a chat with the Abbot the other day . . . (then he explained impatiently, hating explanations): that new Russian general, the mysterious one, the one who looks like . . . well . . . an abbot, I suppose.

His odd twisted smile undisturbed, Jozef said: General Zarubin likes to chat.

—I wouldn't know, said Tarski. I understand he made a comment about the Bolsheviks' possible intentions, something that might suggest what they're planning for us . . .

—His exact words were: *It's better for you not to know, believe me, if you knew it would drive you mad,* Jozef said, then added: I don't know what he meant by that, and I'd rather not know.

—Well, dammit, man, don't you spend a lot of time with this Russian fellow? Can't you find out? Your little nocturnal visits to the Abbot's office have been noticed, you know.

—By Major Benedykt, no doubt, Jozef said, still smiling, turned to go, added: When he sends for me, I go. He seems to like intelligent conversation.

—What's that supposed to mean?

Jozef laughed without joy or pleasure, a parody of laughter, said smiling: Do you like guessing games? Do you like ironic situations?

—I'm not interested in intellectual word games. All I want is to be told why they're keeping us here. If we knew what we were to them we might be able to make an intelligent guess about their intentions.

—My guesses are no better than yours but if I were you I'd believe Zarubin.

—That nonsense about being driven mad? That's nonsense! Men like us . . . what nonsense. But I suppose you have your reasons for keeping your suspicions to yourself.

—Not really, Jozef said. It's just that all this guessing about the Bolsheviks' intentions has become rather academic for me. You see, I'm to leave here today.

—Oh? Tarski said, feeling a touch of envy. You've been selected for repatriation?

—Not a good guess, Adam. As a matter of fact, I've just been given ten years at hard labor.

—Good God, Tarski said. Whatever for?

—Suspicion of anti-Semitism, Jozef said, pale as death.

Three sparrows settled on the iron handle of the water pump. Tarski groped for his slingshot, thinking about breakfast, thinking that (surely) Jozef was trying to make some sort of a joke. He turned to call out after the limping man and demand explanations. Then someone shouted to him and he saw that Dr. Poremba was hurrying toward him.

—Caught in the act, eh? Dr. Poremba said. Well, try for the one in the middle, he looks the best of the sorry lot.

Tarski drew back on the rubber, sighted, fired, and missed. The sparrows took off. Tarski swore. He tried to understand what Jozef had told him. Someone shouted angrily from across the courtyard. Dr. Poremba laughed.

—Well, you hit something. Can we eat it, whatever it is?

—It's probably another middle-aged reservist.

—Be kind to us, Adam, Dr. Poremba said. We can't all be heroes.

—There's just too damn many civilians in this camp, Tarski said. Invalids, for God's sake, long retired like Jozef. Useless as officers. Why the hell couldn't the Bolsheviks have left them alone? All these civilian experts, who wouldn't be able to march a platoon to the cookhouse, picked up at their jobs, arrested in bed, crammed into their antiquated, ill-fitting uniforms, and, dear God, here they are with us, officers no less!

—Oh, you professionals, Dr. Poremba laughed. Can't you ever relax just a little bit? Must you try to turn even a prison camp into an officers' club?

—It helps, Tarski said. And when Dr. Poremba continued to laugh he said irritably: But you look healthy this morning. Where did you spend the night?

—In the pursuit of science, Dr. Poremba said, and added with mild satisfaction: There was some tea to go along with it.

—That means that you were with the Ox again, Tarski said, not hiding his distaste. What the hell do you do with him every night? If it were anyone but you I'd say that you were getting ready to join the Red Corner.

—Pure science, said Dr. Poremba. I've introduced the Ox and the Gorilla to phrenology.

—I don't know how you get away with it, Tarski said.

Dr. Poremba blew out his round cheeks, laughed, and blinked rapidly. —There's really nothing to it. Phrenology is a very Soviet science, you know. After all, as I point out to my students, who has as many lumps on his head as a Russian? The Ox's head is a little thick but he's certainly getting some wonderful lumps.

—You spend too much time with the Russians, Tarski said. People are beginning to talk about that.

—That's to be expected. *Obgadywanie* . . . talking about others, is a particularly Polish science, I believe.

—Don't say things like that. I don't like to hear anything derogatory about us. We have enough professional detractors as it is.

Dr. Poremba laughed, waved his arms. —My dear, dear Adam, remember your Clausewitz, or perhaps it was Der Grosse Friedrich or some other eminent military psychopath. *People who would defend everything are defending nothing.* Some positions can't be defended, they can't even be justified. I was only saying that our national bump of morality is very well developed, particularly when it comes to criticizing others.

—Is there really such a thing on the head? Tarski asked, grinning despite himself.

—Good God, how should I know? I invent my sciences as I need them. Astrology for children and officers of the General Staff, phrenology for the Ox, the Gorilla, and the Gondolier. That particular science requires a little forcefulness, you see; you can't just poke a potential bump with your finger to get your point across. On Comrade Ox's head I use that iron ruler that he swings so masterfully during interrogations.

Now laughing, Tarski said: Everyone'll catch on to you one of these days and you'll really get it in the neck.

—I don't plan to be here that long, Dr. Poremba said.

—Oh? Are you on the repatriation lists?

—No, oh no! I'm making other arrangements for myself. But you are on this morning's list, that's why I hurried over.

The nightmare was immediately back: the mute, five-jointed serpent, that was the train of course: the same five prison coaches which left the camp siding each nightfall to return empty the next afternoon. A sudden swell of nausea rocked him back and forth.

He didn't know why he should feel such anxiety, even foreboding, at the thought of leaving. He would have done almost anything to be allowed to go. But he feared, unreasonably, without any basis for his fear, that the supposed repatriation was yet another Russian lie. He wanted to believe that the nightly transports which carried off groups of cheering officers on a mysterious journey did, indeed, go to Poland, to whatever freedom was still available in his tormented country, even if it were only the freedom to escape from Poland, to go to France, the Army, to his duty . . . but he could not bring himself to accept the truth of Russian announcements. Unlike most of the others, he thought the repatriation to be a cruel hoax.

—So it was not pure science after all, he said, struggling for control.

—Information is the whole point of science, said Dr. Poremba. The satisfactions of research are incidental.

—Who else is on the list?

—Our whole mess group. Abramowski, Langenfeld, young Jurek Bednarski, the Colonel, your friend Benedykt . . .

—Not my friend, Tarski said.

—Three hundred and sixty men altogether, the biggest transport yet.

—But not you.

—Well, I was on the list. But I persuaded the Ox to scratch my name off it.

—Then you don't believe either that we're being sent to Poland on the damned little train.

—I don't know what to believe, Dr. Poremba said. Therefore I don't believe anything I hear around here. Whatever a Russian tells me I assume the truth is the exact opposite.

Tarski nodded, muttered: It would be too good to believe that they'd send us home.

—I've thought about it for five days, Dr. Poremba said. Ever since the first transport, when they took our generals and all the best, the most resolute and determined of the regular officers, Solski and those fellows who made a joke of Berling's Red Corner . . . It seemed odd that the Bolsheviks should be rewarding those who gave them the most trouble.

—Damn odd, Tarski said.

—But d'you remember that night? All that delirious hope suddenly restored, everybody cheering . . . My fortune-telling business disappeared practically overnight! Even I was ready to believe it.

—We'd all like to believe it, Tarski said. Couldn't you get the truth out of the Ox, or some of the others you poke on the head?

Dr. Poremba looked suddenly uneasy. —Well. Hmmm. Yes. That's part of the reason why this business makes me so very nervous. None of our regular keepers know anything about it. The only one who might know is the Abbot himself, or that popinjay who arrived here just before they started talking about this . . . ah . . . repatriation, that fellow Szymanski. But I wouldn't try any of my tricks on them. They both make me nervous.

—The train commander is sure to know where he takes his cargo.

—And that's another thing, Dr. Poremba said. They don't allow the train crew anywhere near the monastery. The convoy guards aren't even permitted to get off the train! Besides, the only answer a Russian would give us would be another lie.

—But if they're lying, why the masquerade? Tarski said, and knew as he said it that to expect a logical explanation for illogical behavior in a world where nothing seemed rational, nothing real, and all events conspired to undermine reason, was a civilian luxury and, as such, beneath him. Still, he went on: They even march us to the train behind a military band playing Polish marches, and those damn interrogators line up to wave handkerchiefs. And why the special travel rations wrapped in clean white papers? When did you ever see white paper in this country? It's as if they were to serve champagne in Sing Sing, for God's sake! And why urge those of us who are staying behind to write letters to our families, in Poland, that those who are leaving can take to deliver? It just seems too elaborate for a Russian hoax. It's too elaborately cruel.

—What do you think, then? Could there be anything to it? They certainly act with admirable correctness.

—And that's what makes *me* nervous, Tarski said.

They started walking up and down the courtyard, heads bowed and hands clasped behind their backs, having no goal, no purpose before reveille and roll call.

—And why haven't they taken any of the Red Corner gang? Tarski said suddenly. You'd think they'd liberate their stooges before anybody else.

—Ah, that's something I *can* tell you about, Dr. Poremba said, and grinned at the sky. Our interrogators are really unhappy about their indoctrination program. They've managed to convert only six shaky souls out of our five thousand, and five of the six are Jews. The Ox is keeping the whole Red Corner here to help infect a few more of us. You ought to hear the Ox on the subject, he comes close to choking. They had a regular production quota here, twenty percent of all available human material, the way the Ox states it, at least one thousand men. The Ox has no idea how he'll talk his way out of that disaster.

—They shouldn't even have got six, Tarski said.

—Hunger can be quite persuasive, Dr. Poremba said, then shook his head and spread his hands as though he were about to relate something unbelievable. —But there's a new wrinkle now, a five-year sentence for anti-Semitism if you turn down the overtures of Berling's Red Corner. Can you imagine that?

—Good God, Tarski said. So that's what Jozef was mumbling about.

—He was the first they've tried it on. He refused them twice. So they gave him five years for each refusal. His personal history didn't help him much.

—That poor old bastard, Tarski said. And what about you? Do you still think you'll find a way out of here and then go off searching for your family?

—That's still the idea.

—You ought to get yourself a job in the cookhouse. Half of it is on the other side of the wall. You come in at this end, go out at the other. I don't think they'd have a sentry at the other end.

—For some reason I can't convince anyone to make me a cook. But science is sure to come up with an answer sooner or later.

Despite himself, and the moment, Tarski smiled, said: I have an odd faith in your scientific mind. But what I'd really like to know is something concrete about that repatriation.

—Speaking as a magician and a scientist, Dr. Poremba said, I'm afraid that's only an illusion.

Tarski nodded, said: Agreed. So what's the worst thing that they could be doing? Shipping us off to the tundra to look at white bears? Kola . . . Kamchatka . . . some ice hole like that?

—In twenty hours? Don't forget, that little train comes back every afternoon.

—Ah, that's the point, Tarski said. That's no more than a ten-hour trip each way, say eight, with two for unloading. They could get us to Poland in eight hours, couldn't they?

—It doesn't seem likely. We are about . . . oh, I'd say . . . two hundred kilometers southwest of Moscow, somewhere in the old Kaluga Governorate, not far from the Bryansk railroad. If we were going to Poland we'd have to go to Moscow first, then switch over to the Smolensk line. So it's more likely that they unload between Smolensk and the Polish border.

—Smolensk? Tarski said. Now what is it that I've heard about Smolensk?

—But since the railroad siding is five kilometers away, and we don't actually see that little train going anywhere, and since we don't know which direction it takes, south or north, we're no closer to knowing where it goes than we were before.

—Wait, Tarski said. There's something about that Smolensk area, something I remember . . . some kind of a forest?

—Either way, it sounds like just another camp.

—Wait, Tarski said. I remember now. I was in Warsaw last summer, an intelligence seminar, one of those damn courses the *ekspozytura* people ran for field-grade officers. My colonel loved sending us to things like that, thought it would make intellectuals out of us, though they always bored the hell out of me . . . Someone said something about this mysterious forest, some sort of secret Russian installation northeast of Smolensk . . . some sort of special prison? I wish I could remember.

—Well, that's it, then, said Dr. Poremba. I never could believe these bastards would send us home.

—They'd be insane to do it, Tarski said. Think what it would mean to the underground, or for our new army in France, to have five thousand officers, not to mention the other qualifications around here. There are twenty-one university professors in this damned monastery, six hundred and fifty-four other teachers, three hundred medical doctors, at least a regiment of lawyers, more journalists and assorted scribblers than fleas on a dog. We had twelve of the fourteen captured Polish generals here too, remember? Granted, most of them were retired old gentlemen, a little hazy about modern warfare, but they couldn't have forgotten everything they knew. Even if the Russians were insane enough to release such people, their German allies would never let them do it.

—Those lying sons of bitches, said Dr. Poremba.

The sparrows were back, unconcerned. Black smoke unfolded above the bakery like a funeral banner. The NKVD officer whom the internees called the Gondolier, because he always stirred the noon soup before it was ladled from the rusty cauldron into jars and cans, so that the grease, the thin gruel, the rare piece of fatback, the accidental fragment of the marrowbone would rise from the bottom, came out of the abbot's refectory and began to beat the ornamental bronze bell with an iron bar. The bell hung on a gibbet. It was reveille.

The roll call in the rain lasted through midmorning as the Ox and the Gorilla counted ranks, miscounted, lost count and counted again, and the officers stood talking to each other.

It was cold. Tarski's teeth were chattering. The Nervous Colonel was darning a sock. Major Benedykt was toying with his monocle. Jozef Abramowski was massaging his knee. Dr. Poremba was staring at the sky.

. . . It's not the cold that bothers everyone, Tarski thought, it's this everlasting dampness, the reeking wetness of everything we touch. Walls, bodies, and the untrimmed pine bunks in which the officers were stacked for the night. Never the sight of the sun. He didn't know this part of Russia, in the penumbral hinterland of Moscow, in a southwestern plain bordered by pine and birches where, he supposed, spring would be sunny, mild. But in the meantime there was rain, and gray sleet at nightfall, and illness and hunger.

—Well, it'll soon be over, said the Nervous Colonel. It looks as if the Bolsheviks are keeping the agreement. A little late but better lat than never, is what I always say.

Tarski said: Can we really believe it?

—Of course we can believe it! What's more, we must believe it! Oh,

I know what you're thinking, Tarski. Don't think like that, that's defeatist thinking. The main thing is to have faith in our destiny, always do our duty, and remember who we are.

—There's something else I'm trying to remember, Tarski said. Have any of you gentlemen heard anything about a forest near Smolensk? There were some staff studies done about that place, our intelligence people were interested in it.

—Well, there's the Katyn Forest, the colonel said. That's over there somewhere.

—That's the one, Tarski said. Now, what is it about it that I'm trying to remember? It was a special zone of the GPU, barbed wire, dogs, patrols . . . a forbidden area . . . something about all of the local population being moved away from it . . .

—Well, you know the Russians, said Major Benedykt. They make a state secret out of everything.

—Yes, Tarski said. Our intelligence tried to penetrate it in 1938 but it was sealed so tight that a snake wouldn't have wriggled through. There was something odd about that place, but I can't remember what it was.

—In a few more days we won't have to give a thought to any of this Bolshevik nonsense, said Major Benedykt.

—Yes, gentlemen, said the Nervous Colonel. Tomorrow we shall be rolling through Polish fields, seeing Polish birches . . . And then I shall invite you all to breakfast at the Georges in Lwów.

—That seems almost impossible to believe, Tarski said. They can't afford to let any of us go home.

—But they're obliged to do so by the terms of the capitulation, said the Nervous Colonel. Timoshenko and Khrushchev both signed the agreement that all our officers would be allowed to go abroad or to stay in Poland. Do you think any of us would have laid down our arms under other terms?

—No, I suppose not, Tarski said. It's just that I don't believe that these new kinds of Russians bother to keep agreements. Even the Tsar's commanders weren't good at it.

—One must believe in something, said the Nervous Colonel. One must have faith. Hasn't that always been our way?

—Our Via Dolorosa, Dr. Poremba said.

—Let me tell you something, said the Nervous Colonel. Nations, like people, have their fates. There's nothing to be done about that. We have a certain destiny among nations, and all we can do is be true to ourselves, have faith in the justice of our cause, and believe that God is always watching.

—And what about the Devil? said Dr. Poremba.

—That goes without saying.

Jurek Bednarski, who reminded Tarski so much of himself as a young man, began to sing a parody of a sentimental military song about Lady War, that cruel and enigmatic mistress of the Eternal Lancer.

> . . . *Wojenko, wojenko, Little Lady War*
> *Some die for your smile*
> *And others meanwhile*
> *Stay in bed and snore . . .*

Then, suddenly laughing, he said: And now a verse about our going home, hoping that we are truly going, that this isn't only a dream.

> . . . *Czerwonko, czerwonko*
> *Cóżeś Ty za pani . . .*
> *Jednych transportujesz*
> *Dru-u-ugich internujesz*
> *W przeklętej otchłani . . .*

He sang in a clear high voice and other young men joined him while the preparations for the convoy got under way. Those who were staying behind congratulated those who were about to leave. There were envious faces and disappointed faces and there were mutterings of *why him, why not me, if I can't why can he?* and backs were slapped, hands were shaken, embraces were exchanged. Notes and letters were hurriedly written for delivery to families in Poland and pressed into the hands of the fortunate. Yes, we're the fortunate today, Tarski thought, at least we are leaving. No matter where we are going it is motion, it is not stagnation, it is something new. Whatever lies ahead may, perhaps, be better. Perhaps, finally, our status will be defined . . .

He took handfuls of brown paper scraps, mechanically stuffing the messages into his greatcoat pockets; he watched himself, as if from a height, making the expected gestures of confidence that he didn't feel. Yes, of course I'll send this on, dear friend, as soon as I'm back in Lwów, you can depend on it; yes, Julku, I'll be happy to tell your mother you're well; certainly, Romku, I'll tell your lady that you'll be home soon, how can you even wonder? Calculating at the rate of three hundred men a day, all of us will be home by the end of April.

Up to that moment he could count the lies he had ever told on the fingers of one hand. But why crush hope on the evidence of night-

mares? And maybe, after all, despite the portents and the probabilities
. . . Perhaps one should believe. Faith has never been difficult for men
of our kind. Perhaps one should pray . . .

(. . . Well then, we'll see each other in France. Ah, *stary*, let me tell
you, Paris at this time of the year . . . And they say our army there is
totally mechanized now, just like the Germans . . . three divisions already, I am told, won't that make a difference! Well, certainly, to be
sure, that's where we'll see each other . . . It's your turn today, lucky
devil, maybe my turn tomorrow!)

There were warning voices but nobody listened. No one wanted to
hear anything that undermined his hopes. The troubled moon face of
Jasio Poremba appeared briefly at the chapel window and Tarski bowed
his head as if to acknowledge inaudible warnings as he wandered about
the chapel unable to find a place for himself. The cheerfulness set his
nerves on edge. He stretched, yawned, silently cursed the cramped bunk
in which he had slept. Four men to a wooden box on straw, and that's
for field-grade officers. Only the old, retired generals had had cots to
themselves. The privileges of rank had considerably diminished but,
even so, the Bolsheviks seemed to be making an attempt to be civilized.

One had to be calm. Doubt had to be subdued. Looking through a
stained-glass Byzantine Madonna and a Bleeding Heart, he saw that
NKVD soldiers had surrounded the chapel with fixed bayonets.

The midday meal was a feast. No one had seen anything like it in the
camp before: thick gruel and a length of sausage, and hot sweet tea
ladled out of tubs by big-breasted smiling women in NKVD uniforms.

—Tea, gentlemen, and with sugar too, well, really, said the Nervous
Colonel. What is one to think?

Jozef Abramowski, who had been staring into the fatty gruel as
though it were a miracle, finally smiled and said: Well, obviously,
they want our last memory of Russia to be a good one . . .

—I'll settle for any kind, sir, just so it's the last one, Jurek Bednarski
cried, then blushed and averted his face while the others laughed.

—Ah, gentlemen, gentlemen, said Major Benedykt, who had once
more embedded his polished monocle in place. Can't we afford a little
charity at a time like this? A little tolerance? They're really not so bad,
you know, if it weren't for this Communist disease . . . a bit boorish,
perhaps, a little backward, hardly on our level . . . but blood is thicker
than water and old roots sink deep. It's the same old Slavic stock, you
know!

—Well, there's no doubt about it now, said the Nervous Colonel
with obvious satisfaction. It would seem, gentlemen, that we shall soon

be home. The only question now is just how quickly we can get to France. The sooner the better, you know, before all the good appointments are given away!

—The question is where we are going, Langenfeld said quietly.

—I don't see the point of asking such questions.

—I see that you are also going, my dear professor, Major Benedykt said, laughed, tossed his monocle, retrieved it, replaced it. Planning to see Paris?

—No, said Langenfeld.

—I didn't think so. No need to ask why.

And Tarski said quietly, so that only Langenfeld and Jozef could hear: Then you don't believe that we're going home either?

—If I told you what I thought you'd think me insane, Langenfeld said calmly. And to tell you the truth, I hope that I am.

—Is it ridiculous to hope, then? Tarski asked.

—Hope? Of course one must hope! Where the devil do you think we'd be without hope? That's what we've always been able to do, that's been our greatest strength, our faith in the ultimate resurrection of our country, our single-minded pursuit of impossible dreams! Oh no, my friend, don't denigrate hope, just don't confuse it with wishful thinking. We are no longer living in a civilized world.

The chapel had darkened. Everyone but the officers who were to leave that night, whose thoughts had preceded them to freedom, who sang and joked or rested with their minds at ease, who did their best to mend and clean their worn and mud-stained uniforms, who polished their buttons, who traded cracked and broken boots for more presentable footwear, had been locked outside. Again, looking out, Tarski saw Poremba; he watched him pacing worriedly outside the chapel windows.

The Ox and the Robot joined the Gondolier to list personal possessions and to take away odds and ends of camp property, and a representative of the State Jewelry Trust began to make offers for cigarette cases, lighters, fountain pens and watches, and after the Gorilla had finished the headcount, consulted with the others and agreed that there were indeed, three hundred and sixty internees present and ready for transport, two other NKVD officers came into the chapel.

One, slim and elegant, darkly handsome, with a finely chiseled authoritative face, said nothing. The other, a shapeless, graceless man, whose features seemed blasted out of concrete, said in coarse guttural Russian that his name was Zarnov, that he was the train and transport commander, and that anyone who disobeyed his orders, or any other orders while in his charge, would be shot.

The Nervous Colonel stood up, cleared his throat, said importantly:
I have a question. May I ask a question?

The elegant Soviet officer nodded pleasantly.

—What's all this nonsense about being shot? I remind you of the
provisions of the Geneva Convention regarding treatment of officers
who are prisoners of war!

—Thank you for the reminder, the NKVD officer said in unaccented
Polish. I remind you, in turn, that the Soviet Union is not a signatory
of the Geneva Convention, that no state of war exists between the Soviet Union and your country, and that, therefore, you are not prisoners
of war.

—What are we then? Tarski cried.

—Think of yourselves as our guests at the moment.

—Thanks for the hospitality, Jurek shouted, and several other young
men laughed.

The elegant officer raised his hand for silence, and Benedykt said
approvingly: Change uniforms with him and he could be one of us,
eh? Blood will tell.

Langenfeld looked up, opened his mouth to speak, closed it, averted
his face.

—The man's a fool, Professor, Tarski said swiftly. Tell me what you
think.

—Gentlemen, said the elegant Soviet officer. Colonel Zarnov's disci-
plinary announcement is routine, it needn't worry you. It's merely a
matter of discipline and order. You know how it is, gentlemen, when
you must move large bodies of men. Absolute obedience is a must, isn't
that correct? We wouldn't want anything to happen to our guests.

—And your men will really shoot without warning? asked the Nervous Colonel.

—I'd rather expect it. No one, however, expects to do any shooting.
We are just as anxious to see you gentlemen returned to your homes as
you're anxious to go. I'm sure that we can count on your cooperation.

—Professor, Tarski said once more, urgently. Please tell me what
you're thinking.

The gaunt, stooped reservist, who had borrowed a fountain pen from
the Nervous Colonel, and who was writing on the sheet of white paper
in which his traveling rations had been wrapped, looked up at Tarski,
said: Why do you always call me by my academic title rather than by
my military rank?

—I don't know, Tarski said. Somehow it seems . . . more natural.

—There is the clue to what you want to know, Langenfeld said.
When in doubt, people always do what is natural to them. It's really
too bad.

—Then you think that what the Russians have in mind for us is natural to Russians?

—Yes, to the specific kind of Russians we're dealing with here. Russians don't change much, they were a closed society long before their Revolution, they've never been self-conscious about being brutal . . . And there's an odd, mad streak of mysticism in the best of them . . . But this new lot that we're dealing with, well, it's almost a new species . . . Nothing quite like them has ever been seen before. Even among Russians.

—It's only Asia with a thin European veneer, Tarski said.

—What is natural to this new breed of Russians would be unnatural even under Lenin.

—What's this about Lenin? Benedykt said fiercely. We don't want to hear Bolshevik propaganda here. This isn't your Red Corner, my dear professor!

Langenfeld nodded, folded and pocketed the paper on which he had been writing, returned the fountain pen to the Nervous Colonel.

—The trouble with *some* people, Benedykt said, looking at the ceiling, is that they have a natural inclination to disloyalty. In due time this will be remembered.

Tarski got up. He tugged at his greatcoat and straightened its collar. He glanced regretfully at his cracked and muddy boots, the stains and the patches. He pushed his way to the front row of the massed officers and the impassive group of NKVD men in their blue-banded caps. They were about to leave. The Gondolier was pounding on the door, the Robot was shouting. Tarski caught the elegant Commander Szymanski by the sleeve, said softly: Sir, one more word?

—How can I oblige you?

—What is it that you are really going to do with us?

—What do you suppose?

—I don't know. But I know that you are not repatriating us.

—And how do you know that?

—Call it a soldier's instinct.

—Instincts can be wrong.

—Agreed, but I've been eating soldier's bread since I was a boy. One learns to smell danger.

—You doubt us, then?

—Yes.

—Why?

—Again, a soldier's instinct.

—Your colleagues don't share it.

—I can't speak for them.

—You lived in Russia before the Revolution, didn't you? It's all in your file.

—Yes.

—Did you take part in the People's Liberation?

—Only so far as the Polish national liberation was concerned.

—You didn't have your independence long.

—Long enough to remind us who and what we are.

The finely formed head bowed briefly, the eyes were half closed, the casual voice said: Yes, this is quite familiar . . .

There was a moment during which the elegant NKVD officer appeared to be thinking, weighing alternatives, and Tarski thought how easy it would be to say to this poised officer in his well-cut tunic, this civilized man: You and I speak the same language, we understand each other; can you forget your threatening uniform, the distances between us, can you remember the blood in your veins? May we speak to each other as brother officers? But before he could piece together an adequate phrase, the pale blue eyes so near to his own were suddenly narrow, the thin lips were smiling.

—By this time tomorrow you will have no doubts.

—But what does that mean?

—It means that you'll be perfectly at ease about everything.

—I have your word for that? Tarski said, insistent, hearing his own antique absurdity. The Soviet officer's courteous manner had almost disarmed him.

—I already gave it.

—A gentleman, Tarski blurted out. —Your word as a gentleman?

The Soviet officer's eyebrows went up, he stifled a smile.

—That too, if you wish it.

—And Katyn, Tarski said. What will you do with us there? That *is* where we're going, isn't it?

And suddenly the darkly handsome face was fixed in a shocked gray smile. It was no longer handsome, and the eyes were slitted as the smile died.

—No one known to have been taken there has ever been seen again, Tarski said, remembering the forgotten lecture.

—Outside with them, Szymanski ordered in Russian. Quick. Outside. And don't let them talk.

—Move! cried the Ox, the Robot, and the Gondolier. Everyone outside! Form fives, face the gates and absolute silence!

They marched to the train surrounded by a double file of NKVD soldiers with fixed bayonets, the long traditional Russian *shtyki*, on long Mosin rifles. Long Russian greatcoats flapping at the ankles. Leaping guard dogs. The shadows were falling. In time to the beat of the drum, the long-remembered rhythms, behind the NKVD band playing Polish marches.

The sun was poised above the western rim of birch crowns, spruce and pine in scarlet and gold. Soon it would vanish under the horizon.

The ancient music tugged at memories.

Tarski felt his throat tighten, his eyes were suddenly filled with tears as the musicians threw the promise and challenge of the *Varsovienne* into the chilled and darkening sky.

His country's history with its grandeur, treasons, triumphs, and heroic follies soared in that music: lost wars and desperate charges, the nation's funeral pyre; righteousness, prayers, taps, artillery salutes . . . In their graves, should dead soldiers lie as they fell, like broken dolls and hamstrung puppets? Or at parade rest . . . ?

> . . . *'Tis the Day of Blood-o-od and Glo-o-ry,*
> *May it be our Re-sur-rec-tion Day* . . .

Jozef Abramowski's huge body and tormented spirit lurched beside him, limping on old wounds, the source of all his physical agonies and spiritual anguish. I never really liked him, Tarski told himself. Silent and unforgiving, he had allowed himself to be nominated as Jozef's only friend. Too many gulfs of nature and of culture lay between them, Magda stood between them. Nobody loves the man who walks alone because no one knows him, and Jozef, despite his craving for acceptance, would always be alone. His home had been unbearable: a place without joy or the simplest pleasure. How Abel could have grown up whole in such bitterness was beyond Tarski's understanding. Jozef and Magda had not spoken to each other in his memory. Jozef was a twisted and tormented man, driven by fears and yearnings that made acquisition the core of existence. Any object, no matter how trivial, became a rare treasure when heaped upon innumerable other objects which filled and overflowed every level surface in his home. Each day brought something new to be handled and pushed about the shelves: a book, a figurine, an ornate letter opener, cut-crystal ashtray, or canister for toothpicks; all to be fondled for an hour or so and put aside to be immediately replaced with a new possession. This was an obscene hunger, as if the huge man with his colossal appetites and conflicts was permanently frightened, always dispossessed. He was a terrible and terrifying man; he suffered from that blackness of the soul which four thousand years of littleness might inflict upon a giant and which deformed him and marred his spirit like a crooked scar. In all other physical respects he was what he had longed to be in the years of the antique photograph which Abel carried with him about the world: successful lawyer, manufacturer of surgical appliances, popular speaker at nationalist rallies, contributor to patriotic weeklies, retired officer of the reserve, and gallant former legionnaire of Jozef Pilsudski, a man of good name, property, and acceptable tradition who happened to have been born a Jew. No matter where he went, Tarski couldn't forget that raging, soaring voice, imperious yet uncertain, while one impatient hand beat upon the air. His physical strength was enormous and his excesses were exorbitant. They made him a hateful parody of what he pursued: a religious convert who was, indeed, *plus Catholique que le Pape*, a supernationalist contempuous of minorities who would walk a mile in order not to buy from a Jewish store. Everything about him was an exaggeration, so that he embarrassed and upset the temporary captives at his entertainments: in turn a tyrant and fawning sycophant, a cruel caricature of national character at its worst.

Tarski had envied Jozef the possession of Magda, or rather the illusion of possession, the privilege of familiarity. She was, he supposed, the most successful of her father's famous thoroughbreds, quite overwhelming for a man like Jozef, who was always waiting for someone to call his bluff. She never had been like any other woman. A woman gives her man freedom to do as he would with his life; it remains for men to lead her to bed, stand or fall under their country's flag, and dominate the planet; it remains the woman's problem to find the man to whom she may safely make her enormous gift. But Magda was an elemental force. Who was poor twisted Jozef to think that he could ever be more than a shadow beside her? And how like him, colossal in his innocence, to try.

The beat of the drum was one with the pulse. The immemorial call of silver and brass which had sent countless generations of young Poles to the barricades and foreign battlefields, deaf to reasoning, beyond the reach of argument or logic, blinded to all but the messianic vision of their country's inevitable resurrection: the Phoenix summoned up from pyre after pyre. We cannot die, the bugles assured him. We can be overthrown but never defeated. We are beyond any means of subjugation known to man. No enemy has ever mastered us, new life is always surging in our ancient body. One thousand Polish years stand ready to assure us of eternal life . . .

He was immensely moved and he no longer minded if his emotions showed, and clutched his own sudden memories to himself. The vanished hopes of youth, when life had a meaning imposed by direct action, danced joyfully before him. Slogans and exhortations had been unnecessary. He was again running away from home to join the Legions. (His mother had made sure that he had packed extra handkerchiefs; his father had given him ten rubles and a speech.) And he was

now, as he had been then, ready to jump over the moon at the call of
the bugles.

The train was waiting at the siding: five long prison coaches, an intimately Russian institution that anteceded Revolution by more than
half a century. The single locomotive meant that the journey wouldn't
be a long one. There was a hiss of steam. Tarski had no more questions.
In the long run, it wouldn't matter where they would be taken. The
centuries had defined the character of the march and created their
own rituals. There would be detours and delays but the goal was
fixed, the principles were eternal. The ranks of blue-capped soldiers
parted and the dogs retreated and the loading started in all five
coaches at once.

Langenfeld was the first to vanish beyond the narrow door at the
edge of the coach. Jozef mounted next, then the Nervous Colonel.
Then the boy lancer. Benedykt came next.

A narrow passage ran the length of the car against the far wall, separated from a dozen cages by a thick wire mesh from ceiling to floor. A
ventilating hole, screened with chicken wire, was set near the ceiling.
Twenty men crowded into each cage. The doors in the mesh were
padlocked. Guards settled in the passage. The single door into each car
was bolted outside. There was a shout, a single answering blast of the
locomotive whistle. Couplings clanged, the train lurched. The train
began to move.

—There is some writing here on the wall, said Jurek Bednarski.
Can't make it out too well, but I think it's a list of railroad stations.
Smolensk is the last one.

—Here's something else, said Benedykt. Listen to this: *We have
been brought somewhere to a forest. Looks like a summer resort. A
thorough personal search. Rubles, belt, and pocketknife were taken.* It's
signed *Adam Solski.*

—That's Major Solski, said the Nervous Colonel. He went with the
first transport, with all the generals. But what the devil is he talking
about? A summer resort!

—This wall is covered with writing, Langenfeld said. Here it says:
*Gniazdovo. We are outside a small station, loading into trucks. Two
and a half companies of NKVD. Trucks leave and return in half-hour
intervals. Forest on horizon.*

—Here it says: *Windows of the buses are smeared with cement,*
Jurek read.

—What the devil does cement have to do with anything? asked the
Nervous Colonel.

—I don't think this train will take us to Poland, Langenfeld said.

—Ridiculous, said the colonel. It's perfectly obvious what this is about. The Communists are supposed to have turned this country into a paradise, correct? The Bolsheviks never let their prison trains outside their own borders, it's bad propaganda. They're going to transfer us in Smolensk into a proper train to take us to Poland.

—I think that we are going to be killed, Langenfeld said, and Tarski knew that no one understood him, that no one would listen because such words could never be believed. The words seemed to hang suspended, like monstrous flares; he felt the shock of the others' silence.

—That simply couldn't happen in the twentieth century, Major Benedykt said. Has he gone mad? Or is this some sort of provocation?

—We must accept the possibility, said Langenfeld. Otherwise we shall have no chance.

—But listen, Tarski said. Think of the violence of their civil war . . .

—And now even you've become contaminated! Benedykt cried.

—Well, said the Nervous Colonel. I'll grant you one point. The violence of a civil war could be one thing. Certainly. It might possibly justify excesses. But cold-blooded mass murder in a time of peace and comparative calmness? What sort of mind could come up with a thought like that?

Langenfeld shrugged, said quietly: We are in the hands of professional practitioners of terror.

The lurid words drifted across consciousness, burned themselves out and vanished, yet a kind of afterglow of nausea remained for some moments. It was an inconceivable idea, Tarski knew, and wondered if he had allowed his suspicions to overwhelm his reason. The thought violated every concept of human behavior, it could not be believed.

. . . The summer resort, the camp in the forest.

Yes, that was one possible explanation of the Russian riddle. It was acceptable, his mind did not recoil. The trucks or buses make the round trip in a half hour, do they? Say, fifteen minutes each way; say . . . five kilometers at twenty an hour. That is about the normal distance from a railroad for a Russian military installation.

But, Tarski thought, we can't allow them to lose us in a forest. Someone must hear about this. Who? How? He would have time to think about that in the long hours of the night and no doubt some idea would occur to him. He longed suddenly for the conspiratorial talents of Dr. Poremba, who would have a plethora of ideas at his fingertips. Thought of the moon-faced amateur magician's shrewd buffooneries . . .

. . . Listened to the monotonous clatter of the wheels, stuttering on switch points. Hollow on bridges. The talk of the others. Before he knew it he had fallen asleep.

Then it was morning: red sun, gray air, the cage was still dark. He was awake as suddenly and completely as he used to wake on all those mornings between wars that were so difficult to imagine now, coming into the day without a transition, taking the gulf between the darkness and light in one stride. Night would end and the orderly routines of the day would be already unfolding and he would step into them as though they were his boots. It was always the same small bachelor apartment no matter which town it happened to be in; never farther from the regimental barracks than a street or two, and not much in it in the way of furniture. He wasn't a man for possessions, he collected nothing. His vices were uncomplicated: good wine (in moderation) and English tobacco. He had the good sense to pick his women in the same age bracket as his own and, after Magda, he had avoided complicated women; not because he feared their problems or resented them but because other people's complexities weren't his specialty and, since he could not help, he didn't pretend to.

His life was simple, as far as he could tell; nothing about it was going to surprise him or threaten him with mirrors that might reflect a doubt. Oh, certainly, certainly . . . there had been some moments that were far from simple: there had been Magda, who had turned several worlds upside down for him; but all this was part of the barbarity of youth . . . And with youth put away, the memories in mothballs, events and people sorted out, cropped and pasted in that memory as lifeless as photographs in an album, the dreams dismissed, the hopes compromised, the dedications narrowed to their sharpest focus, life had become no harder to handle than an infantry battalion in a garrison town. You wake, and the orderly is working with polishing cloths, and the aroma of fresh coffee blends with the smell of leather and brass polish, and dust specks revolve in the sun, and you know exactly what the day will bring. It will not litter your private landscape with claims on compassion or drain your spiritual energies or obliterate your values or challenge moral concepts. It will not disturb the sleep of your certainties; you will see no specters, hear no gibbering ghosts.

. . . To refine your commitments, filter the dross of emotional involvements, discard the nonessential, is to hold the essence of your life in your own hands. All is reduced then to sharp planes and hard delineations; the several facets may be read as one.

And this is good, this is as it should be; when you've thrown off the weight of others' personalities you have independence; and like all true freedoms everywhere, it is always under attack and must be fiercely defended. Magda had been the greatest threat to this independence; she had swept through every aspect of his life like a hurricane and left it in shambles. At times she had seemed to be a plague which followed him around, withering everything he touched. She squeezed him till his bones cracked, racked him with fevers of distraction, and drained him of substance until he finally fled back into the Army, civilian possibilities hastily abandoned, as men might have entered monasteries in another century.

He had fled from her, and knew that this had been an act of cowardice. Yet it had also been an attempt to save himself from disintegration, even though he had never fully managed to escape her. The Army had brought peace. His sense of order could be nourished there. Predictable routines created contentment. Magda was always with him, even now, but she could no longer touch anything important. In the Army, life had become simple. It had acquired order and delineation. He measured it in regiments rather than in years: first this one, then another, all much the same and yet each distinct in his memory. The last decade was called in his private calendar the Twenty-first Regiment, and that was enough. His little company of years paraded past and he took the salute.

In the gray monochrome of morning the forms of men were blurred. The train was standing still. Jurek Bednarski was up on one of the benches, peering through the ventilation hole. During the night someone had punched out the chicken-wire screen.

—Hell, what's this? Tarski said. Where is Langenfeld?

—They took him off at Smolensk, Jozef said.

—What for?

—Who knows? Zarnov came in with a couple of ugly new faces in blue caps, called out his name, and took him away.

—We're better off without him, Benedykt said. I detest the type. Neither one thing nor another, neither beast nor bird. Can't put your trust in a fellow like that.

—He did a damn funny thing, Jozef said. See the ventilation hole? Well, it was Langenfeld who pushed out the screen. I think he was getting ready to throw out messages. He was writing something just before they came to take him away . . .

—Can't trust those scribbling fellows, Benedykt interrupted. Who knows what he was writing, or to whom, eh? Well, if they ask me about that chicken wire I'll tell them right off. What loyalty do I owe to a Langenfeld?

Nobody answered. Tarski yawned. Jozef shrugged, said: Whatever

Langenfeld was writing is in your pocket, Adam. He didn't have time
to throw it out before they came for him.

Tarski said: He put it in my pocket?

—Exactly what I mean, Benedykt said. Imagine putting something
in another man's pocket. But then, what could you expect from an odd
bird like that?

—I'm more concerned about where we are right now, Tarski said.

—Well, Jozef said. We were in Smolensk just before sunrise, we
waited there only a few minutes and then moved on a few kilometers.
The shadows of the telephone poles indicate that we're traveling northwest.

—And that, gentlemen, said the Nervous Colonel puts us right in
line for Vilno. Beautiful city, do any of you know it?

—I was there in '28, Tarski said. The Fifth Regiment . . .

—Always a delightful atmosphere, the colonel assured them. Wonderfully charming people. Nothing quite like it in the country, except
Lwów, of course, but that, as one used to say, is *incomparabile dictu.*

—And you really think, sir, that we're going to Vilno?

—Well, heading northwest from Smolensk, where else could we get
to? (And then, to Jurek:) Well, boy, what do you see there?

—We seem to be outside a little station, sir, Jurek said off his perch.
There's a big square, partly covered with grass, and there's a dirt road at
right angles to the railroad track, skirting the left side of the square.
Nothing but woods on the horizon, sir.

—Nothing more, eh?

—Well, sir, there's an old bus in the square, the wood-burning kind.
The windows, sir, have been covered with black paint.

—Gentlemen, Tarski said. I think that in one way or another we've
come to the end of the journey.

—Oh, not again, Benedykt said. What's the matter with you?

Tarski leaned back, closed his eyes, wished that he could relax, that
he could agree. It had always been like that in his memory: the sense
of comradeship, the solidity provided by a uniform world which
assigned him a clearly discernible place and fixed his position; the
sense of time extended beyond natural boundaries by its monochrome;
an order of things in which the elementary became the elemental.
One could like or dislike this or another member of the community
but one didn't question the tenets of the faith. He was quite ready
to believe that, when in doubt, people will do what is natural to
them, but no civilized man could accept Langenfeld's conclusions.
We are, after all (Tarski told himself), a civilized people. And so
are the Russians. There may be more than just a whiff of Asia about
them but they did once have a culture and the Bolsheviks couldn't have

destroyed it all. There would still be some men of conscience among them. What he had been suggesting to himself was simply a reflection of an unstable mind. Lack of discipline. A civilian's approach to reality, of which he was ashamed. Nevertheless, he was quite sure that this somnolent small station in the middle of nowhere was their destination. He wondered what kind of camp it would prove to be.

Jozef was looking at him strangely and Tarski wondered for a moment whether this caricature of them all had ever suspected his mesmerized enslavement by his wife. It didn't seem possible. But nowadays, in these incomprehensible new times, one could no longer be sure about anything. Was anything still true? Were the bright absolutes still in place? So much seemed to have changed in just a few months, and change was always a disaster.

. . . No, I was wrong, he thought. She couldn't have loved me. Needed me at one time, perhaps . . . She had cried out to him too late, when he had been already in full flight, his hands over his ears. She could love no one, not even herself, and yet . . . possibly . . . at one time . . . No, he thought, it couldn't have been more than a reflection of his own need for life.

He realized that he had not touched his traveling rations; looking around, he saw that all the others had been eating theirs. He took the white-wrapped package from his pocket. A folded square of paper fell out with the package. He smoothed the white sheet on his knee. It was covered with Langenfeld's cramped writing.

Benedykt looked at Tarski with something like pity, shook his head and said: A little message from our absent friend? No need to ask what's in it.

He began to write on the wall.

—There's something happening now, sir, Jurek said at the window. There're three more buses coming down the road. And soldiers are coming into the square.

—What kind of soldiers, boy?

—Blue cap bands, sir. NKVD with rifles and fixed bayonets. And there's that Colonel Zarnov walking about too.

—Now what the devil could that be about? said the Nervous Colonel.

—There are now four buses in the square, sir, Jurek said. The three new ones have their windows covered with cement. One of them is backing up to the first carriage and there are NKVD soldiers all around it.

—What's Zarnov doing?

—He's up there with the bus, sir.

Benedykt had finished writing and looked about him with satisfaction, then handed the pencil to Tarski with an ironic smile. The sil-

very metal tube was puzzling for a moment; Tarski didn't know what
to do with it. He leaned across Jozef to read what Benedykt had written
on the wall.

—You really believe that? he asked in a low voice.

—I am certain of it.

—How can you be certain? What reason can you give?

Benedykt shrugged and began to inspect his monocle.

—What I don't understand is this damned cement business, said the
Nervous Colonel. And the black paint. Didn't you say, boy, that one of
the buses had its windows covered with black paint?

—Yes, sir. It's on its way now to the head of the train. They have the
first car open and they're beginning to load our people into the bus.
Shall I count them, sir?

—Count them?

—I mean, sir, to see how many they're putting in at a time. How
many to a bus, sir.

—Certainly. Go ahead.

—Thank you, sir.

—You're a smart young man, the colonel said. I'll remember that.

. . . Langenfeld had written on the crumpled white paper, among
the stains left by the smoked fish, in carefully blocked Cyrillic letters, in
a language that Tarski had almost forgotten: *To be delivered to the
Ambassador of France in Moscow. Large reward is promised.* And then
in French: *Your Excellency, the undersigned is a Polish officer who has
reason to believe that a monstrous crime is taking place near Smolensk,
where Polish officers, prisoners of war, are being systematically murdered by the NKVD* . . .

—What's going on now, boy? said the Nervous Colonel.

—They're still loading the bus, sir. They're searching all our people
before putting them into the bus one at a time.

—That's just what Major Solski had written on the wall, Benedykt
said uneasily.

—Cement, black paint, and now a personal search, said the Nervous
Colonel. I don't understand this at all. Does anyone have any ideas?

Suddenly every man in the cage looked at Tarski, who averted his
face, and then everyone began to speak at once: doesn't mean anything
. . . could be anything . . . who can keep track of all the Bolshevik
nonsense? . . . gentlemen, remember who you are, what's all this sudden nervousness? . . .

—They're an odd bunch of birds, Benedykt said, but they *are* brother
Slavs . . .

. . . *I urge Your Excellency to inform your Government and the Polish Government in Angers that Polish officers are transported in groups*

of fifty to three hundred and sixty to a wooded area, about six miles northwest of Smolensk . . .

—That's it for the first bus, sir, Jurek said. Twenty men inside. The bus is driving off down the road.

. . . loaded aboard buses and taken five kilometers in a northward direction to a forest . . .

—The second bus is loading now, sir, Jurek said. The same procedure, sir.

. . . and killed. Six transports adding up to 1,800 officers of all ranks, including twelve generals, have been dispatched in this manner through the first week of April from the camp at Kozielsk, and it may be assumed that the same extermination program is in progress at the camps of Starobielsk and Ostashkov, where between 12,000 and 15,000 Polish officers, or approximately 40% of the Polish Officers Corps, have been imprisoned, in violation of agreements, since Oct.–Nov. 1939 . . .

—It looks, sir, Jurek said, as if they're loading one compartment at a time, sir. I mean a train compartment, sir, like this one. The second bus is loaded now but it hasn't left. I see that other Russian officer, sir, the well-mannered one who speaks Polish.

. . . in charge of the transports is a Col. Zarnow. In charge of the extermination program is an NKVD officer known as Commander Szymanski . . .

—Well, it's all rather odd, no doubt, said the Nervous Colonel. But I'm sure there's a reasonable explanation.

—We all know how the Russians are, said Benedykt.

—How are they? said Jozef.

—Well, if they can't turn everything into a secret they can't get it done. It's that old Slavic instinct for melodrama, I'm afraid. We must ignore them. The main thing is control, isn't that so? Iron self-discipline is the main thing. We mustn't give way to idiotic fancies. Anyone who undermines our confidence should not retain ours.

—Quite right, said the colonel.

—The first bus is coming back sir, Jurek said. And now the second bus is leaving. A third bus is loading up. And now the fourth bus is backing up toward us.

—Odd that they should be sending only one bus at a time, said the colonel.

—Ah, said Benedykt. One bus attracts less attention than a convoy. It's that obsession of theirs about secrecy!

—And that, the colonel said with satisfaction, explains this damned cement!

—Well, sir, they're all around our carriage now, Jurek said.

—I think it's our turn, said the Nervous Colonel.

*. . . I estimate that by the end of April at least 10,000 Polish officers
will be murdered in this manner and beg your urgent action (Signed:)
Langenfeld, M. Maj. Res., Polish Army.*

The door, the outer door, was unbolted. It was opened. NKVD soldiers began to crowd into the passageway. The door to the neighboring
cage was opened. —Outside, shouted Zarnow.

—Remember, gentlemen, absolute self-control, said the Nervous
Colonel.

—What would you do if you were a Russian worker, say a railroad
repairman, and you saw a piece of white paper on the ground? Tarski
asked Benedykt.

—White paper, in this country? Need you ask? I'd pick it up at once.

—That's what I thought, Tarski said.

—Is that the stuff that Langenfeld was writing? What did he write?

—What he's been saying all along.

Tarski crumpled the white sheet in his hand, began to juggle with it,
looked once more at what Benedykt had written on the wall. —That,
what you wrote on the wall, he said. You can't say such things without
proof.

—I've all the proof I need. I have my convictions. I think that Langenfeld is an agent provocateur planted among us to spread despond-
ency and fear. I think this should be known.

—No, Tarski said.

—He also happens to represent an element which is totally untrust-
worthy, Benedykt went on. A community which welcomed the Bolsheviks to Poland in 1919, in 1921, and again in 1939, and which will undoubtedly do it again if it gets the chance, which forms the Red Corner
. . . Only a fool would trust a damn Jew. He's a Bolshevik agent, a
traitor like the lot of them. Why else would they have taken him off at
Smolensk?

—I don't know, said Tarski.

Suddenly he got up and threw the crumped message through the ventilation hole, then stooped and wrote on the wooden wall of the carriage, *Katyn, April 1940.*

An NKVD soldier unlocked the huge padlock in the iron door, drew
the chain through the metal loops, swung the door open, and motioned
them outside.

The sun was pale yellow, hanging above trees. The sky was cloudless,
clear as the September sky had been during the thirty days of war, so
that he felt himself transported for a moment back to the chaos of
those thousand hours, the days of blood and glory which had brought
about a crucifixion, not a resurrection. Rise, O rise, White Eagle, he

whispered to himself, blinded by the sun. There was a fresh breeze off the woods, whipping up the dust, and the dust swirled overhead like the yellow carapace that had hung above the Polish roads, and the black clouds that coiled above the vertical exhaust pipes of the bus were like the columns of smoke that had soared above burning Polish cities; so much death, so much devastation, a part of the immemorial march, the cry of the song.

Two soldiers seized him as he stepped into the glare of daylight and turned out his pockets, and all the brown paper messages of a quick homecoming, confident words of love, flew about like moths. His watch was whisked out of his pocket and his wallet vanished into a potato sack.

He had been seized by robots whose faces told him nothing, and he saw nothing around him except a mass of soldiers who formed a thick, sour-smelling corridor between the door of the prison carriage and the door of the bus. He smelled their unwashed stench and the reek of charcoal, heard angry cries, felt impatient hands pushing him, fell, got up again, and began to climb the five steps of the short wooden ladder propped under the door of the bus. There was a metal wall between the driver's compartment and the passengers, and all the windows had been smeared with cement, and the men stood pressed together in a gray air that resembled twilight. The wooden floor of the bus was wet as if freshly scrubbed. There was a strong acrid smell of carbolic soap, the roar of the motor. The bus shook and shuddered, pitching the men about on the slippery wet floor. He had been the last to ascend the little wooden scaffold and the door of the bus was slammed into his back. *Dum spiro spero* rattled through his brain as the bus lurched and began to move and the mass of cursing men rolled against him, crushed him, then fell away again. No, no; it couldn't happen, it just couldn't happen. This is the twentieth century. *Dum spero spi* . . . no, it was the other way around, although it would do just as well this way . . .

The bus stopped. The men were hurled forward in a heap: a mass of tangled bodies, arms, and boots righting itself among curses. The bus is shuddering now and the motor coughs. Bolts squeal, the door is flung open . . . Tarski leaped outside, took the first stride of what he was determined would be a sprint for the woods, saw the rifle butt swinging toward him, and a blaze of light exploded in his head. His mouth was filled with blood, vomit, and smashed teeth. He rolled away from the plunging bayonets, struggled to his feet.

. . . My name is Adam Tarski, major, the Twenty-first Regiment (Warsaw). Born: nineteenth century. Died: twentieth century. Cavalier of the Virtuti Militari with twenty years' service, no known survivors. *Dulce et decorum est pro patria mori* . . . Frenchmen, remember that forty generations are looking down upon you . . . Caesar, we who are about to die, salute you! Carthage is overthrown, her fields are plowed with salt, she shall not rise again. Rise, O rise, White Eagle . . . With the Smoke of Fires we raise our Voice, O Lord/give us our country's freedom once again . . .

He heard a distant shout and thought it was his own, and hands had fastened to his arms and shoulders, arms embraced his legs, and other hands were clawing at his mouth; then he was down again in the dry sand, his mouth stuffed with sawdust, and two men were sitting on his back wrenching his arms together, and two men were hanging on to his legs as he bucked and kicked, and once more the rifle butt exploded in his skull.

White light, streaked with scarlet, then a booming echo. Nostrils full of blood. Shouts and the thud of rifle butts into flesh and bone filter through cracked eardrums. Ears full of blood. Huge bells are ringing, bugles cry. The silver trumpets call across the centuries: Rise, O rise . . .

He threw himself against the weight, heaved it off his shoulders, broke free and rolled away, but his arms had been tied behind his back and when he struggled to his feet his knees collapsed under him. He remained kneeling as the first bayonet entered him from the back. Oh, the swift burning, and then breath is gone. But he could see, yes, he saw through the salty redness in his eyes: Jozef had wrenched a rifle away from a soldier, the rifle swung and splintered, cracked a skull . . . Benedykt was on his knees, vomiting blood, he was red with it from heel to monocle, spouting like a fountain from a dozen wounds . . . Jurek was down, bayoneted . . . the Nervous Colonel was down . . . soldiers and prisoners were fighting in the bus, and then Jozef was down, on his face in sand, while bayonets pinned him . . .

The trees were near and dark. Again the swift burning, the scarlet flare revolving in a fiery aureole, hands grasping and pulling. He was thrown on his back against a pile of sand, among empty ammunition boxes. Dark spruce, festive pine were all around among long yellow mounds of sand, six feet high, ten feet wide, a hundred feet long . . . lines of mass graves receding among the trees.

Darkness fell on him suddenly. He heard distant crackling, flat reports beating out a slow and regular cadence, measured as a muffled drum. Then darkness left him and he could see again through the corner of one eye.

. . . Murders, wars, massacres, betrayals . . . (Do you hear me, Abel?) When these things happen, people wonder why. That is to say, intelligent people wonder . . . The self-satisfied, complacent, docile brutish mass, those part-time human beings who so successfully mas-

querade as people, never wonder . . . never have to wonder . . . to such
grotesque parodies of the Divine Image all things are known, rational.
All can be explained in social, political, economic, or historical clichés.
An act of violence inspires a variety of feelings depending on the myths
by which different people live. Seen through a thousand eyes, it may
have five hundred separate and distinct realities . . .

Hands grasped him, dragged him by the heels. He was lifted upward,
heaved and thrown against angular wood. So we are going home, after
all, he whispered to himself, and at once Magda's bitter face and Abel's
contemputous eyes presented themselves. He tried to think of someone
who might have loved him. A son or a daughter. Somone to live beyond
him, to say by being: He was here. A child to light the way of the
human race, as all parents expect their children to do. But mostly something to point to with pride. You can't exist without the thought of
continuation. Families may fall apart, nations themselves may sink like
Pacific islands in the huge volcanic upheavals of war, the tidal
wave of invasion, but the human race will continue and there is no
worry. When you are so alone that you are the very last of all, and you
cannot die without your own spirit, your blood, your kind, left in a vacuum, what you want most to remain, even for a little while, is your
memory.

Black trees, red sand, and the innocent blue sky. Oh, they are so
bloody now, the executioners. Then darkness again. Weakness. Loss of
blood. The flat reports continue, coming, it seemed to him, across
infinite time . . . then consciousness abruptly returned.

. . . Jozef, my gallant and tormented friend, is struggling at the edge
of the pit so slippery with blood that they cannot hold him, and so he
kicks and butts and tosses them aside with his gigantic shoulders and,
yes, he would be bellowing with that familiar, towering rage if a felt
pad hadn't been tied around his mouth, and his arms would be flaying
the air in that familiar gesture that spoke of metamorphosis, that terrifying blend of fury and despair, if his arms had not been roped behind
his back; and they fall back from him, astonished, and rush him with
their bayonets and rifle butts, their boots and their fists, but he is still
erect, still living, and this enrages them. My gallant friend has per-
formed a miracle: he has transformed mute robots into a blood-mad
mob. Each splash of his blood renders them more human. Now they
shout and curse as they swing their rifles and stab with their *shtyki*, and
each blow brings the crack of a broken bone but it is not enough: my
Jozef is still standing. Forgive me, Jozef, for every evil thought, for having wished you dead, for not having loved you; for thinking you a caricature and not the substance of the best of us, for having thought you

smaller than you are. Stand, Jozef, you are standing for us all! I want to wish you everlasting life . . .

But Jozef's feet slipped in the excrement and blood and sodden sand of the execution pit, and they slid apart, and finally the executioners had him beaten to his knees and grasped his tied hands with a practiced gesture and jerked him forward on his face into the steaming, reeking sand where the flies were swarming, and another soldier stepped forward, planted his boot in the small of Jozef's back, pressed the muzzle of his pistol against the bottom of Jozef's skull, and fired. The huge corpse leaped, voided itself, subsided in filth, quivered, and lay still. The cursing soldiers heaved on the great body, lifted it, and pitched it forward into the pit. The pit is brown with layers of uniformed corpses. Should the dead lie like soldiers at attention or like the butchered animals in a slaughterhouse that they really are? Stiff with virtue, history gives its orders, and the dead obey, but Jozef has fallen athwart the orderly rows of dead men, perversely ruining the effect, and the cursing soldiers climbed into the pit to stretch him out in line with all the others.

. . . He had so wanted to be indistinguishable from the rest of us, but even in death there has to be a difference . . .

Then it was a cavalry underensign with a face which was no longer recognizable, but, for all that, the Eternal Lancer kissing his lady's hand. His eyes had been so completely trusting in the train. They had choked him with ropes and now dragged him by his feet, the massacred face leaving a bloody trail in the sand . . . A senseless sacrifice. He was probably already dead but the executioner was loading his pistol and so they lined him up at the edge of the pit. The executioner fired into his brain. The body lay still. They threw the body into the pit and the executioner called for ammunition.

There were three empty ammunition boxes near Tarski. (Yes, sir, three boxes, count them, sir: five hundred rounds to a box, GECO cal. 7.65, manufactured by the Genschow Company of Durlach, Germany, in 1938, export under license, equals fifteen hundred rounds, equals fifteen hundred officers in five transports of three hundred each.)

A shot. A body is pitched into the pit and a noncom shouts for Nikita and Ivan to get their asses down in there, into the pit, and straighten out the legs.

. . . The colonel comes next. He is no longer nervous. The colonel is smiling. His head is erect. He has been bayoneted but he walks unaided. He stands at attention at the edge of the pit, salutes, kneels, is stretched out and shot. His brother officers are waiting. He has died with honor.

. . . Benedykt is dragged by the heels like a slaughtered ox. A shot. A stench. The death of a dinosaur. The soldier loads his pistol.

It seemed to him then that his consciousness was ebbing once again because the trees had started to move, and how could that be? But yes, the pine and spruce had picked up their roots and were in flight across the parallel yellow mounds that had scarred their forest. Young trees flowed over the graves but now he could see that they were carried by soldiers in blue caps and that the soldiers were women, and that the women were planting the trees in the new graves, as older trees had obviously been planted over older graves. In five or six years no one would ever know what had happened here.

. . . And still the patient rhythm of the shots. Still the pitching bodies. And now he thought that he could feel hands grasping his own shoulders, lifting and hoisting, and huge red circles had begun to revolve before his eyes, and a far-off surf resounded in his ears. But he had never heard a sea and so, perhaps, it was the hiss of bowed banners. The beat of ancient drums, perhaps.

His regiments were lined up for inspection; he counted them, found them all in order.

(Permission to pass in review, sir? Permission granted. Gladly.)

And may there be music?

The wind supplies the music, the dark Russian wind.

. . . The Twenty-first Regiment presented arms and vanished, and Warsaw vanished with it: the years of his deepest personal peace, with the images of the mercurial Magda subdued, if never entirely dispersed, his compromises made in a city where commitments are a way of life . . . the purposeful energy of Warsaw had been a merciful drug; the Fifth Regiment saluted with the easygoing charm of Vilno, the conservatory where he had spent off-duty evenings studying, of all things, musicology and the flute . . . in the poetic Lithuanian air all things were possible even though his superiors took a dim view of it; the First Legion Infantry, offspring of Pilsudski's original 1914 band of desperadoes, reminded him of Abel because it was in the years of the First that he had thought that Abel was his son, and so the First took longer to march past than most of the others. The Nineteenth and the Fortieth had been his refuge from disintegration, his personal Order of the Spirit had been founded in their Citadel, they had been his first family which had defined him and fixed his place in an unchanging, reasonable universe; and they cried out to him with all the joyousness and passion of the gayest city in the Commonwealth: Lwów, *incomparabile dictu*, as the colonel had said, and since they carried the portrait of the Leopard Baby on their white and amaranthine banners, they took the longest of all to pass from his sight.

All present, all accounted for.

Very well. Dismissed.

His face was in the sand, his mouth sweet with blood, his nostrils rich with the acrid reeks of offal. The executioner trod upon his back. Lord, in the hour of our death, remember our country.

The Magician

NOT EVEN RUSSIAN DARKNESS can be absolute. The night, a cool night in June, was thick with ground mist, so that it seemed to him that he was walking among ghosts and clouds on a mountaintop, but the sky was clear. The trains had disappeared, swallowed by the Great Bear. There were many stars. The flares were nailed to the firmament like illuminated signposts and promised safe passage.

. . . Tarski, Langenfeld, young Jurek, Abel's father . . . not much in common there, to be sure, and even less for him; but each had something in his life that he liked and liking begets liking. Now they were gone, spinning among strange stars, and the dark birds of fantasy swooped and croaked. The oracle was struck dumb. The bright and glittering knowing-by-daylight had given way before the equal and opposite unknowing-by-night.

The lights on the guard towers began their nervous sweep of sacerdotal domes, the courtyard was empty. It was colder now and, for a moment, Dr. Poremba stood undecided in the ecclesiastic gloom, then headed for the only lighted windows.

He thought of Mann-Bielecki without hatred. (Odd how you can loathe a man who merely annoys you, but understand and forgive a mortal injury, as though pettiness itself could make a man pitiless and encouraged hatred.) It was an old story. Survival must take precedence over morality. The aging enfant terrible of café society, the bon mot and the lordly gesture, had sold him to the NKVD along with Father Zenek and was immediately forgiven but his *pretensions* were . . . how was he to say it without exaggeration . . . ah: *unforgivable?* Something of that kind. Zenek and he had shaken hands without words in the courtyard of the Kharkov prison: mute partings had still been a novelty then. He didn't know what had become of the young priest after that, didn't think about it . . . Perhaps Mann-Bielecki had bought himself a

cup of hot water with his denunciation . . . So may he survive one day
longer. To a believer everything is said to be an act of God, and not to
be questioned . . . But for him, Jan Poremba, the husband and father,
Lake Sergin had become a punctuation mark: the sudden loss of his living constants and his determination to find them again.

God only knew where he was to begin his search, although the Devil
probably knew his way around this country of the damned much better
than God . . . What mattered now was that he, Jan Poremba, had not
been destroyed.

The monastery was silent now, the chapel was abandoned, only two
hundred and forty gray, shadowy figures still wandered about the courtyard between sunrise and sunset, and the morning roll call took merely
half an hour. The others were gone, taken away by the malevolent little
train, and they were gone forever, and he knew that his own end was
hastening toward him. The Red Corner had not grown noticeably; it
still numbered fewer than two dozen, and the Russians' patience was
exhausted. What to do, how to save himself, how to remain himself in
this devilish land where only traitors got enough to eat? His cheeks had
caved in, his belly had disappeared, and the last of his hair had fallen
out through scurvy. The little train wouldn't come back again, he
knew; it had not come back since the end of April, there was no one
left in the monastery who couldn't be broken. The men who were left,
who had not marched to the train behind the NKVD band that played
Polish marches, were Red Corner people or candidates for Red Corner
people, and himself. Any day now, he knew from the Ox and the
Gondolier, all of them would go to another camp in yet another train.
The name of the new camp was Pavelitchev Bor, and there the final selection would be made. The choice would be either the Red Corner or
extinction, the Ox had made it clear.

. . . Now that Tarski was gone, there was no one with whom he
could talk about things like that! No, not about the nerve-racking personal anxieties of lost wife and children (each man had more than his
just share of that sort of grief), but about the threatening unknown,
the dimly suspected, the unimaginable . . . And suddenly he craved intelligent conversation, always an antidote for sagging spirits. To talk
about the books he loved, to explore ideas without fear of denunciation
or imbecilic comment . . . Ah, but my brother officers are somewhat
limited in that respect, he muttered into gloom; like all men reduced to
a singular view of the universe, they live in deathly fear of the egocen-
tric who lives for ideas. The Abbot was a polished man, give the Devil
his due. He had brought a library of five hundred French, English, and
German books to the monastery and it was sometimes possible to borrow something good to read. An affable, civilized man, to be sure, yet

Dr. Poremba felt an odd revulsion. Call it a premonition, he concluded, based upon no fact. Zarubin's mask (like his own) was not quite good enough to withstand careful scrutiny but adequate to soothe fearful and frustrated men whose eyes were turned inward. When people are too busy with their own insubstantial dreams to pay more than a semblance of attention to anything outside themselves, you can make them believe anything you want.

To see the Abbot, or not to see the Abbot? V. M. Zarubin was a true enigma, no one knew what to make of him, how to define his position or the role he was playing in the monastery. The Ox, the Gorilla, and the Gondolier were careful not to talk about him; they tried to pretend that he didn't exist, and perhaps he didn't: a product of an imagination thirsty for mystery. He was an NKVD major general but he was not the prison commandant. That was the Robot's function. The Abbot had no function that anyone could see, he was as much a mystery to the NKVD men as he was to the internees, and so perhaps the time had come to crack his secret? Mysteries are much like Chinese puzzle boxes: you unlock one and discover another and so on to the core of the matter.

Well, what about Zarubin? He had admitted to being fifty-five, which would account for his Old World courtesy: otherwise utterly impossible in the brutal service whose uniform he wore. The unexpected frankness, the ease, and the tact were aristocratic, perhaps. He had obviously traveled about the world. But in what context? He doesn't speak, he rustles like an ancient parchment. (The word *cyrograf* leaped immediately to mind: the document of folklore by which a pact was made with hell's managing director and signed, invariably, in blood.) There is a chilling timelessness about him, despite the genial smile and the benevolent hand. His white curly hair is trimmed like an amateur's wig, complete with imitation tonsure; lots of deep wrinkles in the soft skin of an ancient baby. Each gesture is a ritual, a blessing or a curse, and it's a sharp man who can tell at a glance which is which. Oh yes, the archaic eyes do laugh but with detachment which states clearly, undisputably, that the joke is antique and has been heard many times . . .

Dr. Poremba shuddered, cursed the sudden chill, made a tentative sign of the cross across his chest and shoulders. What I am thinking is impossible in the twentieth century. It's just this damned uncertainty about what the Bolsheviks are foisting upon our imaginations . . . ! The only reality which offers hope of reason is that the Allies will move in France in a month or two and crush these devils or, at least, persuade them to let us leave their hell.

. . . I live too close to madness, he panted, out of breath. Nerves

frayed, as in the old Spenserian form of *affrayed*, tattered by the dry
whip of paralyzing thought . . . A cold wind blew across the courtyard
from the north, he ran toward light.

It was late but the Abbot kept Moscow office hours; the insomnia
that kept the Greatest Living Man, the Sun of the Nations, wandering
all night through the halls of the Kremlin, had given the whole of this
dark subcontinent that air of conspiracy that exists among men who do
their work at night and go home at sunrise.

Zarubin's name effected the necessary magic, the sentries acquiesced.
One of them went along to see that the Polish prisoner made no unauthorized detours through any other office. The soldier was mute, his
face impassive as though all emotion had been siphoned out of him,
but his little eyes glittered with suspicion. The halls were not silent.
The Robot was droning, the Ox was bellowing, and the Gorilla roaring,
and occasionally there was the thin, uneven voice of a prisoner trying to
explain the inexplicable facts of his existence. This was the dark time
for special interrogations, the cathechism of rank, professional affilia-
tions, standing in society, attitude toward the Soviet Union and the
Communist dialectic, religious beliefs, and all else likely to lead to arrest, pain, disappearance . . . One didn't have to be an avowed enemy
of the people; potential for animosity was enough.

His mind went searching for the vanished convoys. The sinsister
quintet of prison cars rattled through his skull, all switches thrown,
heading for the edge of the world. He had no doubt that he would end
up as part of similar cargoes unless he came up with a stroke of genius
and became invisible . . . Or, he thought suddenly, to be *so* visible that
no one noticed him at all! Abracadabra, Dr. Poremba muttered to himself. Now you see him now you don't. It's all done with mirrors. Magic.
To be seen as something other than what you are is not to be seen.
Create an illusion. Yes, comrade, that's a wonderful bump of credulity
you have there . . . ! And, in the meantime, he had come to Zarubin's
door.

The soldier watched him as though he were an object whose use he
didn't understand, an artifact from a bygone era which would have
defied his comprehension anyway. Well, comrade, you defy my comprehension too, if that's any comfort, your icy planet is populated by
ghosts, maniacs, and warlocks, and all of them are one. Give me some
relatively human sign, you museum bronze. To see a smile on that
graven face would have unhinged his reason, Dr. Poremba thought, and
knocked upon the door. The Latin words *magna mater* were hissing in
his head.

Round-faced and smiling, his wide-set eyes on the move, looking for a doubt to settle, Zarubin filled the narrow entrance and beckoned him forward.

—Come in, dear doctor. I've just been thinking of you.

There was a smoking samovar in the corner, a bottle of Baczewski's Atlasowka and Crimean wines, Lithuanian liqueurs and Polish Krupnik on a lacquered tray, a pretty box of Latvian chocolates and a carved Ukrainian casket full of long black cigarettes in fearful symmetry, an elegant table lighter with a family crest, and a cracked plate of thin biscuit wafers. And was there mockery in the dry voice, a sketch of a smile?

—What will it be this evening, Doctor? Some Chinese tea and Victor Hugo? If tea and Hugo are not strong enough, I suggest your excellent Polish Atlasowka and Thomas Aquinas.

The antique leather chair must have been part of the original furniture of the abbot's quarters. No, not this abbot but the real one: the long-dead-and-buried murdered man who had nodded here over ancient texts. Dr. Poremba wondered how the ornate chair could have survived the disappearance of its owner's religion, the transubstantiation of spirit into an iron age of matter, lowered himself carefully into tattered leather, and stared at the floor: an alternating white and crimson checkerboard gouged by neighboring peasants for building materials. Black holes were yawning among red porphyry and white marble, a large white moon had swung itself into the sky and sent its beams through fragments of stained glass. The room was long, vaulted, groined, and ecclesiastic. The carbide lantern hissed like a disapproving old serpent no longer able to shed its final skin. The air was damp. Tendrils of yellow mist curled into the room through holes in the brown paper that patched the shattered window. Even so, it was all palatial. Books gave it richness, liquor gave it warmth, the samovar added a reassuring touch of the commonplace. A bourgeois melancholy hung among the arches, the sense of doom was momentarily displaced.

—I'm always anxious to please my guests, Zarubin said. When you gentlemen come here you must feel as if you were visiting a friend. Why don't you help yourself to a cigarette?

Dr. Poremba took one, lit it, said: Thank you very much.

—And a drink? Please pour yourself a drink.

Dr. Poremba filled a small crystal goblet for Zarubin and a large metal drinking mug for himself. Zarubin nodded in approval and went on: Yes. Friendship is essential. Understanding is the first step toward brotherhood and love. Without them a man is particularly naked. He is completely vulnerable. We Russians understand this better than anyone else.

—Friendship is like poverty, General, Dr. Poremba said cautiously.

It's always being redefined by people who are neither poor nor friend-less.

—And the poor are always with us, said Zarubin, nodding. Isn't that so?

—So Christ is said to have said.

—And the poor always suffer. And from their suffering comes the cre-ative truth we are all suffering no matter whether we're rich or poor. And from this universal suffering comes universal friendship. We Rus-sians suffer more than anyone. We understand the need for friendship better than anyone else. People who have not suffered can't understand the meaning of friendship.

Zarubin studied his visitor, nodded, reached for a book and opened it to a passage marked with a piece of straw. —Do you know Hold Your Heads Up, by Aseyev? he asked softly. He wrote it for you Polish gentlemen.

—I'm afraid I don't even know Aseyev.

Zarubin nodded and began to read in his dry, persuasive voice so redo-lent of time, lost continents, vanished peoples, and Dr. Poremba felt his head beginning to sag. He was immensely tired, he realized, and now a throbbing headache added to his feeling of oppression. It had been a mistake to come to the Abbot. There would be no opportunity here to come to terms with his uncertainties while Zarubin was in his apostolic mood; nor would he crack that imperturbable old shell. Soft Russian words rustled around him and he thought of chants, miracu-lous icons, and candlelight processionals, and the reading man seemed to change, to compress his bulk into the frail illusion of an ancient monk droning liturgical consonants amid incense: *The Landlords' Flag has been trampled underfoot / but you, Polish people, have not been humiliated. / Do you believe the tale that we have stepped forward to add to your sorrows?*

—Well?

Aware of sudden silence, lost in the gloomy wastes of his own fa-tigue, Dr. Poremba murmured quickly: Heaven forbid! Such a thought would never cross my mind . . .

He made vague gestures which he hoped would appear disarming.

If we have crossed the frontier, Zarubin read softly, remote yet insist-ent, *it isn't to make you afraid. / We do not want your fear. Proudly you can hold up your heads.*

. . . Yes, thought Dr. Poremba. We have always done so, and what good has it done us? High heads stretch the neck, invite the knife, and offer temptation. His mind seemed suddenly sheathed in cobwebs. He raised his head and looked toward the ceiling where vaguely troubling shadows had began to dance.

Zarubin put away his book and picked up another. He clasped his hands behind his back and began to pace up and down the wounded square white and red slabs, in the hissing glow of the battle lantern, while the slow shadows advanced and retreated overhead. This too was a processional of a kind, Dr. Poremba thought, groping among images: a ceremonial dance pacing in and out of memory. Stiff and proud, the costumed puppets of his imagination bowed and dipped.

—Why should we want your fear?

Off guard, he said, unthinking: Why indeed? I should have thought you have enough of your own . . .

He closed his eyes, finding no relief from the throbbing pain, and added quickly, making a vague gesture:

> *The cat watches me warily.*
> *I say to him: You have nothing*
> *to fear from me, Brother!*
> *But the cat runs away.*
> *Perhaps he knows my imperfect nature*
> *better than I.*

He noted that Zarubin had halted again and was regarding him with an odd intensity, a look in which knowledge of human folly competed briefly with a greater disappointment. Then the Russian shrugged, said: Who wrote that? and resumed his pacing.

—The poet's name in Abel Abramowski. I doubt that you would have heard of him, General, he is very young. He may have had an interesting future . . .

—I've heard of him, Zarubin said abruptly. In another context. Nothing to do with poetry at all.

—A professional context? I'm sorry to hear it.

—The young man has nothing to worry about if he shows good sense. That could be said about almost anyone, wouldn't you agree? Even about yourself.

—Certainly, certainly . . .

—You tell me *Yes!* But what do you tell yourself?

. . . It is not I who am telling myself anything, thought Dr. Poremba, and saw himself again at the lone, frosted mound of piled-up scree and ice, the white taiga tomb of his friend Modelski, having become an inheritor of a dead man's vision.

But the Russian waited. Slowly, hardly hearing what he was saying, Dr. Poremba murmured: Get thee behind me, Satan. (Then went on, with caution:) I don't mean to imply that we (the dead and the living) wouldn't respond to genuine Russian friendship. (Witness the number of tombs in the taiga.) But all too often we've found in the past that we had made yet another mistake.

Zarubin halted near the table and studied him as though he too had suddenly become a frayed bound volume that might be read and quoted, then picked up his glass, drained it, and smashed it against a wall.

Angrily, as though what he was saying was a personal insult to himself, an undeserved and ungracious lack of gratitude, he said: The way you people write history, Christ could have died as easily in an electric chair.

—I don't understand.

—Why do Poles always think that there is a worldwide conspiracy to destroy them? What makes you think you are important enough to command such attention? If you have no active enemies you invent them, as if you're able to find a reason for existence only in someone's hatred. I don't know of any conspiracy against your people because there's no need for one. Your leaders, of whatever vintage, are doing such a splendid job in that regard, convincing whoever still can stand to listen to them that all Poles are the reactionary dolts that they are said to be, that adding fuel to this suicidal fire would be, indeed, a waste of energy. Given enough of a stimulant to his injured pride, a Pole will always set fire to his own head.

Dr. Poremba stared about, seeking nonexistent exits, unable to meet the Russian general's stare.

—What have *you* to do with such people? the Russian went on softly. You, a man capable of thought, a humanist, a patriot . . . Politically they're just to the left of Julius Caesar; intellectually, they make adequate librarians. I should think you'd find such company insulting.

Dr. Poremba stared into his metal cup. You must know, said the proud receding shadows, that a man can only have one invulnerable loyalty, the inheritance of history and icy visions and old men's memories notwithstanding: the loyalty to his own concept of the obligations of manhood. All other loyalties, no matter how appealing, are merely the deputies of that one. So if you're making your decision with that guide in mind, and if centuries are to be any kind of guideposts, you should learn to read them in the language of your times. The Polish ritual of atavistic passion is only one of many melodies; hear it against the measured ruthless cadence of the Germans, the desperate excesses of the Russians . . . Centuries tell their lies like pensioners on a park bench. And we, being the most ingenious of the creatures, are always the engineers of our own entrapment . . . He shuddered in genuine distress. Unlike his gallantly fallen countrymen, he knew, he would play dead when outnumbered or surrounded.

Dr. Poremba filled and drained his cup. Zarubin was smiling. It was his function, then, to smile and to reassure, to suggest that civilization had not been totally abandoned. And, in the meantime, there was his other function and that was something that Dr. Poremba still could not bring himself to think about.

—For your own sake you must keep trying, the Russian said, remote but insistent. Don't you think that you should keep on trying? Isn't that the primary message of your literature, man's evolution and humanistic progress through the centuries? Isn't that what your entire civilization has been about? We, Russians, I admit, are not as you are, we are fulfilled in another manner. As a people, we have never benefited by Europe's humanist tradition . . . But if you claim to be a man in the Western sense you must keep making the attempt.

—Perhaps so.

Zarubin had resumed his patient walk, stroking the paper spines of books in bookcases made of empty ammunition cases, the Gothic script of caliber designations making its own commentary to the works of Schiller.

—In Russian history, man has always been a means and never an end. This can't be changed. We aren't really able to do great things except at moments of national exultation. This is the dark flaw in Russian blood. We are undisciplined, we drink too much, we must be tyrannized. That's why we do not like to see neighbors who are different. It makes us insecure and insecurity has driven us mad. This is why we must go far into the past in search of our answers. We need the old forgotten secrets to give us a new means for achieving a sense of exultation that might lift us again beyond our limitations . . . The authoritarian system is natural for us. It's the most efficient order of things and we're used to it. Despotism has been with us since the times of Ivan the Terrible. We are too big, too chaotic, too uncontrollable, we Russians . . . If we got democracy tomorrow we would fly apart.

—But no one can hope to control others by fear alone, Dr. Poremba said. Fear breeds discontent, doesn't it?

—Fear discourages action, said Zarubin. Thus it's an antidote for discontent. Oh, I know what you'll say. All you people say the same thing. You say that people resent feeling helpless, that they feel degraded, and that when this resentment has boiled long enough it turns discontent to anger, and when the anger becomes desperate enough it overcomes the restraining influence of fear, and so, you say, fear breeds its own destruction. Perhaps so. But I will answer you in simple Russian peasant terms. Kiss the horse and he'll bite off your nose if he's used to the whip. The main thing is not to confuse the people with ideas which are foreign to them.

—I don't know much about this business of controlling people, Dr. Poremba said. It seems a bit unrealistic to suppose that anyone could control anyone else long enough to make any difference. But I do wonder what you have in mind for us since, as you've said, you've no way to control us.

—You have no reason to be nervous.

—Sometimes, not having a reason for something is reason enough. We are not used to being afraid without reason, and we are not used to being manipulated. For some of us, for me at any rate, that's sufficient reason to be nervous.

—Have a drink, Doctor, said Zarubin. Try some of these chocolates. They're made in our new Latvian S.S.R.

—I'm afraid they'd be too rich for my stomach . . .

—Then have a drink. When you drink you don't think and then you don't worry. Wonderful people, the Latvians. We have great hopes for them.

—And for us, General? said Dr. Poremba. What do you have in mind for us?

—Let's drink to friendship, an end to suspicion.

—An honest answer might dissolve a doubt better than a drink.

Zarubin closed his eyes. He seemed infinitely old in moonlight strained through a fragment of blue glass, and for a moment Dr. Poremba wondered if he hadn't totally slipped his hold on reality. And who was he suddenly to demand honesty, having sailed under dubious colors all his life? But any reasonable idea of reality seemed out of the question. Of all the Polish realities only good manners were left in his arsenal and perhaps the time had come to discard them too.

—To start with you, could you tell me what really happened to my friends. Is that too much to ask?

. . . The old eyes opened, regarded him; he felt himself recoiling. He thought: This man can't be much older than I am, why does he seem so ancient? Byzantine shadows mocked him with their arches. He said: A simple courtesy . . .

—Doctor, the Russian said. Are you attempting to manipulate me?

—How would I dare?

—Doctor, Doctor, Zarubin said with a cold mocking smile. How could you help trying? One does what one thinks one can. Sometimes one plays the fool, raps on tables, reads palms, pokes about the heads of credulous idiots, but one is always shrewd, always manipulating. But how ready are you for really deep waters? Tell me . . . (and he paused for a moment and averted his face from the light) have you ever studied any of the ancient texts on the Shamballah? What would you say to that kind of manipulation? This should be entertaining.

—Can I believe my ears? said Dr. Poremba.

—I don't see why not.

Dr. Poremba blinked, cupped his ear, leaned closer while the flickering idea in his mind burst into lurid incandescence and flooded his brain. —General, he said. What are you telling me? Or are we suddenly back in the Middle Ages?

—Always manipulating, aren't you? Zarubin said, smiling.

To protest that human realities must be, necessarily, *human* since they relate, no matter how remotely, to human possibilities, would be futile, he knew. That is the language of another world. Bereft of reason, we are left with either black magic or mechanistic logic, a choice–no-choice, any way you see it.

Once again he asked for a simple answer.

—Believe me, it would have been inhuman to tell you. You Poles have always been a threat to us, few as you are among us, because you represent all the things we are not. You are an irritant, a disturbing element; we have never been able to absorb you or digest you safely. Speaking as a Communist, the problem becomes acute. Yes, that's a serious matter. We are the world's first socialist state, you see, and we are living in a state of siege. We must protect our people from such influences as yours. You do see my point?

Dr. Poremba sighed, nodded with his face averted: A blind man would see it . . .

—The outside world is always trying to undermine us, the reasonable dry voice went on with remorseless logic. Our vigilance must be ruthless. Personally, I regret it. But individual tastes are only a distraction! An ordinary man is such a little thing, so insignificant . . . He must be lifted despite himself, unknowing . . . As Russians and as Communists, we have little choice. As Russians, we are driven to emotional extremes, our vision is orgiastic. As Communists, we are pragmatic and direct. Combine the two and you'll find the only reality that our history permits. And a true realist, Doctor, faces his realities as they are, not as a he would like them. They may call for solutions which defy your humanist traditions.

Dr. Poremba said, cursing imagination: Are you suggesting inhuman solutions?

Zarubin said, remotely: Well . . . let's say suprahuman . . . Beyond the reach of ordinary comprehension.

—But not beyond the reach of our imaginations?

—Well, that too, perhaps.

Bleak, dwarfed, resentful and afraid, Dr. Poremba sat in silence staring at Zarubin.

—What? Nothing more to say? the Russian said, smiling.

. . . *Magna mater.* He knew what the words meant, the invocation of Roman initiates who believed that only through spilled blood could they achieve spiritual transubstantiation and ascend into a new reality.

—I was thinking about what you said. The Shamballah . . . the City of Evil . . . Mass human sacrifice to draw the attention of . . . how shall I put it . . . demons? Secret powers? Obviously my thoughts stray. Please pay no attention.

—Would something like that be very surprising?

—Yes. No. I don't know. But to kill five . . . ten thousand men like that, not out of malice or even as a matter of some monstrous policy, men who mean nothing to you, in an attempt to invoke the interest of some imaginary power . . . I may be naïve for my age and experience, but such depravity . . . it's hard for me to believe.

—Aren't you alarming yourself unnecessarily? You've nothing to fear if you accept our friendship.

And Dr. Poremba argued through his blinding headache: But you can't possibly believe in demonic possession?

—Why not? We have some political trials now and then and the subject occasionally comes up. The world is invariably aghast, it asks *How could such a man do such a thing?* and it refuses to look at the obvious. Yet it's only a matter of transposing two words, a new one and a very ancient one: responsibility and possession.

—But that would mean that no one could ever be blamed for the most horrible crimes!

—Quite so, said Zarubin, nodding slightly in red glow of moonlight and stained glass. Then he was smiling, nodding, saying gently: Believe me, dear doctor . . . I wouldn't want to cause you a moment of unnecessary concern . . . Please fill your glass again. And I would much rather talk about Victor Hugo . . .

Dr. Poremba was also nodding. He had filled his cup again and began to drink. He grinned at the demons dancing in his head. He wondered how much they would give for the soul of a very frightened literary editor, an angel of doubtfully guiding mercy.

—Quite so, he said, and Zarubin smiled.

—And would you like some tea?

—Tea would be . . . ah . . . delightful.

Stained glass and moonlight striped the floor in scarlet, blue, and yellow; so might a man change colors by shifting positions. Despite himself, Dr. Poremba groaned.

Busy with the samovar, the Russian general said: I asked you earlier why you felt that you had anything in common with people who can justify their lives only in the moment of their death. They are made for sacrifice, they are brought up to it, they have no other expectations.

—What sacrifice, General? Dr. Poremba said, although he thought he knew.

—Any sacrifice. Their own, in the name of whatever drives them to their own destruction, or another, arranged for them by the imperatives of history. I asked, what do you have in common with people like that?

—I am . . . a human being, Dr. Poremba said.

—Exactly. And human beings think. They consider choices, they choose what's best for them. They cooperate with others. A human being is a social animal, useless by himself. He knows instinctively that he is nothing outside his society, less than nothing. Only as part of his society does he have any meaning. If he doesn't serve his society, he has no right to exist at all.

—I would serve, said Dr. Poremba. But how . . . ? Where? What? (He did not ask *Why?*, was careful not to wonder *Whom?* The Abbot was a formidable antagonist at the best of times.)

—Your own country's interests. Isn't that your patriotic duty? The kind of Poland with whom her neighbors would be able to live in peace . . . surely, that is obvious. That is the kind of Poland that real Polish patriots are constructing now. They look to the future. We are creating a new Polish government, we shall form a Polish democratic army, we shall finally put an end to the hostility between us. Can you think of a better cause than that?

—A government! Dr. Poremba said, astonished. An army? Are Berling's twelve men enough for all that?

—We have tens of thousands of loyal Soviet citizens who are of Polish blood . . .

—The Polish government and army are in France, said Dr. Poremba.

—Oh, haven't you heard? Zarubin asked quietly. No, I suppose you haven't. I must have newspapers sent into the camp tomorrow. France has fallen. The English have fled. Lemon?

—Lemon?

—In your tea.

—Oh, yes, certainly. Lemon.

—And sugar?

—Yes, sugar.

He listened to Zarubin explaining the disaster but he didn't really hear what the Russian was saying; the words were sounds, no more. All that he himself could think of in that moment was: How can there be a Europe without France? Then he thought: How can I remain a European? One needs a continent for an identity that might resist Asia. This was a blow beyond anyone's capacity for resistance, he knew; it would shatter the strongest of his companions in captivity. The ruin of

France was even more than a nightmare repetition of the fall of Poland. Then, even in that unbearable disaster, there had remained the faith that France, with England's help, would restore them all to life, would put an end to torment; there could be no appeal with France overthrown. Each civilized man had two countries, he thought in terror and confusion, two sources of his spiritual being: the country of his birth and France, and never mind that it had been a Frenchman who had coined that phrase. He knew that time was running out for them all, that moral constants had ceased to exist, that with the fall of France something essential had left humanity, that years, not merely months, of dreadful captivity were ahead, and that these years would grind them all to dust.

He could have sworn, then, that he heard distant laughter. It was the wind, of course, the high whistling wind. Dr. Poremba heard the soaring music of the *Varsovienne* played by the Russian military band as Tarski, Langenfeld, that poor ass Benedykt and the Nervous Colonel, Jurek Bednarski and five thousand others marched out to their deaths. Such a splendid concert. They had marched so beautifully, with such bold precision, led by their tune of glory . . . Such a brave show of faith in a monumental lie. And had they died well or badly in the Katyn Forest? Had they struggled, did they beg? Will others like them fight, elsewhere, unpleading? Will any of them have an inkling of regret? It will matter to them how well they can die, they will be conscious of the eyes of history, listening to the centuries, while he closed his ears . . .

What did he ever have in common with such people, he who had never wanted more than to be civilized, as he understood it: to stand above prejudice and hatred, which, to him, were barbaric. If anyone had demanded a statement of his convictions he would have said: to transcend savagery. This was lofty enough to have been meaningless. He would not have said: to cultivate my tastes, to learn from art the meaning of detachment . . . to play the game of living as joyfully as he could. To have confessed impractical ideas would have rendered him open to suspicion. Ideals weren't allowed to soar beyond the reach of pharmacists and dentists in this egalitarian age. Everyone was supposed to have his mind tuned vertically to some sort of slogan but it all had to fit the practicalities of the moment. To suggest that there were higher forms of animated matter than lawyers or professors . . . or, God help us all, retired major generals, former ambassadors, pensioned politicians . . . well, really, my dear fellow . . . next you'll be questioning achievement as the measure of Man!

What grandeur could such narrow lives permit? Titles, degrees, professional societies, an exaggerated sense of courtesy which transformed every small-town lawyer into a Maecenas! An infinity of clubs which spawned legions of Presidents and Chairmen (sonorous honorifics for visiting cards), a certain hopeful sense of righteousness, a moral and ethical code based more on good manners than on spiritual convictions . . . Napoleonic dreams of destiny, ornamental rhetoric in place of consciousness: all of it a clamorous anachronism, turned inward upon a vanished past. And under it: the quicksands of sentimentality in place of the senses . . . what could it all amount to in the end?

(*Tombstones,* the Modelskis' cousin, Wlada, said emphatically, and he said to himself: Why is she always so emphatic? Why is she . . . why are we . . . always emoting? We have all lived as though we were collecting aphorisms for an epitaph.)

The twilight abbot had made it very clear. The unimaginable had been practical, the inconceivable had proved to be true. Dr. Poremba sat perfectly still but his mind leaped into fantasy. Suddenly he was driving through the gates in Zarubin's car, saluted by the Robot and the Gondolier, having somehow managed to hypnotize the Abbot into a change of clothes (or would it be simpler to bash him on the head with the Atlasowka?), then he was boarding trains with nonexistent papers, slipping through controls, overcoming every difficulty, finding Alicja and the children, and, in a variety of disguises, through various daring strokes, glib impersonations, outwitting an infinity of simple-minded Oxes, arriving in Persia; then it was just a hop and a skip to Ankara, Turkey, the Polish legation, and a ship to . . . somewhere. In Paris . . . No, not in Paris, for Paris had fallen, but in London? in New York? in the Andes of Peru? Wherever Polish soldiers would be gathering to fight, to resist, to die for their country behind tunes of glory . . .

(Two lumps?

—Lumps?

—The sugar for your tea.

—If you'd be so kind.)

. . . He was reporting to General Sikorski. The world is aghast, some other gallant allies make a demarche, which is a lot more practical than marching . . . Roosevelt makes his inevitable appeal to a monster's conscience . . . The world holds its sides.

But the realities of the moment were considerably different. His wits had always been his most reliable weapon. He was an optimist, a realist, a manipulator . . . he would have made a splendid confidential agent. It was ironic: he had so wanted to be a secret agent and he did have a crack at it, after a fashion, in the strife-torn Silesia of the early twenties, the surreptitious comings and goings of a patriotic Polish student underground at war with the Germans. And to think that a man of such dramatic possibilities should have become a bookman and (God forgive me!) critic. Ah, the comedy had become burlesque. Was there to be no end to irony?

And literature seemed particularly useless at that moment. No amount of poetic inspiration could put a dent in such a reality as this.

Yet he would think of something. He had never failed for an idea when he needed one. Somewhere between the rustling complexities of the Abbot and the witlessness of the Ox a hole could be found. Martyrs of history, bats and secret shadows, devils and magicians cavorted in his head while Zarubin began talking about Victor Hugo.

The night was passing. Dr. Poremba counted his gains. He had cracked the Abbot's secret, he had mourned his friends, his vague notions of escape to search for Alicja had crystallized into a determination to reach her with his skin intact. Certainly, there was some thoughtful planning to be done. Truth can afford to be spontaneous, it can come on like a magic lantern and it did not matter whether anyone believed it! But a hoax must be believed or it isn't a hoax, and a spontaneous hoax is a contradiction, and that means time, and time had to be bought, and Dr. Poremba thought that he might find the necessary time, only slightly soiled, in Berling's Red Corner.

The thought was repulsive. Berling himself may not have been so bad, he supposed: a "wrong idealist" nevertheless may have some ideals, may follow a sense of personal destiny *pro bono publico*, may nourish a dream; the others were despicable opportunists. (And what am I? he had to ask himself.) True, to hoist false colors is a recognized subterfuge of civilized warfare, despised as treacherous only when done successfully by the enemy. *Paris is worth a mass*, said Henri of Navarre, but no historian had ever recorded if the French king had enjoyed his first *Te Deum* there.

And must one be totally cynical to be a realist . . . ?

But the appearance of treason tastes no better than the real thing, and when you think of my entire life, its course and direction (no, not the comedies and the melodrama but the . . . ah, how is one to put it . . . the *poetry* of it!), well, this kind of thing jams itself sideways in the throat.

He did choke then and covered it up by coughing. He made a vague apologetic gesture and the solicitous Zarubin offered him more tea.

—This night has been a revelation to me, General.

Zarubin smiled and smiled, looked at him with eyes that were utterly indifferent, eyes that were cold with distance, a look that spanned centuries. —Indeed?

—You could say, he began, that I've been . . . magically transformed.

Zarubin nodded, turned away. —We must talk again.

—Oh, I intend that we shall, said Dr. Poremba.

—And you should get to know our Colonel Berling.

—Oh, I intend to.

—Believe me, it will all turn out for the best.

—Yes, yes.

He wondered if he had overplayed his hand, too weary to think. The dancing shadows had left the ceiling, waited in the corners. He watched Zarubin's face, looking for an expression, listening to the hammering of his heart.

Then he was in the corridor again, among shadows grown gray. The Abbot's door had closed behind him, the demon of temptation or salvation had vanished, and his mind was paralyzed.

He was wet with sweat and shaking in the cold gray hour before dawn. The mist had lifted. The bats had hanged themselves for sleep. The dark watchtowers were defined and threatening. The stars had retreated. He started walking toward the ruinous chapel, a torment in stone, a home for the demented winds, for lost hopes, for faith and illusions, each of his steps more difficult than the one before.

Then he began to run.

Then he was running. Blindly. Eyes fixed on memory. Whispering *Non Omnis Mortuis*. God have mercy on me. His dead friends pursued him out of the shadowed corners of the Abbot's quarters. The colonel blew an invisible whistle and uttered an inaudible command, the major had embedded a monocle into an eyeless skull, the underensign was looking for his lance, the centuries were marching up and down and demanding passwords. No, not to me, not to me, he whispered; no, it wouldn't happen to him. Well, well, how does it happen? They open your door at night and you are looking upward, you look up in the direction of skies and stars and clouds and suns and planets and God and endless space, in the direction of eternity and continuity, you look into light and see eyes pointing downward with metallic hardness, and they begin to shoot . . .

Eastward, beyond the edge of the muddy plains, red light streaked upward, torn shreds of cloud caught fire.

He heard a shout, a command.

He had stopped, he was no longer running. He stood rooted in fear and superstition and in the faith of dead men like a plaster saint, hollow and full of stale air. Heard footsteps and curses. The Ox (gigantic, bull-necked, red-eyed in the morning) was shaking fists manacled in watches.

—And where d'you think you're going, you son of a bitch?

(Either to heaven or hell, he muttered, what choice do we have; and heaven wasn't likely.)

The Ox swung a boot, slowed by a sleepless night of questioning and cursing and shouting and tormenting. Dr. Poremba managed to dodge aside.

The red eyes regarded him madly. A red sun appeared in a tumbled gap between the monastery wall and the strands of barbed wire and hung, suspended like an eye in ambush.

—Into the cookhouse, you son of a bitch. I'll teach you to walk about enjoying yourself when poor men are working. You think you're still in Poland, you son of a bitch?

He ran toward the cookhouse, hearing harsh laughter off the watch-tower near the gate, ran past the grinning sentry at the cookhouse door, ran into the cookhouse, ran past the iron stoves, past the vat of gruel, past the bags of millet and the piles of turnips, ran through a mire of potato peels, ran past the bleak-eyed broken men who were quartering potatoes, ran past the cook and the assistant cook, ran past the overseer, ran through the back door of the cookhouse into the open air and he kept on running. He ran among bushes and among shrubs, under trees and branches, into and out of fronds, into and out of a small stream, across a green meadow. A shout, a shot behind him. A string of firecrackers popped and rattled in receding distance. He ran among trees.

His breath roared in his ears and his heart was pounding, and scarlet circles revolved before his eyes, and scarlet fire had filled his eyes and he was choking in salt, in sweat, in tears perhaps, and he felt nothing and thought about nothing and was aware of nothing and cared about nothing. A huge flame hung bloodily in the sky, fully armed, and a white palpitating light rushed toward him through the trees among which he was running. It was like something solid and hard-edged approaching at great speed: a mighty army with its glittering banners, its horsemen and crosses . . . He ran until he fell. He listened to a vast wind roaring in his ears.

Then there was silence. The wind had died down. He pushed his head cautiously out of the leaves and dry fronds that he had piled about himself, on top of the little chasm in which he was crouching, and peered about.

He heard a dog barking in the near distance. There was nothing else. The woods were still. The sun was gone, it had moved behind him and the shadows were beginning to return. As far as he could tell he had got away with it, he was in the clear. If they were still looking for him it would be nearer the camp, they wouldn't be able to believe that he could run so far. He had come through the woods, he must have run for miles, a mad and unremembered gallop that had just about exploded his lungs, and now he was on the other side, at the edge of a long plain of rye swept by a rolling wind, and two thin feathers of smoke beckoned in the distance to a diminutive village. Plain simple people there, to be sure, and that's what he needed. He had the advantage of his civilian rags, remnants of the suit that he had worn in Lwów when the net of deportation had swept him up, and which he had been wearing six weeks later when he was arrested near Lake Sergin, the river station for the barges of the upper Ob, and sent to the monastery.

He breathed slowly, patiently. His heart had grown quiet. He found himself grinning. The Ox must be ramming his head against the cookhouse wall. It might improve his bump of precognition, he thought, weak with silent laughter, but it wouldn't save him from paying with his life for losing a prisoner.

. . . A cold mist crept through the undergrowth and coiled about his shoulders.

The dog barked, persistent, and another answered, and for a few moments the furious challenges rolled across the plain. Then, just as suddenly as they had started their savage exchange, the dogs gave it up.

He sighed, sneezed. The dry fronds were powdery in his nose. He itched. He scratched himself, cursed his lice, envisioned a bathhouse and a meal. He tried to picture the bed in which he would sleep. He would not sleep on lousy straw in a tumbled shed, among accusing ghosts, among the remnants of his spectral past. He would never stand for roll call among the gallant dead. He had nothing to which he might return. He would be free, he knew, until he was killed.

. . . So much for modern magic, he whispered to himself. Into the cookhouse with you, you son of a bitch. Open Sesame. Abracadabra, he whispered to himself, laughing. Now you see him, now you don't, and devil take the hindmost. He dug himself out of his burrow, sniffing the fresh evening air, brushed off the dust of desiccated leaves and spread out his resources. Only in a Russian prison does a man live with all his worldly goods hidden about himself, otherwise he soon ceases to have any goods at all. Well now, what do I have? A nine-inch loaf of white bread, courtesy of the Red Corner (although Berling's people were not aware of their courtesy), a crude map of the monstrous landmass that contained him (torn out of a school atlas in the Ox's office), five smoked and salted fish, twenty rubles, a Russian dictionary and a handbook of conversational phrases (sample: *where is the nearest bathhouse . . . a delousing station . . . a post of the People's Commissariat for Internal Affairs . . . ?*), the stub of a pencil, a candle end, a needle fashioned from a fishbone, a spool of thread, a watch. Add to that a pound of optimism, he thought, a pinch of confidence, a ton of faith in the impossible, and something might be done.

He circled the southern shore of Lake Sergin on the map. That's where the search would start. East, north, south, it made little difference; he would search until he found Alicja and the children. Whole nations had been swallowed up in the depths of this gigantic country, but with France fallen, and the hope of rescue no longer possible, he had years to spare.

And he, miraculously, was free.

The sun finally fell into the woods. He could begin to move. The sense of freedom, even though it was still limited to his imagination, was exhilarating. He said clearly, loudly: *I am free!* and immediately asked: *What is free?* (It had been so long since such a thought could have occurred to him.) To be free is not to be under the power or control of another, being able to move in any direction; free as verse, free as a translation, free as spending without reckoning the cost; free as a road clear of obstacles, free to use freely whatever freedom falls into my grasp; not, perhaps, free as in frankness . . . that would be catastrophic in the Soviet Union . . . but, anyway, free as in free thought . . . as a freebooter might be free with no limits set to his adventure and no constraints other than his own.

He didn't know where he was in reference to his map. It was so small that a pencil point would cover a hundred square miles. But, he muttered, as I live and breathe and God is my witness: Columbus had a lot less than that when he set out to find a new world. At least I needn't worry about falling off the edge of the ocean.

He pocketed his visible resources and set out briskly through the rye toward the distant village.

A dog barked at him.

Zdrastvitie, Comrade Dog. Where is the nearest delousing station . . . warm stove . . . a bottle of vodka? And are there any other final thoughts before the masquerade begins? A thought for the poor Ox? *Magna mater,* comrade. Your blood is necessary for my life. Not one thought for the Abbot, thank you very much. And now, how about a place for the night? To turn away a *starets,* mystic and wanderer of Russian legend, is the worst possible luck. Even in these enlightened times of the Great Stalin, a *starets* is a *starets* . . . as Russia is Russia . . . Lenin had said that civilization equaled Communism plus electricity . . . but Russia is Russia and dogs still bark at strangers.

He combed his beard with his fingers to make it seem fuller and entered the village. The moon had come up again, this time as a friend. The dog was still barking. A woman came out of a badly whitewashed cottage and cursed at the dog.

He paused, looked at the woman, caught a glimpse of a grimy face in the harsh white light splashed down by the moon, and immediately recoiled. A Gypsy hag, or what? You can't fool a Gypsy. He sensed her weariness, smelled animal terror, saw two dark eyes shining. He had never seen anyone so totally resigned, as though the years had taught her, beyond doubt, that her every act, no matter how trivial, would end in disaster . . . She may have been fifty or forty . . . or perhaps only twenty-five . . . perhaps he had just imagined the aura of tragedy? This was no time for his imagination to be playing tricks.

She saw him. He stepped nearer, searching for a smile. Her fist flew to her forehead and froze there, the sign of the cross uncompleted.

She cried out a name.

He saw wild weeds tangled in her front yard, withered sunflower stalks. The picket fence had rotted away in sections and had not been repaired. The hut shone whitely with reflected moonlight: ghostly and dead. The house stood alone at the edge of the village, surrounded by overgrown graves and fallen Greek crosses, a dozen cottages clustered together farther on. Inside the woman's house, a child began to utter dull, rhythmic cries.

—Praised be the Lord Jesus Christ, Dr. Poremba said, coming forward.

The woman said nothing. Her clenched fist remained at her forehead.

—A guest in the house is God in the house, Dr. Poremba said, wondering if Polish proverbs still worked in the Ukraine.

The woman cried out a name once more. Her fingers moved to touch her breast and shoulders, and went on to inscribe crosses again and again.

There was something here that plucked at his nerves . . . something unspeakable. Tragedy shouldn't be that obvious, he muttered to himself, cleared his throat, felt his eyelids twitch, stepped forward once more, tried again:

—Praised be the Lord . . .

. . . And felt like an idiot.

The woman's mouth hung open. Her teeth, he noted accidentally, were white, even and strong . . . an incredible discovery in a Ukrainian village where teeth were like manners. He handed her the little white loaf, felt his false smile slipping.

—I've come a long way, he said, tried to step around her so that he might look into the hut, to see if it was safe to enter. She took the bread, then stepped aside, her eyes fixed on his. He heard her hoarse whisper.

—Yes, yes, Ivan, he said, repeating the name she was whispering.

One name was as good as another and he needed a new identity. —A man of God, he added, and went on rapidly: I can tell the secrets of the stars . . . Are you alone? Is anyone with you?

She shook her head once, twice.

—May I go inside?

She nodded, said nothing, stepped aside. He entered the cottage. She followed him, breathless. He felt his chest constricting, suddenly uneasy.

—They took him, oh, so long ago, she said.

—Ah, hmmm. Did they? Well . . .

—But now you've come back.

—Ah, said Dr. Poremba. Hmmm. Did I? So I did. So they took your man away, did they? Well, well.

The woman's eyes were suddenly filled with tears; then the tears spilled over.

—Oh now, come, come, he said. Don't be afraid of me. I won't harm you. Here now, stop this weeping, come now, stop.

—Oh, my dear! she cried.

—Eh? What's that?

—Oh, my dear, my precious, the woman said, her fearful eyes searching his face as though the secrets of salvation might be read there. How I have waited! It has been so hard. They were so cruel and they laughed so . . . no, not about you, they didn't laugh about you, they laughed about me . . . And then there was the child . . . They said such terrible things about you, such lies. After they took you there was nothing, nothing! But I waited. I knew you would come back.

She made quick darting movements with her hands but her eyes were fixed in a dark shining stare. Her face changed in the pale light, transformed by shifting shadow. She was a crone, a tremulous young girl . . . a shaking gray hag . . . —I prayed and I prayed and I prayed . . . ! Sit, rest, you must have come such a long way. I knew you would come. They said you'd never come again but they are always lying. God has brought you back and they say there is no God. They are always lying.

Her hands went to her face, wandered hopelessly about the leathery skin as if to transform it to what it might have been. Her eyes begged and pleaded.

He tried to interrupt the flow, to explain, but she could not be stopped. All those years, she said. Day after day and it was all the same. But it would all be different now, wouldn't it? It would be like before. Didn't he think it could be like it was before? Did he still remember? She hadn't forgotten, no, never, even when . . . ah, but he would understand even that, wouldn't he? You see, she said, there was no food and she could not work and there was the child . . . and what the people said, what they did . . .

Oh, she said, in terror, have you forgotten? How could you have forgotten? But it will be all right, my precious, my love, he had to believe her.

—Rest, you must be so tired . . .

The child cried out in quick animal bursts and she cocked her head, suddenly smiling, looking at Dr. Poremba out of the corners of her eyes.

—The child, she said, shyly. He wasn't even born then. Do you remember?

—Ah, the child . . .

The huge bulging head wobbled on a thin gray neck, scaly as a turtle's, over the edge of a crate; the vacant eyes regarded him blankly, the bony fingers clutched air, opening and closing like the talons of a stricken bird, and the short animal cries had changed to a murmur. The boy was perhaps ten years old. An idiot.

—You see, the woman said. He knows you. Children always know.

Then she bent over the crate and began to feed the child small pieces of bread —There now, my precious, my treasure, my little jewel. Everything's going to be better now, it'll all be different.

The great child gulped and gurgled and the woman crooned and Dr. Poremba felt the hair rise on the back of his neck. Weariness settled upon him like a boulder come to rest between his shoulder blades.

—Oh, I waited, I waited, the woman cried. So many years. They said that once they take you there's no coming back. And they lied, how they lied, one day they came here and said you were dead, yes, that you had died. They showed me a paper . . .

He looked around the bare hut, saw leaping shadows cast by a tallow candle, wondered if the woman would try to stop him if he ran away. The wooden walls glowed a violent pink. There was a plain bench, a stool, the child's crate and a cracked clay stove covered with rags and paper, a wooden bucket and a wooden tub, a broom made of gray straw wired to a stick. There was the long pine table at which he was sitting.

Innumerable questions crowded into his mind, a mad procession of shadows grinned and mocked. Out of one madhouse into another, well, wouldn't you know it. He had been a fool to expect anything else. And yet there was something else in this cottage that made him sit still: a primeval force that clamored for attention, a primitive instinct for survival that could conquer reason. He had the normal fear of madness of the unmad man but pity overthrew the horror. He was suddenly too tired for anything but pity.

. . . The idiot head had vanished in the crate; it gurgled and snored.

The woman stood before him, her hands twisted in a soiled apron, her eyes fixed on him. He smelled her terror. Her mouth was trembling and spilled words.

(Had she changed much, did he think she had? Her hand went up to her streaked grimy hair, fell hopelessly. It had been so . . . difficult. The animal eyes were full of fear, she waited for judgment. She spoke with an intense inner concentration as if to pierce a screen. —If you could only know how hard it had been . . .)

—Listen, he said gently. I'm not who you think I am . . .

(Then she had changed too much! But so had he, couldn't he understand? People change a little when it's so hard, so long, but they are still the same! He would see! Her hands smoothed the furrows on her forehead, rubbed the dead gray cheeks. He need do nothing for her, only wait a little. They could go away to the Mari country where nobody knew them, where no one would know about him, where they could find work. And she could make him real comfortable . . . and he didn't need to do anything for her . . .)

Then suddenly she stopped and cocked her head and listened, her face contorted, and looked at him fearfully, a mute appeal for mercy, as a drunken voice began to shout outside: Anulka, hey, Anna, you old bitch, open up, you stinking bag of bones, hey, you gray death!

. . . And a fist pounded on the door.

—There was no work, she whispered to her twisting hands. They wouldn't let me work after they took you. And there was the child . . .

—Anna Dimitrevna, the drunken voice began to plead. Open up, it's Igor, I got bread and vodka. The vodka's for me, ha-ha, and the bread's for you. Hey, don't you want to eat? Come on, you old witch!

. . . It was so hard, she said.

—Open up, you old whore, or I'll burn your house down!

—I waited so long . . .

Glass broke outside, curses flew, a boot kicked the door, the fist pounded. A twisted smile of agony had split the gray face. The idiot child woke and barked shrill cries again. The dark eyes had grown dim.

Dr. Poremba got slowly to his feet. He went to the door. He drew the wooden bar. The black night and the spangled sky were all he could see. An icy hand passed across his face and the white moon danced. The reeling old peasant stared into his face, his mouth hanging open. Dr. Poremba brought the wooden bar heavily across the peasant's skull.

The thick, drunken man scrambled on hands and knees among broken glass, blood streaming from his head, and then he was at the sagging gate and staggering away. His eyes were awry.

Then they were quiet, alone.

The woman had not moved. Her eyes were dark and empty as dry wells. She was as still as silence. Whatever had animated her before had now disappeared, and she herself had stepped into an inner world where no one could follow. He sat at the head of the table, his head in his hands, and alternated between fits of trembling and bursts of silent laughter. The madness of the moon had followed him inside, he felt the terror of the fleeing peasant as if it were himself who was now bellowing in the distance. Had the drunken peasant been a strong young man the story would undoubtedly have been different, but a soused old peasant weaving in the moonlight . . . well. It couldn't have gone better if he had arranged it. And yet his rage had been genuine. He had not gone to the door for any purpose but to crush an obscenity. Something in the woman had cried out to him, he had peered for a moment into a pit of tragedy, saw lonely years of anguish, heard the indignities and abuse and mockery, measured the depth of terror. Before he had thrown open the door he hadn't known if he would face a superstitious old drunk or a young man who could floor him with one blow. He had been seized by an inner tremor, a concentration of will that was beyond willpower, and the wild light of the moon had set him ablaze. It was a kind of madness, he supposed; a woman had been rendered mad by loss; her mad grief had brushed against him like the wing of an invisible bird . . . And he had responded.

Now the brief luminous delirium had passed. He was spent and empty. He looked at the woman. Had she seen, had she heard, who could tell? Whatever she was seeing and hearing at this moment was a secret shared only by the moon. The child moaned and wailed.

—Anna Dimitrevna, he said. Anna Dimitrevna.

The woman seemed to come awake with a great inner shudder and focused her eyes on his, asking a mute question. Her face was still, composed, and the terror was gone. What had replaced it was a resignation as deep as peace, and yet her questions still had to be asked.

—Please sit down, Anna Dimitrevna, Dr. Poremba said.

The gray face trembled, the wrinkles dissolved, and two great tears rolled through the grime unheeded. She came toward him stiffly like a somnambulist, stood still as if listening, then seized his hand and kissed it.

—No, he cried as if touched by fire.

—I love you, she said.

—No, he cried. You must understand. I am not your husband.

She nodded, sighed, touched her hair. The two tears had washed soft lines on her cheeks. She looked away from him, smiling secretly, her head lowered. —They said he died ten years ago, she said softly. He was crushed by a tree, they said. But they always lie.

Then she remembered something, went outside. He heard her moving about among broken glass. When she came back she was carrying a small gray loaf of bread, asked if he was hungry. No, he said, and took the five small fish from his pocket and put them on the table.

—Taran, she said. Where did you get Taran? Ah, but that is what they give you for the journey. I remember.

She cut the bread into slices. Gave him one. Put one on the table for herself. Wrapped the others in a yellow piece of newsprint and hid them in a coffer under the deal bench.

—Eat, she said. Eat.

But he shook his head.

—When you come home you must eat, she said uncertainly, and once more the grooves of insupportable worry sliced horizontal lines into her forehead.

—I've tried to explain, he began, but she jumped to her feet, backed away, her hands rising feebly.

—You know how it was first for us, when they took us both. Do you remember? Of course, how could you forget! And do you remember what we told each other, over and over, through that year, over and over. That no matter what they did to us, no matter what happened, we would never change.

. . . All that they needed, she said, was a little time. Time to see each other as they truly were, not as time had made them. It really wasn't very much to ask for . . . Just a little time . . .

He made a vague gesture, surrendering. He knew that he should get up and leave immediately. Out into the chilling night, the unnerving moonlight . . . ! But his legs seemed rooted to the floor.

. . . The dogs were barking once again.

—When I came back alone, with you staying up there in those terrible woods, I thought I would die, she said. There was nothing to live for. The child was coming and you weren't here. All of them told me that you'd never come back, that when your five years were up they'd give you five more, and then more and more, and that our whole life was finished. They said if I divorced you I could work. Maybe not teaching again but something else. But I remembered what you said. I have never forgotten. Surely *you* couldn't have forgotten? No, of course you couldn't . . .

. . . As for *that*, she said gesturing toward the door and the debris left outside by the drunken peasant, looking down: in time he'd understand even that, there had been nothing else that she could do . . . could have done. —There was the child, you see.

He nodded, stared into the fire.

—Please sit down, he said.

—All that we need, she said, is a little time.

. . . And would he like some vodka?

He nodded, sighed, closed his eyes. The long run through the woods was still very much with him. His heart was still pounding and his knees were weak. Whether it was the wild cross-country gallop from the prison camp or the rage with the drunken peasant that had made him violent and which now disarmed him, he didn't know. She handed him a cracked glass; he sniffed the vodka, tossed it down, and grinned at the first star that had suddenly appeared, as a boy in Poland would at Christmastime: the traditional signal that he might begin to open his gifts . . .

. . . Was he quite sure that he wouldn't eat just yet?

Yes, he was, thank you.

—Perhaps later, she said.

His mind was dulled, sheeted with lead. He thought he was drunk: never before on one glass of vodka. Better have another. The remnants of exhilaration, anger . . . hatred, he supposed . . . had vanished, leaving him exhausted. Someone would come to the house as soon as the terrified old drunk had spread the word of his arrival (. . . It was the Devil, I tell you, comrades! The Devil himself!) . . . It would probably be a humorless militiaman, if they had one in such a small village . . . Even the Devil couldn't travel in this paradise without a passport . . . identification . . . He would cope with that emergency when it came. At this moment thinking was impossible. He was falling asleep. The Abbot and the monastery, the Ox and the train . . . Alicja and the children crowded into his thoughts.

He looked up, found the madwoman watching him, saw her secret smile, shook in sudden terror. She had decided something, that was clear. She was no longer afraid. Whatever she knew, all the good and evil that life had inflicted upon her, was . . . *were* . . . matters that he was too tired to imagine. She had stepped into herself and found there the necessary magic and now she was smiling, and it was only in the tentative motions of her hands, as if she were gathering an invisible substance and offering it to him, searching among her memories for the recipe of safety, that he could see doubt.

His thoughts spun away.

. . . He was once more an actor, waiting for his cue, listening to shrill and threatening voices in the gloomy amphitheater of a ruined chapel . . . The Abbot was rustling . . . The bats darted, mocked.

(A man must believe in something, said the Nervous Colonel.)

Sleep, he thought. Rest.

Only for a moment.

He could no longer remember such moments of oblivion.

. . . The Devil never sleeps; the proverbs, legends, folklore, old wives' tales are positive about that. He was alone, in a void, Alicja was calling.

Mann-Bielecki whispers to a Russian, points. The Russian is shouting
. . . The priest (and why couldn't he remember the name of this
young friend?) is kicked to his knees . . . *You'll get ten years for
religious propaganda, you son of a bitch! And you, you were an officer!*
(Never had the honor, said Dr. Poremba.) Alicja's eyes were dry, as
were the eyes of Janina Modelska. He tried to speak as he was being
kicked and shoved toward the prison coach . . . no, not the sinister
small train which had stolen Langenfeld and Tarski, no, the *other* train
. . . wanted to tell Alicja that she shouldn't worry, that he'd find her
again. She should wait for him, he wanted to say. She should not despair. She should remember other times. Wait. He wanted to say all
that and more but there wasn't time for even one word. At one inexplicable moment he was standing by Modelski's grave while the gray wind
whistled through the scree and, in the next, he was inside the cattle car
and the doors were sealed . . . He could still hear Alicja beating on the
doors. Calling him. He was only half a person without her. She was the
portion of their common body which contained the heart. Without her
he was nothing, less than nothing . . .

He woke, startled, looked around. A cold wind was seeping through
the insufficiently sealed windows where many panes were missing and
others were cracked. He was shuddering but he knew that his chill had
nothing to do with the temperature outside.

Something was missing. He had to think hard to remember where he
was.

He looked for the woman.

The child wailed suddenly, gurgled, grew silent, was still.

The woman was singing.

She was kneeling in front of the coffer, lifting out white linen. Red
glass beads took fire from the tallow candle. She knelt before the coffer
as though it were an altar, touching sacred objects. Then she was moving quietly about the room, touching other objects as though they had
become unfamiliar. Her eyes were dark with terrible concentration. She
nodded, looked at him, her lips moved. She said nothing. She picked up
the wooden bucket and took it outside. He crossed his arms on the
table before him, put his head on his arms. Thoughts drifted and dissolved. He was a young man again running among slag heaps while bullets whined around him in the black night, hoarse shouts pursued him,
his cargo of clandestine leaflets winged about like doves. Silesia has
been Polish, is Polish, will be Polish, cried the doves to a black and
unresponsive sky. The shouts were close and scarlet. *Heilige Sakrament
von Teufel, where could he have got to?* while he crouched in the coal
pit. *Well, he can't have grown wings* . . . The long night passes, the
shouts boom and echo in the black corridors, then recede, the search is
given up, and he crawls through the darkness toward a faint light.

Quick, inside, says the young girl, have they hurt you? He grins into sky-blue eyes, auburn hair: not as much as I've hurt them, *Panienko*, but perhaps I'm wrong, perhaps they killed me and I am in heaven . . . She shakes her head: how dirty you are, you look like a devil. How can a devil get to paradise, he grins as she brings him water, how can he meet angels? Stop this silly nonsense, she says but she can't help smiling. What's your name, *Panienko*? Alicja Komarowska. Will you marry me immediately, but no, that would be a misalliance on a celestial scale, an act of miscegenation, wouldn't it; how can a devil marry an angel? Oh, stop this nonsense, hush up, wash up, are you hungry? Starved for beauty. You'll have to settle for some bread and ham. That is no substitute. Then you will have to practice abstinence, it purifies your thinking. I'm up to here with abstinence. Then eat the bread and ham, and do hush up or you'll wake my parents. Will you meet me to-morrow in the park? No. Day after tomorrow? No. The day after that? Hush up and eat. I am starved for beauty, will you meet me the day after the day after tomorrow? Hush up and go, you will wake my mother. The day after the day after the day after tomorrow? All right, but go now before you wake my father. A kiss before I go? Don't be silly.

Someone was singing a delicate sad song. He heard a rustling whisper. He raised his head, momentarily displaced, saw the bright red flash of a forgotten shout . . . glass burning like rubies . . . the pink walls. The woman was singing softly as she swept the floor with the gray straw broom. Her hair was washed and combed and tied behind her head with a scarlet ribbon. She had put on a wide-sleeved yellow blouse that had once been white and the insufficient little flame of the candle picked out the rich blues and reds of her embroidery, the red and yellow edging of her wide blue skirt. She had set fire to a small dish of aromatic herbs.

Her face was scrubbed and shining and her eyes were calm with a distant knowledge that cried out to him suddenly: I am a woman, the immemorial luminary; I bring you forth and I take you in. I am the beginning of the mystery and I am its end.

She heard his movements and was immediately still, poised for flight among memories that she could not erase; her eyes glassy with uncertainty, then clearing. He saw the doubt and the uncertainty; the lined gaunt face could not hide her from him. The dark tormented eyes pleaded and commanded.

—Will you eat now? she said.

He nodded.

She sighed, her body filled. She had already put the wooden platters on the table and now sat down beside him to divide the bread and the fish.

Catherine

THE PAINS WERE SHARP, insistent. There was a moment of sudden clarity akin to cold fire observed from a distance; no, nothing monumental, unimportant really: just a matter of being lucid and aware in the half-light, of seeing the litter of the human garbage still tangled in sleep while she was awake. The stupor of exhaustion was momentarily displaced: that's all there was to it. She was crouched in the wet brown corner by the urine bucket, coiled about the various sources of her pains, looking up, saw King Whore (Her Criminal Majesty, absolute ruler of this airless, reeking outer province of hell) sprawled naked on the high shelf near the only window: her bloody turban of cotton waste and rags had slipped over one eye, giving her a look of particular depravity; saw (still aware of her privilege of silent nonparticipation) the waxed severe disapproving mask of Pani Mosinska (gray hair bunned neatly in place, tweed suit tightly and correctly buttoned, hands of a General's Lady folded like battle flags in a museum case), the suddenly aged, worn delicate face of Wanda Sierocka, who had confessed to her that she had once loved Abel . . .

Pictures at an exhibition, hung in the anteroom of hell. The half-light lay upon them like a film of dust, blurring detail. Some thanks were due for small mercies but the pains were becoming frequent and robbed her of breath.

The heat was stifling, even then. Her thin cotton shift (Pani Mosinska's venomous insistence on modesty at all costs) was glued to her body; her belly was a bulging veined balloon that seemed suddenly obscene . . . her thin dirt-streaked legs were unrecognizable, and hadn't one become shorter than the other? She inspected herself casually with mild distaste as a discarded object, a piece of meaningless and quite useless refuse that she might have come across accidentally in a place where she had no business visiting: some squalid tenement alley, per-

haps a forbidden shortcut home from school: some desperate street of
hopeless poverty, the quintessential ruin of whatever dreams its people
might have had . . . She would immediately forget it in her parents'
warm and comforting apartment, where her own dreams and yearnings
would be always safe . . . Gray-skinned, gaunt naked women snored
and muttered on the communal wooden pallets.

Her child moved suddenly and she touched her belly. It would be
born today. Somehow. In this place. Her child: the moment of her supposed fulfillment as a woman, traditions assured her. So much for traditions. And how could IT possibly survive longer than an hour in this
place where even the most unshakable traditions died in moments? She
willed herself not to think about IT: no difficult matter in the rapidly
returning stupor of exhaustion. They had said yesterday that they
might possibly move her to the infirmary for the birth but the *bolnitza*
(which, to her, sounded like a warehouse where pains might be stored)
was full at the moment, indeed the sick women were piled in the corridors, and it all depended on whether someone in one of the beds died
to make room for her. And why for *her*, she for whom, she was told, the
days of privilege were over; this was a transit prison, she was to
remember, Butyrki no less, where she was one of twenty thousand people waiting for their transport (criminal scum! socially unacceptable
material!), and *they*, the uniformed representatives of Mankind's Most
Perfect Social Order, were not obliged by regulations to shower privileges on enemies of the people. And anyway, the irritated *lekpom* said:
women had been giving birth without infirmaries for thousands of
years. Drop your whelp like any other bitch.

Someone would help. She didn't know much about having babies: it
wasn't part of the knowledge guaranteed by a convent education; in
fact, long lines of ashen-faced nuns, melting like wax candles impaled
around plaster saints, nodded their heads, wagged fingers, clicked
rosaries and tongues, said: I told you so (except that they had never
said a thing about it!). She had allowed herself to be defiled, she had
stepped beyond permissible bounds, she had in fact leaped so joyfully
beyond them! So now, of course, a terrible punishment was due, but
perhaps the harassed liquored *lekpom* had a point: it wasn't anything
that she had invented. This business of having babies had been going
on for a considerable time and not too many people were the worse for
it. When it came, it came. She would do her best to have it properly
and, perhaps, someone could be found to help. It was ironic that there
didn't happen to be a doctor in the cell at the moment. Only a week
earlier there had been one of the best obstetricians from Lwów, there
had been a gynecologist, but the medical contingent had been whittled
down by several midnight transports, and now she had a choice of

poetesses, minor journalists, a radio announcer, and some military wives.

But there was still some time, she knew. There were supposed to be some signals, advance warnings; something about breaking water. And then someone had said something about timing the pains. With what? Nobody has a watch . . . ! And there was supposed to be plenty of hot water . . . Well, on that point she could set her mind at ease. There would be hot water. They brought it every morning with the bread.

. . . Gray walls: the light is pale blue: strange fevers consume her. Exhaustion brings about a certain peace, a form of acceptance, a mildly contemplative resignation, and, for a moment, apathy has won over her determination. Not even enough strength to cry out with the pains which are becoming frequent . . . and so she did nothing, drifting in half-sleep. No real sleep is possible between bouts of pain. It's best to lie still, make the mind blank, dissolve in the heat. Her life is ebbing, her thoughts are cast adrift and float in circles away from their safe moorings, and because of the stench of rot and the drone of the flies she thinks of a beach which is now littered with sea-bleached objects too heavy for the tide to carry away: the moaning grunting mass of women sunk in sleep. The beach stinks of offal and dead fish. The putrefying mass mutters and heaves about. The flies rise and fall in heavy black waves; their drone is soporific.

She would come through this as she had come through everything else: the endless questionings at Zamarstynow, the shouts and the beatings, the indifference of the guards, the humiliation of having her body poked and probed and peered into in a public hallway, the reduction of her status from Human Being to valueless object . . . I have no fears about myself, she told herself formally, I am invisibly sustained. If there were any real fears tormenting her now they would be all connected with her child.

Someone would have to take care of it after it was born, and she searched among the hag faces for a possible recruit, heard a deep groan (her own), sat up on the pallet struggling against massed bodies.

What day is this?

What month is this?

What year is this?

What had she really wanted? Dreams, hopes based upon assumptions that two people who could love each other, among whom a certain bond spanning time and space could be supposed to exist, could create a life which, while excluding no one and welcoming everyone, could be self-contained. Yes, we are larger than ourselves when each supports the spirit of the other. Souls linked in tandem like power generators (Abel had once said) pumping energy. The pain was suddenly enormous and she did cry out but nobody heard her. She would resist this staggering sense of loss, the loneliness that drained all strength out of spirit, that undermined determination and destroyed the will. Perhaps this was nothing that she would ever be able to explain to anyone but Abel, who was in need of so many explanations, for whom nothing short of perfection would ever do; certainly, it was nothing that anyone else could be expected to understand with their compromises made, their treasons painted over.

People . . . well, people. Each of them translates the universe into a private pasture where only he or she is permitted to graze, where the winds must always be benign and the rain is gentle. Each of us creates that awful loneliness which is a shield against everybody else. We tell ourselves: I am all there is, all else is incidental: part of my setting, meaningless without me, and nothing is important in itself; all things, from mud to miracle, exist only in their relationship to me . . .

. . . You see that so clearly in a place such as this. This is the jungle. And you see the other. On one hand the terror before King Whore, the ferocious rule of the criminals, thieves, and murderesses for whom all life is an unending war, a continuous assault on the human spirit centered on the preservation of Self if only for an hour. On the other hand there is the ice-cold contemptuous aloofness of Pani Mosinska, for whom life is surely only a disagreeable theater performance, where if one only plays one's role, nothing else could matter. Then there's the overwhelmed intensity of Wanda Sierocka and, somewhere between all of them, herself.

Sleep.

If only she could count on the mercy of oblivion, the illusion of a miraculously melted flesh.

Whatever sleep may have been possible between the shards of pain was gone for the day. The sweat-drenched stinking body, unwashed in six months, the veined balloon with its cargo of swift pains, had been recaptured, pinioned on its pallet in blue-gray light; and even thoughts, flung so far and wide, so freely, must recognize the illusion of their temporary liberation.

I'm here again, she told herself, awake and aware. Cell No. 22, M to S (IV), and in a moment the others will be awakening, the terrible day would begin all over again, and she would step across the threshold of an imagined silence into the daily scene that she would not have been able to create in her wildest nightmares; the grotesque faces, the dull distended eyes, the clutching fingers, the screams and curses; out of her private self-contained illusion of silence into a pit of sound. By noon,

this small gray room with its forty women will be a furnace boiling with
naked and half-naked bodies tormenting each other.

Thoughts were a refuge of a kind.

What was it that Abel had said in those lost days that were removed
from her by so many centuries? (Because, yes, centuries seemed to have
passed in what was obviously no longer than nine months, an entire
civilization had already been forgotten; a new Creation had taken
place, perhaps, and the remorseless process of evolution was grinding
down the weak and the helpless.) Odd words appeared, vanished, had
no further meaning. Gentleness. Love. Consideration. And that other
one, the one she had made such a fetish of at one time: tenderness.
Affection . . . the mutterings of a madman. Dear loving madman. He
couldn't help striving for perfection in all things, whether it was his work
or his human relationships, and the closer he stood to the person or to
the idea, the more insistent he would be that it, or they, be perfect. It
was that poetic longing for perfection without the shadow of a blemish
that made him an artist.

They were awakening now.

The vague screened grunts and muted mutterings were giving way to
curses.

. . . Get your fat filthy carcass off here, scum!

. . . Kill you, bitch!

Outside a transport convoy was forming. She could hear the dogs
rounding up the herd, and the guards' curses; the dull roar of several
thousand voices, men pushed and beaten into head-count formations
(saw them in her mind's eye, massed in their fives, facing gates, their
bundles on their backs, their heads lowered, their boots thudding on
the cobblestones).

. . . Keep your lines, there!

Crack. The whistle of leather.

. . . Silence!

The ravaged flock of women, or what might possibly have been
women at another time (if there had been any other time, if this was
not all that there was to reality!), clung to the bars, peering at the men,
shouting obscene invitations.

Laughter.

The triumphant howl.

. . . Could Abel be one of the men outside?

. . . They had begun something, he and she, something that was too
fresh, too newly planted to produce an identifiable bloom. If she
believed that this new organism was true, that it could not be withered
by distance and time, that it could carry her above the terror, filth, the

howling triumph of obscenity and fearful disappointments, then surely it would grow whether either of them, he or she, was there to nourish it.

Such a dear madman, swinging among principles like a runaway pendulum, yet surely reaching higher in each swing . . .

And how was one to live with a man like that? It could be damaging, certainly; one had to exercise the most gentle guidance when living with an elemental force, a man whose life was limited only by the bounds of an imagination, who recognized no constraints on his spirit and who could never, not in a million years, not with a thousand cautions, ten thousand commands, accept anybody's yoke.

One had to be cautious, patient. Not to demand too much too soon. Look at him with more than the pygmy vision of a rational mind. One couldn't pin production schedules on a notice board. (Did Mrs. Mickiewicz really expect her Adam to come home for dinner every night?) Ludicrous. There was that lovely word again. And yet (and wasn't it ironic, wasn't it absurd?) this wholly irrational madman spent his life in search of a yoke. Think of Gawain in search of the City of Light . . .

. . . I'll kill you, bitch, I'll tear out your eyes, a woman was howling.

She was alone, without him.

No, she didn't need him for a crutch. It was more than that. And it was suddenly clear to her in the chaos of a new brutal day that she would probably always be alone because he, like all his kind who insisted on giving so much (each a Prometheus chained by his own demands upon himself: commitment to perfection), was able to give her only a fragment of himself and she would never know what fragment it would be.

She clutched her swollen body.

. . . Yesterday, or perhaps it was the day before (all these days having run into each other like streams of ordure from the leaking bucket), one of these gargoyle beings, surely nonhuman, possessing none of the characteristics one has been taught to associate with women, had bitten off the ear of King Whore in a fight. Bitten it right off! And then ran off into a corner and cut off one of her own to make amends . . .

(Why can't there by any unity among us? Wanda had asked in her first weeks there. Someone, she said, had written in a book that companionship in adversity was supposed to create certain bonds . . . Whoever wrote that book had never been in a transit prison. And they said that up north, in the camps, it was even worse, that since no one could hope to survive for more than two years there, all semblance of human thought and human sensibilities was totally abandoned . . . King

Whore ruled one segment of this jungle with an iron hand, the iron will of Pani Mosinska controlled another segment. Between these two inflexible antipodes, what was left of forty human lives struggled for survival.)

And now one woman, or what once had been a woman, howled: Get your fat belly out of the way there, bitch!

Said King Whore, carelessly, straddling the brown bucket: Shut your filthy hole there, scurvy bitch! (And then to Catherine:) Goin' to pop it today, are you? Huh?

Catherine couldn't speak, nodded.

—Well, you don't have to look like the world's coming to an end. There's nothing to it. Never had one before, did you?

Catherine shook her head.

—You scared?

This time she looked up fiercely, met the one visible eye of the huge Ukrainian woman.

—No.

—That's right, said King Whore. Nothing to be scared of. Not a goddam thing you can do about it anyway. When it comes, it comes. I've had a few, I know. Best way's to squat, like you was takin' a shit, and out it pops. After it's all over you'll never know what the fuss was about.

—She ought to be in the infirmary, said Wanda Sierocka.

—Is that so? said King Whore. In-*fir*-ma-ry. Am I sayin' it right, got the accent or whatever the fuck it is in the right place? In-fir-*marry*, maybe? Well, if a tree fell on her, or if she got run over with a tractor, or if she was the camp commandant's little doll, well, then we could talk about infirmaries. Some of them camp commanders in the North have regular harems, see? So far away from anything, all on their own like they are, like they was gods up there, well, you can see how they do it. Then when the *komandir*'s done with you there's the guards. Then there's storekeepers or the cook. The cook's a good one to get. Every time I go up I get a storekeeper or a cook. Point is always to get yourself a man, see? Try to get yourself one of the work-squad leaders too. They're tough, they been around the camps a long time, they know their way around and they'll keep all the others off your ass. So what article you got?

—I don't know, said Catherine.

—Well, it don't much matter anyway, said King Whore. Most of you fine ladies go up on Article 54, and that's five years, and nobody lasts that long in the camps.

—King Whore, hey, King Whore, said one of the women. Can I have the bucket?

—Now goddammit, didn't I tell you to shut your trap? Now I'm tellin' this nice little bitch here what she's got to know so she can survive and all you can think about is the goddam bucket? Shove a cork up your ass and wait till I'm done. All them fine ladies, them politicals, don't have a chance in hell unless it's put to 'em right, and who can do it better'n me? Eh? (And then to Catherine:) I been up three times. Take it from me, I know all about it.

—Goddam stupid politicals, said one of the women. How stupid can you get?

—I'm not sayin' they're not stupid, said King Whore. It's stupid as hell to get sent up for nothing. What difference does it make who says what about anything? Them's just words and words are shit and it's goddam stupid to get sent up for shit, but if you're going up somebody's got to put it to you right or you don't last six months. So if I get this nice little bitch here straightened out a bit she might last a year. Hell, she's no older'n I was the first time I went up.

—So maybe she's your daughter, said one of the women.

—She could be, said King Whore. One of 'em was a girl, they told me.

—How many children have you had? Catherine asked.

—Jesus, I don't know. Five, six, maybe. The only one I remember is the first one. Up in the Kola, it was, building a camp in the forest. Colder'n a bitch. Fuckin' water froze when it broke. The little bastard was hard like a log, damn near split me in half, but all it took was a day in the *bolnitza* and I was back at work next morning. You're lucky you're poppin' it here, not in the snow behind a tree somewhere. Nice and warm here.

—Will you help me when it's time?

—Who, me? Shit now! You want all these here to laugh at me for a fuckin' midwife?

Then she got off the bucket, yawned, scratched herself, found a louse and cracked it.

—A cook's the best bet for you, she said. Or a storekeeper. All right, I'm done with the bucket, but that bitch that did all the yapping goes last, see? She don't go till I say she can.

. . . Thoughts fly away. The women are fighting. Most of them are Polish Ukrainians or Carpatho-Ruthenians who had moved joyfully in whole villages into Soviet-occupied Poland, to be arrested for illegal border crossing, but there are also many Russian women, some Asiatics, a Jewess who had been chairman of a revolutionary tribunal in Stanislawów that had sent hundreds of people to the prisons, and another who was a member of Mendeltort's Hargan; there is a Chinese crone and three wraiths who are said to have been Russian Orthodox nuns (who are as still as plaster statues, only their lips moving silently all day). There are nine Polish women in the cell, mostly wives of officers, though a few, like Wanda, are writers, journalists . . . Two are still dressed in the evening wraps and high heels they had worn for the cultural reception in Lwów, given for visiting Eastern Ukrainian poets, to which Mann-Bielecki had invited Abel and herself. . . . Abel was to have given a speech (not more than five minutes, Mann-Bielecki said) as a representative of the younger poets . . .

—Are your pains regular now, do you think? Wanda was whispering then. Her ringed sunken eyes were enormous in a face stamped with permanent terror.

—I think so.

(And had she imagined the look of compassion in the stern bitter eyes of Pani Mosinska?)

Wanda began to wipe her face with the hem of her sequined skirt.

—What can I do?

—Nothing, she said fiercely. Who can do anything?

—There must be something that somebody can do. Perhaps if we all began shouting for the *lekpom* . . .

—Nothing would happen. You know nothing would happen.

She felt a sudden hatred, as bright and intense as her pains, for the compassionate and ineffectual Wanda in her ruined ball gown, for all things decent and unsullied, for undefiled altars, for all the men and women everywhere who were not suffering at this moment, who had never suffered, for the complacent and well-meaning givers of advice in a world which was not beautiful, not human, which was a world of sham and drudgery and broken dreams, for the obscenity of the murmured consolations, for the pretenders and the liars, for the untormented, for innocence, for everyone who was safe, for all enchantment and rhetoric and magic, for those whose young souls had not been violated, for the unimaginative old, for any kind of faith or ideal in a world which recognized only entries in a ledger, for life and for living.

Her pains and nausea had become transformed into contempt and hatred for all the sanctimonious people who lie in the name of truth, for whom affection is expediency, for those who close their ears to the distress of others, for those who regret that they are too busy to help, for those who damage others' opportunity to hide their own weakness, for those who leave another stranded among indifferent people, for those who are exalted because they are rich, for the ineffectual who smile sadly while another drowns, for those who say *What can I do alone?*, for all of her kind.

She could be scornful now about all her lost worlds: they had never existed except as flights of fancy hurled by the imagination of a loving madman.

She would win. The meek and the mild shall inherit graves in a snowy wilderness, and the flies and the burrowing rodents shall inherit the meek and the mild, but she would not be anyone's inheritance. She would be triumphant.

Suddenly she was wet and flowing. Something had constricted within her, something had given way. There was a moment of ease in which consciousness ebbed, or perhaps it was her life which was ebbing (she was indifferent to either possibility), then came resurgence.

—Well, here's the water break, someone said.

—Is she going to have it now? Wanda asked, tremulous.

—Are you as much of an idiot as you seem? asked Pani Mosinska.

Catherine felt like laughing.

The monument had spoken.

The embodiment of all the stiff-necked virtues, the unforgiving, bitterly contemptuous symbol of reproach, had stepped off her high-backed judgment seat. Was there a woman inside that graven image, after all? In six months she had never spoken to Catherine, never looked her way; Catherine had been judged by a glance, condemned by an idea; she was beyond the pale, unredeemable; her presence violated all the notions of propriety, and the punishment for this most terrible of all the transgressions was banishment from the consciousness of right-thinking people.

And now humanity? Would the statue creak? Would the stiff iron joints grate as she began to move? Would the neck finally bend? The General's Lady was taking tactical command by virtue of her position as judge and prosecutor and museum piece, and suddenly Catherine heard quick animal bursts of hysterical laughter (her own) and the merciful curtain of exhaustion fell on her again.

Strength could be found for anything, she knew, everything could be endured. There was no such thing as humiliation unless one surrendered and no longer spoke one's truths whatever one conceived them to be, and strength of spirit could be nurtured, torments could be dismissed at least as easily as the flies, if one could rise above them. Mere survival is an insult when one can be triumphant.

> . . . To see a world in a grain of sand
> And a heaven in a wild flower . . .

Had she really said such things at one time? And how could she have forgotten them so quickly?

And then there was a moment of what could pass for sleep.

Moments, minutes, perhaps hours later there was a rhythmic roar: the sort of thing that you might hear coming from a football stadium. Lwów had been slightly insane about football but she had never gone to a match; there was supposed to be something a little too physical about that sort of thing . . . not suitable for young ladies of good family. Too . . . ah . . . *sweaty?* Was *animal* the word? Perhaps too absolutely male for good taste. But this particular roaring was very much female. It meant that the cell door had been thrown open and that the warders were hurling in quarter loaves of bread. Forty mouths roared and eighty hands rose as each brown-crusted ration loaf arced overhead, fell among the clutching hands and tearing fingernails, and immediately vanished. So many ration loaves were thrown in for so many women, each woman tried to get as many as she could (for the moldy bread was not only food but currency). If you didn't catch one, then you didn't get one; as far as the hooting warders were concerned, forty loaves thrown among forty women meant that everybody had been fed.

Wanda was whispering.

—What can I do to help?

—Nothing, Catherine said.

—Oh, I wish there was something.

—So do I, said Catherine. But there isn't. So why don't you just forget about it and jump for your bread?

—Pani Mosinska said I was to stay with you.

—I don't need you.

—Oh, please don't say that, Wanda said.

—Oh, my God! said Catherine.

—You're hurting my hand, Wanda said. But that's all right, hurt me if it helps you.

—Oh, my God, said Catherine.

—Pani Mosinska says that it's our duty to ourselves to look after each other.

—What shit, said Catherine.

—Otherwise we're all reduced to the status of wild animals, don't you see? And that's what they want to do to us and we mustn't let them.

—Go write a poem about it, Catherine said. Oh, but that one hurt.

—It can't go on much longer.

—I hope not. I really hope not.

—Would you like to pray?

—Shit no, said Catherine.

—What can I do?

—Nothing. Stop talking. Hold my hand. Help me up.

She made an effort to sit up, look around.

No, she would not give way. She would not surrender to the luxury of her suffering. She would have no self-pity, or any other kind of pity, or sympathy or piety or commiseration. Everything that happens to anyone forms one total fabric, she thought suddenly, and if it has any meaning whatsoever it is only in the context of the whole. Our lives are allegorical. To look at any one of us as if each of us were everything, able to form some kind of a totality, is like trying to understand the meaning of a forest by studying it one leaf at a time.

The pains came swiftly now; it would not be long. Pain is not a particularly allegorical experience. The gloomy nuns cowled in piety, ignorance, and a denial of all non-allegorical experience, whispered admonitions. Father was shaking his gentle muddled head, and Mother was saying: to be a woman in a society such as ours is an absurdity, but some people's absurdities are greater than the total achievements of others; Emil was peering, snickering; Abel was declaiming (looking a little like a demented Christ); the Angel of Death smiled, beckoned, but she shook her head.

There will be nothing to it, King Whore had assured her. It's like taking a shit.

The pains made her dizzy, made her vision shake.

—What can I do? said Wanda.

She shook her head, heard her teeth grinding against each other, wished to be limp, pliable, and formless. But she had been carefully and responsibly designed (she remembered).

. . . *I will praise Thee/for I am fearfully and wonderfully made* . . .

—What did you say? said Wanda.

She looked about, trying to clear her vision.

A crust of bread struck her in the face.

. . . *Behold the fowls of the air: for they sow not, neither do they reap, nor gather into barns; yet our heavenly father feedeth them* . . .

—What *are* you saying, Catherine?

—You wouldn't believe it.

. . . In cell No. 22, M to S (IV), in the great transit prison of Butyrki, Moscow. The birth of a child. Normally, naturally, painfully in an immemorial ritual, amid love and hatred, with gratitude for the sudden cessation of pain and the swift descent of a comforting darkness, the stupor of exhaustion. Now, in this magically transformed year of 1940. To serve as a symbol.

—Well, said Pani Mosinska from a great height above clouds. Well. Not a bad-looking little fellow, is he? Bite off the cord, tie it off. Now mop up all this mess. Bring up the water. Clean her up. Get that clean cotton waste packed in well. That's right, that's correct.

—She looks so pale, someone said.

—Normal.

Someone was sobbing hysterically very far away, perhaps in a cave.

—Stop that at once, said Pani Mosinska. Or I shall slap your face.

—I can't help it, Wanda said. I just can't help it. It's too terrible.

Then there was the soft wet leathery sound.

—I told you to stop it.

—I can't help it, really.

—Ridiculous. Clean up the child, wrap him in my jacket. Clean up the girl and cover her up decently. After all, we're not animals. And stop this hysterical exhibition in front of that scum! Don't you have any feeling for what's expected of us?

—I'm sorry, Wanda was saying then. I am very sorry.

—Ah, Catherine said.

She had been climbing a mountain on a narrow path, alone and unguided, and she had lost her footing and now she was falling down the side of the cliff. She could hear the wind whistling in her ears, and a distant ringing, and the booming echoes of calls among the crags, but nobody was calling out to her, she hadn't told anyone where she was going and nobody would be wondering where she had gone or why, no one would set out to look for her and, probably, she would never be found at the foot of the mountain where, in the dark motionless silent peace of mind and of spirit, she would be able to rest.

Abel

THE DOOR WAS THICK AND NARROW, an iron rectangle that resembled the lid of a coffin. He thought the shape appropriate; one could say (if, like Avrum Mendeltort, or as Avrum Mendeltort would say, *one was still given to saying things like that*) that the Lubyanka was something of a graveyard, in the way that the pyramids of Egypt were resting places for dead pharaohs awaiting resurrection. The difference was that no one entombed at the Lubyanka was entirely dead. They breathed, ate or dreamed of eating, sometimes defecated in their iron buckets, did not sleep. Cried, wept, went mad. Heard and answered questions. Faced huge lights. Forgot about the feel and comfort of darkness. Signed statments scribbled on brown wrapping paper and the flyleaf pages torn out of books, made confessions. Denounced and were denounced, pointed accusatory fingers with and without fingernails, were tried and condemned, disappeared. Became something unrecognizable in nature: not quite an animal but certainly not human, and could never hope to join Osiris or anybody else in whatever world.

The yellow-brick prison was a warren of long narrow corridors and small cells; each cell folded about its solitary prisoner like the wrappings of a bud around a flickering germ of life, silent and impenetrable, lifted above time. Impersonal, not malevolent. You (Abel told himself again) must always remember that there is nothing malevolent about this. No more than an erupting volcano, earthquakes, continental floods, buried mine shafts are malevolent. Icebergs bear no ill will toward the ocean liners that they ram and sink. It's a natural disaster.

Abel had no idea where he was in the vast complex of floors, corridors and their branches, cellars and vaults, the silent galaxies of isolated planets quietly going mad; nor which of the innumerable constellations housed his diminutive gray world.

The Honeybear—that is to say, the man who emptied the latrine buckets—whom he had never been allowed to look at but whom he glimpsed now and then behind his turned back out of the corner of his remaining eye, glimpsed as a small scurrying shadow, who (if the duty turnkey was the blue-eyed Yakovlev) occasionally whispered, whose soft and persuasive voice had reminded Abel of the young priest he had come across in Catherine's apartment, had once said (whispered) that there were fewer than three hundred cells in the Lubyanka complex, which was hard to believe. Because, whispered the Reverend Honey-bear, this wasn't a prison in the proper sense, that is to say a place where prisoners were imprisoned, but only a passing phase in a prisoner's journey to his Golgotha.

But Abel knew better.

This wasn't any phase, a disintegrating organism isn't concerned with phases. This wasn't even a location. It was an idea, a monument to silence, sleeplessness, and a great white light which went down all the way to the molten heart of the earth and then soared upward to brush against the sky.

He no longer knew how long he had been there. There were no longer nights or days, or hours. It had begun to seem to him that he had never been anywhere else; that his whole life (whatever that might have been at some forgotten, unimaginable time) had always pulsed under the ever-glowing light bulb, between the iron bucket, the gray walls which occasionally told him the seasons of the year, the narrow ledge of pine plank sunk into the wall, and the door . . . A lifetime measured in fifteen-minute intervals by the dry metallic click of the judas window.

(Click: and an eye regards him. Blank, impersonal. What color is the eye? Is it black, gray, or blue? The color of the eye has an important bearing on what may happen later.)

Click: and the eye is gone.

In fifteen minutes: click.

. . . The huge antique iron key begins to turn in the lock. He gets to his feet, turns. Faces the gray wall. He is not allowed to look at the guards, turnkeys, escorts, anyone.

He has seen single eyes in the Judas window. He has heard some voices. And shortly . . . shortly, it appears, he will hear more voices . . .

He will see two bright lights; even brighter than his ever-glowing light bulb . . .

The door opened. Or he thought it opened. Perhaps it was only a door of memory which was opening. (Footsteps are remembered.) A hard hand grasped his shoulder, turned him to face the door, the man behind the hand turning with him so that he (the man with the hand) remained hidden behind his (Abel's) back. The other necessary man has hidden behind the door.

—Outside!

. . . He is outside, or thinks that he might be. The corridor is long and narrow, a white line is painted down the center of the corridor and he places his feet carefully on the line, watches the line and thinks of phrases like *the party line, the line of least resistance,* and then *stand in line, family line, lifeline* and *cue line* and *the thin red line.* A thin red thread of continuity runs through his consciousness but its ends are lost in shadows which press in upon him and urge him to sleep. The two guards fall-in half a step behind him, where he cannot see them. —*Move!* He moves or perhaps he only thinks that he is moving. The feet move. He can see the feet walking on the line. He hears their shuffling movement, the slurred whisper of his gutted shoes on the concrete floor. He hears the snapping of the two guards' fingers in ragged rhythm, keeping time with the shuffling whisper. Snap-snap, whisper-whisper. They come to a corner. —*Halt! Close your eyes!* He closes his eyes. One of the guards goes forward and peers around the corner. —*Come up here! Turn right! Open your eyes!* He steps around the corner, takes his place on the white line, the guards take their places. —*Forward march!*

Snap-snap.

Forward shuffle.

Forward . . . What is *forward?*

It is motion from one point to another. *Ambulo, ergo sum.* From which point to what point? There is no point, that's the point. The motion is pointless.

Forward.

Snap.

Down the long corridor where everything is blurred.

Snap-snap.

Blank doors on both sides, mute iron rectangles. Then steps that lead up and steps that lead down. Up and down, snap-snap, the endless corridor. Snap. Turns and twists, many corners. —*Halt!* A halt at each corner. Why do the guards snap their fingers or jingle their keys? Oh, but he knows, of course; that is the red thread of continuity which parallels the white line, the signal to any other pair of guards who might be escorting another prisoner. The prisoners are not permitted to see each other. When a confrontation becomes inevitable one of the prisoners is put in a *kishka,* a long stone closet that starts about three feet below the level of the corridor, a niche in the wall for the invisible saint, a stone coffin that rises vertically twenty feet toward an invisible ceiling where there might be some diffused light from an invisible grating, and the prisoner, having been made invisible, waits in the *kishka* until the other prisoner and escorts have passed (equally invisible); he stands in the excremental darkness of the *kishka* and all its walls touch him simultaneously, and sometimes it may seem that the walls are moving inward, pressing the prisoner, and then the prisoner starts screaming . . .

Then, *forward* once more. Head down to watch the white line. (See the scaly brown bird's claw clutching the beltless waistband of what used to be trousers.) Must watch that white line. Toe the line. No, it is not a lifeline or a line of poetry or a comic line. A step to the right or a step to the left is an attempt to escape, thus it is more a death line, if there is such a thing, the one beyond the last line of resistance, the only reasonable line for a prisoner to take on his way to the interrogation room.

. . . The interrogation room is large and deep in shadow and the walls are whitewashed. There is something startling, even painful, about a clean whitewashed wall; it is so unlike the gray moist wall to which you are accustomed: one of the four gray concrete boundaries of your world . . . The whitewashed startling walls upset your equilibrium. (Forever afterward you will associate clean whitewashed walls with interrogation, you will associate a question with pain.) There is the wooden table, a cupboard for the straps and the metal rods, the broomstick, the hoe handles, the three-legged stool. There are the automobile headlights mounted on the table, the lights that burn red circles deep ino your brain, that blind you so that you may never see the face of the interrogator, that set your inflamed eyes on fire.

—Face the lights!

Always face the lights.

—Keep your eyes open, you son of a bitch!

. . . The faces hide behind the lights but the voices can't. The voices have color. There is a sharp red voice (Comrade Reitbaum) and the voice that bores into the brain with a yellow ice pick (Comrade Interrogator Grubov) and an insidious blue-green voice that drowns and suffocates (Comrade Assistant State Prosecutor Trepov).

. . . Of the three of them I'll take the ice pick any time. I've heard that they do it here . . . sometimes . . . at the end. When it is all over. Put the point of the ice pick up against the bony roof of the eye socket parallel with the nose and then wham! Two inches. Takes only three minutes. Called transorbital lobotomy . . .

(Never again feel anything afterward: no pain, unhappiness, fear, illusion, hunger, doubt . . . Never think or wonder. You function: you do what you are told.)

. . . Comrade Assistant State Prosecutor–Interrogator of the Second

Class Zaslavsky has a glaring white voice, as white as the headlights. That is the voice which stamps the scarlet circles on the brain. But there is something untrue about that voice, something fearful; its terrible intensity is marred by something secret, watchful, and withdrawn; it wavers at times, its beam becomes unfocused, and then one can rest. The white voice becomes particularly uncertain when yet another voice, this one a dark voice without definite color, is there to whisper to Abel in Polish. The dark voice is like a shaded night-light and whispers of sleep; it promises oblivion: rest and peace . . . it is the most dangerous voice of the lot. It isn't often that the featureless dark voice is there, but, when it is, then the interrogation is particularly painful. Not in the sense of physical pain inflicted but of mental agony endured. By this time there isn't much more physical pain that can be inflicted but there still seems to be an endless number of things to be endured: a part of the game.

(The voices take their turns in playing the game. The white voice begins it: name? occupation? nationality? father's name? occupation? mother's name? occupation? father's nationality? mother's nationality? religion? *Don't lie to us, you son of a bitch: we know all about you!*)

. . . That is the beginning of the game each time the game is played, and the game is played for minutes or for hours, each hour on the hour, or not at all for weeks at a time, and you are never allowed to suspect when the game might be begun or when it might end, but eventually the voices do get to the point and the point is inevitably painful if the dark voice happens to be there to whisper in Polish . . . It's not that the dark voice ever orders that pain be inflicted. On the contrary. The dark voice is never anything but a background presence. But this presence has a violent effect on the other voices.

(*When did you see him last?* Seven years ago. *You have seen him since then, we know that!* It's not true. *Don't tell us what's true, you son of a bitch, just answer the questions! What did he talk about?* How can I remember what happened seven years ago? *Answer the question, you son of a bitch.* I don't remember what he talked about. *We can remind you, want us to remind you?* You can try but you won't remind me of what I don't know. *You'd be surprised, you son of a bitch, of what we can remind you; what names did he name?* I can't remember him naming any names. *We know the names, you son of a bitch, now you tell them to us if you know what's good for you.* Sleep would be good for me. *You'll never sleep again until you tell us what we want to know; what were the names?* He never named any names to me. *But YOU'RE going to name them!* How can I tell you something I don't know? *We'll show you how, you son of a bitch, you were working for him.* That's not true. *Don't tell us what's true and what isn't, you son of a bitch, we know what is true!*

—Does the name Absalom mean anything to you? the dark voice asked softly.

—Certainly, in the Old Testament . . .

—Fuck the Old Testament, the white voice shouted, quavering. We know all about that, you son of a bitch!

—Then why is he asking?

—Shut up! said the red voice.

—Don't ask questions! said the blue-green voice.

—You're here to answer questions! said the voice like a yellow ice pick. Not to ask them!

—When did you see him last? Where?

—I told you . . .

—You told us nothing, you son of a bitch!

—Tell it to us again, you son of a bitch!

. . . And now that featureless, toneless dark voice said softly, patiently: Bring him around again, pick him up, stand him up again; and the white voice, grown pale, said immediately: Immediately, Comrade Commander! Stand up, you son of a bitch! Face the lights!

. . . And the dark voice said, reflectively: It seems to me that you yourself, Comrade Assistant State Prosecutor–Interrogator, could answer a few of those questions . . . And the white voice cried: I? I? Comrade Commander, how could I answer them? Well, said the dark voice but this time in Russian, weren't you one of Mendeltort's people at one time? Never! cried the white voice. Oh, I may have come across him here and there in the old days . . . Precisely, said the dark voice: Where? . . . Why, I don't remember, it was years ago, but many people knew him here then . . . ! Name a few, said the dark voice. Why, Comrade Commander, I wouldn't know where to begin! There were so many people! Even Comrade Stalin . . . ! *That,* said the dark voice, *is the one name that you need not remember, Comrade Interrogator,* but think of some others . . . I would advise you to give it some thought. He has been seen in Moscow . . . Does the name Absalom mean anything to *you?*

And the white voice cried, explosively: Certainly not! Except as something out of the Old Testament, as the prisoner has said . . . Why, is it important?

—That is the name that he used in Kiev, the dark voice said. I'm sure you'll remember with a little thought. It's part of his password.

—I'd . . . hardly know about anything like that, said the quavering white voice. And . . . Comrade Commander . . .

—Yes?

—May I go on with the interrogation?

—Certainly. Forgive me for interrupting your interrogation.

(*All right! All right, you son of a bitch, stand up, face the lights, when did you see him last? Seven years ago? I'll show you seven years ago, you son of a bitch!*)

And the dark, pleasant, cultivated voice, redolent of something that Abel could no longer entirely remember, a scene which included two old men hanging from a tree, said gently in Polish: You had begun to tell us about Absalom.

—Absalom . . . ?

—Yes. Don't you remember?

—Yes. Absalom . . .

—What do you know about him?

—Well, the quotation . . .

—Which quotation?

—Well, from the Old Testament . . . I can't quite remember.

—Could you refresh the prisoner's memory, Comrade Assistant State Prosecutor–Interrogator? You should remember a quotation from the Old Testament.

—Why should I, Comrade Commander? What does the Old Testament have to do with me? I am a Russian! cried the pale white voice.

—I beg your pardon, said the dark voice. I must have misread the personal statistics in your employment file. Such things do happen, even in our files. Remind the prisoner of the quotation, the first few words will do.

—*But Absalom sent spies,* whispered the pale voice.

—Where did he sent the spies? said the pleasant dark voice.

—*Throughout the tribes of Israel,* Abel said, or thought he was saying. *Saying, as soon as you . . . ye . . . hear the sound of the trumpet, then shall ye say . . .* say . . . ye say . . . shall say . . .

—Say what? said the dark voice.

—*Then shall ye say, Absalom reigneth in . . .*

—In what? Where?

—I don't know, said Abel.

—In Lwów? Was it in Lwów?

—Yes, perhaps, in Lwów.

—And in Warsaw? Tell me about Warsaw.

—Perhaps. It was. In Warsaw.

—And in Hebron?

—Absalom rules in Hebron, Abel said.

—You see? said the dark voice quietly, dangerously. He knows all about it. Isn't that the password?

And the white voice said, unfocused: I assure you, Comrade Commander . . . I *beg* to assure you . . . that I don't know anything about it!

—Well, said the dark voice. Please give it some thought, Comrade Assistant State Prosecutor–Interrogator, I'd strongly advise it. Comrade Zarubin isn't someone to trifle with, you know.

—Certainly, certainly, Comrade Commander, said the ill white voice. And if that son of a bitch knows anything about it I'll get it out of him!

(*Well, you son of a bitch, what do you know about it?* I don't know what you're talking about.)

—You know quite well, said the dark voice quietly. Otherwise how would you know your dear uncle's password?

—I don't know what you're talking about, Abel thought he said.

—Amazing, said the dark voice. Here is another one who doesn't know the password. Mendeltort certainly knows how to pick his people. But please go on with the interrogation.

(*Well now, you son of a bitch, are you going to talk? You must still have an unbroken bone somewhere in your body! You still have one fingernail left. You still have one eye!*)

. . . I don't know anything about him, I don't know anything about his organization, I don't know anything about passwords, I don't know any names, I don't know where he is or what he is doing, I don't know what you are all talking about . . .

(*Don't tell us what you don't know anything about, you son of a bitch! We'll make you tell us things you can't even dream of!*)

. . . Or would you like to stand at attention for another nine hours with your nose one centimeter from the wall, not touching the wall, no part of you allowed to touch the wall? After fifteen minutes you'll swear you're on the deck of a small boat in a hurricane at sea . . . and if you move without an order, if you sway out of line, if your hand trembles, if you touch the wall, or fall . . . that's an attempt to escape!

(*You son of a bitch!*)

He wondered if it was night or day and, if it was day, if the day outside was sunny or cloudy, or if it was raining, or if it was snowing, and thought how good it would be to feel the sun or the rain or even the snow on his face and body, and of how good it would feel to take a long walk in wide empty streets, to see the sky, a tree, an animal, a bird, and thought about wind and how that would feel in his hair and beard. All these were no longer part of his reality, they were the stuff of dreams rather than memory. He could no longer recall the feel of rain or sunshine, the tug of the wind. The thought of voices, people talking, laughter, a conversation, sweep of argument, exchange of ideas, or a moment of emotional and spiritual closeness with a human being, lay beyond all bounds of comprehension.

If such things still happened to somebody somewhere, and if they had ever happened to him, they were no nearer to him than mythology, legends, fairy tale: witches and spirits, warlocks and hobgoblins, *krasno-ludki*, Pan Twardowski contemplating his sins on the moon, unicorns and maidens . . . things read about, heard from a menopausal aunt but never seen, never experienced. He was quite sure that he had always been here, in this gray stone box under the merciless light bulb, while an eternity had clicked by to the measured opening and closing of the judas window.

. . . There is something the matter with a prisoner if he thinks he can get away with flights of fantasy, claims of innocence, silence . . . that he can break the rules of the game.

(*Comrade Reitbaum has a right to know what he wants to know. It is his duty to know. He wants to do his duty. What makes you think you may deprive him of his rights?* There is something seriously the matter with a prisoner if he thinks that *he* has any rights.)

. . . What my interrogators are saying is that I owe them my cooper-ation. If I refuse to give them what I owe them I am depriving them of what is rightfully theirs.

(*Talking to that son of a bitch is like talking to a wall!*)

Face the wall! Not touching the wall! One centimeter away from the wall!

(*Stand still, you son of a bitch!*)

. . . What the wall in my cell is saying is that the wall and the pris-oner have become wholly dependent on each other; without each other, neither would have a socially useful function. If it wasn't for the pris-oner there would be no need for the wall, and if there were no wall there'd be no prisoner. The prisoner wouldn't be there, and if he wasn't there he would be nowhere, because there is no longer any other place.

The wall was sweating.

His fingers were dry.

He sucked the spatulate dry fingers and spat at the wet wall. Love the wall, honor the wall, was what the wall was saying. He took excep-tion to what the wall was saying. He couldn't spit well without his front teeth.

. . . A prisoner who doesn't fear his jailors is an unnatural prisoner, he's not a socially useful object, he's not playing the game. If I break the rules of the game it is their duty to punish and mine to be punished. (*Get up! Stand up! Face the lights! Face the wall! Stand*

still! Answer all the questions! You son of a bitch!) Fear is to prisoners
what . . . ah . . . monuments are to heroes; they aren't supposed to
have a choice in the matter. If heroes and prisoners were offered a
choice there would be neither fear of jailors nor respect for heroes, instead there would be anarchy . . . Think of what would happen to civilization if there were neither prisoners nor heroes.

Honor Thy Interrogator and Thy Prosecutor: that's what the wall
was saying.

. . . Face the wall! Listen to the wall! Pay attention to what the wall
is saying! The wall is a socially useful object! You can learn a lot from
listening to the wall! The wall is mute and yet it makes a statement.
The walls and you are one, indivisible, mutually sustaining.

The finger left his mouth and pointed to the wall.

Hello, finger.

He looked at the finger.

The finger was mute, yet it made a statement. It had no fingernail.
All fingers have nails but Abel's had none; they had been punished for
not playing the game.

(*Comrade Zaslavsky knows what's good for you! He wants to teach
you that every man gets what he deserves!*)

The finger pointed at the light bulb. The light bulb glared down
from its wire cage. I only want to destroy you a little, said the glaring
light bulb.

. . . What the light bulb was really saying in its wire cage was that
there was no longer any night or day, nor were there weeks or years, and
that the prisoner had better make his peace with that or he would be
destroyed.

I'll make my peace with that, Abel told the light bulb, or I shall be
destroyed. You really will, you know, the wall said. The bucket murmured in agreement. You must become an object in harmony with all
the other objects, or you will not be a socially useful object and you will
be destroyed.

. . . If I can't sleep I shall be destroyed. And I will never again be
able to sleep because the light bulb won't permit it. That's why it is
there. The light bulb is a socially useful object, a part of the procedure
for repairing objects that aren't working right. And if I should have the
temerity to defy the light bulb and to close my one remaining solitary
eye even for a moment, the Judas window will betray me (that's why it
is there) and the guard will come in to wake me again.

None of this is malicious, the light bulb was saying. No one wastes
malice on a useless object. Malice is a useful instrument of terror,
wasted when misused. All that concerns us here is the repair of an object that isn't working right.

—I understand, said Abel.

You must become a socially useful object, the bucket yawned and said. The only useful function of an interrogated prisoner is to answer questions. A malfunctioning object is unnecessary and will be destroyed.

—Of course, Abel said.

He looked at his finger.

The finger pointed at the bucket.

. . . It's too late now, finger, you had your chance and you didn't take it. If you had done your pointing at the proper time you'd have a fingernail, all of your fellow fingers would have fingernails, you'd be proper fingers. As it is, you're no longer much of anything. You look like a sausage hit with a sledgehammer, run over by a steamroller . . . I wish you were a sausage so that I could eat you.

Yes. They were right. Of course. There was something seriously the matter with him. He was not afraid.

—There is nothing heroic about this lack of fear, he was quick to say. Please don't consider me at all heroic, I am not heroic, I leave that sort of thing to my monumental uncle, and to my late lamented military mentor. I am certainly imaginative enough to anticipate ordeals in my imagination and that, as anyone can tell, is what fear is mainly about. But for some reason I am not afraid. I am not cooperative about answering questions, a matter of my natural perversity, perhaps. It doesn't matter what the matter is because everyone has agreed that something is the matter, thus it is necessary to teach me the rudiments of fear, the foundation of respect which, in turn, is the basis of civilization.

There is nothing wrong with that particular idea.

The trouble was, perhaps, that he had always been an unresponsive student when the subject failed to interest him. For example, he had never been able to understand the point of algebra, he had never understood the need to solve problems in arithmetic. Reitbaum and Grubov and Trepov and Zaslavsky had a variety of ways to make their lessons memorable, they were responsible for his missing fingernails. The light bulb was responsible, indirectly, for the missing eye. Neither the light bulb nor RGT&Z were responsible for his missing teeth.

—That, Abel told the wall, is an ironic and unsolicited legacy from Major Tarski, my former military mentor, who couldn't keep his archaic consciousness from erupting on a public highway, who beat a deserter in a leather coat, which set in motion a series of later events.

But that was neither here nor there, at the moment. Correction. It was there. Everything that had happened there could be attributed to

the will of God. Everything that had happened here could be attributed to RGT&Z, although there was something about Z which
didn't quite put him in the same impersonal category as the rest of the
firm . . . something, ah, elusive . . . a quality of frenzy which was personal, which introduced an unexpected factor into this equation.

   . . . It is unthinkable for a prisoner not to answer questions. When
he doesn't have the answers at his fingertips, as it were, they are extracted from him one fingernail at a time, or beaten out of him across
the kitchen table with thin metal rods, and if the answers are unsatis-
factory, if the unnatural prisoner continues to violate the interrogators'
rights, he is introduced to the hot tar and the three-legged stool, and
straps and the leather vomit mask, and quite soon he begs to be allowed to answer every question. This is the natural procedure with unnatural prisoners and, with the inexplicable exception of Zaslavsky,
there is nothing personal about it. There is no malice. They are not malicious. They may seem inhuman but inhumanity is older than humanity, it is humanity's original condition, it is deeper-seated in mankind
than whatever humanity mankind had managed to learn, it is more
profoundly satisfying, it is emotionally more fulfilling than, even, affection . . .

   There is nothing cruel about the hot tar and the fingernails, the quarter rations and the 200-watt light bulb crouched in its wire cage, because one cannot be cruel to an object. There is something frightening
about Zaslavsky's wavering white voice because it is frightened but,
even there, I fail to see malice. Reitbaum and Grubov and Trepov and
Zaslavsky, and even that infinitely dangerous soft-spoken dark-voiced
senior partner, that Comrade Commander who terrifies Zaslavsky, only
want to repair a malfunctioning object. They're skilled technicians pursuing their trade. It is their duty to make such repairs. It is everyone's
duty to function as a useful object.

   (*Answer the question, you son of a bitch.*)

   . . . Well, perhaps, perhaps . . . What question . . . ?

   (*You're not to ask questions, you son of a bitch, you're to answer
them. It is your duty to answer the questions.*)

   . . . As things stand, Major Tarski said somewhere near the wall, you
never have been a very useful object. You failed to perform your functions as a soldier, you disobeyed my orders, you showed me disrespect
. . . You haven't done so well as a man either, have you; you haven't
been exactly successful as a human being . . . Stop asking questions
and start answering them, to yourself if to no one else . . .

   —Yes, sir.

   . . . And stand at attention when you talk to me. I am your superior
officer, you are a junior officer, and a reservist at that. When you ad-

dress a superior officer, you stand at attention. And why don't you ever do what is good for you?

—Because it is someone else who tells me what is good for me. I haven't yet decided.

—So many people know what is good for you, why haven't you decided?

—A matter of natural perversity, perhaps.

—You're a fool.

—I'm a human being.

—Ah, so that's what it is.

—That's what it is, Uncle.

—I hope you come to some decision while there's still some time.

(What time? There is no time. Time, in its proper sense, no longer exists. It has been abolished by the light bulb which makes it impossible to guess whether it is night or day.)

Abel stood at attention and looked at the light bulb. The light bulb was a most superior object. It had erased night and day, the hours and the seasons, and this gave it a natural superiority over every other object in the cell.

Abel's finger pointed at the light bulb. He said: Pow.

The light bulb spat at him.

I have no resources to cope with superior objects, Abel told himself. Hey, Brother Light Bulb, how about some compassion for a fellow object?

The light bulb spat white fire into his only eye.

The judas window clicked.

. . . It's all right, I'm awake, my eye is open, try in fifteen minutes.

Ha-ha, said the light bulb.

The eye may not be closed, said the judas window.

The wall leaned forward, the bucket gaped and whispered its dry secrets to the wall. They must be saying that there is something the matter with me, I have to be repaired.

. . . There must be something the matter with you for making them feel that you are not afraid, for failing to fear them, for shaking their belief in themselves, their power, and their function . . .

Be sensible, whatever that might mean, said the wall; accept the necessity for compromise, it is a necessity. And, besides, who'll know whether you talked or not? Walls don't gossip about people's secrets, they'll respect your problem. Why don't you tell them what they want to know? Be fair. Torturing is hard work; Comrades Reitbaum, Grubov, Trepov, and Zaslavsky don't enjoy it any more than you do. Their terror is as great as yours when the dark soft voice is present.

. . . Consider the dark voice which whispers to you in such flawless Polish..

Tell them something.

There's no need to think and no point in trying to remember . . .

(Except for one moment you can't quite forget and can't entirely remember: someone . . . an old priest or perhaps a military mentor . . . somewhere . . . saying something about the difference between an animal and man.)

. . . And now get up, walk up and down the cell, sit down and rest, breathe deeply, close your eye, concentrate on breathing. I am here and that's all, and eventually I shall be put elsewhere, and that is all that a prisoner in solitary confinement may safely allow himself to think.

Abel got up, did his best to stretch without falling, walked a few paces up and down the cell, felt dizzy, saw the floor revolving, sat down on the hard edge of the plank and got up again.

. . . Eight paces forward, march. Halt. About-face.

The gray wet wall makes another statement. It orders Abel to honor all superior objects, and follow the example of all his superiors and begin to perform socially useful functions. The floor in the interrogation room creaks instead of whispering, it is a brilliantly polished oak parquet that reflects automobile headlights and the gleaming white-washed wall . . . In the cellars . . . because he had also been led through the execution cellars to drive home a point . . . there is dripping water. The corridor personnel is changed every two hours, so that the worried Yakovlev isn't always there . . . the eye in the judas window isn't always the curiously compassionate cornflower-blue eye.

(*You'll tell us things you can't even dream of, you son of a bitch!*)

Tell them anything, said the wall, buy a little time.

Abel laughed.

. . . How can you buy something that doesn't exist? Time is an absurd concept in solitary confinement.

But tell them . . . something. How else can you prove that you have learned to fear them and will now obey them and that you're finally ready to be socially useful? And if you don't know anything about Mendeltort, why don't you make it up?

Nobody tells the truth in Russia, anyway.

The light bulb hissed in its wire cage. Listen, hissed the light bulb. I really feel like hurting this son of a bitch. You can't feel that, said the wall, we are not malicious, we feel only what we are permitted to feel and the regulations forbid us to feel malice; there can be no malice toward a prisoner, the regulations for the treatment of prisoners in the correctional institutions of the Soviet Union forbid malicious torture, the regulations are quite clear about that.

But I am going to hurt him a little, anyway, the light bulb whispered. Well, just a little then, said the wall.

Now came the nausea. His body was a black void begging to be filled. His stomach had become a tightly wound, intricate knot of pain twisted about nothing, like the quipu cords of the Incas, foretelling the future. His body was contorted as if to make itself smaller, reduce the emptiness, and his breath was rattling in its cage of ribs. Strange objects bobbed and weaved in the corners of his shrunken vision but he knew that they were only the fevered products of a starved body and a mind that was escaping the bonds of time and place. Some dusty groove of memory played festive music while visions of heaping dishes, smoking tureens of borsch thick with sour cream, Easter confections, the gargantuan twelve-course spread of a Polish Christmas, mocked him and tormented. He gnawed his fingers wishing that he might sleep and forget the hunger.

Then he was numb, beyond thought or feeling, an ecstasy of pain and illumination that made him mercifully fleshless. His face was wet and icy. Since he was no longer able to sweat he knew that the freezing wetness must have been made by tears. He heard a distant malevolent chuckle and knew it was his own and this sound, as much as the iced tears, brought him for a moment out of the void in which he was spinning.

First you talk to inanimate objects, says the prison lore, and that's all right, that does no harm; you talk to yourself and that too is harmless as such things are reckoned. Then you weep consciously or unconsciously and that, while harmless in itself (and in fact somewhat beneficial as an outlet for everything that you can't express and don't dare to feel), is a forerunner of the end. When you start chuckling you will soon be laughing at the top of your voice (Yakovlev had been quite explicit about that) and then it's only a short step to screaming, and once you start to scream you can never stop.

So, Brother Wall, he said wearily, let us continue our dialogue; lend me your imperturbable surfaces, give me the mercy of your blank imperviousness, or I will start to tell you such legends and myths as will undermine us both.

I do not wish to crumble.

It is, you see, essential to make some sound, otherwise I become a prey to thought, visions, and imagination and that creates cravings for the unattainable: the sensations which can no longer be permitted to exist.

. . . And now the antique key is rattling in the keyhole. A bar is dropped. A bolt begins to slide. They are about to open the door.

Abel took up his prescribed position with his face to the gray wall opposite the door, hands folded behind him. (It is forbidden to look at the guard.) In six months he had never seen one except the puzzled Yakovlev: a greenish blur, a silent though not ungentle machine that shook him awake. (It is forbidden to sleep until you are condemned; a prisoner under interrogation may not sleep.) He had not seen another prisoner, except a stolen glimpse or two of the Honeybear-priest. Perhaps there were no other prisoners. Perhaps he and the Honeybear and the invisible guard, a demonic though impersonal presence like the dark voice which no longer whispered, were all that was left of a lost human race.

And a world well lost, I should say.

Catherine had made it clear as she whispered her poem across the ruin of their hopes. She had seen the eternity of things that pass away and the infinity that lies hidden in the finite. He (Abel, poor fool) could only see the diversity of things: divisions, limitations.

And in the meantime they were opening the door.

. . . Catherine had been emphatic about it in that intense moment; she had been offering him a part of herself that he hadn't supposed anyone still possessed. The supernatural power of an active love. The alchemist's stone. Perhaps an early Christian, unburdened by the dreadful shadow of St. Paul, could have expected it; to Abel it had been a shocking revelation. They had looked across the body of the little man kicked among broken plates, and neither the bulky Russian nor the pale young Jew in the leather coat nor his sweating round companion with the face of a ruined boxer could distort the message. In that moment which was the end of one reality she had begun to construct another.

He laughed.

Click.

Should he pretend to stretch, yawn . . . turn his head a little and look at the eye?

The eye would be regarding him for some moments before the door was opened. Then the door would open. Then his rations would be laid on the floor just inside the door. If the eye was blue, the guard would be Yakovlev. Then a rolled and lighted cigarette would be laid on the floor. There'd be no cigarette if the eye was of another color. A gray eye, flecked with green, would mean a convoy to the interrogation room but that hadn't happened for some time. He could turn slightly around before the door was opened and look at the eye and know whether or not to expect a lighted cigarette, a moment of oblivion, but he didn't want to see the eye if it was not blue. If he didn't know the color of the eye he could continue to hope for his cigarette for a few minutes longer. When the door closed again (and the dull booming slam was now as much a part of his consciousness as his pulse and heartbeat) he'd be allowed to turn around, face the room and door, and run toward his rations and his cigarette. The eye would watch him until he had finished with both.

. . . Well, it is either seven o'clock in the morning or seven at night. Otherwise they wouldn't be opening the door.

Had he been on full rations he would have been able to tell night from morning. A blue-enameled cup full of thick black coffee and one hundred grams of black rye bread would mean that it was morning. One hundred grams of bread and a tin bowl of turnip soup would mean that it was evening. But, although he was no longer questioned very often, he had not yet been officially condemned; he was on quarter rations, the necessary mental and physical conditioning for interrogations. There was no soup, no coffee. And fifty grams of bread in the morning looks just like fifty grams of bread at night, and the nights and the days had become blurred in the white glare of the light bulb and in the hands of the invisible guards who shook him awake.

The door was opening. Abel put his forehead against the sweating wall and heard the door opening. He heard a footstep, then he heard another, then he heard a man breathing. The door closed, the key rattled again in the keyhole. The iron bar fell into its twin hooks and the bolt slid home. The guard rapped on the door, the judas window clicked to accommodate the eye, and Abel turned around, saw the eye (it was cornflower blue), saw the clumsily rolled brown-paper cigarette which lay on the floor with twin thin plumes of blue-gray smoke curling toward the ceiling, noted the piece of brown bread which lay on the floor. He stumbled toward them, seized the cigarette before it could go out and drew in a lungful of bitter harsh smoke. He was immediately dizzy. He sat on the floor. The smoke filled him, masked the emptiness. After a long moment he lay on his back, unable to sit, and smoked until the gray ceiling ceased to pulse, the light bulb stopped revolving in chaotic circles, and the blood began to return to his head. The coal of the cigarette was wedged redly between the yellow blisters and black burns on his thumb and forefinger but he still sucked at what was left of the thick black *mahorka* and the coarse veins of tobacco leaves.

The frosted concrete flowed like lava, forming globules, bubbles of gray air that seemed to be eyes that stared at him with chilly indifference. Cold frosted walls meant late autumn or the start of winter.

If this was really autumn, yet another autumn, then he had been in Lubyanka for about eight months, which meant that he had been imprisoned for at least a year, which made next to no difference to him at this point. Time was a game, a conspiracy like civilization; neither existed without an agreement between philosophers and policemen. He believed that he had not been out of his cell for at least five months. Perhaps it was six. Late spring or early summer (a hot day in the cell, and the wall was dry) was the last time that he had been asked questions about Uncle Avrum. At least, he *thought* that this had been the last time; reality had acquired totally new dimensions and all events had become superimposed on each other. His uncle had been seen in Kiev, on his way to Moscow. Or perhaps it had been the other way around. Or perhaps that interrogation had taken place only a few days ago, and he was thinking about another interrogation. His private calendar was totally confused, entire blocks of pages had been lost, the entries had become illegible, and all the names and places and voices and faces—with the exception of one face, one voice, one whispered poem —had become disarranged. He thought that he must have been arrested about a year ago, and thought that he remembered the first of his prisons, the old Polish military prison of Zamarstynow in Lwów, which the NKVD had taken over, and where he stood on his feet for ten days in a twelve-man cell that contained more than eighty men. But perhaps that had not happened at Zamarstynow, perhaps that happened in the train which carried eighty men wedged upright in each boxcar, upright and frozen to each other as the transport crept through a month of nights across the Russian winter. Out of the hundred boxcars, or eight thousand men, only a score or two had still been alive when the dead and living were pried away from each other in a Moscow night. Then there had been another prison, a transit prison, probably the prison of Butyrki (although he didn't know what prison it had been), but all that he thought that he could remember from that prison was the unending roar of twenty thousand voices, the crush of bodies stacked and piled in layers, a Babel of languages, fights to the death over crusts of bread. Then there was the silence and isolation of Lubyanka. When he could still be bothered to remember this and all that followed, it was with a sense that it had not happened to him, that it had happened (if it had happened at all) to someone whom he had met in one of the prisons, someone whom he didn't know and for whom he felt little sympathy or concern. His interest in memory was mild, as though he were leafing through typescripts of old plays in which he may have acted in some other lifetime.

And now he noted that the ceiling had acquired ribs which moved in and out, so that he felt himself contained in the gut of a large beast.

He had been swallowed and the beast was digesting him. The wisps of smoke from his last cigarette could no longer be there. Surely, he hadn't had a cigarette for at least ten hours. But he could see the smoke, thick as cables, luminous and pneumatic in blue-green neon and fluorescent purple. The light bulb pulsed, the white light bored into his brain, and blinded him to all but the distorted fragments of a memory he wanted to forget, his last remaining memory of another lifetime, his final link with a reality other than his own.

He lay on the plank, hidden within himself, while the white light trod upon his head, grinding down the images. There is one! Hunt her down, stamp out her memorable face, the feel of her body. Exorcise the last residue of my myth. If I think about her, I shall be destroyed.

. . . They had kicked down the door, flooded us with light while the ghosts of our hopes and new affirmation, the magical animals of silent communion, scampered and squeaked. The ruins of our Last Supper, the sacramental pledge over the bread and the wine, grated under their iron-studded boots in shards of crockery; I couldn't face the sudden ice in her eyes, the lost half smile that would have frozen summer. The little Hungarian had felt it coming, you could tell, he had become uneasy as four o'clock drew near, he would have known that this was their favorite time for kicking down doors (all scientifically worked out, don't you know, as the time of a man's deepest sleep, the hour before the dawn that is called the nadir of oblivion) and he had been nervous; and they, the modern Temple guards complete with a Judas, went about the ancient ritual and led him from our Last Supper to his imitation Golgotha in the snow outside.

She had been turned into a statue of crystal and ice and I was full of worship I couldn't express. Dostoyevsky had talked about a White Christ coming out of Russia but all we had was a little Red Hungarian in a cracked oilskin coat . . . No Great Passion there, don't you see, no capital letters, just a small personal act of faith for him and for us.

I had wanted to pile flowers at her feet, light candles, offer pennies to the poor. In that climactic moment she had become the focus of all my ambitions. If there had been bronze bells to ring I would have swung on ropes like Quasimodo, I would have chanted, I was ready to declaim, but so much had become compressed into that moment that there was neither time nor will to do anything. We had such hopes, you see, we had silently arrived at such a conclusion; and suddenly it was all chopped down in one invisible stroke, that unexpected and unearned bolt of lightning that never fails to strike, the whim of the supremely ironical entity, the Monstrous Comedian, and both of us knew it. We looked at each other but whatever we were mutely saying was lost in the roars and crashes of a collapsing world. To tell the truth, I could think of nothing to say until she began speaking; she seemed to say much more from the start: she made a definite promise. Love is a sustaining energy, she said; compassion is triumph. All I could say then, and later under inquisition arc lights, was that I had made a mistake to bring her to Mendeltort's apartment, but who could have guessed what would happen there? There had been nowhere else to go. Nowhere else for her to come later.

She had been eloquent in her silence. My silence had been incoherent with apologies, wild leaps of the imagination that denied reality. She made the promise and I echoed it, a vow of commitment to a principle which is still unclear . . . But to the devil with principles; they can be melted down and poured into whatever mold suits the convenience, personal pride, and prejudice of the moment; what matters is People, and that was part of the promise she was making. Yes, she was distinct. We were no farther than ten feet away from each other but this distance might as well have been the breadth of the universe; we both knew, you see, that we would never again come closer to each other. Deserts and ice wastes were opening between us; it was the final nearness we would be allowed. There was an instant affirmation of our pledge: a defiant refusal to play at a game where everybody cheats, a furious insistence that there was something else . . . what, where, it didn't matter at that moment. We were the alchemists of the twentieth century, yes, we could change the nature of man.

The moment was intense. Then it passed. That stairwell was like a ladder driven into the bowels of the earth. I fell into that bottomless pit, out of the brightest light imaginable into the deepest imaginable darkness. On the stairs, that pale little swine in the leather coat suddenly remembered where we had met. I had recognized him from the start, although he had been far less martial when Tarski had attacked him, responding to God only knows what archaic impulse. (Oh, he said. He beat me like a dog, like a dog. And I said, perversely, that Tarski would never strike a dog or any other worthwhile animal. I said that Tarski might, occasionally, accidentally, step on a piece of dogshit. And he had shouted, *You will pay for this, you will all pay for this, and for so much more,* as if he were an accountant for history, as though he carried lists of injuries engraved on stone tablets. And I said something foolish, something proud, and he said something equally foolish and quite as proud, and that set in motion a sequence of events that led to loss of teeth. Such a gratuitous little injury after the thunderbolt.)

. . . But what I'm trying to say, Brother Wall, is that the moment when Catherine and I were one, when we knew that we were facing our last instant together, when we spoke to each other despite the icy galaxies suddenly thrown between us, it was like taking a ride on a comet!

Click, went the shutter of the judas window; less a sound to be heard than an impression of an eye.

Then he was seized and shaken. The great white light revolved and settled into place on the bridge of his nose. The light bulb crept back into its wire cage. The wall no longer flowed, the bubbling eyes had closed. The concrete had stopped breathing. The cables had dissolved. The ribs of the beast had withdrawn, he had not been crushed.

He got off the bench, each of his movements separate and distinct, as if to rise in any other way might confuse him, and took a slow turn about the cell: a matter of discipline so that he would no longer throw himself on his food like a starved animal.

Eight paces up and down, three across. And watch the empty bucket in the corner. He kept to an imaginary white line painted down the middle of the floor, as he would do if still escorted by the shepherds of pain. A step to the right or the left of the center line . . .

His posture was characteristic, he supposed: the shuffling walk, head down to watch the floor, left hand holding up loose trousers. No buttons, of course. That's the first thing they take away from you, along with any belts, suspenders, braces, shoelaces, and the lining of your coat. Odd bits of string gathered in transit prisons, twigs threaded through the waistband, and one bent pin (a closely guarded secret) held his clothes more or less together.

Three times up and down the cell and he began to lose consciousness.

I must look like a skeleton, he thought . . . must exercise, must learn to breathe properly again, must not think and must not remember anything but an existence bounded by the wall, the bucket, and the light bulb, the iron door and the judas window.

He took up the little piece of bread, halved it (careful not to spill and lose a single crumb), wrapped one half in a torn-off fragment of his shirttail. He began to eat the other piece. Mindfulness was the key. I am chewing, he told himself. This is nourishment. The mind's diffuseness must be overcome, the mind must always be the contemplated object.

Shaking from head to foot now, but perfectly aware of what he was doing, he licked his fingers until every crumb had disappeared. He unwrapped the bread in the shirttail, looked at it, and battled temptation. He wrapped the bread once more and stowed it safely in his trouser leg.

Transports are called without notice. A meal might be missed. Once missed, a meal can never be replaced.

The bread would stay inisde his trouser leg until he was given another piece in twelve hours.

Mendeltort

THE THUNDEROUS TATTOO BEATEN UPON HIS EARDRUMS resolved itself into sharp knocking on his cellar door, and gradually the dim room took shape around him, the shadows firmed. Night and the dawn assault of uncharacteristic thought, the residue of illness, began to recede. He struggled out of sleep and the morass of fever, feeling as though he had been struck between the eyes with a sledgehammer; nothing was fresh and new, the day had not brought a virginal beginning but only a continuation of what was, surely, an endless night in which time, space, and nature obeyed ironic rules, most of them hideously complex. The endless spiraling shapes of his vanished friend-ships escaped him again.

. . . And in the meantime, the knocking had awakened him, contin-ued, the door opened slowly. The toothless old woman stood there, smelling of potatoes, looking like chaos and old night.

He sat up on the straw pallet while she averted her eyes with the false modesty of an ancient hag who had seen everything, to whom nothing could ever be new, who couldn't be astonished. He took the tin cup of hot black acorn coffee, said, as each morning: Any news?

She cackled, threw a stained pile of newspapers onto his bed.

—That's not the news I mean, he said.

—It takes time to find people in this town, she said evasively.

—And it takes money, right?

She grinned, said nothing. He took his wallet out of his shirt, drew out a bank note, held it out to her. She clutched at it but he drew it back, out of her reach.

—It's a big town, she said.

—It has to be today.

—Yes, yes, today, she assured him. Or perhaps tomorrow . . .

—Or perhaps you already know where he lives and how I can find him but want to keep me here, paying you, for a little longer?

She grinned, cackled, and clutched at the bank note. —It's sure to be today. You can't stay here much longer. Too many people know.

—It's good to know we understand each other, Zinaida Natanovna, he said.

—Why do you want to find this man, anyway? she said.

—He's an old friend.

—What's a friend? They come and they go.

—I need him for something.

—You might get more from him than you're bargaining for.

—You don't know what I'm bargaining for or what I need him for. Just find him, he ordered. It has to be today.

—Yes, yes, she said. Today. I know.

She went out.

He sipped the coffee in the gray room. The dull flyspecked window had darkened imperceptibly and large drops of rain began to splash against it.

The newsprint blurred before his eyes, told him little: the eight-hour working day and the six-day workweek had been reintroduced by order of the Supreme Soviet, which meant that industry was being put practically on war footing, while *Pravda* was reassuring Germany that she had nothing to fear in the east and could turn her entire attention against England. *There is a deliberate attempt to cast a shadow on Soviet-German relations,* said the editorial . . . *wishful thinking on the part of certain British, American, Swedish, and Japanese gentlemen who seem incapable of grasping the fact that the good-neighborly relations between the Soviet Union and Germany are not based on temporary motives* . . . Sir Stafford Cripps had been appointed the new British ambassador in Moscow, and that could mean something . . . and Trotsky had been murdered in Mexico City. The arm of the *kinto* was long and his vengeance was implacable, but Mendeltort didn't need *Pravda* to tell him about that.

A note on the back page, announcing the promotion of V. M. Zarubin of the Commissariat of Internal Affairs to lieutenant general, sent him off on a speculative track.

Today, perhaps, he would know. As in the old days, in the magic years of certainty and action for the sake of action, not in these years of plotting and maneuvering, everything would depend on David.

He finished his cup of coffee, lit a cigarette.

A great human drama was unfolding at the moment over British skies but Tass was trying to hide it in statistics. Again he felt a measure of regret: without warning, with no logical transition, he seemed to have lost his capacity for excitement.

It'll pass . . . it'll pass, he assured himself. His illness had probably much to do with it. This new icy coldness was probably not the human failure that he imagined it to be. And even if it were . . . well, what is failure? . . . even death may have a living purpose in it. Passion and excitement always die a little when innocence is lost.

He got off his pallet, the lumpy sack of straw and wood shavings that combined the functions of the rack and the wheel, and made a perfunctory search for fleas and lice. This had become a ritual of a kind, a stylized ballet: each movement conventionalized and precise. The fingers danced along seams, probed in cuffs . . . but the night phalanx of insects had marched off before dawn. The ants were still staggering up and down the north wall under their immemorial little burdens, but there were few thoughts to spare for the destiny of ants. He put on his boots.

The old woman was sweeping out the narrow passage outside his door, a strip of paving stones looted from a Jewish cemetery; he could decipher the sign of the owl underfoot, a worn six-pointed star: the mystery of its harmonious flow out of and into itself, the interwoven continuity of all things, was a kind of omen. The old woman stared at him, astonished, then the gray lines dissolved, the rheumy eyes retreated into their ambush of wrinkles, and only the toothless mouth gaped open in a sly idiot grin.

—You're going out?

—Yes.

—Are you coming back?

—Well now, Zinaida Natanovna, he said, grinning in his turn. Who can tell?

—But you never go out, the old woman said.

—I'm going out today.

—But it's dangerous out there.

—Maybe it's not as dangerous as you say.

—But don't you want to wait until we find your friend?

—I think you've found him. If I go away for a little while maybe you'll remember where he is.

—There may be something to that, the old woman said. But how will I tell you what maybe I'll remember if you don't come back?

—Tell me now and you won't have to worry about it.

The old woman cackled, blinked, and hunched forward, leaning on her broom. —Listen, she said. I will tell you one thing that is truth itself. It is no good for you to be in the streets. Don't go out in the big streets. You stick out like a sunflower in a cabbage patch.

—Maybe I'll walk on my knees, do you think that'll help?

—Laugh, laugh, go ahead and laugh, but I'm telling you, I know. First time I saw you I knew. Anybody can tell about a man like you. And it don't help what you walk on, see?

—Don't tell me you're worried about me, Mendeltort said, and laughed.

—I don't worry about anybody but me and I don't worry much about me either. What's an old woman like me got to worry about? You live a little longer, then you die. You die and you don't have to worry about living. So what's there to worry about? But not even a turkey puts his head under the ax.

—As you say, Zinaida Natanovna, they have to catch the turkey first.

—Well, it's your neck, she said. But if you come back tonight I'll know about your friend.

—I'd rather you told me now. It's time to be moving.

—You have that feeling, eh? Well, sometimes you can tell by the feeling, and sometimes you can't. I know about men like you, you see a lot in time in a place like this. You're not the first who stayed here and you're not the last. Some stay long, some go quickly, that's the only difference.

—It's best not to stay too long in one place, Mendeltort said. Isn't that so?

She shrugged, evasive. —That's what they say. But who's to say they're right? The hare runs from one place to another and the dogs get the hare. The gray fieldmouse sits quiet in a hole and the hawk doesn't see it. But a man like you . . . well, who can tell . . . yes, I think it's better that you go away.

Then she said with sly wonder: But what luck you have! It isn't always the same with men like you, but if you have this luck it lasts.

—What luck is that? he said. To be sick as a dog?

—You have changed, changed . . . You wouldn't know yourself if you saw a mirror. You're thin, you look old. The fever's taken a lot of your hair. You're yellow like a Chinaman. Your beard's all gray. You could walk up to one of them headhunters right now and they'd never know you.

—Have they been looking for me around here?

—Well, she said. You must know how it is. You've been here a long time. Nobody around here talks about anybody else, but when you're a long time in one place . . .

He nodded and she also nodded, sitting huddled in her shawls and kerchiefs, the voluminous gray skirts, looking down while he got some money from his pockets and handed it to her. He couldn't read the expression in her eyes. It lay somewhere between derision and pity.

Whatever she knew or had guessed or merely supposed would remain with her unless she chose to share it; it would do no good to ask her, he knew well enough.

She had sheltered him as long as she could, or thought that she was sheltering him, which was the same thing; she had kept her end of the unspoken bargain of the shadow world.

—Where will you go? she said, and when he merely shook his head she added: Take my advice, leave Moscow. Rest up in the country. It takes a while to get right, ill as you've been. I got a cousin, lives up around Orsha . . . an old woman like me . . .

—Maybe I'll do that, after I see my friend.

She thought for a long moment, looked away, then said: Are you sure about this man? That he is still your friend?

—Sure as I think I can be.

—A man could change . . .

—I have a need to see him, Zinaida Natanovna, he said carefully. That's all I can say.

She nodded, took a scrap of paper from under her shawls, deep from the pockets of aprons and skirt, and handed it to him, but he had never heard of the street or its quarter. —Where is this? he asked.

—Behind the Lubyanka, she whispered.

—Is it a new development, or what?

She nodded once, said: Your friend has gone up in the world. But tell me one thing.

—What?

—If you have such friends, why are they looking for you?

—Such friends as what? he said, feeling his heart beat up, but she only stared at him curiously, shrugged, and looked away. —All right then, he said. Now you tell me something. How long have you had this address?

She grinned, cackled. —How can a poor old woman remember everything?

—So it's not such a big town after all.

She nodded.

She brought his cardboard suitcase out from behind the door and handed it to him and said: May you have a wide road, as they say in Poland.

She was no longer looking at him but beyond him. It was a look he knew. He had once more become an invisible man, a shadow within shadows.

He went up the short flight of worn steps to the upstairs passage, through the motes of dust revolving in the sunlight to the door, and so on, out of shadow and out of the house. The quick violent October rain

had washed the morning clean and the air was clear. One might see far
off a mountain peak on a day like this. The still sadness of a Russian
autumn conjured up memories, resurrected dreams. Each shadowed
cave of memory was suddenly clear.

. . . A loudspeaker croaked remotely: *The German losses were one
hundred and eighty-five planes, the British lost twenty-five . . . ten
British pilots bailed out over England* . . . and another voice, this one
nonmetallic, chuckled and said: Well, at least those German bastards
are getting it in the neck from somebody . . .

And another said: The longer they're busy there, the longer it'll be
before they look at us . . . And yet another said: Well, Stalin knows
best, it's all in his hands . . . Still, to be allied to those bastards,
well . . .

The city glowed before him like a dome of light. His feet moved mechanically along the railroad tracks, and his brain ground out absurd
images: Mendeltort, traveling with a cardboard suitcase stuffed with
counterfeit, is met at the Smolensk station by the ghost of his
unlamented youth . . . a collage of Meyer, David, and Anatole Lopatsky . . . who laughs into his face. He also laughs, grimaces, makes
lunatic gestures . . . Because who but a madman arranges his own capture? Insanity will have come full circle when he insists on choosing his
own executioners.

He breathed easier once streets closed about him and the remnants
of the work-bound morning crowd enfolded him in numbers, but this
protection was illusory, he knew. Moscow had its own timetables of
safety yet they had never made provision for the surreptitious man.
How to avoid one band of pursuers who would be after him for what
might be called purely routine reasons, as natural as breathing in this
new Byzantium, and simultaneously bait a plausible trap for wholly
different hunters, was a difficult matter. He would have to allow himself to be caught by Zarubin's people while avoiding the *kinto*'s routine
executioners, and only a genuine capture would convince Zarubin that
he held all the cards in whatever game he wanted to play. Mendeltort
didn't know why Zarubin's men had tracked him across Russia, why
Zarubin pursued him with such determination; he had never had anything to do with Zarubin and with the subtleties of power that this
shadowy Russian represented. If what he suspected of Zarubin's function was at all possible in the dark and brutal labyrinth of Russia,
where cold dissembling and intrigue were the only political realities,
then getting to Zarubin was necessary for him. How to get to Zarubin
was another matter. (The Devil isn't listed in the telephone directory.)
And since in Russia, since time immemorial, only the fallen and imprisoned great had ever received respectful attention (since all important

Russians, from the times of Ivan the Terrible to the Great Stalin, always expected to be themselves sooner or later among the fallen and imprisoned) Mendeltort led his pursuers step by step toward his own capture. It was a risk, he knew, but it was hardly the first risk he had ever taken, and the prize, he thought, justified the possibility of a dreadful error. His own Moscow friends had vanished in the execution cellars of the GPU and in the Gulag camps of the Arctic Circle, along with twenty million others who had to be killed to make an example that no Russian would ever forget. Legend and time had turned these victims of the *kinto*'s terror into benevolent Santa Clauses whose hands were only accidentally crimson, yet to deny some virtue to these men would be to apply criteria as narrow as those of Stalin. Whoever had not vanished, had diminished. Mendeltort knew that he had no one on whom he could depend, other than himself. Meanwhile, the dull uncharacteristic ache he had noted in the roof of his skull had become a pain. Time and the self-perpetuating deceit of the twilight world seemed to have eroded the traveler as well as the road. Certainly, the star-blown northern sky had blurred, his mouth was parched with the residue of fever, and his skin crackled like dry parchment when he stretched his lips.

An old potato seller, a brown crone, stared at him with knowing eyes and winked. He hurried away.

He was alone and conscious of aloneness, suddenly detached from that procession of tormented and dispossessed people in which he had wanted to be the link between vanished thousands and the millions who followed without even knowing that they were in motion. To be a lone shadow among lesser shadows was no new experience; indeed, there was a certain blessing in aloneness. But loneliness was something else again. One had to have some sort of faith in life, the process couldn't be entirely without meaning, and faith needed a sense of purpose and commitment, an irrational ideal with which to counter the myths, ghouls, and vampires of a lunatic reality. This needs companionship, even for the strongest.

For the lonely man, he knew, there is no greater disillusionment than life itself, and he had guarded himself against this paradox of idealists with the memory of friendships. Now mountains seemed to have fallen on the long devious path behind him, the landmarks were buried; his friends had stepped into another world and left him alone. He would have done better to have placed his faith in callousness, cynical brutality, and the denial of the humanity of others, to look at terrorism as an artistic and international profession in which the art of perfidy is practiced for its own sake, but to have done that would have destroyed his purpose, as he understood it.

And now he was feeling really ill, he had to sit down and rest for a moment.

He entered a small park, picking up several newspapers from a wire basket to serve as disguise. In the park, six small boys were playing war. *Bang, you're dead!* They saw him coming and watched him with a sudden quick solemnity. He averted his face. Fatigue and illness made him tremble. Old scars were aching deep under his skin. His replacement, that next necessary lunatic, was long overdue. An oppressive silence filled him with foreboding and he blessed the small warriors for their resumed noise; their bloodless little massacres kept his senses working. He couldn't afford one careless move, an amateur conspirator quickly became a dead one. (*Bang bang.*) He had long suspected that there were twin ideologies at work in the *kinto*'s Proletarian Paradise, an exoteric one for the masses, and a highly secret esoteric doctrine for the inner circle, something that would appeal to the primitive Georgian superstitions of the Greatest Living Man and Father of the Peoples, something suited to the madhouse and house of horrors that Russia had become. One only had to look next door at the Nazi madhouse, with its theories of a hollow earth and eternal ice, and Germans had never been less rational than Russians. In Russia, the crackpot genetics of Lysenko had already dismantled modern science, so why should not the other, the unmentionable, be possible too? It appealed to Mendeltort's sense of the absurd to suppose that a system based on science and history, where all was reduced to matter and man to a machine, where morality had become expediency and terror was the logical system for administration, should contain a semi-mystical core above the reasoning intellect. How logical, he thought, how very Russian to abolish God in order to elevate a Devil.

He picked up a newspaper and hid behind it from the little warriors. Out of the corner of an eye he saw another man approaching and watched him until he sat down on the bench, took bread and sausage from a paper bag, and began to eat. The sudden smell of garlic made his stomach twist.

The headlines told him nothing that he didn't know. In the west, England was besieged, her lifelines torn by bombs and torpedoes, and the Western Alliance had fallen apart. *We now see,* last week's *Pravda* told him, *how great is the responsiblility of the English imperialists, who, by rejecting the generous peace offers of Germany, set off the Second Imperialist War in Europe.*

There was some frantic speculation about Hess in England and, as if to compensate for an unmentionable fear that England and Germany might be negotiating peace, the Supreme Soviet had created new military ranks. There were to be no more comrade commanders of whatever class, officers without badges. The Red Army was now reequipped with generals and colonels. Mendeltort wondered how soon the hated Tsarists shoulder boards would be introduced to the People's Army, and when the new religion might be proclaimed, and what would end as the last vestigial remnant of the Revolution. The violence of the newspaper attacks on Great Britain, now identified as the imperialist agressor, had the kind of frenzy with which primitive man must have appeased suddenly awakened spirits of evil . . . All of it had the surreal quality of a rain dance, the fearful stirring of primeval doubt.

Young men in baggy blue serge, young women in white berets, were walking self-consciously up and down the gravel and concrete paths, stiff as puppets, their faces puritanical. They seemed at great pains not to touch each other. The small boys' war had given way to an armistice of boredom and dwindled to skirmishing around an ornamental pond. There was a quick silence. Mendeltort looked up, saw an urchin studying him intently, was immediately aware of his foreign clothes.

The park had suddenly become as dangerous as the streets, the boys weren't smiling. It occurred to him that he hadn't seen a smile for months, neither in Kiev nor here, nor anywhere else along his road from Lwów, as though the process of expressing joy was as foreign in Russia as his overcoat.

Unsmiling, he said: Whom were you fighting?

The boy looked at him as though he were insane.

—The hereditary enemy, who else?

The man who sat on the bench beside Mendeltort had finished his meal. He looked at Mendeltort with mild curiosity. He laughed. Mendeltort cursed the uncharacteristic diffusion of his mind, forced his attention to the boy, aware of sudden danger.

—Yes, who else? he said, and then, before he could stop himself: And did you win?

—We always win, the boy said, suspicious. We're the Russians. What's wrong with you, anyway? Who are you? Why do you look like that?

—And who is now the hereditary enemy? Mendeltort asked quickly. Still the Japanese?

—That was last summer, stupid, the boy said.

—Of course it was. What can I be thinking? It wouldn't be the Germans, would it, or the Poles?

—That too was last year. And anyway, we conquered the Poles.

—And who is it now?

—Why, the boy said, are you stupid or what? England is now the hereditary enemy, everyone knows that.

—Of course, Mendeltort said. There's always the hereditary enemy.

—Well, I should think so, the boy said, indignant.

The man on the bench laughed again, slapped his knees, said: There's a little soldier! A sharp little monkey, eh?

He regarded Mendeltort curiously out of pale blue eyes. He was short and stocky. His neck was shaved high up his round skull, his red good-natured face was shining, and there was the smell of a uniform about him. The long black boots that stuck out from under his shabby Russian raincoat suggested a soldier but whatever cap might have identified him was hidden in his paper bag.

—Hey, comrade, he said suddenly, and nudged Mendeltort. Seems like I've seen you somewhere before.

Careful not to smile, his eyes full of authority, Mendeltort said harshly: If I'd seen you before I'd remember you.

The boy was staring at Mendeltort in somber appraisal.

—There's something funny about you, said the boy.

His five companions were lined up behind him as though on parade. They were alike as copies of each other in white shirts and scarlet neckerchiefs. Their twelve dark eyes were pointed at him like weapons, and Mendeltort wondered how quickly they would go in search of the militia. How else could it be in a country where children don't laugh?

—Funny? he said. You think I am funny?

—Where d'you get those clothes?

—Oh, Mendeltort said. These? You mean this coat?

—That coat, the boy said. It's a foreign coat. What are you, anyway?

Mendeltort heard more than saw the man beside him shifting uneasily on the bench. He winked at the man.

—Shh, he said. You mustn't tell anybody, promise?

—Well, the boy said.

—Your word as a Young Pioneer. Nobody can know.

—Well, the boy said. Ah, well . . .

—I was on a mission to a foreign country. You understand me, little comrade?

—I still think I seen you somewhere, comrade, said the blue-eyed man. If it wasn't you it was someone a hell of a lot like you. And a man your size . . .

—Where did you go? the boy said.

—To the country of the hereditary enemy, Mendeltort said, and frowned.

He got up. He gathered his newspapers. The wooden lovers marched back and forth under the arc lights. He walked out of the park.

The dark suspicious little eyes of the Young Pioneers seemed to have followed him into the streets where no one was smiling. Gray people hurried past him with averted faces, no eye met his own, no one looked at anybody else. Liubov Orlova smiled off a poster, touching her fingertips to a captain's cap: *Volga, Volga* was playing at the Metropole. *Yesli zavtra vayna!* a loudspeaker crackled in his ears and he hummed the sadly stirring music as he walked along: If war should come tomorrow . . .

He was suddenly convinced that the suspicious little Pioneer had been Jewish and wanted him to know unrestrained joy and innocent curiosity. Time had formed a capsule around him, insulating him in all his loyalties and faiths, but beyond that shield civilizations crumbled. *Bang, you're dead!* had become the only alternative to Eretz Yisroel, not merely an imaginary sanctuary, a terra incognita of comfort and well-being and a visionary's dream, but a powerful nation able to inflict its will upon its enemies.

He walked quickly, head and shoulders lowered to reduce his size, feeling time itself hurrying toward him, and heard the rapid footsteps coming up behind him and forced himself not to break into a run.

—Hey, comrade. Hey?

He stopped, turned. The blue-eyed man who had been sitting in the park beside him had now put on his green military cap, with its dark blue band and red star. Grease off the garlic sausage had smeared the patent-leather peak.

—You sure you don't know me? I'm sure I've seen you somewhere.

He was too young to have known Mendeltort in the old days which now rushed toward him, too old to be put off with stories about missions.

—I told you. I don't know you.

—Good memory, eh?

—Good memory, good eyes, that's what I'm paid for, Mendeltort said harshly. You know what I mean?

—Ah, hmmm, so it's like that, is it? I should've known you'd be in the service, the man said quickly. Sorry to've bothered you, Comrade Officer. It's just that I thought I'd seen you before.

—You haven't, comrade, understood? Neither now nor ever.

—Sure. Of course, comrade. Seems like we both see a lot of people in our lines of work, mine's not so different. Maybe I seen you in a crowd somewhere.

—What crowd? Mendeltort said.

—Any crowd, comrade, in the street or something . . . Sorry to mention it. It's just that a man your size sticks out, see . . . I see a lot of people where I work . . .

—Where do you work?

—Well, the man said, touched his cap, moved uneasily. I'm not supposed to talk about that, comrade.

—Then why are you talking?

—I just thought I'd seen somebody like you not so long ago, can't remember where. A man's got to keep his eyes open, that's all that I'm saying.

—Your eyes stay open longer if you shut your mouth.

—Ha, isn't that the truth? No need to be a big-dome professor to know that. Well . . . I'll be seeing you.

—Maybe you will, Mendeltort said darkly.

—Sooner or later I see everybody in the place I work.

He touched his cap, shrugged.

—A man your size is hard to forget. But if it's not you, comrade, then it's somebody else I seen. Can't remember who, so that's why I was asking.

Mendeltort nodded in dismissal. Turned, walked away. The man was not a soldier, after all; his cap identified him as a prison guard.

Then he was standing before Lopatsky's house, the house of an old friend. Ah, but did old friendships still mean anything? Ten years had passed since he had climbed these stairs but it seemed to him that he had left the house only yesterday. The damp walls appeared to be what they had always been and at each landing the smell of cabbage soup reminded him that he had eaten nothing that morning. But everything else had changed, from men to ideas. His gnawing loneliness was making breathing difficult; this sudden need for reassurance that friends still existed, even though all their dreams had long turned into nightmare, was new and alarming. He had never confused a common cause with friendship; some of his best allies had been his enemies. Whatever human closeness he might have needed came to him accidentally, his friendships were profound because they were few. It was this providential quality of affection that had made his friendships so memorable and lasting.

He rose through silent gloom, each step a memory, among the ghosts of impassioned arguments and plans that had been splendid and exalting. This house, the source of disappointments, he thought, ascending into his own past. It had been here that he and David and Meyer and Anatole Lopatsky had met in dim days that seemed to have passed beyond imagination. He could recognize in each worn stair a part of himself and hurried as if to a meeting with his own beginnings.

And suddenly he was sure that he had come to the wrong door, perhaps the wrong house. How could he have made such a stupid mistake? (Monumental heroes are infallible, they make no mistakes.) His life didn't permit too many mistakes. He must leave swiftly, he thought, before the door opened and he faced a stranger, but he knew that he

would face one now no matter who opened the door at his knock. The
yellow piece of pasteboard tacked under the doorbell assured him that
he had come to the home of the Litterateur Anatole Lopatsky, that his
instincts had not failed him, that he had made no error. He rang the
bell, heard footsteps and waited for the door to open, and thought with
neither bitterness nor grief about Anatole Lopatsky, who did not open
the door and who said, from behind the door, in a voice that removed
all doubts about a mistake: Who is there?

—It's Avrum, he said, listened to the silence.

—Avrum who?

—Avrum Mendeltort, of course.

The door remained closed.

A key turned, a chain rattled.

Bolts slid back: one, two, three.

The door opened just enough to show white hair awry, a pink skull
gleaming wetly, and a hand unfolding with the caution of an octopus
testing a new environment.

(The eyes, he thought; at such moments the eyes are always
unbelieving.)

—What's the matter, old friend? Mendeltort said gently. Have I
come at an inconvenient time?

Eyes dull as ashes blinked, then fixed themselves on threadbare carpet slippers. They rose to peer beyond Mendeltort's shoulder and
scanned the staircase.

He waited for the greeting that could no longer come, said, to his
own memory of the man: Whom were you expecting? You look as if
you were going to have a heart attack, Anatole. What kind of a way is
this to greet an old friend? I'm real, touch me, I am not a ghost.

—You look like a ghost, Lopatsky said softly. (Then, fussily, like a
pensioner arranging his mementos on a mantelpiece, the old man
said:) Come in, come in. Don't you know any better than to talk on
the stairs?

His face was yellow, the lines were deeply etched. He closed the door
behind Mendeltort and locked it and bolted it, and looked at his visitor, at his carpet slippers, at his entwined fingers; a patient man humble
before disaster. Gently, because no matter how often you have seen life
escaping from an old friend's eyes, hope put away, courage and determination buried like rusted pistols, and ideals burned along with every
other youthful manifesto, the pity is always original and new, Mendeltort said: Are you ill, is that it?

—Why should I be well? said Lopatsky. The whole world is dying of
the plague, am I to be spared?

—Can I at least take off my coat?

—Oh, Lopatsky said. Oh. Yes. Take off your coat.

. . . A rare and precious light had been extinguished even though he had expected nothing else; the resulting darkness was immeasurably deep. Anatole had been a spiritual source, as David had embodied a particular future. A dried-up fountainhead didn't leave him much, David would take the rest. The ancient pits were open before him, glittering with skulls. Fallen prophets. Each of us must find his own illumination. No one could be blamed. Not even vengeance could make up for his sense of loss. —Is something the matter, then?

. . . And again, as in the park with the little Pioneer, he was looking into bewildered eyes that were accusing him of madness.

—Matter? Lopatsky said. What could be the matter? And (he stared at Mendeltort as though he had only just realized to whom he was speaking) where have you sprung from, anyway?

—Kiev, Mendeltort said. And before that, Poland.

—Ah well, Poland. Yes. Of course. Well, hang up that coat, come in, sit down. Ah . . . and how have you been?

—I'm coming down with something, Mendeltort said. But I didn't come here to talk about my health.

—You're ill, eh? Yes, you look terrible. What is it, do you think? Typhus? Pneumonia? We're having quite a lot of typhus and pneumonia.

Lopatsky led the way into the small apartment, musty with stale air, shuttered and barred, piled high with old newspapers and books in brown wrappers, dusty gimcracks, odds and ends of antique furniture.

—Well, he said. Well.

He sighed and rubbed his forehead. —I've been quite ill myself, he confided. Maybe you shouldn't stay too long, you could catch it from me.

—What is it, old friend, a touch of the plague?

—Ah yes, the plague. We've been having quite a lot of plague. The times, you see, are so difficult just now.

—Were they ever easy? You used to tell us that achievement without effort was contemptible, that compromise was the easiest habit to acquire. You used to write about historians who never make history.

—Oh, that, Lopatsky said, and waved a vague hand about his head. That. A defenseless man can only surrender. That's a fact of history.

—You taught us to make history, not pick its dead bones.

—Did you come here to remind me that I was a fool? Lopatsky said.

—I came to see an old friend.

—All your friends are dead, Lopatsky said. Dead or as good as dead. When you are powerless to influence events life becomes a matter of staying alive. To be alive is enough of a reason for living, believe me.

—You taught me better than that, Mendeltort said. You taught us to seize control of our own lives or die in the attempt. History is useless unless there is a future.

. . . And it's not that I'm being prophetic at the moment, Mendeltort told himself; I don't believe in oracles, traditional or new, never have, never could. It's merely a matter of learning the lessons of history, of living and seeing, sensing and experiencing, of having moved about at a crucial time, the time of an emergence of an extraordinary race. The future can be read in the bones and entrails of a gutted nation. Survival may have been an alternative while old men's values offered civilized solutions. That had been the great appeal of Marxism to them all: the assumption that man was on an upward spiral and his eventual ascent only a matter of time. Time read as faith in history before it was made. But history is more than time and mere survival is no longer a possibility, and faith in man's ability to transform himself was a terrible delusion, and hope and a faith in a sympathetic Deity were as unreasonable as prayer. Persecution, whether imaginary or real, painfully suffered in one hemisphere and artificially maintained in the other, is an insulting way for a Nation to identify itself. Power is bought with blood, no matter how bitterly the sentimentalists complain; the world doesn't respect the slaughtered, it only honors and obeys those who fight, and only fools and children and professional martyrs advertise their own infirmity.

Lopatsky had sat down.

—How can you still dream anything so foolish? A man's ability to control his life is limited to his power to defend it.

Mendeltort laughed, said: And if God had wanted cows to fly he'd have given them feathers, is that right?

—Well, Lopatsky said, and a trace of an old smile appeared on his face. Do they fly?

—I remember everything you told us, Mendeltort said. How humanity staggers forward, whether or not it's aware of motion or direction, lurching from one aspiration to another on the shoulders of inspired eccentrics, these necessary lunatics whom God never fails to provide. They fall and their skulls mark the milestones of the journey; doomed by their poetry and their prophetic mission, condemned by their own people as likely as not, they stagger through centuries of night and their dumb burdens mouth obscenities. Every journey has two kinds of travelers, you used to assure us: the burden and the burden carrier who blesses the night because it gives him stars, his bearings beyond pity, morality, or logic; he who is moved, whether or not he knows it, and he who does the moving; he who cries *Save me!* struggling and protesting, and he who marks the trail with his bones so that the next necessary lunatic might know where to begin.

—And now I'm telling you to suppress your daydreams. Poets make no more history than historians. And . . . did I really talk about blessing the night because it gave us stars?

—Once an old Jew, always a quotation, Mendeltort said, laughing.

Lopatsky's eyes had begun to sparkle and he chuckled a little, and looked around as though he were no longer quite sure where he was and what he might have been doing there. —Ah, Avrum, he began, seeing you . . . (Then the light vanished.) What are you doing in Moscow?

Carefully, considering each word before he let it fall, Mendeltort told him: I came to get myself arrested.

Lopatsky nodded, a thoughtful man in a time of madness. —We don't joke about that in Russia, he said. Yezhov is dead and the Terror is supposedly over but people still disappear every day. Don't you know how we've been living here?

—I know. And I make no jokes. I also want to make contact with some of our old friends. I was in Kiev for a few weeks, looking for Isaac Brodsky, but he seems to have vanished.

—He's gone. They've all gone one way or another.

—What could they find against that poor old bird?

—What kind of question is that? Lopatsky said softly. What moon have you come from? Article fifty-seven covers everything from the cradle to the grave . . . from the erection to the resurrection, as the Russians say . . . ah, you see? I *am* smiling . . . but they don't need even that one any more. The NKVD can now hand out a five-year administrative sentence. It simplifies everything. There are no trials, no records to keep, the man just disappears. We are living in the times of the Pharaohs again.

—Not a bad time for another Moses, Mendeltort said, smiling.

—Don't look for him here.

—Then there is David, Mendeltort said carefully. Does he still live in Petrushevsky Lane?

—He did five years ago.

—An old friend like that, so many shared dreams, so many adventures, and you no longer see him?

—He has new friends.

—He isn't likely to forget an old one.

—No, Lopatsky said, then cried: Why don't you ever listen to reason? Why can't you learn from your own experience? Why can't you leave us alone? Who needs you? What good can you do now? You're a corpse in search of a firing squad. Must we all go with you to the wall?

—You used to tell us, when we were shooting others, that a Jew puts his back against a wall the day he is born.

Lopatsky stared, his eyes were full of tears; he threw his arms upward, let them fall and hang, said in that cracked new voice that had greeted Mendeltort: Leave Moscow, I beg you. You are only bringing disaster to us all. It's too late for what you're trying to do, perhaps it was always too late. We do have plague among us, I wasn't merely playing with metaphor, and you've become a part of it. Leave Russia, go away, go to America where nobody gets hurt making other people's revolutions. Why should we all die before we have to?

His stare was wide with lunacy, his gestures punctured the flat, stale air with minute explosions; his voice was climbing his personal Golgotha in wrong gear, lurching from one hiatus to another.

—I have to see David.

—David has made his choice about survival, Lopatsky said. He's one of the worst of them now.

—David, Meyer, and now you, Mendeltort said, and shuddered despite himself. This house is full of ghosts.

—You're the only ghost here, Lopatsky said. We have all made our peace with our realities. We don't have to think as one, we are not a monolith, each of us is unique in our definitions. Had we all been the stereotypes that our own people imagine, our enemies would have found a way to wipe us off the face of the earth four thousand years ago. Ah, it's not what you think, I haven't forgotten anything, I can still remember. If it was only for myself . . . well, who can say? . . . but I've a wife and children and a grandchild coming . . . Do us all a favor, Avrum, in the name of that old friendship that we used to share. Go away and leave us alone.

Mendeltort rose, took the other's hand. Goodbye, unrecognizable old friend, he whispered to himself, you've fallen into the hands of the hereditary enemy, that sense of doom that has sent generations to the pits. Each time the eyes are different but the fear is the same and who can blame a man for wishing to remain alive? Lopatsky's hand jumped from his grasp, flew sideways, clenching and unclenching.

—I'm too old for this, Lopatsky said. And I've become suspicious of romantics, heroes . . . They live in search of martyrdom, you see, and that means death to too many others.

Aloud, walking toward the stairs, the short square wooden landing which had become a stage, he asked over his shoulder, wanting to know: What finally broke your spirit? And please don't tell me about your wife and grandchild, that might do for someone who didn't know you in the Revolution . . .

—You think I am broken?

—Why else would you be trying to commit suicide?

—Is it that obvious? Well, who knows? I did too much thinking, I suppose, trying to understand what we were all doing to each other here, and to ourselves, of course . . . It's so impossible to account on any ordinary hypothesis for our centuries of abuse, all those revolting acts of blood which you and I had tried to imitate, that the mind turns to the occult . . . myths of the Dark Ages . . . How do you explain unremitting evil? You might feel better about genocide if you turn it into a national tragedy, or hope for the advent of reason to cleanse the world, or become irrational yourself! It doesn't matter whether times were ever easier, the point is that they will always become more difficult. As men know more, they comprehend less. Teach them the narrowness of organized religions, and they'll invent movements which are even more restrictive and hysterical. Cure their diseases and they'll find new methods of killing themselves. Offer them libraries and they'll stay up all night plotting how to burn them. What is the point of struggling if nothing can change?

Despite himself, Mendeltort was moved to pity, the luxury that no conspirator can afford. The black Moscow night was crowding up the stairs. The day had passed unnoticed. The light bulb over the landing turned a sickly yellow. Anatole's lips, he noted, were gray.

He nodded. —Goodbye, Anatole.

—Goodbye.

The light Moscow twilight darkened at breakneck speed; it had already thinned the hurrying gray crowds. Ghosts of dead friends made room for him and whispered urgent warnings, and two policemen went by at a run.

In the small square outside the park, where a cigarette vendor was wheeling a barrow piled high with multicolored packages, the old woman was still roasting her potatoes in a charcoal burner. Mendeltort bought one. It burned his lips, filled his mouth with ashes. The toothless brown hag winked at him again and grinned and he thought, suddenly, that this was the first smile he had seen in Moscow.

—Want some more, lad? A big man like you ought to get half a dozen. It'll take at least that many to fill up a man big as you.

—Give me three, Mother. That's enough for now.

—Take three more for later. You'll never know when you'll need them, and if you don't have them, what then? Can't get them from thin air. Take my advice, I'm an old woman, I know a few things, take half a dozen while you can and save three for later.

—That's good advice, Mother.

—That way when you need them they'll be right there for you.

She wrapped the hot black tubers in a sheet of *Pravda* and handed him the little cornucopia of starch and propaganda like Mother Earth herself bestowing nourishment and wisdom.

—That's right, lad, the old woman said, cackled, blew her nose in her fingers, turned to her potatoes. —You only have what's in your hands. If it's not in your hands then you haven't got it. And it's even better to have it in your belly, then nobody can take it out of your hands.

There were still people in the street, moving quickly with grim un- smiling concentration, and a pair of belted and greatcoated policemen began to pace majestically underneath the arc lights. He was suddenly out of breath, his mouth choked with ashes, thinking about David.

—Thank you, he said.

But she was already wrapping a potato for somebody else, saying: You had better take another one for later, you only have what's in your hands, my lad.

Then he was standing in the shadow of a building which heaved up- ward out of gloom in a mindless and chaotic profusion of minarets and spires, knobs, protuberances, urns. What kind of mind, expressing what kind of art, reflecting and illuminating what kind of life, could conceive anything like that? A nightmare in cement, glass, parquet flooring; a wedding cake to be eaten at a wake (if, aesthetic comrade architectural worker, you have the stomach for it). He entered this drunken dream, climbed stairs, came to the door, and knocked.

. . . And he was trembling. Faces and memories ascending and de- scending this spiral of carpet, wood, and imitation marble.

The year is . . . well, forget the year, time has stepped aside. Do you remember the cold? When I'm broiling in hell I'll remember the cold. And the hunger? That, my friend, is something you never forget. Not that kind of hunger. Start with a broad white plain, and two young men sitting in snow among stunted shrubs, the dwarf pine of the tundra, regarding each other with the yellow eyes of tigers. Manic grins. Each is triumphant but each triumph is a wholly different celebration. Between the young men lies a providential find: the carcass of a snow hare, frozen hard as iron. Remember the hunger. Remember that these two young men are the survivors of a far more numerous group which has died, for the most part, of hunger. Next to their shambling stoop, what strikes most forcibly about starving men is their eyes. There is nothing like them in human experience. They have been pressed into the skull with hot irons that blackened the flesh, and in those scorched wounds, running from black to purple, lie glittering yellow pebbles star- ing across fleshless noses that resemble beaks. Between the eyebrows deep vertical grooves have been carved, as if from unsupportable worry, but these are faces far beyond such trivia as worry; they are so predatory that, in comparison with every other known or suspected condition of man, they are utterly unique. In comparison, every other condition of man looks merely harassed, no matter how rapacious. Note this fact of absolute rapacity, the essence of the predator . . . The younger of the two young men has found the snow hare while digging for roots and by the universal law of Hunger the hare belongs to him. It is his, absolutely, beyond argument. Nothing is shared under the laws of Hunger; the idea is inconceivable. That is how and why these young men have become Survivors, by no means incidentally. There can be no discussion at this point; neither of the two young men would even attempt it. And so one pair of yellow tiger eyes says *I shall live today and perhaps tomorrow* and the other says with equal triumph of a different nature *You will live today and perhaps tomorrow* and then the younger of the two very young men takes up his saber and hacks the frozen carcass in two equal portions, laughing as he does so (and it takes him a considerable amount of time to split the frozen hare, since he hardly has the strength to lift the heavy Cossack saber), and the slightly older of the two young men, who doesn't question universal laws, says to remind the other of the law *If you share this with me today, what will you have tomorrow?* and the younger man says with his brilliant smile, which illuminates matters far beyond the law, *Well then, tomorrow we will share the hunger.*

. . . Knocks on the door, remembering.

The voice is strangely shrunken and uncertain. But recognizable. (The years, cried Mendeltort. The years! How else could it be? The old resonance is there.)

—Who's there?

And Mendeltort, finally. He. Who had hesitated for a moment on the edge of shadow. Edge of reason. The wholly anti-Roman buccinator blowing the assembly on the edge of reason. Wilderness. Contemplating excrescence in concrete, carcass of snow hare. Said joyfully and clearly as if to invoke and summon the spirits of the shadows: It's Absalom, David, come to rule in Hebron. Can't you hear the trumpets?

—That is a name out of antiquity, the voice said.

The silence continued, an infinity of icy disappointments. (The shock, cried Mendeltort. There's bound to be a certain shock. Time and its effects on human reflexes.) The door remained closed. There was a sound beyond the door: a sob or a deep breath, or a chaotic something in between. The silence deepened, darkened. Once again, the shadows. But finally bolts began to creak like bones of old men bending, one by one, and the door opened just enough to show an oddly aged and suddenly defeated face, and from this face of puzzled resignation two dark and bitter eyes peered over Mendeltort's shoulder.

David Zaslavsky stared into Mendeltort's face as though a message of deep meaning could be read between its many lines; he began to make a gesture which was both pleading and peremptory . . . his arms hung half-spread like the crooked wings of a shotgunned crow, still poised for flight but falling.

—Well, David, what is it? Mendeltort said.

Nothing. Everything, said the pleading eyes.

—Aren't you going to ask me inside?

No, said the bitter eyes. The mouth opened, said: Ah yes, of course . . . come in . . .

It was the shock, of course, what else could it be? Except that it *was* something else, of course. Mendeltort felt tension ebb, said, beginning to laugh: For a moment I thought . . .

—Come in, come in! Zaslavsky said quickly. We'll talk inside.

—It's so fine to see you, David, Mendeltort said. So awfully fine to see you.

—It is . . . *extraordinary* . . . to see you, said Zaslavsky.

—You look as if you've seen a ghost, Mendeltort said, and laughed and heard the unconvincing note.

—Do I?

—Well . . . something like that.

—Well, you know, it is something like that.

—It's the shock, of course, Mendeltort said. I understand that.

—Well, yes, it is a kind of shock. Yes, I suppose that's right.

—After all, it's been so many years, and then right out of nowhere, unexpected . . .

—No, Zaslavsky said bitterly. I've been expecting you.

. . . You listen for inflections, guideposts. This is natural. This is part of the way of life, the immemorial journey through the twilight, by now second nature. So you listen, hear . . . Even though you know very well what is happening here . . . But this is David, your brother, mirror of your soul, with whom you have feasted on carcass of snow hare, hunger, the dreams and hopes and glittering illusions of a vanished youth, a strangely twisted, dwarfed and tormented David . . . perhaps a corrupted David . . . nevertheless you listen for the resonance in the muted voice, see the brilliance of the nonexistent smile . . . Time, you say: it is only Time, the gravedigger of hope . . . it changes us all. This is only natural. It's only natural to harbor illusions.

David closed the door carefully, sliding bolts into hasps with the mechanical precision of a soldier in a firing squad chambering his rounds.

—You say you've been expecting me?

Zaslavsky nodded, still facing the door, then said without bitterness but sadly: Why did you have to come now of all the times? They know that you are here.

—Nobody followed me, Mendeltort began, I'm sure of that . . . But the younger man, who seemed so much older, whose fleshy face had collapsed about itself, shook his head impatiently and said: No, I mean in Moscow.

—And you're afraid that I'll bring them down on your neck, is that it? Well, I'll go at once!

—No, no, Zaslavsky said, waving a vague arm, his face still carefully averted. That doesn't make the slightest difference now. Half measures . . . you know what you always used to say about half measures . . . it's too late for that now.

—What's too late?

—Nothing, nothing . . .

Then David started to laugh hysterically, a thin spiraling giggle choking on a half note: You might say that they have heard the trumpets!

—Ah, so it's that again, is it? Mendeltort said. What is it this time? Zionism? Separatism? A cosmopolitan orientation? Devotion to interests other than those of the Socialist Motherland?

—Take your choice.

Zaslavsky passed both hands across his eyes as if to smooth out crumpled images, shook his head as if to awaken from an intolerable dream, cleared his throat, and smiled briefly, fleetingly, over Mendeltort's shoulder. His face was gray and mottled in the dim light of the diminutive hallway, and the smile was a grotesque parody of a remembered brilliance. Perhaps synopsis would describe it better, Mendeltort thought suddenly, because that abbreviated twisting of the lips condensed invisible volumes. They had been standing in the hall for several minutes and they had yet to shake hands, or reach toward each other (not to speak of the brotherly embrace that could have been expected), and Mendeltort knew that neither of them would ever try to touch the other again. Time, that implacable enemy of love, had suspended its streaked and spotted barrier between them, yet something of the old unity—that essential human bond of mutual dependence—might be forced to pass between the clouded crystals.

—Come now, take off your coat, Zaslavsky said abruptly. Go into the room.

—I think I should leave.

—What's this? And suddenly Zaslavsky's violent laugh was harsh and mocking. Indecision from Avrum Mendeltort? The world must be standing on its head.

—When there is vagueness from David Zaslavsky . . .

—Forget it, cried the other. Leave? Why should you leave? It won't make any difference. Take off that coat. Go into the room. Sit down. Tea! Would you like some tea? What a question, when have you ever been known to refuse a glass of anything? But I can do better than tea; tea is for every day and this is like no day that has ever been. I have a bottle of Crimean wine. And a cake too. The cake is two or three days old, but there is no vermin in these new apartments, you never see a rat, so it's still good cake. Go in, go in, sit down! (Then laughing, shrugging, he went on as if unable to stop:) Yes, it's true, you do stir up the ancient plague wherever you go but if they hadn't had that old Absalom business to dig up it would have been something else. Isn't there always something? When have they ever run short of an excuse? So sit down, man, sit down, make yourself at home!

In the sharp yellow air of the white-painted room, a five-meter cube cluttered with possessions, Mendeltort could get a better look at David. Yes, he had aged and changed but in a manner which defied understanding. He had thickened, coarsened . . . but perhaps that was a trick of the light or his own faulty eyes unable to focus. His head was shaved high at the back in the military manner, but he had not shaved his beard for several days. The silver stubble on a face that Mendeltort had imagined as perpetually young, always lifted toward the sun of ideals and adventure, made him look threadbare. He wore a pair of khaki Soviet military breeches stuffed into wool socks, soft leather slippers, and a heavy sweater, and certain clues could be read in that but, at the moment, Mendeltort had decided to ignore the warnings. They were unnecessary, anyway. An odd weight, summing up the images of the day, was settling upon him.

In its own way the weight was comforting, it offered a certain illusion and a restfulness, and this, he knew suddenly, he could no longer do without. Invisible filaments were spinning around his body, anchoring him as firmly as any Gulliver. He allowed them to do so.

David was talking, asking questions, supplying his own answers, the sharp words leaping about Mendeltort in a manner which was painfully familiar, yet he could no longer identify the curious singsong intonation and the quick sharp cries. That is the way that interrogators speak.

. . . From Poland, David was saying then. I spent three months in Lwów last winter . . . many changes now . . . Poles simply can't understand what is happening to them, leaving it up to us . . . Did you look in on anyone in Kiev? Nobody there now, of course . . . Know about Lopatsky? Twenty-five years, that's what's coming to him, and he has all imaginable kinds of papers, remember how he was about documents? Much good they'll do him . . . Brodsky got five years' "administrative," extended indefinitely on the spot . . . after Krimsky's defection everything started going to hell for us, especially when Reiss got it too . . . but there are some very strange new things happening here . . . did you ever hear of V. M. Zarubin?

—Can't place him, Mendeltort said. The name sounds familiar.

—Well, no matter . . . just thought you might illuminate a dark spot for me. Drink up, have another. Have a piece of cake. Everything is so damn dark nowadays . . . Not that I'm complaining, you understand, I wouldn't complain!

—Of course you wouldn't.

—You mean the apartment? Well, of course, that's part of it all. Believe me, I had thought I had covered the old tracks pretty well. Believe me, it cost a lot of money, our comrades at the Commissariat for Internal Affairs don't sell themselves cheaply, but they do sell themselves . . . Then *you* jump from the grave! Oh, they've heard the trumpets.

—You don't seem to be doing badly.

—How would you know? You're like the wind that tears through a forest and goes on. I've been suspended for five months. Each time the bell rings, or somebody knocks . . . well, this time it was you, next time . . . well, what the devil, I had a good run. No, you're not going to bring the Collector down on my neck, he's on it already.

—I'm sorry, David.

—To hell with it, drink up.

—I am truly sorry.

—You're sorry!

—Well, what else can I say?

—That's what they all say, but they always end up saying a hell of a lot more. I know what you could say and I'm glad you're not saying it, so please remember not to say it. Nobody could say anything now that could change anything at all, do you understand? It's all moved far beyond anyone's ability to change it, stop it, anything. Drink up!

—It's good wine.

—The best! The best for the best! The perks of the service. Let us liquidate my remaining liquid assets. The midnight callers won't appreciate it much.

—Well, here's to whatever's coming, Mendeltort said quietly, and Zaslavsky choked, laughing suddenly: Don't drink to that, my friend.

—Why?

—Because you know what's coming. You knew the moment you stepped in my door. Maybe you didn't know you knew it but you always know. Isn't that the secret of your long success?

—Meyer said something like that to me recently, Mendeltort said.

—Now there's a man with a future, cried Zaslavsky. When did you see him last?

—It was sometime in November 1939, still in Lwów.

—Yes, said Zaslavsky. I remember hearing about that . . . Well, you will hardly know him now, when you see him. He's gone up in the world.

—I heard that said about you a few hours ago.

—Oh? Whoever said it must have a cockeyed view of the world. (Then suddenly:) Who said it? Where? When?

—An old woman. I had her looking for you.

—Aha . . . and what was her name?

—I don't remember, Mendeltort said softly, and knew why David's singsong cadence and quick stabbing words seemed so terribly familiar.

It all made perfect sense, of course; the signs were all there; and the inevitability of it, the timeworn formula of the ritual gave him a certain reassurance. It was not the reassurance that he had been seeking but, he thought, it would do. It *will* do! It took great effort to remember his lines because this *had* been David.

He said, slowly: Do you remember that time in Odessa . . . ?

And suddenly David was on his feet and shouting: No, I don't! I don't remember anything! Get that in your head! If you remember things out of your past they'll just get in the way of our present, they'll trip you up flat, and then what's the future? I am not talking about any special kind of future, destinies of nations, nothing ambitious for any-one, certainly not myself, just a continuation of whatever there is. If you've got that then that is enough of a future. So come on, drink up.

—When I remember what you used to say, the things you wanted, the things you believed . . .

—Forget it! How many centuries ago was that? In what lifetime was it? You're talking about the shadows of dead children, not the flesh of men who must go on living.

—They were magnificent children, David, they can still be magnifi-cent men.

—They are dead, Avrum. They never were any more than dreams. You are the only one who has never woken up to the new realities.

—I've never pleaded with anyone for anything, David, but I'm plead-ing with you. Remember what you were.

—Why should I when I know what I am?

—And what are you, David?

—An officer under suspension, waiting for the midnight knock, or for the bell to ring at four in the morning. And right when I had it fixed so good you wouldn't believe it . . . It was nothing that you could understand, Avrum, nothing heroic, bigger than life, grandiose, or significant . . . but down here, on this level where ordinary human

beings live and die, eat and get eaten, it was good enough. Do you
know what I've been doing for the past six years?

—I can read the signs.

—You only get one life, Zaslavsky said. Drink up.

—Don't worry about the old woman, Mendeltort said. She's safe.

—An old woman, eh? David said in a soft wondering voice that was
suddenly remote. Not very discreet for an old practitioner, wouldn't
you say?

—There was no other way.

Zalslavsky nodded, reflected for a moment, then sighed and smiled.

—Well, what's the difference, right? Drink up. *Raz kozie śmierć*, as
they say in Poland. How many times can you kill a goat?

Then he got up, opened the sideboard cabinet and took from it a telephone, put it on the table between himself and Mendeltort, refilled
the glasses, picked up the receiver and dialed a number. The metallic
answer was immediate and Zaslavsky said: Is that you, Vladimir
Stanislavovich? . . . Zaslavsky here. Got an old friend visiting, dropped
in out of the sky, so we're celebrating. Send up a couple of good bottles,
all right? You know where I live. (He shielded the mouthpiece slightly
and said to Mendeltort in Polish:) What do you feel like drinking?

—Don't go to all this trouble just for me, Mendeltort said softly.

—No trouble. I need it anyway. What do you want them to send?

—What they always send.

—My friend says for you to send what you always send, Zaslavsky
said into the telephone. Fine. Good. No hurry.

He slammed the receiver back into its cradle and left the telephone
standing on the table and reached for the bottle. This time he filled
only his own glass and downed it at once.

—Drink up, Avrum, he said.

Mendeltort said: How much time do I have, David?

—Time? Why, the whole night, man. Stay the whole night, we'll
make a party of it.

—How much time?

—Ten minutes, said Zaslavsky. Maybe fifteen if the motor's cold.

—I'm sorry, David.

—Right now it's best not to say anything, Avrum. Be like your
nephew and say nothing at all.

—Abel? Mendeltort said sharply, on his feet. You know something
about my Abel?

—We've got him at Lubyanka. Or rather *they've* got him. I don't
have anybody anywhere any more.

—What in God's name would they want from him?

—You, said Zaslavsky.

—But he doesn't know anything about me.

—Go and tell them so.

—Have they hurt him much?

—Oh, you know how that is.

—No, damn your black soul, man, I don't know how it is with you people any more! So tell me how it is.

—They do what they can.

—How is he?

—Alive.

—Is that all you can say? Alive?

—Isn't that enough? People pay a thousand rubles just to hear that word.

—You've got to get him out, Mendeltort said.

—*Me?* Zaslavsky said, and started laughing while large tears began to roll down his fleshless cheeks. *I've* got to get him out? I'm going to be right in there with him, don't you understand?

—Not after that telephone call, you're not.

—Don't give a thought to that telephone call. That's what they call insurance in capitalist countries but it doesn't protect you from an act of God. All right, we've abolished God and capitalism, so let's throw dice instead. I made a throw but the dice haven't stopped rolling yet.

—Tell me just this. Would you have telephoned if I hadn't told you about the old woman?

—You don't have time to waste on questions like that.

—I know that. Answer me.

—Forget it. Have a drink.

—What the hell have they done to you? You're not the David that I used to know.

—I couldn't agree with you more, Zaslavsky said, pulling on a pair of tall, polished boots, taking off the sweater. Call it an occupational disease, call it the ancient plague, but there's no point in telling me about it.

—I have enough money to buy Abel out, Mendeltort said. In gold. I have enough to help you if you need it. Just tell me whom to see.

—You're going to see him in about three minutes unless the motor was cold. But at this time of the year that's not very likely. They'll come quickly for you. The Collector has been turning Moscow upside down to find you.

—Whom do I pay, David?

—Nobody, Avrum. There isn't enough money in the world to buy out your Abel. He belongs to the Collector. That is like saying that he belongs to God, or the Devil, whichever you like. He is beyond all possibility of help. Please try to understand this while you still have time.

—That's the third time you've mentioned this Collector. What kind of new Devil is he?

—Fourth time, not third time, Zaslavsky said. You're not as quick as you were in the past, Avrum.

—And you're not as drunk as you pretended to be five minutes ago, David. So tell me very quickly about the Collector.

—I really was getting a little drunk there, until you told me about that old woman, Zaslavsky said, pulling on and buttoning a long-sleeved gray military shirt without a collar. That old woman was the last pebble on the scales, you understand that, don't you?

—It doesn't matter now, Mendeltort said. About the Collector.

—The Collector is exactly what you called him, a new kind of Devil. There is some very special devilry going on that nobody knows anything about. You hear this and that, but you know how that goes . . . it isn't thought safe to ask too much about it. If I knew more about this kind of deviling I think I'd be able to cook myself a very tasty dish. I also think that you have about two minutes left at most.

—So don't waste them for me. What is his name, his rank? What's his function?

Zaslavsky had now taken a military tunic of soft wool from under the divan, where it had been folded in newspapers on a wooden rack. He put on the tunic, buttoned it to his chin. He passed a nervous hand across the stubble on his chin and cheeks.

—To hell with it, he said. I'm not going to the Kremlin.

Mendeltort said: For the last time, David, about the Collector.

—Ah yes, the Collector . . . I really can't tell you very much about him.

—His name?

—His name is Szymanski.

—Polish?

—Not so you'd notice it. I think his father was Polish, from somewhere near Smolensk or Vitebsk, those old Polish Kingdom territories from way back before the Partitions . . . there are a lot of Poles, half Poles, and quarter Poles still living around there. His rank, well, that's quite a question. We have a new system of ranks now and no one can quite figure out what anybody is. Under the old system he was a commander but even that didn't mean anything. In that whole Zarubin group, those new devils you were christening here . . .

—Never mind that now. How much does he cost?

Zaslavsky laughed, shook his head, and began to strap on a broad leather belt with a holstered revolver.

—You just won't believe me, will you? he said. You can't buy this man.

—There never has been a time in Russia when they had a man who could not be bought, Mendeltort said. Some of them take strange coin but they all take something.

—Not Zarubin's people. Not the Collector.

—What makes them so special? What do they do?

—I told you, I don't know. There are many stories about a sort of secret core within the core, if you know what I mean . . . something almost mystical . . . It's nothing ideological or political; it's a lot deeper and darker than that.

The bell was sharp, insistent.

—Is there another way out of this apartment?

He said it only because it was expected of him and he would leave no details to chance.

—Only the window. My poor friend, after all, this *is* Moscow!

—No fire escapes, no way to the roof?

—Fire escapes could imply criticism of the efficiency of the Fire Brigades, which are a government department.

Mendeltort looked out of the window to the darkening and deserted street below, the black asphalt and gray concrete, where two black cars were parked at the curbside and a large man in a belted raincoat was reading a newspaper in insufficient light.

—Four floors, Zaslavsky said. You'd break your legs.

The bell rang again. Zaslavsky drew the Nagan revolver from its shining holster, cocked it, and pointed the ugly octagonal barrel at Mendeltort's stomach.

—Walk to the front door, he said.

—You don't need that, David.

—I know it, but you know what they say about appearances.

Mendeltort laughed, said: No, David, tell me what they say.

—Appearances are always important. You really shouldn't have wasted all that time with questions.

—Did you think I could just walk off once you mentioned Abel?

—Not for a moment, Zaslavsky said, and opened the door.

It was, of course, what he had expected: a moment of a minor arrival, what the Americans call a whistle stop . . . a part of a journey had come to an end. What would come next might not seem visibly different but it would be different. Something had been decided in this moment, was concluded. An end is always a beginning but in such moments this is remarkably scant comfort. He would not judge David. He would not judge the sensation of the moment. It was a new sensation yet it was also familiar in an undefined way . . . something, perhaps, always expected though never believed . . . a homecoming of a kind.

Rest ye now, weary traveler. Wary traveler. It was perhaps the death of an idea, a sharp turn in the road, though he would never go as far as to accept finality. Nothing is ever final; even death poses questions. Tombstones should be shaped like question marks. So not death . . . no . . . say it was rather the closing of a well-thumbed book . . .

And in the meantime everything was moving very quickly. There was no sense of motion. His vision seemed to be suddenly split in half, the left side of the canvas jogging up and down, filled with men in raincoats, while the right side, stretching the canvas sideways, focused on the still mask of David: itself a white canvasy screen across which vanishing memories flickered and jerked. The flat eyes reflected fragments of illusion. Who could say where love ended and hate began? Still, I bless you, brother. Had there been jealousy in those forgotten times? Yes, there was jealousy. Love and jealousy seem to operate the same glands . . . and, certainly, isn't the notion of a wrathful jealous God, our God, the rough and oblique way for us to reassure ourselves of His love for us? Thus even in betrayal the seed of love can be found . . . The stairs spiraled downward, suddenly liquid. A whirlpool of imitation marble, sucking down. No light at the bottom. The elegant officer was motioning politely toward one of the black Zis limousines (David, relieved of his revolver and his ghastly smile, was getting into the other one, having served his purpose) and Mendeltort blessed him silently and dismissed him from his memory. His thoughts were grotesque puppets dancing woodenly on invisible black threads. *Quo vadis*, puppeteer? Your cross has been replaced by a question mark, and all *our* burning crosses are no more than a ritual sacrifice to an absent God.

The shadows flowed softly past the windows. Smooth asphalt gave way to cobblestones before the iron gates. Bars of shadow. Two huge brick warehouses formed a tunnel . . .

He knew where he was.

Cobblestones, flagstones, doorways, stairs with and without a carpet, the squeak of a pencil scribbling on a flyleaf torn out of a book, the cornflower-blue eyes of a turnkey regarding him with instant recognition but without surprise, then the barren brightness of a cell.

The cornflower-blue eyes were no long curious, and not at all surprised. —They said to give you anything you want, you are a Special here. Do you want some coffee?

Coffee, Mendeltort said, would be good to have.

—D'you want a smoke? I'll roll you one.

Certainly. Why not.

He was immediately relaxed on the hard wooden bench against the harsh gray wall, under the glaring light bulb in its wire cage. The puppets were still, dangling motionless, their strings entangled; a certain lucidity beyond knowledge is possible at such moments: a kind of peace, almost a contentment. Once tripped, his stride broken, the long-distance runner must begin all over again. Innocence might be regained, passion could be reborn, and all questions are rhetorical at best and need not be answered. The blue-eyed turnkey was handing him a bright-enameled mug, also blue, full of a hot dark liquid without taste, rolled him a cigarette, lighted it and placed it on the floor.

—Anything you want to know? the turnkey said. About what the regulations are, and like that?

He shook his head. He had no further questions to ask of anyone. He knew that this night he would sleep like an innocent man.

—You remember me, eh?

He nodded.

—It'd be best if you didn't mention it, the turnkey said softly. You never know what people would think.

—I won't mention it.

—And I remember where I seen you before, or another like you. There's a young man a lot like you, down the corridor. It's a small world, eh?

And shrinking all the time. Shrinking and expanding. Breathing. Living. The road dips and rises but it is never wholly out of sight. People, ideas die only so that they may be replaced. There is this continuing process of replacement. Regeneration. The rattling last breath of an old man becomes the scream of a newborn infant. God will know when it's time to send down the next necessary lunatic. In the meantime . . .

—Sooner or later, the turnkey said, smiled, shrugged, nodded at the walls, retrieved the empty cup, picked up the used match. —You see them all in a place like this, and sometimes you learn something. Listen, you want something, just shout, see? They said you was to get whatever you wanted.

Mendeltort nodded, closed his eyes; he heard the booming slam of the iron door closing behind the guard, the parting click of the judas window. A soft sound like a kiss, infinitely tender. Sleep fell upon him like a black marble slab; he was no longer coldly monumental.

PART FOUR

IN THE WILDERNESS

The Magician

HE OPENED HIS EYES, thankful that the wind had stopped and he could see again, and saw the stars low on the horizon, and knew that it was time to halt for the night. The white Arctic night reflected the vast sea of snow over which he had traveled. The stars were surely an illusion. Real stars would be pale white in these latitudes and these were yellow and bright.

There were no more forests.

The forests had seemed endless, green-black depths pitted with swamp that promised to go on forever, but they had fallen far behind many weeks ago, and now the Great Siberian Plain itself was coming to an end. He had come at least four thousand miles on his wandering course, or so his schoolboy atlas and the birch-bark maps that he drew informed him. The Ostyaks would, most likely, go no further with him and he would have to start all over again with some other people. He wondered what lost tribes and nations lived in this wilderness, what language they would speak, what animal or fish or ancestor they worshipped.

Ahmer would know, of course . . . *Perhaps* he would know. The little Ket hunter had wandered over the Siberian steppe farther than most of his people. But even he had never come as far north as this because (as he had said a few days earlier) there was no reason why any man would ever want to come here. There were no bear or elk to hunt here. Another people lived here, though distantly related to his own; there were ghosts and demons. You could hear their spirits crying in the wind . . .

The icy wind had died down during the short day and now the small brown men were making motions to him, suggesting a campsite. Soon Ahmer stood before him, looking like a diminutive bear in his robes and furs.

He pointed to the yellow lights ahead of them, and to more distant lights where the pale beam of a searchlight swept over the horizon.

—It is time to camp.

Dr. Poremba nodded and watched the little column of reindeer sleighs spread out in the rough crescent that custom demanded, and the first birch-bark tents began to go up. The Khanty of the Ob and the Ket of the Yenisei were not used to traveling such distances in winter and had been uneasy for some time about going so far away from their own territories. Dr. Poremba thought that very soon they'd want to turn back.

He watched the imitation stars in the near distance.

Some went out as he looked at them but new ones immediately appeared, so that he knew that he was near another settlement. The distant searchlight told him that a camp was near, and that would probably mean more Polish deportees and so, perhaps, something of what he was seeking: news, rumor, a suggestion, it was all one to him; sooner or later he would pick up the trail. The settlement would be no different than the hundred other scattered, isolated villages he had bypassed or visited in the months of travel; cut off from the world, each was a world unto itself: islands of Ukrainians, Russians, resettled Jews, rebellious Uzbeks, Tartars, Kazakhs, and Turkmen spilled over thousands of kilometers in this white wilderness of the Ostyaks and the Samoyeds. The wandering hunters, herdsmen, and fishermen of the tundra burrowed their homes under the ground for winter, so these yellow lanterns, if that was what they were, would not be theirs.

Ahmer had watched attentively, followed the direction of his glance, and now said shrugging, nodding his round, furred head toward the lights: Russians, master.

But this meant nothing. Anyone who was not an Ostyak or a Samoyed, with all their clan and tribal subdivisions, was a "Russian" to the men of the taiga and the tundra. If you were not brown and small, stood taller than five feet in your birch-bark boots, if you could grow hair on your chin and if your eyes were round, you were a "Russian" to the Khanty, the Ket, the Selkup, and the Samoyed of the north, and to the Komi, Zyrian, and Permyaks of the Pechora, Mezen, and Vychegda basins, the Votyaks of the Vyatka region, the Cheremis and the Mordvins who lived between the Volga and the Oka, and the Vogul of the middle Urals. There were a hundred and thirty nationalities in this gigantic country, and the less that most of them had to do with any kind of "Russian," the better they liked it. Ahmer had been as far west as the Urals, so he knew something of the difference, and he knew the difference between free settlements and camps, but even so he followed the bias of his people.

—What kind of Russians would they be? Dr. Poremba asked.

—We don't know yet, master.

—What kind of place is it, then? Is it a place where one can enter, or is it one of the other kind? Is it a new place or an old one, can you tell me that?

—I don't know, shaman, Ahmer said. But it would seem to be the kind of place where a man might go in. I have sent the men with the Message.

—But there are the other kind of places near as well, isn't that so?

—Oh yes, Ahmer said. North and east of here there are many places. Many Russians. They dig in the ground. But we have never come this far north before. This isn't our country. We are the first of our people to come here, so there isn't even legend to tell us about it.

There was some pride in the hunter's voice but also a doubt.

—You are a traveled man, Dr. Poremba said, scorning his own unsubtle flattery. You have seen some of the world and now you're seeing more.

—There are some places that nobody should see.

—Are your people talking about going back?

—Who would talk against you, shaman? Ahmer said, evasive. But it is true that the Khanty want to go back to their nets and weirs and seines. They do not want to sleep in birch-bark tents in winter.

—And your own people, Ahmer?

The small brown man shook his short horn bow, the quiver full of reed arrows tipped with flintstone. —We are the Ket, the hunters. We hunt the squirrel, the fox, the bear, the elk, and the hare. But here where you have brought us, shaman, there is nothing to hunt. Nothing lives here, only Russians who dig in the ground. Why do they all come here?

He was polite enough not to include his shaman in this category of incomprehensible Russians.

—None of them want to come here, Dr. Poremba said.

—Then why are they here?

—They are not free like you to go where you wish.

—What kind of way is that for a man to live?

—No way at all, Ahmer.

—And you, shaman, you want to come here. Why? And how much farther will you want to go?

—I don't know, Ahmer, Dr. Poremba said.

—You don't know?

—Ah. Hmm. Well. It's a manner of speaking . . . There will be a sign.

—A sign? Ah yes, a sign. The people will be pleased to have this sign at last. We have come far from our own country and this is the season when we drive the reindeer.

—I am your shaman, Ahmer, Dr. Poremba said, trying to make his voice sound stern and remote, knowing that he could cease to be a shaman as easily as he had become one. The tribesmen would follow him only as long as they wished to.

Ahmer said nothing, waiting.

Dr. Poremba said: I must know what kind of Russians there are in this village.

—I know what must be done, master, Ahmer said. We have done this before. As I've said, your Message has been sent to this settlement.

—And if its the kind of Russian that I'm looking for I want to speak to one.

—Yes, yes, Ahmer said. And you will want to know when they were brought here and where they have come from. How many times have we done this?

—Who can count that high?

—And who would want to? Ahmer said. But it is true about the people, shaman. We want to go back to our own country soon.

—I am your shaman, said Dr. Poremba.

Ahmer sighed, bowed, withdrew.

The birch-bark tents were up around him now and he got off the sleigh. He was stiff with cold, his dogskin robe was frozen. His furs crackled when he stretched his arms. Anna Dimitrevna was already squatting in the snow, having cleared a small space for the cooking fire. She was striking sparks off a flint with a bent hobnail and the dry lichens would be burning soon. The child still slept. The Ostyaks were scattering among the low shrubs hidden under ice, their short bows at the ready. The lights of the settlement went out one by one.

. . . There had been so many tribes and nations since he had begun. He had traveled with Yakuts and Siberian Tartars, the Soyots, the Kamasin, and the Kazagas of the upper Yenisei River. The Khanty had been the first clan of the Ostyaks with whom he had shared a birch-bark tent in summer and a buried log cabin in winter, then he had come among the Ket of the lower Yenisei and these had now brought him to the edge of their world. So many peoples, faiths, languages. Distances greater than all of Western Europe. With each new tribe he had done the necessary magic, made prophecies, sung, acted as a healer, consulted stars when they were to be seen, exorcised demons, offered sacrifices to the appropriate fish, animal, or ancestor or spirit, told tales and legends. They had passed him from one free wandering tribe to another. Vast territories lay behind him now. He had had no idea how many different peoples there would be. He and the madwoman and the idiot boy had come by train as far as Cheboksary on the Volga, then they had gone up the Volga into the Mari country, then eastward among the Mordvins and north again to the Pechora and Vorkuta regions, where he had searched among a hundred camps. Sometimes whole months passed before he saw a European face: some Polish Jews resettled in the forest villages of the Mari, transplanted Volga Germans, thousands of Ukrainians buried in the taiga since the middle twenties. He had crossed the middle Urals into the lands of the Vogul and first came among the Ostyaks where the rivers Irtysh and Ob flowed into each other, then followed the frozen Ob to the gulf that empties into Kara Sea. The Ket of the Yenisei had kept him the longest. No official ever ventured among these wandering tribes which recognized no authority other than their shaman's and moved about their vast spaces at the shaman's will.

He had been traveling more or less northeast from the mouth of the Yenisei, following frozen rivers: the Pyasina and the Kheta and the lower Khatanga (or so his atlas told him) and now he supposed that he was on the southern edge of the Taimyr Peninsula, near the vast lake, where in an area greater than France and Germany together, clasped in the icy grip of the Kara and Laptev seas, another vast complex of convict camps lay hidden. Wandering Yakuts told of fleets of barges which covered the Khatanga every summer, bringing people here. No one had ever been known to return. And further east lay the dreaded delta of the Lena, and beyond that, beyond a hundred rivers without names lay the legendary goldfields of Kolyma, the river of death, where a whole galaxy of camps was supposedly buried under eternal ice. And what about the unknown islands of the East Siberian Sea? Twenty million people worked and died in the huge secret arc north of the 65th Parallel, one and a half million of them Poles (each of whom might have seen Alicja and the children, might have heard of them, might suggest another corner of this ice hell to explore). The wind-swept snowy wilderness that stretched from the White Sea to the Bering Strait contained a nation of slaves, and how was he to make his way to them all? His atlas and his birch-bark maps told him that he had covered only a fraction of his journey.

Doubt and a sense of hopelessness rocked him for a moment. He had been wrong to think that he had infinite reserves of time, that only perseverance and determination were needed. A million people were said to die in this wilderness each winter.

He shook off the stupor, blamed the cold for the momentary doubt.

(What else can I do?)

Ah, nothing is ever hopeless until you yourself decide that it is. The dreadful names were ringing in his head: Kola Peninsula, Cheshskaya Bay, Pechora, and the terrible Vorkuta. It's all a matter of economics really. Fifteen per cent of the heavy industrial production had been assigned to the NKVD, hence the need for slaves.

. . . Severnaya Zemlya and Kotelny Island. Kazachye.

The Yana and the Indigirka.

Magadan . . .

Sooner or later, he muttered to himself.

The woman stooped over her little fire, turned the strips of dried and frozen squirrel meat laid like a grate across it. She didn't look up. In her rags, robes, and furs tied with rawhide thongs she seemed even more shrunken and wasted than he was, but he knew that she was hard as iron. He envied her the insensitivity of madness. Unable to imagine the end of the journey, she was beyond the reach of either fear or doubt. She was totally concentrated within herself. Her world was closed to him and he felt a sudden unreasoning longing to enter the absolute safety of a mind without thought. No doubts, no goals, no purpose. And an assurance which he didn't understand. She was humming, crooning. The child awoke, moaned, and was immediately still. Snow leaped about them in sudden flurries, drifted, suspended brief curtains.

—You are all right? he asked.

She looked up, nodded. Her mouth was hidden under rags but it would be smiling. Only her deeply luminous mad eyes showed among the strips of cloth and fur folded about her face. Their light was milky; he thought of black water under three meters of transparent ice in the middle of a frozen river.

—You are content? he asked gently.

—You are not?

He shrugged in turn, sighed. He knew she was smiling. He was aware of her hard, supple body under the cloth and furs, and knew that she knew that he remembered her; they hadn't spent all their nights in sleighs. Alicja seemed no more real then than an idea, the children a dream; Anna Dimitrevna hummed a very old song. Except for her height, the breadth of her shoulders, and the roundness of her opaque, knowing eyes, she looked no different than the Ostyak women busy among their tents. So might we live among these gentle people forever, he thought: the past and the future equally forgotten.

Nothing lasts beyond memory, isn't that so? If you forget your horrors they'll be gone. Old loves vanish only so that they might be replaced and who's to say in these times, in this faithless country, what constitutes true loyalty anyway? The old world is gone, never to return; the classical notions of loyalty and betrayal no longer apply. Now it is all a matter of juggling with possibilities, walking on a tightrope, lies and trickery, and each day finds its own justification in survival. So tell me, he muttered to himself, why go on with it? There are too many icy miles ahead and at their end there's likely to be nothing except disappointment, a renewal of that desperate sense of loss which had begun to fade, the resurrection of pain. Why not consign the whole thing to the devil and forget about it? If you have someone, anyone, to share their life with you, the world is far less dreadful and it no longer matters if you fail to find what you want. It's dangerous to get what you want, anyway, he told himself once more; it sets you up for loss and tragedy. Want nothing and nothing will ever be taken away from you.

. . . And for a moment he couldn't remember what Alicja looked like. He thought of auburn hair and black eyes. No, no, Alicja's eyes were blue! His woman looked at him.

The child had sensed him near and gurgled with pleasure. He stooped over the idiot boy, stroked his grotesque head. The vacant face was glittering under frozen spittle, the eyes were frosted shut, and Dr. Poremba knew that the idiot boy wouldn't live much longer. Luta was dead, Ziuta was lost, the idiot was dying, Alicja's eyes were blue; I shouldn't have brought him and the woman here. Should, shouldn't, what did that mean? What did it matter? All the old concepts have been overthrown. He didn't owe the woman anything just because her son would be dead in a day or two. No one owed anything to anyone or to anything. He picked up the child's heavy body and carried it into the conical little tent where the Ostyak women had spread out his furs, laid the boy on the pallet, wrapped him in dog and otter skin, went outside again. Anna Dimitrevna speared a strip of burning meat on the end of her knife and handed it to him. The meat was black. The globules of precious fat were instantly frozen. He didn't taste it until it was gone.

—The boy, he said, and gestured abruptly, avoiding her eyes, as though diplomacy and vagueness could be of some value.

She was immediately still, very like a small wild animal on a tether with danger approaching. With their mouths hidden from each other, the smiles and trembling lip equally concealed, and gestures an interruption more than punctuation, their eyes had become suddenly eloquent.

Then her head dipped, bobbed up and down, and the acrid smoke stung his eyes. He jerked his head aside, stepped out of the smoke. Watering eyes would freeze immediately.

—There isn't much that anyone can do for him.

—He has been dying a long time, she said. My jewel. My precious. Such a life it's been . . . But it is all going to be better now.

She held out another spitted strip of burned meat toward him but he waved it impatiently aside.

—You have to understand that nobody can help him.

—Not even you?

—Good God, he said. I least of all. You shouldn't have come here with me. I didn't want you to come.

—It's not your fault, she said.

—I know it, dammit! I don't want him on my conscience too.

—It's not your fault . . .

—Nothing is anybody's fault! You have to understand that a child like that, an idiot, doesn't survive long, anyway.

—Why are you angry with me?

—I'm not angry with you.

—You are angry with somebody. With yourself? Why should you be angry with yourself? Eat, don't be angry. The boy is now eleven years old. He has been dying for eleven years. For all those years he was all that I had of you. But now you are here. How could it be your fault? So why are you angry? Come now, eat.

—If I hadn't brought you to this ice hell, if you hadn't insisted on coming . . .

—How could I not have come? And, anyway, I've seen you cure others.

—A hoax, he said. Lies, tricks! I can't cure anybody who is really ill. I can't bring people back from the dead!

—Then why are we here?

—I don't know what you mean, he said. Knowing very well, his voice suddenly cracked. She looked up at him for a long moment and he turned away from that deep steady knowing stare that challenged the last of his truths, telling himself that she was mad, a raving lunatic, that she couldn't read him as easily as that. Oh, but she could and had! And who was she, anyway, to point out his own insanity? He had to cling to some sort of faith no less than she! And what difference did it make that it was wholly unreasonable, that it made no sense? No faith makes sense, it is all a matter of hope and delusions, the slant of light imagined in darkness. Faith and sense, whatever *that* was in this time and place, are mortal enemies. One will mock the other. Reality is a matter of the moment, this moment, not another: with no past, no future. I am I and I am here, and wasn't that the way it had always been for him, and how could he have forgotten it, blinded by an imaginary beacon? And who was she, this madwoman who was surely the most unmad person in a world peopled with obscene shadows, to tell *him* with those unanswerable eyes that saw right through his subterfuge (she, of all people, who could step so easily from nightmare to dreams!) that he was following stars of his own creation? She was mad, of course. Her truth was real in this world, she shattered illusions. Lost in the frozen swamp of her own saving myth and beckoning to him. Come join me, be with me, I am real; eat, it is not your fault, close your eyes, your stars are a hoax, your tricks are good for others but we both know that they're unnecessary for us, we don't need them, we know what is real; we are we and we are here, the past is only the memory of a dream but we have bodies which are tangible. Do you remember my body? Yes, I can see that you can remember. That is reality, it is not illusion. Why search for fire with a lighted lantern? We are alive in a charnel house; we are the lone survivors. The living can only live with the living, life calls out to life! The dead and the dying have no right to intrude.

—Eat, she said abruptly.

The burned black meat seemed wooden between his frozen lips. He tasted nothing as he chewed it and the roof of his mouth registered no pain.

The child wailed suddenly, a short sharp bleat buried in a whimper. The woman cocked her head, listening as though from a distance, whispering something that he couldn't hear. (My jewel? My precious? Some automatic endearment that she used as her own invocation, a spell against disaster.) I'm not responsible, he whispered to himself. It would have happened anyway, here or there, it doesn't make a difference. A crackling parchment voice unfolded in his head. *Magna, mater* . . . Bats swooped remotely in his consciousness, an ancient eye regarded him thoughtfully. Death is the natural order of all things, more reasonable here than living; the dead and the dying are not to be mourned. They are to be forgotten, buried like ideals. She knows it too. She is so young, so old: immemorial. I bring you forth and I take you in . . . I am the woman, somebody had said it. He caught her steady gaze and again averted his face.

The child was quiet.

—He would have died anyway, he said.

She nodded. He didn't look at her but he knew that her eyes were still fixed on him. Shrill red cries reechoed through his head. A white body plunged streetward, shattered on snowy cobblestones, exploded and was gone. He was whispering, whispering. The dead were gathering to bury the dead. A bowing mute processional.

—What did you say?

—Perhaps we can have another.

—That's callous, he cried. How can you be so callous?

She looked at him, untroubled. —What is callous?

—This! Everything! No, forgive me, nothing. I keep forgetting where

I am, do you know? How we are living, what matters here . . . You're right. There's no such thing as being callous here.

—You always were a gentle man, a kind man, that's how I remember you. And you haven't changed. But it is better to have pity for the living than for the dead.

—I know it.

—It is because you spoke against the arrests and the killings that they took you.

—Is that what happened then?

Now she mocked him quietly. (Ah, what an innocent you are!) He thought of Langenfeld, Zarubin, the malevolent train pulling away from the monastery siding . . . Shuddered. Death had come by trailing her icy wings and brushed him in passing. Suddenly he was sweating. She was laughing, nodding, saying: Have you forgotten, then? But you are right, so right, it is best forgotten, best not thought about. Perhaps it didn't happen? They'll never find us again, we can see to that, and they'll never take you away any more and we shall be together, and we shall find a place for ourselves, you'll see, where nobody knows us, and it will all be even better for us than it was before. Do you remember how it was?

He nodded, sighed, said: Nobody could forget that.

But she insisted: You remember, then?

—Yes, he said. I remember.

—I could wait for you, she said. All those terrible years. Because I knew it could be like that for us again. They said you were dead but I *knew* they were lying!

Her voice was high, triumphant, uncontrollable in the upper registers. He thought: I can't destroy her faith without giving her something to replace it; knew his compassion to be yet another hoax, said: Such faith must be rewarded . . .

—We can go anywhere, live anywhere, it's such a big country.

—Well, not quite anywhere, he said, seeking obstacles, and jerked his head toward the settlement and the pale lights beyond it.

—Why not? she said. Earlier I saw a dog. If a dog can live here so can we.

Right on cue came a distant barking: and so he knew that the Ostyaks had reached the settlement carrying the birch-bark scroll (the Message), part of his magical paraphernalia.

. . . *Litwo, ojczyzno moia,* he had written on the flat-pressed, rolled strips of birch bark, *Ty jesteś jak zdrowie* . . . lines that any Pole would immediately recognize: the lonely patriotic fervor of Mickiewicz's Parisian exile, the messianic vision of a lost Poland that couldn't possibly have ever existed, was (he had told the Ostyaks) certain protection against the half-wild wolfhounds of the north.

. . . Thou art like health, my country; only he knows you who has lost you . . .

Strong medicine for an exile.

If there were any Poles in this settlement, and he had yet to come across one of these future Soviet cities, hacked out of the wilderness by convicts and exiles, which (still speaking of the settlements) didn't contain a Pole or a Jew from Poland, he (the exile, the deportee), magically drawn by the antique elegy, wondering what the devil the Ostyaks were doing with Mickiewicz, would come to have a look. Then more words: questions, answers. And the dogs (it was true!) hadn't bitten anybody either.

The small brown man had waited patiently, squatting on his heels. Now he got to his feet, whistled between his teeth, made himself noticeable, peered upward into the magician's face. His own flat placid mask communicated nothing but Dr. Poremba knew that something had happened. The bark and wicker screens were up at the far end of the encampment to protect a council.

—The men return early today.

—Yes, shaman, Ahmer said.

—Those were not my orders.

—We are not Russians, shaman, Ahmer said politely. We come and go as seems good to us.

—Did it seem good to any of you to go to the village?

—Yes. Some men went. They took the Message. They will be back before very long.

—Why didn't you go yourself? None of your men speak Russian.

—There is a council, shaman, Ahmer said.

—I didn't call a council, said Dr. Poremba.

—Nevertheless there is one.

And so he knew that his stay among the Khanty and Ket had come to an end when he could least afford it. Without them he would be immobilized and, to be sure, frozen stiff and dead in less than a day. To go on would be a declaration of intent to commit suicide yet, out of force of habit, he started to marshal images of future dupes. Whom would he mystify next?

Some sort of effort must be made to regain control. Why? To what end? The search was hopeless. Give it up, turn back! Accept the inevitable, which, please admit it, Jasiu, wouldn't be so bad anyway. The year was ending, a whole life had ended, let the dead mourn the dying, let us go on with the sorry business of living, which, to be sure, wasn't quite as sorry as I'd like to make out. All kinds of possibilities remain and, as the parchment abbot had rustled at the close of a former lifetime, the dead can't manipulate. My first responsiblility is to remain alive.

He made his voice heavy with foreboding:

—The spirits of your ancestors will be angry. To hold a council without your shaman is the worst possible luck, you know that. No self-respecting spirit can forgive anything like that.

Ahmer bowed, said softly: It has occurred to us, shaman, that our ancestors can't truly tell you what they wish.

—Why not?

—They do not speak Russian.

—Do the stars speak Russian?

—We do not know about the stars, hands, bumps on the head; all that is new to us. We do know about the spirits of our ancestors. We always know what they wish because they never wish us to do what we don't want to do. Perhaps it's different among your people.

—No, by God, it isn't, Dr. Poremba said, and began to laugh. That's perfectly normal for ancestral spirits, you can't fault them there.

He would come up with something in a moment.

—So the people want to go back to their own country, is that it?

—The spirits command it.

—Very wise of them.

If he could survive a day or two alone and on foot he might be able to reach another tribe, supposing he knew where to look for one. There should be Selkup herdsmen between the Khatanga and the Yana and his mind leaped at once into quick catalogue. Another branch of the Ostyaks, which is a Russian name for several nations (much as American Indians bear a general label not of their own making). Exogamous society, patrilineal clans, speaking yet another version of a Ugrian language thought to belong to the Paleo-Arctic group (not unlike the Eskimos of the Bering Strait) but more likely a survivor of a vanished Sino-Tibetan subgroup . . . there was a lot to be said for a good European degree in philology. More Yakuts were said to live in the Yana and Lena basins. Orthodox, ripe for miracles, and (fortunately!) on a good shamanist substratum. Pastoral, which was rather less convenient . . .

(They might have lived on the far side of the moon for all the good they were likely to do him. If the Ostyaks left him he'd be dead in a day.)

The idiot child whimpered quietly and Ahmer was waiting.

—Didn't I tell you there would be a sign?

—Has there been one, shaman?

—Shortly, shortly. You can't hurry that sort of thing. The boy is dying, you know that, don't you?

—The boy who is touched by the spirits.

—He belongs to the spirits. When he dies we shall be given a sign. I've no doubt that it'll point back to your country, but we have to be sure.

—Will he take long to die?

—Not long. A day or two.

—There is no hunting here and the food is coming to an end.

—What is a little hunger to such men as the Ket?

—Perhaps he could die quicker, Ahmer said. Shaman, the people are not going to wait two days for something that maybe won't happen for a week.

And because Ahmer looked troubled, his standing as interpreter threatened by his shaman's fall (the surrogate voice of the spirits would be unnecessary), and because they had both come to depend on each other in their weeks together . . . and mutual dependence, need, and self-interest were the cement of friendship . . . and because there was, perhaps, a glimmer of personal affection between them and they understood each other (the small brown man being older than Dr. Poremba and playing his own cautious game: today's disciple could be tomorrow's leader of his people) and, finally, because he himself stood on the threshold of an unthinkable act and couldn't find his way to his own private subterranean refuge where there'd be a plethora of distractions to dull a moral ache and, in sum total, because he knew that being rational is no guarantee against stupidity, Dr. Poremba said, in a voice that surely couldn't have anything to do with him, couldn't have come from him but was, most likely, imposed on him by his imagination (rustling like crumbling parchment, hissing as the wind): He'll die as quickly as he can.

—There is a saying, Ahmer said. Fathers must eat their children to grow strong.

—He'll die tomorrow, said Dr. Poremba.

—Shaman, Ahmer said. It would not be good if I told the people that the sacrifice would be made tomorrow, and that there'd be a sign, if tomorrow there is neither sacrifice nor sign.

—Are you doubting me?

—There can be no mistake.

—I've taught you a lot, said Dr. Poremba. But I haven't taught you everything.

—There are some things that no one has to teach me. I know that if a body is left outside the tent, and the furs are removed, the body will freeze. It is a quiet, easy death.

—No, said Dr. Poremba. Not yet.

—No? Well, you're still the shaman today, perhaps you know best. But the people will not wait longer than tomorrow. A shaman is a shaman only if the people want him.

—I know all about that.

—Surely, surely. But may I tell the people that tomorrow there will be a sign?

—Yes.

—It will be tomorrow?

—Yes.

—And . . . do you wish me to help?

—No.

—There are some things I could do. It would be a small matter.

—No, said Dr. Poremba.

Ahmer bowed, said: You are the shaman.

—Yes.

He closed his eyes, feeling what must surely be the most terrible loneliness of all, filled neither with terror nor with boredom but with self-contempt. To be trapped like this between two impossibilities . . . But he knew that he was only deluding himself. Nothing was truly impossible, it was all a matter of choice: this act or the other or no act at all . . . and every true choice called for a sacrifice of something (comfort, ideals, peace of mind, whatever) . . . and it was only men who lacked the courage to choose and then to act who talked about impossibilities. Act, do it now, do not think about it. The antique gods of self-preservation were waiting for their sacrifice, and one couldn't depend on a last-minute announcement that it was all some sort of a test of loyalty or that there would be a convenient lamb trapped in a nearby thorn-bush . . .

A sacrifice had been made in Poland. A country had been placed upon the pyre in defiance of logic, so that one had to search for reasons beyond the beginnings of civilization. But had the victims given their consent? Or had they been led, drugged by the fumes of history, marching jerkily like puppets up the steps of illusion with flowers thrown before them and songs at their backs?

That too was surely a matter of murder.

. . . They (WE!) talk and talk.

Endlessly.

Question and consider.

Try to position ourselves in a reality greater than our existential circumstances allow . . . and miss the point entirely. Perhaps only a Russian, with his spirit rooted in the soil, could understand this desperate need to define ourselves in a universe larger than our own. Others would ask: How can you excuse such detachment at a time like this? Your world has ended, your country has fallen, you have been cast adrift in a hurricane, and you send your minds on hyperbolic flights into the abstract! It's your wives, mothers, fathers, lovers . . . *that's* what you should be in torment about. Are they dead? Will they live? Can you live? Anyone else would ask that, why don't you? We can't. We feel too much, you see. We feel our love so deeply. And so we feel all of their pain as well as our own. Their wounds are our wounds, don't you see? I cannot bring myself to think of these lost loves . . . Alicja . . . the children . . . And always, always, don't you see, underlying this apparent flight into the fantastic, the hyperbolic refuge of a shocked mind, is the bleak and rapturous Polish truth that dazzles the senses, that is beyond the grasp of a foreign consciousness: This is not the first time! All this has happened to us before and it will again; we are following in the icy footprints which make our past and future into One. We must assume that our lovers, mothers, fathers, wives and children and lost friends will survive, will not be badly damaged in this trial by ordeal, will emerge from the holocaust: the senseless affirmation of a destiny of doom. Perhaps only a Jew could understand something of this knowledge in which death, like our borrowed lives, is only one more hostile incident on the march . . . Yes, perhaps a Jew: harried, driven from one disaster to another, always living in a land of strangers. They do at least have their terrible God to whip them through the desolate valleys of their history . . . While we . . . talk. Question endlessly.

. . . We had been taught to think that an act, any form of action, could bridge all the discrepancies between what is and what should be. Fix bayonets, sabers out, charge, and to the devil with the consequences . . . ! But action is just as likely to leap from fear and evasion.

(At least old Abraham had been wrapped in mysticism and the hysteria of senility. What a luxury! The final refuge of an infirm mind.)

He opened his eyes. The small brown man had stepped aside but watched him carefully.

The child wailed suddenly, whimpered.

He caught Ahmer's eye, nodded toward the child, assenting.

The woman said nothing; he was careful to avoid her eyes. She was looking at him across the edge of an unbridgeable pit.

The dogs had stopped barking. He noted what at first sight seemed to be a clump of dwarf pine surrounding an oak, moving swiftly. So, not inanimate in this desolation. He saw men: Ostyaks surrounding a European, coming from the settlement.

The wind picked up suddenly, rustling in the birch-bark strips.

Don't mock the finally infirm, he muttered.

(*Magna mater*, comrade. The Abbot was smiling.)

. . . This isn't I, he said; I don't do such things. I am (was, used to be) a civilized human being, an arrow shot into the blue trailing the sum total of a people's knowledge, culture, and experience. Did I say something about being callous? The last vestigial stump of his former being, as an inhabitant of another world, had crumbled away.

Welcome, welcome, whispered the memories of bats. Crackling black lightning. The message was clear.

Catherine

IT WAS EITHER OCTOBER OR NOVEMBER, most probably November. It might have been even the beginning of December, there was no way to tell. Time had lost whatever meaning it had had; it seemed to be a long night, a mindless automatic progress between imaginary hours from a remote beginning, now scarcely remembered, through a blurred series of events which erased friends, people one knew, mysteriously by the barrackful, falling upon them like destiny . . . a time to get up and a time to eat and a time to march, a time to work and a time to return, and times for all other routine motions without thought or plan, all hooked upon an equally dim necessity, with instinct doing the work of the will, and determination a matter of habit.

The air in the barrack was icy; each cautious breath seemed to crackle in her lungs. She coughed (she was always coughing now) and the painful hacking stabbed her deep inside. The walls and the stacked sleeping bodies were filmed over with a glittering white frost.

She had wrapped all her clothes about herself, indeed she was never out of them: stiff rags worn thin as paper, shredded, torn and split. Burlap, straw, canvas, and tar paper but, nevertheless, an armor of a sort. It was important to be armed and armored inside as outside: hard, brutal, cruel, and determined, whatever all that was, giving nothing and taking whatever she was strong enough to get, the sadness of Father Boguslawski notwithstanding. Gibbering Ursuline ghosts no longer had to be appeased, their sallow disapproving faces had burned down like candles. Prayers were words, undelivered messages sent through an intermediary, and she negotiated directly with the Angel of Death: so much for so much and payment on the barrelhead, a day at a time.

She had no overcoat and there were no blankets. But Wanda had a coat, Alaskan sealskin of all things (and don't ask how she had hung on to it, why King Whore hadn't ripped it off her back, why the *komandir* didn't give it to Ziuta or some other member of his harem; she had it, that's all: you couldn't even be sure of robbery and murder), and Wanda was dying and if only she, Wanda, had the goodness to die when she, Catherine, was present, if she would finally waste away and wither on the daily diet of seven ounces of bread given to the sick who were no longer strong enough to work, and if she'd do it at a time when Catherine was not away at work or on her way to work or marching across the four miles of ice and scree back from the day's work, or getting food, or trading, or stealing, or forgaging among the day's dead, then the coat would be another inheritance.

Much could be made of it. Little was left of her Lwów finery. Nothing had been stolen, she knew how to defend it.

. . . A black padded jacket (*had* once been black, was now gray and green) was an inheritance from an unknown man—a tall, skeletal Mongol, she remembered. He had frozen to death, or perhaps only near death, in the sludge of the mine; and she had burned the jacket accidentally, having dragged it (and the Mongol in it) nearer to the fire so that she could thaw it out sufficiently to get it off the corpse . . .

(He had said something in a voice that threatened credibility: a rocking plaintive gurgle, the wail of a child, cradled in the body of a man. A one-dimensional cardboard man with a red dream throbbing in his temples, his face a black inverted triangle resting upon a point. Something about the banners of Lehistan, and minarets and a prophesy . . . all the while looking up at her with his frozen eyes. He might have thought that she was trying to save him.)

. . . The quilted pants, patched with stolen canvas, were no inheritance. They had become hers through a combination of theft and trade, a matter of properly capitalistic enterprise if you like: demand and supply and the exploitation of a workingman. She had traded a small personal commodity of no value (herself) for a commodity of enormous value, corrupting and exploiting the bathhouse attendant who had to steal the pants from somebody else.

. . . The worn felt boots, enormous on her bones, had burst on the frozen legs of their former owner but she had mended them with a flint needle and wire (one found, the other stolen from the storehouse) and canvas and tar paper torn, at the risk of death for sabotage, off the roof of the machinery storage shed. And the straw in the boots came out of a crate of surveying instruments, and the burlap, soft as the gray rye flour it had brought up the river in summer, was the result of yet another trade. She had sewn the baby's clothes out of it, and her own underwear.

Up early of her own will in the Arctic night, she had seen the lights of Krasnaya Gorka, a derisive beacon. Well, no . . . No . . .

No longer derisive, no longer driving home comparisons. Her condition, prospects were beyond any comparison. Those kerosene and tallow stars no longer tantalized her with illusions of freedom; she had no more envy for the relative liberty of the people in the free settlement; she was no longer bitter about their furnished houses, varieties of work, their school, the milk and potatoes, Esterka's weaving, Mama Rashevsky's jars of preserves and pickles (no two-hour marches to and from work there! No twelve hours in the pits! No need to rob the dead!), the forty-eight-hour working week, the commissary, the practical nurse and midwife with her aspirins and bicarbonate of soda, the semblance of normality, the unbroken family; the luxury of jealousies, hatreds, feuds, intrigue, and complaint; the continuing dialogue of love, the practice of passion. The three kilometers between Krasnaya Gorka and the first gaunt spider-legged watchtowers of the camp could have been measured in light-years; only a fool with time on her hands would envy the inhabitants of another planet.

There was at least a whole hour before rising time, said to be at four o'clock or thereabouts. One more hour of a deep, energizing Nothing: the peace of oblivion, the only privacy in which she could experience whatever perceptions, sensations, and meanings were still possible, that illusion of a personal autonomy necessary to stay sane.

But she had things to do, her day's routine was already unfolding. Privacy, thought, sanity, escape were luxuries; that way lay relaxation and *that* was destruction. She had to find someone with whom to leave the baby, a woman weak and ill enough not to go to work but strong enough to survive until Catherine returned. Someone died in the barrack every day. She didn't want to find her child once more blue with terror locked in the rigid arms of a corpse. Starving on their half rations, the wasting women followed her with hopeless pleading eyes, reaching out, struggling to sit up to show how strong they were, mute in their lying assurances of competence, their minds and souls and entire beings fixed maniacally upon the five ounces of bread and sips of birch tea with which she paid for their services. She peered into their extinguished masks, fingered the cracked dry skin, felt the bones, judged and discarded, much as a woman might do choosing vegetables for dinner. Here is an eye that still reflects something like hope. Is hope a sort of strength? Does it mean energy? It's probably just fever . . . None of them spoke; each of them knew that words were not to be believed. Sympathy, compassion, any kind of feeling, the idea of friendship played no part in anybody's life. Ludicrous expectations! They know it and they know I know it better than anyone else, so why say anything? To stretch the ruin of their faces into a lying smile wasted

energy and accomplished nothing. All smiles were lies, only the deep-
etched frown was true.

The huge eyes pursued her even if the heads were unable to turn;
skulls gleamed through gray skin, long yellow teeth tempted her
knuckles like the dead keys of a mechanical piano. She thought she
could hear the crackling bones in the fluttering hands. They were tools,
objects, something that she might use, worthless except for that. Amaz-
ingly, irritatingly, Wanda looked the most promising of the lot.

. . . Up and down the barrack; once, twice. Peering, judging.

She heard the mute pleas. Her choice would be a verdict of a kind.

Suddenly she was short of breath and struggling for air. She heard
the deep, contented, knowing sigh of bodies settling back, heard the
snap of teeth, the rattle of dropped hands. She couldn't stop shaking.

Oh no, she told herself through the dizzy fog: not I, not yet. I *can*,
therefore I *will*. My life has an object. No abstracts. No obscurantist
myths but a living being. A child. And anyway, it hasn't been two
years . . .

. . . Dry rustling breath, a cackle of coughing.

She walked back to her bunk, careful to place her feet correctly on
the rotten boards, rummaged in her bundle, found the frozen lump of
milk wrapped in a footcloth, located the blue-black rock which was a
potato (blessing Janek Stypenko, knowing that she must march to work
because she had to meet him, suddenly conscious of her dry breasts, the
open mouth of the sleeping infant, cursing her body for betraying her).
Swift hatred sustained her. She took the lump of milk and the frozen
potato to the stove, kicked aside the pile of drying boots, squatted and
stirred the embers, placed the potato at their edge. The milk wouldn't
melt but she would push slivers of it into the hot potato.

She heard a distant uproar: one of those desperate mindless fights
that were constantly erupting in the men's barracks. Never a reason for
them, who would need a reason? To crack a skull, gouge an eye, snap a
limb, hammer another body into the ground, extract submission, extort
a scream of pain, inflict an injury to another spirit could be an affirmation of one's own existence. Fear touched off by futility, spontaneous
combustion. Victims seek victims of their own. And was it Father who
had said that all oppression was only a matter of opportunity? The
meek stay mild only until they can find someone meeker and milder
. . . Here, in her barrack, only the sick and dying could keep sleep at
bay. The others were sleeping. Down each long sidewall of heavy timber caulked with moss and clay stood fifty three-tier bunks, with three
women on each, huddled together for such warmth as they could find

in each other's bodies. Only one of the three sheet-iron stoves was working.

She gave her body orders: first, to control the quivering knees and thighs, then to subdue the ache and shift the weight (a ton of stone, a mountain of ice, a desolate windswept wilderness compressed into a burden) that had settled on her head and shoulders. Terror subsided and dizziness ebbed. Her roots went deeper than the ice and shale! She unfolded upward, waited. Opened cautiously to a harsh idea. Now looking down into the twin brown pits of Wanda's eyes, she saw them as a mirror. The yellow-gray cracked ivory skin stretched over naked bone was *her* face as much as the other's; the pursed black mouth was inflamed like a bullet hole. A life was seeping through it, full of clotted dreams. The pits glowed, unblinking. What was left of a woman's spirit made a feverish response to the dictatorship of the flesh.

—You'll take him, she said, and turned away from the eyes that suddenly became not hungry pits driven through skin and bone but pools reflecting her imagined mercy. Their light was ringed, turned inward, like a wreathed symbolic candle thrown into a well.

The black mouth gaped, exhaled decay, clattered an affirmative, exposed the tombstone teeth leaning upon each other. The sunken eyes drowned in a hiss of breath. A small brown animal seemed to be crouched at the bottom of the pits; it trembled under the weight of accumulated darkness.

Burned on the outside, frozen on the inside, the potato was as ready to eat as it would ever be. She broke it open, cracked shards of milk off the lump, mixed the two. She fed the child with her fingers. The small mouth was blue. The little wizened monkey face was yellow. She forced herself to make her motions dispassionate, remote from her being, stuffing the broken little puppet as though it weren't a child but a toy. There had been miniature Sèvres cups and saucers, Lilliputian spoons, tea and milk, currant cake, a slanting August sun between muslin curtains, and the mechanical Mama-croak of tilted artificial babies; real silk yellow hair, gray-green eyes painted in porcelain faces (Mother had done that because Catherine's eyes were green, or gray when she cried), fat simpering smiles molded between the bulging apple-red cheeks, eyelids that clicked open. And all the time in a safe predictable never-to-be-changed universe between lunch and teatime.

The child made no sound. It never cried, never gurgled. She had never seen it smile. It hardly ever moved. Tilt it all you want: the inflamed eyelids stayed open, naked and angry like flesh about a wound. The crumpled gray skin clung to a face as tightly clenched as an old man's fist. It stared at her with a mindless dark solemnity, an antique

resignation that made her vision tremble. No, she said fiercely: you're
not going to die and neither shall I. Those who live for someone shall
survive, and listen to Father Boguslawski in that matter, please. You are
a part of me, a fragment of Abel, a heraldic beast (part lion, part
eagle), you have all the resources of mythology and who's to say how
much of it's a lie? Bird or beast, you'll learn that necessary ferocity of
the only animal that can make promises, and you'll sprout the predatory beak and talons along with your pinfeathers. Then the poetry of
flight might be safely imagined.

She had to hurry; the bell clanged, commanded. (Well, not a bell,
not exactly, and absolute precision of imagery had become essential: it
was the only constant. So . . . not a bell. A yard of rail swinging on a
chain, now beaten with an iron bar.) All around her the harsh cracked
wind-burned faces snapped open, snarled obscenities; boots hit the clay
floor. The door flew open, slammed against a wall splintering icicles.

—Up, bitches!

The sudden blast of cold air made her ears ache.

Boots and curses flew. Sowinski ducked them, laughing, slammed the
door, was gone.

She put the child beside Wanda, folding the woman's stick arms
about the child's small body. The woman was fleshless, soft in helplessness, terrorized, defeated. A wax tear had frozen at the corner of an
eye.

Catherine looked into the crushed cadaverous face ridged and
grooved around enormous eyes, studying the topography of disaster as
though her own path might be marked upon it, read a smug promise,
rejected premonition, denounced an icy certainty: the harsh idea of
dying which had risen earlier like a cold Arctic sun. No, she said, and
saw the glint of malice flickering through the destroyed woman's
pathetic gratitude. Yes, there would be malice; the dying can't help it.
Time was about to fall upon her too, dismantling her defenses; her own
bleached skull peered at her out of Wanda's eyes. The skull grinned
and beckoned. The knowing eyes were mocking her across the ice wall
of the ultimate experience; they made a definite appointment. No, she
said, numb with certainty, not if I can help it! But you can't help it, the
twin brown pits informed her casually: this month or the next, today or
tomorrow, you are doomed. Surrender. No, she said. Cease the useless
struggle. It is not useless! Yes, it is. The struggle itself makes the end
inevitable, or do you think that the struggle is an end in itself? If so,
God bless your naïve soul and the Devil take it. I don't know, she said,
I don't care, leave me alone! Oh, come, come on now, that's out of the
question; why should you be left alone? Nobody else enjoys that luxury.
Damn you to hell, Catherine said. (Ha-ha-ha!) . . . She could swear

then that her own skin crackled and creaked, stretching like dry leather. Her skull was signaling to the other. This was treason. The skeletons were exchanging pleasantries, making pacts. Her skin—she suddenly thought of coarse-grained envelopes—was tight with hatred and she envied Wanda the luxury of defeat, but only for a moment. Hatred sustained her once again. Sympathy was weakness. Compassion, understanding, fellow feeling never failed to become a sentence of death. The dead and the dying must lie on the far side of pity. She had none to spare even for herself.

. . . An elbow, shoulder (something bony, sharp: a blow as mindless as a prayer, pointed as a curse) stabbed her between the shoulders. A wooden hip cracked against her own. She was spun immediately into another reality, the dimension of animal survival, and flowed as part of the black-brown-gray-frosted mass, harsh as the day, through the open door. One set of thoughts snapped shut, another sprung open. Her hands leaped up automatically, pulled down the earflaps, fastened straps and string (losing your ears is an easy business at fifty below), donned mittens. Her brain clicked off the necessary catalogue: spoon in boot, crust of bread in one pocket and tin bowl in another, flint needle up her sleeve, outer rags secured, inner shell in place. Her boots were pounding through fresh snow.

The snow was powdery, loose as flour, but it ran like water. Ironically, the wind had become almost tangible, thick as sand. Memory crackled warning signals (danger, danger!) and the mind took note. The danger is deadly. The march to work becomes twice as difficult and doubly exhausting when the snow is powdery. It becomes a nightmare. The legs pump frantically. You lean against the wind as though it were a wall. The feet can't find traction and the body sinks in the terrible quicksand stuff, and each forward step is a distinct and separate effort: a huge lurch upward and a sliding backward. Dialectical materialism at its finest: two steps forward, one step back. And in the meantime blood vessels burst, the brain is starved of oxygen in the thin Arctic air, lungs fill with moisture which freezes instantly, lungs become congested, sweat freezes on the body, tears freeze, the mouth fills with vomit which also freezes immediately, nostrils are clogged with bloody ice, people suffocate. They faint, fall, freeze, and are trampled and finally provide a solid surface for the boots . . .

Her heart beat up suddenly. Ah . . . The icy air lay like a band of fire along her cheeks. She wrapped her face in sackcloth. It was, as Mann-Bielecki would intone, an ideologically perfect moment to make a commitment . . .

Her feet slid out from under her and she fell.

Everyone was running.

Five thousand men and women had poured out of the barracks, huts, dugouts, and sheds around the square, making for the cookhouse. Pani Mosinka had said that there were five thousand. Professor Kukla had confirmed it, though *that* was no proof! King Whore had said that there were twenty camps just like this in the seven-hundred-and-fifty-kilometer mass of the peninsula, and that meant a hundred thousand men and women (nine out of ten of whom would be dead by spring) now in full morning gallop . . . The birch tea would be hot for the first two or three hundred in the lines.

Then she was sobbing, choked on hysterical laughter, wiping the swift tears before they could freeze. She struggled upward, ran. The signal crackled in her head. Tumblers fell, the gears creaked, revolved . . . The brain had finally come to terms with the message of the morning gallop and a ghostly calendar was fluttering open. Birch tea in the morning meant that this was Sunday, which, in turn, meant that three large dried and salted fish would be issued to every working prisoner at night (no point in wasting good food on the dying!) and the workday itself would be only six hours instead of the normal weekday twelve! For on the Seventh Day the Proletariat rested . . . And this was clemency, mercy. (She blessed the absentee gods of the ice world.) This would almost make up for the dangerous new snow.

But it could not be Sunday!

Catherine definitely remembered birch tea and salted fish three or four days ago. So . . . not a Sunday. No. Some other special day of divine interest in the inhabitants of hell. The gift of rest (six whole hours!) wasn't bestowed lightly. And it was not an anniversary of the October Revolution, it wasn't October. It was either November or December, most likely December. What happened in December? There was the birthday of the Christ, but this was not his kingdom; so . . . perhaps Stalin's birthday? God bless the great and glorious leader of his people, the wisest man on earth, Father of Mankind; if only he could have twelve birthdays a year! If Abyssinian Christians could celebrate Christmas every month, why not a monthly homage to the Great Red God? Salted fish, *ukrop* (boiling water), only six hours of work . . .

It could even be some kind of a mistake, the result of rumor . . . God himself knew well enough, having been a convict: there were always enough of *those* to go around!

God be praised for a little elbow room. Two men before her flailed at each other with insufficient fists, one fell. There was a sudden gap in the tight black mass: she darted forward, reached the bottom step.

Her own fists, elbows, knees, and boots were at work. Never mind the curses. We are no longer human and less than animals, we'd devour each other if we could. Obscenity is the language of the ice world, the lingua franca of the wilderness.

—My dear man, Professor Karolewski was arguing hopelessly with someone. You are pushing. Stop pushing! I was here before you!

—I was here before *you*, you Polish prick! a huge voice shouted. Two years before you!

—Well, if you take *that* tone . . . Well! I must say . . .

—Get the fuck out of my way!

She saw familiar faces in which everything was new: Pani Mosinska, no longer monumental, stained and darkly haggard like an icon in which nobody could believe; the narrow yellow smile of Mann-Bielecki, which demanded instant execution; Kepi and Kobza (Prrr-prr, *this way*, little lady!); and the thin sallow mask of Itzek Fogel, suddenly brilliant with malignant fire (vowing what frightful oaths of what unspeakable forms of vengeance?). She heard the hollow panting of Professor Kukla (treacherous and corrupt, he was making promises that he wouldn't keep) and she knew that she was standing among the survivors. Each of them had found something to sustain them: hatred or whatever twisted form sympathy was still able to take, resourcefulness or cunning, animal brutality or the subleties of treason.

On the top step, Surma and Sowinski were breaking foolish heads with ax and hoe handles, keeping the doorway open for the Unknown Criminal. (When he arrives and enters we shall be able to go in.)

Kobza spat, said: No way up those steps, I'd say. Prrr-prr.

—No way? said Kepi. Let me tell you, I've gotten into tougher places than that.

—Friends, comrades! Mann-Bielecki said. There's no need for a riot today, I assure you.

—No reason at all, comrades, said Professor Kukla.

—Whenever I hear this *comrade* shit I know I'm going to get hit in the ass the next minute, Kepi said.

—There'll be lots to eat for everyone today, Mann-Bielecki said. Special rations. I have it from the *nachalnik* himself!

—Tea? Coffee? *Ukrop?*

—Coffee. Real coffee!

—Soup? Gruel? Fatback? Bread?

(So might they have said Justice? Dignity? In another context.)

. . . She was suddenly light-headed. Darkness claimed her eyes; time was beating heavily toward her, death stunned her with a promise. She was immediately detached from her bony prison and seemed to be wheeling among bruised clouds. The smoke of the cookhouse fire snapped and crackled below her in the wind.

—Gruel *and* fatback *and* a full four hundred grams of bread, said the Archangel Gabriel. And that's just for breakfast . . .

—You lying crock of shit!

The steps were high with ice. Now she was standing on a mountain-top, looking down, and a dark man twisted from wind and smoke was showing her the treasures of a world, grinning from ear to ear with his mouth shut tight. She saw a life, reached out toward it, asked about the price. It seemed so little in the currency of the realm.

—I have it from the *nachalnik* himself . . . !

—As I love God, said Kepi. Stalin must've croaked!

—The Tsar's pulled off a resurrection.

—Has the war begun?

. . . A yellow smile glittered between beard and mustache like the Judas lights in a thicket above swamps; a leathery hand fluttered, two pebble eyes were wet with excitement. That was Mann-Bielecki. She could see far beyond that dark insistent vapor. There, on the edge of the world, the gaunt watchtowers rolled and strutted among graves like the drunken soldiers of an occupying army, the black smoke scrawled new laws in the leaden sky . . .

We are a law-abiding people, are we not? (argued the panting hollow voice of Zbigniew Kukla.) We always do our duty. It is our duty to survive. And everyone's ultimate allegiance is always to themselves . . .

Back to earth, numb with the effort to control her fear.

Mann-Bielecki's little wet eyes had become chips of quartz. Up went the leathery black claw, the furred gloved finger waggled; the yellow grin had split a frozen beard.

—It's as we've been trying to tell you all along, Mann-Bielecki said. The Russians are not our enemies. Theirs is a deep and passionate humanity that exceeds anything we've known. Our new commander has a heart . . .

. . . He has his duty, Zygfryd Bunt went on authoritatively. And duty . . .

. . . Is harsh sometimes, Professor Kukla fervently assured. Isn't it sometimes necessary to be cruel in order to be kind? We ought to know about *that!*

—No, no, there's no cruelty involved in this! Mann-Bielecki said.

—No, no, of course not! said Professor Kukla. We have been justly punished for our crimes against a higher reality, a higher philosophic concept, you might say, than our historically narrow nationalism . . .

—No, Mann-Bielecki said impatiently. Not punishment. Education . . . !

—Certainly, the professor said. That's just what I said. We're being educated in a new reality, the greatest good of the greatest number.

The Soviet people bring us a new alternative, it is *our* fault if we don't understand it. Such opportunities may not come our way again for a hundred years!

—And you have never missed an opportunity, have you? said Pani Mosinska.

—I mean our *historical* opportunity vis-à-vis our obligations to *all* peoples. Dear lady, you're being quite obstructionistic. But then what could we expect from your kind? That middle-class, parochial, provincial, egotistic sense of national identity has no further meaning! We have abolished such separatist concepts!

—I'm going to abolish you, you son of a bitch, unless you get on with it, Kepi said. We've heard enough of your committee bullshit.

Zygfryd Bunt clenched a fist, raised it, cried: You have no right to insult the Committee!

—The Committee has no right to insult our intelligence, cried Pani Mosinka.

. . . Just to get through the day was no longer enough. Yes, she would go to work, meet Janek Stypenko, who . . . oh, she remembered: If this was some sort of holiday Janek wouldn't be there! The people from the free settlements didn't work on holidays and Sundays. So . . . no potato, no frozen lump of milk. Suddenly she was cursing the Great Red God as fervently as she had praised him a moment ago. Weak with hunger, she was suddenly struck by the certainty that the child would die. And with him herself. Because the one life was dependent on the other, one sustained the other; faith in the survival of one was hope for the other. She must do something to get the necessary food; someone must help. If she took a man . . .

If generosity and goodness were out of the question, she'd settle for strength: inner or outer (any kind!). Raw animal power. Brute force to throw in the path of that brutal existence that could overwhelm her . . .

But they were only snapping at each other like small dogs.

—You don't know how much you owe the Committee! Zygfryd Bunt was shouting. If it hadn't been for us . . .

—Prrr-prrr. Some good men would've been alive.

—You'll get five years for this, you obstructionist bastard!

. . . Harsh as granite, comtemptuous as time, Pani Mosinska said: And what are *you* getting out of it? Traitor! Opportunist!

. . . The narrow yellow smile had become its own grotesque parody. Red eyelids fluttered, the hard chips of quartz had become compressed. —Such words, said Mann-Bielecki. Such *meaningless* words. And such foolish and dangerous words too, under the circumstances. Who is the traitor here and what is his treason? Will your cockroach concepts of loyalty keep you warm? Will they feed you? Will they feed anybody else? The General's Lady doesn't think of that! You can't eat ideals. I think it's time for us to find new alternatives. The classic notions of loyalty no longer apply. The General's Lady says, so rigidly, so unbending, so uncomprehending: *What are you getting out of it?* Well, I'll answer her! How about *Life*, comrades, isn't that worth getting?

—You filthy swine, said Pani Mosinka.

—Words, words, more words. You can't wrap them around yourself like a blanket, can you? They don't keep out the wind. What are we getting out of it? No one is going to get anything they don't earn, and that includes the privilege of living.

—To crawl on your knees . . .

—Better than to rot on your back, Mann-Bielecki said.

—Life is *not* a privilege, cried Pani Mosinka. It is an honor and a duty!

—Honor, said Mann-Bielecki. Duty. Three cheers for the General's Lady. And all the other generals and their ladies, and all the comfortable gentlemen who ran away to France.

—Our men went to France to fight! They're fighting in England!

—Dear lady, said Professor Kukla. Who fights in France? And what does England have to do with us? We must accommodate ourselves to our own reality. We aren't drinking tea in London at this moment, are we?

—Exactly, said Mann-Bielecki. The point that we on the Committee of Cooperation are trying to make is that the Russians also have a point of view. We must make an effort to understand it. We musn't condemn something just because it seems to defy our immediate comprehension. It may prove to be something beneficial! We must extend ourselves, examine the alternatives, search our conscience, and, finally, seize our opportunity!

—What opportunity? Catherine said.

—A chance to play traitor, said Pani Mosinska.

—But what opportunity?

—To show our Russian friends that we are worthy of their consideration!

—But what does that mean?

—We must extend ourselves! said Professor Kukla.

—God help me, Kepi said. If these sons of bitches don't get to the point I'm going to extend the whole fucking lot of 'em.

But Mann-Bielecki, Zygfryd Bunt, and Professor Kukla were no longer there.

There *was* gruel *and* fatback *and* a full four-hundred-gram ration of gray bread. One bowl of watery gruel, about half a ladle; the fatback was a rubbery lump, the size of a matchbox. A feast, though. A veritable triumph. And there was a cup of birch tea to take back to the barrack.

She kept her bowl clasped tightly under her chin, bowed her head over it, tried to make herself and her food invisible. Her eyes were watchful, trying to encompass everything and everyone with each suspicious glance. This was the Northern Glance, the key to temporary survival: partly sentry duty in case some brutal, hunger-crazed animal stronger than herself made a desperate attempt for her bowl and her pockets, and partly hopeful reconnaissance. Someone might drop something. Someone might suddenly give way to weakness and collapse, leaving a partly filled bowl. Someone . . . a gang boss, naturally . . . might feel like throwing her a piece of bread. Not likely, true, but it was known to happen, a sign of royal favor. Once could miss no chances . . .

She spooned her gruel rapidly, careful to spill nothing although her hands had resumed their trembling. (Mustn't show the trembling! Mustn't show that the eradicating process has begun!) The bread and fatback were stowed in her pockets. (Must get them to the barrack!) Her stomach leaped and churned, her insides were coiling and uncoiling like a chopped snake. She belched, blew huge farts. She found it difficult to focus her eyes.

Some camps, it was said, had regular mess halls: tables to sit behind and benches to sit on. But this was a comparatively new camp, only three years old, and the construction program hadn't got around to luxuries like mess halls. There was only one table. Two benches, no more. Her eyes were fixed most often on the fifteen men and the solitary woman eating at the table . . . a grim fraternity on which her life most likely depended . . . King Whore, the Unknown Criminal, Surma and Sowinski, and a round dozen of the pioneers—survivors of the original band of seven thousand which had built the camp out of the wilderness and which had long gone under. Harder and stronger, leaner and bigger than their buried comrades . . . more ruthless, willing to jerk crusts of bread out of sick men's hands . . . willing to kill for a bowl of soup, denounce for a cigarette, they had stayed alive through two winters such as this. It was a staggering accomplishment, worthy of respect. (Some of *them* were said to have been engineers, officers, Heroes of the Revolution). True to the laws of nature, the dozen murderous survivors had been elevated, honored, and rewarded. They were the work-gang foremen, work-brigade leaders now: the lesser gods of this particular creation. They drove the pit gangs and made the work assignments and were thus in a position to decide who would survive the day. They weeded out the sick, which was a death sentence. (No way to hide a trembling hand from those eyes! They harried the desperately ill men and women until these wrecks stopped pretending that they were fit to work and surrendered to the luxury of their inevitable end . . .

Catherine squatted on the floor just inside the door, brushed by an occasional warm stench drifting from the stoves. She stared for a moment into her empty bowl as if expecting manna. There were no miracles forthcoming on *this* journey. She sighed, hid the bowl, looked over the hunched silent group at the Table of the Gods, made her choice, advanced, struggled through the mob to the presence, and waited.

—King Whore, hey, King Whore, she said.

The woman's red-rimmed eyes flipped upward, a coal chip in a fire, blank with the contempt of offended majesty. Catherine knew she had to be careful: never presume on the goodwill or memory of princes, in this world or the next.

She had placed her hands behind her to conceal their trembling, now brought one forward, sunk it in a pocket, found the lump of fatback (thought of her child, who could have sucked some strength out of it . . . ah, but this was better in the long run!), put the greasy-gray offering on the table. King Whore regarded it, dismissed it and Catherine. Her heart was beating fast, fluttering in her throat. Surma looked up and grinned, his mouth a deathtrap full of rotting milestones. (He hadn't yet learned the art of royal scorn.) Sowinski licked his lips. The Unknown Criminal reached out and swept the offering to the floor. She bent her back to find it. The twelve originals were swabbing out their bowls with bread, lighting cigarettes . . . She had pleaded, the jury would decide. The best thing to pray for here would be that life be mercifully short . . . but her whole life hadn't been long enough for that kind of plea! The jury wasn't to be allowed to guess what she was thinking.

(. . . Ah, but they know what I know: that if a man or woman knows that he or she is going to die, and there's no shadow of a doubt about it, the soon-to-be-dead person will spend his or her last days, or even weeks, in as much comfort as can be bought.)

That wasn't what she had come to buy; she must make sure they knew it. King Whore might realize it (she was sure to know it!) but she gave no sign. Nor could one be expected.

. . . *Two years, it hasn't been two years!* she wished to remind them. She had not yet reached the outer limit of possible survival.

(. . . Those who live for others shall survive, said Father Boguslawski.)

. . . Ah, but the nuns died first!

Wanda was dying, finally liberated; her sentence was over.

(. . . But I'm *not* dying, I'm *not* going to die. This isn't that sort of bribe, gentlemen and madam of the jury. And please don't tell me what kind of a bribe it is. It is . . . an offering and an application. Draw your own conclusions. Think of it, if you like, as the opening bid. I can go higher, like any other woman. Why not? Currency is only as good as what it can buy. I'm starting off with fatback, not a bag of bones, but the implied promise should be clear.)

She jerked up her head, stiffened her spine, pushed her shoulders back. King Whore grinned suddenly. Huh, said the Unknown Criminal. Sowinski was whispering to Surma, who was also grinning and shaking his head.

She saw Kobza in midstep in the doorway. His face was expressionless, or seemed so in that fragile moment, then he was gone down the steps. She caught a fleeting glint of derision in Itzek Fogel's eyes, noted the waves of anger coming from Kepi's back . . .

Listen, she wanted to shout at them all. I don't want a savior-hero! Who can trust a hero having seen so many suicidal fools? You know camp lore! When luck has vanished, when there are no more illusions to believe, when even an old priest's mysticism no longer works, when Lady Fortune shows you only her bony ass to kiss, you're better off with someone who knows the geography of *that* region! . . . And who the hell are you to condemn anyone for wanting to live?

(. . . Father Boguslawski had said once that we can trust our lives only to someone who values his good name, wants to live with honor, wants the rewards of honor. But she knew that an honored skull smelled no better than the other kind. The real truth is that we can trust only a fragment of our lives to anyone. And if we're interested in living we must choose someone whose life is demonstrably valuable to himself!)

Surma was grinning, chewing bread, little pig eyes fastened upon a memory of rape. (That was how Zuita had begun her career . . .) King Whore toyed with a notion, her eyes were scrunched down among speculations. Catherine silently assured her that *she* would be no threat to HER position . . . now.

King Whore shrugged.

Thank you, whispered Catherine.

Sowinski pushed a spatulate black finger back and forth inside his bowl. The Unknown Criminal poked a black tooth, picked a splayed nose, scratched a tangled beard . . . She couldn't help a shudder. King Whore laughed.

She heard the first of the shrill whistles for assembly piped outside, turned and ran. Laughter followed her, laden with threatening promise. Her heart had leaped into her throat and fluttered there like a caged canary. She was as cold inside, then, as she was outside.

She scooped up snow as she ran, cleaned the piece of fatback and began to chew it. The baby had no teeth worth talking about, so it would suck the fatback. Perhaps she could trust Wanda not to pry it out of that little bleak purse of a mouth and eat it herself . . . Yes, she thought she could. Helpless, hopeless Wanda . . . so much for fragility, gentleness . . . ! Wanda was dying of her own free will. The will to live is measured in what you will *do* to live. Conscience is a weakness and scruples are futile.

Pani Mosinska called to her angrily across the square. Catherine waved an arm, pointed toward the barrack, ran on. She didn't want to hear that harsh voice or look into those eyes. Later it wouldn't matter. Now it would shake her purpose.

Coughing, she lost the gummy lump of fatback, scrambled for it in the snow, found it, clenched it in her fist, ran into the barrack.

The birch tea in the metal cup was cold and thick with ice.

The whistles pursued her.

He who does not work, shall not eat!

Oh, be still, she whispered. I know.

In the barrack, the Priest scrawled a small cross in the vapor of her breath. She was convulsed with hatred.

—What are *you* doing here?

. . . And why is her trembling voice out of control, leaping among cracked stars? The smile lay on his bruised and broken mouth like a moth on dark glass.

Don't dare to reproach me.

Damn you, damn you, she whispered. Why do you have to resurrect my gentle dead today? I've just buried the last of them!

. . . His voice is so low that she must lean into it as though it were a hurricane . . .

The Priest said: Your child is in my barrack, sleeping.

—What?

The whistles cut into her back like whips. She jerked under them like a puppet. (A moment! A moment!)

—Where is my baby?

—It's quite safe with me, the Priest said.

—He, she cried. He! Not *it!* But why did you have to . . . ah.
Wanda, she saw, was dead.

. . . Outside: Whistles fracturing icy air. Boots drumming. Shouts.
(I'm coming, oh just a moment, please . . .)
Inside she was focusing her whole being around a solitary spark.

—What do you know about children . . . Father?

. . . The shaggy head tilts backward, the eyes are confident and calm.
Eyes now colder than mirror glass, indifferent to secrets, now deep as
water under ice and glinting with silence. Long beyond the solitude of
youth, he need never again depend upon himself.

. . . Had been a missionary.

(China, Tibet, was it not? So Abel had told her. His hands lay hidden in his sleeves but she had seen them often: twin knotted fists with
which to hang a symbol in the air, grip an ax, divide frozen berries
found under the snow, chill a fever, close vacant eyes, and consecrate a
day.)

. . . Had been a scholar, exorcist of hatred.

(Tokyo and Vienna and Warsaw, I believe? A luminary in his own
right and dimmed only by an act of his own will. Proud as the Devil at
one time, it had been said . . . until he found that the harsh light of a
missionary's zeal, the self-warming flame of the scholar, was not much
different than the fire of an auto-da-fé.)

. . . Had been a parish priest.

—I can do at least as well as a dying woman, he said. At least I'm on
my feet.

—Aren't you going out to work today . . . Father?

—It seems that I'm not.

—If you are strong enough to stand you're strong enough to work!

—How quickly you've learned hatred, the Priest said.

Yes, she said. Haven't I? And why shouldn't I? That is the language
of the country! And haven't I had wonderful instructors? Ice walls keep
out the icy wind; would you have me naked? There is a corpse under
your hand; *she* would not learn the language but she is colder now than
I am, icier, stiffer. So who is proved right? And, by the way, can I have
that coat?

—I didn't say that you were wrong to hate, the Priest said.

—Thank heaven for small mercies!

—I do not even say that you should try prayer.

She laughed, her head cocked swiftly to the shrill call of the whistles,
the pounding of boots. Bleak sunken eyes regarded her from the bunks
of the sick who could not go to work.

—Well, that's good, she said. Because as someone just said, you can't eat prayers, they can't keep you warm. And love doesn't seem to hold up very well at this temperature. So I'm grateful for your tactful dispensation.

She worked the fur coat from under Wanda's body, struggled into the arms and searched for strips of hemp to plait into a belt. Later she would make holes, sew on bone buttons, make clasps out of twigs. The whistles were insistent, the column was forming. She had to hurry now. Wanda's dead body hung half out of the bunk, the face upturned, and suddenly she stooped, peered into the mouth, and stepped back, laughing.

—So you can't even trust the dying, she said.

—What do you mean, my child?

—She choked on the potato, Catherine said. I left her with a potato for the baby. She stole the potato. Look in there, you can see it sticking in her throat. It never did melt all the way into the center.

—So she was learning the language of the country, after all, the Priest said quietly.

—She learned it a bit late. The damn thing is, it wasn't necessary. I brought her bread and some tea for the child. If she had only waited she'd have had bread and tea and a piece of fatback. The fatback was for the child but I suppose she'd have stolen it. You said that you'd look after my baby today?

—Every day, as long as I can.

—Then you take the bread, the tea, and the fatback. No, not the fatback. I'll take that along and give it to the baby after work. And not all the bread. I hope you'll forgive me this inability to trust anyone.

—There's nothing to forgive.

. . . Now the eyes glow and shine like faith or rotten wood. The smile is no longer tentative with the moments of age: the red moth has spread her wings and the flame enfolds her. The Priest is a ghost of the men he had been; ghosts don't have anything to fear.

—You trust me with your child, he said. But you won't trust me with a few scraps of food?

Swift as truth, having learned her lessons, reciting all those declensions of misery whipped into her at the grammar school of hell, she said: Well, you can't eat the baby.

And ran for the door.

And now the voice is harsh. It comes at her in splintered multicolored shards, fills the dark naves of consciousness with the thunder of a falling mountain.

—How can you be sure?

—Don't mock me, you! she cried, frozen in midstride, then turned and ran back. —Here! Take the food! Eat all you want of it!

—Keep your food, Catherine. I have enough for myself . . . and your baby.

—There's never enough!

—Old men need very little.

—If you don't eat you'll die!

—That seems probable.

—If you don't work you won't be given anything to eat, she began to argue, and strained to hear the whistles which no longer came.

—That seems to be the rule.

—Do you want to die, then? Is that it?

—I believe that a priest has more reason to resist death than anyone else.

—What is it that you're doing, then? What are you after? There's no difference between a martyr and a suicide . . .

—It wasn't my decision, the Priest said.

—Oh, Catherine cried, running for the door. Well then, protest it!

—I've never known my God to change his mind, said Father Boguslawski.

. . . Can't trust a saint; he has too much to gain. Talk about love for enemies (and that will come next!) is a threat to nature. She fled at once into a world of childhood, babbling nursery rhymes; the old priest couldn't follow her there.

Abel was dead, she was sure. She'd know if he was still alive. Wanda had choken to death. Ziuta Poremba is the camp whore, her little brother is her pimp, Mann-Bielecki and Professor Kukla form their "progressive committees," and Father Boguslawski preaches sermons of forgiveness . . .

Then she was at the gates where the columns were forming and looked for her own squad.

(—Form your fives! Face the gates! Get moving, you bastards!)

—Hey Kaśka!

No one had ever used that crude, contemptful form of her name before. It meant nothing to her, no more than the rest of the language of the country: one name's as good as another when the whole ritual of living is an obscenity . . . One quick glance framed the Poremba boy: to some he was pathetic, to some as natural as syphilis and plague. He rolls toward her with an old man's stagger, takes up a wide-legged stance, and jerks up his head. His tongue is flickering around a twist of newsprint and *mahorka* and it is difficult to remember that he can't be much older than Emil.

—Hear you been talking to the bosses, Wiesio said in his thick little mercenary voice; the small triangular face was momentarily open.

—I didn't say a word, she said over her shoulder.

—Wait. What's your hurry? There's a big search at the gate today.
You've got lots of time. I want to talk to you, might have something
for you.

—Expanding your business?

—Why not? Meat is meat.

—Is your little sister getting tired?

—She's got no complaints. She eats every day. How's your belly rumbling these days, Kaśka?

She shrugged, turned away, hurried on. He cried after her:

—What do you want for that coat? Spirits, tobacco . . . ? You want
some white flour? Hey, you dumb bitch, how'd you like a place of your
own to sleep in? Nice and dry. How'd you like a job working in the
kitchen?

Then he cried, as she plunged into the crowd: Your kid might even
make it until spring.

She burrowed into the forming column, a mass without names or
faces, histories or identities, a past or a future. A work column is
defined in density and weight, not in memories. Raw, windburned, hard
as soil under ice, heartless as the tundra, splashed with the ghostly
sheen of frostbite, gangrenous and keening, reeking of future boneyards,
gutted and endlessly renewed. It is always arriving down the river and
vanishing in the pits. Without names or faces there can be no victims.

(She thinks of ice floes inching toward a frozen sea, glaciers on the
move.)

. . . No room is made for her. The mass is in motion. Think of an
avalanche growling down a valley. Oh, but she *will* tunnel her way to
the head of the column! She has brought all of herself into one sharp,
bright pinpoint flame of will.

—Well, little lady, you've cut it pretty close today. Prrr-prrr.

—I'm here, aren't I?

(—No talking in the column!)

The crowd pressed forward, silent and malevolent. Perhaps, she
thought, it *creaked* at such times; it rumbled icy promises the way the
frozen earth did above the pits. No strength to waste on curses. Breath
was strength! The trick was to keep one's mouth shut tight, though she
might froth inside like the Dnieper cataracts; life could depend on
reaching the head of the column.

But Kobza was talking. She glanced at him sideways because he
surely knew better than to waste his breath. And why was he telling her
what she knew at least as well as he?

. . . I've done this one hundred and eighty-eight times!

—Got to get up front, little lady. The good jobs go to the front files every day. Did I say good? Well, they're good enough if the back files get the pits. Not that there's ever any choice about it. Did I say choice? That's *some* word, eh? Some word. Choice, huh. All you can do is get yourself in the right spot where, if you're lucky . . . and for sure, little lady, you make your own luck, that's true enough, and you got nothing to be ashamed of about the way you make it . . . where, I say, you're *there*, as they say, for the easy job. Did I say easy? They're easy all right when you think about them goddam pits. Once you start going to the pits . . . well, the next thing's the last.

—Did they ever get you in there, Kobza?

And at once she was cursing herself for talking, wasting breath, wondered what job she could hope for today if she got as far as the first hundred files. The word was out that a hundred new barracks were to be built by spring. If she could work right in the camp, without that four-mile march in freshly fallen snow . . . well! If not that, then perhaps one of the jobs where a fire was needed.

. . . Burning scrub to soften the ground for digging at the construction sites. The ice above ground was two meters thick. Under the ice the ground was frozen at least two meters down and it took half a day to warm it enough so that two or three feet of a hole could be dug . . . Or tearing frozen *gubka* in sheets off the dwarf pine. Then boiling the thick fungoid growth, drying it. To make a fire maker. All you need then is a flint and a bent nail . . .

But to get into *those* work squads you had to go without the morning *ukrop*. You had to wait at the gates before reveille. You had to be in the first fifty files of fives.

If you started the morning march deeper in the column the best you could hope for was the crushing labor of carrying sacks of ore out of the mine shafts. The water-soaked, frozen sacks weighed up to eighty kilos . . . normally twice the weight of the men and women who carried them up rickety ladders, ran with them to the collection point, ran back, and slid down icy ropes for another load . . . Carrying ore, you had to meet a quota of fifty sacks a worker in a twelve-hour day. People ran and carried until they dropped and froze. But even this was better than the bucket brigade draining the pits, where you worked twelve hours knee-deep in frozen water. Still, the water *was* only knee-deep! So if you were lucky . . .

. . . And if you had no luck . . . Or if your courage left you . . . If you were beyond the spur of your own will, numb past the reach of instinct . . . If you no longer had the strength to push, kick, and claw your way into the leading files before the column lurched out of the camp in the morning, if you could no longer summon reserves of energy and alertness to work your way up the column on the march (and oh, you had to keep your eyes on the guards and the dogs when you were breaking ranks . . . a step out of ranks is an attempt to escape, and that means a bullet), if you could no longer find someone, *anyone*, weaker than yourself . . . someone whom you could pull down, push behind you, trample if necessary . . . if, in short, you were among the weakest . . . ah, then you were marched to the pitheads, driven down the ladders into Stygian darkness where every groan boomed like a drum, and there you crept on hands and knees into narrow tunnels where, bent in half as though for beheading, shoulder-deep in black water and frozen sludge, you hacked with a dull-witted numb despair at a precious seam while rotting timbers creaked overhead, stones crashed into the water all about your head, and torches guttered in foul air.

Folklore: *Once you're in the pits you'll never work your way up the column again.* Twelve hours in the tunnels and you could never hope to reach the first five hundred files again. And that meant . . . the pits. And no one within living memory had ever lasted in the pits longer than one week.

—No, Kobza said. They'll never get me in there.

Then Kepi was there. Itzek Fogel with fresh blood black against the leather of his face.

(Pani Mosinska turns away when she sees Catherine coming . . .)

—Jesus, I thought you'd never get here, Kepi said.

—Had to wait for the little lady, see?

—The little lady knows how to look after her own ass, I'd say.

—You shut your face. Hold your tongue. That's all I got to say.

—Ha! Seems to me, Kepi said. Seems to me as I live and breathe, that old Kobza, that stupid old fart, is thinkin' of getting himself a little camp wife. Could that be? You think an old fart like that would know what he's in for, takin' on a woman and a kid . . .

—Seems to me, Kobza said, I heard somewhere like them Arabs used to cut the tongue out of some of them legionnaires.

—Tongue and balls, Kepi said happily. Tongue and balls. Then they'd put one in one place and the other in another. Switch them around. And sew them on as pretty as a picture. You never saw such a goddam sight.

—Seems to me like I might see it any minute now. If somebody around here doesn't shut his face.

—Ho ho ho, Kepi said. Ho ho ho ho ho.

Pani Mosinska turned her head to stare and Catherine recoiled. (Damn you, she whispered, don't damn *me!*) The woman's voice was dry, cold, compressed. —Enough of that, she said.

The men grinned at each other.

—Wanda is dead?

Catherine nodded, drew the sealskin coat tighter about herself.

—Who is looking after your child today?

—Father Boguslawski. He said he wasn't going out to work today . . .

—He's been forbidden to work.

—But if he doesn't work . . .

—He will die. That is the idea.

—But why? He does no harm . . .

—He does his duty.

—His masses were always secret . . .

—He was denounced. There are no secrets here, you know that.

—Who denounced him?

—A man who came to him yesterday and asked him to hear a confession.

—Who? Do you know who?

—Mann-Bielecki.

—But Father Boguslawski knew all about him! He knows all about
that committee. Everybody knows it. To perform a religious service in
front of an informer, well, that's suicidal!

—He is a priest, said Pani Mosinska. He can't refuse to hear a confession.

—Why do they do such things? Catherine said.

—Who? said Pani Mosinska. Why do they do such things as what?

—Mann-Bielecki, Kukla, Zygfryd Bunt, Banda-Cyganowski, Agnieszka
Dlapanow . . . selling people, betraying people. You know who!

—Why did you do what you did? said Pani Mosinska.

—I haven't betrayed anybody!

—You've betrayed yourself.

—Ah, now, wait a minute there, lady, Kobza said, Wait a minute.
Everybody's got to look after hisself. And if it don't do no harm to
nobody else . . .

Pani Mosinska turned her head, a gesture of dismissal.

—It's not like that at all, Kepi said.

Itzek Fogel smiled with his broken mouth.

—We all know about them committee bastards, Kepi said. Isn't that
right? We know why *they* do it.

—It's not just to eat, Kobza said. Not to live.

—Not for an easier job, Kepi said.

—They do it 'cause they're bastards! Kobza said.

Itzek Fogel laughed.

—What are *you* laughing at, you flea-bitten Yid? Kepi said.

—I can tell *you* about bastards, whispered Itzek Fogel.

—You can tell me about bastards? You? Didn't you bastards sell us all to the bloody Bolsheviks? Didn't you all jump up and down (pissed yourselves with joy!) when they came to Lwów? Who was down at the city limits with flowers when *those* bastards came? Was it me?

—It wasn't me, Itzek Fogel said.

—Stop laughing, you bastard! And the goddam Red Militia, *them* bastards, who set that up in Lwów?

—It was some other bastards, Itzek Fogel said.

—Stop laughing, I tell you!

—*Nu*, why not? said Itzek Fogel, laughing. I'll oblige you. Why shouldn't I oblige you? It's all in the family, all among us bastards.

Then he choked, coughed, spat blood which froze instantly in ruby-red droplets and intricate glinting threads woven through his beard. His swaddled hands crept up and lay upon his narrow wasted chest as though to warm themselves . . .

—Stop that, all of you, said Pani Mosinska. The Russians can hear.

—Ha ha ha, laughed Itzek Fogel.

His hands were still upon his chest, like a badge of office.

. . . Now the column moves. Lurches forward. A step at a time. Stops. Moves again. Stops. Moves toward the gate while the wind whips up. Beyond the gate the long white day lies coiled and waiting. The gate yawns. The day is motionless and pale and hissing with flurries. The crooked gate is the maw of the day. It is a coarse trellis of barbed wire wrenched to the side so that a gap may be created in the barbed-wire fence: a puny obstacle. (Five Boy Scouts armed with pocketknives could take it in open assault, Catherine thought.) The gate is not a gate but a clumsy weave of wire and snow, and the fence is not a fence but a wall thick with ice. It holds back the wind. In places it is down for yards under the weight of the ice and snow. The weight of the wind. Easy enough to climb over the gently rounded white battlements which keep out the wind . . . But to what earthly purpose? Escape is impossible. (That is to say, she corrected herself formally, conscious of the need for precision, for the exact image upon which to focus a mind and sidestep madness for another day: *successful* escape is impossible; to vanish in the tundra is no problem at all.) Escape must be an arriving as well as a departure but here the *distance* is a prison wall . . . Who could cross a thousand miles on foot . . . and such miles! Miles of ice, wind, and snow that lie beyond the fence . . . when only four miles strike the mind with terror? The tundra and the taiga are more of a wall and a fence than any amount of barbed wire and stone . . .

(Now near the gate, she can see through the wry gap and beyond the fence-wall. Sees a squad of soldiers, their long-bayoneted rifles slung across their backs, searching the files of fives as they march up to the gate. Hears the shouts and the curses. The soldiers poke and rummage among frozen rags, snap carefully hoarded strings, tear cloth, fling aside bits of canvas, sacking . . . make no sound of their own. Dull routine of a morning. The files of fives howl, scream obscenities, but are careful not to raise a fist or even to clench one. Coats gape, layers of loosened clothing whip in the wind, blue flesh is revealed. A man has been stripped to the waist and freezes to death while uttering short high-pitched yelps like an injured dog. A dog which had been run over by a truck, perhaps. Crushed under the wheels. But no, not a dog, not here; because a dog is valuable here and a man is not.)

Catherine peered between the files of fives to see what was being confiscated this morning. It's one thing one day, something else on another. You could never guess ahead of the search which of your precious treasures (the wooden spoon, the tin mug, the bowl, the hidden flint needle, the scrap of pencil sewn into the boot) would land you in the bunker. The bunker was the only concrete building in the camp: a prison within a prison. No stove there. Not even a pallet. Only an icy concrete floor. Few people ever came out of the bunker after a week in it.

—Prrr-prr, Kobza said. They're going all the way today.

He sniffed the air like a country dog brought into the city, tasting its composition, moved his head carefully from side to side, small eyes watchful. —Something's up.

—Big search today, the bastards, Kepi said.

—Ah, said Itzek Fogel.

She looked at him squarely for the first time, saw a frail little man knotted out of wire, the wind might knock him down. Magically twisted out of sand perhaps, like Pan Twardowski's fairy-tale whip, to confound the Devil. A bitter little man, harsh and unforgiving as his own laughter, who knew, not merely supposed, that cruelty was only a matter of opportunity, that passive victims created their own oppressors, that vengeance was sweeter than confectionery sugar, that suffering was an insult. An honest workman who won't cut against the grain mixing tears and laughter . . .

The skeletal small Jew grinned his frozen smile, his face a ragged sheet of parchment crowded with notations: a record written by innumerable hands, none of them his own. So might she read something there if she understood all the languages. (She doesn't.) But the eyes spoke dark volumes anyway.

She tried a smile, thinking about Abel, feeling her own face as blank as paper waiting to be written on, hearing a murmur of consolation (nobody's blaming you, little lady, you got to make your own luck), sought answers in eyes as black and deep as the barrels of a shotgun.

Itzek Fogel hummed, twitched, unfolded his mysterious message. People can offer much harm and little good. For when it's a matter of life and death a man will always choose his own life over any other.

. . . Big Search, Big Search: the warning voices rustled down the column. (Two or three hours standing in the wind, comrade. That's what!) Not just the ordinary morning search: the perfunctory prods and pats by bored hands, the careless swift kick-and-shove as the files of fives march up to the gate. A big search today. Big Search . . .

—Prrr-prr. What's up then? Something's up.

—Somebody must've stole something . . .

—Stole what? What's there to steal?

—Bastards're scared we're carrying their goddam camp out a piece at a time.

—Who'd want the goddam thing?

—But something's up, Kobza said.

—You feel it, eh?

—I feel it.

Kepi spat, said: I'll tell you what's up. It's all up with our six-hour workday. Can't trust those bastards ever. Two hours search now, two more when we get back from work, and there's four goddam hours up the spout. So what does that leave us?

—Leaves you two hours, Itzek Fogel said.

—Two hours isn't six!

—It's two more than you'd have had on a regular day. Ha ha ha.

—You crazy bastard, Kepi said.

—Ha ha ha, said Itzek Fogel. Happy New Year, comrades.

She saw the angular old trucks shaking and rattling at the head of the column, their long vertical chimneys belching smoke. Trucks, she thought, numb. Smelled the reek of charcoal and wood smoke.

. . . Trucks out today, the word crept down the column. They'll make grooves in the snow, pack it, make the march bearable. Trucks, trucks . . .

—Well, I'll be goddamned, Kobza said.

—Well, isn't that something, Kepi said. Hey, maybe them committee bastards weren't lying!

—Well, but look, there's the trucks.

—So they'll want something from us. How many times did they get out the trucks since you been here?

—Twice, three times. I don't know.

—It was twice. Every time they do it they want something from us. The first time they done it, you remember it?

—That's when they come around with them goddam passports.

—Now your head's working. They run the trucks to soften us up, make us feel good about their goddam passports, show us how good they can be to us, the bloody sons of bitches.

—They got pissed off when nobody took their passports, Kepi said, and laughed. Doubled the norm at the pits, I remember.

—Some people took the passports, Itzek Fogel said.

—Yids took the passports, Kepi said. Bastard Yids.

—There's no Yids on the committee, Itzek Fogel said.

—No Yids? What d'you mean, no Yids? They got to be Yids if they took the passports. Who'd want to be a goddam Bolshevik if he wasn't a Yid? Sure they are Yids, everybody knows that! And how come *you* didn't take one of them Russian passports, you crazy bastard?

—Maybe I'd rather be a Yid, Itzek Fogel said.

—Now I know you're crazy.

—Let me tell you, Kobza said. *They* don't do anything for nothing. Either they want something from us or they're scared of something.

Kepi sighed, regretful. —There isn't going to be trouble here. They got everybody just about starved.

Kobza said: Them people on Chelyuskin Island didn't eat no better, but they burned down their camp all the same. Listen, let me tell you, when people got nothing left to live for they don't care about dying.

—I got something to live for, Kepi said.

—What?

—I don't know, said Kepi.

Itzel Fogel laughed. Catherine saw the small Jew suddenly as locked in terrible loneliness, a prison beyond terror, past the bars of boredom or the dank cells of mere survival . . . Wanted to touch him but he was out of reach. The little man made of antique parchments, old rags, and steel wire was doubled over in a paroxysm of soundless laughter.

—What are you laughing at, you crazy little bastard? You laughing at me? Kepi hissed.

—No, Itzek Fogel said. I'm laughing at me.

—Maybe you think *you* got something to live for?

—I got nothing to die for, Itzek Fogel said.

—Well, you'll die here all right, Kepi shouted. Everybody's going to die here. What d'you think about that?

—Who can think about that?

—Well d'you *feel* anything, for Chrissake . . . !

—Lost, cold, and hungry, Itzek Fogel said. Ha ha ha.

—By Christ's holy wounds . . . So help me . . . !

—Ha ha ha.

—Leave him alone, Catherine said.

Itzek spat, contemptuous. —Who's asking for your help?

She said: Maybe, perhaps, I'm asking for yours . . .

Itzek Fogel shrugged, muttered: I can't hear you and you can't hear me.

Pani Mosinska said: Keep quiet, all of you. The Russians can hear you!

—So let them hear me, Itzek Fogel muttered.

—Raise your heads! Get your backs straight, damn you, stand erect . . . like *people!*

—Like people? Itzek Fogel said. Ha ha ha.

Catherine said: But I *do* hear you . . . I hear you very well.

Kepi said: Who wants to hear *him!* What I want to hear is dynamite going off, them fucking barracks burning . . .

—No, Catherine said automatically. There's been enough of that . . .

—Better that than to die by inches, said Pani Mosinska.

—I am not going to die, Catherine said, heard the older woman's harsh, contemptuous voice (could it truly have been soft and gentle, had it ever whispered, had a troubled young man ever found it soothing, had it sung to a child?): You'll die. Your child will die.

—I will not, said Catherine. He will not.

—Today, tomorrow, or next week. This month or the next.

—Then let it be *then!*

—Why then rather than now since it's inevitable?

—Because it is . . . *then.*

—No chance of anything happening here, Kepi said. Too many women, crazy Yids . . . them committee bastards . . . You got to have *men* for something to happen. Look at all them corpses, they can hardly stand up on their feet.

—Listen, Kobza said. You think nothing's going to happen here. So maybe it won't. Everybody thinks it'll never be him, always some other man but never him. It's always like that. That's how *they* keep everybody down until everybody's down for good. But maybe one day something happens, see? I don't know what, something. Some little thing that don't mean much of anything by itself, see, and it don't mean much to anybody either. What thing? How do I know what thing? It hasn't happened yet! But when it happens, let me tell you, it's like the biggest thing that ever happened to anybody and everybody knows it. It's like a spark, see, only a little thing and you don't see it until it's so goddam dark all around you can't see anything else! And thats all you need. And it don't matter what the hell you got: men, women, Yids, or what. And then things get started.

—So let's get things started, for Chrissake, Kepi said.

—You don't get things started. They got to start all by themselves. But when they get started . . . Prrr-prrr. That's all I got to say.

. . . Now she is at the gate, the ice wall is behind her, the wind is in her face, and her eyes are burning. Nothing will happen. She will last through the day and all her compromises will be justified. And treason and betrayals, if such things can still be talked about—if there still *are* such things—must be weighed in the scales of the times.

Here right is never wholly right; a wrong can't call down instant lightning; good and evil have become one, each is a vital fragment of the other and perhaps that is just as well.

Then she was through the gate, running toward the others, hauling her clothes together about herself. Nothing had been taken. If nothing had been taken then nothing's been lost.

(Form your fives! Silence! Forward march!)

The trucks heaved forward under streamers of black smoke. The soldiers and the dogs set off beside the column.

The Magician

THE MAN WAS LARGE AND BEARDED. He walked among the Ostyaks much as a bear might move among circling dogs, arms loose at his sides, head outthrust, hunched and dangerous. From time to time he'd stop. He would look around. The Ostyaks would draw together then and make polite, encouraging gestures with their bows. The man came on and Dr. Poremba took a few steps forward to show a good intention.

By this time he supposed himself an old dog at the game, he knew all the tricks. The visitor would be frightened of him, dragged to the Ostyak encampment by curiosity but wrapped in suspicion as though it were a magical cloak which might protect him. Watchful, sniffing air, likely to think Poremba a Soviet official. . . . Well, we've been through this half a hundred times, Dr. Poremba muttered to himself: the poor bastards are always on their guard, the Message notwithstanding. *Litwo, ojczyzno moia*, that's one side of it. They can never resist the challenge of that riddle, they have to know what it is all about . . . but they've been taught to step with caution in this godforsaken country where no one trusted anybody else if they still had a shred of their wits about them. They've been taught to approach any suggestion of authority as though it were an unstable explosive: an equal compound of malice and madness. Up here, in the archipelago of the Gulag, in the huge secret continent of the NKVD, a smile was not a smile, an outthrust hand wasn't to be shaken. Nothing here was quite what it was anywhere else and one false step was always the last. So, he thought, getting ready to greet the new arrival, no one walks confidently into anything and everyone tries to keep his eyes open in every direction at the same time because the unexpected is more likely to represent disaster than anything else. After a time, that is something that you can learn to live with.

He gathered his routines around himself as though they were a shaman's regalia, launched into his performance.

He watched the large bearded man, thought him young despite the painfully hunched shoulders. A bent back and a heavy foot were the stigmata of the North. But the man wore good felt boots and that meant that he was still able to defend them. No sign of frostbite on the windburned face, and that also meant something. A hard young man, tough as tanned leather, coiled within himself . . . Still able to feel anger, still tense, ready to lash out with fists and boots, still conscious of himself as a man of some kind, not yet crushed by the awful weight of time in the wilderness, still remembering, not yet sapped by overwork and hunger, still snapping on his chain like a trapped timber wolf, not yet ground down into the rock and shale, the ice and the snow . . . He hasn't been up here longer than a year, Dr. Poremba thought.

. . . Watched him coming. Saw the arrogance of youth made weary. Saw that at least that much was left of a youth that could no longer be believed. Youth without future is no better than old age. Saw no innocence in young eyes that had become ancient in less than a year but that still were able to reflect the monumental anger of the dispossessed and the disillusioned.

And then he stared in disbelief, having recognized the man.

(He was immediately back in the Lwów apartment of the dead Modelski and the whole careful structure of his masquerade had been blown apart; the grotesque fragments of the fraud he had committed against himself only a moment ago were raining about him. What a fool he had been to think that he could make decisions . . . Events make decisions! Anna Dimitrevna was gone, wiped from his memory; her idiot child had become an unspeakable mistake frozen into his spirit; the Ket and the Khanty had vanished, as though they had never been, and their foolish and discredited shaman disappeared in a puff of smoke. Several thousand miles were suddenly compressed into the dark dimensions of a shuttered city flat, and the forgotten was suddenly real.)

Why now? he thought. It was all over and done with; a choice had been made. Murder is no less murder for never having left the heart, betrayal is no less a betrayal for having been no more than an idea. Are dead hopes and illusions to be brought back to life after all? And who is this angry young man to play my deus ex machina? I'm the manipulator here.

(. . . And Jurek was there, the Eternal Lancer angrily denouncing the end of his life as he had been taught to understand it. [He had apparently brought more recent ghosts along for company.] That lovely gentle girl, the Modelskis' daughter . . . what was her name and how could he have forgotten it? Catherine, of course . . . Now, *there* was innocence! Catherine and Abel . . . The Jewish family from Zywiec, whatever they were called . . . ah, the Rashevskys. The Patriarch and the girl Esterka for whom *this* unexpected apparition had yearned . . .)

(Traitor, deserter, Jews' errand boy! Jurek was shouting out of the rubble of his shattered pride, the ruin of his dreams . . . And there had been others, hadn't he forgotten? St. Francis of the Kremlin puncturing the mornings with his tubercular explosions . . . a servant girl named Bronka and a boy named Emil . . .)

And why couldn't he bring himself to name the remainder: the blue-eyed, auburn-haired woman, the two flushed excited young girls who had carried conspiratorial messages about the occupied and violated city, the boy to whom he had once talked about the vicissitudes of life as endurance contests? Their names had become an incantation.

Alicja, he whispered. Luta. Ziuta. Wiesio.

Ave Satanas, he whispered in terror.

Don't tempt me again. Temptation offers yet another choice. I don't want to make any further choices. There's to be no more trust in the invisible. Hope is never more than a lying prelude to the inevitable disappointment. Only a moment ago it was all over and done with: a fool's game had been exposed to vanish in the snow along with the body of an idiot child. Only a fool turns his back on his own conclusions . . .

And, in the meantime, the young Ukrainian and the Ostyaks had entered the encampment.

. . . Comes now in answer to the incantation. There must be something to that magic business. Hard eyes are suddenly wide with recognition, the stunned young man leans against the wind. He had not yet arrived at an age when the flesh has shrugged off the future and the spirit halts to look at the past with longing. He stood astride the present, staying off that awkward humility that men learn to wear in prisons, fighting against the stoop of the exile, the diminishing resources of hope, anger, and the knowledge that his own survival was impossible. The bearded head jerks back, the mouth circles in astonishment, hangs idiot-slack . . . the eyes leap to the Ostyaks, who have certainly never seen such a successful show. Their shaman is worth his keep, no question about that: the large bearded "Russian" has been turned to ice.

Dr. Poremba raised his hands, dropped them on Janek's shoulders.

In Polish . . . (not even Ahmer would be able to make sense out of that): *Janku, kochany chlopcze . . . !* In a voice as harsh as the flurries whirling about their heads, a tone as whitely pointed as the disappearing stars: —Don't speak to me in Russian, one of them understands it!

The young man shook his head slowly from side to side, his mouth hanging open.

—There's nothing to be afraid of, said Dr. Poremba, the words thick and awkward; nothing that either of them could say to each other could be believed, he knew. But the young man must not be allowed to leap from shock into suspicion and then into fear.

Suspicion was already rising between them like a mist, distorting and confusing normal images. The morning fog had been much like that on the innumerable rivers he had crossed; particles of light would hang in it, mocking the chilly curtain with multicolored crystals.

—Are you hungry? Would you like to eat?

This was the infallible icebreaker: none of the northern exiles could resist an offer of food. He looked around for the madwoman and her cooking fire, caught her empty eyes and muttered soft curses. This too was an incantation of a kind. How did she always know what he was thinking before he could be sure himself? But the young man had not moved, he was still silent and shaking his head. Ahmer's watchful eyes had almost disappeared behind slits.

—You know me, don't you?

The young man said, as though dreaming: I remember you.

—I know you remember! Dr. Poremba cried expansively. And you know that we've always been friends!

—We weren't friends, the young man said. We only lived in the same house for a while.

—We weren't enemies, that must count for something.

The young man nodded.

—We are countrymen, Dr. Poremba said.

—We shared a country, the Ukrainian said. We weren't countrymen.

—Well, neither of us has a country now, so that gives us something else that we might share, don't you think? Call it a brotherhood in adversity, if you like. Perhaps we weren't able to share much before, but there's nothing to stop us being countrymen now.

—That may be, said Janek.

—So you see that you have nothing to fear from me. You can trust me.

—I'm not afraid of anything, the young man said quickly.

—Oh, of course, of course, said Dr. Poremba. Who'd suggest such a thing? But come into the tent where we can talk in comfort.

—And I don't trust anything, either, Janek said. If you want to talk, we'll talk in the open.

—It's cold out in the open, Dr. Poremba said, pretending to shiver.

—I'm used to the cold.

—I'll never get used to it, Dr. Poremba said in a thin, whining voice
which he hoped would sound like an old man's complaint. They've lit a
fire in the tent. There is salted fish, dried meat . . . There's reindeer
kumis . . . But what is all that to an old man? When his time comes, it
comes, and that's all there's to it . . .

—Come on, then, Janek said. Let's go inside the tent.

—Ah, but you said it's safer to talk in the open . . .

—It's cold out in the open! Janek said. God, you old men are really
something, you know that? You don't have the sense to get in out of
the cold.

—God gives us wise children, said Dr. Poremba.

—Are you laughing, old man?

—No, no, it's a cough . . .

Inside the tent, dog and reindeer skins were already stretched on
their short birch frames in the shaman's circle around a small fire where
reindeer chips were burning. A miniature Ket woman, all of four feet
tall from her leather traveling mask to the tips of her felt boots, squatted by the fire. She was melting snow in a birch-bark cup. Strips of
dried fish, stiff as barrel staves, were thawing near the fire. The woman
had piled them in a little pyramid around the black cup. Dr. Poremba
was suddenly hungry and, as suddenly, hunger was the last thing on his
mind. He peered into the thick aromatic smoke of burning dry dung,
saw the leather flasks, didn't see the child. Janek was holding up the circular leather flap so that he might step into the tent. He looked up and
around but couldn't see Anna Dimitrevna anywhere. He caught
Ahmer's eyes. The little Ket hunter's flat Mongolian face communicated nothing. He knows, though (Dr. Poremba thought at
once): you can see he knows.

He pulled the entry flap out of Janek's hands, pushed the young man
into the tent. —Get in!

—Hey, not so rough! And what about you?

—I'm right behind you, with you in a moment.

—All of a sudden you don't seen as old as you did a moment ago, the
young man said. What are you up to, anyway?

—I have remarkable powers of recovery, said Dr. Poremba.

He dropped the entry flap behind the Ukrainian, hurried to Ahmer.

—Where is the child? he said. I don't see the child.

Ahmer said softly: I caught your eye, shaman, I know what to do.
But the council says that we shall start back tomorrow for our own
country, whether there is a sign or not.

—What if I forbid it?

—Then you will have a lonely journey for as long as it lasts.

—Do you feel ready to challenge me? Dr. Poremba said. Let me advise against it. I haven't taught you everything I know.

—Everything will be done as you want it, shaman.

—Not as I *want* it! As it must be done!

—Either way, there will be sacrifice so that the people may have the sign that custom requires. That is all that should matter to a people's shaman. The shaman is a keeper of a people's customs.

Dr. Poremba swore heavily, kept still for a moment, glared at the small brown man, found that his hands were shaking. Irresolute? There's nothing like losing control of a situation in a critical moment! A fine time for personal surprises! Something would have to be done to awe the Ket again and he (damnation!) was fresh out of magic. His bag of tricks was considerably depleted.

He heard his own curses, thought them impotent. And he heard someone else's curses behind his bowed back.

He looked around, saw that the young Ukrainian was already half out of the tent, hurried toward him, pushed him in again and climbed in after him. The little Ket woman looked at them and fled. He thought that the infuriated young man was going to attack him, launched into his story (the monastery, his escape, the long search) while looking for a weapon with which to defend himself. Janek glared, cursed, mouthed threats. Well (though Dr. Poremba) that's reasonable, that's fair; I've tricked him and his puerile pride is a bit askew. Young men always take themselves with such ferocious seriousness. Hold up a mirror to their foolishness and their brains blow up.

He passed the first of the leather flasks, watched the young man's eyes watering and the anger dimming as the powerful alcoholic mixture of fermented wheat, reindeer milk, and urine exploded in his head . . . Knew he would have to wait before asking questions until suspicion had dissolved in the *kumis*, until a bridge of confidences had been suspended between himself and the Ukrainian . . . He would wait, had the patience. Had done this before. But there were some questions that anyone could ask even this early in the game.

—What's the name of that settlement of yours?

—Mine? Janek cried. What makes you think I've anything to do with that Russian shithouse?

—Don't ask me, said Dr. Poremba.

—Damned Russians, Janek said. Called this place Krasnaya Gorka, and isn't it just like the damned stupid Russians to call a flat white wilderness a *Little Red Hill*?

—There are many places called Krasnaya Gorka, said Dr. Poremba. I came across one in the Pervomaisky Uchastok, in the Mari country.

The young man wouldn't meet Dr. Poremba's eyes. He had been angry and confused in Lwów, as who hadn't been, but he had loved someone then and that had made a difference. Now he had narrowed, a love had turned to hatred. He could not be rushed into anything.

—What kind of people live in that settlement? Russian Jews, or what?

. . . The broad mouth is immediately tight. The voice seeps from it like pus from an infected wound. The eyes retreat. The face is pinched, deprived.

—Well, mostly Jews from Poland, Janek said, and drank from the leather flask until it was empty, and Dr. Poremba immediately tossed another to him.

—About six hundred of them, Janek said. Seventy-two complete families, grandmothers and all. A few bachelors. I got to share their hut and their lice in summer. You've never seen so many lice as we've got here in summer. There's one Ukrainian family, but not out of Poland. No damned Poles at all, thank God. That's all we'd need here, some lousy stiff-necked Poles with their noses up in the air, giving themselves titles! There's one crazy Czech, a Jew like the rest, who came to Russia because he thought it was a paradise! There's fifteen Russians, all that's left of the lot they sent up here to build the settlement. They're the foremen now. They've been here ever since that trouble the Russians had with their collective farms.

—That would be when? About the middle twenties? Dr. Poremba asked, passing a leather flask.

Janek Stypenko drank, shrugged, wiped his mouth. —Who gives a damn? Twenties, thirties, forties . . . New people come here every summer when the rivers thaw. They die every winter.

—It could be worse, said Dr. Poremba. Couldn't it?

Janek said nothing, drank.

—You could be in the camps.

Janek nodded, drank. Dr. Poremba sighed, reached out, stroked the unkempt head, felt the young man shivering under his touch. Poor driven and tormented bastard . . . still struggling, still refusing to acknowledge his inevitable end. When they still think that they have something left for which they might live (and anything would do: a woman, an idea) they can still feel threatened. As long as they are able to feel a threat they can be dangerous.

And suddenly he was tired, weary of the game which he had played too often in too many places exactly like this one, so that it seemed to him that he was treading water merely to keep himself afloat. The young man's bowed shoulders had slumped even further.

—Have another drink, said Dr. Poremba. It's all right. There's a lot more *kumis*. So where do you work?

—All around here, Janek said, waved a vague arm around his head, drank from the leather flask. —Unloading the barges that come around the cape in summer. Everything has to come around by sea, like we did ourselves. There's no roads, no railways for three, four thousand miles. Nothing moves here until the ice thaws.

—Yes, I know that, said Dr. Poremba.

—I suppose you do. You were on the train last December, weren't you? I thought I saw you there. Burying Catherine's father. Jesus, think of it, last December, a whole year ago . . .

—They took me off the train at Lake Sergin, Dr. Poremba said. Or I might have been up here with you.

—Not at Krasnaya Gorka, you wouldn't be. We don't have any Poles at Krasnaya Gorka.

—Yes, I remember, Dr. Poremba said. You said the place was full of Jews. Were they on the train?

—Most of them were.

—Do you remember any of the others who were on the train? They all must have come north with you.

—Maybe they did, maybe not. A lot died on the way.

—I heard the people at Lake Sergin were made to march last year.

—It must have been some other people. If you march, you die. We stayed a month at Sergin, waiting for more people. Then, when the ice started breaking up in April, they put us on barges, then we went down the Ob to the Obskaya Guba, then around the Gyda Peninsula to the mouth of the Yenisei. Some more people came down the Yenisei at about the same time. There must have been twenty thousand people there in May, it was like being back in Poland again.

—I know, I've been at the mouth of the Yenisei, said Dr. Poremba.

—Yes, I suppose you have. A lot of our people were put ashore there. They're building a port and a railway, I hear. We're going to be building a port on the Khatanga in summer.

—You or the people from the camps?

—Well, I don't suppose it'll be us. That kind of work, well, you know how heavy that is . . . And we're a free settlement, we have Russian passports . . . A lot of the people at the settlement have them, anyway.

—Tell me about the people who were on the train and who came up with you to the Yenisei.

—What's there to tell? A lot of our people were dead by the time we got there. It took two months to get there on those open barges. We went all the way around Taimyr Peninsula, put some people ashore on Severnaya Zemlya, on Bolshevik Island, some more on Maly Taimyr, some more on Cape Chelyuskin . . . You know what happened there two months ago? When they burned the camp?

—Did that really happen?

—It happened, all right. They tracked down the last of those poor bastards right around here less than two weeks ago. Fed them to the dogs. So that accounts for some more of our people.

—But some of the people from the train came here with you in June?

—Maybe it was June, maybe the start of July. It doesn't make that much difference around here. It took more than three months to get here from Sergin, that's all I know.

—How many people got here with you?

—I told you. There's the six hundred Jews at Krasnaya Gorka . . .

—I don't care about the Jews at Krasnaya Gorka. What about the people on the train who died on the way here? Do you remember any of them?

—There was that Polish priest, Janek said. The young one, the one that used to come to Catherine's house in Lwów. A schoolteacher, or something. You know the one I mean?

—I know him, I know all about him, said Dr. Poremba. But he didn't die on the barges. The NKVD took him with me on the train from Sergin, then took him off in Moscow.

Janek grinned, nodded, spat. —Trust a Polish priest to find himself a soft spot. Moscow, is it? Well, wouldn't you know it?

—Not as soft as all that, said Dr. Poremba. They gave him ten years for praying over Professor Modelski's grave.

—Is that right? Janek said. Well, what did he expect, the damn fool? Everybody knows what happens to you for making religious propaganda. You ought to see all those Jews at Krasnaya Gorka, they're ready to burst! Hell, you won't find me feeling sorry about a damn priest.

—Or for Jews either, it would seem.

—To hell with the Jews.

—You didn't always think like that. It seems to me that in Lwów, as I remember . . .

—Never mind about Lwów, Janek cried. That's all over and done! None of that was any good, anyway. It was all shit, I tell you!

—Easy now, easy, said Dr. Poremba.

—Easy? I'll tell you about easy! Janek said, drank from the flask, laughed harshly. You want to know about Lwów, you want it back again? Stay here until the ice breaks and the barges can come around again! You'll have all your Lwów friends around you right here!

—Well, I might just do that, said Dr. Poremba. Do you remember Catherine? Of course you remember. Is she also dead?

He watched the black eyes dimming, the face turned away. The young man was about to lie and made it quite clear.

—I don't know. I know about her mother. She's dead. I helped to bury her, like you buried the father. Hey, is there any more of this fermented piss to drink? I'm cold. And can't you make that fire a bit better?

Dr. Poremba shouted and the diminutive Ket woman came into the tent to tend to the fire, and he pointed to an empty leather flask, which she immediately took away and replaced with half a dozen full ones. The young man was making clumsy gestures toward the tiny woman. He was very drunk. Dr. Poremba knew that it was time to move the game along.

—How did she die? he said.

—Who? Catherine? Catherine didn't die.

—Catherine's mother.

—Starved herself to death, giving her rations to her little boy. Little Emil. He and that snotty cousin of theirs, that Pani Wlada who was always talking French, they got put ashore on Maly Taimyr . . . Bronka, the maid . . . do you remember Bronka?

—The one that used to say *Honest to God?*

—That's the one. They took her up the Ob when we went downriver. I don't know anything about anybody else.

—You lied about the priest, said Dr. Poremba, leaning back, and smiling. You lied about Catherine. I don't want to hear any more lies from you.

—I don't have to tell you a damn thing, Janek said, shrugged, spat, drank from a new flask. —What's your game, Poremba?

—I want to know about my wife and children. You've been very careful not to mention them.

—I don't know anything about your wife and children.

—You're lying again.

—Why the hell should I lie?

—Because you're a lying, stinking pisspot of a Ukrainian, said Dr. Poremba. And I'm going to have your insufficient Ukrainian balls cut off and shoved into your lying mouth And then I'm going to give you to my little people to play with for a while. They need somebody to be sacrificed, and you're just the animal for that. But perhaps you're lying to save me from bad news? Are you that considerate? Are you feeling sorry for me, you Ukrainian pisspot?

—I don't feel sorry for anybody, the young man muttered. Least of all, for a stinking Pole . . .

—Lying again, Dr. Poremba said. Do you think it's enough to turn yourself into an animal in order to survive?

—Leave me alone, Janek cried. You try to live up here for a year, and then talk about brutality . . . animals . . . Try it and see what happens to you!

—I know what happens, said Dr. Poremba. And it isn't worth it. There aren't many people who are born with hatred. That's something you must teach yourself. Brutality only guarantees your own eventual destruction.

—You know so much, don't you? Janek cried. Well, there are some things you don't know about. You want to know about your wife? All right, I'll tell you. She is dead. Now do you feel happy?

—Where did she die? said Dr. Poremba.

—In the barges. I told you, a lot of people died on those open barges. Is that what you were waiting to hear? It doesn't seem to have moved you very much. God, what a cold bastard you are. But maybe this will move you. D'you want to know where she's buried? You might want to put some flowers on her grave or light a candle on All Souls' Day.

—Yes, said Dr. Poremba. Tell me where she's buried.

—Right in the middle of the Vilkitski Strait. You know where that is?

—Yes.

—You'll have a long swim with your flowers and candle.

Grief would come later. Later still, perhaps, the grief would lessen and then disappear.

. . . Now think of a long time ago when you had lived so successfully disguised as a human being. When it was still possible to have friends, to love a woman, to hope for your children, to take the generosities of life for granted, or to feel sympathy for anyone other than yourself. A time when the only justifiable contempt was for the impossible.

He supposed that he had always known that Alicja would not be able to survive loss of civilization as she understood it: the gentle normalcies of a wife and mother. Death stepped aside, indifferent. *Magna mater,* comrade. He heard himself asking the young man how his wife had died but didn't hear the answer. It didn't matter how she had died, not really. First Luta, then Alicja. He had lost one half of his possibilities. The parchment abbot rustled in his head. New lives for old at small cost, a matter of a soul . . .

—How did Alicja die? he heard himself asking.

—Christ, why do you go on with this? the young man said. Do you enjoy hurting yourself as much as you like to hurt other people?

—Not particularly, said Dr. Poremba.

—What difference does it make how she died? She's dead, that's all. Isn't that enough? Look, I can't stand to talk about it any more.

Still struggling, he would be broken soon.

—Oblige me in this matter, please, said Dr. Poremba.

—All right, you heartless devil! She starved herself like Catherine's mother. Feeding your goddam children. Now do you feel better?

—Then Ziuta and Wiesio are still alive?

—Yes, Janek cried.

—They're in that camp with Catherine?

—All that I'm going to say is that they were on the barges. They came around the cape with us that summer. Everything comes here that way, there's no other way. Unless the barges go down the Yenisei from Krasnoyarsk to Karaul and then around the Taimyr . . .

—I didn't come that way, said Dr. Poremba.

—I don't know how you got here, then.

—Think of it as magic. I came here the same way that I'll be leaving tomorrow, having all the way come all the way across Russia, some three thousand miles . . .

—Well, that's impossible right there, Janek said.

—Think of it as magic. Think about the cloak of invisibility and seven-league boots . . .

—You're mad, that's what it is, you crazy old devil! That is what it must be.

—It would be a comfort to believe it.

He peered at Janek through the aromatic smoke of the burning dung cakes, saw him as a blurred reflection of his own discredited humanity, brushed his wet eyes; saw pain and fear and anger and humiliation branded into a darkly etched image of a face which had now turned toward him as though for reassurance . . . Saw in his mind's dark eye a rescue and pursuit, and then an alternative to pursuit: the flames and riot of a possible diversion, and a means whereby to awe and enrich his Ostyaks beyond their wildest dreams and, at one awful stroke, to bind them to himself with the insoluble ties of men on the run.

He would need a plan. Small plans have no magic, they can't stir men's blood. His plan would be stark with the fire of forgotten lightnings, harsh with ancient music. So might we yet hear chariot wheels thundering in the tundra . . .

—Now tell me who else died, Dr. Poremba heard himself saying. Don't miss anyone.

—Why should you care who else died, you crazy old devil?

—I'm keeping a record.

—Nobody'll ever read it, it'll be too heavy to carry around.

—When you can think of dead thousands it's easier to forget about one or two.

—A lot of the Jews died, Janek said after a long silence. But you don't care about the Jews, you said. Esterka's mother fell into an ice hole last winter, froze to death; her father went crazy.

—Some men can't shield themselves against grief.

Janek shrugged, indifferent.

—Did the grandfather die?

—Him? Janek said, and laughed. Hell, he'll live forever. He just about runs Krasnaya Gorka! He's probably the only Jew there who wouldn't take a Russian passport. They threatened him with camps but I don't think he even heard them when they did! They knew damn well they'd have a revolution on their hands if they sent him up.

—You think the people at Krasnaya Gorka would rise up against them?

—It wouldn't take much, Janek said. They're like a powder barrel looking for a match. But the Old Man would never allow it. He wouldn't allow anything that's against a law.

—The younger people could be goaded into it.

And now he knew that he would start upon a wholly different journey, having come too far from his discernible beginnings. He reached toward a future, in which he would not be able to live with himself, across a present that he must soon fill with blood. That is the price of man's humanity. No, it was not a question of wounds, battles, struggles. Life had somehow dwindled to a series of last stands in desolate places. He knew that this terrible desolation was his own.

What happened then, he supposed, was the coming together of forces which compressed time, fused thoughts, and illuminated in their dark imperious glow the unimaginable distances through which he had passed.

While it is happening, the change is imperceptible, it lies unnoticed deep below the surface. Symbols drift out of sight. Truths reassemble their structural components. There are astonishing new perspectives. What may have been your bright and motivating factors, the causes of each of your predictable effects, vanish and no longer illuminate anything, and what had seemed the inconceivable, submerged in the murk, is suddenly seen with the clarity of the obvious. It acquires the hardened gleam of crystal because it stands in absolute isolation, free of the sawdust and excelsior of civilization.

No, it was not a question of wounding disappointments; these had dried long ago. But he was suddenly and painfully aware of the coarse abrasive tissue of the scars which armored every thought. The body still was competent enough, but the spirit limped on crooked stumps of mutilated hope.

. . . And gently, softly, he asked the next question.

—Is Esterka there?

Suddenly tearful, hurt, and pinched with hunger, Janek said: Oh, she's there all right.

—And is Jankele there?

—He's there, Janek said. Kamila is there. The whole damn lot of them are there.

—Did they take Russian passports?

—How could they if the Old Man wouldn't hear of it? Janek cried.

Quietly, Dr. Poremba said: Esterka would know what happened to my children. I'll have to talk to her.

—Maybe she would, Janek said, and twisted his fingers in his beard. Don't ask me what she knows. All I can tell you is what she doesn't know and that would take all day.

—I thought you loved her once, said Dr. Poremba.

—Love? I've had it with the lot of them! Give me a chance to get away from here and that'll be that. She can freeze her ass off here for all that I care.

Dr. Poremba smiled with an averted face, thought and remembered a long-gone time of his own youthful dedications, dismissed it, said: Where would you go?

—Nowhere without wings.

—But if there was a way?

—Why talk about it, Poremba? Do you like to beat your head against a wall? Nobody's every got away from here!

—I might think of something.

—You and whose army? Don't be such a fool. D'you think if there was any way to escape there'd be anybody here? It's not that drunken NKVD *komandir* and his three dimwit helpers that keep this place going. It's ice and snow, and three thousand miles filled with wind. Think of a wall a thousand miles high! Hey, do you want a laugh? I didn't have to come here. I could have stayed in Lwów. I'm a Ukrainian. I could have joined the goddam Red Militia now that they've cleaned the Jews out of it. Could've gone home to Kolomyia. But I wanted to stay with her . . . Thought she'd come around . . . thought, oh hell, what do I know what I thought? And here I am and she's got no use for me, she's as cold as you.

—You can leave tomorrow, with me, said Dr. Poremba.

—Stop laughing at me, you son of a bitch! This isn't anything to laugh about! You talk about leaving this place as if this was Poland, where all you need to travel is money for a ticket . . . Going away from here! Just like that! You tell me that you're leaving and I've got to stay?

—You can come with me, said Dr. Poremba. Others can come with

us if there is anyone at the camp or at Krasnaya Gorka that we want to
take along . . .

—But nobody leaves here, Janek cried. Nobody, ever . . . There's no
way . . . ! All right, I know, you got here somehow, so there is a way
. . . But I don't believe it!

—Stop struggling, Janek, said Dr. Poremba. Give up your will. Let
me do the thinking.

—It'll be just like it was with the people at the Chelyuskin camp.
They rose up, burned their camp, escaped, and this is as far as they got
before the chasers caught them. They're buried all around you here,
under ice.

—Stop struggling, boy, said Dr. Poremba. You don't have to leave
Esterka behind. She can come with you, you can rescue her. She can
owe you her life and the lives of what's left of her family. It's quite a
classic case, you know, the knight and the lady, the free man of the
steppes abducting his maiden. Very romantic, very Ukrainian . . .

—Stop laughing, you devil!

—How many firearms are there at Krasnaya Gorka?

—The *komandir* has a Nagan . . . His three men have rifles . . . But
you are mad, of course . . .

—Call it the madness of necessity, said Dr. Poremba. How many soldiers are there in the camp?

—Which camp? There are twenty of them in the Taimyr alone.
That's ten . . . maybe fifteen thousand soldiers!

—And they have ten thousand square miles in which to get lost, and
a hundred thousand people to control. People who'd tear them apart if
they got a chance . . . People beyond mere desperation. Not one of
those ten or fifteen thousand NKVD troopers is going to stir a foot
from his own camp, and you know it! How many guards are there at
this nearest camp?

—Four or five hundred . . .

—And how many people?

—I don't know. Five or six thousand, maybe a lot less now. There's a
hundred people dying up there every day. How am I to know how
many there are?

—That's right, I forgot, said Dr. Poremba. You don't go near the
camp. You work in the village.

—That's right, Janek muttered, drank, slumped among the furs.
Don't go near the camp . . .

—Oh, that's too bad, said Dr. Poremba. I'm really sorry about that.
I would have liked to take you with me tomorrow, you see. You and Esterka and the old grandfather and the little boy . . . What was his

name, by the way? I seem to have forgotten it. An old man's memory, you know . . .

—Jankele, said Janek.

—Of course, Jankele. I remember the little red star you gave him in Lwów. You and Esterka used to walk him to school every morning . . . We'd start southwest tomorrow, first thing in the morning. Then we'd travel south along the Yenisei . . .

—There's nothing south of here for three thousand miles, Janek was muttering then.

—That's right, said Dr. Poremba. No towns, no roads or railroads, not a single telegraph post, no NKVD. Nothing but thousands of miles of space, forest, and grasses taller than a mounted man. You could lose a continent or two between the Taimyr and the Chinese border. Entire nations wander about there and nobody knows anything about them. Do you know that there are still whole peoples east of the Yenisei who think that Russia is ruled today by Alexander Romanov? They've never heard of the Revolution, never see a Russian. I don't suppose they see a European face once in fifteen years . . . They wouldn't know a Communist if they stepped on one. We would be as safe there as behind your old grandmother's stove.

Janek stared with eyes that had become askew. He shuddered. His breathing was chaotic. Sweat had begun to blister his forehead with frosted white drops.

—Three thousand miles as free birds might fly, said Dr. Poremba. Add another thousand and you are in China.

—Could we really get there?

—I got here, didn't I? It's just about the same distance, I'd imagine. And once you get into the Evenki country there are crops, forests, animals, rivers so full of fish that you can walk from one bank to another and never get your boots wet. A country bigger than Poland, Germany, and France put together and fewer than a hundred thousand people in it . . . We'll be there before the ice begins to break up along the Khatanga.

—How are you going to get across the borders?

—One ought to leave God something to take care of, Dr. Poremba said.

—I want to go with you, Janek said. I want to take Esterka and the Old Man and the little boy . . . (Then the broad mouth was tightening again, the eyes reflected the facts of the young man's anguish: eyes as hard as plate glass, the lenses suddenly fractured by a quick white light.) —There is a price, I suppose? Nobody does anything for nothing.

Dr. Poremba could see that the young man was trying to resist him. Pitiful young fool. I have taken him to the top of the mountain in the wilderness, showed him all the pathetic treasures of his world, the glittering illusion of a love, a life. Such perishable tinsel. Poor fool, to throw aside his shield for a promise.

He listened to his own voice as though it were a stranger's: a toneless gray dishwater bucket of a voice leaking words, coming from a distance. Vaguely familiar, an echo of a rustling memory. Someone whom he had met once and feared very much.

—Whom can you contact at the camp? Do you see Catherine there?

The young man would make one last futile attempt in the name of reason and the lessons of reality.

—I told you. I don't go there . . .

—Of course you do. Stop lying to me. Stop resisting me, because you are only struggling against yourself. Who hauls the pit timbers to the mines and supplies to the camp? Don't you think I know what these free settlements are for?

. . . The young man tried once more, surely for the last time.

—That's summer work. When the timber comes around in barges and the ore goes out . . .

—And now it's odd jobs around the camp. What do you do there? Drive a truck, or what?

—Sometimes I drive a truck, Janek said. Carry the tools behind the column . . .

—Not sometimes, lad, every day. Isn't that correct?

Janek nodded. —Whenever they use trucks.

—And who do you see there? Catherine?

—I see her sometimes. I give her food, she has a baby now. Sometimes I see Kobza, the janitor. You remember him?

—That's better, that's much better, said Dr. Poremba, and passed the last leather flask.

. . . Listening to the harsh, brutal voice of another stranger, a voice like a battering ram. (No mercy, no compassion.) He heard the crackling flames of tomorrow's diversion. Saw the dead men and women: a necessary sacrifice, I am sure. Said:

—Drink. Listen. There is a lot to arrange before tomorrow morning. Escape equals freedom. A diversion equals no pursuit. (Janek was nodding, understanding nothing.) Escape is impossible without a diversion. All that you have to do is to convince your Jews to attack the camp.

—They'll never do it, Janek said.

—You just told me that they are ready to explode. Let them think that they are joining an insurrection already in progress. If the old men refuse to listen to you, incite the young men. Insult their courage, sneer at their manhood . . .

—They will be massacred, Janek said.

—All these people would have died before spring anyway, wouldn't they? This way, at least, their deaths will be useful. So let's bestow a final meaning on their otherwise unimportant lives. Let them go out in a blaze of glory, or any other blaze. At the final moment, and God will do. God only knows what they've lived for, let them die for something. I would consider that a boon under the circumstances. Think of them as already dead, what do they have to lose except their lives? And what lives! A matter of a month or two at most. And a month of what? Sometimes, my lad, death can be a blessing.

—You want me to lead them to their deaths?

—You are not God, you are not responsible. Nobody makes anyone a victim, victims create themselves. Life is survival and lies are a part of life. Nobody is responsible for anybody else. People create their own unhappiness, they suffer if they want to suffer, they believe only what they want to believe. But the choice is yours . . . China . . . Esterka . . . years of peace and plenty . . .

—Oh, Christ, Janek said. Oh, Christ. Give me some more to drink.

—Yes, that does help sometimes, said Dr. Poremba.

The Rebel

OUT OF BREATH, his head filled with chaotic visions—the roar of distant thunder and crackle of flames (a remembered battle), green miles of a safe beguiling wilderness, Poremba's cracked whispering drone and his own illusions—he stopped outside the long log meeting house at the beginning of the street, at the point where the street became a tortured track winding toward the woods. Twisted and crooked as his own disappointed spirit, leading out of one kind of wilderness to another.

They were inside, he knew. Discussing his story. Unwittingly preparing for their deaths. At prayer. Invoking their own immemorial sense of tragedy. Cherishing antique grief, they could not live without it. He cursed the harshness of their dedication, their incomprehensible cohesion, their complete preoccupation with themselves that excluded him.

. . . Eretz Yisroel—God's eyes rest on it forever, said the very old voice.

Janek Stypenko was suddenly shrunken grey with hatred.

. . . Eretz Yisroel—that is the very *Shekinah* itself!

He pressed his hot face against the coarse roughhewn logs that locked him outside, always the outsider, even as he prepared to lead them to their deaths.

How did they dare to deny him his dreams and his substance? He could not reach them where they lived: each man locked in himself, each his own fortress. How could they live so thoroughly within their own visions, each man (and woman!) alone, not needing him at all?

. . . Come all of you in a common bond (said the very old voice), linked together in one soul, in love and brotherhood and comradeship . . . to resettle the land in its entirety . . . that the Nation may be born at one stroke . . . !

(No room for him among them, except as a beast of burden, a weapon or a tool. The icy bark was freezing to his forehead.)

. . . This is the day we have been hoping for, let us be glad and rejoice with our beloved land . . .

He listened to the resonant old voice that locked him forever outside.

. . . For it is for you and for us to rebuild the House of the Lord . . . For the doings of the Fathers shall be inherited by the sons.

He felt pierced and wounded.

Esterka danced away in shadows which now turned and mocked. He had hoped for so much from her but, to tell the truth, she had never made him any promises. The ringing promises he thought she had made were made by him to himself on her behalf without her even knowing anything about them. He had formed a vision of her and of what he wanted her to be, and he had convinced himself that this was what she was or could be: all the myriad things that his private demonology demanded; and he had told himself that she could agree with this view of herself as wife, lover, mother, and apparition out of legends, a paragon of virtues who would follow him out of her dream and into his own.

Esterka had never made him any promises. He had made them for her. And what's the old proverb about promises? A man who would trade horses for a promise ends up with tired feet.

. . . for great are the deeds of our Lord!

. . . This is the day for which we have been waiting.

And someone was coming crookedly down the street.

Man, woman, child. Who could tell. A bundle of shawls, wraps, patched alpaca, felt boots, thrifty gabardine; an apparition from the turbulent years of earnest illusions. Bitterly lamenting. A mourner, then? There were many mourners in the white nights, and more every day. By this day's end there would be many more.

Poremba had made everything marvelously clear. The Devil! The tempter! (But who could resist that particular temptation?) Who would have thought that babbling moon-faced man capable of such calculated cold brutality? (Who would have thought me capable of mine?) The madwoman was still squatting over her frozen child in the blurred periphery of his vision. (What happened to the child? And who was she to grieve as if she had invented suffering?) The fumes of the *kumis* had blown away in the new icy air. Five hundred people would be dead by nightfall. Maybe more. It was sure to be more. Frontal assault, the tempter had explained, whatever that meant. Diversion. Well, that's all very well! So many private scores to be settled in the camp, so many insults (disappointments!) to avenge in the settlement . . . so: fire, smoke, chaos and confusion. A natural conclusion. And, in

the meantime, the dead and the dying. And the swift little brown men
vanishing in the tundra with whoever managed to cling to their sledges.

. . . And then there would be the rich green wilderness of the Evenki
lands. Rivers so thick with fish that a man could walk from one bank to
the other and never wet his boots. That's what the tempter said.

But first: the fire.

The dead and the dying.

Mourners. Oh, there were always mourners among these damn Jews.
This lamenting child hugging his misery to his shawls. Icicles glitter on
his chest like ornamental fringes.

. . . And China, perhaps? The Devil had said: China. Just think of
that. Don't think about mourners . . .

He knew the boy at once, how could he not know him? And quailed
before his own dumb brutality, coldly anticipating no fewer than five
hundred deaths to provide diversion (knowing that hatred is another
name for envy and fear), and cursed the need to inflict any kind of
pain, and listened to the droning chant of the old man in the long log
house. Up and down, hypnotic. He found himself swaying, as they
would be swaying.

. . . For the doings of the Fathers shall be inherited by the sons.

—What are you sniveling about, boy?

Jankele ignored him.

—Look at me, damn you, when I'm speaking to you. Has somebody
died?

The boy shook his head.

—Won't talk, eh? All right, then. Don't tell me. I don't want to hear
any more of your Jewish sorrows. You think your people have a monopoly on grief? You think nobody else ever suffered? You think we don't
feel nothing, eh? And what are you afraid of, anyway? It's only life, boy,
don't you understand?

The small bleak face regarded him with blank solemnity.

I want to love you all, Janek cried inside himself where no one could
hear him, where he would be unable to hear himself crying. I would
have loved you so! But hatred is easier, it's more natural than love,
don't you see? You don't have to *make* yourself hate anyone, you don't
even have to know anything about them, it takes no effort to manufacture hatred, it's as natural as breathing, and you don't lose anything,
hating someone, because you risk nothing. You only lose by loving.
Then nothing is safe. Then there are no alternatives to truth, no rocks
to hide under. Truth is too difficult and it's dangerous. Lying is easy
when you can hate someone.

He tried to force a soft cajoling note into his suddenly creaky old-
man voice (And will you stop sniveling? I'm not going to eat you!) but

the boy had already learned all the varieties of hatred and would remember them as long as he lived.

—Well, am I? What am I to you people, some kind of a bloody cannibal? An animal, eh?

And thought with a savage joy that astonished him: you'll need those tears tomorrow.

There'll be death, terror. And enough grief for everyone. Even for himself. All the fears unchained, hates unshackled. Lots of time for tears. No time for prayers. No more droning voices. No difference between any people: we'll all be united! There'll be only two kinds of people here tomorrow: the dead and the dying.

—Answer me, damn you, when I'm talking to you!

The boy turned away.

But then (he thought) even hatred is a luxury that I can't afford. Hatred is a feeling and you must hate *something*. Once you hate something you must be conscious of it, you must think about it. And I don't want to think about anything. Unawareness, that is what I want. Don't think, don't feel anything, Poremba had told him as the dark accusing eyes of a madwoman pointed at his own. Be a stone. To think is disaster, no revolution is made by thought alone. Not to think, to feel nothing . . . that way lies success. Don't think about today or even tomorrow, about the necessary killing time, the dead and the dying. Because it is necessary, don't you know, there can be no escape without the dead and the dying, especially not without the dead and the dying. If you must think then think about the day *after* tomorrow: the whole vast wilderness of freedom. Liberation. The emptiness of an uncluttered space. The soft hissing of the Ostyak sleighs across the frozen water . . . And China, perhaps?

. . . Think about China. In China men get to live to a ripe old age. Think about Esterka.

He pushed open the door of the long log house where the old men of the settlement were nodding and swaying.

A soft warm darkness. He thinks of a womb. Perhaps a damp fruit cellar stinking of wet leaves. Bodies never completely exposed to light, never fully washed. Old age. Rotting apples. Piss. Oh, who'd be able to count all the stenches?

A table, benches.

Books and innumerable old newspapers too tattered to read but religiously preserved in this long dark room that they, the bowed men, called *switlica* in curiously corrupted Polish: the Place of Light, in an accent that demanded darkness. Light . . . or illumination. Or maybe the Russian *svet* had certain special meanings here. *The Life of Lenin* in forty-two volumes, a poster of an underground railway in Moscow, a grotesque Polish nobleman on a bayonet . . . Windows, glazed in fish skin, admit a blue-gray imitation light.

Gloom framed in resignation and in something else: a warm and argumentative insistence that every moment of a life, even such as this one, have huge significance. For lament, for protest. And this (he thought, shrugging in their way and aware of it) they call a religion of joy? He had lived among them for more than a year, and didn't understand the first thing about these voluble strange men who could claim that their lives were simple but for whom the smallest event was filled with mysteries. He had learned to tell a *chnyok* from a *zaidener yinger manchik*, and knew all about the powers of letters and figures, and he knew that the armpiece of the tefillin had a knot in it that was never covered (because it symbolized the man without guile, among other things) but all that only made these people more inaccessible.

He peered among the shadows of bowed, swaying men, prepared for the journey but not yet sure that they were going to take it. Old Moishe had brought with him a feather bed and a pillowcase, thick socks, underwear, aspirin and insect repellent, postcards and stamps and a writing tablet, a thick book and a thin one. Uli's father had thought that the less there would be to carry in the wilderness, the better, and had brought four huge sandwiches. Yehuda, the bald, plump postal clerk and father of six children, anxiously cracked his lice; they would go with him whether he wanted to bring them or not. Small, thin Haim, who had operated with a cart and two horses in Lublin, and had a mouthful of silver teeth, displayed a fearsome smile in the indefinite light. Janek identified the Old Man, Esterka's grandfather, and moved up beside him.

There were a dozen others. Some were young among the swaying old men in the room, barely visible in shadow. To his surprise, he noted that some of the assembly were women. A shock, then, a surprise. These people never consulted their women about anything, treated them like domestic animals or children, and stupid ones at that. But here they were this time, rustling like anxious hens with the fox circling outside the coop, so he knew that no decision had been reached, that a world of argument had to be conquered first, and that what he had heard outside had not been yet another prayer but an exhortation.

The women sat in the darkest corner of the room as if veiled, as though the old men wanted to conceal them or, perhaps, wished to hide themselves and their old-man thoughts from women. He couldn't tell in the electric gloom whether he knew any of them (he would have known the younger, prettier ones, by sight anyway) and wondered if Esterka was among them and what she thought of him, and if she'd ever know that what he was doing was done only for her (and, if she did find out what he was really doing, if she would ever be able to forgive it), and what she thought of what must have spread and flown like flame among the thatched roofs of the settlement: his news that the Lake Camp was going up in its own flames at nightfall, and that they (the people at Krasnaya Gorka) could join the uprising and the mass escape.

He didn't think the old men would approve any kind of violence (though didn't they always say that violence was their people's heritage?) but the young men (Shlomo and Ariz) could be goaded into it and that would be enough. Now he peered into shadows, searching for their faces, pinched with a year of hunger and centuries of insult, saw Ariz and Shlomo and the other young ones, saw the Latvian Jewess who taught in the one-room school, didn't see Esterka (but knew she was there!). He sensed excitement, smelled anxiety and the promise of violence (searching for whatever message these might have for him), felt their curiosity and occasionally the red lick of anger, but true clues continued to elude him.

He was impatient, angry with himself, and he wanted this masquerade of his to come to an end. Dealing with Jews was worse than dealing with the Ostyaks; they wouldn't tell you anything until they were ready and they would make a ceremony even out of that.

—Is there more news?

(He had told them, as Poremba had told him to tell it, that they were joining an uprising, not beginning one, that the camp guards would have their bloody hands full, their machine guns busy, that the slaves and convicts would take care of their own keepers, the guards and the work-brigade leaders. With a vengeance. That the camp uprising would provide diversion. That they, these desperately thinking Jews, could only profit by such a diversion [and yes, even that silver-mouthed Haim to whom no one listened without a wry smile said, understanding nothing, that he could understand the benefits of diversion], and that all that they had to do to effect their own liberation was to overcome four men: the drunken *nachalnik* and his idiot helpers [a matter of three rifles and a six-shot Nagan revolver], and that, then, it would be just a matter of collecting their women and children, their food and their belongings, and marching to the camp, where the self-liberated convicts and Poremba and the Ostyaks would be waiting for them, so that the joint escape to freedom could begin.)

—What more do you want to hear? Janek said, and listened to the creaks and rustlings among the hidden women. Was she there or not? And what was she thinking?

—That the Messiah is coming, perhaps, said an irreverent young voice, and another laughed in the swift shocked silence.

—Speedily in our days, said another young man.

And Ariz, surely it was Ariz although he was once more invisible in gloom, the butt-shaped, bullet-headed blacksmith from near Pinsk, a wild Jew from a village (as the others called him), one of those rare Jews who were from a village (one of those rare wholly Jewish villages which nestled uneasily in the eastern marshes among the Poles, the Byelorussians, and the Ukrainians), a sour and embittered suitor for Kamila's terror-stricken hand, the youngest son of an enormous family which had disappeared one by one, a day at a time, the coarse survivor of a plague, whom no one in his right mind would ever call a silken *zaidener*, neither pious nor virtuous nor tractable nor scholarly nor desirable as a son-in-law (even for Kamila!), who was said to have been a Zionist (whatever that was) and then a Communist after the Russians came, and was now, in final definition, merely a Survivor, laughed again and said: Well, that's the news if anybody wants to hear it. That we are still waiting.

—Nothing has been decided, then? Janek asked him.

—Well, what do you think? said the younger Shlomo. This is the waiting room.

—We are the Waiting People, Ariz said, and laughed. That is what we were chosen for, to wait.

—That is why we have waiting rooms, Shlomo said. Haven't you learned that much about us? We wait for decisions.

—And such decisions they make for us in these waiting rooms, Ariz said, not laughing. You wouldn't believe how important these decisions are.

—This is where they decide whether we should eat two or three kreplach on Shavuot, Shlomo said.

—Or one, said Ariz. But such a big one that it should equal the volume of two.

—So don't expect anyone here to make a decision about an escape, or anything else that doesn't include a thousand years of waiting, until the Messiah comes, Shlomo said while the old men muttered and began to stir.

—And even then we'll have to wait in line for tickets to the grandstand, Ariz said.

—What is this? Moishe shouted from among the old men. What's wrong with you, you anarchist? To talk like that in front of the *ger*?

—He isn't as much of a stranger as all that, Ariz said.

—He isn't one of us, Haim said with his ghastly smile, and that is enough!

. . . Enough, Janek thought. No more. And to Ariz he said swiftly above the rising roar of old and young voices: But what about the escape? I thought you'd be for it.

—I'm for anything that doesn't include waiting, Ariz said. But you don't get swift decisions from old men. They have to find a law that covers everything they do and that, believe me, can drive a horse crazy.

—Is your mouth still open, you Bolshevik, you anarchist, may your father never know such shame! old Moishe shouted, waved his arms. We live by the Law!

—We live by the Law! Haim echoed with a flash of silver.

And Ariz said, with uncharacteristic mildness: Well, uncle, that's hardly news to anybody here. And that's why we're waiting for you old men to make a decision, since you know the Law, but if you don't make a decision before we are all as old as you are then the decisions will be made for you.

—And anyway, said Shlomo, who had wanted to be an electrical engineer but whose father (now dead) had apprenticed him to a shoemaker in Przemysl, who read everything that he could get his hands on, who was called the Student: Isn't there some kind of law about helping strangers?

—There is certainly one about young anarchists with big open mouths, Moishe said.

—There's one for everything else, Shlomo said bitterly.

—Respect! old Moishe cried. You will show respect!

—You will not speak against the Law, said Grandfather Rashevsky.

—There are laws and laws, Ariz said.

—For us there is only one Law and all other laws come from it. We live by all the laws. We are law-abiding. We can do nothing which is against a law.

And from the women's corner Esterka said clearly (and Janek felt his heart lurch, and his stomach fluttered, and he saw his clasped hands beginning to tremble): Grandfather, you are confusing the Law with authority.

And the Old Man rose, leaned forward, and said harshly into shadow: I am confused? I? Have you forgotten who you are? And how we have lived? What is the meaning of our lives in all our thousands of years, in all our wanderings, in all our tears, in all the prayers of good men, if we have come to disrespect? How have I deserved this in front of my friends?

—And doesn't it always come to this? Shlomo said. We want a ruling, we want a decision!

Esterka said from the angry shadows in the women's corner: We are nowhere forbidden to resist oppressors!

—Don't shame me, girl, said Grandfather Rashevsky.

Haim said (brilliantly): The young have no respect. How have we deserved it?

Uli's father sighed, shook his head, ate the first of his four sand-wiches, said: To join in this madness will only bring us trouble. Do we need more trouble?

—So you're not going, then? old Moishe said. So why did you come here?

—I changed my mind, Uli's father said. Things could be worse for us, we could be in a camp, God forbid such a thought. I should go and put a rope around my neck and then take it to the *nachalnik* and say: *Please, will you hang me, and save me the trouble?* Let them do what they want in that camp, and is it our business? What do we have to do with convicts, criminals? Let them kill each other. The more of them that kill each other, the fewer there'll be to give us trouble. And who would want trouble? Maybe a crazy man, or an anarchist who has no respect.

He shrugged, sighed, shook his head. He ate another sandwich.

—It's not our land, Haim said. They are not our people.

—If we do nothing here we'll never deserve a country of our own, Es-terka cried. Isn't that what you were all saying a moment ago?

—Be quiet! The grandfather said.

—No! Esterka said. *Come all of you in a common bond, linked to-gether in one soul, in love and brotherhood and comradeship . . .* Isn't that what we're talking about here? *For the doings of the Fathers shall be inherited by the sons!*

—Nothing, you notice, Haim muttered, is said about daughters.

—Enough of this! cried Grandfather Rashevsky. You will not speak! You will not shame me so!

—This time, Grandfather, there must be an inheritance, Esterka said quietly. Not words, not the wind.

—My sons are damn well going to inherit something, Ariz said, then added with a dark and crooked grin of complicity toward the women's corner: And my daughters too.

Grandfather Rashevsky said, wearily: We obey the Law.

Old Moishe said: We must have more time.

Haim cried, sending silver signals through the gloom: What do we want with more time? The Law is the Law and it is all decided!

—The only thing that's been decided here, Ariz said to Shlomo, is that somehow the fact of being a grandfather instead of a grandson changes the way you look at everything. Well, I still have to make my first son, not to mention grandsons, and I'm tired of looking at the world through an old man's eyes. I say we do it.

—We have to do it, Shlomo said. But we must take everybody with us, we can't leave anyone behind. So we still have to wait for the old men to make their decision.

—When the Messiah comes? Ariz said, unsmiling.

—Maybe he'll hurry.

. . . He had thought that the younger men would have to be taunted into an uprising, or perhaps it had been Poremba, the tempter, who had thought it, said it . . . Thought that he would have to humiliate them as Poremba had humilated him. He had practiced insults. He had armed himself with the necessary hatred so that he could wound them. But they were doing their own provocation, making him innocent of their deaths, their dying, and they were talking about an inheritance . . .

He thought about Esterka, closed his eyes, listened to her clear and angry voice, didn't hear the words. Wanted to say something to her now. Immediately. While there was still time. Could find no words. It was like trying to make a gift of flowers and ribbons and finding nothing in your pocket but a handful of dull stones. Looking for something that was wholly his . . . a woman, a country . . . that had eluded him for years. Twenty-four years of meaningless living. Now these had turned upon him, taunting him and wounding.

The gloom around him was sparkling with anger. Shadows were leaping up to confront each other. He didn't know which of the several possible kinds of men he wanted to be. Were these the kind of people that he hadn't thought of? And how could he become one of them, being forever an outsider to them? And, anyway, they would soon be dead.

(I want my children to inherit something! Ariz shouted then.)

—It's our right, said Shlomo.

—Listen to him, old Moishe cried. What is happening here? Is this a revolution? Are you a goy to talk like that, you Bolshevik you? Is the world coming to an end?

—Such disrespect, Uli's father said. What is the world coming to when a *kind* like that tells people what to do?

—Perhaps it's the best way to get the kind of world we want and will have, Shlomo said. And this time we'll have it!

—You want! You want! Who are you to want anything? Is God to listen to the likes of you? Now I know the world is standing on its head!

—You shame us all! Moishe cried, then muttered.

—It's your shame, uncle, Ariz said. Let it be your shame.

—My shame! You do the talking and I'm to be ashamed?

—Hey, uncle, Schlomo said. Weren't you ready to escape with us?

Why did you bring all this stuff, that feather bed, those books, if you weren't going?

—I am not going anywhere with young Bolsheviks!

—You shame us before *him!*

Haim's mouth gleamed and glittered in imitation light. He pointed to Janek. —That one of *them* should see such things among *us*, hear such things . . . If you must show disrespect, why don't you do it in a language the *gerim* don't know?

—Because you old men are deaf in two hundred languages, and Hebrew and Yiddish are only two that you can't hear!

—Enough! said Grandfather Rashevsky.

And Ariz said, nodding: Yes, we've had enough.

—It was probably enough four thousand years ago, said Shlomo. And that's quite long enough to make a decision.

—It's time to stop thinking about what outsiders may be thinking of us, Esterka said angrily, and Janek's heart constricted. (Then, to her grandfather:) This is not a world for reason and logic and humility and patience, no one understands that sort of thing, no one will ever listen. We are not turning upon your ways, Grandfather, the Law will govern us in a spiritual sense, but what we want we shall take because that is the way of the world that we live in. And now is the time to make a beginning. What we want, we take. As for other people and what they think about us . . . well, they will never love us and never respect us for the way we've lived, in humility and patience, taking for ourselves only what others have decided that we may have. From now on let them fear us, that'll be enough.

—We are a law-abiding people, Grandfather Rashevsky was whispering beside Janek, but (Janek thought) the Old Man was speaking only to himself.

—Then remember the laws of the *ger*, Esterka said quietly. *He who befriends a Gentile and converts him, it is as if he created him.*

—Genesis Rabba thirty-nine, Shlomo said.

—*The same law shall apply to both the native-born and to the* ger *who is living among you*, Esterka said quietly.

—Exodus twelve, forty-nine, Shlomo said.

And Moishe said, nodding: When a *ger* settles with you in your land, you shall not oppress him . . . because you were *gerim* in Egypt . . .

And Haim said, beginning to sway: When you reap your harvest, you shall not reap right into the edges of your field, neither shall you glean the fallen ears; you shall leave them for the poor and for the *ger* . . .

And Uli's father said: You and the *ger* are alike before the Lord. There shall be one law and one custom for you and for the *ger* who lives among you.

And the Old Man, Esterka's grandfather, said softly, barely audible in the suden flow of quotations around him: The Lord your God is . . . no respecter of persons . . . and loves the *ger* among you . . . You too must love the *ger*, for you once lived as *gerim* in Egypt.

—Deuteronomy ten, Shlomo said. Eighteen and nineteen.

—Is there really a law about everything? Ariz said. Is there a law about helping out in a camp uprising?

—*You shall not deprive* gerim *and orphans of justice*, Grandfather Rashevsky said firmly.

—Deuteronomy seventeen, Shlomo said.

—*A curse upon him who withholds justice from the* ger, said Moishe.

—Deuteronomy twenty-seven, I think, Shlomo said.

—Well, what about it, Shlomo?

—It all depends on what they think is justice, Shlomo said. But I'm willing to bet there's some law to cover what we want.

Moishe said, rising: *Deal fairly with one another; do not oppress the* ger.

—Jeremiah? said Shlomo.

Uli's father put aside his sandwich, wrapped it, wiped his mouth, shouted: Jeremiah? I'll give you Jeremiah! *Deal justly and fairly! Rescue the victim from his oppressors, do not ill-treat the* ger . . .

Moishe shook both his fists at Uli's father, shouted happily: *You shall give the* ger *his patrimony!* And Uli's father cried: *I will appear before you in court, prompt to testify against* . . . ah . . . *those who* . . . ah . . . *thrust the* ger *aside and have no fear of Me!*

—So there really is a law for everything, Ariz said, surprised.

—There may even be a law about the uprising, Shlomo said. But Law or no Law, I'll give you thirty rubles if these old *bekishes* decide on going with us to the camp. There's such a thing as custom and tradition as well as the Law.

—Suddenly I'm an old believer, Ariz said. Make it forty rubles.

And Grandfather Rashevsky rose and waved for silence, said: *And when the Gibeonites said to Joshua: "come quickly to our relief," Joshua said: are we to bother the community about these* gerim? *The Blessed Holy One said: "Joshua, if you spurn the distant ones, you will end up alienating the near ones; besides, are you not yourself descended from* gerim?"

—Numbers Rabba eight, Shlomo said bitterly. I should have known it.

—Well then, old Moishe said: So it is decided?

—It is decided, said Grandfather Rashevsky. We live by the Law.

—And here's your forty rubles, Shlomo said.

He also wanted a country of his own, although his idea of a country was vague and ill defined. Nation, state (and all the other multipurpose words that Esterka used as part of her dream, and that Ariz and Shlomo and the other young ones repeated so often), these meant little to him. He saw them only as labels for an area where everyone, from postmen and policemen to presidents and priests, was . . . or rather, were . . . his own kind, whatever that was. Where each name above a display window was his kind of name, written in his kind of alphabet, and where he'd have to use his own language to order a meal from a restaurant or a ton of coal delivered in autumn. *Country* was a better word than *nation*, for what he had in mind. It included land, and space in which to feel at home, and a special kind of air under a pure blue Ukrainian sky. The blue sky and the golden fields provided colors for a banner. *Country* and *land* denoted seasons of the year: winters and summers under his own Ukrainian sun. This word was magic, surely, if true magic existed anywhere; it contained all that he had ever wanted for himself and set no limits to his possibilities.

. . . To cease being a stranger wherever he went. To be able to say: *I am this, I come from here . . . My country is this . . .* To be at home in his own house, where everyone would know who and what he was without an explanation.

(Was there anything more . . . uh . . . *degrading* . . . than to be forced, always and forever, to make such explanations?)

. . . And no one for whom he cared, whom he loved and wanted, would ever ask him there, in that country: Why don't you stay with your own kind?

Because that would be exactly where he was.

—Goddammit all, he muttered, following the others: Esterka, Ariz, Shlomo, at the head of a ragged, wrapped and bundled mob, and all of them alien. *They* were the outsiders. It was for *them* to make the explanations.

. . . Inheritance, they said. Their Eretz Yisroel . . .

None of them owned anything but the shawls and bundles, the pitchforks, spades, and axes in their hands, a dream and an idea.

He hated them for having such a clear idea of their dream, their talk of cultural and biological necessities: complete with time and place. He also wanted to inherit a name and a future. There they were, around him. The Old Man flowing like a river of quotations, not a Rebbe in the proper sense but exercising some sort of an authority as the oldest Jew in the community; Ariz, the blacksmith, shouldering his hammer; Shlomo the Student, with a cobbler's awl stuck into his belt and a heavy piece of timber in his hands; Moishe, unarmed, pulling all his

belongings on a makeshift sledge; Yuval, a poultry farmer, tripping over
the skirts of his long *bekish* (the black cloth slick and smeared with the
traces of a thousand eggs that he had wiped on it); Uli's father, carrying
a shovel and his remaining sandwich; small, unhappy Haim, flashing his
ghastly smile, no longer protesting; the oddly silent Russian Jew,
Lopatsky, a thin, stooped man who was forever losing his spectacles, always waving papers, said to have been a personal friend of the drunken
NKVD *nachalnik* (who, in turn, was said to have been a disgraced interrogator); terrified Kamila and Jankele (huge-eyed, remembering
everything); Jankele's Latvian teacher, who was said to have been the
wife of a cabinet minister . . . And ahead of them all, her kerchief gone
and her black hair spilling on the icy wind like a Tartar banner (somewhere there, because he couldn't see her), was Esterka.

Now they had come to the end of the street where the glazed track,
trodden into the wilderness by a thousand feet, fell toward the river, became an embankment, where buried crates and bales had become white
mounds under snow, and where the old iron barge lay frozen in
midriver. Here, the only real glass windowpanes in Krasnaya Gorka
reflected the angry red midmorning sun in the windows of the drunken
nachalnik's kantora. He peered uneasily through the powdery whiteness
of new snow driven along the street, looking for Esterka and Ariz and
Shlomo and, beyond them, at the scarlet windows and the squat black
door of the *kantora,* and beyond these buildings toward the houses
where the Russian foremen lived, and saw nothing there. Silence and
stillness although there should be something. Someone should be there,
something should be happening to keep the mob moving forward by its
own momentum. (Had the NKVD detachment and the Russians fled?
They would have heard from an informer of what was to happen, there
were no secrets in a place like Krasnaya Gorka.) But no one moved at
the end of the street; there was silence, whiteness. Nothing but the
harsh crunch of snow under the flowing mob. He had to keep the people moving as a mob. Once they had halted, the people would no
longer be a mob but individuals wondering what the devil they were
doing there, imagining the dangers, coming to their senses, then slink-
ing away.

He listened to his heartbeat. Thump-thump thump. Clearly in his
ears. Like a drum. It ought to be the bell of a Judas goat, leading them
to slaughter. He wanted to say something (a shout, a battle cry which
might mean something to them) but the snow had caked and frozen in
his beard, and his icy breath was rattling in his chest. His mouth was
sealed. He stared wildly around but he couldn't tell one person from

another. All were white, silent, patient and enduring, marching to wherever it was they were always going no matter what the name of the country where they happened to live, heads down against the icy blast sweeping down the street, capped in snow, wrapped in desolation.

He strained to hear the sound of shooting from the camp, as they were all straining (wishing and believing . . . and would they hear what they wished to hear, could they create a fact simply by believing?), and saw their heads turning, cold ears cocked for the sound that they wouldn't hear, eyes searching each other's . . . Three miles away, in this wind, impossible to hear, is what they were saying; the wind is carrying away the sound of the diversion. He listened anxiously for the sound that he knew he would never hear: the soft, distant tapping of machine-gun fire blown down from the camp.

Ah!

Well . . .

They hadn't been *forced* to believe him, had they? Not by him . . . not much of a lie . . . And whose fault was it if people believed what their own legend had made believable?

Thump-thump . . . It ought to be a bell.

He heard a shout, then, at the head of the column (which, he swiftly argued, was *not* a column but a mob in motion), which had slowed down, then halted, and which no longer sustained its individual particles with mindless resolve. The mob was once more turning into people.

He hurried forward, searching for someone who would be able to turn these people back into a mob. A word would do, a cry out of history . . . .

The sound of a shot. Near, not distant. Here. Whipped away by the wind roaring from the river. More shouts. A curse. The dry familiar rattle of a rifle bolt. People turning, thinking, looking at each other, wondering, shaking heads and moving away . . . Must keep them moving forward, can't let them stop to think, must think of something, can't le them become people, must see to it that they remain a mob. Mindless, flowing. Unable to believe that they were individually in danger . . . Must get Esterka away from the head of the column.

The Russian Jew, Lopatsky, caught his sleeve.

—Where is the diversion?

—The wind, Janek said, waved his arms. It must be the wind . . . Blowing away the sound . . .

—The wind is coming *from* the camp, not away from us. Tell me immediately, what have you done?

—It's too late either way, Janek said. Get these people moving.

He knew that they had to be told at once that they had been betrayed, so that they could scatter. Run. Save themselves as best as they could in the wilderness. Before the soldiers came down from the camp, as they would surely come, with rifles and machine guns. Once that had happened, it would be too late to save anyone. The soldiers wouldn't listen to pleas of innocent or guilty. They would kill anybody they could find. Mindless, unquestioning, shooting, bayoneting until they grew tired. (Briefly, in a moment of his years that he tried never to remember, he had been a soldier in a war that had no meaning to him, mindless, unquestioning, shooting, bayoneting until he was tired.) Whoever was still on his feet after the killing ended would be herded to the camp, to the slower death there.

—Can you get them moving? They can't stop now. It's too late, whatever happens at the camp. They have to keep moving.

. . . And peered into sad, contemptuous eyes framed in gold wire, narrowed behind glass.

And then the Russian Jew had vanished in the crowd and he was running forward.

. . . And heard another shot. Then there was another. And a dreadful blow.

Oh no, he said, terribly disappointed. That wasn't supposed to happen. Not part of the plan . . .

He ran, or thought that he was running, as he began to lurch and stagger toward Esterka.

She had stopped as if puzzled. Listening. All of them had stopped and listened to the wind. They were no longer looking at each other but at him. He hurried, blind with sudden pain, caught her eye, raised an arm, and finally managed to open his mouth and forced a harsh strangled sound out of his smashed chest.

—Don't stop now . . . Forward!

She was looking at him.

Holy Mother, help me. And the Archangel Michael.

The pain was immense.

No.

The pain was en-or-mous.

No.

The pain was huge.

Ah . . .

It was a great pain.

Why?

Me?

No.

Oh.

It wasn't supposed to happen . . . to *have* happened.

He knew what it was. (He had been a soldier.)

He didn't believe it.

(How can you believe it? You never can believe that this could happen to you. Others, yes, why not? This was for the others. But You? Never. Never.)

Of all of them he was the only soldier. Had been a soldier. True, not much of a soldier. A deserter from the Kolomyia Regiment of Infantry, whose famous number he couldn't remember. Such a famous number! There seemed to be a great deal . . . much . . . that he couldn't remember . . .

. . . As he could hardly remember that awful Polish war where he had been a soldier . . . the bloody thousand hours of September (which, surely, had nothing to do with him . . . absolutely! *They* were not his people . . .). He was . . . what? Where? Something. Something else. He couldn't remember. There was a battle that he had forgotten and suddenly remembered. It was in a forest. No. Not a forest in a proper sense. But woods, yes. Janów Woods. A swamp. The Germans had trenches. A sandy track had led them through the thick black Polish night toward the sleeping Germans. (Oh, such machines they had! But they too were sleeping.) The three famous Ukrainian regiments of the Polish . . . uh . . . Eleventh Division (You'd be a Royal Guard if we had a King, their general had told them) falling upon the unsuspecting Germans. The number of his regiment was 49. Yes. (He was suddenly delighted.) Or was it 48? Or was that the Stanislawów Regiment? Or the Regiment of Stryj? So much blood. Yes. He would certainly remember. If he tried. In a quiet moment. Shorly, shortly. He had to remember. The pain is sharp. Hard to breathe. A bubbling noise in his ears. Mouth frozen. The blood freezing on his chest. (Another shot . . . oh, from so far away!) The others were looking. They were no longer moving, they had stopped. Esterka was looking. Esterka . . . ah. He had to keep them moving (Forward! the Leathery General had said. Urrra! said the Ukrainian soldiers.) They had to keep moving. Once you start something like that you have to finish it. There is no turning back once an attack begins. Forward! It would be either *forward* or straight into the ground.

—Come on, people!

. . . Come on!

. . . He was beside Esterka, Ariz, Shlomo, the Old Man, the carter and the postal clerk and the poultry farmer, the boy (dry-eyed and wondering, remembering, learning and forgetting nothing), the teacher (said to have been the wife of a cabinet minister . . .), a hysterical woman, a girl who whimpered, Uli's father. Moishe was sitting on his feather bed and holding his stomach. His stomach was red. The windows were burning in scarlet and gold. The black door was open. They had come outside, the three of them. Snow was falling on them. They were white with snow. White. Scared out of their wits. Well, so (goddammit all!) they should be; this was a regiment with a famous number. Numbers fifteen, fourteen and sixteen, as Shlomo would say. *You and the ger are alike before the Lord*. Got to get them moving . . .

The sun was gone.

Lifted beyond the highest cloud, sheathed in snow.

Why were the windows red?

With the sun gone, what were they reflecting?

Dreams.

Blood.

The dead and the dying.

. . . He thought then, in this near-to-final illuminating moment, his application for membership in this brotherhood accepted, sealed and stamped (but never to be delivered): Some men are marked for destruction at birth; nothing that they do, or anything that anyone else may do on their behalf can alter this cruel and irrevocable verdict. I am one of those; I bear the secret sign of blood on my forehead: the mark of the Chosen.

Old Man, I know the secret of your magic.

It has come too late. One can acquire a taste for betrayal.

I am what I am. Don't think I have any illusions about that.

I was a soldier.

(Oh, not perhaps in the way of the red-faced major or the Leathery General: *Pan Major* This and *Pan General* That . . . But for all that a sort of a soldier.)

And . . . as a soldier . . . I don't believe in starting battles I can't win.

(Yehuda, the bald plump postal clerk, was dead at his feet. Moishe was dying on his feather bed. Esterka put her thin arms around him and pushed him gently to the sleigh and seated him beside the dying old Jew.)

—You must go on, he said. The camp . . .

—Don't talk now.

—Nothing there, you see . . .

—Don't talk.

—It was for you . . . !

—I know.

—No . . . it was for me . . .

—Don't talk.

—He said . . . it was the only way. Liberation . . . China . . .

—Never mind all that. Don't talk.

—Tell them to scatter. They must . . .

—Don't talk. We know about all that.

(. . . *For anyone who sins inadvertently there shall be one law, whether native Israelite or resident* ger. *But he who sins presumptuously, native or* ger . . . *shall be cut off from his people.*)

Someone—the odd silent Russian Jew, Lopatsky—stood forward, shouting:

—David!

The three NKVD troopers had backed away against the walls of the *kantora*. Their rifles pointed forward but their hands were trembling. The long bayonets shook from side to side.

—David, cried Lopatsky.

The dim white, swaying figure of the *nachalnik* Zaslavsky appeared in the doorway.

—This is for all of us, Lopatsky said. Come with us. It is not too late.

The *nachalnik* clutched a frosted bottle to his chest. His face was wet with frozen tears and spittle. —Come, David, said Lopatsky. We need you now. This is the day we've been waiting for.

—Nobody can escape forever, Zaslavsky said thickly. He raised the Nagan revolver. The ugly octagonal barrel pointed at Lopatsky. Moved from him to the Patriarch, to Ariz, to Shlomo, to Esterka . . . To the teacher who had been the wife of a cabinet minister. It moved back and forth. Zaslavsky wasn't looking at any of them. He looked at the revolver.

The Old Man said then: *For any Israelite or* ger *settled in Israel who gives any of his children to Moloch shall be put to death!*

—Come with us, David, Lopatsky cried.

Zaslavsky raised his head. The red eyes looked beyond Lopatsky. Far beyond the people. Across the street, past the squatting little timber houses, past the white wilderness.

—If you came with us, Lopatsky said, I would be able to believe that we could succeed. It isn't only that you know how the NKVD operates in cases such as this, but it would be a sort of confirmation that what we had all set out to do so many years ago, you and I and Mendeltort and all the others, was what had to be done. We can't change, David, it isn't possible for us to become something that we are not. We follow an idea, no matter how many detours are necessary to remain alive. Mendeltort made that clear to me in Moscow. There is no escape for us from our destiny, but it is up to us to decide what our destiny can be.

—I betrayed Mendeltort, Zaslavsky said thickly. Did you know that?

—I knew that you would. Mendeltort also knew it. We all have a purpose in each other's lives. Indeed, our lives would be meaningless without that. And no one can be held accountable, by other people's standards, for everything that he must do to remain alive. Come back to us, come with us, and you will see that your entire life has made perfect sense and that there is nothing that you must regret.

—How good it would be to be able to think so.

—Hey, *komandir, komandir,* one of the soldiers said. What are we to do?

—Throw down your rifles, said Zaslavsky.

One by one, the three soldiers let their rifles drop, raised their arms, and, one by one, grinning stupidly, they knelt in the snow.

. . . And now the crowd . . . no, not a crowd, the people . . . were laughing and shouting, and from the north, carried on the wind, came the faint tapping sounds of scattered rifle fire, and another sound as if a sea had stirred, as if trees were groaning . . .

I have not lied to them, Janek Stypenko whispered in joy, and looked at Esterka.

Zaslavsky looked at his revolver. He raised it, placed it in his mouth, fired and fell.

THE SECOND
INTERLUDE

Killing Time

ONCE MORE THERE WAS A FANTASY. She was adrift in a black acrid cloud, her eyes and ears were full of blood, her breath was gurgling outward in pink froth, and the corners of her eyes and mouth were cracked wide open under ice. Abel was smiling, making promises in candlelight, and her heart was pounding. She had to hurry to him before he averted his face and turned into granite and vanished down a booming stairwell, but the black trucks were already roaring through the streets and the windows splintered with red morning light, and the kiss which she had placed so delicately on the frozen air had drifted past his head.

She was bent forward into the swift wind, unable to move; her boots were sliding under her in the powdery new snow; she would have fallen if a hard arm hooked around her waist hadn't pulled her up and on. Her feet were finding their own way into the deep ruts pressed into the snow by the equipment trucks. These coughed and stuttered at the head of the column. In her fantasy she was flowing down a great black river dotted with islands, fairy castles, palaces and temples. She was free of fear. Invisible and magically supported, she drifted toward a sun.

Again she was light-headed, trembling, out of breath, crushed beneath a weight.

Once more her mind and her body had parted company. Huge red suns were dancing before her in remorseless circles, a great black wing swept between her and the sky, and an icy drum had begun to boom in her chest and ears but she was deafened by a whistling wind and didn't hear the rhythm. Nothing to do with her, these chaotic rhythms.

. . . It is midmorning on a day which could be a Sunday, the last day of the year, yes, it is 1940 in a country with no name, a white space bounded by invisible rectilinear markings of latitude and longitude (about 150 miles south of the 75th Parallel, so they said, roughly between 100 and 105 degrees, whatever that meant), and she, the disembodied Catherine, is only remotely connected to the sharp pain that slices through her chest and deaf to the roaring in her ears. Thick clouds of charcoal smoke pour out of the trucks and are immediately flattened by the wind along the column. A black wall of five hunched backs has narrowed her horizons, five fierce faces and ten thudding boots pursue her and she is swept along on the hoarse whisper of four thousand breaths.

. . . No, it is not midmorning; little more than a quarter of the morning had passed. There is so much more time to go. There are white miles ahead. There is a sudden cry, a brief eddy around a fallen object in the hurtling black mass ahead of her, and the sharp familiar crack-crack-crack of a rifle butt connecting with a rib cage.

A hollow moan, the flat dry crackle of quick rifle fire.

A dog barked and leaped.

But she, the disembodied Catherine, flowed above it all, past the black crumpled rag bundles flattened with rifle butts and torn with bayonets, past the discarded mounds spilled out of the column (broken dolls and puppets, toppled scarecrows, covered so swiftly by the drifting snow).

The careless shots seemed to her to be an exclamation of compassion. Not one head turned to look.

What in this particular corner of the earth could make anybody care? Death was part of the morning march to work, part of the work quota; not even the return from work to the camp could be accomplished without it. And as long as it was someone else's broken body which finally gave out, this natural event shouldn't worry anyone. Incurious, unconcerned, the column struggled forward to fill the vacant places in leading files of fives.

. . . Perhaps in some other unimaginable lifetime, in a century which she would never see, someone would stop, take notice, offer help or sympathy or prayer, but this is 1940 in a nameless country and to pause is to be thrown down, to be trampled and hauled out of the column, cast aside. Yes, the year is ending as it has begun, marked by the humped black mounds sinking in the snowdrifts.

You fall and that's the end of everything. Then there is only the shot in the back of the neck or the impatient, resentful bayonet and, in less time than it would take to murmur a prayer, the ragged black mounds vanish under snow.

II

Dwarf pine appeared not a moment too soon.

Catherine's knees buckled outward, Pani Mosinska noted with contempt. And Kobza's strong arms hauled the thin girl upward, an undeserving girl who could turn her back upon ten centuries of decency and civilization, the one being the cornerstone of the other.

Such people, she thought with distaste: how dared they continue living while so many others, brave and noble and proud and suffering and true to the immemorial principles which made them human and respectable, rather than animal and contemptible, died in their hundreds every day.

Halt! And the stalled column closes upon itself like a concertina.

(First five files of fives! Out of the column! Move!)

She stared at them through a red haze that turned the snow scarlet. The hatred and the envy around her were tangible as the twenty-five skeletal bundles of rags, bone, and transparent flesh galloped into the snow, among the conical little trees festooned with ice, and stood there shivering, triumphant beside the rudimentary bonfire.

They would work near a fire!

Kepi was cursing in a dull monotone.

—Sonovabitching bastards!

Pani Mosinska closed her eyes and tried to close her ears and to withdraw into that inner fortress of her mind and soul where she could also stand entrenched and triumphant.

—Just the luck of the game, Kobza said without conviction, and anxiously began to count the scurrying scarecrows who were already clearing space for the other bonfires that would melt the ice off the little trees and expose the precious fire-making fungus.

—What's luck got to do with it? Kepi snarled and muttered. What's luck? Bastards lined up at the gate two hours before reveille . . .

—Nobody stopped you from joining them, she said.

—What? And miss my rations?

—You had a choice to make, you made it, Pani Mosinska said. Now stop complaining about it. If you can't act like a civilized human being at least try to act like a man!

—And isn't that always the way? Itzek Fogel said.

—What is, for Chrissake? Kepi said.

—To make a choice, of course. Ha ha.

—Ah, you crazy bastard . . . Well, at least they'll be hungry all day.

—So will you, said Itzek. But you'll be cold and hungry and they will be warm.

Kobza had finished counting the twenty-five fortunates and now scratched his nose. —Prr-prr . . . Can't say I like this much . . .

—Damn right you don't like it! Sneaky goddam bastards lining up at the gate two hours before anybody else!

—I don't mean that at all. Look, there's only twenty-five in this work brigade today, see? And they didn't leave anybody in the camp. Most days they'd leave a hundred people there and take fifty here. Seems to me we'll wind up damn close to the pits today.

—Jesus Christ, said Kepi.

. . . And Kobza, that secret self-sufficient man who seemed to live so wholly for himself, whose eyes occasionally betrayed him with an intelligence and a comprehension he should not have possessed, with sardonic knowledge which rendered her helpless . . . whom she detested so unreasonably (such an utter peasant!) . . . said to the girl, the weak and undeserving: *How do you feel, little lady? Not so good today?* And made that awful sound.

Pani Mosinska watched as the young woman shook her head, feeling her own narrow, shrunken chest constricting with envy and anger, while the roaring in her ears receded and her bitterness subsided, evenly with her breathing. But the endless white wasteland still seemed to her to be streaked with a bloody rain.

—I can work, Catherine said fiercely.

—Prr-prr. Who said you couldn't? Of course you can work. But at what? Doing what? You ought to stay right here, that's the best job today.

Catherine said: Why should you concern yourself with me?

—Shut up! Pani Mosinska said furiously. You are all disgusting!

. . . And closed her senses to the human degradation, the rut and the lust, the greed and the brutality and the . . . oh, sheer lack of decency . . . that threatened everything she wanted to hold dear.

(And why would they not remember who they were, these contemptible weak people? They had forgotten—and how had they dared to forget?—that life was not worth living if there were no longer principles for which one might die.)

Ah, once more (trembling with disgust) I will attempt to reason with these contemptible weak people, Pani Mosinska thought. I will do my duty. When all that we have left is our own consciousness of honor, when memory provides the only acceptable reality, each one of us who degrades herself destroys us all.

She felt Catherine's elbow turn under her fingers.

—What do you want? Catherine said.

—The first degrading step is not the hardest, she said while her own harsh voice crackled in her ears as though from a distance comparable to history. It is the easiest because you can't imagine where it leads! But once you've stepped across that invisible line that separates an animal from a human being you can never come back.

The girl said, dully: I am not going to die.

—What nonsense! Pani Mosinska cried, angry and contemptuous. Of course you are! We will all die, you fool. But if we die with dignity, with honor, with a pure conscience . . .

—We will be just as dead as if we died without them, Kobza said suddenly. Prr-prr.

—Pride is life! said Pani Mosinska. Dignity, courage, contempt for the impossible! I should have thought it unnecessary to say something quite that obvious . . .

—Anger is life, Itzek Fogel said suddenly into the bruised sky. Memory . . . and anger.

—I am *not* going to die here, Catherine said.

—I'd see to that, if you'd let me, Kobza said.

—Keep quiet! she shouted above the roaring in her ears. Keep your disgusting lusts to yourself! You don't know any more about decency and honor than this idiot child!

—A man don't have to be a general to know what *you're* talking about, lady, Kobza said.

—Perhaps not! she gasped, her eyes on fire with fresh freezing tears. But he must be a man! And a woman has to be a woman, not an idiot child . . . and we must all retain our decency, our sense of goodness, our ability to tell right from wrong, otherwise we are animals!

—But what if we are helpless? Catherine said. Don't you know how fragile that makes us?

—You become helpless only when you admit that you are, Pani Mosinska said.

—That is exactly what I mean, Catherine said.

—How . . . contemptible.

III

Hating, the woman whirled away. Catherine knew that this was her true way of relating to the world, and her true sense of sight. And it was no use saying that mediocre minds always cling to flagpoles . . . slogans . . . testaments; there was the matter of good personal habits and a faith. A way of life riveted to an undeniable sense of grandeur. A sense of self in absolute commitment to a principle, as if the hottest, most persistent fire were raging in her chest. Catherine knew her, understood her; like the quaint ugly trim of artful ornaments in her father's study—the gimcrack and the antimacassar and the gilded frames —this woman represented epoch rather than character.

Through the revolving scarlet circles that distorted vision, Catherine watched Surma and Sowinski pacing along the column, peering among the ranks.

Smoke began to rise thinly among the scrub pine, the dwarfed and ugly trees of the taiga glittering with ice . . .

She had made her move in full consciousness of what she was doing, or thought that she did. She regretted nothing. While there was still a fragment of a life to be lived there could be no regrets. To be alive is the most important thing that anyone can do. Faiths, symbols, and ideals are only the ritual trappings for the act of living . . . and she *would* live, the quiet sorrow of Father Boguslawski and the iron contempt of Pani Mosinska notwithstanding.

Such a small price to pay for so much.

And if the first payment is difficult to make . . . well, the second would be easier.

Kobza's encircling and supporting arm fell away as she stepped closer to the outer edge of the column, her back erect, head high, shoulders pushed as far behind as she could get them . . . and, unaccountably, wished herself invisible.

She heard distant laughter. An icy image of brass cupids, ritual candelabra, a sudden flash of light, a melting explosion, a pentagram and a declamation, a pledge sent silently across the wreckage of a vanished morning, a pair of empty military boots sagging at attention, trembled uncertainly at the edge of vision, dipped and bowed and vanished.

Abel was dead, she was quite sure of that, and she owed him nothing. You can't trust the dead, they are the worst of all possible blackmailers. You can't trust the dying, the living, anyone. It may be that we are all alike in the way that a white wilderness filled with snow can be called freezing, powdery, wet or dry, and endless, but each snowflake is different from every other, separate from the other, and all relationships are accidental at best.

Sowinski saw her, pointed.

Surma grinned.

Catherine watched them coming toward her, felt the sudden fire of ice along her upper cheeks, heard (but didn't feel) the sharp crack of an open palm splitting her upper lip. Looked up surprised into the hate-filled eyes of Pani Mosinska. Why did she have to do that? What I do doesn't diminish her. She is what she is and I am what I am and what does the one have to do with the other? She heard the whistles, cries, barking dogs once more alerting the column.

. . . Saw the encrusted pebble eyes set too close together, a pitted nose, the thick loose grinning mouth, the wide-legged stagger. Saw the black-rimmed horned callused thumb jerked commandingly toward her and out, shrugged off restrictions and restraining fingers and stepped out of the column.

She heard a sigh, a whisper, thudding boots; felt more than heard the forward lurch of the black files of fives. She did not look back.

. . . Heard the dry loose snick-snack of a rifle bolt chambering a round because she had done the unforgivable in stepping from the column, bowed before the expected bullet.

Surma's slack lips twisted, mouthed words near the soldier's ear. (Hooo-ha-ha ha-ha!) The soldier shrugged, slung his rifle, and trudged past her without a glance, indifferent.

Perhaps she wasn't there after all? Having become suddenly invisible, perhaps she was safe.

She didn't move.

. . . Saw the smoke of the bonfires coiling about the ice cage of glittering dwarf pine. Saw Surma and Sowinski on each side of a cadaverous man, rushing him into her place in the column. Heard his cries of protest. Comrades! People! I waited! I was first!

So (Surma said, smashing the side of the man's jaw with a blow, scattering gobs of blood and pink crystals of bone) now you'll be the last!

(Hoo-ha-ha-ha!)

—You tell 'im, Surma.

—You tell 'im, Sowinski.

. . . No, the man cried, wept. No, she has no right . . . You have no right . . . I was first to form up at the gate this morning. (Right: what is right, and why should anybody care?) Help, people, help! I waited! I was first! Comrades, don't do this to me! I beg you . . . by Christ's living wounds, by the tears of the Immaculate, if you want Salvation . . . I am of the people! I have a child, a mother . . . only another two years and my time's up . . . served ten, you know what that means . . . Comrades, have mercy! I beg you . . . Comrades, people!

They threw him bodily into the churning black depths of the column, where he fell, staggered forward, cried, and ran out again into the open field. A step to the right . . .

—She has no right!

The first bullet struck him in the side. He raised both his hands high above his head, staggered sideways. The hands swooped and fluttered. He sat down in the snow.

He started to drag himself slowly forward toward the first bonfire, one arm folded against his chest like a broken wing, the other a crutch.

—I was first . . . waited . . .

The second bullet struck him in the head.

—Stupid sonovabitch, Surma said.

IV

Then it began to snow and horizons vanished. Catherine had also vanished, along with the dwarf pine, the smoke, and the bonfires, and Kobza heaved a great sigh, plunged through the thickening curtain of whirling white powder which made him so deceptively alone. Each time that he had chosen to involve himself in the life of others (and God only knew that he had sworn often enough never to do that again) the result had been violence and chaos, and he, old enough to have known better at the start, found his self-contained little world in shambles. And that's the way things would always be, he muttered to himself (prr-prrr), as long as he kept finding people weaker than himself, people who needed his help without knowing it, people who asked him (without ever saying one word about it) to take care of them, and as long as he, ignoring all his long and hard-won experience, continued to involve himself with others. Catherine may have been thinking that she did not need to account to anyone for the choices she made for herself, but each choice that a person made involved everyone who cared for that person. If Surma and Sowinski laid a hand on her he would have to kill them and *that* would be only a beginning; there was no way to hide a couple of dead gang bosses, the other gang bosses would see to that. He had watched Catherine in the mess hall, as she made her bid for the criminals' attention, and he knew then that he would have to kill somebody before the day was over. When Catherine stepped out of the column it was a confirmation of someone's death sentence. Surma . . . Sowinski . . . perhaps both. And then there'd have to be many others before they killed *him*.

He didn't blame Catherine for making her choice; it was her choice to make if she wanted to live a month or two longer. He didn't blame the terrible old woman, the General's Lady, who staggered beside him, for the fuss she had made. He had watched Catherine, in pleasure and wonder, growing up in a house where no one had ever given him a thought, where no one had ever spoken a quiet word to him, a word which was not an order or demand, where he had been invisible inside the black cellars (which was what he wanted), where no one had asked who he was or where he had come from, or if his unknown life had ever contained anything that they would understand. He had been Kobza, the janitor who spoke in an accent that no one could place, who made a strange farting sound through some missing teeth, who wiped his nose on his sleeve, who shoveled the sidewalks, swept the yard in autumn, carried coal. His name itself was a joke, an improbable allusion to mountains and goats. As long as no one cared to know any more than that about him, or to give him more than a passing glance as he scrubbed the stairs, he could be content. Who ever looks at janitors or asks about their lives? It was the best way to be invisible. He lived in a world he hardly ever had to think about, a world centered on a cellar and the packing crate in which he slept under old newspapers, in a landscape of crumbling yellow newsprint piled to the ceiling, old slogans, ancient exhortations, the daily history of turmoil and trouble, in a valley bordered by black slopes of coal sliding down upon him, dark escarpments in a dusty vault, in the squeal and scamper of gaunt rats with whom he had signed a personal armistice, among the piles of broken hobbyhorses spilling sawdust, ruptured teddy bears, headless dolls and rusty bicycles, himself an ignored piece of debris, a discarded household object which, once in a while, may have been useful but was generally forgotten. Outside the still center of his hidden world was another, which he had abandoned, where men struggled until they were broken, where life ebbed out of ruined bodies instead of harmless sawdust, where the debris had breath. There God and human destiny were locked in combat more hideous than anything that his private underworld could witness. He was alone among all those other people as he would be to the end of his days, having been born into a loneliness beyond comprehension of those who feel they live in loneliness; those recognitions of success and failure by which other men lived were meaningless to him.

(One day Catherine's father had come to the cellars to ask for help in searching for a now forgotten item in the old newspapers, a record of futility if ever there was one, and said across the mountains of coal, in the near squeal of curious rats which had banded in a corner to watch the intruder: Do you know that I envy you your solitude, the sense of order you bring to this world by your will alone? When did you first discover that people do not really need each other as people, and that our passion for organizations, the mania for belonging, is less a sign of a social conscience or historical imperative than a reflection of a fear that we, incompletely developed, might be obliged to spend an evening in company as dull as our own?)

. . . To have replied in kind to this man who, in memory, sounded as ineffectual as a card player in a cherry orchard, would have revealed him as something other than he wished to seem. And so he said then (and muttered wryly to himself now, as he struggled to keep his feet in the shifting powder): A man's got to look after hisself . . . think about hisself, nobody else'll do it . . . And he had quickly wiped his nose with his dirty sleeve.

The image which he projected so successfully that it had become a part of his nature was that of a peasant, the kind among whom he had spent his youth, a dull and primitive being whose known world could be traveled in three days, whose life revolved between the fields, the marketplace, the church, the tavern, and the graveyard. The folklore which he had come to collect in the villages had taught him how to be a peasant whose strength, shrewdness, native wit, inventiveness, and cunning could overcome human cruelty. Humiliation had to be borne with patience, according to folklore, so that the tables might be turned upon the tormentor when he least expected it, but revenge was a waste of time since punishment was worse if it was self-inflicted. The trouble with fairy tales was that no one was able to recognize them while living within them.

He had schooled himself to be what he appeared: deceptively simple and relying only on himself. That was the peasant image not the peasant substance of brutality and crudeness beyond comprehension, but who but a real peasant would know that? Not a trusting fool enamoured of legends.

Beside him, Pani Mosinska fell. He stooped and picked up the crumpled bag of bones that had been a porcelain figurine, a clockwork ballerina, a jeweled bird, a rose pressed between the pages of patriotic poems, a silhouette cut from tinted cardboard. He set her on her feet as easily as though she were a child who had tripped and fallen while exploring his dark and dusty cellars, noted indifferently her wrench of revulsion as she pushed herself away from his arm . . .

. . . A woman made of stone or perhaps of iron. Forged under a hammer, cast in a furnace or quarried but surely not born. Her face a chart of journeys, pilgrimages, marches; well-traveled peaks and dark valleys. The high ridges of pride cast a veil of shadow over sorrow. Because to her sorrow is self-indulgence and must be concealed. A thickening, coarsening woman whose delicate small bones tell that she had been lithe and quick and knows about laughter, had danced, had made love, birthed a child, knows how high to lift the foot in the gavotte, had nursed a young husband through his first wounds and knows that when a wound heals there will be a scar, knows that before one may be generous one has to be frugal and that before there may be mercy there must be bravery, has learned that sorrow can etch stainless steel as deeply as acid. Sorrow does not ennoble, it makes people ugly. There is no nobility of spirit in sorrowful endurance and beauty is *not* in the eye of the beholder. A compact, narrowing woman, the size of a boy, as tough as tanned leather and scrap metal stitched with bone and steel. The hands are small, square-fingered, blunted, crippled, blue, dark with calluses which lie on them in layers. Hands hard as gauntlets to be flung down, or picked up. Hands not to be ignored. Eyes to avoid as mirrors are avoided. A mouth which is a wrinkle, some fault in the mold. Not a mouth for kissing, for soft words, for music, for prayer or confession, but an instrument for sipping icy air, a weapon cold and dry as the edge of destruction itself.

—You all right, lady?

—Don't touch me!

—Save your breath, he said.

. . . And thought, without pity, of himself as a younger man with all *his* delusions; a foolish fellow who had carried a silk pocket handkerchief *and* a cotton one (and who wouldn't have dreamed of wiping his nose on a sleeve), who had become enamoured of simple peasant virtues and married a peasant girl because he thought her redolent of immortality like the earth itself—fruitful, enduring, self-renewing and renewing him—and who had murdered his stupid, emptyheaded peasant wife and her loutish lover. Retribution had come in true fable fashion: no one can murder another without killing a part of himself.

Beside him, Kepi mumbled blind obscenities, Itzek Fogel grunted, Pani Mosinska slipped again and lay without a sound as the next dark file of fives bore down upon her with churning boots and snow. He picked her up again, felt her futile struggles.

—Let . . . me . . . go!

—About a mile more to go, lady. Prr-prrr.

—And must you . . . make . . . that obscene . . . noise!

He laughed. In fairy tales laughter was a gift.

V

Camp people have no curiosity. The fires were smoldering. Ice cracked and melted. Catherine moved among the stunted trees, reaching out, grasping, tearing off strips of gray frozen fungus, carried them to the boiler. Big black kettle balanced among flames and the white rim of instantly freezing steam growing ever higher. The frosted rim curves inward, the opening grows smaller. The water is sluggish.

Surma and Sowinski were gone but they would be back. The rest of the work brigade had scattered over a square mile and she was suddenly alone. She could see far across the symmetrical white cones and humped billows of deadfall under snow, as far as the blinding glare of whiteness permitted. The column was gone, vanished in the north, and wind-whipped snow hissed along its path, covering up all traces. She could no longer see the dead man; he had disappeared. But the flat indifferent double crack that had signaled his death was echoing in her ears, and the historical beasts of childhood, the glittering pantheon of her own mythology, were scattering in terror.

Again slow tumblers moved and fell, frozen gears ground forward. Her head was ringing with double explosions; a red mist settled about her head and cushioned the echoes. A chorus of soft disappointed voices had become harsh in a litany of fear and chanted a warning: a hairline crack had appeared on the glossy forehead of a monument carved from ice and crystal. The Angel of Death stepped forward, unsmiling, and opened her arms.

From where she crouched beside the kettle and the fire (her face, arms, hands, chest, and knees scorched and her back and neck coated with thin ice) she could see far across the humped white wilderness where small groups were moving, saw beasts of burden, memorials and statues, landmarks and signposts . . . Read the directions carved in ice, saw the roads unfolding like banners among flames and knew where they would take her. She heard footsteps crushing the soft snow behind her.

. . . Heard the granite voice thundering on the edge of a precipice and took a backward step.

. . . An old priest was babbling about universal love, the brotherhood of man (the eternal dream!), and called for forgiveness, but she was beyond compassion for anyone but herself. Her eyes were deep in the chasm before her, a chasm or a void. She had passed through many, skirted an infinity of others in the company of Abel, for whom a void had been peace and refuge, who had sought extinction, who had become enamored of his own cold interior spaces, hollow as a bronze. The seasons of her childhood were never so present as her inner winter. Here the sky was part of the landscape, a mere curve in the earth's hollow surface, sweeping harshly upward. And then she was focusing her unseeing eyes on her impossible idea.

Alone (no, not alone, that's the point: carrying her child) she would never manage an escape. Nobody escaped; ever. It wasn't even anything to daydream about. Only the mad would do it. Think of invisible walls fashioned of some impenetrable translucent material. Think of time and distance. No, this is not a literary game or poetic fancy. There really are such walls! Reduced to a kernel, the will is shackled even if the body is more or less free.

. . . And anyway, nobody can believe that, in the end, anything really dreadful will happen to him or to her. To others: certainly, why not? They probably deserve it. But the essential I? Unthinkable.

Because God is Just, is He not? HE knows that Goodness must always be rewarded and that no man is evil. (It's just all his neighbors who deserve hellfire.) And God sees everything, does He not? Not a single sparrow, and all that . . . HE can't remain indifferent!

. . . It's just a matter of enduring, of working and waiting and buying my days one small compromise at a time, of making the effort, of willing my survival, of believing that I shall be saved . . .

And dying with everyone else!

To stay here was to die. Sooner or later. Pani Mosinska was right about that. She was probably right about a lot of things. And compromises only bought a day, a handful of hours.

Motion was life, she had said. There was something to that. If she were suddenly to get up and start to move. Walk. Southward. (Where is south?) Anywhere. She wouldn't last the night.

(But what if *many* were to go?)

And it wouldn't matter *where* they went from here. Nor how. That (the *how* of it) was the least important. What mattered was to get away from here, where, she could tell with absolute certainty, everyone would die.

Behind her, there were no more footsteps.

They . . . her new masters . . . had arrived to collect their tribute. Catherine held her head down, thinking: It isn't really going to happen, is it? How can it? It can't possibly happen unless I will it; if I will it *not* to happen then it won't! If I drive every thought about it out of my mind then it simply won't exist! If it doesn't happen I shall believe in God again, I shall pray. If I don't acknowledge their silent multiple malevolent presence at my back, if I resurrect my faith, if I refuse to hear their heavy breathing (how many will there be? Just Surma and Sowinski or all of them?), perhaps they'll vanish. Disappear. Not *be* there when I look around. The main thing was not to look around; until she actually saw them she would be able to think that they weren't there.

. . . And suddenly thought that she would have to have her child baptized and christened. Soon.

Before he died.

. . . And thought of Abel, who had averted his face when she most needed him . . . and could no longer remember what he looked like.

Now.

. . . And thought of Kobza, unaccountably, as she had glimpsed him in that roaring street of icicles and bayonets, in that imagined city she would never see, and saw him wrapping neighbors' children in yellow newspapers, stuffing them into his own sleeping crate like fragile ornaments packed for a bumpy trip . . . He could have spent those moments looting an apartment; he could have wrapped himself in foxes, sables, bearskin, the stoat and the otter. We had no time to take them . . . Oh, hurry, she told him. Help me! The bellying dark sky was about to give birth to some sort of a sun. An icy claw had clamped itself to her bones, she was spun around.

. . . St. Theresa of Avila said then, emphatically: *Que rien ne te trouble, que rien ne t'épouvante; tout passe, Dieu ne change pas.*

No change in the abstract.

Tout passe, rien ne change pas.

The Nothing is not changed.

I am inviolate, impervious, a part of the void.

Death is a door between two rooms, one cold and the other colder,

said the passing spirit of a murdered man who had tripped on the
threshold of his own illusions and who was now being buried by the
drifting snow. Eternity is assured, said Father Boguslawski.

(Yes, but, she cried, an eternity of what?)

. . . And Mann-Bielecki was bowing with his yellow smile, a tulip
made of chicken feathers in his buttonhole, saying: As I said, an
enchanting idea . . . Or at least it may have been until a prolific journalist wrote a sentimental French profile about lost illusions . . . Since
then, ladies and gentlemen, all assurances of permanence, even on the
celestial level (ha ha ha), have become political rhetoric . . .

(Ha ha ha! Heh heh!)

—Well, who goes first?

—Who d'you think?

—Now, listen, Surma . . .

Tout passe.

Her memory had become a time bomb, ticking backward, and she lay
helpless as an open city inviting occupation. All the bloody-handed psy-
chopaths of history caracoled their chargers among the ruins of her
temples, and the feathered beasts of other men's imaginations crowded
into the bombproof shelter where her spirit crouched.

No comforting illusions leaped up to avert the decree. Her masters
laughed and bickered and confirmed her sentence. And knowing what
she did, having learned that one can be right and lose, that force can
conquer spirit, that hatred always makes its point while love is seldom
heard, that dedications and ideals aren't their own recompense, would
she do it again?

Yes, if her existential circumstances were the same, she argued in
chaos. All that we do, don't you see, is made reasonable by the inspired
chemistry of time and place upon ourselves; all our thoughts and actions are coherent as a distillation of those hideous and revealed forces
under which our whole future lies ready to embrace us, as a banner exists while still furled, as a devious road is hidden by its bends . . .

No! she cried.

Circumstances never repeat themselves! And people who claim that
they do delude themselves to justify their own failure to achieve a
transubstantiation, their lack of vision, spiritual infirmity and impoverished minds!

. . . The cowled agents of retribution nodded and smiled then. A
land mine had blown up the gates of paradise and the flaming angel
swung his Teutonic sword to keep the crowd moving. Please don't
block the entrance, said the Virgin Mary.

They were swelling, swelling . . . Huge, bulging, they fell on her like
mountains. They were all hands and teeth. Her stately myths were

trampling stacks of incandescent dead, an icy day had opened its yellow maw and swallowed everything in sight; she reached out, clawed a bony wrist, took the pulse of a dead civilization, heard a booming heartbeat thudding against her own and understood the meaning of martyrdoms. A harsh gray fog swept across frozen water, covering everything, and the earth turned slowly on its splintered axis.

. . . Cold lives, soft as new snow, form their passing dunes, dissolve in the wind: men, women, lovers, friends. The stars were splintered. Her blood was uttering pale rhythmic screams and her bones were leaping. The Recording Angel grimaced in disgust. The golden quill fell, turned to chicken feathers, drifted, and was lost. The imitation Arctic sun was crudely orange in the cracked fragmented eyes bearing down upon her, and her captive shadow was striped in blue and gray.

She was in flames and freezing, blind with sudden blood, impaled on a column of ice. There was a sudden cry, a churning of black shapes, the wind howled. Be silent, cried the animals of history. Her mind snapped shut, escaped and soared. She had leaped upward and found herself falling. The nuns were in full flight, their eyes extinguished so that they need not see a nowhere-near-virginal naked creature, descend to the grave.

. . . And saw the pure spirit springing from torn flesh and ascending to light . . .

. . . Heard and saw four cursing men hold down a dry-eyed, silent struggling girl whom they have gagged with her imaginary pigtails and sailor collar, while another (Hoooo-ha!) launches himself between her thin legs. She is split and momentarily rigid in terror and shock, then lurches upward. Whee! No, goddammit, I'm not hurryin', wait your turn. Ooooooh-ooooooh! Ahhhhh. Jeee-*zus!* That's *prima,* I tell you . . . The ice is white and milky underfoot. A mile further into the lake the ice is clean and clear and the black water stares upward like a malignant eye filled with infinite knowledge, the wisdom of patience.

Silent as death, and icy, she hurls her body away from her. Their hate spurts into her in great arcs and she feels exultant. Her absent spirit wanders off to bow over the drifting grave of the man who had died by mistake. The black eye of the lake is wide with satisfaction. Hadst Thou been here, Lord, she chuckles, and creaks with frozen laughter, my brother would not have died . . . My Son is with you always, says the Mater Dolorosa.

Not a single sparrow. Not a pebble.

Wait your turn, goddammit!

Ugh-agh!

. . . I am the Resurrection and the Light.

Wheee! Jeee-zuz! Ahhh!

Who's next?

. . . I am with you always.

The gurgling rapist sings.

The brutalized body curves into the snow.

—Hey, Surma, hurry up! Somebody's coming!

—Well. (Hoo-ha-ha!) It isn't me.

—Ah, you bastard, hurry it up, will you? They're coming up fast! For Chrissake, they got axes!

—Who? Wha-a-a . . .

Then cries, curses, the thud of an ax. Howling black bundles wrapped about each other are rolling in the snow.

—Jeee-ZUS!

The crack of wood on bone.

—Prr-prrr.

—Ah! Ahhh . . .

Once again, teeth and nails. Fists and boots. And the whirling axes.

—One's getting away! Get 'im, Kepi!

—I'll get 'im! Ha ha.

—Comrades, mercy! Mercy . . .

—Die, sonovabitch.

She was dry, gutted, scorched, cauterized, healed, and purified: all grief and sorrow had melted and evaporated in the fire; all the wax statuettes of the deadly virtues had bubbled away. Her body heaved, replenished and fertile, ready to populate the hell of her imagination, assuming the burdens of every murderer who had pumped his poison into her. The dead man's spirit blew away in a pathetic spiral of powdery snow. She, incandescent, blinking amaranthine eyes, glittering with hatred, burned like a naked beacon in the snow.

. . . Let us pause, said the poet. Let us rest now, for we have looked into tomorrow's sorrow.

Ice, wind, and snow.

Cries and the thud of footsteps.

Then she was wrapped in ice and cradled upon stone. The cradle was rocking. She heard a muted crooning, looked up into the granite gray face of the General's Lady.

Leaning thoughtfully on his ax, scarlet to the elbows, Kobza bowed his head. So might a woodcutter rest, she thought, at the far edge of the first of many clearings. His hollow eyes were black with the distance of millennia, turned to a private calendar of his own within him. He stood astride her history. She knew him then, understood him, read the scrolls etched into his forehead, sent him a personal message of complicity across his dark centuries; the past, the present, and the future had suddenly come together.

—Which one escaped? asked Pani Mosinska.

Kobza shrugged, embarrassed. (Oh yes, a craftsman who is shown a flaw in the finish.)

—Prr-prrr, can't tell. The way this lot's been done . . . Ah, lady, you can see for yourself . . . No way to tell who any of them were.

—Surma's the one that got away, Itzek Fogel said.

—Well, let's get this lot on the sledge, get 'em out of sight. Put your back into it. Toss 'im in. Christ, that's a big one. Which one the hell was he?

—Sowinski, Itzek said.

—One of yours?

—One of mine.

The slaughtered men had bled very little, the spurting blood had frozen as soon as it had appeared, sealing the wounds, and now snow drifted across the bits and pieces, restoring symmetry. Once more she thought of trees and lumbermen, a pause for rest in an honest working day. One moment more and even the sledge had begun to vanish. It dwindled in distance, pulled by Kobza and pushed by Itzek Fogel.

She was aware of nothing other than a certain deadness and detachment: that moral insensibility which is the legacy of months rather than of moments. She had become as arid as a desert; empty, with all her fires extinguished, she was herself a void without horizons.

—Can you walk?

She nodded.

. . . Heard the sound of shots: flat and dry in the thin Arctic air. Not memory, not imagination . . .

Saw a man, running.

Saw a man who plunged through the snow on horseback.

Saw a staggering woman, then two men walking quickly.

A smudge of smoke crouched over the near horizon.

A dull humming roar.

The sky was strangely tilted, like a saucer draining her horizons. She was not surprised.

When you have exhausted all the possible varieties of feeling, and people and ideas, and material objects, there comes a pause, a sort of gap in time. What is left to fill it? A mystical experience? She thought that she would probably have to settle for madness.

The wilderness had a certain softness where it was blurred and vague, and definition was something to avoid . . . It was enough to say in this fleeting fraction of her total moment that Pani Mosinska's face looked sad. The harsh lines had dissolved, the day's page had been blackened. So might a dissolute and ruined Pope look on Judgment Day.

And in the meantime the woman had taken her arm.

There were many people, running in the snowdrifts.

She heard a shot, another.

. . . Heard a drawn-out, muffled howl: hatred breaking the re-straining bonds of terror, flattened in the distance.

. . . Saw the wide-open gate without guards. Saw yellow flames curling from a barrack and small brown men darting in and out of smoke. Saw a dark, faceless mass stamping in total silence on a spread-eagled red and brown object. Scarlet snow.

. . . Heard a short, dry, despairing shout from a man carried over-head by others before they pitched him into fire.

And there was Kepi, saying. Bastard got away.

—It doesn't matter now, said Pani Mosinska.

VI

Father Boguslawski closed his eyes to pray. He was terribly afraid that no one would hear him. Forgive me, Father. Please, please hear me, Father. Please forgive us all.

—Get some men together, Kobza was commanding. Get into the naphtha store. Set that watchtower on fire, and the cookhouse too. Burn them all out of there.

—For God's sake, no! begged Father Boguslawski.

—For our sakes, yes, prr-prrr. Get on with it, Kepi.

—You bet! We'll fry the fucking bastards. There's just the gang bosses to worry about anyway, you know? The guards fucked off as soon as them Ostyaks showed up and the people rose . . .

—They'll be back. Get going.

. . . God, the priest prayed. Father . . .

Turn your eyes away.

Forgive us.

We have all betrayed you.

You made us in Your wonderful image but there are other spirits which You have created and these are in us as much as You are within us, and we are helpless against their terrible need to take us from You. Give me a sign that we are as You wanted us to be. The beast within us is tethered loosely on such a slender thread . . . And all of man's his-tory has been written by murderers for so many centuries! Surely a sign, a miracle, a rain of blood, a whirlwind carrying Seraphim and Demons . . . or something smaller, something less demanding . . . now, at this dreadful time . . . Oh, must I also doubt You?

He heard a wail of terror, a cry, supplication, a howl from the pit, and Mann-Bielecki ran past, his hands about his ears. Blind with fear, the poet headed for the wall of snow and barbed wire pursued by the mob. He slipped in stained snow, lay squealing. They threw themselves upon him and wrenched his head backward. Glass glittered redly in the hand of the executioner and Mann-Bielecki screamed.

—Oh, stop it, stop it, the priest cried, said, whispered to a sky made violent with fire and smoke. —Will you listen to me?

—Stop it? Why? He betrayed *you*, didn't he?

—God has forgiven him! Don't you see what *you* are betraying?

The priest closed his eyes. It's no disgrace to be betrayed, a great voice assured him. It is a privilege, a mark of My favor; it brings you to My notice in a form and fashion that guarantees a welcome.

Father Boguslawski tried to pray. He thought of his two old friends hanged so carelessly behind their manor house, betrayed by their dream. (To fashion a new man, to seek out the embers of the human spirit among the ashes of selfishness and greed, to destroy prejudice, to make all men human.) The dream had seemed so possible in the treasure house of Zygmunt's study, among the books and music: all that accumulated evidence of man's evolution out of darkness . . .

And Mann-Bielecki continued to scream.

Mea culpa, Father.

He couldn't believe that his life, as he had imagined it principle by principle, faith by faith, could come to an end so easily. He had never been able to believe that anything existed unless God wished it to exist. And all that needed to be done, he had thought, to bring about God's kingdom on earth, was to restore and reconstruct His image, reaffirm His will.

Mea culpa, Father. In your great mercy, help me to forget my terrible presumption.

Mea maxima culpa . . .

Under the sawing shard of glass, Mann-Bielecki was finally dying. A clatter of yellow teeth, a drowning gurgle, the pewter eyes began to turn to ice.

—Get a rope, someone shouted. String up the fucking bastard. Where's the rest of them committee traitors?

. . . There must be a way to make amends for this, he muttered to himself.

—What? said the moon-faced man, the leader and commander.

—I'm sorry, he said, shrunk into himself. I didn't know that I had spoken aloud.

—I'm also sorry, said Dr. Poremba. Believe me, Father, there is no other way. Cruel, merciless, inhuman, all that is true. But when everything is reduced to the question of dying or living then all your humanistic arguments become rather foolish.

He cried: You can't believe that, Doctor!

—I can't?

—No man of goodwill can believe anything like that!

—Man of goodwill? What does that mean here? If there is any goodwill in this hell it's purely personal. Goodwill to me, to hell with the others. All that counts is success, if we fail we die. There is no right or wrong.

—How can a man like you believe such a thing?

—A man like me? said Dr. Poremba. I'm sorry, Father I no longer know what kind of man I am.

—But don't you even see what you are doing to yourself?

—Only the pure or innocent or the simpleminded can assume that there is anything gratuitous about an act of violence. Such acts, believe me, are more meaningful than poetry or prayer.

—No, he whispered. No.

VII

It was the wind, of course: the high Russian wind. Dr. Poremba heard exultant voices roaring in his ears.

Laughing gaunt men or women (they could have been women) seized the body of the butchered poet, the civilized man, the man of the imagination, the enfant terrible of café society, and hanged it by the heels. Still now, the black protruding tongue; dead, the pewter eyes.

And they were shouting: kill the fucking traitors. And they were singing, singing. The tunes of Blood and Glory. And was the NKVD military band ready at the gate?

The parchment abbot rustled in ecclesiastic gloom, and he looked desperately around, hearing songs and voices, and caught the bleak question in the eyes of Anna Dimitrevna. Such acts, he hastened to explain, can be read as messages to mankind . . . !

Magna mater, comrade.

Tarski looked at him worriedly and Langenfeld was smiling, and the Eternal Lancer sang of Lady War, and Mann-Bielecki swung quietly overhead. The priest was praying, and Catherine seemed asleep with her eyes wide open; eyes as extinguished as the black pits in the dark face of Anna Dimitrevna. The older men were silent, nodding. Nobody protested the massacre that he had begun. No one seemed able to see that anything was amiss. Their harsh, gaunt faces, slashed with horizontal grooves, were closed and turned wholly upon themselves. He hadn't gone far enough in his new awareness to pity them but he thought that he could finally begin to understand himself. Without their many props they had not diminished in their own conception of themselves; he seemed to have shrunk without his. Perhaps there was still something that could be taken from him, but other than life, which had become a burden without purpose, he couldn't imagine what he still had to lose. His children? Yes, his children; he had already heard about his children, he knew what they were. As long as a man isn't deprived of everything he may still cling to dreams, to some illusion of purpose and personal worth. But when he has been stripped of all his treasured visions, when life has become an accident without meaning (a wry, contemptuously bitter comedy where only irony is apparent, where even poetry has become cruel,) and when all faith and trust lead only to betrayals and to violence, then each man becomes a living lie. He thought that if there were still something for which he might hope it was that he might end this suddenly incomprehensible life in a manner that wouldn't turn it all into a lie. To give some posthumous substance to the role that he had tried to play.

He tried to think of friends, moments of laughter, couldn't remember any. There seemed to be crowds of men and women moving in his mind and each, at one time or another, had been called a friend, but now these friendships, like the friends themselves, seemed unbelievable. Passing illusions, transitory fancies, hinged upon a day. He remembered leaflets but not what they said. He had a clearer recollection of slag heaps, secret handshakes, passwords, and clandestine meetings than of the burning, glittering young men and women with whom he had met. Events stood stark and vivid in his mind but the men and women who had helped him to fashion these events had blurred, their names were forgotten. In the sudden loneliness of this new incomprehensible life in which he could no longer recognize himself, it seemed that whole great ceremonial parades of people had crossed his course as small boats might on a foggy night, blinking out an occasional recognition signal, hailing him in passing, then disappeared in his luminous wake. He could remember a part of Alicja's body, a gesture or a characteristic movement, an old phrase or two, an idea that she had conveyed to him about herself, but the woman herself had ceased to exist.

His children, as children, had vanished. What had been his daughter was a mindless whore, her soiled empty eyes as bleak as a bruise; his son was a monster. A madwoman had been his conscience for a moment and now she was destroyed, her idiot child was dead. Even those old friends . . . well, let's say it: *brothers* . . . whom he had believed to be immortal in his memory were remembered only as physical fragments attached to a day which, in itself, had become a dim fragment of a larger incomprehensible event. No, no examples, no need for examples. But they intruded: Tarski, Langenfeld, Jozef Abramowski . . . Rows of disembodied faces stared at him, cowled in shadows, as a procession of monks ascending and descending an endless staircase; his mind swept across a panorama of words, letters, scenes, and forms that merged continuously into each other, collapsing and emerging simultaneously, as though time had become a cylinder on which his beginning and his end flowed into each other.

Dr. Poremba stared at fire and smoke.

He looked about, unable to decide what he should do next. There had been something that he had forgotten to tell the Ukrainian boy whose name had vanished from his memory. Time had betrayed him and enlisted among his enemies, and now his mind betrayed him. It refused to function. The beads of his experience had run together and formed one icy pool in which the past and the present couldn't be distinguished. A watchtower flamed like a torch, toppled, fell in a roar of sparks and burning timbers. The barracks burned in tiers like votive candles, and did he really hear the beginning of a hymn?

> . . . 'Tis the Day of Blo-o-od and Glo-o-ry
> May it be our Re-sur-rec-tion Day . . . !

A totally naked woman, her hair on fire, ran whooping into snow with a red and yellow turban unfolding behind her.

He watched a huge hag dragged out of a window, then saw her metamorphosis into scarlet snow. (Hey, King Whore! Whose turn on the bucket?) Starved people, too weak to move without help, stretched skeletal claws between burning logs, crying their tunes of glory. He recognized the man he had known only as the Unknown Criminal, hanged upside down from a burning timber, saw someone else whom he seemed to know, dragged by his heels toward another beam. Looked with dispassionate interest at an act of murder. Viewed mindless mayhem. Beheld looting. Remarked upon bestiality, watched an evisceration followed by a gouging. Noted the beginning of a massacre. Observed a mutilation.

He saw his whole life in terms of pure logic, but it seemed to have missed a universe of feeling. Yet there had been feeling, there had been a love. The hollow man was too recently gutted to be able to forget what it had felt like to contain a heart. But now all of his interior processes, the mind and the spirit, had become one darkly intricate woodblock print superimposing night upon day; his years were suddenly a clock which never ticks, a blank round surface without numbers, and he a man who had never known the time. . . .

Ahmer was speaking to him, and, for a moment that seemed to spill beyond its natural boundaries, he couldn't understand what the diminutive Ket hunter was doing in this place of captivity and carnage where Tarski, Abramowski, Langenfeld, Jurek, and the colonel would shortly blow their invisible whistles and utter their inaudible commands. The NKWD band was late at the gate with a tune of glory.

—The people from the settlement haven't come, shaman, Ahmer was reporting.

He made an effort to respond.

—Where are the camp guards?

—Guards, shaman?

—Oh, for God's sake, Ahmer! The Russians with the guns.

—They are at the river. They will kill all the people from the settlement if no one goes to help. . . . My people can't do anything like that, we must leave at once.

Petulant as an old man, irritated, Dr. Poremba said: Well, leave then, go!

—And what about you, shaman?

—I don't know.

He had become old without warning, felt evil and corrupt, saw himself as something ancient that lived in the pits (the saurian eyes of Anna Dimitrevna searching for her child), and wondered what had happened to that nice old gentleman he had planned to be: a gentleman of the old school who would never have been able to understand that the old school had been swallowed in an earthquake, that the humanist traditions of his ancient Europe had been shot at dawn, that the truths he had lived by had emigrated, never to return.

—Well, are you still here?

But now someone else had come up to him, clothed in quilted patches. He looked into eyes that seemed frozen in their scarlet sockets. The old priest waited like an overdue debt.

—I want to know what you have in mind, the priest said.

—In mind? I don't know.

—You are the leader, you are the commander!

There was a long distant tapping of machine-gun fire, somewhat plaintive in the icy sweep of the afternoon. Tap-tap-tap. Insistent. A penitent was begging at the gate. Tap-tap-tap. Please let me in to join your celebration.

—That's out toward the river, Itzek Fogel said. What the hell is going on out there?

—Well, it's the Jews, said Dr. Poremba.

—What about the Jews?

—They're coming here. From the settlement. That's where the camp guards are, you see. That is our diversion.

—What Jews? Kobza said. What diversion?

—There's something that I forgot to tell that Ukrainian boy, Dr. Poremba said. I can't remember what it was. There's something wrong with me, I am not thinking well. Perhaps I am tired. Perhaps they can break through to us, in which case, as I said, everything can still be all right for everyone. But I don't quite seem to remember what I am doing here.

—God help you, said the priest. What have you done?

—I don't know, Dr. Poremba said.

—Someone had better go down toward the settlement and see if they can help, Kobza said.

—How? Itzek Fogel said.

—How the hell would I know? Kobza said. Give the Russians something else to shoot at, give those poor bastards from the settlement a chance to break through.

—Just stop it, Father Boguslawski said. Stop this awful slaughter.

—It's too late for that, Kobza said.

Pani Mosinska said: We mustn't weaken now. Our main concern must be with ourselves. If you men can take the west gate, the cookhouse, and the towers, we can still succeed! Isn't there one among you who isn't afraid?

—No one can go beyond fear until they're beyond conscience, Dr. Poremba whispered.

—And what about the people from the settlement? Itzek Fogel said.

Dr. Poremba shrugged. He made his way toward a group of barracks that had not yet begun to burn.

His murdered friends were calling out to him. They beckoned and waited. He had to hurry, it was time to join them. When pure courage no longer brings victory, when effort and endurance can't provide that miraculous chemistry which transmutes aspirations into more than a vague shadow of achievement, when faith itself had become only an endless argument, then death by violence must surely be an accolade. The murderer fires the bullet into the flesh we love and reaches us through what we love the most: ourselves. The loving traitor whispers denunciations; Judas kisses Christ. The blow is struck with the kiss, the whisper and the bullet, and it is the same blow. It may even be the ultimate act of love. . . .

The priest followed him, begging for the impossible: the end to the killing. The priest was pleading that he should remember Christ, Golgotha, crucifixions. . . . Whatever the priest wanted to talk about, whatever he was still able to cling to, was no affair of his. His voice was

old, dry, dead, coming from a distance as he asked the only question
that he had.

—Do you know my children?

The priest didn't answer. Dr. Poremba felt grief, not for the priest, or
the children, and not for himself, but merely grief that such things as
destruction of living human beings should happen at all. But such
things happened every day. One could live and then one could do so no
longer.

VIII

. . . In the barrack, the blind old Ukrainian who had been a Hero of
the Revolution, who never stopped talking about his son to anyone
who would listen (the son who was a lieutenant in the Red Air Force,
whose memory was the only thing that kept the old man alive), was
begging someone, anyone, to read him his son's letter. They had all
read the letter in which the lieutenant cursed and renounced his father
as a dog, a traitor, an enemy of the people, a counterrevolutionist, a
kulak saboteur, a wrecker, and a snake fit only to be crushed. No one
would read that letter to the blind old man and he was always begging
someone, anyone, to read it to him.

Father Boguslawski looked out through the broken door at the flames
and shadows. A mute mass struggled to be heard. Emaciated corpses
grasped and grappled, trampled and tore the last rattling breath out of
each other's throats, settling long-forgotten scores.

Poles, Russians, Ukrainians, old Mongols, the last of the Uzbeks, we
are all the same. All mere individuals incapable of sustaining our ties of
affection, duty, loyalty, reverence, and responsibility when overwhelmed
by chaos and destruction. All little people despite the boundless sweep
of our pretensions, denied the pursuit of private peace and ideas by the
crush of public wars and ideologies. We are all innocent and we are all
guilty and our executioners are in each of us. And if that is so, then
each of these dreadful parodies of the divine image is in me, and in me
is the same rage, the same loneliness, and I must struggle to understand
these shared emotions.

Dr. Poremba's face was yellow-gray and he looked unhealthy; he
seemed to find it difficult to draw a full breath. It was less a face than a
skull over which a waxy yellow skin had been stretched unevenly. He
turned his head a fraction of an inch at a time, as if the movement
were an agony, and the face which was no longer capable of expressing
feeling was shuttered and cold. He went on turning his head until he
was looking over his shoulder at the smoke and fire beyond the broken
door. Looking at him, Father Boguslawski realized that the conniving

moonfaced man was seeing nothing, that his eyes were shut, that tears had frozen over them, that he was showing the back of his neck as if inviting someone to draw a pistol and shoot him at leisure.

The suddenly old and emptied man beside him was still alive, Father Boguslawski knew, but he could no longer be considered as one of the living. His children had been the last half of his possibilities. He waited for the sound of a bullet entering his skull; Father Boguslawski knew that it was so. And when the man finally lowered his head into his hands he was sure of it.

He held the girl's hand, locked within himself, attempted to pray. He listened to Catherine's hollow lifeless voice, thought of the waste, the folly, the hopes, the disasters, the moments of brightness, the cruel fate, the undeserved and unforgivable triumph of evil, the destruction of a precious human organism, the ruin of a work of art, the death of a soul. The lifeless voice and the dead hand had erased all meaning from his life and threatened his reason.

—There was a time when I had a sense of my own rightness, Catherine was saying.

It didn't matter what the girl was saying. What mattered was that she was saying something. As long as he could keep her talking her wounds would be draining, the poisons seeping through the broken barrier. And then, perhaps, a healing process could begin.

He was careful to say nothing to her, knowing that there was nothing she wanted to hear.

—Rightness, she said. A sense of being part of a wonderful design. I had a feeling of access to life. As if it would all open up to me in its own time. All I had to do was wait, I was that sure, you see.

He tried to keep absolutely still, as if the slightest movement on his part would suddenly remind her of his presence and dam the healing flow. She must not be startled. He cursed his tremors, tried to still his breathing, prayed: Help me to find the words which I may use later, a phrase that a human being could believe despite the evidence of evil's dreadful presence. There must be something that a priest can say . . .

Catherine's words fell like stones into a well and sank without a trace.

—Why do we all invent such a silly lie for ourselves? Why is it necessary to learn that there is nothing in which to believe? If only priests could be made to tell the truth, if only we'd all stop lying.

He looked at Catherine and began to shudder as though in a fever. He began to pray. Our Father which Art. In Heaven. He became confused. Catherine's child was lying on the floor. Give Us This Day Our Daily Bread. He picked up the child. He heard the screams outside. And Deliver Us. From Evil. The sound of fighting had diminished near the gate but now it flared up in another quarter. And Forgive Us Our Trespasses. Someone began to titter. Someone else began to sing in a clear young voice. How could they be singing? Such an old anthem, such an ancient plea to be repeated through the centuries . . .

He crouched lower, humbler, while symbols and legends leaped into flame above him and beckoning crosses opened their bloodred arms. As We Forgive, he prayed in confusion, Those Who Trespass Against Us. The cracked young voices were singing in the barrack then, while watchtowers toppled.

> *Z dymem pożarow, wznosimy błaganie:*
> *Ojczyznę wolną, Racz nam zwrócić Panie . . .*

In one way or another, one people or another, our prayers are sent to heaven on columns of sacrificial smoke, and the offerings of the pious have become no more subtle than ritual murder, perhaps more meaningful as a philosophic abstraction than in their avowed purpose.

> *. . . In smoke of fires we send Thee the word:*
> *Return our Country's freedom, O Merciful Lord!*

Sooner or later such dreams become forests of gibbets and burning crosses, the fetid breath of the arena, the roar of the beast. They carry their own atavistic wish for self-destruction.

He knelt in prayer but he could not pray, fearful that this time he would not hear the great voice which answered his daily litanies of self-humiliation, waiting (he thought with self-contempt) for an engraved invitation to make his ascent. A cross was waiting but not for him.

Conscious of vanity, doubt, ancient anger, impatience with those who couldn't understand the true geography of God's heavenly kingdom (who looked for it in clouds, in manuals and mortar, in a parish office), and of his own small treasons in the name of his own earthly conception of an approachable God, he had believed in an illumination at his final moment and had gone on, eyes fixed from the beginning on this final signature and seal without which, surely, a life could have no meaning.

He felt no more alive than the hand he was clasping in his old, cold fingers, and thought that not to be ignored by his merciful Master in his final moment would be accomplishment enough. Perhaps only by experiencing some kind of death can we be sure of any kind of life.

—It's all such a stupid and unnecessary lie, Catherine was saying then. So evil, so misleading . . . so destructive.

He clutched her hand as though to will it back to life, and knew that his own touch was a form of treachery; it was a promise that he would never be able to keep.

But, he whispered bleakly above the screams, the howls, the crackle of flames, the stray shots, the long slow crash of falling timbers, the clattering shards of ice melting off the ceiling: couldn't this treachery be seen as grief and as caring? If we had not been taught to interpret the story of Christ's passion would we be able to tell, by their actions alone, whether it was the jealous and treacherous Judas or the violent but cowardly Peter who had truly loved Him? Suddenly, he understood what Dr. Poremba had said to him earlier, and lowered his own head into his hands to hide his distress.

—God only knows why all my certainties have disappeared, Catherine was saying in her terrible flat voice. Tell me, is this all some sort of an experiment? Are we specimens in a laboratory of some kind?

—I don't know, he said, conscious of betrayal. All I know is that we are never more inhuman than when we know, beyond all doubt, that we are right. That is the essence of human cruelty, don't you see? It is a craving for peace with one's own awful conscience in whatever name. What is done by one man is done by us all and each brutal act is a plea for mercy; it is a cry in which to say that we are lonely and afraid or simply bewildered. It is a terrible attempt to signal God, perhaps. We are all lost, in terror of ourselves, fearing the unknown, unable to bear the frightful burdens of all our uncertainties and doubts. We steal, we lie, we murder each other, we betray each other, seeking a final safety, reassurance. But while we think that we can still beg for God's attention we are not without hope! The ancient sacrifices are repeated over and over through the centuries to draw His attention to our unendurable loneliness! Could this possibly help you just a little?

—Help? How? Toward what?

Accidentally, he had turned his face upward, stared into the dilated, broken eyes of Mann-Bielecki who looked down at him, and, for a moment, he thought that the corpse was about to speak. The hanging man had gone beyond death to the other side of the mystery, finally beyond the reach of everything.

—Each act of violence maims the perpetrator far more than his victim, Father Boguslawski said. So that the perpetrator may acquire the visible scars upon his soul that he needs to plead for divine compassion, hoping, like a medieval beggar, that these self-inflicted wounds might provoke pity in some unimaginable source of power and peace. . . .

—What? Catherine said, incredulous, and looked directly into the priest's eyes.

—All I can say is that death is repulsive and that in the midst of death we are all diminished.

She laughed then; at least the terrible thin sound might have passed for laughter.

—But what does that mean?

—I really don't know, the priest said.

—Well, she said. At least you're honest, that could be a start. I'd hate to have you telling me about forgiveness and the love that must exist between enemies if there is to be peace upon Earth. About being fashioned in some greater image. About immortal souls, and all that. About God and mercy and about how the meek shall inherit and about patience, faith, and charity, and about how virtue is always triumphant. Thank God or whatever that none of that will ever be believed by anyone again.

He listened for the great voice in his inner silence; outside, there was still sound enough. He heard nothing. No one spoke to him. His thoughts were settling dreamily into a slow-motion dance of shadows in torment. There was one last short splutter of machine-gune fire, then a huge new cry.

He looked around in that moment of intense awareness at the gaunt wasted faces, noting, as if to list details for an auction catalogue, the scars and the craters, a country's history written in horizontal grooves of privation and pain, in the predatory beaks of starving men, the hard line of cheekbone and unnaturally bright eyes sunk in hollow circles but fixed upon a vision, the white frostbitten lips compressed as sharply as the edges of a cliff, and he saw them all and himself as if for the first time.

Despite ourselves, we are all one people. Neither good nor evil. Not holy, not profane. Because in the infinite mercy of the Man on the Cross, in the absorption of all these helpless human particles into the Universal Spirit, no distinction is made by what these fragments might have done during their brief span of agony on earth. There are no saints, no monsters: neither blame nor virtue. God's will is always done.

Outside, a great hoarse voice shouted a command in another language from antiquity, the broken door was full of fire and light, and as storm lanterns suddenly appeared—and as the gang-bosses, trusties, quota-makers, murderers, thieves, denouncers, masters of life and death, careless executioners, the kings and judges of the underworld, the professional survivors at whatever cost fled into the newly fallen night—the survivors of the camp uprising staggered across their barricades to greet the newcomers. Boots pounded in the snow, and the cries were joyful. An ugly, bearded, barrel-shaped young Jew appeared in the frame of the broken door, a Mosin rifle in one hand, an ax in the other. Soon after, the shouts and the screaming dwindled, then were gone.

PART FIVE

RESURRECTION

A Leader of His People

THAT NIGHT, looting and killing, some shrill dimensions of despair. Kobza came awake coughing. He had been lying for some hours in what had been a barrack, wrapped in a padded dogskin coat taken off a corpse; he had slept, he thought.

The camp was gutted and spilling survivors. He looked around the scorched space, beating his arms to restore feeling to his body, some notion of reality to his disordered and reluctant mind. The people, what was left of them, wandered among the ruins or crouched under temporary and insufficient shelter made (like his own) of debris, burned timbers, fallen roofing, a section of tar paper, even frozen bodies. Kepi was bent over a small fire made of rags and splinters in a kerosene bucket, Pani Mosinska had ignited an unbroken lamp, an Ostyak tried to warm life into a red-glazed arm.

Professor Karolewski was handing out Taran, raw millet by the handful, tins of American bully beef from the Russians' store; his narrow toothless mouth made rubbery sounds.

—*Smacznego, smacznego* . . .

—Is it *likely* to taste good?

—Offhand, madame, I'd say it is a sensation comparable to eating a dead dog.

—Ap-p-*pall*-ing!

Kobza tried breathing through his nose, his throat had constricted about a larynx scraped raw by the abrasive wind. There is a lot to be said for silence, for keeping one's mouth shut instead of shouting in a windstorm, he should have known better.

Awake now, in control of his memory and imagination, he looked about, waiting for someone to give him an order. The cold made thinking difficult. Men dying, frozen stiff as historical artifacts, had assumed the weight, consistency, and role of cement blocks, a definition both concrete and final, to be stacked as walls against the wind and spread in interlocking layers as roofing material. Dr. Poremba's woman keened and whimpered, summoning his attention.

Why to die here in a howling wilderness, in the wind as bitter as a memory, out in the open now, everyone squatting around smoking piles of split timbers, wrapped in burlap, canvas, coats looted off the dead, lice-filled sheepskins, quilted prison jackets? Foul breaths, rancid with fear, escaped in snowy vapor as they struggled toward the river on feet wrapped in sacking.

He was walking along the frozen highway of the river before he was aware that he was in motion.

People were suddenly visible as people; made animate by an unreasonable hope, they were no longer objects. He envied them the comfort of their pathetic optimism, wanted to warn them, then shrugged, turned away, thinking that people hate to be reminded of what waits on the far side of their last illusion.

He looked for Catherine, conscious of his own illusions, found them contemptible, then found her walking beside a sleigh, carrying her child, distinct and unique . . . as was the priest bending and mumbling among the wounded on the sleighs, as was the suddenly radiant face of the granite lady (Pani Mosinska looked a decade younger), as was the Russian madwoman who had lost her child and peered into snowdrifts. All the surviving litterateurs were trying to make themselves invisible or, at least, forgotten: the toothless and apologetic Professor Kukla, Agnieszka Dlapanow, Sobiepan Bogomily, Banda-Cyganowski, Zygfryd Bunt . . . And the recently violent Professor Karolewski, and grinning Wiesio, and mute-dazed Ziuta (whom he had *not* used in the storehouse, on the gunnysacks, which had made *him* unique . . .), Esterka and the Patriarch and little Jankele and the few Jews from the settlement who had made their way through and around the machine-gun fire (Ariz and Shlomo, Brodsky and Lopatsky, and the odd one with the witless smile of the purest silver) and Dr. Poremba with his twisted smile . . . all nodding, their heads wrapped in scarves, moving so swiftly through the powdery snow that they seemed to be floating an inch or two above it.

Since no one seemed to be giving any orders, he began to do so.

—Keep moving, faster.

Later they turned westward as the river turned, sat under a tall glazed bank, hidden from the wind. He feared what he would find on his left foot when the time came to cut away the boot and the rotted footcloths; his toes had frozen together. He imagined the stench of gangrene in the Arctic air. Poremba's Russian madwoman was hiccuping in sorrow, her face was set in an expression of tranquility unusual in the living. Life, death (he concluded) seemed to be ruled by a drunken conjuror. He looked about for Dr. Poremba, unwilling in this last extremity to assume responsibility for others' disaster, yet sure that he must do so. He found him sitting in the snow, gloveless hands clasped before his face, his eyelids seemed frozen. One thick thumbnail, a miniature turtle shell, rattled against another.

—Mmmm. You . . . You . . .

—It's too soon for a halt, Kobza said. We must . . . ah, we got to . . . move, keep moving.

—Why?

Looking down, past the frosted glance of the muttering magician, he thought of the morning as his last, and all fear left him. There was no longer any need to contemplate the future.

—We didn't burn the camp to die in the snow.

—Nevertheless, we'll do so.

—Not if I can help it.

—Ah, a hero, then, Dr. Poremba said.

Kobza would share his tired contempt with no one. The sad stale smell of a defeated life mounted to his imagination; and was that all that could be said, at the end, of personal loss? This staring into nothing, a loss of will to live, a time when a man's only assets are his secrets, no matter how ugly . . .

He asked, holding his throat with both hands gloved in dogskin, thinking that it would be more appropriate to bark, how long they would be resting under the riverbank. The Ostyaks were taking the wounded off the sleighs; the wounded died in the snow in uncomplaining rows.

Petulant as an old man, Dr. Poremba said: Well, what do you expect? There's no room in the sleighs for everyone.

—So some must be killed?

—It's better that some should be saved than that all should fail. What's the matter with you? You're getting awfully particular about killing people, aren't you?

—I always have been, Kobza said.

—You're talking about the idiot boy, eh? Is that what it is? Well, don't blame me, he died in the snow on his own.

—I don't know anything about any idiots.

—You're lucky. I do.

—At least have your Ostyaks pitch their tents.

—You have them do it and, oh, by the way, they aren't anybody's Ostyaks, least of all mine. Perhaps they'll be yours? Who are you, anyway? Did the Abbot send you? I think that shortly, shortly, very soon I'll have a message for him.

—I don't know about any Abbots. As for who I am . . .

—Kobza, isn't it? For a minute I thought you were someone else, from another lifetime, an apparition so to speak. Kobza, is it, now?

—Kobza. Sir (he added, opting for humility; it had served him in the past and might do so again).

—That's what you call yourself now, is it? A good name, two syllables, perfect for a leader, easy to chant in chorus. Sta-*lin!* Le-*nin!* Kob-*za!* It's a lot easier to remember than some of our antique, lost polysyllabic gentlemen and ladies . . . Kobza, you said?

—Kobza, prr-prrr.

—Well, let it be Kobza, if that's what you want. You'll do for a symbol. People are perishable but symbols are immortal, they can be followed even when they're dead. That other name that you used to have, the one I can't remember, wouldn't have done at all.

Looking about, he asked: What makes you think I had a different name?

—I don't think, Dr. Poremba said. There will be no more thinking.

—What's all this? Kobza said. Have you given up?

—No, on the contrary, I know exactly what I have to do, but the remainder of my journey has nothing to do with yours. My transformation, you see, is just about complete. An ancient debt is waiting to be paid, there must be sacrifice, an offering, it's part of the ritual. It is a most exciting moment, I assure you.

—It sounds as if you're planning to stay here.

—Does it really? How extraordinary. But then, you see, I am badly wounded.

—Where? I don't see anything.

—Ah, that's the question, isn't it. Where. A beast becomes a beast only after it has learned how to act like beasts. Still, once you have relegated all morality to its proper place you can accept responsibility for everything you've done. You and I, Kobza, will be graves together soon enough and the dogs shall piss on us both, but if we have always done what had to be done we shall be remembered.

—I'll see about the tents, Kobza said.

On his way toward the Ostyaks' cooking fires, he passed the priest kneeling in the snow. The priest was praying for the wounded who had not yet died. He skirted huddled groups which looked less like people than flocks of carrion birds hunched about their meals. He looked at Catherine and his chest constricted and, suddenly, he felt that he would shortly be unable to breathe at all. Responsibility for the lives of others had been the last of his wants. He doubted his ability to command beyond the moment when the people refused to be commanded, the point at which commanders sometimes became leaders, and didn't trust them to find their own way. Without a leader, they would all die in the wilderness; she along with the rest. He knew that one can command others only if they, in all their complex varieties of cravings and hatreds, had something to fear. What did these scorched and harrowed beings still have to fear, having lived through every variety of fear? Nothing could threaten them now, death least of all. Death had ceased to be fearful to us all, he thought; it had been such an ordinary event in our lives, as unremarkable as the pulse and heartbeat . . . Solitude and his responsibility only for himself had never been so appealing or so impossible.

He moved toward Catherine, then changed his mind, turned away. Life, in its proper sense, had ended for him long before he had found refuge in the cellars, and now he saw himself as a dead man on leave. That is what made the difference, that is what made it possible for him to make his decision now; only a dead man could dream of a new life, resurrection was not available to the living.

Very well, he thought. First we'll go to the Yenisei. We'll avoid Karaul. We shall go up the Yenisei to the Angara, these are our natural highways at this time of year, and our food supply. We should be at the confluence of these rivers in a month or two. They say it's a fruitful country there, with fewer than a dozen inhabitants for every hundred square kilometers; it's like an empty house with a full-stocked larder . . . More than enough to rebuild ruined bodies . . . We could go west-southwest then, toward Kazakhstan, but there'll be too much going on at the southern edge of the Ural Mountains. Railheads mean telegraphs and that's the last thing we'd want to trip over . . . So, we'll follow the Angara eastward, then turn sharply south to where the Ilia and the Oka join it in a lake, then we'll head east again to the northern tip of Lake Baikal, then move south into the fertile and forested backlands of the Ust-Barguzin, well to the north of the Trans-Siberian Railway, where we should be safe. The Khanty will teach us about skeins and weirs, the Ket will show us how to use a bow. The people, no longer skeletal, will develop their own natural leaders, that's also something that Darwin made clear . . .

Then he was among them, the people, his people although they didn't know it, by virtue of his natural succession. Father Boguslawski was bending over the wounded, Janek Stypenko had been lifted off a sleigh, Pani Mosinska made youthful, optimistic sounds, and the Jews were silent. Professor Kukla (also silent) was trying to make himself too insignificant to notice (he who had been so significant in the camp); Professor Karolewski, wrapped in what Kobza recognized as

Mann-Bielecki's old scarf, last worn by Surma, was grinning like an idiot; Catherine's child made a human sound.

—Hey, Kobza, Kobza, Kepi said. We're going to have a celebration!
—What celebration, for Chrissake?
—Don't we have a reason to celebrate? I'll say we have a reason!
—Prr-prrr, Kobza said.
Celebration?

Here in the wilderness, on this endless white stage in the pale Arctic light, among the conical black birch-bark tents of the little brown men, with all the stars gone. They had been promised a return to life and they insisted on it, all these wasted skeletons belted with old rope, held together by their frozen rags; they were suddenly insisting that all the promises be kept. They were too new to the idea of freedom, the possibility of survival, no matter how remote. Each of their sudden hopes had to be immediately confirmed, otherwise the wilderness would overpower them, the interminable distances would kill them as surely as bullets, the madness of their enterprise would become apparent.

—Well . . . for Chrissake . . . why not?

Professor Karolewski wanted to make a speech. He said that what he had in mind would be very funny: a parody of the speech they had been given at the camp so often (a speech which would have been given by Professor Kukla, who would now be careful to say absolutely nothing), about the wisdom of accepting Soviet passports, the need to obey the orders of history, fulfill historical imperatives and the Destiny of Man.

Agnieszka Dlapanow would recite the *Reduta Ordona* (*Nam strzelać nie kazano!*), not too apt under the circumstances, the story of another lost redoubt, a war poem written by a patriotic poet who had been careful to avoid all the patriotic wars, who had never heard a bullet whistling over his head, but solemn, soaring, patriotic, redolent of graduation ceremonies, schoolboy recitations . . . Itzek Fogel would play the violin.

—All right, then, Kobza said. We'll do it at the next halt.
—All right, then, Kepi said. Are you going to do something?
—I know some stories, Kobza said. Folk tales, and like that. I could tell a story.
—And the Ostyaks are going to play their flutes. Hey, Kobza, now's your chance to dance with the little lady, ha ha ha.
—Prr-prrr, said Kobza.
—I'll be good and damned, Kepi said. The old fart's blushing.
—Ha ha, Itzek said.
—Blushing hell, Kobza said. It's the goddam wind. I'm just natu-

rally concerned, you might say, about the little lady. She lived in my building back in Lwów.

—Sure, Kepi said. And her old lady had you to tea and cakes every Friday afternoon, a friend of the family, you were.

—Well, prr-prrr, no. I just fired the furnace.

—And now you'd like to fire her little furnace, eh? Kepi said.

—Stop it, keep quiet now, said Pani Mosinska.

—It never fails, Kepi said. I must've seen it a hundred times. An old fart lives alone all his life and he don't know how good he's got it, just got hisself to look after, and you'd think after all them years he'd know to leave well enough alone. But all of a sudden like he gets the itch, the old capon wants to be a rooster, and in no time at all you've got the biggest damn fool you've ever seen. Shit, Kobza, get your brains up from between your legs.

—You've had your say, Kobza said.

—Damn right.

—So one more word about the little lady and I'll kick your ass right out through your ear.

—Hey now, look, Kepi said.

—No, you look and listen. I didn't always sweep stairs and shovel the sidewalks. You want to keep walking to where I'm going to take you, you'll keep your mouth shut about the little lady. In fact, goddammit, from now on you'll keep your mouth shut about everything unless I tell you to open it. That goes for all of you. It's getting so that one word from you is one word too many.

—Hey, Kobza, hey . . .

—Ha ha ha, Itzek Fogel said.

And Kepi shouted into the scarred, furrowed parchment face that mocked all grief and fear: What are you laughing at, you flea-bitten Yid? You think I'm scared of old fartface here?

And Kobza swung a scarred, corroded fist (remembering, remembering) and heard a dull, wet, thudding blow like the sound that a paving stone might make when hurled against a mud wall, or a small head, a woman's head (a shapely but such a fragile and bewildering container for a man's vision of himself) might make when struck in hopelessness and terror with the flat side of an ax, and Kepi was on his face in the snow and Itzek was laughing.

—Jesus Christ, what was that? Kepi said, sitting up and clutching his head.

—That was one word too many.

—Jesus Holy Christ.

Then he was shouting, ordering the march to begin.

Catherine

LIGHTS, WINDOWS. The pale nocturnal glow of the settlement had fallen behind. The sky was red above the camp below the horizon. Still seeing flames, hearing screams and shots, the very recent past, she felt nothing. She had come to the edge of her possibilities, had looked over the side, and now moved away. But to herself she seemed motionless, held by the past as though it were a vise forged out of ice; it was some kind of shoal, perhaps, and she a wreck aground on memory.

The past can do nothing for us except to release us, she knew beyond argument. But it can only do that if there is a future. And *that*, she thought, was suddenly a concept as vast and incomprehensible as the sky. The stars, for all their pinpoint glitter, were like a cluster of frozen tears, and the coarse bloom of fire gradually turned into a thin pulsing line shining out of a distance beyond reckoning, and the inky-blue miles of snow without end were like the polished surface of a marble tomb, and the harsh Arctic night lifted above her like a vast hand opening in blessing or a curse. Then all man-made light disappeared.

She was adrift on an unknown wind among strange animals and even stranger people. Her mind was tightly furled, putting out no shoots. The real and the fantastic had become one; each was tangible but oddly just beyond her reach. The stars were not stars; they were chips of ice, distant and cold. The flames were now a memory of something that she might have merely imagined while ill and in fever. The reindeer had become mythical and each of the other bowed and trudging shadows, like herself, had become opaque and insubstantial.

. . . Plodding, falling. Getting up unaided. It was too soon for people to remember that they might help each other. The conscious processes of thought and perception slowed down, then drifted like a bird's feather to the ground. She heard her own rasping breath coming from behind her, the slow hiss of sleigh runners, the patient creaking thud of boots . . . thought of a whisper thrown across the ruins of a meal . . . a mock Last Supper . . . a promise, then a birth. Fell, got to her feet, leaned on Janek's sleigh, went on.

. . . Thought of rest, drifted.

Opened to a thought, tried to accept an impossible idea. Life had become desirable again in whatever form it might be made to manifest itself; it was no longer a vague theory that had to be proved.

Memory returned. She could look up beyond the cries nailed to the sky, saw faces, recognized King Whore crucified on barbed wire and burning to death, the Unknown Criminal patiently trampled into a muddy flat obscenity, Mann-Bielecki turning on his rope . . .

Dr. Poremba's face was suddenly askew; it was lopsided, flowing as though a mask had melted, or a sculptor's clay had slipped downward before it could harden. She had the swift urge to reach out and straighten his inverted smile . . . Looked into the dark intense luminosity of Esterka's anger. Shook with quick envy, wondering if she herself, driven to her limits, was to be wholly beyond feeling from now on.

Esterka snapped commands, ordering the lives of her family. The old grandfather was present only as a body, abandoned by whatever spirit had made him unique; the little boy was cursing like a man. Esterka's eyes, like dueling pistols, were aimed at Catherine.

She focused her own eyes on that difficult sheen, then the glances locked. They carried all the possibilities from a passionate friendship to a mortal hatred; the choice seemed her own. Esterka had changed beyond recognition and Catherine felt the sudden searing heat of the other's commitment to a new identity; the pale dark self-effacing quiet girl had become transformed, and Catherine thought of the lava heart deep inside the earth erupting in fire, and felt her own inner tremor begin at the knees. The Jewish girl seemed to project a circle of shadow which no one could enter; she was staring outward from a dream where a burning legend had become an obsession. Now her body seemed to be gaping open like a wound, her face resembled an abrasion.

. . . Thought unexpectedly of Abel.

She could no longer feel his interior life.

She had slept through a year of nights hoping to wake to see him in the morning, to hear mocking laughter which would tell her (gently) that her abandoned body had survived its period of uselessness, that life is never a matter of chance. But he was gone, vanished, part of her inner night but no part of her morning. She would have known if he were still alive; he was dead, she knew. But if he were to appear suddenly in this mute swaying crowd, among the hurrying animals and sleighs under the translucent lid of the Arctic day, she would be able to laugh into his face.

Esterka seemed to understand, turned her face away. Father Boguslawski looked at her with troubled eyes. He sighed. His hand rose, hesitated, tapped his chest three times, scrawled a shaky cross on the wind. The priest closed his eyes.

Janek Stypenko, black with his own frozen blood, seemed to have made his choice between consciousness and conscience; he slept, battling nightmares, on the sleigh beside which she was walking, his head sloped on the edge of a dead Jew's shoulder. So she would fall asleep . . . *had hoped* to fall asleep in future fact as in her dead and discredited wishes . . . with her head uneasily angled on Abel's shoulder. Or his hard chest. None of that mattered any longer.

All the unnatural light was gone then: the light of windows and the memory of fire. The forms of animals and men were becoming clear, each edged with a cold white glow: the dark new day reflected by frost and by ice. The long Arctic night was ending only in her mind. The blue-gray monotony of the winter plain would not be swept clean by daylight for several months. She thought that soon it would be time to stop.

A small heart was beating close under her breast, the child in her arms stirred infinitesimally; she thought of a need for baptism, shrugged it off . . . Thought of a boutonniere of yellow chicken feathers, pewter eyes, and a corpse turning round and round like an upturned lighthouse . . . And food for the child. Life had become a very small word.

She heard some other words, looked down, saw that Janek Stypenko was trying to speak, bent her head to hear him; for all she knew these were his dying words. She wondered what her father's dying words had been; he would have said something. Mother had probably said nothing at all. Cousin Wlada had probably whispered *Incroyable!* Had Abel declaimed? What had Jurek said? Mann-Bielecki's last clear word had been *Please*.

—What did you say?

The Ukrainian choked.

—It's the wind, she said, the hum of the column. You'll have to speak louder.

—A fool will believe anyone, Janek said.

—You have to stop talking.

—And dying?

—You won't die.

—Best thing to do, he said.

—Stupid nonsense.

He was choking, laughing.

—You know what you sound like?

—What? she said, uncurious.

—That old lady there.

—Who? Pani Mosinska? What nonsense.

—Stupid nonsense, he said, mimicking. You're even starting to look like her. Soon there won't be a way to tell one of you people from another.

—If you'll just keep quiet, she said. Rest. Save your strength . . . you'll be all right, you'll see.

—Not in this world, he said. And there's not another.

He had risen to his elbows to make himself heard, a fresh flow of blood erupting on his beard, and now dropped back to the skins and furs and the flat chest of the dead man on which he was lying, staring upward, no longer haunted by his ghosts or dazzled by his own disappearing stars, and laughed and laughed while icy red tears were streaming down his frozen white face.

. . . Four in the morning, give or take an hour: less than twelve hours since the killing time. Call it an Uprising. Must dignify it with a word, another lie. One set of straw dogs had merely been butchering another; she didn't think that a single keeper had been scratched. The guards had disappeared at the first sign of trouble. It had been just prisoners murdering prisoners. Settling private scores in the name of a Great Idea. Everyone can always find some sort of oppressor to prove himself a victim so that they themselves, in turn, could become oppressors and victimize others. Well, why not? A killing time needs victims who expect no mercy, having no idea what it means. The history books had made it all abundantly clear. Tumbrels, drums, knitting needles were merely confused metaphor.

(In her mind's ear she could still hear Professor Kukla denouncing Mann-Bielecki as traitor and betrayer, and Banda-Cyganowski had held one thrashing leg, and Zygfryd Bunt had sat on the other, and Kepi had sawed on the yellow throat with a piece of glass, and Agnieszka Dlapanow had been trying to vomit. Impossible to do it on an empty stomach. Pani Mosinska, wrapped in her patriotic indignation, had paid no attention. Dr. Poremba was issuing commands which no one could hear. She, Catherine, had been saying something to somebody. She didn't remember what she said or to whom she said it. Pity. Or perhaps not. It couldn't have been anything heroic. Not for a moment did she think that what she remembered would ever become part of the National Epic of Great Words.)

Meanwhile there was to be a halt in the march and even more confusion. It would take historians to end the confusion. There had to be some way for everyone to be able to agree about what had really happened, and so the Great Uprising of the history books wouldn't really happen until Banda-Cyganowski wrote a book about it. And Professor

Kukla would annotate it with the proper footnotes. And the survivors
of the Great Uprising would be supplied with scholarly facts under
which to hide from what they might have done in a killing time.
Zygfryd Bunt would write an epic introduction about man's imperishable spirit, the struggle for liberty and justice. Human Dignity. Of
course. And about how only a selfless struggle for human dignity can restore a people to their destiny and give them a more coherent image of
themselves . . . The Great Words might even construct a new Great
Idea . . . Truth didn't matter much if the lie had literary merit.

And in the meantime, people had stopped walking.

She could tell at a glance who had been in the camp and who had
come from the settlement at Krasnaya Gorka. The camp people stood
motionless as statues; they wouldn't dare to step out of a column for
months, perhaps years. Perhaps mentally they'd never again be able to
break ranks and strike out on their own. The people from the settlement straggled all over the landscape. Neither group was curious about
the other. Nobody seemed to understand where they were or how they
had got there, or whether this arrival was the start of something or
merely the end of something else. They had been in one place, now
they were in another, tomorrow they would start for somewhere else
. . . If she were to tell them that their march was endless, that distance
could no longer be measured in miles, that the wilderness that they
would have to cross lay in each of them, and that their time was more
than history, they'd think her insane.

White empty miles were behind them, others were endlessly ahead.
The small brown Ostyaks were making camp. She thought it too soon.

Then she remembered that no one was likely to pursue them. No one
had ever escaped from an Arctic camp and lived to talk about it, and if
they ever did, to whom could they talk? The NKVD would know that
better than anyone; they could depend upon the wilderness to silence
an inconvenient witness. And as for getting out of Russia and talking
about it . . . well . . . people had a better chance of reaching the
moon.

She wondered if the survivors in the camp were already forming at
the gate to march to the pits. Nothing could interfere with the day's
work quota. Two or three dozen of the weakest, least able to work,
would be chosen at random for the firing squad so that rebellion could
be punished. Then there'd be a quick settling of accounts with the two
or three hundred Jews and Russians who had refused to leave Krasnaya
Gorka, fearing the unknown more than what they knew would happen
to them if they stayed behind. They would replace the dead, the missing, and the fugitives at the camp. The camp would be rebuilt in spring
and, in the meantime, it didn't matter if everyone froze. In spring, after

the ice had broken on the lower Ob and the barges could sail around the peninsula again, the camp and the settlement would be abundantly refilled, and no one would ever know that anything out of the ordinary had *ever* happened there. By spring the old camp would have been empty anyway; she and all the others would have been dead.

Impossibly, life had become possible again.

She was suddenly sure that in time she would arrive somewhere and be someone else. And that this journey, march . . . whatever anybody called it . . . would have nothing to do with miles and years. She and all the others who were now spilling from the halted column had destroyed the column. They were no longer numb mute particles of matter but people brought to life. She wanted to laugh, thinking: Resurrection! Imagine: we are people, what a strange and amazing idea. And she was to be one of them: distinct and unique, moving, talking, arguing, crowding about the Ostyaks' dung-cake cooking fires . . . The endless self-renewing work column had been replaced by people and in that lay all the clues to her possibilities.

The sound she made then, surreptitious as a thief, startled her. She listened to it long after it was gone, then identified it.

. . . Would you believe that I can laugh? In time, she knew, it would sound like laughter. Kobza had heard her, paused.

—You all right, little lady?

She nodded; it was such an astonishing idea that anyone could be free, or think of life as something that could happen the day after tomorrow.

—That's good, Kobza said. And the little fellow? He looks all right. Hungry, though, I'll bet. Prrr-prrr. Well, that's all right too. We'll eat soon. These little brown bastards got more food than I seen in a year. There's going to be a bit of trouble with it though.

She said: Trouble?

. . . Thought: There is nothing astonishing about that idea.

—It's meat, Kobza said.

Kepi said: Jeee-zus!

Itzek Fogel laughed.

—Dried smoked meat, Kobza said. Hard as iron. And I don't think there's a dozen teeth left between the lot of us.

—Shit, Kepi said. Here we've been living on cold air all this time and now there's meat and nobody can eat it.

—Ha ha ha, Itzek Fogel said.

—Goddammit, Itzek, what d'you always find to laugh about?

—Me. You. Everybody. Besides, I have teeth.

—You? Shit. You haven't had a tooth in your head for a year.

—Ha ha, Itzek said.

He took a fractured set of dentures from his pocket, clicked them shut and open, laughed, grimaced, turned, walked away.

—What a world, Kepi said. Dogs live in houses and the Yids have teeth.

Catherine choked, made a sound.

—Hey, little lady! Kobza said. You can laugh. You'll be all right!

—Certainly, said Catherine.

Time, the manipulator of Historical Moments, was rushing toward her with great strides, carrying a future, and she was on her way to meet it, as she had hurried once before, in another context, on All Souls' Day, defiant and eager and anxious to effect a transformation, fearful but determined.

Something had started very suddenly, an idea had arrived without an announcement, and it would have to run its course. Things that start suddenly don't stop suddenly, her father had said, and people who make things happen can't stop them from happening; once started, the mechanism of the future can't be stopped. No command in any language can stop an idea; it can slow momentum or divert a course, but the idea leaves a shadow that people will follow after the idea itself, its author, or for that matter the freedom to have an idea, have wholly disappeared.

. . . And they, these odd creatures around her who were suddenly people in contact with themselves, whom she could see stark in the glare of their wisdom and folly, compassion and hatred, brutality and beauty—the shabby remnants of their towering past—were free of the past. Dear God, she thought, how simple it could be. If only people didn't complicate things so.

Some of them tried to laugh. They staggered about in skeletal imitation of well-fed peasant dances. She couldn't have told them anything if she wanted to. They were eating, moving, cursing, grinning, boasting, lying, arguing, and alive. The certainty of death was no longer there.

The Magician

HE HADN'T THOUGHT THAT HE'D BE ABLE TO SLEEP despite the *kumis* the young woman brought him; he remembered having struggled against thick oblivion. But he was suddenly awake, aware of the cold, and saw that the small brown woman had fallen asleep and that the fire had gone out. He reached the embers of the charcoaled dung chips and managed to fan them, once more, into flame, just in time to warm his hands before they were frozen.

He heard a howl of laughter, shouting, the music of flutes; it was the wind, of course, the cold Russian wind, it could not be music. The band had played the *Varsovienne* as they were marching out . . . *And had they died well or badly in the Katyn Forest?* How they died would have mattered to them. They were alive to all but touch, immortal, eternal, and he had become an ill-tempered crochety old man who fed on the pap of his disappointments. In them, yesterday and today and tomorrow had become forever. The antiqued young reptilian eyes of his son and daughter mocked him with their terrible indifference; the youthful eyes of his old friends closed with final compassion in the Katyn Forest.

What had he to do to be saved, was there anything that could be done so late in his time. Eyes fixed on mountaintops, his head in the clouds, he had climbed into his abyss one step at a time, until he learned that he, too, was an agent of destruction. Yet surely, surely, he who strives upward, although headed downward, must also be saved. A dog howled and howled; the wounded died one by one in the wilderness. The day, if it was day, was full of shouts, hootings, footfalls, creak of leather tackle, bleating grunts of reindeer, the hiss of moving sleighs. And they were in the tent, creating the shadows: Tarski, Abramowski, Jurek, and the colonel . . . And where was Langenfeld? Why had he not come to visit and to comfort a sick friend? People like Langenfeld

must be found and saved. There are only so many decent men allotted
to each generation, and we who are not decent, who live through deceit,
must turn our lies into truth by saving the decent.

Alicja's death, she who had starved herself to feed his unspeakable
children, was just such an act of violence and love rendered in reverse,
he was sure, and saw in it a hope of his salvation. Her blow may have
been a way of saying that not even love was so alive as she had been
alive; that Christ himself was not so present except as he lived in her
. . . Or perhaps she was trying to say that being a wife and mother was
a torment to herself as a woman, lethal to the man. There is no way of
summing up the variety of things that her act meant to tell me . . .
this act of violence rendered with the heart rather than a bullet, thus
being loving. We have forgotten how to listen to our women, gentlemen, he shouted silently to the waiting shadows. We no longer hear
them. They must signal to us in the only language we seem to understand.

He was immediately enraged and shouted for Ahmer, the Ket hadn't
woken him before all the others. The small brown woman woke,
squealed, fled into the day. His children lay still. He had been careful
not to look at them, thinking that if he caught a reflection of himself in
their destroyed eyes it would drive him mad, but now his eyes had
dimmed, it was dark and getting swiftly darker, and he called for
torches.

—How can I save you fools if I can't see what I'm doing?

—The best things happen in the dark, Wiesio said, and sniggered.

—What? What? What did you say?

—I can see what I have to . . . Father. What's the matter, afraid of
the dark?

—Get out, you animal! cried Dr. Poremba, but the boy chuckled,
spat, rolled a cigarette, and turned to his sister. They were whispering.
They snorted with laughter. A sudden roar of wild, delighted laughter
came from the outside.

Something had happened, he could see a crooked shadow, then knew
it for his own. He was aware of time as a mordant weight pressing on
his shoulders, and sensed a terrible new urgency as if the merging corridors of his personal history had suddenly become too narrow for him.

The children (he would have to stop thinking of them as children,
they had ceased to be children when they became subhuman, when
they ceased to indulge in innocence, when the rot of their corruption
had consumed their souls) snorted, hissed, giggled, whispered, nudged
each other, sat in knowing silence, looked at him with a mild disinterested derision, some sort of tolerant contempt. He was rummaging
among his bark-strip maps and notes (the journal of his journeys), una-

ware that he was doing anything at all, then looked up, tried to focus his disobedient eyes on their shadowy indifference.

—When do we eat? Wiesio said. You got any food here? Father?

(Then laughed, as if the title of Father were a crude and cruel gibe. Ziuta's grating giggles served as his applause.)

Dr. Poremba shook his head, at a loss for words, trying to find a language in which he could address himself to these dangerous and primitive beings who had been his children, who emanated an aura of primeval menace, hatred, and suspicion. What could he say to them, how was he to say it?

—Listen, he said. There has to be some way for us to understand each other.

—Why? Wiesio said.

—If there is nothing else between us, if there is nothing of mutual worth, a common ground on which we might meet, then surely, surely, your mother's death can give us grief to share. Grief is a terrible thing to share, I admit, when there is nothing else, but do you really want your mother to have died for nothing?

—What is this? his son said, spat into the fire. A lecture? A fucking sermon? Send for the food. Or don't people obey you any more?

Lately, in fact, they hadn't. Kobza was commanding, and he, the false shaman of the Ostyaks (the *former* false shaman!), was a pensioner living off his merits, carried in sleighs and looked after in a birchbark tent until such time as Ahmer, or his elders, decided that they need not carry him any longer. Even so, he went through his shamanistic paces; he would try again.

—She died for you, he said.

—That's the story, is it? Well, nobody ever gave me enough to eat, I got it for myself. Ziuta's ass is worth a lot more than you think. Hey, listen, would you like a piece? It's all right with Ziuta. That fatherdaughter shit is nothing, anyway. Nobody pays attention to that stuff any more. Well, what about it, want some?

He shrank in horror, he felt himself shrinking, heard his daughter's simpering giggle, his son's contemptuous guffaw, craved instant death, prayed for their annihilation, for lightning and fire, for God's clean wrath, for the end of the world. He could not come to any terms with a life which had borne such fruit.

Still he would try. —Have you no feeling for your mother? he whispered. (He did not dare to ask: for *me*?)

Wiesio shrugged, Ziuta looked at him expectantly.

—Everybody does what they have to. She did what she wanted. Either you eat or you get eaten and that's all that happens. Well, old

man, what about it? You getting a piece or not? Ziuta's ready to go, hot
as a baked potato, can't wait for you forever.

—Oh, get out, he whispered.

—Suits me, Wiesio said. There's a lot of good business outside.

He wanted to pray for mercy, for forgiveness, for death, for an end to
existence, for peace, for instant lack of being, felt the ice slicing
through his wet cheeks, cutting past his beard. But where to send such
prayers, who would hear them? Powdery snow blew in through the tent
flap, then he was alone.

. . . Peace. That's all I ever wanted. An absence of strife. Peace of
mind, absence of distracting images. All conflicts resolved, the contradictions of my life reconciled, and the universe itself in order, unobtrusive. No alarums, trumpets; all drums discreetly muffled. Perhaps I
wanted to live in a void. Who can tell if I can't? And I can't. I have
never been able to explain it. Certainly I would never understand such
an explanation. I think of a woman walking in darkness with her arms
outstretched. Why? What does that have to do with the peacefulness I
am trying to talk about? Nothing. I don't know why I thought of it.
Perhaps because the woman is in darkness, seeking. Seeking to avoid,
not to embrace, accidental shapes. To shrink into a self-contained impervious grain, kernel or morsel, is my aspiration. To cast no shadow.
To draw beyond the range of the slingshot. To purr like a cat. To be
minuscule and beyond observation. To be unaffected, undisturbed in a
remote dream, suspended between heaven and earth, thoughtless and at
peace. Not to be troubled. Not to be stirred into ungentle acts of
rebuke, discipline, correction, regulation, decision, assignment, and
proscription. Not to impose my will and to be out of reach of every
other will. My inner environment unpolluted, secret; and I the only inhabitant of a terra incognita: the kernel globe of my own thoughtless
mind at peace. Kernel or morsel, I have said. A revealing slip. Perhaps a
longing to be eaten and digested, the fulfillment of an atavistic prophecy, the national longing for the cosmic gulp? Whatever it might be, it
is our truth, the final distillation of all our blundering footsteps in the
dark. It is our essence. Is it fragrant? Does it stink? And who wants to
know? To withdraw into this inviolate little temple of the mind is to
dream of paradise: is it not? To be what we seem to be is the object of
all culture. (Oh, my primitive professors!) To be what we are is the object of civilization. To exceed our possibilities is to prove the unlimited
. . . ah . . . possibilities of Man . . . Ah, but that's exactly the kind of
thought that I have always wanted to avoid . . . No easy labels for people, if you please; no slogans and no definitions, because, in the meantime, one did have to exist in some fashion, one did have to justify
one's own justifications . . . The strange woman, perhaps a saint (per-

haps a symbol of a prophecy, a ghost risen from the rubble of racial memory), has long ascended from my shadows in a spiral of snow. She has fallen skyward on a column of ice. Doors have been slammed upon her, each of their ornamental nails is a sun in nova and I . . . and I . . . lost, flaming, burning out, descending into the void, finally consumed. Beyond hope, beyond dreams, beyond the range of the historical cannoneers, out of reach, out of time, out of mind and context: magically removed from the worlds of chaos and illusion and placed, as gently as a petal landing upon water, in the absolute No.

He got up in the gathering darkness, which, he knew, was his own and not connected with the time of day, geography, and the seasons, wrapped himself in furs, went outside. The cold seemed warm to him, the wind had become a prop that he might lean against. He found the priest moving among the wounded, scrawling the sign of the cross in the vapor of their breaths, closing the eyes of those laid out in the snow. He waited for the priest's protest, an argument, an appeal, and the inevitable denunciation, but none came. No plea for mercy came from the dying wounded. He looked for Anna Dimitrevna, failed to find her, came across Ahmer and told him to bring the mad Russian woman to his tent in the event that a tent were left for him when the march resumed. He watched the preparations, the hitching of the reindeer, the packing of fur robes. He caught Kobza's eye but Kobza turned away, making his absurd sound, and moved swiftly out of sight among the milling people. He saw a group of Jews huddled around a row of frozen corpses, recognized the dead face of the Patriarch Rashevsky. He saw the dead and emptied body of Janek Stypenko, looked into the living, still mask of Esterka's anger, felt (or thought he felt) the heat of her hatred laid upon his forehead like a brand. It would endure beyond them both, he knew. In Jankele's pinched face he read a promise of enduring vengeance. Someone called out to him but he turned, as slowly as if he were performing a complicated turn on a tightrope above a sea of faces which were hungrily watching for his fall, went back to his tent.

The tent was empty, the furs had been taken away, but the fire still burned anemically under the birch-bark pot and a flask of *kumis* had been tossed in. He gathered the scattered bark-strip evidence of his travels, his journal of hope and determination, the record of his last illusion about life and himself, and fed it, piece by piece, to the fire.

Then the priest was there. —Yours is a heavy burden at the moment, perhaps I can share it.

—Are you also anxious to share the responsibility?

—If that's what you need, said the old priest, and Dr. Poremba swore softly, shook his head, said: I need a miracle.

—A prayer to St. Dymphna had been known to help.

—Is she any good for frostbite of the soul? Which saint runs the heavenly travel office, where do these people apply for compasses and maps? Who arranges for the daily manna? And who the devil is this Dymphna anyway? I've never heard of her.

—She is the patroness of those in emotional distress.

—Obviously she's professionally unqualified. There are a hundred and forty people here who have gone far beyond the laws of probability. There's no use telling any of them that they are indestructible, imperishable, and irresistible because they are unique, or that willpower and determination will overcome the normal shortages in human equipment. Tell them to grow a camel's hump to carry the water, sprout some wings and fins . . . Hope is no substitute for a highway system! We are only what we ourselves can manage to create, and it's at such times as this that we can see what a poor job we are able to do. Faith is all very well on a Sunday morning.

—Determination can be a sort of faith, said Father Boguslawski.

—Spare me your contemptuous jokes, said Dr. Poremba. Man is badly designed to cope with everything he insists on doing to himself with or without determination. What is possible is rigidly defined.

—God didn't set our limitations, Father Boguslawski said.

—The devil he didn't! He may not be the author of our lives but He's the director. How are *we* supposed to cope with the impossible?

—See it as growth into something greater than ourselves, a challenge to our human possibilities.

—And a mind closed to the cruel realities of the moment?

—A mind turned inward as the heart reaches outward. Acceptance of the unbelievable. And a grand design. You must have had some plan when you began this action.

—Plans die when reality takes over. No plans can be lived.

—Yet the people trusted you, they were following you.

—Trust? That word is meaningless. Only people incapable of thinking for themselves or running their own lives feel the need to follow anybody else. Trust is a word for children . . . and I am obviously not talking about mine.

—You can trust God's mercy, the priest said.

—In which world, may I ask? said Dr. Poremba.

—It all depends on how we face ourselves, our fear, our disappointments, wanting and desire, our impatience with human imperfection, our bitterness, our anxiety to lie down in the snow, surrender and die.

—I told you I needed a miracle, Dr. Poremba said.

—God will grant it if you ask Him for it.

—One has to ask? Am I to make a general confession? I've nothing to confess. I've never injured anyone, cheated anyone, betrayed anyone, used anyone for my own ends, killed or consented to the killing of anyone, led anyone into a deathtrap, schemed, plotted or connived, judged or condemned anyone, coveted my neighbor's ass or lied to a priest. I think I've qualified for canonization.

The priest smiled, nodded, said: What counts is that you believe in God.

—How could I believe in the Devil otherwise?

The priest smiled, bowed his head over folded hands, said: I suppose that you aren't speaking metaphorically.

—That, Father, is an insult, said Dr. Poremba. I'm a respectable literary editor, you won't find a metaphor anywhere about me. The most incriminating piece of evidence you might find is ten percent of a hyperbole.

After a long pause, Father Boguslawski said: Before the war I lived in a small village near Lwów. I had two friends there and, along with them, I had a certain dream. One of them was a very fierce old man, called Jakob Mendeltort. He was ninety-four years old when he died. He always talked about me as *that youngster*, although I was sixty-one at that time. He used to say that he had been a father three times before I was born.

—The name rings a most alarming bell, said Dr. Poremba.

—You knew Jakob's son?

—One of them, yes. Young Abel's father. He's dead.

—You never met Avrum?

—Never had the pleasure. Hope never to have it, particularly if the survivors of Krasnaya Gorka ever get to see him.

—No one will blame you for what happened there.

—And elsewhere?

—I don't know. I think that you can answer that better than I.

—Quite so. And I assure you that there is one man who blames me for one hell of a lot of very nasty things.

—Is that yourself?

—I've never met the fellow.

—Well, when you do, tell him that he's a fool, said Father Boguslawski. Love and hatred have become one for us and no one is to blame for anything. Besides, everything was paid for a long time ago.

—Yes, yes, a very long time ago, in the month of Nisan, Dr. Poremba said. We've managed to accumulate quite a debt since then.

—Perhaps it is time to pay some more of it. Why are you staying behind with the sick and wounded?

—It's too soon for me to tell you that, Dr. Poremba said.

—Yet you knew I would also stay. You've made the arrangements. Why did you think that I would have to stay? Why did you decide that you and I were bound to make that choice?

—I thought that you were contemplating martyrdom, my friend.

—The Church made a conscious seeking of martyrdom illegal some centuries ago.

—Very wise, I'm sure. Otherwise you'd have run out of Christians before you were ready, and you'd have had to double the length of the calendar to make room for all the surplus saints, and all the lions would have indigestion. It must make things rather awkward for people like you, whose lives acquire a meaning only at their end.

—We manage, the priest said, and smiled.

—A matter of chance, isn't it? Circumstances? *Deus vult,* and all that, and in the meantime someone turns up to make the arrangements?

—It seems to work something along those lines.

—Always?

—I don't know.

—Well, we do seem to have whole nations which are forever trying to nail themselves to some sort of a cross.

The priest smiled. —No metaphors, you said?

—*Touché, mon père.* A slip, an indiscretion. Not a mortal sin. God will forgive it. *C'est son métier,* as somebody has said.

—First we must learn to forgive each other.

—No simple matter, that.

—And before that there is another lesson to be learned.

—I don't know if I can stomach any more lessons today, said Dr. Poremba.

—Perhaps what I've been trying to say, said Father Boguslawski, and saying it badly, is that the deepest love and the most implacable hatred are one and the same. It's hard to tell where the one ends and the other begins. One who has really suffered at the hands of others finds it quite easy to forgive. He even finds it possible to understand the people who caused his suffering, and then there comes the recognition of the most creative truth; because from honestly endured suffering and grief flows an instinctive sense of privilege. You know at once what Christ was talking about: forgiveness for others, as for ourselves, for we too do not know what we do.

—And so, Dr. Poremba whispered to himself as much as to the priest. You suggest a sort of spiritual cease-fire? It sounds like surrender.

—No, of course not surrender. But a sort of emotional armistice, if you know what I mean, while the shocked human organism struggles up again . . . that's what I'd tell our people now if we were going with them.

—More patience? More endurance? It's a bitter diet.

—It may mean more in the long run than passing gallantry. I am suggesting reasonable rather than emotional solutions, a retreat into our own inner fortresses where we might patch our spiritual armor, sharpen the blunted edges of our hopes, and try to position ourselves against larger meanings. Hasn't that too been part of the Polish way? To leap beyond the boundaries of disaster . . .

—We have no say in what happens to us, Dr. Poremba said. There is no way to change our lot, we struggle blindly to no other purpose than that, eventually, the struggle might cease. That is all that we have a right to expect: the end of conscious struggle. No victory, no failure, neither decay nor growth, but the sudden end of all activity. But even then . . . even then . . . who can tell? Perhaps the struggle is moved to another plane and goes on, unchanging . . .

—In one way or another, Father Boguslawski said, each of us must manage the impossible and reach some sort of understanding with himself. We must reject a consciousness of grief. Think of it as a way to separate hatred from love and to liberate your love. Hatred withers quickly unless it's kept alive by some unreal, imaginary, artificial means . . . one of these so-called historic truths that enslave every generation . . . And once there is love among enemies then peace on earth becomes a possibility.

—There isn't that much love in the entire world.

—There is, if we can learn how to forgive ourselves.

The priest was smiling quietly to himself, his argument concluded; Dr. Poremba noted the passage of a moment of rare understanding.

Smiling, nodding, delighting in the final irony, once again able to find amusement in his own mountebank performance, he said: I am mad enough to have believed in romance, I was sick of this sycophantic age, tired of the miserable mildewed things people racked their brains about, wrote books about, called Life . . . Maundering academics, silly little journalists with their endless memoirs, literary poseurs unable to create anything that they had not experienced, and (the worst of the lot!) Artists with a Message . . . There's no message in life but the message of splendid living, I thought. It meant the things that our primitive forefathers were contented with, things that their overly refined descendants would rather forget as they sit about, picking scabs off their souls. I mean things like battle and murder and sudden death, with plenty of good friends and an absolute callousness about cracking the ungodly over the head . . . Primitive chivalry, if you like, Gawain before the Holy Grail, Bayard on the bridge of Garigliano, Roland at the gates of Spain . . . And a damsel in distress, and virtue triumphant, and a wholesale slaughter of villains at the end, and a real fight running through it all. Maybe that wasn't very true to life but I thought it was, or should be . . . And a lack of bitterness, of course, a joyous fatalism, each man a champion of lost causes fought with a smile . . . And now a saint and a sinner are going off together into a frozen sunset, and God's will is done. I wouldn't have accepted such a theme in my for-mer professional capacity.

He heard himself laughing. The priest also laughed, then said: A saint and a sinner, yes, but which is which?

Then Ahmer was back, bowing. —The woman Anna will not come.
—Why not? I have a fire here.
—She says she must stay where she is, she is waiting for her son.
—Tell her that we can wait together.

Ahmer bowed, withdrew. The priest got up, smiled at Dr. Poremba, made a small sign of the cross that seemed to embrace them both, and left. The water boiled in the birch-bark pot. Dr. Poremba added the last of the dung chips to the feeble blaze. He threw a handful of dry lichens into the steaming water to make Ostyak tea. Outside, ap-parently, someone else had died, for the dog was howling once again. He heard his son's croaking laugh, tried to think of him with pity, was suddenly dazed. Breathing had become almost impossible in the confined space of the conical tent. He closed his eyes but all his ghosts were still there, as they would always be. He got up to lace down the tent flap, looked into the gigantic glare of the morning, saw the eternal day of the Arctic winter, a night-day reflected in millions of prisms, glit-tering miles of snow without end.

. . . And she was back beside him, incandescent among exploding suns, leaning from her historic pedestal of ice: the mother-daughter of his secret dreams soothing the reflections of each man's desire; a myth embroidered upon the north wind by his imagination . . . a mural daz-zling with white cloaks and galloping horses. Her eyes were wide with cries and blood, enormously open; her icy chains rang against the cracked firmament of his consciousness. Such stirring music! May the dead rest in peace, he whispered in the ecstasy of submission: the final resistance. May this frozen earth be light. We walked past you each day, our animal eyes fixed on the small print of our guarantees while new worlds were plunging to collision overhead. Dreams, ideals, the fires of our hope died under your ashes. Looking inward, we never saw the stars. Passing you, as a man might pass a tree and ignore God's presence in it. Deafened by our centuries. Hearing a private music. Too certain that the endless miracles of resurrection were ours for the asking. We saw our private images stained into your glass and thought reverence sufficient to avert disaster . . .

She had not been trying to avoid contact, this vision of a life and country he had lost, she had not sought a void. Her arms were open to embrace, she was the child bride of a vanished youth extravagant with promise. Her smile was fixed in scarlet. Death's silver luminosity crackled among her amaranthine banners, saying: Follow, follow! Gone, cried the bronze bells, she is never to be seen again. But while he lived, she could not be lost, the anthem assured him. She would live in him and he in her, whatever vision of her he possessed in this final moment of saying goodbye: mother and daughter, family and home, lover who reconciled his contradiction at the dawn of the century . . . Myth, mural, banner, incandescence. The massed artillery of a thousand years thundered in his skull. Spirits smiled and beckoned. She stepped toward him out of legend and song, a handful of nails forged out of frozen tears were her wedding gift. She was smiling. You give Death too much honor, said the God in the tree.

Kobza's Way

SPRING: MARCH OR APRIL, and at last a village. Smoke curls above roofs thatched with old gray straw, reinforced with bark. Thick logs caulked with dry mud make the walls, and the sun reflects redly in the glass of windows. Barking dogs. The ground steams at morning. Women shield their eyes as they look toward them under snow-white kerchiefs. A field cleared for planting. Brown pliant soil where footsteps leave footprints. Darkness at nightfall and moonrise and hard rains.

They had traveled through a season of white nights, marking their miles with their dead. Now they stood on the edge of a civilization, neither believing nor disbelieving their accomplishment, neither confident nor fearful. They were alive and sure that life would continue as long as it was necessary, that the machinery of annihilation may occasionally fail before the will to live, that life's tangible solidity occasionally triumphs over the mania that men have called history. They had been able once to look upon horror with innocent eyes and ask for explanations, then learned to ask nothing; the banality of evil, as of good, made them immune to both.

In this month or the next, depending upon which month of a new spring this was, he would be fifty-one, a marked survivor of an Odyssey, having descended to mankind's darkest sources and then stepped beyond. He would no longer look back, no longer consider that which had made him as he found himself in a new decade of an extraordinary life —a life which was so richly studded with great and small disasters as to appear a blur of lost causes, retreats, but never indifference. His hair and beard and mustache (he knew by inspection) were as black as coal except where white tufts sprouted with majestic carelessness from his ears and nostrils. He walked slowly. He leaned heavily on a staff. He knew that the toes of his left foot had frozen together in another lifetime and would have to be cut off.

From where he stood on a hillock among pine, he could look east and west across the vast yellow-gray Siberian Plain, the birch forests behind him. Small groups of women were at work in the fields among the mounds of winter potatoes. His own people straggled across the flat and grassy landscape, squatting in fresh furrows to dig for buried tubers and roots, crying out at an occasional providential find.

He looked down, found an edible object, weighed it in his hand, and passed it to Catherine, who smiled and nodded in mute gratitude. Words had become largely unnecessary, the vocabulary of survival is designed to conserve every energy. He nodded toward the women in the fields, the village beyond.

—A small place, he said. Isolated. Not much chance of an official there.

—A hunters' settlement, then? Catherine said.

—Most likely.

—We'll go in there, then?

—Most likely, he said.

He pointed to a crude wooden shelter, a shepherd's lair, the remnants of a hundred fires where tea might be brewed, shifted his pack off his back. They could hear a stream in the pines below them. —This will do, he said. Later, when the hunters come back to the village, we'll go in. There is no point in scaring the women.

Catherine said: Women are not as easily frightened as you think.

She was looking out across the fields, looked up for a moment, a flat, dark look cold as death that made Kobza think of legends, ancient tales of how warriors dreaded being taken alive and turned over to the women of the enemy. Made for mercy, they could show less mercy than a reptile.

He grunted, looked away, turned, and looked at the twin struggling lines behind them. Each day of the march the lines had grown thinner, longer; each night there were fewer people assembling around him. Forty-two last night. They came from the limit of his vision, his farthest horizon, following snowy footprints. Now snow lay about in patches, soft wet puddles in which grass was beginning to grow, now there were fewer footprints. He tried to count them, stopped at thirty, his vision had blurred. Thirty, forty people bowed under their burdens, the hardest, the strongest; each carried a spark of an idea that propelled them forward, each spark unique and belonging only to that man or woman, that sense of vision, different from every other spark. Should they ever burn together, he thought, they'd make a conflagration that would illuminate the world. Poles on the right and Jews on the left, the lines advanced steadily from the edge of vision, oblivious of each other. Each difficult step increased the distances between them; as the frozen miles fell away behind them, as they grew stronger in themselves, as their memory of death grew dimmer, as each day's survival became a possibility rather than a desperate attempt, as they could turn their thoughts from the moment in which they found themselves to the past and future, they were returning to those notions, memories, suspicions, superstitions, envies, jealousies, hatreds, fears, and contempts that had created the distances between them. Now at night, he knew, they would make two camps, light two cooking fires, and at each nightfall it would take him longer to pass from one to the other.

Kepi came up then, puffing, then Pani Mosinska and Poremba's children. The litterateurs had some way to go.

—A village, eh? We're going in?

—Later, he said. After the men have returned for the night. No point alarming them, prr-prr.

—Women, Kepi said. Ha. Look at 'em there . . . Let's go down now before the men get back, get a little something going for us, eh?

—Would you rather fuck than eat? Kobza said.

—Both, if I can get it.

—Well, maybe there'll be a time when you can do both, right now you've got a choice of one or the other. Start playing with the women and we'll spend the night running from the men. Settle down and we'll go in later, get some food. What do you think they'll have there?

—Meat for sure, Kepi said, smacked his lips. Those fields could be millet, potatoes for sure. Maybe groats. Hey, did you hear that? A rooster! They've got chickens, by God.

—A chicken, cried Professor Karolewski. Now you are really talking about miracles. A chicken . . . an egg! That is too much for my mind to cope with.

—It's just food we can trade for, Professor, Kobza said.

—What do we have to trade? Kepi said.

—We'll have to give these people something that they want, the professor said. Does anybody have a watch or a fountain pen? That, as I remember from my student days, is what you give to peasants.

—How the hell would anybody have a watch after two years in Russia? Kepi said.

—We'll give them something better than a watch, Kobza said. A moment from the past, something that only the oldest of them can remember. A peasant will trust nothing that comes from a city . . .

—Religion? The professor was immediately alarmed. —Be careful! We're not out of Russia yet! There's still such a thing as ten years for religious propaganda.

—Well, I'm not going to lecture on good manners, Kobza said. I know village thinking. For me a peasant isn't something you find in a book. He lives close to the soil, he clings to what is old, hates every-thing that he doesn't understand, looks with suspicion at anything new. Offer him something that he already knows and he'll listen to you.

—Well, I could argue about that, the professor said.

—Tomorrow, Kobza said. You can do your arguing tomorrow. In the meantime, we have to get something to eat.

—I really miss our good Dr. Poremba, the professor said. He had a way that . . . well . . . what can I say? He could make people do the most unlikely things.

—Sometimes it's easier to fake a miracle than make one, Kobza said.

—What do you have in mind, then? Kepi said.

—Legends and tales, something the peasants can whisper at night. Something old, from the forests . . .

—Superstitions? the professor said. In the age of Communism and electricity? Not even Russian peasants can be as stupid as that.

—It's not a matter of stupidity, Kobza said, and sighed. Look, there are villages in Poland and the Ukraine that've belonged to the same people for a thousand years, but here, in the Siberian Plain, there was only grass a hundred years ago. The people here have nothing to remember, they came here from somewhere else in Russia after the Rev-olution. They brought nothing with them from their old lives, not even the stories that they tell each other. Their stories belong elsewhere, they don't fit this place, and if there's one thing that every peasant needs it's a feeling that he belongs to his soil, that he has always been exactly where he is, if you're following me. You, Kepi, do you know what I'm talking about?

—Shit no, Kepi said. I'm not a fucking peasant. I come from a city.

—They want something older than their lives, Kobza said. You give them that and they'll give you everything you need.

—Well, I'll believe in chickens when I see them, the professor said.

—You'll see them, Kobza said, then swept his arm in a circle to em-brace the hillock, the pine grove, the shepherd's shelter, and the invisi-ble stream. —We'll make camp here. Let's get some water up from that stream, get a fire going. No need to put up shelter, it doesn't look like rain.

—And then what? Kepi said.

—Then we'll have some dancing.

—Dancing, for Chrissake!

—Don't you feel like dancing?

—I feel like dying!

—That wouldn't make those peasants curious. They wouldn't come up here to see what *that* noise was about.

—All right then, Kepi said. We'll dance for our supper.

—Now go and see Itzek Fogel, see if he still has his old fiddle with him. Then go see Esterka. Tell them we're making one camp tonight, not two. Tell everybody that we're finally having that celebration they've wanted since we burned the camp. Dancing, singing, card tricks, storytelling . . . the professor can make another speech . . .

—Why do we have to make camp with the Jews? Pani Mosinska said. We've done very well on our own, I don't see the need to change everything.

—A speech, well, hmmm, the professor said. I suppose that something patriotic, something . . . how shall I put it? . . . uplifting, perhaps . . .

—One camp, Kobza said. Either we go on together from now on or everybody can split up and go his own way.

—I d-d-disagree, said Pani Mosinska. Who are you to make autocratic decisions?

—One camp, Kobza said. Go tell them, Kepi.

—I p-p-protest!

—You're free to go off by yourself, Kobza said. Do you want to do that?

—Alone? Are you mad? And how dare you speak to me in that tone of voice? I know that I can't expect decency, good breeding, manners, or civilized behavior from a man like you . . .

—Oh, shut the fuck up, lady, Kepi said.

—Prr-prrr, Kobza said.

—And stop that vulgar noise!

—If I could only think of something funny, the professor said. Some absurd little thing to make people laugh . . . I think it'd be good for us to laugh, perhaps at ourselves . . .

—Say what you like, Kobza said, and sighed. People will hear only what they want to hear anyway. Get on with it, Kepi.

Later, alone (the others gone about their business, making camp), he sat on a tree stump, massaged his aching leg, wondered how soon he would find the courage to take off his boot, unwrap the rotted footcloths, and inspect the source of his pain. Each day it seemed to reach further up his leg, he cursed himself for having let it go for so long.

He had become a leader by default and there were still many hundreds of miles to be crossed before he could cease to be responsible for the others. Yet he had no illusions about their affection. If they had followed him so far it was because he walked ahead, offering a direction which they had not been able to decide for themselves, having no idea that there were choices they could make. He was a signpost, a banner carried at the head of the column, an image of a leader, not a man who led. He knew that it was never more than an image of their own desires that any people followed.

Dragging his ruined foot, he moved painfully through the rudimentary encampment. In his mind's eye he could see the birches stripped of their leaves and this, in turn, reminded him of his skeletal existence as the disembodied, depersonalized heaver of coal and sweeper of stairs, an existence which had never seemed more appealing than now. Children had wandered through his dusty dreams, hiding before seeking. There are, he thought, so few ways to shut out memory, to reconstruct abandoned beginnings; why should he not make use of whatever moments of forgetfulness life, herself forgetful, placed in his path? In Catherine's company he had felt, at times, as if his aloneness was an artifice, the remains of a romantic landscape not composed of cinders, slag heaps, mounds of coal, yellowing newspapers, and sawdust. He was touched by the childish purity of her pride as she, dressed in a purple curtain and enthroned upon an upturned coal scuttle, a humming top in one hand, a whip in the other, presided over a royal levee. (Respectful rodents scurried in dark corners.) He could watch over her then as if she had been entrusted to his care, and felt, at such moments, most like himself: benign, wise, virile, and beyond upheavals. His need for her was crippling; it seemed like an answer to all the prayers that he had never said. It was a need that eroded last, God be thanked.

In his mind's ear her voice was still girlish but she was not a girl, no longer a child, having gone beyond the deepest experiences of age in less than two years. She used a dull, flat voice without resonance, a voice for brutal statements, for denials, for hoarse and grating confirmation of events that had grazed her bloom.

He looked for her, found her spreading her bedding near the top of the hillock next to the door of the shepherd's shelter, which he had reserved for himself. A fire was lighted at that moment. The thought of her as a lonely aging woman, sitting in future years by an empty window, touched him even further. Her youth, concealed and perhaps discarded, was still clear in his memory. And knowing the unimportance of youth in the scheme of things, why did he, at this time of life, seem almost ready to sell his life for youth? It serves only as one minor introduction to old age, he knew.

Could he go back to any kind of life that would not include her, and such means of forgetfulness as her disguised youth promised to provide? Could he? He could not. He would not.

Later, toward midmorning, the sun began to give imitation warmth. The crude encampment had been made. No tents, no other shelter. Bundles flung down on dry patches of earth marked the double helix in which they would sleep. They had moved closer together, as ordered, but retained two circles: the Jews (he could hear Esterka's harsh voice issuing commands) lower down the slope, nearer to the marsh grass and the stream, the others (all the others) at the edge of the pines that crowned the small summit. He knew without looking that the Jews would lie facing outward toward the fields and the village, their backs to the others, who would be facing inward on the summit of the little hill. If they could make themselves invisible to each other they could ignore each other, could claim innocence, could accuse each other, could declare their various monopolies of martyrdom at each other's hands.

Kobza suppressed a groan, counting the cadences of his pain, and looked toward Catherine. She was walking in the direction of the stream, a smile passed across her face like sunlight on a plowed field. Professor Karolewski's steady smile was a parapet (he thought) behind which his personality waited, crouched in isolation, peering with bitterness from the depths of his disappointments.

Kobza rose, leaning on his staff, and moved down the hillside. The day was warm and the grass had steamed itself gray under layers of mist, so that it resembled the frost that would harden there before dawn. Sunlight spread like seed from one field to another. A wind arrived, sprayed pale pine needles into his mouth, then left with its cargo of clouds. The ravens cawed, wheeling. An owl trod with shortsighted dignity into a nest, the mouse in its beak caught the sun with eyes that were dark with the death to come. Hunched in the green frame of the pines, he hobbled down the slope seeing things take shape, separate from their shadows. Smoke lifted above a thatch, drifted into the fields, a group of boys was crossing the furrows. A rooster called his harem to attention. A door slammed, a goat rang its bell, a shotgun pop-popped in the near distance. On the horizon, parting this hour from another, the stacked clouds waited with a cargo of rain they would spill at nightfall.

Someone, probably Jankele, was playing *Krakowiaczek Jeden* on an Ostyak flute, someone was keeping time with stones rattled in a kettle. Agnieszka Dlapanow was combing her hair. Pani Mosinska was hectoring Ziuta once again, each of her angry words a plea for the return of certainties that had disappeared. She dangled them before the sullen girl like overcooked carrots, nourishing but tasteless, and the girl, who had been lusty once and vibrant and now was merely pudgy, as if she could make up in quantity what she lacked in quality, bedeviled by the accident of birth, scanned an interior night. Wiesio, who had been fat and now was merely narrow, raised bright blue calculating eyes as Kobza walked past him. Blows from Ariz's ax were shattering a tree.

Catherine and Esterka were talking near the stream, made invisible by ferns.

—If we could only talk about these things, Catherine was saying. Truthfully, openly. If we could finally learn to listen to each other . . .

—No, no more talking, Esterka was saying. And as for listening, well, *you* had better learn to listen to someone other than yourselves, we've listened to enough. We've heard enough abuse, insult, enough of our own pieties, enough of everything except what *we* want to hear . . . And no more feeling either, no more emotional distractions . . . And, anyway, why don't you leave me alone?

—We used to be friends.

—No, never. Your friends are people who share your opinions.

—But you must have someone to whom you feel close, someone with whom you feel warm, with whom you are free, Catherine said, then explained impatiently: Everyone must have somebody like that.

—No, not everyone, Esterka said harshly.

—Yes, everyone! Everyone who is a human being! Because if you don't have that connection with your own humanity you have no idea what being human is about.

—It needn't be a person, it can be an idea.

—Not if you are human!

—I will never again care for anyone who can't be immediately replaced, Esterka said.

He had stopped to listen, leaned against a tree trunk, realized that he was eavesdropping on a dialogue that had run unspoken for centuries and that was coming to an end of its own dead weight like a blighted tree sinking in a swamp. He had apparently wandered into a personal interlude in an argument that resumed at once.

—Our journey began in Lwów, in Poland, Catherine was saying, and it will never entirely leave there. We were all searching for something that we didn't have. We deplored every gulf between all our peoples but we didn't really do very much about it. We could only communicate on the level of formal political ideas. We collected facts but real questions went unanswered. We never tried to get to the pain and joys of each other's lives. If one of you married one of us she was mourned as dead, if one of us tried it she was regarded as some sort of traitor to a national ideal. If any of you ever took a real interest in the country in which you were living it was less to learn about your country, and about how you might be a part of it, than to see whether we were any readier to allow you to continue in your isolation. I am sorry if this doesn't suit your legend of oppression but it is the truth. I think that we'll continue not knowing each other and lying about each other wherever we go. You keep complaining that your oppression is endless and, in the end, we feel that your complaints, and only your complaints, are endless too. Surely, whatever is still keeping us apart can be resolved. We've all been through so much that, surely, we've learned something. We are together now, going toward some sort of resolution, can't we use our shared time to share each other's lives? That could be a beginning.

—No more beginnings, Esterka said. At least, not with you.

—We could at least learn to talk to each other.

—We've talked now, Esterka said. Did we answer any questions? And what is this about being together, sharing time? We aren't even sharing this journey! For you the arrival will mean more than the journey. For us, it's more important to keep going.

—We could at least . . .

—No! Esterka said. The purpose of *our* journey is that we need never talk to you again, that we need never even have to hear each other.

He caught sight of Esterka then, she had moved up the slope from the stream, stepped from among the ferns, naked and clutching a bundle of clothing. Her hair was a wet black helmet, her face held pride and anger, a blind bronze.

—There isn't a gravestone big enough to summarize our life among you, she said.

The gleam of beauty he had noticed in her had been absorbed by hatred like something swallowed by a reptile. She spoke with a remembered grief that had become malignant.

He looked toward Catherine, found her watching him or perhaps merely looking in the direction which he happened to occupy; he stood in the way of her gaze, an object which was not herself in her reality. High overhead a hawk hung suspended on bent wings.

Lead them, lead them. To what, to what, to what . . . If anything was going to keep these people alive it was love, the love between people who do not permit a shrinking of their vision of a human being. Their agonies had destroyed the old beliefs in human solidarity on which life depends in the face of history, they must find new beliefs which could make each of them more than monstrous, foolish, or unnecessary in each other's eyes. Love between people in camps, under bombardment, in the presence of a massacre, in deportation trains, in ghettos, despite fanaticism and terror and paralysis of will. We must be known to ourselves, he muttered. What makes love possible is that we don't know anything about each other. Everything about each of us counts toward some sort of a total, but we don't have to know it all. The pain, for those who are in pain, is the sum of moments in which only the total affects reality; the fragments of the various agonies that add up to the total are surely unimportant.

He turned away, stepped into the light. Again the sun, white like a plate with gauze spread over it to keep out the flies, again the quick wind. The landscape had changed. It seemed more melancholy, wider, less abstract. It stretched between dark forested horizons like a living substance with the power to inflict injury and to suffer it. He staggered, lurched, yes, he was lurching now, away from the voices which seemed unreal even when they spoke a truth, hearing the others who stood and lay about in disconnected attitudes among the pines, in shadow, like purgatorial souls waiting for orders. People sometimes feel terribly guilty only because they've been terribly punished, he thought, and guilt causes hatred.

Eyes like dry caves, full of skulls and gnawed bones, cold and lightless as the eyes of corpses, regarded him from among the trees. Sitting down, extending his leg, he closed his own eyes to count the thawed seconds of his pain.

Later, the sun moved under clouds, the air became heavy; the sky was gray again, and cold like a winter's pond. The land had flattened out. Behind him, when the trees thinned out, he could see the dark arch of the hillock, the feathery ribbon of smoke marking the camp. The bare branches of single birches scattered among the pines veined themselves against it, forking down to white and naked trunks.

He was trembling, his pulse full of pain, but he ignored his body. If you don't think about your pain it doesn't hurt as much. His body was numb with the pain, and his soul was too tired and hungry to feel. A dog kept barking, made braver by his silence, as he stepped into the field where the children waited. They greeted him with silence, solemn eyes; blue eyes regarded him out of dusty faces, small mouths were round about grubby thumbs. He lowered himself carefully to the ground, sat on the stream's bank and stretched his leg before him. Ah. Whooo. Tssss. The children were suddenly in motion like a flock of starlings wheeling away from him, then stood still again, watching. He had an empty ache in his stomach and the spit came into his mouth just from thinking about food. He closed his eyes, leaned against a tree trunk, began to hum a tuneless song. Bum-bitty-bum, bum bum. He felt the dog before he could see him, felt the cold nose and hot carnivorous breath. The dog's head came under his fingers. He scratched it behind the ears. Good boy, he said, opening his eyes. The dog slipped from under his hand, backed away and stood alert, wagging a shaggy tail. A boy called to the dog. Come here, Vanya. Here. The dog looked at the boy, ran a few steps toward him, then turned and came back. Here, Vanya, I said! He closed his eyes again, hummed. Whooof, said the dog. Vanya, cried the boy. His hand groped ahead, meeting nothing, and he wondered where the dog had gone, then his foot touched the soft hide and he realized that the animal was lying down before him. Good boy, he said. Good Vanya, good dog. He could hear the thump of the dog's tail beating against the ground. Good dog, I'd give you a bone if I had one. Yes. But I don't have a bone. Have nothing to eat. Whooof! That's right. Maybe I'll have something for you later. Then he could feel the dog's hot tongue sliding along his foot.

—What's wrong with your leg? a boy said at some distance.

—I hurt it a bit.

—Going to cut it off?

—Most likely.

—When're you going to cut it off?

—Don't really know. Soon, I expect.

—Can I watch you do it?

—Why not? Maybe you can help.

—Yes, yes, the boy said. I can do it. I've seen it done. Last winter, there was this man, he got caught in a deadfall. They cut off his whole leg and I watched them do it. Then they put a red-hot axhead up against the wound to stop it from bleeding, and that's when he died. You going to put hot iron up against the wound after they cut off *your* leg?

—I expect I will.

—Hmmm, the boy said, closer.

—Where are you from? said another child.

He opened his eyes, pointed to the western skyline where the sun had dipped; soon it would be peering over the edge of the world like a red eye in ambush across a wall, a shocked and angry eye with murder behind it. Out of the tired cloud of his mind a woman's face appeared, a young contemptuous face seeking definitions (You've always treated me as if I were more than a human being!), then changed and dissolved into another face with dark watery eyes, the broad nose, the pinched mouth, the sad look of labor and dependence. He saw the whitewashed cottage wall, the worn fence, smoke trailing from the chimney. She would be readying for supper, cooking groats and fatback, potatoes, cabbage soup, sour milk in pitchers. The bread would still be hot. Most likely, if she were still alive, she would be thinking about him now and worrying, as she always worried, an old woman, a mother. Most likely he'd never see her again, never eat her cooking, would only remember, seeing her face turned in dumb obedience to her angry husband. A woman has no soul, his father said clearly through the massed ticking of his clocks, mad as a bull and ready to strike with whatever lay close to hand. Good luck to you, Ma, Kobza said. Home would be to the west and south, to the right of the sun. He faced that way, hearing the whisper of his father's clocks, three, four hundred sets of gears sliding in unison, a hundred black hands moving, an aviary of wooden cuckoos ready to explode. Time itself had seemed to be imprisoned there.

—What are you doing here? the boy said.

—Resting.

—How come you're not working? The sun's not down yet.

—I work when the sun goes down.

—What are you, then? A thief?

—I'm a storyteller.

—What kind of stories do you tell?

—Any kind, lots of kinds. About the Devil who wrestled with a bear, and about the Foolish Youth who looked for Fear, and about the Drowned Man in the magic swamp. And about wizards and magic tables that spread themselves with food, and about the enchanted princess on a mountain made of glass.

—Will you tell us some stories before they cut off your leg?

—I expect I will.

—What else can you do?

—I can tell the future.

—Ah, the boy said, uncertain. Nobody can do that.

—There's a few who can. Ask your grandmother about storytellers, about fortune-telling.

—Grandmother died last year, the boy said.

—Then ask your grandfather.

—I got no grandfather, the boy said.

—I do, I do, a girl cried.

—Then ask *your* grandfather. Tell him to come up to the hill tonight, after supper, there'll be dancing, singing. And I'll tell stories and look into the future.

—Are you a Gypsy, then? Or what? You don't look like a Gypsy.

—Hard to tell what anybody is just by looking at him.

—Because if you're a Gypsy you better look out, the girl said. Don't try to steal nothing. Grandfather told me all about the Gypsies.

—They steal children, the boy said. But I won't let them do it.

—There's a brave boy, Kobza said.

A woman shouted then, a long impatient cry from the village, and the children stirred. The dog leaped up, barking, and at once other dogs replied. From the trees behind him came the thin chirping of a bird preparing for nightfall, then there was a swift brief silence and he heard the rustling of the wind among the dead corn stubble, the small echo of a voice, the hoot of a screech owl.

—You'll come up later, then? he said. I'll tell you a story.

—Yes, we'll come, the children cried. Yes. Later.

—And ask your grandfather about people like me who can tell the future.

—I will, the girl cried, running through the furrows.

They ran home across the fields calling to each other, as all children did in every village in each country of the world, as he had done, as he had hoped his own children would do. They pranced, skipped and hopped, laughing, to the village. In the west, the sky had caught fire. Stars began to wink whitely overhead.

Night, and a white moon running in a witch's sky. A time for tales, legends. The fire around which they lay glowed and died, glowed and died, as the breeze played with it. The camp was silent, except for the now-and-then mutter of one man to another, a sigh rattling up from a skeletal chest, the crack of burning logs, hiss of sap. The world had faded to a dark rim, far and dim as clouds in the night sky. Lights appeared as small yellow squares in the village, cold as votive candles at a graveside. Good luck to you too, Ma, he whispered, thinking of the woman who had never known one moment of joy in her entire life, whose worn face had known only hardship. Before he could stop it, a sob escaped him and his eyes were wet. Oh, dammit all to hell. He was cold and stiff clear to his bones, eased his leg forward and kneaded his kneecap, an old man reconstructing his realities from pain. After a while he sat up, safe and unseen in the dark shepherd's shelter, and gouged tears from his eyes.

—Are you all right? Catherine asked, outside.

—Yes.

—Are you in much pain?

—Yes. No. It's all right. It's been worse.

—Where? she said, and he had to smile. Where had it been worse?

—It'll all be better where we're going.

—Where will we go from here?

—We'll know when we have to.

—We'll . . . none of us . . . will ever forget you for what you've done for us all, she said, invisible except as a shadow.

—We'll see who forgets who (whom!) when things change, little lady.

—Change to what?

—Hard to remember, isn't it, how it was, how it will be.

—Oh, that, she said. I don't even think about things like that. To live in a city again, to know what every day will bring, to be sure of tomorrow . . . I can't imagine what that could have been like.

—To love someone again? (He added, apologetically:) I heard you talking to Esterka . . .

—That too, I suppose. Why didn't we ever know each other before?

—We did. We used to talk when you came to play in the cellar.

—But since I grew up, since childhood.

—There was no need for it.

—I never thought about you, one way or another, while I was growing up. Never wondered anything about you. Just a nice man in a cellar who slept in packing cases.

—A nice old man, he said carefully.

—I never thought of you as being old. Or, for that matter, as being a man. You were a presence, an authority, a voice in a crate. You are much more visible to me now.

—In all this darkness? he said gently, feeling the need to be gentle with her.

—It's not all that dark. I know now that in all your sharply focused will for survival there is a contradiction. Your thoughts seem wholly centered on yourself but you know, and I know you know, that as soon as a man begins to care about himself, to the exclusion of all other people, he is finished as a human being. You are not a young man, you are safely beyond the narrow selfishness of youth. You can accept total responsibility for yourself, for all your actions and thoughts and feelings, past, present, and future, and so you can become responsible for others.

—Whooo, Kobza said. Tsss. I don't think I'd want that.

—I suppose that's what maturity is about. I suppose that's why people trust you.

—Such foolishness, Kobza said gently. Prrr-prrr. Everybody's got to look after himself . . .

—You are . . . dependable, she said. Durable, rooted in the soil. A man who cares about his own life and so can be counted upon to care for the lives of others. Not a pendulum perpetually swinging between hostile extremes, not a self-styled Messiah searching for his cross. A man at rest within himself, at peace with himself, and so equipped to struggle and to conquer exterior disasters. And not at *all* old, not at *all*.

—Such foolishness, he said, needing to believe it.

A spark arced high out of the fire, a star swooped and fell. She was silent and he listened to the night sounds, heard calls across the fields, watched Itzek Fogel (carrying his fiddle) and little Jankele with his Ostyak flute coming from the shadows.

—Hey, hey, Professor Karolewski cried. Well, why not? When there is nothing else we might as well have music.

—Hey, Kobza, Kepi cried. When are those peasants coming?

—Soon. After they've talked about it for a bit.

—If you say so, I believe it. Damned if I know why.

The people from the village came in perhaps an hour, perhaps a little more. They stood in the shadows, listening to the music, whispering, shuffling about, and clearing their throats. Hooo-ha! cried Kepi, hopping around the fire with Agnieszka Dlapanow. Hooo-ha! Ha! Hey, Hey, cried Professor Karolewski, uncorking a bottle. Itzek Fogel bowed over his fiddle, Jankele piped tunes of his own invention, Professor Kukla pounded on an upturned kettle with a wooden spoon. A polonaise, if you please, said Pani Mosinska.

Kobza smiled, looked quickly at Catherine as the pairs began to form for the processional, then shrugged. Pain stabbed him through the leg with a touch of fire. She sat by the fire, her back straight, her hands folded in her lap, smiling to herself. He got up, hobbled toward her and the child, which lay still and mute beside her in wrappings of burlap.

—A polonaise, I said, Pani Mosinska ordered. Three beats to the bar, surely you can manage.

—You're not dancing?

—No, Catherine said.

She bent over the child, adjusted his wrappings, her body supple in his imagination, moving strongly under the worn prison clothing, and Kobza was suddenly aware of her fresh scrubbed smell. He moved toward the waiting Russians: five women, none young, all respectfully quiet. Dark careworn faces splashed with moonlight, hands hanging stiffly at the seams of jackets or hidden in aprons. Small acorn eyes regarded him blankly.

—Welcome, he said.

They murmured an inaudible reply. He looked beyond them, saw no men and no one who could be any kind of government official. There would be no *komandir* in a hunters' settlement so far to the north but, even so, he had to make sure. The moon hid behind a cloud again, the dark faces vanished, he felt the quick sharp breeze tugging at his beard, thought of past days, the needs of the present. The women stood uneasily, shifting from one foot to another. Then one nudged another.

—God be praised, he said, waited for an answer. (None came, of course, nor did he expect one.)

One woman, the oldest, stepped forward, said: Who are you? Where are you from?

—Later, he said. We'll talk about that later. Now join us, warm yourselves.

—Well, all right. We heard you were here, came to see, that's all. You come from the west?

—Yes, yes, and other places too. Join us, dance if you want to.

The old woman giggled, covered her mouth with a hand as black and gnarled as walnuts. —Me dance? Ha, and who'd sweep up the old bones?

—Then take a drink of vodka, it comes from your village.

—Well, one then. Does no harm, drowns the worms. Ha, you tell stories, huh? The children were talking.

—Yes, stories, wonders. A man sees a lot.

—And the future, she said cautiously. I heard you look into the future, tell how things will be.

—Sometimes I do that, when everything is right.

—In the old days there were many like you. But now it is different.

—Maybe the old days are coming back again.

—Praise God, the old woman said.

Then they were whispering among themselves, looking at the dancers; one giggled like a girl, one sighed and brought her hands together as in prayer or wonder, another belched and was immediately hushed. The clearing on the hilltop had filled up with people who laughed, danced, hopped about, drank from vodka bottles, hooted, spat into the fire, slapped backs, threw arms around shoulders, said *Ho* and *Ha* and *Hoo-ha* and *Ha ha ha* and *Wheee* (Kepi opening bottles) and *Pairs forward, please* and *Take your places*, while Itzek's violin soared and swooped and summoned and commanded, and courtly pairs dipped in the polonaise. TUM-tata-ta-ta-ta-ta-ta Tum ta-ta. *Pierwsza para!* cried Professor Karolewski, and Pani Mosinska advanced on the arm of Professor Kukla, curtsied, while he bowed. *Kto nie pije ten nie żyje*, shouted Kepi. Drink to what is coming. Wheee! Hoooo! Haaa! TUM-ta-ta. More men and women were coming from among the trees, and Kobza wondered about how quickly it was that people who were worn and wearied, hungry and weakened by disease, bitter and hopeless, violent in their angers, could cross into life. *Drink!* shouted Kepi, and *Ladies to the left*, cried Professor Karolewski, and *Get the fuck up from under my feet*, roared Banda-Cyganowski to a fallen dancer, and the trees swayed and rustled and perfumed the clearing.

—Do you want to join us?

The peasant women looked at each other, murmured, sloughed their boots in the dry pine needles, smiled at the bottles glinting in the moonlight. —If it's no trouble, said the largest of them. If you want us to . . .

He nodded, made a sweeping gesture toward the fire and the warm, cleared space where Catherine was sitting, turned and limped toward

her. The women followed, murmuring, smiling their difficult smiles.
—Greetings to you, child, one of them (the oldest) said to Catherine.
And hasn't it been a hard winter? And is that your child, said another,
and does he always sleep with his little eyes open to the world?

—He closes his eyes only when he is afraid, Catherine said softly.

—When he's afraid, you say? Isn't that a wonder?

—Ah, well, there's much to be afraid of in the world, said the oldest
woman.

—And have you come far?

Ahhh, Kobza groaned despite his best efforts, hissed, lowered himself
to the ground beside Catherine. The pain had mounted to his belly and
rode him like a horse. And I, Kobza thought through the sum total of
his weariness, am as hungry as a bear in spring.

TUM-tata, sang the ancient music, the centuries advancing and re-
treating, bowing to each other. A rooster, late to sleep, crowed to him
from the village and the dogs were barking. Wet wood hissed in the fire
like a soul in torment, and a screech owl hooted. He stared gloomily at
the remnants of the salted dried fish, the parched strips of Taran,
looked at the peasant women seated about the fire, thought of their
unrewarding days, their lives of sad labor, their daughters and their sons
who would abandon them to fulfill their destinies, saying, as all people
of all time have always said when inflicting cruelties and hoaxes: We
are the humans, the others are just Man. He shrugged, cleared his
throat (hurrumph), said harshly: Terrible days are coming.

—Ah, said the women, nodding like mourners at a wake. Yes, yes.
Yes . . .

—The young no longer listen to their elders, they go their own way
. . .

—Ah, said the women in a sighing chorus, a wind that passed
through husks in a barren field.

—The old are scorned, ignored, no one listens to them . . .

—It's the truth, the oldest woman said, and stared at Kobza with
glittering eyes.

—It wasn't always like that, Kobza said.

—No, no, it was not.

—The world was better when we were all younger. We knew how to
respect our elders, and what could be wiser? Who knows his way home
better than an old horse?

—No one, no one, said the oldest woman.

—True, true, so true, said the other women. Ah yes, ah yes, they said,
making stricken gestures, their voices soft with pleasure and self-pity.

—Now there are signs in the sky, Kobza said. Prr-prrr. Death walks in the forests and people turn to ice. Terrible signs, if only we could read them, none of them promise anything good, prr-prrr.

—Ah, signs, said the women.

—There were always signs when I was a young girl, said the oldest woman, her small eyes fixed and brilliant in the firelight. Always. Always.

Kobza sighed, peered sideways at Catherine, who had turned away, bowed over her child. To hide a smile? To take no part in what was taking place? Softly, he said: But maybe the evil can be averted, eh? If a man sits under a tree and the tree falls on him he is crushed to death . . . But if he knows that the tree will fall he can sit somewhere else.

—Yes, yes, if he knew . . .

—When I was a girl, the oldest woman said, a *starets* came to my village. In the Ukraine, it was, a land of milk and honey, oh, such a land, so wide, so beautiful . . . We were so happy there, we were all so young . . . Men such as you went about from village to village, telling stories, telling about the future. The *starets*, the one who came to us when I was a girl, could read the future in salt and in the sand . . .

—Ah yes, Kobza said. Prr-prrr. Salt and sand . . . Well, everything's changed since then, and salt and sand don't work too well any more.

—Yes, yes, the woman said. Everything is changing.

—We live in new times, after all, Kobza said. We are not muzhiks, we are educated . . . Sand and salt, well, that could have been good enough in the ignorant old days when the future was easy to tell, you know that. Now it's a lot different.

—You can tell the future, then?

Kobza nodded, looked up, saw Professor Karolewski approaching with a bottle, sighed, said: It's different these days but it can be done.

—Well then, the oldest woman said. What do you need to do it? What must we bring you?

—Bring? Well, prr-prrr, maybe because we are becoming such good friends . . . because you are so generous, so kind, such good honest women . . . But tell me first, where are your men, and why aren't there any young people with you?

—Young people run away to the cities, the oldest woman said. The men, well, you know how it is in these times, they want to keep away from strangers. You never know what can happen to you if you talk to strangers.

—And what about your *nachalnik*? Even a village as small as yours must have a *nachalnik*.

—Oh, we have one, yes, the oldest woman said. He's gone to the city with the winter furs, two, three months now since he went to Irkutsk. He'll be back before the planting's over.

—What a pity, the professor said. There are some things we'd need from the *nachalnik*.

—Well, said the oldest of the women. I'm his mother, he left all his stamps with me. I'm the deputy *nachalnik*, you might say. So if you need a paper with a stamp, I'll stamp it if you have the paper.

—A man can't have too many papers nowadays, Kobza said.

The cock crowed again and Kobza heard his stomach rumbling. Catherine was looking at him, smiling to herself. Professor Karolewski was rubbing his hands, smiling at the women.

—Well then, I'll do it, Kobza said. Is that a black rooster that I hear crowing?

—White, the old woman said.

Nodding, with what he hoped would pass for evidence of wisdom, he turned to consult. —What do you think, Professor?

—Eh? What? Hrumph, the professor said. A black one would be best. (Then added swiftly, smiling:) Of course, there are ways of doing it with white ones, any color really . . . Of course, you understand that unless we have the best possible equipment . . . (He spread his hands, shrugged.) It is like every other science, you know, your results are only as good as your equipment . . .

—We only have two roosters, the youngest of the women said. I don't suppose that rooster will be in one piece when you've finished with him?

—Even roosters aren't what they used to be, Kobza said. Especially young roosters. But what's a dozen hens without a young rooster? If you can't spare a rooster, a dozen hens will do.

—Twelve hens! the youngest of the women said. The *nachalnik* will have us up for that! He'd make it hot for us.

—I am his mother, said the oldest woman. I have all the stamps. Let him think a fox got the hens, let him arrest the fox. And I haven't forgotten what it's like to make things hot for *him!*

—Twelve hens! said the youngest woman. We only have thirty.

—Better to have two roosters and eighteen hens than thirty hens without any roosters, Kobza said.

—You can have the hens, said the oldest woman.

—And what about some eggs? murmured the professor.

—And some eggs, the old woman said. These are hard times, and worse times are coming, so take the hens and the eggs and tell us the future.

—Tomorrow, Kobza said. After we've eaten, slept a bit . . .

—And do bring some salt, the professor added. We shouldn't leave anything to chance.

—And the sand? said the oldest woman. Don't you want the sand?

—That is no longer part of the technology.

Later, they ate. They drank and they danced. Head full of stars and vodka, going round. Flat on his back, staring up. Pines waving spectral fronds like overturned spiders. Stars and moons spinning. There were at least twice as many stars as there had been before, and some were flying out of the sky, some were falling, and some were going around in small circles, and most of the others were quivering and pulsing like jellyfish. There were two moons, side by side, and they were changing colors. They were the biggest of the jellyfish. Black up there, lonely, among all the stars. Warm down here and dry. The earth smells of a century of beginnings, of roots that sucked in subterranean rivers, of things that will grow. His fingers were buried in the earth; he felt the currents of the buried centuries shooting up his fingers.

Some of the stars winked then, and he winked back at them.

A cool breeze then, soothing as a ballad.

He felt himself forgiving, warm and sentimental, and he looked about inside himself for a reason to weep.

People, all his people, and about two dozen men and women he had not seen before, were dancing and singing. There were many bottles to catch the light from the moon and the stars and the huge bonfire, to catch the light in the eyes and on the gleaming teeth, the light in the sweated gaunt dark faces and the very red faces of the people who danced and who sang, who were drunk and happy. He was very happy, he was very drunk; he hoped that everyone else was happy and drunk. It was a celebration and it didn't matter what there may have been a reason to celebrate. Or what there may not have been a reason, he decided, trying to view the matter with ob-jec-ti-vi-ty. It was a celebration of life itself, perhaps, he concluded. Of non-death. A celebration is its own reason, it is a celebration to celebrate a celebration, otherwise it is not a celebration, it serves a purpose other than its own. (His leg was not a reason for a celebration.) Ahhhh, he said. He belched. He blew a loud fart. That made him feel much better about everything. The granite lady was giggling like a girl. She said: *Wheeee*. (Women were giggling and squealing and saying *Wheee*.) The men were grunting and hooting and saying *Whooo*. (He said *Whooo*.) They were saying *Oooha-ha*. (He said *Tsss*.) Some other people were saying other things among the ferns and bushes and in the deep shadows among the pines, and they made thrashing and crashing sounds in those shadows, and they made wheezing sounds.

He wondered why so many people had been bringing him vodka all night long and making him drink it. It wasn't even real vodka but a home-brewed distillation of pure grain alcohol that tasted like old horseshoes and had just about the same effect when applied to the head. Kepi had been the most persistent with this *samogon*, and this was most surprising, because for as long as he had known Kepi (and that was now a matter of more than fifteen years) he had never known Kepi to give anyone anything that he could drink himself. But perhaps that's what happened at a celebration. Pani Mosinska, the granite General's Lady, had surprised him even more. She had brought him two large metal cups filled with *samogon* and giggled and said that it was time for them to drink *Bruderschaft* together, use first names and the familiar *Thou*, which, he knew, meant that he had to put down the mugful of *samogon* at one gulp, and they clicked their mugs and linked arms and he threw back his head and drank the *samogon* to the last drop, and then she giggled again and kissed him, and he fell flat on his back. He had been on his back ever since then, unable to get up. Pani Mosinska had not fallen down. She was dancing with someone. She was still giggling and saying *Wheee*. Kepi was crawling on his hands and knees and saying *Woof-woof*. Good dog, that Kepi. Ah well, that's what happens at a celebration.

(Professor Kukla puts a rope around his neck and hands the loose end to Itzek Fogel, who has put down his fiddle for just a moment to have a drink of vodka. Professor Kukla urges Itzek Fogel to do something, Itzek shakes his head. No, the professor is not suffering a fit of punitive remorse, he has not judged himself guilty of past treasons, he is not demanding his own execution, he has an invulnerable ability to live in the present whatever it may be. He has convinced himself that he is a bear, a Russian Dancing Bear, and he wants to be led to the village so that he may dance and earn a lot of money. Itzek Fogel will have none of it.)

Sitting beside Itzek Fogel is the giant Ariz, who is smiling softly and sharpening his ax. Kamila sits beside him and smiles up at him (she has put away her fears of painful violation). Agnieszka Dlapanow sits beside Kamila and her eyes are shining, and her lips are moist and open to the moon, and she is whispering something to the stars; perhaps she is composing a story for good children, or a poem about gingerbread houses and mountains of ice cream, because she licks and bites her lips and totally ignores the large Russian peasant who has buried both hands, to the elbows, under her skirt. Next to the transported poetess sits an unsmiling Esterka, in each of whose terrible black eyes a red flame is dancing. Woof-woof, Kepi says, and comes toward Kobza. He carries a bottle.

—Good old dog, Kobza said. How are you, good dog?

—Woof, Kepi said. Have another drink.

—Had 'nough, Kobza said. Dizzy.

—Never such a thing as enough, Kepi said. Good for you to be dizzy. It's a dizzy world, you wouldn't want to be the only undizzy man in a dizzy world, would you now? Here now, drink this down.

—Whooo, Kobza said. Ahhhh . . .

—Good?

—G-g-g-g, Kobza said.

—Hair of the dog, said Kepi. Woof-woof. You got to have a hair of the dog. Dog is a man's best friend, a lot better than a woman, right?

—R-r-r-r, Kobza said.

—Am I your best friend?

—You are my best friend, Kobza said precisely.

—So have another drink with your best friend.

—Ahhh, Kobza said, sighed, belched. Thasss good.

—Best thing in the world, your best friend wouldn't lead you astray, Kepi said. So now you have to have another little drink, make your best friend happy.

—Best thing in the world, Kobza said. Make my friend happy.

—That's it, down it goes, Kepi said. Have another. Make everybody happy.

(Want ever'body happy, Kobza thought he said. From now on ever'body happy.)

—Want Cath'rine be happy, he said.

(Catherine held his hand, said: I'll be happy if you have another drink.)

—First time I ever heard a woman say she'd be happy if a man took another drink, Kepi said. Now, isn't that something? Isn't that some woman? You got to drink to that kind of woman. Have another drink.

—Can't see, can't hear, Kobza said.

—Not going to feel a thing either, old friend, Kepi said. Now one more drink. There. There.

—Fell a thong, Kobza said. Feel a ahhhh.

—Do you feel this? Catherine said.

—Feel happy, Kobza said. Make ever'body happy.

—And this? Do you feel this?

—Happy, Kobza said.

—He's ready, Kepi said. Won't feel a damn thing. Jesus, what a stink.

—Well, look at it, Catherine said. These toes are quite rotten.

—Phew, Kepi said. Itzek, bring the lamp. Is the water ready?

—Ahhhhh, Kobza said.

—That's right, old friend, you're going to lose a bit of a foot. But that's not much to make your friends happy, is it?

—Mmmmm, Kobza said.

—Hold the light right here, Catherine said. Where's Ariz?

—He's coming, Itzek Fogel said. He's sharpening the ax. Here are all the wrappings we could get from the village, good soft homespun stuff.

—The water's hot enough, said Pani Mosinska. But are you sure *you'll* be all right?

—Of course I'll be all right, Catherine said. All right then, stretch him out, hold him down. Put that block under his ankle, Kepi.

—Jesus, Kepi said. I'm glad it's him, not me.

—Happy, Kobza said.

. . . And heard, from a great distance, from among the disappearing stars, a voice announcing: He's out like a light.

> Sleep. Peace.
> The contradictions of memory and dreams.
> Life making all its rules as it went along;
> life and love denied, love promised,
> death bestowed.
> He wanted his sleep dug as deep as a pit.

(You've always treated me as if I were more than a human being, his unloved wife told him. So what did you expect?)

—Love, he said. Peace. Sleep.

(I needed a man, not a congregation, said his unfaithful wife. I'm not a stained-glass window, I'm not made of plaster. Have you ever felt anything for anyone? Can you ever feel anything for a real woman?)

—Ah, he said. Pain.

(It's time you felt something, his unwanted wife told him angrily. What do you expect from a woman, anyway? What do you all expect? It's time you understood that women are people.)

. . . Time, now, to understand, to regret, to exorcise and then to forget, so that a painful past may be severed and buried.

(Perhaps you thought it flattering, said his dead young wife. Perhaps it wasn't anything that you could do anything about, inevitable in a culture where a woman is either a whore or a stained-glass window. But what does your mythology have to do with me? I'm not a product of your imagination.)

—I understand. I'm sorry.

(Well, it's too damn late, his murdered wife told him. You should have thought about it before you turned me into an illusion. You certainly had a lot of time to think about that.)

—Years and years, he said. Years and years.

. . . Time now to spin among stars, to drift through vast spaces, to feel nothing beyond regret at the waste of years, the death of affection. Out of his mind's incandescent haze came the ferocious ticking of his father's collection of clocks. Tic-tock-tic-tock raised to the power of three hundred, beyond the power of endurance, the pulse of his life as a country child, young man in flight from the rigidity of his definitions, a scholarship student and a would-be scholar returning to seek life's simplicities among the peasants with whom he had been raised. The crash and clatter, the calling and the ringing of massed cuckoo clocks had dominated the first two decades of his life.

—Now do you understand? he said. Why I can't bear to look at a watch?

(Hold him down firmly, now, Catherine said. I've got him, Kepi said. I'm going to be sick, said Professor Karolewski.)

. . . Time to consider the part of the father, having considered the part of the son. A whiskered arrogant drunken gentleman married to a peasant and fiddling with clocks, a gentleman turned potato farmer, turned village clockmaker, a praying and exhorting and churchgoing tyrant, willing accomplice to the tyrannies of time. Time to him had been physical, a tangible machine composed of cogs and gears and pulleys and chains and the occasional shrill manufactured bird; he neither could nor would learn anything that had not existed before he was born. How odd it was to note that the Ten Commandments, which provided the sum total of the crazed clockmaker's verities, had ordered the child to honor the parent, but not at all vice versa, that nowhere in the culture except for the folk tale was it possible to hear a child's complaint.

—But still, he said with that clairvoyance that extreme agony can sometimes bestow. It's better to have been weaned on the gruel of neglect than to have had a parent who had loved too well. That way you learn not to take love for granted.

(Liar, said his wife. You took *me* for granted. So what had you learned?)

—I treated you as I was taught a woman should be treated. You were to be a symbol of all the virtues that I knew I lacked.

(People are not symbols, cried his wife. And women are people.)

—I meant no harm, he said. I knew no better then.

(I hope he's drunk enough, Catherine said, and Kepi said: Oh well, we did what we could, he's sure to feel something.)

—I didn't mean to cause you any pain.

(Yes, Catherine said. All right, then. Are you ready, Ariz? I'm ready, Ariz said.)

—And at the end, he said. In that final moment. When I struck to

kill. It wasn't you that I was killing then, do you understand? Can you
believe me? I was killing time.

(All right, then, Catherine said. All right, Ariz. Now.)

—No, he cried as he had cried then, suddenly comprehending.

(No, cried his unbeautiful, unloved, unfaithful murdered wife.)

—Oh, he cried. Oh my God. Oh.

(A clean cut, Kepi said. Bring up that hot iron.)

Looking up. Seeing stars, now fixed and bloody in a scarlet sky. He
smelled Catherine's stream-washed, sun-dried hair. Looking at her, he
knew that he was looking for an end to despair, as he had looked
for it, in women, time and time again, only to find its inevitable
confirmation. Her eyes had crouched in shadows of tarnished bronze,
the hollows under them darkened as if by stunning blows. Her jaw, he
knew by touch, was small and rounded, the bones in her face strongly
curved. The eyes, he knew, woud continue to confuse him for some
time, mute testimony to a life of reversals and illuminated moments
lifted from their context, an endless process of beginnings in which
each fresh catastrophe became no more remarkable, in time, than old
Latin lessons.

He was asleep, he knew, and dreamed that she bathed his face with
wet cloths, that cold wet cloths had been spread about his foot, which
would have to be amputated sometime in the future so that the pain
and the corruption and the memory of pain might be exorcised, and
dreamed that many persons came to look at him and ask about his
health. The classic laments of man—Pain, Hunger, Death, and Solitude—had abated in his mind and body, stunned by alcohol, shock, and
the contents of the night. The art of the survivor, he thought, is survival with half an inch to spare.

Bum, bitty-bum, bum bum, he hummed or perhaps it was someone
else who was humming for him. Night and repletion. Night and solitude. Night and a mind at peace. Sleep. The stars were steady, bright in
their velvet boxes. The moon regarded him with a wide and benign
stare. Professor Karolewski smiled down out of the darkness behind the
stars, belched with drunken dignity, said: And how is your patient,
Madame Surgeon? Catherine murmured something. Ah, said the professor, it was an honor to assist you in the technique which bears your
name . . . Catherine's laugh was clear and surprising.

(I'll sit with him if you're tired, the professor said. But she said: No,
I'm not tired, at least I don't feel tired, I want to sit with him. Oh, said
the professor, is that how it is? That's how it may very well be, Catherine said.)

—What is it about these heroic amputees that fascinates women? It seems that history is always repeating herself.

—Not always, said Catherine.

—As I remember, there was a young man in your life, young Abramowski, wasn't it?

—It was.

—But it isn't now? You and he were going to change the world, as I remember.

—I had a change of heart.

—About the world?

—That would have been a change of mind.

—Yes. Well. History does repeat herself.

—Seldom, Catherine said.

Later, he awoke delirious with pain and fainted very quickly.

Later yet, he awoke, and Catherine said to him: Is it very bad?

—It's the worst yet, he said. You have to cut it off.

—I'll do it later, she said. Try to get some rest.

—You're smiling, he said. What's there to smile about?

—Lots of things, she said.

—Well, this damn foot is hurting like hell. I can feel every toe screaming at me there. You better get somebody to help you cut it off.

—Get some rest, she said. I'll take care of it later.

But he misunderstood or misheard and said, thinking that he was replying to a question: Yes, we'll rest here, it's a good safe place. And then I have to see about getting some food for the people . . .

—You'll think of something, she said.

He said: Yes. I will.

And he slept again.

The night was almost gone the next time he awoke, cold in the blue-gray chill before dawn, with his leg on fire. He wondered, so remotely that it translated to indifference, how much longer he would have to live with any kind of pain. His head, he noted with surprise, was pillowed on softness; it was in Catherine's lap. Her back was set against a tree and her eyes were closed; he lay perfectly still so as not to wake her. He thought of life that would contain a future, thought of her and the innocent moment of the stream bath in which he had surprised her and Esterka; her gaunt ribbed flesh had moved him to tenderness and pity, he could have done murder to avenge what had been done to her. His childhood, suddenly recalled, was not so Gorgonian as to have frozen him into vengeful poses, nor so caustic as to have sent him down the chattering corridors of fantasy and illusion, nor so idyllic as to contradict the lessons of his own life: the tragedy of waste and fragility of affection. The lessons of his parents' lives had taught him only that death wouldn't be able to rob him of the living he had done. But he knew something else. That if you burned high enough (steadily, not fiercely; with affection rather than with anger) then someone would be able to carry a memory of this warmth to their own grave. And if that someone had voice of their own, and was old enough to have judged with fairness, then you may have lived better than you had supposed and more than you had planned. He understood the need of the dying to manage their own fate, to break down lifetimes of restraint in order to communicate affection while there was still time, to die in the time and among the people they had loved. Poremba's death, at first sight wasteful and unnecessary, had made that much clear. To those whom he was leading and who lay around him under the pines and ferns, asleep now or murmuring, time might prove less kind. He heard two of them now (Kukla? Karolewski? One of them, whichever, interchangeable) ask each other on the edge of sleep: But what if, somehow, this war should be lost and we can't return to our lives in Poland? What will you do then? Will you shine shoes in London, sweep stairs in New York, how will you survive? To tell them what he knew would have discouraged them from doing all that they would have to do to guarantee survival. And, more important, it would have awakened Catherine.

He looked at Catherine's child, its pebble eyes open to the reddening night, thought that he would build a cradle for it as soon as he could. He reached out and touched the scaly brow; the dry transparent skin turned into leopard spots under his fingers. The fire had died out and everyone was sleeping.

He looked out into the dark then. Looked out and listened while he thought: Feels like spring, sure enough. He lifted himself from the ground and looked at the Big Dipper, the pitcher from which the Virgin's milk had spilled as she fled with the Infant from the executioners of Herod, according to legend; looked at the North Star, to which the Dipper pointed, the North Star which hung over the Taimyr country, over Poremba's bones; the mourning light which looked down upon a galaxy of camps in which whole nations died. From high overhead he caught the faint honk of Arctic geese beating to nesting grounds.

PART SIX

NINETEEN FORTY-ONE

Mendeltort

DARK STREETS, SPARSELY LIGHTED in the Moscow suburbs; dark trees in flight, a white moon and the beginning of a warm June night.

The black limousine hissed through rain-wet streets, deserted avenues, a leather-coated outrider trapped in white beams of light. Inside: the heavy smell of Balkan tobacco, cut-crystal ashtrays, two red roses in a fluted vase; Szymanski's yellow eyes were attentive. Mendeltort closed his own to rest them for a moment.

—Where are we going this night?

The slight accent on the next to last word was hardly noticeable, even to himself; this night or another, this *dacha* or another, this or another Soviet officer, it made little difference.

—A house, Szymanski said. A pleasant place.

—They've all been pleasant places. Will Zarubin be there?

—I'm not a fortune-teller, Szymanski said. I only make the general's arrangements.

The classic sculptured features of the elegant Russian officer, so unlike anything one was likely to see above the collar of a Soviet military blouse, would tell him nothing, he knew. He kept his own eyes on the glistening wet trees that hurtled past the windows. There was a quarter moon, the air was soft and hushed and the light vaporous, the clouds had formed pyramids and tombstones. Some flower that blooms in June had scented the air, and the night seemed to hold out challenges and the promise of the unexpected. There was a world in torment beyond this Russian evening, armies heaved and splintered. Serbs and Greeks had fallen under German cannon only a month before, and most of civilized Europe lay under Hitler's feet; and now even the Acropolis crouched under the crooked cross. The darkness, then, seemed vaster than this pall that had fallen upon him.

—Would you care for a cigarette?

A packet of Diplomats had appeared in Szymanski's gloved hand.

Mendeltort shook his head, hunted for his pipe in the pockets of his new light summer coat. He felt his teeth clamp like steel traps around the stem; at least they would no longer chatter with the residue of fever.

They were in open country, Moscow had fallen far behind, only the huge umbrella of light suspended over the city in the rain reflected in the driver's rearview mirror. It was one of the cities of his youth, changed beyond recognition and yet essentially unchanging; stunned and hamstrung like an animal in a slaughterhouse, rendered bleak, and yet still Moscow, still theatrical, brooding and gigantic.

The road on which they drove at breakneck speed, their hurtling flight as much a badge of privilege as the black limousine and outrider, had been a dirt track across the old Tverskaya Street of Eastern bazaars. Now it was a broad asphalt ribbon thrown from the Kremlin toward the Leningrad road. The roadside trees appeared to be the same. The warm wet night had not changed. While still in Moscow, the road had been a street lined with large buildings, elaborate balconies, and vaguely historical heads cemented to the cornices, and it had reminded him, unaccountably, of plush settees and brass inkstands, hallmarks of that vanished era from which he had grown. Now these were gone as if their exiled years had crept back in the wet night to find what they had left behind in flight from revolution. Now he was carried at ministerial speed past the abandoned private parks of murdered merchants, past fallen arbors, rustic fakery imported from France and strangled by weeds. The wooden gates yawned open, sagged; the former owners of the parks and the private villas were not even remembered. Coarse, noisy, vulgar, and pretentious (as he remembered them), the parvenu manufacturers of cardboard army boots, mine owners and speculators in railroad stocks (so universally despised even in his days) were buried, scattered to the four benign European winds. The plaster rattled off their shuttered villas of barbaric splendor. In one such villa Mendeltort had spent his unlamented youth.

The night was melancholy, suicidal, its gloomy theatricality unchanged. Unthinking, he reached for a red rose in the fluted vase, caught the sardonic gleam in Szymanski's eyes, knocked out his pipe instead in a crystal ashtray. He was sitting in comfort beside his father's careless murderer and the torturer of Abel and he was suddenly convulsed with the wish to kill. His dead father's children gibbered and pranced and demanded vengeance: Avrum (himself), the decadent Russian princeling who had vanished in the murk of the Revolution; Yuval, the oldest brother, who was no longer Yuval but Jozef Abramowski, a Catholic and a Pole; Mordecai, a bruised and dazed deserter from the Kaiser's armies, coughing at the gallows; Aaron, in flight from his father's visions across the Atlantic. Ruta was dead in childbirth, mangled by a midwife; Ruchla had followed Aaron to Brooklyn, U.S.A., and disappeared in the fire and smoke of a burning sweatshop; Edyta, the youngest and the prettiest of the sisters, ran off with a German. Sarah, the wife of Jakob Mendeltort, who had abandoned another man in Vilno, died of a woman's sadness, finally comprehending what her life had been all about. It was a family that had been less divided than ripped to shreds by the fact of its existence, unraveled by eternal exile, turned inwardly upon itself by the demands of other people's histories, a family of suicides that had stubbornly refused to turn into dust.

The soft, clear voice beside him laughed. —On a night like this a man should either put a bullet in his head or go to bed with a beautiful woman.

—Really? Mendeltort said, and suddenly thought of Abel, who had grown up to his own awful destiny, who had had a girl, who would have said that sort of thing were he there to say it, whom he had missed in Lwów on a night much like this one (except that it was far, far colder, he remembered), whose destruction had taken something vital out of his own vision of himself, and who was never out of his thoughts for long. Wishing that he could break his own rules and demand a favor before his opponents had shown him all their cards, he said in a voice made cold and indifferent by a lifetime of partings and departures: Is my nephew still alive? By the way.

—Is he important to you? the Soviet officer said quickly.

—No. Not important. We're a divided family. I haven't given them a thought for years.

—You're thinking of them now?

—It's that sort of night.

—It's been a dry summer, the Russian remarked. We need the rain. It's as dry between Moscow and the Polish territories as it was in Poland two years ago.

—They called it Hitler weather then, Mendeltort said.

—They still call it that.

—Are you expecting an invasion?

—Who would be stupid enough to invade the Soviet Union? No, there won't be war this year. But we must always be prepared for one.

As if on cue, as though their appearance had been prearranged, hooded blue lights were suddenly flashing on the right, a silent, waiting convoy of army trucks was visible under the trees, half off the road, half on it. The motorcycle outrider turned on a red lamp and a siren wailed, and for a mile or so the limousine and escort flew past line after line of open, flat-back lorries, each lorry burdened with rows of silent soldiers, silent and motionless in the rain, their blankets rolled across their backs, their long and narrow bayonets fixed to their rifles, orderly and mindlessly obedient; row after row of stolid backs, white faces. Szymanski had given them one incurious glance, hummed a few bars of a military song.

—No, not this year, he said, and stared at Mendeltort as though expecting an argument.

—You didn't answer my question about Abel.

—What Abel?

—My nephew, Abel Abramowski.

—I thought it didn't matter about him.

—It doesn't. Tell me anyway.

—I don't know anything new about him. I can make inquiries if it's important to you.

—It's not important, Mendeltort said, and turned to the window.

One mile and then another, and then the trucks were gone. The rain fell steadily. The night was dark and vast and his eyes were blurring. His mouth was sour with anger and his stomach heaved and knotted about its own emptiness, and he was wearily aware of another fruitless day, a difficult day of meetings which decided nothing. The damp night's cold had passed into his bones.

To ask where he was being taken, with whom he would be meeting, whether Zarubin would finally put in an appearance, would only bring a question in answer to his questions, and would tell him nothing. In Russia, things had always happened when they happened and no one asked questions. He was quite sure that he had seen Zarubin anyway, dressed as Death at a masquerade, while he had been roasting in his fever.

Szymanski hummed his song, his eyes fixed on the weaving brown back of the motorcycle rider, a shining figurehead at the tip of the converging headlights. *Yesli zavtra vayna*, the song played every hour through every loudspeaker in the Soviet Union, but he had said that there would be no war.

—Please stop that noise, Mendeltort said suddenly, and Szymanski stared at him in swift bewilderment, then fixed his eyes rigidly ahead. He was no longer humming.

Mendeltort was aware of his foolish pleasure to have annoyed Szymanski.

There had been days, nights, weeks, months, seasons, a winter and a spring. Cold gray walls and carbolic soap. An ancient gray-frocked crone, face of *terra d'ombra*, a blue-eyed turnkey, a scurrying surreptitious little man with a dangling stethoscope. Rubber umbilicus and interchangeable placenta, the fires of a fever. Faces peering, mumbling.

Words falling upon his ear like stones on a coffin. Typhus, pneumonia
. . . And Mendeltort choking back his own words, drowning in his
fever . . . to keep the secret of the names and places which had become
his history (Kiev, 1922; Hamburg, 1933; Allenstein, 1936 . . . the men
of Antonowka, that most secret of Polish Secret Service operations
which trained fighting Jews toward the moment when some future land
of Israel might require their terrible profession . . . Stern's best people
had come from Antonowka, and so had the staff men of the Hagannah,
and so had his own . . .); thinking of Langenfeld, wondering where he
might find his next reliable liaison with a General Staff and a Secret
Service, looking far ahead . . . his next professional machine-gunner,
dynamiter . . . a good man with automatic weapons . . . a young man
he might train as his own inevitable replacement if he could not free
Abel in time to save his body and his mind . . . wiping his mind clean
of all he remembered of how an Action Group was formed, willing his
own unconsciousness, defying the questions (and all the time full of the
alcoholic's craving to spill it all and be rid of it) . . . And now. And
now . . . on the threshold of yet another action, cold as death on a
warm summer evening.

He knew that this time he himself had come closer to extinction than
ever before. He was aware of death as a distinct possibility before he
was ready, sensed the acceleration of his time. The gap between his purpose and its accomplishment narrowed with painful slowness; each of
his devious steps had acquired its own cautious systems, with each he
pitted all of his experience against an overwhelming urge to risk everything in one swift forward leap . . . But patience, carefulness and care,
attention to detail along each step of the way, were the most valuable
pieces of a revolutionist's equipment. So . . . *nitchevo*. No leaps.
Twists and turns. Delays. Introspection, the checks and balances of his
internal systems. A thought for Fallen Heroes: straws cast upon a hurricane or relics for a legend? A Moment of Silence, as in Armistice, and
flowers at the Tomb . . . Each time, the young men he had led died
unheard and he, disappearing, wondered if next time their fall would
make a sound.

Now he was approaching yet another crisis, and prepared to settle accounts with himself. The Last Will and Testament was just about
signed but he was still searching for a beneficiary. He had hoped, indeed he had worked and planned, to keep his vision in the family, had
kept it bright for Abel, but the boy had been imprisoned for too long,
he would be virtually destroyed. He wondered if there were any more
reliable young men, remembered Berg, whom he had left in Warsaw, a
promising young man full of necessary anger; thought of young Traurig,
whom he would see later. Stern had been hanged by a Pilatic decree, a

victim of his own people's machinations. The old professionals had withered, aged, retired. Jabotinsky was selling life insurance now, if such an irony could be imagined. Betar's Begin was not yet ready to kill. Of the young men brought up in the spirit of the Bund and of the Halutz pioneers only a few deserved to come to mind. His own Hargan was shattered, would have to be rebuilt. A brighter beacon had to be lighted for the scattered Nation, and monuments of bones had to be flung into hostile skies, the Nation's night was too bewildering without them. Ah, but the cost, the cost, he cried out to himself. All those young lives.

Once more, Szymanski appeared to have read his thoughts, or perhaps his own dark thoughts had paralled Mendeltort's in the doomed introspective melodrama of the Russian night, and he said softly: A night for witchcraft . . . for ritual murder . . . (Then added, unexpectedly in Polish:) Whistling doesn't help.

—What whistling? Mendeltort said, irritated.

—In the dark.

They were staring into each other's eyes, speaking a common language to which each had been born but which had become foreign to both of them, saying more than could be said in any language, sharing a momentary closeness as profound as that which sometimes binds lovers, and so, in the end, saying nothing that could be understood. They were a feral pair circling about each other and each of them knew it, and each knew that the other knew it too. A thought had passed between them, it had hung suspended like a monstrous flare, then went out. Looking into the Russian officer's un-Russian face, its hard male surfaces drawn over bones as delicate as a woman's, Mendeltort saw something of his own; he saw a soul in hell, for hell is the spirit locked up with no place to go, it is time trapped in nothingness between two states of being; its destiny is death.

The moment passed. Then they were driving at high speed into a narrow alley, its wild grass high among cracked cobblestones, and the limousine had stopped. The house was dark and tall and appeared abandoned, an empty shell cast on the beach of a revolution. But there were silent men standing around it in heavy leather coats and others walked up and down leading large dogs on chains.

Mendeltort got out; Szymanski held the door for him politely but he was quite aware of the ironies that this ritual contained. Several men hurried toward them, then stopped and backed away, having recognized Szymanski.

—What is this place? Mendeltort asked, determined to exorcise the memory of the shared moment.

—A guest house. It's quite pleasant inside.

—Does it also have a pleasant set of cellars?

Szymanski smiled whitely in the uncertain light of torches and head-lights. —*These* cellars, he said, contain wine.

—And who's inside the house?

—Guests, Szymanski said. I told you, it's a guest house.

—And who are these people? Mendeltort waved an arm toward the groups of silent, watchful men (he counted more than a dozen of them) who stood about bareheaded, glistening in wet leather; each held his right hand in his pocket, he noted in passing.

—These? Szymanski looked about as though the question were a dis-appointment. These are my men, what else would they be here?

He walked toward the house and smiled as he heard Szymanski mut-ter and then stifle an obscenity behind his back.

He heard no signal; indeed, he hadn't thought that one would be necessary, other hard eyes would be watching from the house. The heavy wooden doors, studded with black iron, opened from inside as they drew near. Two very large men in black overcoats stepped out and held the doors open. Mendeltort heard the limousine start up and then the motorcycle coughed and stuttered; the sound of their motors dwindled on the Moscow road. Then the doors were closed behind him and Szymanski, and he was standing in the light of a round vestibule, an Italianate rotunda paved with white native marble, and a circular balus-traded staircase, polished and carpetless and chipped, rose at his left and curved into invisible upper floors where he could hear men's voices, the shrill artifice of a woman's laughter, and the "Blue Danube Waltz" played on an old gramophone. More male voices came amid the clatter of cutlery and china from behind a door set in twin marble columns directly before him, and the thick smell of cooked meat and boiled vegetables came from yet another door, ajar and leaking steam under the staircase, and then a flushed and fleshy young woman, with thick yellow braids wrapped around her head, crossed from the one door to the other carrying a porcelain tureen. Her large breasts were loose and bouncing in a drawstring blouse, her legs were white and bare under a thin black skirt, and she threw him a measuring blue-eyed look as she trotted past.

—A guest house? he said.

—Some of our younger guests call it Villa Bliss, Szymanski mur-mured as he led the way up the staircase. Mendeltort followed, said: Am I to say here, then?

—It's possible. I've made a variety of arrangements.

—I'm sure you're very good at making varieties of arrangements.

—Trying to irritate me is a waste of time, Szymanski said coldly.

They ascended toward a dusty chandelier amid simpering plaster cherubs and Napoleonic eagles, past a wry-mouthed bust of Cicero, bunched grapes and grinning fauns, past centaurs and satyrs in pursuit of nymphs through an undergrowth of long brown watermarks; the paint had cracked into trees and branches. Hera (it had to be Hera because of the wheat) was looking for her husband's thunderbolts while fat Danaë spread her legs for a shower of gold, and a tyrannical Victory extended a cheap wreath; and now the "Blue Danube Waltz" had come to an end. The aura was of damp dust and wood rot, and broken drainage pipes, and there were furry scamperings behind the paneling, and dance music (this time the "Tango Miranda") came out of the invisible gramophone.

Then a large upstairs hall shuttered in steel and curtained in brocade; it would have been a sunny morning room in another era. Now a solitary light bulb in a pink cardboard shade cast an anemic light on a parquet floor painted with creosote. Armchairs, overstuffed couches, a dozen young men in odds and ends of uniform, a half dozen middle-aged men in cavalry boots, one elderly thin man who peered myopically into a newspaper, one very young man who cranked the handle of a gramophone. Spanish guitars and moonlight, palm fronds and castanets, a memory, an illusion. Eyes closed, as if to open them would confront him with an empty mirror, a plump balding middle-aged second lieutenant of the Polish Army's Judge Advocate Division pillowed his cheek on the jouncing self of a large woman's breasts and guided her, with the fanatic dedication of a prosecutor, through the intricacies of the Valentino turn.

—Advocate Apfeld, Szymanski said in passing.

A bald fat man looked up expectantly with a buttery smile.

—Father Pudlo, Szymanski said.

—A priest in a whorehouse?

—Guest house. All privately arranged services by the staff are the guests' private business. And yes, a priest, complete with book and candle. No Polish officers' corps would be complete without one.

—Have you a rabbi, then?

—There had been a couple we wanted to invite, but they died. (Then, like a dedicated keeper guiding a provincial tour in a zoological park, he pointed, said:) Captain Pawloski (the elderly thin man got with some difficulty to his feet), retired but anxious to cooperate. Good evening, Captain. That's Lieutenant Hirshner, the tall one, Captain Binder, Captain Kurylenko . . . You'll meet them all before the night is over. Please don't stop to talk to anyone just now or we'll never get out of this room. Our guests become so enthusiastic about a new arrival.

—I've noticed that before, Mendeltort said. Treason makes men lonely.

—Treason? Szymanski said. These are the real Polish patriots. They serve the best future interests of their country.

—They serve their own best interests, and you know it.

—I wouldn't advise you to advertise such views.

Moving his interior game (it was time to move it) Mendeltort said harshly: I think you know very well what I mean. I think we understand each other very well. I don't think I fool you for a minute, you certainly don't fool me. You, me, Zarubin, or these Polish traitors, everyone wants something from everyone else and they pay for it with the appropriate coin. Everything other than that . . . is hot air, a waste of my time.

He couldn't tell whether the Russian had taken his words at face value, his face was averted. But Szymanski did say, with feigned carelessness over his shoulder: Well, they do say it takes one to know one . . . There, by the way, is Captain Feldman, a dentist from Warsaw, so he should be a good one. Lieutenant Grossman is also a dentist, that's him behind the *Izvestia*. Lieutenant Berman is beside him behind the *Krasnaya Zviezda*, we have great hopes for Lieutenant Berman. That one, in the pince-nez, is the poet Haussner, Teodor Haussner, you may have heard of him. He certainly looks as if he recognized you, doesn't he? Hello there, Mr. Haussner. That's Underensign Glowacki cranking the gramophone, and over there, beside the table with the bottles, are Lieutenants Burda, Osobka, Samolubny, and Wasilewski . . . no relation to the poetess Wanda Wasilewska, of course, but equally cooperative. And there is a new face, someone I haven't met.

Emaciated to the point of illness, the man rose, made a sound between a whisper and a cough.

—Hoch it is, then, Szymanski said. Where are you from, Captain?

—Pavelitchev Bor, the man said in a voice that had begun to tremble. Before that, Starobielsk . . . They closed it up . . .

—Yes, we did, didn't we? We repatriated everyone who wanted to leave us, we wouldn't want anyone among us against their will. We're glad to have you here, Captain.

—Glad to be here, Colonel, the man whispered while beads of sweat appeared below his hairline. Very glad . . . to see you again.

—We've met before? Szymanski said sharply.

—In Starobielsk . . . You came to supervise the . . . repatriation . . .

—You are a regular officer, I see?

—Yes, sir. Yes, Colonel. Yes, I am.

—Then we are very glad to have you here with us. We need regular officers for the new Polish Army. Is there anything that I can do for you? Have you had some food?

For the first time a smile appeared on the worn and worried face of the emaciated captain.

—Yes, sir, he whispered. Yes. I have had some food.

They went on, past other men, toward another door.

—Would you like to wait here, with our other guests, or would you like to be alone? If so, there's the library.

—Is there a window in it?

—Why do you need a window?

—To open it, to breathe some fresh air.

—There is a window in the library. There'll be time for you to meet everyone later. The others are downstairs, at dinner, I imagine.

—How many have you here?

—Fifty-two, Szymanski said. Until the fall of France there were only twelve, then there were fifty. Once Paris fell, twelve other Polish officers suddenly remembered their German origins, and so we sent ten of them to the German Army. Two decided that they would rather stay with us. So there are fifty-two.

—And are you really going to form a new Polish Army?

—I've every reason to believe it, Szymanski said softly. And this is the library.

He turned on the light.

Again the pale solitary light bulb, again the pink shade that, in that room, looked tragically obscene, like a child whore posturing in a marketplace. A small room, then, claustrophobic. Not the vaulted chamber piled to the ceiling with leather-bound volumes which the melancholy night and his own past had led him to expect. There was one shelf of half a dozen volumes of dubious authorship, the collected literary output of J. Stalin; one Karl Marx bound, like holy writ, in black imitation leather with gold lettering; one Russian-Polish dictionary of pre-Revolutionary vintage, huge stacks of newspapers, back issues of *Pravda* and *Izvestia*, carrying the same message. There was a smeared blackboard and a low divan. A bootless, coatless middle-aged man slept there, sprawled as though shot; a cigarette had burned to a long curving ash between his nerveless fingers.

Szymanski walked softly to the couch, looked at the sleeping man as if to check whether he still breathed, whispered: Berling. Try not to wake him. He's been having nightmares.

—Now, why would he have nightmares? Mendeltort voiced contempt that he could not resist and instantly regretted.

Szymanski seemed not to have heard him and looked, for a moment, visibly concerned.

—He is the senior officer among them (a backward flick of his head categorized the others in the house). He may be the future commander of our Polish corps. You and he may have a lot to do with each other.

Despite himself, feeling a sudden onrush of fatigue and the beginning of that bodily tremor that his illness left him, Mendeltort heard himself ask: Out of the thousands of Polish officers in your hands, is that the best you were able to get?

Instantly defensive, as though a child or a protégé were threatened, the Russian snapped: He's an experienced officer. A regular, staff-trained. He could command a brigade without any trouble. With some experienced people of our own behind him, he could look good enough to command an army. He may end up by doing for his people what you'll do for yours. And since you ask, yes, he is the only field-grade officer whom we were able to get.

The sleeping man muttered, groaned, turned over; his eyelids fluttered like a dreaming dog's. In the pale lamplight, his skin resembled wet cardboard, stained and warped. His interior landscapes would be sunless, brown-grassed, leafless, without birds.

Szymanski nodded, said: I'll come for you in an hour or so if the general arrives.

—And if he doesn't?

—Then we'll wait. You've waited before.

—Do I have a choice?

—No one has a choice about anything, Szymanski said, and left.

Beyond the window: gray diagonals of rain upon a dead lawn, weeds and shrubs long returned to wildness. Mendeltort sighed and said to his reflection: Of course I have a choice, I have always had one, if not two. His eyes blurred again and his nostrils filled with an acrid stench. Doubt, he decided coldly, fear; not physical fear in the face of danger, but fear of the price his fearlessness exacted. He had learned how to cope with doubt, self-doubt to be specific, early in his career which, year by year, carried him to his inevitable end. This, he both knew and feared, could very well be useless and, as such, worthless to everyone other than his enemies, of whom there were legions. He feared that he would prove useful to his enemies, who would rejoice in his fall no matter what else happened.

And suddenly, it was always sudden, Mendeltort's knees had begun to tremble, and flecks of whiteness glittered at the edge of vision. He was still far from well, the ceilings still revolved for him when he awoke, and his sleep was tortured by a nightmare no less oppressive than that of the Polish colonel on the leather couch. The dream was one of his own dead face behind glass and a procession of other faces which peered into it. None of his night visitors were people he had known, none were of his race, his kind, a part of his being, none shared either his roots or his destination; all were his enemies, thankful that he was dead. In his glass coffin he was scorched by their terrible euphoria. He had been the last of his kind, threatening to their peace of mind and hopes for themselves; each night they stood in patient lines before his catafalque to reassure themselves, again and again, that he was finally dead. He had not found a replacement for himself; they could go home and sleep without nightmares.

He thought once more of Traurig, who was waiting for him along with Meyer at his hotel in Moscow, thought of Meyer alone and planned to tell him scornfully, for Traurig's benefit: You understand history as profoundly as chickens understand soup. But it's just as possible that we're both right, that is to say, both wrong.

The air in the small room was foul with sweated bodies, chalk dust, old tobacco fumes, and an acrid smell. Could that be cowardice? he asked the sleeping Polish colonel, who groaned in reply. Did treason smell like wet dogs? Ah . . . but now he was feeling definitely ill, light-headed and breathless. Only the weight of his boots, he was sure, kept him on the ground. He was hearing birds' wings, a thick rush of air, and struggled with the wired double windows to open them so that he could breathe. At any moment, he was sure, he might ascend, float free of the floor and so on out into the graying Russian night where the rain had ended. His ears were full of harsh cries, the complaint of widows, the keening of mothers at mass funerals, the white finality of exploding bombs. Battle, murder, and sudden death: he had had them all. Follies there had been. Temptations, cruelty, lies; once a fool's paradise and often a fool's hell. But there were other things, as there must always be, he told his reflection in preparation for what he'd tell Traurig. Not even all that we have done was destiny, young man, not entirely. There must always be more. There could be neither climax nor anticlimax in a life lived at its greatest speed, in the cold upper airs of dedication to a principle. A full life was made up of everything that life had to offer; it was complete, taking everything without fear and giving without favor, and wherever it ended it would always be whole. Everything that a man could do must enrich his life, and for everything that he didn't do his life must be poorer.

This time, instead of leading them to death, he would use his cunning and the vast resources of an enemy to assemble, train, and arm his modern Sicarii, the terrible swift sword. Events were not yet able to suggest how his armed thousands were to make their way to their desert battlefields, but his faith in his cause was boundless, he believed in the future; the Russian song about a coming war was a prophecy, of that he was sure. In the chaos of Russia at war, all things could be possible. And, he confided to his grim reflection, that final and inevitable step in his own destiny as a Jew who fought, a Jew who could kill, would finally bring him to its own conclusion at the wall of execution morning. The legacy of reasoned violence had been his spendthrift inheritance. He had not wasted much of it, held it in trust for Abel as his birthright, would give it to another now that Abel had been taken from him. He thought of Abel as a fallen soldier of a revolution, to be remembered without tears, and he wished that he could make to Abel the last gift that one professional revolutionist can make to another: a clean swift death rather than capture and slow one; but even that munificence was out of his hands.

He heard the soft hiss of his own breath cautiously released. Berling snored and muttered and cried out. Mendeltort stared out of a graying window, saw himself derided by his own reflection, smiled, measured his contempt for death and for dying, felt his tight skin stretch under his beard. How generous of you, his mouth mocked; what a gift you offer. He shrugged. Even accidental generosity was better than nothing.

The sickly light bulb in its flyblown shade also seemed to mock him, reminding him of the artificial suns of Lubyanka which, even now, would be tormenting Abel. Abel and Langenfeld were the two men whom he would demand that night from Zarubin, if this were to be the night to make such demands. The sleeping Pole looked desolate in that anemic light, the hollows burned deep and brown under his twitching eyelids. What price for his own vision of his country had he been willing to pay? And suddenly the room and all its shabby contents, inanimate or human, were sickening to him. Mendeltort turned off the light.

Hours had passed, it seemed, since he had been brought to this refuge for traitors and opportunists. The nervous night would soon be coming to an end. Sunrise in these latitudes would come after four at this time of the year. The house was silent, the dances were over, its guests were mumbling in their sleep; and listening to the hushed whisper of a cold morning breeze among the trees outside, he was conscious only of a dim and distant pulse that seemed to come out of the Russian soil, a fluttering of great wings beyond the horizon, and a grumbling stillness in the west. That, unlike the eastern rim of this awakening continent, still lay in darkness.

. Below his open window he heard footsteps on wet grass, then watched a car arriving.

. . . Listened to Berling sobbing in his sleep, muttering commands on the sprung divan.

. . . Turned around, looked through the reddening light at this former officer of Jozef Pilsudski, a skilled and brave officer with a social conscience who had become a traitor to his country, saw not a man but a generation which had been defeated over and over in a war as obscure as it had been endless; felt a touch of unaccustomed pity (he who had trained himself to be without pity) for dead dreamers of an implausible ideal whose anger and suspicion could turn so easily inward upon themselves.

He hunted in his pockets for his pipe, tobacco, and a match. He had long learned to flow with the unexpected, adjusting progress in midstep and computing all his possibilities before they appeared. Even his illness and delay in his carefully plotted meeting with Zarubin had turned to advantage. Time was his friend at the moment, he was in no hurry without a successor, and the mysterious Russian had given him time.

. . . Slowly, slowly, he muttered to himself, remembering the proverbs. Only a fool hurries to an execution until he knows who is being hanged.

. . . I shall not die today, perhaps not tomorrow, Mendeltort whispered to his own reflection in the blue-gray window of a Russian dawn. I shall be dead for others but I won't know anything about it. If death is not part of my reality can I say that it exists for me? An immortality of a kind can be achieved through an adequate replacement.

Outside, a streak of scarlet had appeared at the edge of the east, and a long drum roll of thunder sounded in the west. Thunder? It seemed more like some sort of an announcement. The sky was clearing, soon the sun would rise and the last of the night clouds would be driven north, the wind was brisk and cool and the air was fresh. It smelled of wet bark and leaves and refreshed soil, and there was a muttering of motors on the invisible highway and a rooster crowed. He took deep dizziness had abated.

The lines were driven deep past the corners of Szymanski's mouth. His eyes were slitted, entrenched behind blue-shadowed moats of a sleepless night, and he had not shaved. A line, something that Langenfeld had told him many years earlier in an ironic moment of an introduction to a powerful man, who had no reason to love him but who needed him, rose lazily from the depths of Mendeltort's memory. A soldier shaves twice a day, Langenfeld had said, a gentleman is always clean-shaven. (The powerful man had worn an enormous mustache.) Mendeltort fingered his beard as Szymanski said: Come quickly.

—He's here, then?

—He's here.

—Flew in on his broom, did he?

Szymanski said nothing. He led the way in silence through the deserted morning room, the dead stale air, the litter of filled ashtrays and abandoned newspapers. Somewhere in the depth of the house a woman was uttering rhythmic cries of artificial joy.

—In here.

Szymanski stepped aside then followed Mendeltort into a small office. The light was pale blue, a lantern was hissing, a lean old man rose from behind a table, extended a hand. His eyes were hooded under lids that seemed to be sinking under a great weight.

—Welcome, he said. Sit down.

It seemed to Mendeltort that he had always known what it would be like to meet the Hereditary Enemy face to face, the substance of his secret dreams of power over the lives of others, that unacknowledged part of himself that was the stuff of nightmares. Nothing that he had ever done had mirrored this moment, nor promised quite so much, nor offered such a certainty of success, but he knew that the rustling voice and hooded eyes brilliant with mad visions had been a part of his reality throughout his terrible career.

Zarubin sighed as though a long and difficult journey had come to an end and Mendeltort fought an overwhelming desire to laugh. The lantern hissed, the thunder rolled and grumbled in the western sky. He felt that peacefulness that comes with certainty. The Russian had leaned forward in his chair, balanced the point of his chin on hands clasped as though he were about to pray, regarded him quietly.

. . . Once more that distant booming then, made special by a particular definition. Szymanski stood like a statue behind the general's chair, his eyes fixed rigidly ahead.

—Summer thunder? Mendeltort suggested, aware that contempt for any enemy was suicidal business; yet he'd allow himself a moment of contempt.

The Russian nodded slowly to himself, his eyes half closed as though he had removed himself by continents and eons from the small cold room where the distant booming, muted by the miles, nudged the morning air. Then he said softly: They say this has been the dryest summer in living memory. But then they're always saying things like that, as though a living memory denoted something particularly long . . . For many men I've known, it had a way of ending practically before it had begun.

Mendeltort also nodded, found his tobacco pouch and loaded his pipe. He noted with amusement how swiftly Szymanski moved forward with a match. Neither the servant nor his master were to be taken lightly; the luxury of contempt had to be put aside.

—So, said Zarubin. We're finally sitting down together. I regret that we couldn't meet sooner. But none of us dispose of our own time entirely.

—Not even you, General? Mendeltort said.

—I least of all. My masters are events. My longevity, if that's what you wish to call it, has been determined solely by my willingness to obey *that* authority. You understand that need quite as well as I. But in the meantime, before either of us is a chapter in a history book, would you like some tea?

As though this were a prearranged signal (which, Mendeltort supposed, it was) Szymanski was immediately in motion, leaving the room and closing the door firmly behind himself, and Zarubin was smiling with apparent candor.

—Some things are best said without a witness, no matter how loyal, and that too has much to do with that longevity I've mentioned. Things don't change much over the centuries here, you know; we still have royal courts with kings and jesters and courtiers and the court magician and the occasional knave. Why don't you pour us both something better than tea? You'll take a vodka?

—Gladly.

Mendeltort poured Finnish vodka into metal cups.

—*L'chaim*, he said.

—You drink to life? Zarubin said, amused.

—I've never had anything else in mind.

—I have, Zarubin said. Frequently. There have been some difficult decisions, some moments when even I had fallen prey to the luxury of feeling. As a Russian, I can hardly be expected not to fall occasionally into some sentimental pit, it's something of a national disease. But reason has never failed to reassert itself in time.

—So I have always found, Mendeltort agreed.

—I know. That's why we're talking here, you and I. Small petty men are ruled by passions, principles of the moment, a poetic longing for perfection. The truly great men of this world operate on levels far beyond the possibility of feeling. To such men as we, life is of small importance. We know that the soil needs to be enriched from time to time so that a new reality may take root and grow.

Mendeltort had allowed his pipe to go out and now took his time to find his matches and light up again: a time in which to judge how much of what he heard was said for effect and how much set the stage for the meeting's purpose. The balance was about even, he decided. He would continue to bide his own time. He had no illusions about Zarubin's candor and felt again a quickening in his pulse that not even all his years of conspiracy could assuage at the edge of action. He watched the Russian's hooded eyes; power and suspicion were the twin mirrors of that particular soul. Fear was his servant, not his master here, but he would never speak a truth if a lie would serve. Lies, half-truths, veiled threats, temptations. It had been so in Russia since Mendeltort could remember; and yes, the man was right: centuries passed through Russia like tourists on a transit visa, leaving nothing.

The curtains billowed and the blue-gray air rushed in, cold as broken ice. A pit seemed to open, he moved to its edge; he fell into the residue of history whose roots lie in massacre, descending mindless as a feather into Babylon and Nineveh, Tyre and Caesarea, and through the gates of Gehenna into the pitiless inferno of the Judaean hills. His city crouched there like a lion in the sun: watchful, vindictive, and ready to kill; the land, drained of color under its shifting shroud, seemed sinister and dead. Once more his heart beat up, he felt the start of tremor in his upper arm and he tasted ashes. In speaking with Zarubin, he would be careful to suppress the only truth that mattered to him, as he had done throughout his life from the moment of his role's first discovery—that contrary thought twenty years before, a moment of capture in a long-forgotten war, when Langenfeld had shown him the lie of the creed that Mendeltort had accepted as an absolute. That moment's sudden understanding of his truth had struck him like a bullet, destroying one complete identity to begin another. Yes, something had to die so that something else could take root and begin to grow. He would lie, he knew, yet in that lie would be more truth than most men spoke in a confessional.

The truth he would be careful to conceal was the tawny city of his imagination, the capital of an empire bounded by the Nile and the Euphrates; no lesser vision was worth his nation's nightmare. Jerusalem, which one may not forget! Pitched in splendid defiance of survival among arid brown hills that rolled in molten ridges against a lead-blue sky, she was a home for ruthless emotions. Hatred and arrogance were her historic truth. And pride above all. If she had not been born of volcanic lava she would have sprung from the fire in men's minds. All the hardness in the rock, and the smoldering fires that had flowed to form it, had made his city, her people, as himself.

The dry voice rustled, but he heard another. Dead generations mourned in solitude for the palace that lay desolate, the Temple that had been destroyed, the walls that were overthrown, and for their own departed majesty . . . The windblown curtains had bared the open window and he focused his eyes on the sun, perched for that moment in the mists of the eastern horizon: an orange bird held briefly in a cage of trees before flight.

Zarubin talked of passion as though it were a terminal disease and, for a moment, Mendeltort felt unmanned.

—Men who are ruled by passion fall victim to passion, the rustling voice went on. Fulfillment in a new reality is possible only when passion is extinguished.

Believing quite the opposite, Mendeltort nodded, said: None of this is new.

—So let me tell you something so new that it hasn't happened. Let me play the prophet, it's a role I particularly enjoy as the years pass. I've searched for you as long as I have because I always search for people of your kind. Sometimes I need them, sometimes I only want to make sure that no one else can use them, often the decision depends on the man himself. I obey the authority of events but, like all good servants, I've learned to anticipate the wishes of my masters. And I believe in coincidences, in the convergence of opposite ideas at a particular moment when both sides profit by cooperation. Both you and I understand the providential nature of alliances. And we prepare for things that may never happen as though they were already recorded in history so that when events issue their commands we may move without a moment's hesitation.

At the sideboard, his back to Zarubin, a brief thin smile was luxury enough. The muted thunder went on drumming in the west.

—When does the prophecy begin?

—Shortly, shortly. But first another toast?

—To the providential nature of alliances? Mendeltort suggested.

—To the fulfillment of your dream, Zarubin said, and smiled remotely into the darkest corner of the room.

—And what is your dream?

—I don't dream, Zarubin said softly. I obey. I accept. I consent. I aid others to rise above themselves whether or not they know it. Occasionally I look into the future so that I may understand the paradox of the present. At this moment I am anticipating an event that may not take place for a hundred years, a new empire's gratitude for the help given to a great man in the realization of his dream.

—You can count on the gratitude of the unborn?

—I've never had any trouble doing that. All men buy future gratitude whenever they can. A sense of obligation distorts vision, rearranges facts, and allows forgiveness.

The massive thunder in the west made the small room mournful with prophetic echoes. Zarubin rose to close the window and to secure the curtain.

—With the curtains closed it is sometimes possible to forget the present, turn your back on the future, and face the past with hope and confidence, he said, then sat laughing quietly.

From the highway came the roar of motors driven at high speed, the clatter of hauled heavy weaponry. Mendeltort watched and listened. That freedom which he had sought so vehemently, with such terrible risk and effort and carelessness about his own existence, had (for all its passion) no possible end in tangible reality; as yet there was no way to transfer his dream beyond Russia's borders, at which point the dream became worthless.

—State your terms, he said.

—So soon? Zarubin said, still laughing. So abruptly?

—If you weren't ready to give me what I want, we wouldn't be talking.

—So be it, then. My terms are gratitude, recognition of my role.

—In a hundred years?

—It is a hundred years after an event that histories are written. There may be also a more immediate future to consider. Events have not revealed themselves entirely, but something has begun to happen. As I said, I like to anticipate events.

—I pay in kind, said Mendeltort. Good for good and evil for evil. If you give me help when I need it, I'll pull you out of whatever chaos threatens to engulf you. If you refute my need, I'll damn you to hell once my hell is over.

—Agreed. You'll have what you want.

Now Abel could be freed, yet he would not allow a personal matter to intrude on his public cause. Sentiment could have no place in a life such as his.

—The first man I want delivered on my doorstep is Maks Langenfeld, Mendeltort said.

Suddenly impatient, the Russian waved his arm, said angrily: Don't bother me with detail. I've never heard of any Langenfeld. Let Szymanski look for him if he's to be found.

Then, reasonably: Wouldn't you rather have your nephew, anyway?

—You'll keep him for a hostage.

—I'm answerable to others in the Kremlin, the Russian explained. A hostage is expected. And for the moment, you'll have to take Meyer. It will make your operation seem less questionable. It's important that you draw no undue attention to what you are doing.

Mendeltort nodded coldly. —I accept.

—I had no doubt that you would. I know you'll be discreet, these are nervous times. With Meyer on your staff you can operate within an acceptable framework, as something that belongs to us. Make your arrangements with Szymanski for anything you need. Now, do we have anything else to discuss at this moment?

—An agreement in principle is enough for now.

—Is it a bargain, then?

—Did you ever doubt it?

—Even I can't foresee every possibility.

—It's a bargain.

Well then, Zarubin said, and raised his cup. To life? To your success?

—It's the most reasonable alternative to the other thing, Mendeltort said.

Zarubin nodded. The conference was over. Mendeltort sat in silence. He drank Finnish vodka and smoked his Russian pipe. He listened to the growling dawn which had begun to quiver in the west. I have been here before, he thought, and asked himself why he had always found those words so profoundly moving. He had no answer, any more than he needed answers to those questions that still had to be asked. Something had happened. Now something else would happen. There was no need to answer questions now, it was enough to know that a beginning could be made.

There was no ministerial limousine for the return to Moscow, no outrider, roses, or cut-crystal ashtrays. The car was an ugly black copy of an American Ford, its rear seat piled to the roof with briefcases, files, and cardboard boxes tied with packing twine. They both sat in the front seat and Szymanski drove. Despite his sleepless night Mendeltort was wide awake. The fields were empty, steaming, gray; the trees were without birds; they met no one and nothing on the road, which unfolded before them with a monotonous sameness that made Mendeltort think that they were standing still and that it was the road, a black conveyor belt, that was in motion and carried them toward the maw of some huge machine. In the pale dawn light the road's mystery was gone, no vengeful shadows clamored to be heard.

Then they were driving into a gray and silent Moscow, still bare of early-morning crowds, but Mendeltort noted more than the usual number of police patrolling the streets. Outside the National Hotel, Szymanski braked hard and stopped. And then, for some moments, they sat quietly in the small square with the Kremlin on its other side, and Mendeltort again remarked on the Kremlin's special personality. Somber, religious, and hysterical, it was purely Moscow. St. Petersburg had been somnolent, reserved, European, but it had been merely Old Europe with German veneer which whole generations of Holstein-Gottorps, masquerading as Romanovs, had imposed on Russia. It was as foreign to the country as drawing-room French. The icy logic of Lenin had seen to it that his brutal and humorless revolution returned the capital to the city of the Ivans. On his right he recognized a neoclassical façade: the fine old riding school of his aristocratic youth, now the Kremlin garage. Facing him across the square was a red-brick building, Byzantine, unremembered, but now a museum. Then the pavement widened into a vast rectangle containing the crenellated fortress wall.

Mendeltort broke the silence then, said: Something has happened, hasn't it? What is it?

Szymanski said nothing. Looking at him sideways, Mendeltort saw anger give way to confusion and remarked again on how easily the self-confidence of these practitioners of terror could be shaken by events beyond their control. Then the Russian officer seemed to draw himself together and said with difficulty: The situation is still . . . unclear. But don't set one foot outside this hotel. When I come looking for you we might be in a hurry.

—I'll be here.

He got out and stood on the sidewalk until Szymanski's car had vanished in the entry port set into the fortress wall. At the edge of vision quivered a mass of domes, large and small, plain and spiraling. Some looked like cut crystal, others like folds in a robe. There was no sense here of European balance and measure; the mood was wholly Eastern and barbaric. The rising sun threw streaks of crimson on the gilded turbans of Vasilyi Blazennyi Cathedral.

He touched a finger to his cap as he passed the old woman who swept the sidewalk in front of the hotel each morning, knowing that she, like everyone else employed by the hotel, was an NKVD informer. She cackled and grinned. She leaned on her broom and watched him until he disappeared in the hotel's doorway. He went to his room. Meyer was sleeping on his bed; Traurig awoke in an old armchair when Mendeltort came in. He went to the window and opened it wide but he could hear no unusual sounds which could explain anything. The square was quieter than on an ordinary morning.

Lenin's tomb was invisible from where he looked toward it, hidden under scaffolding, but the lines of pilgrims were already forming. He heard distant music, the massed bands of an approaching Red Square celebration. A new day, an unusual day was beginning, part of the long and patient procession of days which inched along toward their fulfillment, that explosive fragment of a moment in which their purpose would become accomplished.

In the red morning light the square was changing colors, and suddenly the loudspeaker on the Kremlin wall began to play the "Internationale." *Arise, arise.* To what? From what? He wondered why this music could no longer stir him. Why, it had a soothing quality. The music came as a refrain repeated by the clocks of a medieval castle; it was no longer the voice of a revolution but a chant of a barbaric history.

Below his windows, workmen were hoisting transparencies and posters on a nearby wall. Expecting the usual political faces, he paid them small attention, then noticed something new. White letters were limp on scarlet cloth, and Soviet soldiers charged an invisible enemy on canvas and paper, and a medieval knight (a prince, a saint of a rejected church, Alexander Nevsky) extended his sword. The cold morning air seemed to thicken, the unchangeable historic continuity of this most Asiatic of European capitals mocked any possibility of a lasting change. The riding academy may become a garage but the structure continued under another name, and Mendeltort wondered if change would always be superficial, so that the sacrifice of treasure and young lives would, in the end, invariably prove a waste.

He made a sound he didn't mean to make, a muttered complaint about the permanence of darkness, and Traurig coughed artificially and asked: Shall I turn on the light?

—What?

—The light, Traurig said. Shall I turn it on?

—No, Mendeltort said. You'll wake Meyer.

—Is that possible?

Mendeltort sighed, his chest suddenly constricted. He turned to face the young man and looked him in the eyes. —Turn it on, then.

. . . If there is one thing that I can teach him, he said to himself, it's that life is everything that can't be done twice, and human dignity is to owe nothing to anyone, either as love or as hatred, having paid for everything in full.

And *Thou will give them hardness of heart, Thy curse unto them. Thou will pursue them in anger, and destroy them, from under the heavens of the Lord.*

Traurig was watching him, quiet as his own shadow. His hands were pressed against the seams of his thick Russian breeches. He was leaning forward, at attention. He had thrown off his revolutionary leather as though it were a discredited idea and now looked unarmored. His smashed flat nose, caved-in cheek, hooded eyes hidden in dark sockets were a mask. Here was another young Jew asking for directions to Golgotha. Soon, very soon (Mendeltort thought) he would be ready for the path that leads to the wall. Someone would hang him or shoot him in due time but, in the meantime, which was the only time he had to consider, there was the swift bleak but exhilarating journey of the new

Sicarii, to live with an intensity no Meyer could inspire for as long as the boy's life was necessary. Mendeltort knew that he could train this ready replacement, he had learned how to plant the seeds of disaffection. What mattered now was to fuel the young man's dissatisfaction with his state of being, heighten his awareness of other possibilities; the anger, that precious necessary anger, was there anyway, and that was proof of the intelligence that Mendeltort demanded, and he silently blessed the Hereditary Enemy for creating such abundant quantities of necessary anger. The flesh on the young man's narrow skull was meager, and Mendeltort was conscious of the skull it contained like an ancient bronze wrapped in tissue paper.

Young Traurig coughed then, as if to draw attention to himself, a self-conscious reminder of Mendeltort's own youth bereft of direction, and he smiled, reflecting. This silent lean young man brought to mind the fierce Betar activists of Menachem Begin, but had he grown enough to inherit an imperial dream? Or would he too, after liberation, settle for a plucked chicken of a state, a Palestinian sandbox? And was he ready to learn the final lesson of the homeless terrorist; to fight and kill one day, to rescue the next, to sin one day and to do something heroic the next . . . ?

So may a young man's earlier transgressions be forgiven, he muttered into his reflection in the Russian mirror, thinking of all the old aristocratic mirrors, of ballrooms and boudoirs which a revolution had transformed into committee rooms, interrogation chambers, warehouses, and stables. Feeling again like a free traveler in time, moving backward through the years toward his beginnings, he glanced back, saw Traurig, nodded, saw the young man straighten in his chair as if expecting a command.

Yes, Mendeltort thought. This one has learned how to watch and listen. He has the gift of stillness. He will do.

—How old are you? he asked.

—Twenty, Traurig said.

—Are you sure about that?

—I'll be twenty soon.

—How soon?

—In two years, the boy said, and Mendeltort snorted with contempt. The boy said angrily: I've been a man for a lot longer than that!

—Were you in the Army? No? But if you weren't a deserter why did that officer crack you on the head?

—Who knows why? Traurig asked bitterly. He did it, that's all. He didn't take the time to explain.

—But you were dressed up in a tank driver's leather coat, army boots . . . Where did you get your costume?

—Took it all off a corpse, Traurig said.

Mendeltort knew that he was asking too much and too quickly, not saying enough. The young man struggled to keep up with him, tense under the pressure. He would be solemn, had been diffident, would probably become cruel before the night was over. The young man tried too hard to pretend that he was a killer, and Mendeltort was suddenly of two minds about him. Simple, as an ax falling, the question appeared: Did the young fool have any idea of what was in store for him? It was like watching a child skip and hop on the rim of an open hearth.

He sighed, shrugged, said:

—Where are you from, anyway?

Sullen, Traurig said: I come from my mother.

—Where were you born, then?

—In my father's house.

—What do you want out of life?

—I haven't had enough of it to find out!

—What work can you do?

Injured, the young man said: I can shoe a horse, I can steal one . . .

—If you can also work like a horse, eat like a bird, and sleep with your eyes open, you may live long enough to see a country of your own.

The young man stared and then, miraculously, he laughed. Their eyes met. Traurig's were smaller, harder, fixed on Mendeltort with sudden confidence as though he had already weighed all his alternatives, reviewed his experience, and could be condescending to all former gods.

—I'll learn, Traurig said.

Mendeltort nodded, said, to himself as much as to the young man who stood at attention before him: So be it. (And to himself alone, he added silently: Let it be Traurig if it can't be Abel; we are still less a Nation than a family, anyway.)

The young man released breath, smiled. Slowly, as though to assert a status to which he had not yet become accustomed, he put his hands in his pockets, closed his eyes, raised his chin, and leaned against the wall. His shadow sloped behind him like sand in an hourglass which had almost run out.

The sunrise was brilliant then, in scarlet and gold, and the mist rising from the Moskva River shone with a pale opalescent light, but the room was still dark. The towers were brooding and intense on the Kremlin wall, dark as sacrifice. Their shadow had the quality of a discarded life from which he had barely escaped. Mendeltort drew the curtains to shut out the light.

Then Meyer snored, groaned, gagged, as though a nightmare had filled his throat with bile, and awoke.

—What time is it? he said. Ah, you're back, are you? Did you see Zarubin? What did he say?

—I didn't see him, Mendeltort said carefully.

Traurig shrugged and slumped into his chair, crossed his arms.

—Dreams, God, how I hate dreams, Meyer said, then peered around suspiciously. What's been going on here? he demanded. What have you been doing?

—Talking, Traurig said.

—Talking? It's Mendeltort who's been doing all the talking, I bet. Telling his fairy tales, his damned lies.

Mendeltort smiled, said coldly: The curious part about speaking the truth is that nobody believes it.

—I believe it, Traurig said, and blushed suddenly.

—You believe it? Meyer said. You? Oh, you poor damn fool!

—I may have been a fool once, Traurig said bitterly to Meyer. I'm not one any more. You're the fool here, old man.

—Old man? Meyer said.

His mouth closed, then opened. During the past months he had grown an enormous military mustache, and now he grasped it with both hands, defensively, as though Traurig's contempt for him were a threat to shave it forcibly. —You believe him, then? Don't you know that he'll go to any length to corrupt your thinking? Don't you know who he is, how he makes his living, what he does to people? He is a plague, a killer, a destroyer. He offers empty visions without substance. I've heard him before. He is dangerous, Traurig.

—Not to me, he isn't, the boy said, and spat carefully at the floor.

—Oh, you fool, Meyer cried as though struck and wounded. Have you been blind, all this time, to everything I've shown you?

—No, Traurig said. But you've shown me nothing I wanted to see.

—What is it, then, that you think you want to see, you pitiful child?

—Freedom, Traurig said. A country of my own.

—Freedom isn't something you write on a wall, Meyer said in a voice that trembled and began to quaver. It isn't something you shout into the teeth of a firing squad. It's a business, boy, just like any other, it starts with accounting . . . !

—We are at war, Mendeltort said quietly. Walls, firing squads, rhetoric, and slogans are a part of that.

—So become a poet, why don't you? With *you* war is a permanent condition, because the moment that the killing stops you'll cease to exist! What kind of future is that for anyone? What do you really offer except a hangman's noose?

—Whatever it is, it's more than talk, Traurig said.

—I'd rather talk than be killed, Meyer said. But you are ready to accept his invitation to your own funeral! Listen to me before it's too late, boy. Didn't your father teach you anything?

—My father fed me ignorance for breakfast and proverbs for supper, Traurig muttered then.

In the harsh white light of the single light bulb that dangled from the ceiling, their faces were gaunt, with a bluish convict look, but their eyes (Mendeltort noted, without feeling) were bright, unnaturally gleaming.

—Meyer is right, you know, Mendeltort said to Traurig. You're not being invited to an entertainment.

—I know, Traurig said.

—Are you sure you know? Have you ever seen a bomb go off in a crowded restaurant? Shattered bone, ripped eyes, veined meat, and the other filth . . . you should have no illusions about that.

—I have no illusions.

—Then you are unique among mankind, Meyer cried. Oh, you poor young fool.

Traurig shrugged, looked downward, muttered: I don't think you have to like a war to fight in it, there just has to be something you like even less . . .

—Oh, for God's sake, Meyer said. Not another one. What does romanticism have to do with us? Honorable romantics have been murdering Jews for centuries. Can't you see that this Palestinian empire of his is going to be the world's biggest ashtray?

—At least it'll be ours, Traurig said.

—Ours, theirs . . . Listen to me before it's too late. Do you think a hundred million Arabs are going to cheer while you are stealing their own country from them? Do you think the English are as benign as their propaganda makes them out to be? You try it and you'll have war as a way of life for unborn generations. In Poland, we won't have to fight for anything, it'll be ours for the taking. We have a functioning state, a historical tradition ready and waiting for us if we can only seize control of our own lives. We are Europeans, our home is in Europe. And we don't have to die for it either, don't you see? All that we have to do is pick up our baggage and move in.

—No, Traurig said, fingering his scars. We have to move out.

The light bulb dimmed, glowed a sudden orange, the normal color of a Moscow morning, then it flickered out. Meyer cursed in Russian, lit a match, and demanded a candle. Traurig got up, pulled his suitcase from under the sofa, rummaged in it. There was a black shirt, loose socks, a garlic sausage wrapped in an old *Izvestia*, a thin book (*Questions of Leninism* by J. Stalin) and a thick one (*Ali Baba and the Forty Thieves*), a pair of Polish cavalry officer's riding pants with leather inserts on the inner thigh, a spool of brown thread and a cork with a darning needle stuck in it, a packet of letters, a soiled copy of the Soviet Penal Code, a religious armband, a picture postcard of Sanok taken in the spring, three L. & C. Hardmuth mechanical pencils (red, green, and black) and a leather map case, a saber knot, a fork carved from a bone, a long Finnish dagger, a huge alarm clock with two brass bells on top, an empty picture frame, a ball of wax, and a stub of candle.

—Don't light it for a while, Mendeltort said.

—Light it, Meyer said. How can anybody talk in the dark?

—Will candlelight make you feel like a revolutionary? Mendeltort asked gently. Will it be 1917 for you all over again?

—I am no older than you are, Meyer said. Light the candle, Traurig, I gave you an order.

—You gave me a command, Traurig said. Mendeltort gives the orders.

—Please light the candle, Meyer said. I can't stand the dark.

Traurig lit the candle. In the flickering light, Meyer looked haggard, uncertain, and gray. —Old? I'm not old, he said.

Traurig grinned unkindly, grunted, spat as though a bitter taste had returned to his memory, and said without looking at Meyer: You sound like my father. On Friday morning he went to *shul*, on Sunday morning he talked revolution, the rest of the week he peddled fish and counted his money. Just an old man living other people's dreams.

—To be old and a revolutionary is a contradiction, Meyer said pedantically, as though this were an absolute.

—I'll say it is, Traurig said. But I'm not going to live like that, you can bet your soul.

—So, Mendeltort, Meyer said, you've won again. Corrupted another child. The people whose lives you're playing with haven't even been born yet, don't you see? Why do you want to kill off all our young men, why can't you let them decide for themselves if they would like to live?

—I can decide for myself where and how I am going to live, Traurig said.

—All you've decided is that you're not going to live for very long, Meyer said.

The candlelight illuminated a dirty gray wall, a gray peeling ceiling. A floorboard creaked outside and, for a moment, they were all attentive. The candle flame whipped about, hissed, and drowned in wax. The light bulb glowed redly. Meyer peered sadly at Traurig once again, shook his head as though even such minor movement was painful to him, and spread his hands in a mute acknowledgment of failure. He raised his old, red-rimmed disappointed eyes to Mendeltort. His mustache was quivering. Once more, Mendeltort was aware of danger: this time, a fleeting touch of pity for a man who would want him dead.

—It's not too late to change your mind about anything, he said. We've all made mistakes.

—No, Meyer said, or whispered, looking at the floor, where shadows were rolling about like various tides of darkness, flung this way and that by the flickering light bulb. It would be impossible for him to acknowledge error while a young man was listening.

—The kitchen ought to be open for breakfast, Mendeltort said to Traurig. Will you see if you can get some hot water for tea?

—And sugar, Meyer muttered. Plenty of sugar.

—What if they don't have sugar?

—They'll have it for you. They know who we are.

—If they knew *what* we were they'd give me arsenic, Traurig said.

—And see if you can get a newspaper, Mendeltort said.

—What would you want that for? Meyer muttered. You've read them all twenty years ago.

—I need a *Pravda* to put me to sleep, Mendeltort said.

—Having trouble sleeping?

Traurig left.

The light went out once more and, this time, the darkness had density, weight, a texture of permanence, and Mendeltort was suddenly sure that this was more than just the ordinary power failure, that this was a signal he should decipher as quickly as he could.

—Oh, goddammit all, Meyer said invisibly. How I hate lack of light. Will you please light that candle again?

—Where is it?

—I don't know. Will you please find it and light it? I can't breathe in the dark. No, no don't open the curtains. What's wrong with these damn Russians, anyway? Don't they even know how to run a power station? Can't they do anything worthwhile for themselves? Will you please do something about this suffocating darkness? I can't breathe I tell you.

Mendeltort struck a match, looked about. The "Internationale" was no longer playing and, in the sudden silence of this somber city in which no one went out at night, where gray millions hurried home with the last of daylight, not to emerge until the sun had risen, where only prison convoys hissed through concrete valleys and long trains hooted at cordoned sidings, he heard a roar of distant motors, a near footstep, a dim remote cry. Deep inside the belly of the building, he heard a muted groan, a rumble, the clatter of boots.

—This is more than just a power failure, he said. I think we'd better find out what is going on.

—Whom are you going to ask? This is Moscow. Russia. Sooner or later there'll be an announcement. Nothing happens in Russia without an announcement. If there is no announcement then it hasn't happened.

A distant booming sound rolled through the open window.

—Summer thunder, said Meyer.

Mendeltort listened to the long hushed moments after the rolling sound, felt a slight tremor in the floor under his feet, shook his head. The new day had growled again beyond the horizon and, yes, there would be no one whom he could ask for an explanation.

The room was the best in the hotel, the largest but small at that, sparsely furnished with heavy antique furniture that had been painted white but had become gray. Meyer sat slumped, immobilized by gloom; whatever worlds he had inhabited had proved to be hollow. The thought of giving up his faith was unimaginable to him, Mendeltort thought, and wondered what he would do next. They seemed to be sitting at the darkened graveside of their common past. But while the setting was revolutionary, austere, where was the euphoric herald of new days to come?

Again, the new day replied with its distant booming, again he thought that the floor had quivered, and (this time) the empty square rattled with the echoes of running footsteps and a shout to halt.

—No, Meyer muttered then. Movements can't disappear entirely, they only lose momentum . . . there may be a delay, a detour now and then, but . . .

His huge waxed mustache caught the edge of the relighted candle's insufficient light, it was the only part of him that Mendeltort could see. He thought it less commanding now than artificial, a disguise that Meyer used to hide from himself. And suddenly Traurig's alarm clock began to bang and rattle in the suitcase and, as though this were a signal to hide, to take cover, to seek refuge from approaching danger, Meyer said: You've checked this room?

Mendeltort nodded.

—And you didn't really want tea or a newspaper.

—I thought you might want to say something privately.

—I do, Meyer said. It isn't going to be a confession of ideological errors, if that's what you expect, it's too late for me to start spitting into my own footprints. But I want you to understand exactly where you stand with me. (Then he added slyly:) And that's a lot more than Ben Gurion's people will ever do for you.

—I don't expect anything from Ben Gurion's people.

—Well. That's the first piece of realistic thinking I've ever heard from you. What they *will* do for you is to arrange a bullet in your back, preferably a British one, unless Stern's rope happens to be available. You've no romantic illusions about *that*, I hope?

—None at all.

—Well. Isn't *that* a comfort. You are a lot more dangerous to them than you are to anybody here. In fact, if you're really looking for an enemy, keep an eye on those rural electrification experts in their damned khaki shorts, with their damned mimeograph machines and American money. They'll turn you over to their Pontius Pilate as soon as you're within their reach.

—So? Mendeltort said.

—So for me you're not an enemy, you're not even a competitor, in fact my own future plans would be impossible without you. Zarubin wants to use you for your reputation, this strange authority of yours that I could never understand . . . He's a believer in symbols, legends, monuments, and he looks so far ahead that he makes me dizzy. He'll give you power and resources to organize our people for his private ends. Oh, it'll all sound very logical, believe me, it'll seem very good: a private Jewish empire under Russia's benign supervision, if that's the way you want to look at it. Perhaps he'll make you a member of the Politburo, or promise to make you one. And you'll use his resources to organize our people into an army and a government, or at least some sort of a committee, because that's what you need for your private ends. Am I right? Isn't that what you have in mind?

Mendeltort nodded. —Something like that, he said.

—So, for a time, you will have his ear, the maddeningly logical voice went on. And while you're doing your work, you'll be doing mine. Because, you see, you are going to fail at the end, you won't be able to lead our people out of this particular captivity. There is no way for anyone to leave Russia! You won't even be able to save yourself, because plans such as yours are contrary to reason. But after you have failed, Zarubin will need a replacement for you, to lead whatever you had organized, and I'll be right at hand to be used and to use Zarubin. So, you see, we are walking side by side again, you and I. I'll help you all I can with the Russians because I am your only possible successor.

—What is it that you're hoping to inherit?

—You're dealing with Russians, you know what they'll offer. The stars and the moon and anything else that they don't have to pay for, if that's the bribe that they think you'll take. What has Szymanski been suggesting to you? An army corps? The presidency of an autonomous republic? They have a Jewish Autonomous Republic, by the way, did you know that? It's somewhere near Mongolia, I believe. The Russians have been making such offers in regards to Poland to any Pole who would listen to them, and to most who won't.

—I've met Berling's people.

—Ah, you see? There you are, then. That's going to be the command of Stalin's Polish Army, just as Wanda Wasilewska's Polish Patriots' Committee is going to be the new Polish government. I'm going to be a part of that Committee, and of that Army, and whatever you organize will be that Committee's political-military arm. The Russians know that they can rely only on us to work with them and so we can use them. The Russians plan to move the Committee to their part of Poland and set it up there as a Polish government. The only reason why they haven't done it already is because they don't want to upset the Germans. But if the Germans should ever relinquish their part of Poland . . . well, the Committee will be the government in Warsaw. And then we can help to create the kind of Poland where we can *all* live.

—If that is humanly possible, Mendeltort said quietly.

—Well, of course. A realist deals only in realities.

Again the thunder rolled, muted as drums at a funeral, reduced and made incoherent by distance far beyond the perceptible horizons; again a tremor nudged the soles of Mendeltort's worn boots as though to register a warning, and (this time) a soft musical note came from the trembling glass of the open window.

—You're not the only man with a sense of vision, Meyer said.

—I never thought I was.

—I've followed a vision all my life, Meyer said, and I've been faithful to it. I don't change with the weather. You can turn the head of a young fool with fresh-laid eggs in his brains, that's what such brains are for, but I've a greater sense of loyalty to our people's future. Poland is our country, even if it gives us ulcers, because that's where we were born. Ever since I've known anything about Eastern Europe I've known that Poland is Europe's frontier. I've seen it with my own eyes. Any shrinking of Poland is Asia's advance, and I've no illusions about the Russians' plans for the Poles and Poland. But I am willing to pay the Russians' price to make our country better for our people. Certainly, for some other people, my kind of Poland won't be very pleasant. But I can't be concerned about that. I believe that social justice is not just a phrase. Poland had everything for its Jewish citizens except social justice, a social coherence. When we have created *that* for ourselves in Poland we shall have everything we have ever wanted.

—You've said all that before, Mendeltort said.

—And I'll say it again and again and again, the lone voice cried out of Meyer's private darkness. Others have also said it. Erlich and Alter and the Bund have also wanted to live with pride in the country in which they were born but they refused to pay the Russian's price! So they're in a prison! But I'm willing to give the Russians an access to our lives, I'd give the Devil such an access if he promised me a life with dignity in my own backyard! Isn't that why we were all revolutionaries together at one time?

—At one time, yes.

—Well, I'm still loyal to the principles of my revolution.

—And is Zarubin interested in your social justice?

—I am not trying to convince you, Meyer's voice said sadly, caught up on those streams of feeling that can never surface, which carry a man's best sense of the miracle of life, widespread and incandescent as the light of day. —I only want you to know that someday you will have to take me seriously.

—I do, Mendeltort said.

—It hasn't been easy to do everything that I've had to do.

—I'm sure it wasn't.

—But it was all for us, Meyer cried, then gestured violently toward the chilling gloom and fire of this oddly threatening and suggestive Moscow morning, the far-off drumming across the horizon. —Not for *them!* It was all in the name of our liberation, part of our original international ideal. That much you *have* to understand, you were yourself a disciple of the revolution.

—I remember.

—No, you don't. You've conveniently forgotten. And will you please find something that will make more light! I feel like a ghost, speaking in this darkness. And will you stop that damned noise in that young fool's suitcase.

Mendeltort pulled the rich embossed leather grip from under the sofa, noted the labels of European hotels, Alpine resorts, Mediterranean pleasures, tattered memories of starlit walks in the gardens of Monte Carlo, loving assignations in Baden-Baden, the fallen citadels of leisure and manners which Traurig had never seen or even imagined, which were part of a civilization that had disappeared in the newly loud and booming day. Whose had it been, and where had Traurig stolen it?

Meyer's heavy breathing had become a sob, and again Mendeltort was tasting contempt mixed with pity. Lost in the deep dark spaces between uninhabitable worlds, he could cast no shadow, this man who craved the vastness of an international idea. It was the fear of one's own insignificance that made such men corrupt, but Mendeltort knew better than to waste his time on moralistic judgments. Every truth was true for its believer, part of the structures of his faith.

The candle had burned out. Reluctantly, he pulled the curtains away from the window to let in the light.

A great light flashed then, above the Kremlin wall, and another followed, and then the still-dark morning was split and segmented by sweeping beams of light, and searchlights combed the clouds, and a roar of motors boomed in the hollow square and (moving to the window, hidden behind the curtain) Mendeltort saw black shining Zis limousines with motorcycle escorts converging at high speed on the entry port to the Fortress, and trucks squealed to a halt on the night-wet pavement, spilling platoons of soldiers.

(*Yesli zavtra vayna,* the loudspeaker croaked in his memory, and suddenly all his calculations soared to another plane, and what had seemed hardly possible even to himself, hardly believable in the reality of Russia, had become a probability and he felt prophetic.)

Traurig's alarm clock no longer made a sound. The thunder in the west was identified, had been identified before but now was believable, the dull thuds and boomings were man-made thunderbolts, and he closed his eyes and prayed, and was thankful, and felt his cheeks suffuse with the warmth of tears. *For I am come unto you in thunder and lightning so that you may bear witness to the might of your Lord.*

Watching a war begin, feeling the shock waves of invasion under his trembling feet, he allowed himself a moment of euphoria, feeling something in common with all other people for whom the luxury and trappings of a normal life were abruptly gone. It was inevitable that the war should come to Russia as it had come to less deserving countries, that beast should rend beast, that they who lived by blood should drown in their own, and all his calculations had been based on this probability, for this was the signal for assembly and for exodus. But now that bombs and shells were falling upon these people of oppression he felt, once more, compassion for the dying. He would hug Moscow to his beating heart, he knew, for Moscow was his, his from the first hour of the blacked-out dawn which hid its dreadful beauty until a sun of a distant morning announced the coming of his people's day.

. . . *For this is the day for which we have been waiting,* he whispered in the gleams and flashes that transformed this day, and turned to speak to Meyer.

Still hidden in his shadows, his face revealed in swift brief strokes of light, Meyer had seen and understood nothing of what had happened. His voice, now plaintive in reminiscences, kept up its droning pleas.

—The things we used to talk about, he said. The things we believed. Communism, we used to tell each other, was our own invention, we were going to seek our identity in mankind itself. Nationalism was the

maker of wars and privilege, the killer of our people, the cause of all the
human suffering. The idea of a nationalist Jew was a contradiction. Nationalism was another name for evil until we made another great invention, Zionism, and suddenly nationalism was respectable again, and
flags and wars and corpses and corpse makers were respectable, provided
it was our own nationalism that we were talking about. Ah, don't you
people ever see your own hypocrisy? When you make the corpses, it's
justifiable, moral, a matter of cultural and biological necessity, no less!
When others do it, it's a crime against humanity.

—Meyer, Mendeltort said. Look out of the window.

—Why should I? What's there to see? I don't adjust my ideals to
suit my convenience. I haven't changed. I want our people to live as
part of a civilized mankind, you want to put a boundary around us. So
which one of us has the grander vision and which is the traitor?

—Look outside, said Mendeltort.

—Do you still think me just an opportunist? Do you believe that I
serve the Russians?

—You serve your own image of yourself, Mendeltort said, but Meyer
didn't hear him.

—I don't want to bring Asia into our lives, Meyer cried. I just want to
use it.

—Most people who have thought that have had their necks shot off,
Mendeltort said quietly.

—Perhaps. Perhaps that's what some necks are for. It isn't likely to
happen to a pragmatist, only romantics die on barricades. I function
very well in a pragmatic profession. I am perfectly aware of cause and
effect. I can weigh the degree of risk I'm willing to take.

Wearily now, feeling neither sympathy nor pity, Mendeltort
shrugged, turned his back on Meyer, looked through the window at the
roaring day. And was a giant heart beating strongly in that riven dawn?
Was there indeed a rush of air in his ears as though a mass of birds had
risen in flight? What had begun was only a beginning, what lay ahead
would depend on the complex fears of this self-corrupted man who had
spent a lifetime staring into the mirror of his own frustrations convinced that he was looking through a window at the world outside. It
was vitally important for Mendeltort to know what still moved Meyer,
it was a way to judge the prophecy of his own accelerating destiny: his
time divided by the velocity of events. Meyer had never revealed himself so fully. He had been speaking to excess as a starved man devours
the providential meal, and Mendeltort could smell the Russian *mahorka* on his breath. He heard this man whom he had known for more
than half his years and realized that he had never heard him voice his
thoughts before. Perhaps years had passed since Meyer had been able to

speak freely even to himself and this outpouring was the only way to purge himself, for one luxuriously illumined human moment, of the private torments that peered from his mirrors. He spoke his piece less to a man he knew than to a man whom he could confidently expect to be dead in the near future, and who would not be able to remember. He wanted dreams to come true, he who had professed to hate dreams, who dreamed of hate in the name of loving. He belonged to a dream world, himself consumed within his own nightmare, and Mendeltort was on the point of telling him so when the door was flung violently open. It was Traurig, then, his white face staring as though a cry would come from it at any moment. The corridor behind him was full of candles, torches, shouts, and pounding boots.

—You didn't bring the newspaper, Meyer said accusingly. You didn't bring the tea.

—It's war, Traurig cried. The Germans have invaded. What are we going to do?

—We shall go home, Mendeltort said, and smiled and went up to the trembling boy and embraced him, and understood that indecipherable collision of contingencies that manufactures exaltation or despair.

—War? Meyer said. What war? What are you talking about, you incredible young fool?

—War, that's what, Traurig said. There's been an announcement. Of course, the Russians say they're winning it already but everybody's in a panic, running about like a lot of chickens, and all the big shots in the dining room have disappeared to pack.

—But there can't be a war, Meyer said. How can there be one? There's an alliance between us and Hitler. No, not between *us*, the Russians, oh, you know what I mean!

—That's what they're all shouting in the dining room downstairs but they're running like hell all the same.

—My God, my God, Meyer said. What is going to happen? My God, my God. Oh, my God.

A shout came then from below the window and Mendeltort looked out, saw a Rusisan officer waving his fists at him, and a gray mob of milling NKVD soldiers pointed their bayonets uncertainly at his open window.

Traurig laughed, excited.

Mendeltort closed the windows, drew the curtains, stood in the dark aura of a past, a present, and a future which had become one, heard the lament, the pleas, and the prophecy.

. . . For the palace that lies desolate, his father's strangled voice whispered in his ear, we sit in solitude and mourn. For the Temple that is destroyed, mourned his buried mother. For the walls that are overthrown, cried his murdered brothers. For our majesty that is *not* departed, has never departed, can never depart (he replied, exultant), we need no longer mourn.

The words of a sentimental Russian song broke from the loudspeaker on the Kremlin wall, and the bewildered soldiers in the square had begun to sing, and he tasted the song's terrible irony on his tongue. Never has my breath known such a sweet taste, he thought, never has it been such a joy to draw a free breath. *Is there a land where a man can breathe so freely . . . ?* sang the Russian soldiers, staring at the torn and flashing sky, and he began to laugh.

Abel

THEN IT WAS EVENING.

It must have been evening. Or morning. Perhaps it was morning. Morning and Evening are parts of a Day. A calendar unfolded, and pages were fluttering. A door was opening. Then the door was open. Yakovlev brought food. He placed the bowls and the brownish mass of bread gently on the floor. He stepped back. He grinned.

. . . A pink-enameled bowl, cheerful as a nursery, small yellow grinning animals galloping around the curved metal rim into the refuge of grease spots, and inside this hollow hemisphere a yellow-brown moisture wrinkled into scum. A blue-enameled mug with a portrait of a demented American duck in a sailor collar, full of brown steaming liquid. It is too hot to touch. An implausible memory of coffee on a Sunday morning, the windows of his room opened wide and sunlight slanting across tumbled quilts, and fat flies once more describe lazy parabolas over potted palms, nasturtiums, Mother's aspidistra, and church bells are competing for patrons' attention with streetcars . . . which clang and rattle and whine . . . And four times as much black bread as Abel had seen in one piece since he could remember.

—Have I been condemned?

Yakovlev was grinning. —Eat.

—What's my article?

—Eat, said Yakovlev.

Abel began to eat. Slowly, thoughtfully. Felt his remaining teeth coming free. His eyes were full of tears. That is to say, *one* eye was full of tears and blinded, the other was empty and crowded with visions. He knew that he would have to use all the control left to him not to lick the bowl. Yakovlev rolled and lit a cigarette. —Good, eh?

—Good, Abel said.

The Russian shrugged his shoulders deprecatingly; he might have been a pawnbroker undervaluing a family heirloom. —Turnip soup, from the guards' mess, none of your scum water, and the coffee's real.

—It must be a low paragraph, then, Abel muttered.

Yakovlev sighed, averted his face. —Well, what do you want? You don't get real coffee on Article 54.

. . . Should he be redeemed? Had he deserved redemption? He had been swallowed up, would be regurgitated, thought of vast white nights and enormous spaces, the absence of moonlight, months of darkness and time without end . . . In the end, time would be triumphant.

Yakovlev cleared his throat, rubbed an inflamed eye, hawked, spat into the bucket which shined and beckoned, silver-bright, reflecting the light bulb. He had come alone. He grunted, scratched an ear, rolled a cigarette in a strip of newspaper, offered it to Abel, but Abel shook his head. Mindfulness rejected oblivion even for a moment.

Yakovlev shrugged, sighed, peered gloomily into the corridor and pulled the door almost closed, shook his head as if to clear it of an accidental cobweb. His normally cheerful face was shrunken, dark with worry. He started walking up and down the cell, head down as though to watch an invisible center line which he had to follow, making his turns with the unconscious skill of a prisoner, muttering to himself. Then he stopped, looked at Abel, said:

—Look here, this has got to stop.

Abel nodded, waited.

—You've got everybody stirred up, nobody can figure out what you're up to.

—I'm up to nothing, Abel said, and Yakovlev made a swift pained and exasperated gesture, said: Don't start that again.

Abel nodded, waited.

—It's serious, said Yakovlev. You've pushed your luck too far. You can't do what you're doing and think you can get away with it in a place like this.

Abel nodded, said: You feel threatened?

Yakovlev raised a sudden fist, looked at it, and unclenched his fingers as though he didn't understand what they were: artifacts from another era whose use was unclear . . . and lowered his hand. Shrugged, spat into the bucket, resumed his slow pained walk up and down the cell, said:

—There's been nothing like you on this block before, and we've had some real odd birds here, let me tell you. I could tell you things that'd make the hair fall out of your head, the things some of them do. But it's all natural, it's what people do in a place like this, it's nothing that'll bother anybody. What you're doing has everybody talking, and that's as bad as you can hope to get. You got to stop it, whatever it is.

So far, the word about you is just in this block, but it'll go higher. And when it does . . . well . . . they got a way here with a prisoner that isn't working right.

Abel nodded, smiled, said:

—What bothers you?

Yakovlev spun around, lowered his head like a bull on the point of charging, shook an automatic fist near Abel's face, hissed an accusation:

—You don't even fall asleep any more.

—If I closed my eye you'd only make me open it again, Abel said softly.

—That's not true and you know it! When did I last come in here to shake you up? I'd let you sleep a bit if you'd do it. So would some of the others. But you just sit, never close your eye, never lie down, it's really something to look in that judas and see that one eye and that red hole always staring at you . . . Doesn't the light bother you?

—I don't even see it.

—Well, see, that's what I mean, it's crazy! It's like you were dead. And about the food! You've been on quarter rations for near on two years, you know what that means? A bird couldn't live on it, and you don't even eat most of that a lot of the time . . . Nobody here gives a shit about if you live or die, but it's got to be one or the other, there isn't anything else a prisoner can do, and it's got to be something people can understand. If they don't understand it, you're in real trouble.

—I'm not dead, Abel said.

—Shit, said Yakovlev, it just don't make sense.

Abel nodded, smiled, heard an absent whisper.

. . . Cartesian reason doesn't cover the whole of man or the whole of his knowledge; there is a magic relationship between man and his universe that must be remembered . . .

—Everything's got to be one thing or another, Yakovlev said, troubled. It's all got to make sense.

. . . The truth of the matter, Father Zenek whispered, is that beside this joyless, loveless, materialistic interpretation of the universe is another which is above the reasoning intellect and can't be attained by intellect alone, and in which the universe of matter is merely reflected . . .

—I mean it's either this or that. Everything's got a name, it's all been written about in some book. And it's all either right or wrong, good or bad, black or white . . . and a man's got to know what he's looking at. You got to think about what you're doing. You can last a long time in a place like this if nobody thinks about you, if they forget you're here, but once they start talking . . . thinking . . . shit.

—Nobody is going to do me any harm, Abel said.

—Oh, you think that, eh? Well, let me tell you, I've been here twelve years and I know what happens when a prisoner isn't working right. He don't last too long.

—What happens to him?

—What happens? Yakovlev said, halted, turned around, threw down the brown butt of his cigarette, stamped on it. You know what happens. One day he isn't here any more.

. . . Chipped fragments of eternity passed unnoticed: minutes without reference to a calendar. Injure no one and there shall be no animosity, Father Zenek whispered. Do not lie and there shall be neither cowardice nor malice.

Abel smiled, said: I bow to your judgment.

Yakovlev said: It's too late now, brother.

—Any suggestions?

Yakovlev sighed, shrugged, shook his head, said: I don't know much of anything any more. You and that whispering bastard are driving me crazy. What do you know that I don't know about? What makes you think you can get away with *that*?

—Is that what it takes to shake your whole system? One man refusing to behave like everybody else?

—Refuse? What does that mean? Nobody refuses anything. You do what you're told. If you don't know what you're doing that's all right because *somebody* knows. And what's all this about systems, anyway? Don't give me any of that Big Dome talk. Now, I've seen all kinds here, Yakovlev said, sitting down on the hard plank beside Abel, rolling another cigarette, lighting it, putting the match carefully in his pocket in the regulation manner. —Big Generals. Heroes of the Union. What they call intellectu-als. Real Big Domes. Professors. Think all the time. They break up faster than anybody else. The bigger they are, the faster they break. Talk to themselves, like you did when you first come here. Weep, shout, pray . . . Kill themselves for a fucking cigarette. Well, that's all right . . . that's all right . . . that's what people do. That's what this place is for, to break them. And it breaks them. The Big Domes go crazy with their thinking. But you don't think, do you? I can always tell it when they're thinking.

—No, I don't think, Abel said.

—No thinking, Yakovlev muttered to himself. And it's not that God stuff either, I know when I see it.

—No, it's not the God stuff.

—Well then, what the hell is it?

—It's nothing.

—What d'you mean it's *nothing*? Everything is something!

—I'm sorry, said Abel. I really don't want to cause you any trouble.

—I know that, Yakovlev said. And that's another thing I can't figure out. We're both supposed to give each other trouble. You're supposed to hate me and be scared of me and I'm supposed to think you're a piece of shit. An enemy of the people, a fucking criminal! And that's what you are or you wouldn't be here. But I can't think that any more. Nothing is like it used to be and I can't figure it out. It can't go on like this. What the hell am I doing here, anyway, talking to you? If the block chief caught me I'd be on my way north so fast the ice would melt under me.

—Then perhaps you'd better stop coming to see me. You are a good man, Ivan Borisovich, I wouldn't want anything to happen to you.

—Why should you worry your head about me? Everybody's got to worry about himself, that's all there is to it.

—Then why do you worry your head about me?

—I don't know, Yakovlev said. I can't figure it out. Maybe I don't worry about you at all, maybe I'm worrying about me . . . But I'm getting to think that in some crazy way it's all the same thing. Ah, well. Shit. I've got by here for twelve years, that's longer than most . . . There's no real way out for anybody until they're dead and then it's all the same.

—But a man who is free in spirit is forever free, Abel said. Is this day or night?

—First time I heard you ask, Yakovlev said, grinning. It's night, getting darker. Eat, and then get your things together. Want a smoke? It could be your last one.

—So my time has come?

Yakovlev paced the cell, puffed on his cigarette, and spat out coarse black veins of leaves that refused to burn. —It's come for all you Polish, one way or another.

—Are we all going, then?

But the Russian was pretending not to have heard him, hawked, spat, said: At least you'll go on full rations for a while. So go ahead, drink your coffee, have a smoke too; you won't get better tobacco than this anywhere.

Abel shook his head.

—Come on, now, said Yakovlev. What's the difference now?

—What's my paragraph?

—You want more coffee? I'll get you more coffee.

Abel shook his head. When one still has enough of one's humanity, dignity, and self-awareness left to refuse munificence, a gift of oblivion, the collapse hasn't been absolute. He watched his hands creep about the greasy pink enamel. I will not lick the bowl. I will not accept Yakovlev's cigarette. Whatever else I may be now, I am still my own man. Such foolish, childish proof of . . . ah, how can I say it? . . . vestigial manhood, dignity, independence . . . Yakovlev would never understand it. An NKVD man knows without a doubt, as a priest knows his God, that independence of mind is criminal and that individual human dignity is a contradiction.

—I better go after the rations, Yakovlev said. Got to do my job. I've been sitting here too long anyway. Any day now they'll catch me talking to you and I'll be seeing the fucking white bears . . . Listen, you want me to bring you something special from home, like maybe a sausage? They search you pretty good when you come on duty but when you've been here as long as me there's ways to do just about anything you want.

Abel smiled, shook his head.

—I have all I need, except for some answers.

—The hell with that, Yakovlev said. It don't do no good, asking questions, you just get screwed up. You start asking questions and you don't know when to stop. And the only answer you get in the end is down in the cellar.

Abel nodded, smiled.

Yakovlev smiled, said: You know, there was a time a few months back when I thought you was going to make it out of here. Fact is, I don't remember the last time somebody went outside without coming right back. Except your uncle. That was your uncle, right? Everybody said it.

—My uncle was here? Abel said.

—That's right, that Special down the corridor. But about getting out of here, you know what they say? They say that if you've got somebody on the outside who's really big, and who wants you out, well, then you can do it.

—Then what is to be done?

—Ah, you're having a little laugh, are you? I've heard that sentence before, I am not that stupid. Everybody knows who asked that, but I don't know *what is to be done*. What's coming is coming. Eat, drink your coffee, have a smoke. Stalin's got no better *mahorka* in his pipe. It could be the last smoke either of us'll have.

—So it's that bad, is it? Abel said.

—What's bad in one way, is good in another way. The word is that you've got four paragraphs out of Article 10.

—Treason?

—What difference does that make? Give us the man and we'll find the article, that's what we say here. With Article 10 you get good coffee and soup from the mess.

—Treason, Abel said, laughed remotely. —Well . . . a lot of good people had warned me about it. My father, my late lamented military mentor . . . I suppose there is some sort of justice after all.

—I knew you'd take it good, Yakovlev said. You ought to see some of the others, when they get the word. They break up like children.

—When is it to be, then?

—For you? Oh, it won't be for a while, 'sfar as I know. There's no big hurry, is there? And it's all got to be done properly, so it takes time to set up. But you're going to another cell, another corridor . . . Then maybe they'll move you to another place altogether, that's what usually happens. Either way you'll be on full rations, so that's something, isn't it?

—It's something, Abel said.

—Listen, said Yakovlev. Maybe something can still be done, you know? If you write a letter to Stalin it'll hold everything up for a while. A lot of people write to him from here.

—What should I write? Having a wonderful time, wish you were here?

—How do I know what you ought to write? You're an educated man, you can write something. And that'll hold things up for maybe a month. And then, maybe, if someone was to go to your uncle . . . I mean, supposing he is where everybody says he is, supposing he's big . . . and then, maybe, if that somebody, I'm not saying who, told your uncle that your time's running out . . . well, what do you think?

—That would be treason, Abel said, laughing.

—Jesus, Yakovlev said.

—Would it have made you happy to help me go free, Ivan Borisovich?

Yakovlev cursed, spat. —Happy? What kind of word is that for you to use? Where you come from the people don't even know what happiness is!

—Then why are you so angry, Ivan Borisovich?

—How do I know why I get so angry? I don't know what's happened to me since I've been talking to you. It's my own fault, shouldn't have talked to you in the first place. They don't call your kind Enemies of the People for nothing, they don't lock you up for nothing, the People have to be protected from your kind. The People are happy and then your kind comes along with your talk, your questions, and you poison the air, and than nobody can have any peace. It never used to bother me what happened to anybody. I did my job, didn't give a shit. Don't know why the hell I do now. The more I try to figure it out, the more screwed up it all gets. All I know is that if it's clean business you don't have to do it in the dark, and what we do here, brother, is so fucking dark I can't live with it. So who are you to talk to me about being happy?

—Can't you leave?

Yakovlev laughed. —Leave? What kind of world you think you're living in? Nobody leaves this place, not if you work here, unless it's face-down in the meat truck. You get to see too much in a place like this.

They didn't hear the others coming. They, the others, must have tiptoed in their squeaky concertina boots and waited behind the door, and the door, which had been barely ajar, just wide enough to meet the regulations and not an inch more, was suddenly flung open, and then the cell was full of angry shouting men, and hands seized Yakovlev.

—*Svolotch!* an officer was shouting. *A ty pod stienku pudyesh!*

Kneed in the groin, Yakovlev fell backward across the honey bucket, cracked his skull on concrete.

—And you! the officer shouted, shook his fist at Abel. —Get your things! Outside!

Obediently, Abel stepped into the corridor, faced the wall and waited.

The officer's slate-gray eyes reflected only the emptiness behind them. He could have been a part of the wall. He motioned as if waving away an invisible fly and Abel took his place at the apex of the small isosceles triangle of prisoner and guards. The apex is the prisoner, always facing the unknown; the guards are the propelling base. In theory, the prisoner shouldn't be able to move without being told.

—Move, said the guards in chorus.

Abel moved.

Hope made an unexpected appearance, whispered: You have been re-prieved, a pardon, perhaps an amnesty . . . Experience said: No, it's an interrogation, get ready for the threatening spectrum of multicolored voices. It was just as possible that he was walking to his execution.

His broken boots slapped and shuffled on the concrete floor made smooth by innumerable other prisoners. Slap-slap, shuffle-shuffle. A prisoner is an object to be moved at will, discarded when useless, and I have proved useless even before Mendeltort's arrest.

—Halt, said the guard.

. . . The guard says *Halt* without animosity; there is nothing to be read into that expressionless, uninflected voice, neither hostility nor lack of hostility. It is merely a dry voice which is colorless, which says *Move* again and the triangular formation is set once more in motion. Head down to watch the center line, hold up your sagging pants. Invisi-ble fingers start their rhythmic snapping, the big keys jingle. I hear the grinding thud of the guards' iron-studded boots and my own mindless shuffle. *Left!* Abel turned to the left, noted a narrow slope of ascending passageways. *Right!* He turned to the right. Up and down worn steps that he had never trod, into new corridors. The walls suddenly constricted, the corridors narrowed, white paint (not whitewash) glared from the ceiling . . . So, not an interrogation, not an execution. (At which point the mind boggles, because what other alternatives can there be?) There are two stops on the way, the mind registers them in passing. Moments which could be hours of waiting upright in the silvery darkness of a *kishka,* ankle-deep in dry excrement, in the stench of fear . . . Then *Move!* again.

And so on to a green-painted door.

Behind the door the corridor narrowed even further, became a prone *kishka.* At its far end was another door, this one of rusty iron. Iron hooks and nails had been crudely pounded into its walls . . . that is to say, ah, the walls of the prone *kishka* . . . heaps of torn rags were hanging on the hooks and nails. Further along the corridor some skeletal figures were taking off their clothes, and from behind yet another rusty door came a wisp of yellow steam, the reek of carbolic, and a wave of hot wet air which immediately condensed on the walls and formed rivulets of whitewash.

Razdyavaytes!

Abel began to take his rags apart.

Then he was naked for the first time in eighteen months and watched himself astonished: dry parchment skin, the purple rash encrusted with scabs, the livid marks left on his chest and belly wherever he touched them, the useless and no longer comprehended appendages of sex . . . A prisoner-attendant threw him a minuscule cake of gritty gray soap the size of a matchbox. The rusty door banged open. He was motioned forward.

It was hot, the steam was scalding, but he was shivering. He couldn't stop shaking. He didn't know how to cope with a room full of people. He was suddenly afraid. What saved him from backing out into the corridor, where the guards would have only kicked him in again, was the realization that these were prisoners like himself, which meant that they were no more people than he was a person, that they were creatures of his planet, his true kith and kin. Not human, being prisoners. Animated objects. Skeletons, shadows, ghosts that leaped and pranced. The dead, or the near dead to judge by the evidence of their emaciation, were cavorting in the yellow clouds. They were chanting, surely they were chanting, but he couldn't tell what, couldn't understand them. A gaunt stooped man who was obviously a Jew, who was bent forward like a question mark, was laughing softly to himself as he skipped and danced among spurts of boiling water. Skipped and danced. The general, yes, Abel was sure of it, a man who was or had been the Leathery General, whom he still remembered, also skipped in steam. He slipped, fell, a dozen hands reached for him and set him on his feet. The priest bounced and jounced.

. . . Steam, so much steam. And dirty water running gray in gray iron gutters to open drainage holes where the rats were squealing. His skin was an insubstantial film that would surely melt.

Something was happening other than a shower, in itself a mystery. He heard Latin phrases, saw the Honeybear. It was, then, he supposed, yet another day that would remain engraved in his memory for however long his memory would last: like the Day of the Sparrow, or the Day on Which I Found the Newspaper, the Night of the Hanged Grandfathers, the Morning of the Last Supper and the Whispered Promise, the Day of the Bathhouse Mass would have its own identity. Possibly blasphemous. And the nude mass itself was probably invalid (who ever heard of mass without vestments?) and, certainly, there were no sacramental vessels if you ignored the people, no host and no wine (and transubstantiation was a matter of flesh into spirit, and word into steam) . . . and who had ever heard of a naked priest and a cavorting congregation? And the quiet invocation to an absent Deity and the chorus of murmured responses rolling invisibly while alien fists pounded on the iron door to hurry them on. Prayers were blending with commonplace requests: Give us this day our daily bread and pass the soap, would you? Forgive our trespasses and quit shoving, for Chrissake, for ever and ever, amen. He was struck by the comedy of faith and couldn't help laughing . . . saw tears, was sure they were tears, on the cadaverous gray faces . . . felt the exaltation of an early Christian in the catacombs and did not find this different mass at all remarkable. Forgiveness for others, as for ourselves, for we too do not know what we do.

—*Sursum corda,* said the Honeybear.

—*Habemus ad Dominum,* murmured the leaping men.

If he was laughing then, and someone was laughing, it must have been hysteria: the incongruous had become logical and he was staggered by it. The gaunt Jew dug him in the ribs with an elbow sharp as a bayonet and brought him to his senses.

—The time for levity is over, he said gently. The others are looking.

Abel gasped, choked: What's there to see?

—Disrespect to people's favorite illusions can never be forgiven, that's the ultimate sin in any religion.

—I don't deny them anything, Abel said.

—Let us pray, Father Zenek said.

—*Orate fratres,* groaned the dancing shadows in the yellow steam.

. . . It seemed to him then that the boiling jets were spurting from his body, not against it, that the yellow clouds thick with the acrid stench of disinfectant swirled inside his eyes. An act of faith was taking place around him and generations brayed responses from their graves. Twin lightnings plunged into the bridge of the priest's nose, the general consulted inner manuals, the liquid eyes of the Question Mark dripped perplexity. The rats squealed. The fists pounded on the iron door. (Hurry up, you carrion!) The urgent beat of an invisible drummer summoned to a charge.

He was full of forgiveness for everyone but himself.

. . . For them, whichever of my long-suffering peoples I'm talking about, there must be endless unforgivable suffering to bolster their personal pride, their sense of existence, their legends of martyrdom . . . Otherwise they might be obliged to see themselves just as insignificant as they truly are without the bloody trappings of the hearsay of history.

. . . In their last moment, would they know what their lives had been all about?

Then, peering into eyes which could not see him, hearing the croaking voices, thinking of steaming pools inhabited by demented frogs, by leathery reptiles, thinking of a boneyard in an earthquake, he said: But why are they praying?

The gaunt Question Mark said: It's a service, a mass. They are having a religious service.

—How can this be a mass? Abel said. Is this some Russian joke?

—Perhaps if they think it is a mass, or can be a mass, then for them it is one. Ah, it is hot! (A terrified rat snapped against his ankle, and the man kicked it into the scuppers.) Ah, the filthy beast!

Abel said: How can this be a mass? And why are they praying?

—It's a mass, the gaunt man said. I told you, it's your mass. It's the first opportunity any of them have had to get together with a priest, they're not likely to miss it.

Another gaunt man, not a Jew, hissed: Show some respect, you bastards!

—To what? Abel said.

—God, that's what! cried the man, convulsed in a paroxysm of hatred. Who the hell else?

Abel nodded wisely, his head heavy as lead, his eyes and ears full of steam. He felt his head bobbing up and down, said into steam: Ah, yes, I see . . .

The gaunt man whom he had named the Question Mark took him by an elbow and led him aside.

—You should be more careful, he said. These are desperate people.

—Desperate! Ah, yes. Yes.

—Their faith must be religious, and everything in which they believe is automatically holy.

He listened to the droned rhythm of the prayers, the invocations and responses which each of these men would know by heart, as part of their heritage. To be Polish, to them, was to be a Catholic, was to pray, was to call to God whenever they could. He listened to the sick thudding of his heart.

Then the grim reality of their situation reappeared. He looked around for guards, in sudden panic, said: We've got to stop them. We'll all get ten years!

—I wish we *would* get only ten, the Question Mark said, leaping. Ooof! The heat is more than I can stand, I think. It may be too much for some of the older men in here, there must be some bad hearts in this congregation. Yes, we could get ten years more for praying, or for being present in a place where someone was praying, and that would give me a nice twenty years to think about . . . ah, you know, I can't think of what I'd like to think about for the next twenty years.

—Have you been sentenced, then?

—Yes. Anti-Semitism, a mandatory five. In my case they made it ten and, I think, saved my life. Have you got your sentence?

—Article 10.

—Then why don't you pray?

—To which God? To whose God?

—Don't you have one?

—I have two, Abel said, as far as I know.

—Then you're twice as well off as a man who has one. My name is Langenfeld, by the way. Major. And yours?

—I'm Abel Abramowski.

—I thought you might be.

—We've met before?

—Once. I knew your uncle, you look much as he did at your age. Is he dead, do you know?

—No, Abel said. He's very much alive. What made you think he'd be dead?

—One automatically assumes nowadays that everyone is dead. Your father is dead, did you know?

—No, Abel said. How could he be dead? (Then shook his head, shrugged, made a disclaiming gesture.) I'm sorry, that's a stupid thing to say. How? Where?

—A place called Katyn, I think, said the other. We were together in an officers' camp . . . one of the three camps where the Russians kept our officers . . . They've all been murdered by now, I am sure.

—You saw him killed? How was he killed?

—There would hardly be an eyewitness to a thing like that.

—Why did they kill him? What did he do to them?

—Nothing. At least no more than anybody else. He didn't prove useful.

—But you escaped, or what?

—The Russians took me off the train that was transporting our officers to the execution site. You could call that a sort of miracle.

—Ah, another miracle . . .

—A sort of miracle, I said. A Russian miracle.

—And you are sure about my father? Abel interrupted.

—Quite sure. As sure as I can be.

—How can you be so sure when you weren't there, didn't see it happen? And tell me, then, how you managed *not* to be there, if . . . as you say . . . everyone else in that camp, my father and all . . .

His gesture was the Russian one for a bullet in the neck.

—I'll never be quite sure why they didn't kill me, Langenfeld said, shrugging. They took me off the train for questioning. I had been an economist, I am a reservist, they wanted to know what we knew about their economic problems . . . and there was something else, I think. A Russian miracle, as I said.

—What miracle?

—I had already been sentenced to ten years at hard labor. Having been sentenced, I couldn't be killed. How could I sit in prison if I was a corpse? Their bureaucracy is so terribly involved.

The guards came in then, shouting for the prisoners to hurry. More prisoners were coming, the bathhouse had to be cleared immediately. Their shouts drowned in the steam and the roar of a hundred voices. Everyone was talking at top speed to make up for their months or years of silence, their terrible isolation. They wanted to know who knew whom, who was alive and where, who had been killed and how. And suddenly Abel wanted his silence restored. He didn't want to hear these catalogues of death, deportations, executions, imprisonments . . . the lists of the martyrs that these skeletons were trading with each other sounded to him like one name, one voice, the raging voice of the gigantic disappointed man he didn't want to hear. He was offended by their hungry martyrdoms. Why couldn't they see how offensive they were in their quest for kinship with the dead. As the stooped man, the Question Mark, had said a moment earlier: everyone was dead. Well, almost everyone. Those who were still alive were the cause for wonder.

—Tarski, the gaunt man said, hurrying toward the corridor with Abel beside him. Jan Poremba, he also knew your father . . . five thousand officers in the camp at Kozielsk and twice as many in the other two . . . I tried to warn them but nobody would listen.

—Please, Abel said. I don't want to hear this.

—Well, who could blame them? Langenfeld went on. Who could have believed it? They were soldiers, good men, honest as they could be, honorable people, their one saving grace was that they were willing to die for their country and, perhaps, that's all that matters anyway. But to die for your country is one thing, to die as a mute offering to God is also understandable, but to become a sacrificial offering to an imagined Devil? That's more than anybody would believe.

—What sacrifice? Abel said. What Devil?

—Outside! the guards cried. Move.

A large tubular structure, like a rack of steel, ground into the corridor on iron wheels. Small gray angular prisoner-attendants lifted scorched and burning rags off the rack, began to throw them at the naked men. The rags had journeyed to their own inferno, the delousing furnace. They came apart in Abel's hands as he tried to dress, and survivor lice crept out of the seams.

—There must have been more to it than that, Langenfeld said. There must have been.

—More to what than what? Abel said.

—To that Katyn business. Mad Russian mysticism, yes, that's possible, primitive Devil worship is possible too. There's nothing fictitious about Zarubin, he was certainly there, and so is the gloomy introspective Russian soul, but even so there must have been something else, something touched by logic.

—What kind of logic? Abel said, longing for his silence.

—What I imagine happened is that someone made an administrative error, Langenfeld said. The indoctrination program was a total failure. If the conditions were the same in all the three camps, and there's no reason to suppose that they'd be any different, then they would have converted only eighteen men out of fifteen thousand. No real Pole would ever listen to Soviet temptations. They must have been somewhat nonplussed by that.

—What? Abel said, not listening.

—So someone must have asked Stalin or Beria or Reichman or Merkulov, or some other luminary of the hierarchy, what to do with these recalcitrant Poles and their camps, and the luminary probably shrugged and said: Liquidate them. Perhaps he meant only that the camps should be liquidated, but that word has acquired a very special meaning in the vocabulary of the terror *apparat*, it is a synonym for execution. And since everyone in Russia knows better than to question orders, well, there you are, a tragedy by error.

—Silence! the guards shouted. Move!

—Or perhaps that's what the Russians had in mind from the start.

Langenfeld vanished, marched off by himself. Dressed, grasping shredded pieces of cloth about himself, Abel stood outside the iron door waiting for his jailers. The wall was the color of old bones. The Leathery General passed between four guards, the priest followed in his role of Honeybear, carrying his bucket, and all the other skeletons had marched off behind them. My father is dead, Abel told himself, and tried to feel something. Dead, gone, like the rest, neither loved nor hated. Perhaps they were all a trick of the imagination.

Then he was turned around, positioned facing down the corridor with his guards behind him.

—Move!

Snap, snap. Jingle, jingle.

To yet another door.

And then the door was opening, he could see it opening, once again a door was about to open, and he watched it, waiting. He didn't wonder what awaited him, a prisoner doesn't indulge in wasteful speculations. Then the door was open, he stood in the doorway blinking in sudden light and, for no apparent reason, he was terribly afraid. He made an effort to remember the name or names of the instruments which manufactured this particular kind of light, was sure that he had seen them in another lifetime, then thought: Of course, a chandelier, and those are candelabra! The light reflected in a sheet of glass, stained the top of a great walnut desk, gleamed on polished handles of tall doors that faced each other to his right and left, reflected in buttons. Six double windows curtained in brocade were set in the wall which he was facing, each wall could have accommodated ten times the area of his entire cell. Mirrors the size of . . . what? He couldn't compare. No single object that he could recall even came close to it. An enormous portrait. Stalin, Beria, Molotov in frames side by side . . . The space astonished him. He had forgotten space, as he had managed to overcome the concept of time, and suddenly space and time were both upon him, and he was dwarfed, rendered helpless, some kind of an insect . . .

He blinked but knew better than to close his eyes, blinked not because the light had dazzled him (nothing could ever dazzle him again after the light bulb in his cell, and the automobile headlights in the interrogation room) but because he was frightened and bewildered by the size of the room.

(Is Stalin really eighteen feet tall, he wondered, are we all dwarfs beside him, and is this a room where *people* might be found?)

Again, he was shaking. The guards' fingers had clamped on his upper arms like manacles, and icy sweat was pouring down his face, unseasonable as laughter, and (yes) he knew that they could break him now; all his laboriously constructed defenses had crumbled in the face of the unexpected. He was crushed by all the trivia that he had forgotten: gingerbread mouldings under ornamental ceilings, parquet floors and a Persian carpet. This one was worn in a circular patch halfway between the desk and the doorway where the guards held him upright. He wondered how many hundred broken men had shuffled their feet there . . . Saw gilded peeling chairs, an opulent couch, more worn brocade . . . The round civilian sitting on the couch glanced up at him, then turned his broken boxer's face to a fleshy Russian whose thick neck overflowed his collar . . . Noted the other, a slim and elegant officer lighting a cigarette with a kitchen match as the thick neck bent respectfully toward him . . . Saw the pale young man in the leather coat who leaned against a wall, remembered a beating with a scabbard and his own lost teeth . . . Saw two deep high-backed armchairs turned at a precise angle toward the desk . . .

Someone was whispering. A tall man, made elderly by Abel's memory, was rising from one of the elegant armchairs. The elegant, finely featured Russian officer looked up at him out of the other armchair, tapped the top of the polished walnut with a manicured finger, and two dead old men were immediately revolving on their ropes, and a priest was pleading, and a bonfire crackled behind the manor house and oak tree, and the dark voice of the interrogation room, the voice which had so terrified Zaslavsky, was saying in its flawless Polish: First we destroy the legend, then the man.

Abel watched the tall man rising from the armchair, then coming swiftly forward across the parquet miles. He heard his own gurgle of hysterical laughter, cut short when the guards' fingers tightened on his arms. His months of torment appeared, identified themselves as a gouged eye and plucked fingernails, as hunger, as a light bulb in a wire cage, and laughed into his face. The face above his own, looking down at him with love and with pity, was strangely yellow, ravaged by an illness, and the hair and beard were newly gray, but the black thoughtful eyes were unforgettable. Then Mendeltort's huge hands were about his face (and Tarski shouted distantly: Traitor! Filthy traitor!) and Abel was laughing.

—This is all happening far too quickly, Mendeltort was saying. Don't try to understand it, continue to trust me.

—Is this really you? Abel said.

—There is no time for explanations now.

(A white horse tossed his mane, and a girl was whispering a poem across a ruined room, and the elegant Russian officer was saying *There is no grave here, remember?* And the pale young Jew in the leather coat was muttering *I know him from somewhere,* and the round man with the worried boxer's face said, across years and miles, *Well, we've lost the old wolf but we've got the cub . . .*)

He couldn't stop laughing.

(*Answer all the questions, you son of a bitch!*)

—So it was all for nothing? Abel said.

—There's only so much that I can say now, Mendeltort was saying. Something has happened. Shortly, in a matter of a few weeks, I shall be in a position to help all our people. You'll be set free along with everybody else. Have patience, strength, courage for a little longer.

Abel listened to himself listing his own martyrdoms: I lost an eye, all my fingernails, all that time . . . It was all for nothing?

—You'd know that better than anyone, Mendeltort said quietly.

—All that awful time, Abel said.

—People seldom sacrifice themselves for others, Mendeltort said evenly. Whatever we endure is on our own behalf.

—I don't believe this, Abel said.

—Continue to trust me.

—Didn't you tell me yourself, once, I can't remember where, that trust is impossible once a shred of suspicion has appeared?

—The fact that I am here, in this office, able to have you brought here, to speak to you freely and to assure you that you'll be released, speaks for itself.

—Oh yes, Abel said. Yes. It certainly says something.

The elegant officer began to whisper rapidly to the fleshy one, who pursed his lips and made a steeple out of hairy hands and nodded, and the round man with the face of the disappointed boxer strained forward to hear them, and the young Jew in the leather coat leaned against a wall.

—Your friends, Abel whispered. You know what they are?

Mendeltort said nothing.

—Your father is dead, Abel said. Are you proposing to do anything about it? Do you know who killed him, how he died? I saw him hanged, a sacrifice had been made . . .

—I know, said Mendeltort.

—But there was no consent.

—I know what you've been through, Mendeltort said gently. You won't be here much longer.

—Where will I be, then?

—With me, Mendeltort said. With your own people.

—I am with my people, my kith and my kin . . .

—We shall be organizing soon, recruiting an army, establishing a government in exile, preparing for the future.

—Please, Abel said. I am limited in what I am able to understand.

—Then simply believe me.

—I can do one or the other, not both. Will you make up your mind?

—It won't take long to free you.

—I'm *willing* to believe you, Abel said. But what are you doing with the Russians?

—Trust me, said Mendeltort.

—No, that's too much, Abel said. That I must understand.

He looked at his fingers. One fingernail was better than none and a man was only the sum of his convictions. What can I still believe? Who am I? Why am I here?

. . . And, in the meantime, Mendeltort was whispering about trust and patience.

He wanted to explain to this inexplicably aged uncle of his that, in his mind, he had committed treason, that his mechanism was flawed, he wasn't working right. He had learned to doubt and had to be punished. He had gone beyond the limits allowed by his people, had taken a step off the fixed center line, had proved himself different, was guilty of an attempt to escape his life's mediocrity.

—Use your intelligence, Mendeltort said abruptly.

—Intelligent people become intelligent by satisfying their curiosity, Abel muttered toward Mendeltort, aware that the others in the enormous room were silent and listening.

—You can't get near any truth without the imagination to go far beyond it, Mendeltort said quietly.

—That's why I have to doubt you.

—Good, Mendeltort said. That's very good. I would much rather be doubted than believed. At least that shows that somone is thinking.

—Thinking? Abel said.

—And you have never been afraid of trying something new, Mendeltort said. You and I share one quality, the ability to see a point of view other than our own.

—Are you saying that for me? Abel whispered. Or for *them*? Because if it's for me, it's unnecessary.

—Make your own choice, said Mendeltort.

—It's still too soon for that.

. . . If only my sainted people could learn to doubt their own inestimable virtue, and if my other people, those lost vengeful tribes perpetually wandering through deserts of self-pity, could learn to see a point of view other than their own, a choice might be made.

—It's too soon, and there isn't enough of a difference, Abel said. Don't you understand?

—There is little time.

—Time doesn't worry me, Abel said. I've learned how to deal with it, it's almost a friend. But space, largeness, things like that . . . well . . . that's just too much. Please have me taken back to my cell. Please? I don't want to go anywhere. Does that make sense to you?

Mendeltort nodded, turned away. Abel looked beyond him, saw the pale young man in the leather coat regarding him with curiosity, and a difficult small smile appeared on that pale, narrow face. The face of the ruined boxer turned worriedly toward Mendeltort, who had obviously taken more time with Abel than the rules permitted. The other faces had become merely impatient.

The air was suddenly old and smelled like a bomb shelter in which whole families had spent the night. The light was telling fearful lies. Mendeltort's face had slipped out of focus. The vertical grooves in his cheeks looked like scars inflicted by a personal discipline harsher than saber cuts, and Abel wondered why he hadn't noticed how worn and wrinkled his uncle had become.

—If time is your friend, use it, Mendeltort said quietly. Sooner or later there comes a time when you're standing at the bottom of the pit and someone tells you *Climb!* You're not obliged to do it, but at least give it a little thought.

The elegant commander had begun to whisper again to the thick-necked Russian, whose eyes were wet and whose thirsty mouth was like a ravaged baby's; the mustached round-faced Jew on the brocade ottoman was visibly sweating, and pleading silently with Mendeltort to be done with it . . . quickly, quickly . . . before the Russians lost their civilized veneer along with their patience . . . Mendeltort nodded, beckoned gently toward Abel, pulling a silver cigarette case from his breast pocket automatically, his blurred face changing to a double image like a twice-exposed negative, peering out of his own wintery calendar as Tarski had done on the forest path . . . And Abel felt his spine stiffen, his heels came together (Why? When was *he* ever anyone's adjutant?), but it was the young Jew in the leather coat who hurried forward with a match. Abel was certain that his body had become too heavy to shift. Light lay like dirty water on the windows and in the flat incurious eyes of the elegant commander, which were as sternly righteous as his mouth.

Too many questions were asked of him simultaneously. He was immediately dizzy. The great portrait trembled, tilted, hung askew. His old identity had proved to be a deathtrap; the new was too difficult to imagine. The face in the huge ornamental frame was fatherly, stern yet infinitely loving. Suffering all His children to come unto Him. His desk wouldn't belittle Him with fearful disappointments, the portrait assured . . . And how could anyone be so sure of anything unless He were God? No one since the Creation had had such a father . . . And under Him, reflected in the streaked glass of mirrors as an insect trapped in an isolated fragment of a moment, twittered a hollow gray cadaverous apparition with one stainless-steel eye: Abel himself, brutally restored within the context of time, place, irony, and the vastness of everything that he had managed to forget. The suddenly remembered men and women, the terrible events with which he had come to terms before the reappearance of Mendeltort (in that company and room which crushed his resistance) crowded about him, mocking and appealing . . . He wanted to believe that a choice still could be made about what he was, if not what he had been . . . And that he could say farewell to the dead and the living, those who were so incomprehensibly absent when he needed them most and those whom he invented as a substitute, and to say it not as we say goodbye at the start of a journey but when we are faced with an inexorable and unwanted parting of the spirit and the heart.

. . . And he was hearing someone's insane chuckling and listening to the squeals and creaks and hiccoughs of his own hysteria.

. . . And now the elegant Russian officer was looking inquiringly at Mendeltort, and Mendeltort nodded once, abruptly, as if he couldn't trust himself to speak, and someone . . . the round crumpled man with the hurt gloomy eyes of a defeated boxer . . . sighed as though a difficult bout had come to an end, and the pale young Jew who had not found it difficult this time to recognize Abel, whose eyes had taken the measure of everyone, who peered steadily through eyes as functionally narrow as gun slits in a bunker, who must have passed through other places where faces such as Abel's were constructed, began to study his own fingernails and the tips of his boots.

—Take him out, said the officer with the thick red neck.

. . . And the guards' hands were once more clamped to Abel's upper arms and he was turned around. The turnkey was not poor puzzled corrupted Yakovlev, who could not understand that every man has a right to create whatever illusions his reeling mind required, but a stranger, a being who was utterly remote, impassive as the wall, the typical expressionless Lubyanka guard, a robot in green and gray.

He was still laughing, or thought that he was laughing, someone was laughing nearby (he was sure of that) when the guards pushed him into his cell, the unobtrusive little gray universe where he had thought that he had mastered time, and the door boomed shut and the bolt rattled and the huge key turned and the light bulb glared in its wire cage and the bucket yawned and the gray familiar friendly wall, which had promised him that it would destroy the outer universe, echoed Abel's laughter.

The possibility that there was a world larger than a cell, a space not bound by the limits of the wall, door, bucket, and electric light bulb, had to be considered. The narrowness of his self-made horizons was revealed as yet another lie and he saw himself utterly defenseless.

. . . This is all happening far too soon, Abel told himself; he was terrified at the thought of freedom. He had clung faithfully to the silent, orderly world of his cell. He had disconnected the conscious processes by which man normally exists within time, uncoupled memories, connections with the past, discarded reference points.

(Two hanging . . . One whispering a poem . . . One marching with blind resolution . . . One sobbing in a ditch, beaten with a scabbard . . . One raging among a litter of possessions . . .)

The world, whatever it meant for him at this moment, the temporary physical or the lasting abstract, was growing dimmer; a light had failed again and was continuing to fail, a crisis was at hand. His hold on his liquids (bowels, bladder, tear ducts, and veins) was precarious and sharp. Whether or not he was responsible for being what he was, he had his weaknesses, physical and beyond control, and he was guilty of inability to make up his mind. Blood turned to water in his half-bred veins, there was no reason to suppose that this water would turn into wine. This was a chronic illness, he thought, a national disease which crippled his soul. And despite his praiseworthy curiosity, his determination to remain a doubter and examiner at all cost, he did fear a final and inevitable confrontation with himself. Nothing else could damage him as irrevocably. Behind all his poses, wishes, good intentions, behind his former worship of people and abstract ideas, the fear was always present: fear of an illumination he could not avoid, fear of knowledge which no amount of derision could dissolve, fear of definition. The light was flowing from him through his slack mouth and his vacant eyehole, there was nothing more to do except wait for the final unadmitted resolution, nothing to think of, no one to resent, no one he wanted to love. The concrete was cold and grainy under his threadbare soles, his mind was dry and airless as a waiting room, his tears were invisibly running.

Catherine

AFTER A GUNMETAL-GRAY AUTUMN DAY the night wind brought rain. She was alone in the hut except for her child, sitting in the dark room so as not to waste lighting materials on herself alone, waiting for the other women to come in from the fields, from the cement works where some had found work, from the sheds where they combed raw cotton and stole burlap bags. It was her turn to cook for the women and to watch over their bundled possessions and that was why she had not gone out, at dawn, with everyone else.

. . . Dusk falls early here in the steppe, the heart of our darkness, and night is immediate. Wind comes with nightfall. The wind is colder now and heavy with rain. The landscape tones are borrowed, she recited mentally; Eastern, brown to tarnished bronze to green on the lakeshore . . . The sky is steep and slanted, given to low cloud, mother-of-pearl, oyster gray with purple reflections . . . The lake is vast, of an unmeasured depth; its sand is cool and glittering with mica. At night, the solitude and utter desolation of this village, which war had enriched with an evacuated factory, becomes a physical sensation. Where shall we go from here once it is time to move? Perhaps this is where we will stay, could this be the end of the journey? The men, whatever men are still left in the village, will likely ignore us; we could be on our own, living as we may. The war had already changed much of the people's lives in the heart of Russia but it is too new, too impersonal, to have written new rules for their behavior. To speak to a foreigner in Russia is . . . could be . . . dangerous and all the men know it. They know that Russia's population consists of only three kinds of people: those who had already been imprisoned, those who are in prisons, and those who will be. A foreigner is always dangerous to a Russian's existence. The women are braver, or perhaps more curious, or perhaps more resilient and better able to take care of themselves. We could trade with the women (as we do). We could live here, those of us who can sidestep death. We have been trained not to court eternity and most of us have stopped dying. The old and the weak had died on the journey. A few are still dying, can be expected to die. Not surprisingly. Those who are too ill or too dispirited to forage for roots. And the remaining old. And the very young.

She looked at her child.

I must have it baptized before it's too late. *Him,* not *it,* for he is not an object, not neuter, but a human child for all his silences and lack of human motion. Someone must know something about the ritual of baptism. Perhaps Kobza would know.

We hear of a war.

Remotely, in our isolation.

We wait, for to move about the country now, in the midst of a war (no matter how distant), the movement of armies, the flow of conscripts, the waves of refugees, the chaos and hysteria and summary executions, would bring our greater journey to an unscheduled end.

We hear of an amnesty for people like ourselves, but no one knows what it is all about. How will it affect us? Amnesty, a forgiveness. Are we to forgive? Or have we been forgiven the crime of survival, the sin of not having been born in the heart of Russia? We wait to be told the meaning of forgiveness. Here as elsewhere. In the bleak desert steppe which I must remember. We live, somehow, as birds live, while we're waiting. There are so many new people who had come to join us. Hundreds of men and women lay in the fields, under the few trees that the steppe provided, along the road, along the paths to the lake and also on the lakeshore and all the way to the military camp that others were building. A hundred new walking skeletons arrived each day from camps and from prisons; there were so many Polish people here now that Russian had become a foreign language in the heart of Russia.

She couldn't remember when it had been, precisely, that they had come with Kobza to this village, but it was sure to have been many months ago. Perhaps even as many as three. Under the circumstances of their lives, three months might have been three decades. They had come and stayed because no one among them could go any farther; indeed, too many of them had come to the village only so that they could die with a roof over their heads. The village, or rather the collection of huts, shelters, sheds, makeshift sleeping spaces within the angle of two walls (dead branches had been enough roofing for most of them in summer), was one of hundreds of such villages, she new. The nearest railroad track was scores of kilometers away. It seemed no more permanent than the traces of camel caravans patiently trodden into famous deserts, yet not all the deserts put together could equal the savage spaces of this fragment of the steppe. We're in the country of Samara, she told herself, although it is now called by another name. Its isolation was not a guarantee of safety.

She looked through the window and watched, for some moments, a procession of scarecrows, perhaps three or four hundred in number, march past in threes and fours, supporting each other. There seemed to be nothing human left in these released prisoners of the North, except that they helped each other up when one or another fell face-down in the mud.

Mechanically, she reached out, touched the cradle, rocked it.

. . . Pani Mosinska, who lived on memory, would know the ritual of baptism.

The cradle creaked, it wobbled. It did not rock. The cradle was a box. The rockers had been barrel staves and that's why they were wobbly. The small cross, made by Kobza, hanging crookedly from the canvas awning on top of the cradle, had been carved from fishbones. All Polish people coming to the villages in the heart of Russia, miraculously freed from their camps and prisons, arriving in thousands every day throughout southern Russia, wore crosses made of bone, molded from prison bread, stitched out of thread and string, beaten out of buttons and badges of rank that had been torn off old uniforms, pieced together from cardboard and glue . . .

The child's eyes were closed.

She turned to the window.

She saw four women walking through the mud in the falling darkness.

She wondered if the trading had gone well for them, if they were bringing bread. If they had found a new source of roots, if they had unearthed an old pit of potatoes. It was too dark for her to recognize their faces but she thought she knew them. They walked gingerly, grasping at fence posts and enclosures, for the mud in the wide road passing through the village was knee-deep and treacly, a truly Russian mud, sometimes thick enough to immobilize a horse, sometimes so thin that ducks would drown in it.

She looked into the cradle.

She went to the stove.

Time, now, to light a fire in the big clay stove on which they would sleep later, and the tarred twists of birch and willow which served them for lamps. Light only one torch, there is a shortage of wood that may be used for torches. There is some paraffin, she remembered, but it must be spared to make soap. People still died of overwork and many were hungry, but the typhus lice had all but disappeared and sometimes everyone got enough to eat.

No, not enough, never quite enough; enough perhaps to awake before sunrise and get up for work. Not enough to subdue the pains in the belly, cramps of hunger . . . the fingers which were always shaking, the eyelids that twitched . . . She supposed that none of them would ever say *Enough* to offers of food. In the future, if they were indeed to have the future that rumors of amnesty suggested, they would eat butter by the pound and bread by the loaf. If things were better now . . . and, yes, they *were* better . . . it was only in comparison with typhus and starvation. When people had been dying in dozens every day.

Now only one or two were still dying.

She looked into the cradle; the child hadn't moved. It couldn't eat. Its belly had become a shining gray balloon. Its small mad eyes were mercifully closed. It rumbled with gases. Perhaps it had already died. If not, it—*he* not *it*, she had to remember—would be dead tomorrow. Or the day after.

She set about the stove, lit the kindling wood, put the pot of birch-bark tea on the boil, set out a cooking pot for whatever Pani Mosinska and the other women would bring from the fields. Winter potatoes, boiled roots and berries, perhaps a stolen cabbage, a handful of raw grain. These kept them strong enough for work. The privilege of working in the fields had been extended to them since the amnesty. Work meant a bread ration. They were entitled to half a kilo of gray bread a day as agricultural workers, if they had the money with which to buy the bread in the worker's store. They were not entitled to buy anything if they did not meet the quota for the day's production, which few of them could manage, and they lived on what they found in the fields and on what Kobza's industry provided.

She was hungry but she would eat later in the night at Kobza's hut. She was content, thinking about Kobza.

She looked at her hands.

(Some weeks before . . . oh, a passing moment, no more remarkable than the daily miracles of survival . . . when the news of war and amnesty had begun to trickle into the villages of the Russian heartland, along with dozens of skeletal apparitions who mumbled their litany of terror . . . the names of their camps, prisons, and mines, forests, and islands, continents of ice . . . Kobza himself had set out to nail down the rumors. He had caught a ride to Kuibyshev in an army ambulance full of drunken soldiers, had traded a bottle of vodka for one of iodine, and, thinking of her hands, had stolen a roll of bandages. Her hands were cracked and rotting, the sores never closed. She couldn't bring herself to waste these providential treasures on any part of herself; she had sewed the bandages into headscarves, painted their borders with red-brown animals, exotic blue flowers.)

. . . Such foolishness, Kobza had said gently. Prrr-prrr. Everybody's got to look after himself . . .

Thinking of Kobza now, she smiled, touched the side of her face, shrugged, bent to light the stove.

(Age equals wisdom, says the Old Man's proverb; one does not question the authority of experience!) Youth equals foolishness, says a Polish proverb. The old impose their order, the young must obey.

Yes, she said suddenly, but to what end, what purpose? Am I to be no more than a continuation of some old man's life? And what does age accomplish, other than itself? Some accomplishment! I have my own life to live.

Where? How? She didn't know. But the idea of having a life to live was not entirely an absurdity. She wanted a man on whom her thoughts could focus naturally, a reference point for her own independent spirit . . . Whatever this future life would be, wherever she lived it, she'd keep it free of antique slogans, exhortations: that senseless, selfish Polish glorification of a moldering past, that artificial Jewish pathos of endurance . . . No wonder that old people could point only to the past, they had no future of their own! But somewhere beyond the visible horizons *she* had a future, she was young, alive . . .

. . . Would want a man again sooner or later in her hands and mind, less La Manchan than Cartesian the next time around . . . Whose thoughts described a *flat* trajectory; whose flights of the imagination began and ended on familiar ground.

Wanted one now.

Someone . . . it sounded to her like Dr. Poremba . . . had said something, distantly (being absent), about companionship in adversity, a way to fill an aching and a void, and it might do for her as a beginning; indeed, she questioned, couldn't it do as well for the middle and the end? Perhaps it wouldn't do for a Grand Romantic Idea, not quite enough for dreams of cupids and picture postcards of the Wienerwald, the parabolic leap of the heart beyond the known stars . . . but it suggested kindness, a final filling of the hollow void which her meager flesh contained.

Startled, she felt the sudden icing in her belly, a flutter in her chest . . . then her face was burning.

Her child was dying and her man was waiting, and she was astonished to find her thoughts in order.

There is a certain majesty in surprise, she thought, looking through the window toward invisible stars, conscious of decisions that she had not yet made . . . and caught a shadowed secretive glimpse of herself, an astonishingly chalky apparition pulsing with reflected light. Life calls out to life, she suddenly remembered, makes life, replaces life; nothing else works. The faint glow of light from the nearest galaxy had been en route one hundred and thirty-seven thousand years, traveling six trillion miles a year toward her before she could see it. The ground, luminous with the cold pallor of the sky before moonrise, reflected the chilly emptiness within her . . . And then she was listening to the churning of her inner ice floes, the sigh of the thaw.

Already, she had assumed the position of a penitent sure of absolution, rasped her tongue across her lips and fingered her ribs. Her warmth spread downward. Abruptly, she rose to her feet (off her knees in front of the smoking clay stove) and explored her face as though it were a bruise, and felt her thighs flex with certainty, and her buttocks clenched. *The face you know is better than the face you don't know* had become something of a slogan, but she was turning all her slogans around. All the way to the window she cultivated an air of disinterested objectivity and reason, knowing all along that the light wouldn't be good enough to show her true reflection. Her aura was earth dust, fish oil, paraffin and wood smoke, sweat, damp padded twill, rotting straw, felt boots . . . yet she felt herself to be something more remarkable than the bruised, used body that would confront her in a mirror. She was a woman and knew it again and wanted a man.

Passing the cradle, she looked at its contents; the grotesque little body had collapsed, the gray balloon had emptied, spilling stench; the rubbery cold flesh formed permanent dark hollows wherever she touched it. The shriveled brown toothless face was that of a monkey, the vacant little mouth hung ajar in its own astonishment and, as she watched, a large bluebottle fly landed on its rim, rubbing its legs together in anticipation.

The night was dark over the Volga steppe and a dog was howling. The steppe was flat and endless, its voids infinite, its muddy rivers were heavy with drowned trees. Rain, fellow to the tears she was unable to feel, slanted toward her image in the window, but the sky was clearing. The rain would flood the fields, she thought mechanically. The roads were also flooded. They would be impassable until the first frost.

Then they were there, the women, coming in. Pani Mosinska, gray shawl over shoulders hunched upward like the folded wings of a stooping vulture, reached back a long hand, caught another, pulled. Ziuta Poremba was no longer pretty; her legs were large and stiff under the restitched swinging hem, her chin had narrowed to a thin point, and it seemed likely that she had never had breasts. Under her own fleshless

fishbone chest, Catherine's heart was imitating cannon. A dense unpleasant smell drifted behind Agnieszka Dlapanow. *Dead*, Catherine
said under her breath, and looked toward the cradle. Tereska came last,
one of the new arrivals since the amnesty, a crone who could not have
been much older than herself. Coming in, she kicked out backward
with her heel, slammed shut the door.

—How is your child? said Pani Mosinska. Better?

She hesitated only for a moment, said quietly: Sleeping.

—That's good.

—What's to eat?

The women emptied their pockets on the table; six acorns, a long
tubular root, two blue potatoes, a handful of berries (some green, some
yellow, some black), a handful of brown grain, several leaves peeled surreptitiously off a cabbage head.

—Is there any Taran?

Carefully, Catherine said: Kobza promised to send a few later, as
soon as the professor comes back tonight. Or I'll get them myself.

Ziuta, now virtuous because men were scarce (and she too hideous to
tempt anyone), showed black gums, brown teeth, giggled, said know-
ingly: What else will you get?

—The taiga trots, said the new arrival.

—Get flour, said Pani Mosinska.

—I'll see if Ariz brought some from the mill, Ziuta offered quickly.

—No, not you, child, said Pani Mosinska. Someone else can go.
Catherine. Our Catherine has a way with them, the lice *and* the Jews,
so perhaps she can make both of them remember whom they've been
living off, and who brought them here from the North.

So used to fear, bitterness, and hatred, Catherine hardly heard her.

The old woman had crumpled in her many rages, had lost consistency and coherence. She knew only what she had been and what she
had been born to, and what had been taken from her; she had become
chained to that knowledge and carried it about her like an iron ball; it
was her ballast and stability. In her bitterness she could be blind to the
contradictions between what she knew and what she was saying, Catherine thought, still trying to be charitable. You can't blame the bitter
old for an absence of the sense of the absurd; their own absurdity was
their liberation.

—They have a password now, those Jews, I understand, said Pani
Mosinska. They have secret meetings. They act as though they were
. . . as though we were . . . as though . . .

—We have all changed, Catherine said.

—Have we really? Or have we only just begun to see each other as we
always were? Well, I don't waste my charity on the plotting, conniving,

treacherous . . . (at a loss for words, she attempted parsimonious gestures) . . . I remain what I have always been! But if that's what they
want . . . !

—Nobody wants to hate, Catherine said, aware of her own anger.

—Oh, don't they! Then why do they hate *us?*

—Someone must have taught them, Catherine said.

—Someone? Someone?

—Perhaps they've learned to listen.

—Listen? Listen? That (thin with sarcasm) is practically a *Revela-*
tion! Do you hear voices too?

Catherine turned away, feeling her throat constrict. The old woman
creaked and crackled about Jews. Who . . . and who . . . and who. But
Catherine had heard it all before, had seen it too often; she could recite
that corrupt catechism in her sleep. Old grudges, legends, and suspicions had rested frozen in their northern ice graves, only to be resurrected once Death, the unifying common factor in their lives, had become less present. She thought at once of Esterka, whom she had
envied the possession of a dream and whom she now envied nothing; a
woman burdened with such burning hatred, which was so remote, so
all-encompassing, so knowing that it translated to mildness beyond
reach of argument or reason. The granite lady was a monument to love
beside such silent hatred.

—Can't we still try to treat each other as human beings? she asked, in
search of her own recessed humanity.

—Yes, yes, said Pani Mosinska, replete with antique venom. Your
well-known humanism continues to be . . . well known.

—And misplaced, of course?

The General's Lady slapped the tabletop. A clay bowl (their last)
slipped to the floor, shattered.

—Well? Are you going or not?

. . . She sucks all joy out of the air, Catherine thought, suddenly
short of breath. She destroys oxygen, withers us all with her bitterness.
She was no longer living, so when had she died? In which camp, in
which prison? When did her life become an insupportable burden?
(The dead used to have the grace of immobility and silence!) Why
blame the living for her lack of props, for the vanity that keeps her on
her feet and out of the grave? A terrible old woman, no woman by any
definition: a sexless hulk consecrated to a discredited religion, who
can't forgive anyone else the crime of . . . not being dead . . .

—Yes, persuade your Jewish friends to spare a little flour, Pani
Mosinska said. Ask them nicely.

Ziuta gagged and coughed, wiped blood off her lips. —Ask *Kobza* nicely, she said, propped her shoulders against the whitewashed wall. I didn't have to ask him nicely in the camp. He asked *me* nicely.

—Hush, child, hush, said Pani Mosinska.

—Not one word about him, Catherine said.

Ziuta smiled whitely, coughed, wiped clotting blood. Blood had caked in thin lines downward from the corners of her mouth. No longer fully living, she had become an object of affection for the bitter woman.

—Leave the poor child alone, said Pani Mosinska.

. . . A sound like pebbles rattling in a tin, perhaps a groan. Catherine looked. Agnieszka Dlapanow had fallen asleep, snored, slept on a corner of a bench, her mouth open and accessible to flies. The child was dead, the poetess was dying. Catherine wanted sleep, pinched her arms until her eyes watered, went to the cradle and picked up the dead child.

—You're taking the child?

She nodded.

—On a night like this?

She shrugged.

—It's warm in Kobza's hut, Ziuta whispered.

And now lightning flashed.

She heard a Russian shouting at the end of the street, someone laughed, a woman shrieked and whooped, thunder crumped and crackled on the blackened lake. The white explosions across the huge sheet of water were now a general headache. I wish there was less darkness, she thought, cradling her dead child. She had not asked about the ritual of baptism and now it was too late. But, born in Russia, even an infant would appreciate the dignity of hell, she thought chaotically, and began to run. She had a frantic appetite for light. *This is like being blind!* The mud sucked and gulped at her boots, grasped her by the knees. White sheets of fire flashed among the pines. The fire seemed to burst inside her own brain. Pinpoint red flashes of trees set alight. Thoughts flared like torches. A growling of cannon.

Her path took her past the hut where Esterka lived with Jankele and Kamila. She saw one of the women momentarily outlined against the lighted window, a dark gaunt shadow of a woman who was arguing vehemently with someone inside, someone who was invisible from the road. Her gestures were emphatic; they brooked no disagreement. Each night after work the Jews gathered in Esterka's hut to hear their newcomer, a thin small young man whom Catherine had thought familiar (no, she could not remember where she might have seen that extraordinarily pale face, those dark-burning eyes; in some prison courtyard, probably, awaiting a transport), who seemed equipped with documents and seals that the NKVD *nachalnik* accepted without question, who was some sort of Jewish organizer (it was impossible to conceal such basic matters in a village as small as this one had been before the amnesty), who hardly ever ventured outside Esterka's hut. A tallow candle was burning in her window, and Catherine thought at once: Where could she have got something like that? How could she afford it? Some sort of ceremony was in progress in the hut, it had been decorated with blue and white streamers and a strange Hebrew letter had been painted on the door.

She heard Esterka cry out passionately: *Yes!* as she hurried past, narrowly avoiding the hulking shape of Ariz, the blacksmith, who was hurrying to the meeting.

—Looks like an early winter, Ariz said politely.

Just at that moment one of her boots was husked off her foot by the mud. She stooped to retrieve it and said her own Yes. Yes, she had survived and she would try to live, and Yes, she could love another human being after all. Yes! Yes! Yes! And Yes, she could bring pleasure, perhaps even joy, into another life, and she could fill a life other than her own, and Yes again, in that filling her own body would be reconstructed.

. . . This is an unknown hour after sunset on an unnamed day in August 1941, and she is hurrying to her lover with a muddy boot under one arm and a dead child held in the crook of the other. She is wet and cold and her face is burning and she has never been more certain that what she did was right. The mythical beasts have taken shelter from the rain, their heraldry in tatters, and the disapproving ghosts of childhood have been struck by lightning. Right and wrong are still important to her; after all, she knows she is human; and although the nuns would disapprove of carnal connections, God (she was certain) was delighted. How could He be anything but understanding,, having spent more than thirty years among fools? Yes, she cried, exultant, and Yes again for good measure, for she was a woman possessed of all the graces of her kind despite the dreadful aura; she was a part of that fraction of mankind who could give as well as receive and, in receiving, give again. Gone and forgotten were her other definitions and poetic fancies. No more Raphael Madonnas in a Hermitage, no more heroic fantasies of Liberty on the Barricades. Her breasts, she knew, had risen, and the rain sluiced away the last of her cobwebs and she exulted in the rolling thunder. Lightning followed lightning so swiftly that it seemed like one continuous white glare in which she saw mountains (perhaps they were clouds?) and the thunder struck in cadence to the beat of her pulse.

. . . To share a life, a house, a room, or even a meal without first sharing a greater idea is unrealistic, Esterka once told her. Perhaps that's what nations are really all about, don't you think? Or if not nations, then, at least, a People. No, the inheritance was not of blood, she had said, but one of mutual evolution based on a common need, a growing together, side by side, perhaps separately but toward the same grand objective which is always changing. Everything that lives must change if it is to grow, must evolve. Nothing is ever constant, not even an idea—ah, that least of all. You can't fix the universe in some convenient century of your imagination, you must keep pace with the soil upon which you walk as it spins and hurtles among suns in darkness. Yes, she cried in the riven darkness, and laughed because she suddenly realized that she didn't even know her man's given name. And then the sky was clear and the imaginary mountains had drifted away with the rest of the clouds but she was still poised for flight, impatient and suddenly angry to be alone on the rim of a hostile planet. One of her burdens had fallen in the mud and she felt panic that she had dropped the child. But the small corpse was still clutched, hard and stiffening under her right breast. She stooped to pick up the irreplaceable boot, looked about. The great white moon reflected in a hundred pools. The storm's last mutter had subsided.

Then she was walking past row upon row of dark silent figures sitting on the high banks of the road on bundles, in wet shawls and burlap, strips of cloth and canvas, capes fashioned of tar paper and linoleum hats. She went past them and scanned their faces automatically for someone she had known. Where are you come from? Kolyma, muttered a low voice. Another said: Vorkuta. Yes, but before that? Before *that*? Before that. Ah, well . . . before that . . . well . . . Lwów?
Vilno?
Grodno?
Przemysl?
Tarnopol?
Kowel?
Wlodzimierz Wolynski?
Brzesc nad Bugiem?
And should she then add Poland? Europe? The World? The Solar System? The Galaxy? The Universe? Infinity-in-the-Cosmos? As she had done in schoolbooks as a child. She should have known better than to ask.
—Honest to God, a woman's harsh, weary voice cleaved the darkness, left it notched, and Catherine stood stock-still as if frozen in midstep, and felt her knees beginning to give under her. —Honest to God, they'll be the death of us, the godless scum; to keep people, like this, in

the rain . . . (*Nitchevo*, another muttered, subsiding in mud.) In all my days, said the harsh uncomplaining voice which voiced a general complaint. Never in all my days, honest to God.

—Bronka! she cried, shouted (screamed?). Bronka! Bronka! Bronka!

—What? What? Who . . . ?

—Bronka! Bronka!

—Oh, my sweet Mother Mary . . . !

—Bronka!

Boze mój, o Boze . . .

(Never had soggy canvas felt or smelled so good, never were tears happier!)

. . . When did you . . . and Where have you . . . and How did you . . . And the terrible names fell like clods of earth into an open grave: Taimyr, Novy Bolshoi, the Ob, the Khatanga . . . words chop down forest giants in the Ural Mountains, sink in snow . . .

And do you know anything about . . . anyone?

She did not dare to name them, as if to name them would be to confirm that they had died in snow, crushed under forest giants, starved among mosquitoes on the riverbanks in summer, wasted away in the wilderness, lay buried under ice. But Bronka held her tight against herself, the boot and little corpse were crushed between them, and (miraculously!) Bronka still smelled of fresh bread . . .

—Your parents . . .

—I already know about them! Janek Stypenko was up in the Taimyr, he told me. But . . .

—Emil is alive, Bronka said. Pani Wlada is alive.

—Alive! she cried. Where? Where are they, then? And how do you know?

Because any hope of life had to be immediately confirmed.

—I was with them until a month ago, we were on a train going to Kuibyshev, but I got separated from them. Lost the train, got sick . . . came down here yesterday, walking . . . They were trying to get here, but Kuibyshev is closed to us, none of us are allowed to go in there, so they must've gone somewhere else. But they're alive, wherever they've gone to, they must be. And (and the voice finally broke and whimpered:) have you anything to eat?

—Thank God, then, Catherine said. Thank God that someone's left, I thought I was the last, the only one from our whole family. Thank God!

She clutched her dead child to her breast as though it were an offering she had brought.

—Yes, yes, thank God, Bronka said. But about some food . . . Honest to God, I'm so weak, been living on boiled nettles, bark . . .

She did sit down then, in the mud. Her face was white in moonlight; it looked like a skull.

—Of course I'll find food for you, Catherine said. I don't know where, but I will. You're safe now, you know? You're with us now, sweet girl. If you'll just stand up again . . . that's it . . . that's better . . . (She could drop neither boot nor corpse to embrace the other.) I'll take you to my man.

—Ah, is *he* here, then . . . ?

—What? (Suddenly Catherine realized that Bronka would be thinking about Abel. She saw him then as she had seen him last, read the message that had passed between them, wished him well wherever he might be; if they were ever to meet again anywhere, she knew, it would be with the gentleness of persons who had survived a terrible accident together, who had helped each other, and then returned to separate lives.) —Abel is dead, I think. This is . . . someone else.

—Ah. Well. Honest to God. I don't know what come over me, falling down like that.

—It must be something that you haven't eaten, Catherine said, and suddenly both women were convulsed with laughter.

A cottage door opened.

Kobza got up to welcome her, clumsy as a bear on his stump. She would think of him later while she loved him; she would design his labels: who or what he was to eyes other than his own. Later, after light and food and warmth and her sense of resurrection had restored her reawakening sense of self. Now he was size, and awkwardness and kindness, and that was enough. Firm soil among her quicksands. He took the dead child from her arms without a word, said nothing (she exulted in the wisdom of his silences) as he reached out toward the grief in her face, found none in eyes that contained something altogether different, placed the child in an empty Taran crate.

Kepi rose politely, seeing Kobza rise. Professor Karolewski sat behind the table: stiff, filled with stale air like a lead toy in a painted uniform. But his small eyes glittered.

—I came because . . . well, we found very little in the fields today, Catherine said, and led Bronka to the table. The girl sat down with difficulty on bruised bones.

Professor Karolewski said: We have almost nothing left. I did very badly in Kuibyshev today, very badly. They've requisitioned everything for their soldiers, and people are hoarding whatever they have.

—The fields are full of half-rotted potatoes, she observed. The local people don't bother to dig for them. They take what they need for themselves and leave the rest to rot. We could try to get some of these potatoes.

—Can they be dried? Kobza asked.

—Dried? I don't know. Mushrooms can be dried. There should be mushrooms tomorrow after all this rain.

—Private appropriation of state property, the professor said. Five years' imprisonment minimum. Nobody here is going to risk anything like that.

—We have to have these mushrooms, Kobza said. We have to carry as much food as we can. If that's what it takes to reach the army, that's what we'll have to risk.

—Army? she said. What army? Are we going somewhere else again?

—There's to be a Polish army organized in Russia, Kobza told her then. The professor says that it's part of that amnesty that we've been hearing about.

—An army?

She had to sit down immediately, made suddenly weak.

—We'll be on our way as soon as we find out where this army is supposed to form, Kobza said. Tomorrow morning we have to start collecting everything that we'll need for the journey.

—All this is highly premature, the professor said. I still say that we should wait here until matters . . . ah . . . clarify themselves. There is always time for leaping into the unknown.

Kobza said nothing, smiling to himself. He handed her a small bundle twisted out of kerchiefs. She felt grain move under her fingers and sent her mind on a voyage of magic exploration: wheat? rye? buckwheat groats? And something solid, something more substantial. She opened the bundle, took out a large carrot, and began to laugh.

—A carrot, she said, unbelieving. What sort of an impossible miracle is that?

Professor Karolewski was watching her fingers. —I found that, he said, his voice petulant with hunger. In the truck. It must have fallen out of some woman's bundle. It was the Devil's own temptation not to eat it right there, on the spot, as it were. But (and he gestured vaguely toward Kobza, who grinned and looked away) how could I have done that? Our leader would have found out about it somehow and he'd have skinned me and sold my pelt for army boots. Still, I must say, it was a very tasty and nourishing idea for a while . . .

She looked at Kobza, who nodded and smiled, and she felt uplifted and a little dizzy, and stroked the carrot as though it were an object that called for reverence, and thought of fields full of vegetables and orchards full of fruit, the wealth and natural abundance of the villages

she had known in childhood (impoverished, certainly, by most standards other than those of Russia), and wondered if she would ever take
any kind of abundance for granted. Her hands were shaking. She
placed the carrot on the rough tabletop in front of Bronka and steadied
it to keep it from rolling away, or vanishing in some other manner reserved for objects that were both magical and revered, before the hungry girl could seize it and bring it to her mouth.

Bronka made gurgling animal sounds as she chewed the carrot, and
Catherine closed her eyes. She heard the professor asking where the
bucket was, heard him get the bucket and go to the door, then heard
the door slam behind him. She opened her eyes. Kobza was standing by
the Taran case, looking at her child. She couldn't think of it as anything that had ever had anything to do with her; it had never smiled,
she had never heard it make the slightest sound; it had never seemed entirely human, born as it had been. She didn't know what defect had
made it as it was. She thought that she should feel something other
than relief; surely her sense of calmness, her peacefulness couldn't be
jutified? And *shouldn't* there be grief? Even Poremba's mad Russian
woman had searched through mile after mile of snow for a child frozen
and abandoned days and miles earlier. But, at this moment, she was indifferent to anything outside herself and her immediate feelings. We
can demonstrate only hatred and hunger, nothing more; we are still
strangers to our own emotions. Her inner thaw had only just begun.

She closed her eyes again so as not to see Kobza as he picked up the
child, wrapped it in burlap (an extravagance that seemed to shock her
basic instincts of survival), then replaced the cowled invisible puppet in
the box, covered the box, and moved it behind the crates and all the
other boxes where she would not be able to see it. She was aware of the
child's . . . puppet's . . . presence in the hut but only as a body, yet another body, one of hundreds of such inanimate and discarded objects
which had been part of her reality for what seemed like a lifetime. The
bodies had never been individual to anyone in the camp, they were all
one body, unknown and unremarkable and unimportant, buried and
buried all over again so many times each day, indistinguishable except
in weight and length and the size of the hole that had to be scraped
for them. Why, then, close her eyes? What was she likely to see that she
hadn't seen before? She opened her eyes and knew that, this time, she
would not need to close them again. Kobza was sitting across the table,
facing her again, nodding his large shaggy head, attempting to smile.
He had brought a small clay bowl full of steaming kasha and placed it
before her. He had placed another such bowl before Bronka.

—Eat, he said. There's more when you're done with that.

—Not now. Perhaps later.

—Are you imposing penance on yourself?

—Perhaps. I don't know.

—Your hunger won't resurrect the dead, he said. You come first, you always come first, remember that.

—That's not how we were brought up to think, is it?

—The only place I was ever brought up was in front of a judge, Kepi said, and laughed. It was one hell of a bringing up, I tell you.

Kobza smiled, said: Now there's a truth for you. Eat it while we have it.

—You take half, then, she said. I know it's your own meal for the day. If we're to share anything, then we have to share everything.

—All right, then, he said. I understand that. But what's mine is yours and you've got to take it from now on without thinking about it. As long as I have something, you have something too.

—And what's mine is yours? (Her body, she thought, had clenched like a fist; it closed and opened spasmodically under her; her headache had become a sound in her mind.) I don't bring you much. A child to bury . . .

She looked directly into his large dark eyes, said: And what about this journey? Are we really going to look for this army?

—I think it's very important that we should, he said.

—Well then, tomorrow I'll organize the women and we'll go to pick mushrooms. We can look for berries. It may take us a week or two to collect enough but we shall do our best.

—I know you will, he said. I have a feeling that this will be the most important thing that we will ever do.

—What? she said. Pick mushrooms?

He laughed. —No. To go to this army. Everything can change for us there, I think. We'll never have to think about this kind of thing again.

—This kind of thing?

—This hut, this village, Russia . . .

He put his hand on her shoulder, squeezed it gently, nodded toward his boxes in the corner and what he had concealed behind the boxes. —Never to think of any of that again.

—Someone, she said, Pani Mosinska, I think . . . says that people who don't always remember everything that has ever happened to them are condemned to live through all of it again.

—She has no choice about what she thinks, Kobza said. Her time has stopped moving.

Kepi laughed, said. —Well, what d'you expect? When she was a girl, the fastest thing on earth was a horse!

Catherine could smile then.

Kobza also smiled.

—Easy, isn't it? Didn't I tell you you'd be laughing and smiling again?

—I've smiled quite a bit since then, she reminded him. This isn't the first time.

—No, thank God, he said. You've given me a lot to smile about too.

—But can we really start believing that everything will change?

—Everything? Prrr-prrr. (She smiled again because he had forgotten that, with her, he didn't have to don his janitorial disguises.) I wouldn't know about everything. But we'll make it through this and go on to something else, and then to something else, and so on until all this is over.

—Can we believe that this will ever end? That there really is another life, another kind of life for us somewhere else? That we shall ever *leave* here? How could we ever live anywhere else?

—We'll do it, that's all.

—Can we ever make living a habit, something that we can take for granted? The way that we have made death a habit here.

She would learn someday, she supposed, not to ask questions that no one could answer; she wouldn't really want anyone to answer her questions, only she could know what her questions were really about. Yes, she would believe again that she could go somewhere else and be someone else, coming to life as though it were a destination, the end of a journey and not a beginning; she would be in that life as though it were an imagined city that she had never visited but which she would recognize, instantly, once she had arrived there; a city complete with a glass-roofed terminal where all her arrivals and departures could be noted on a board and kept in perfect order; a life of celebrated moments and unremarkable occasions when time itself could be revered again.

—Honest to God. (Bronka spoke in a voice to which hope had been restored; she spoke from beyond the last milestone of doubt.) I will live. I know it.

. . . I will try to live, Catherine said, smiling to herself.

She introduced the girl (a woman, not a girl, only a year older than herself and therefore eons beyond the simplicities and certainties of girlhood), told Kobza about Emil, Cousin Wlada. Bronka recovered sufficiently to elaborate.

—When they took us from Lwów, we went to Lake Sergin. That's where Pan Modelski died. We were there a month, maybe more. There was no way to tell, even for the women, because nothing inside anybody worked like it did before. We were all sick, a lot of people died. Then, oh, maybe a year ago in winter, maybe it was at the start of spring, they took us, put us on the train. All good people from Lwów and the country around there, mostly well-off Jewish families, a few Polish families, a few Ukrainians. You never saw anybody help each other like we all did then, you'd think we were all one family, looking out for each other in that train. We rode ten days in that train. You know what that's like, so I don't have to tell it. Then we got to a station, a place called Afanasyevskyi Razyezd, in the Sverdlovskyi Oblast. There they took us off the train, and we went on foot about twenty, thirty kilometers into the hills and woods, and there were some old barracks so full of lice and fleas that your legs were black as soon as you stepped in. There we worked digging on a dam. Then we got moved to cutting timber. Pani Wlada worked on the road that we had to build so's to get the timber down to the river for rafting, then she worked on the tree cutting with an ax. I had a job sharpening axes. It paid very little, not enough to buy enough to eat. The best you could get, if you filled your work quota, was eight and a half rubles a day but the quota was so high that nobody could fill it. Anyway, even if you filled your quota you could buy no more than a kilo and a half of gray bread a day, because that's what your ration was for work in the forest, and that cost a ruble and thirty-five kopeks. Emil, the poor little fellow, didn't work, so he had no right to buy anything at all, he ate only when Pani Wlada and me made our quota and when we got paid. There was nothing else we could get except bread unless it was May Day or the anniversary of the October Revolution. We lived on what we had brought with us from Poland that we could sell, but we had brought little, there hadn't been time to take anything, so how long could that last? And we couldn't leave that work and look for other work because the Timber Trust wouldn't let us go. So there we worked a summer and then a winter. In summer the mosquitoes were thick as kasha in the air, we were all swollen like balloons. In winter, well, you know about the winter. Sometimes we worked up to our shoulders in snow. A lot of people died. One old Jewish couple hanged themselves. A lot got hurt when the trees burst in winter and fell on them. And so it went until last month, when they gave us word about this amnesty, and all the Polish people were let go. Pani Wlada and me and little Emil thought we'd come here but we didn't have enough money for the train. So we had to sell everything we had brought from Poland, everything that was still left, even what clothes we had, and even that wasn't enough for the three of us. But there were some good Jews with us, and they helped. They gave what they could so we could go together. I tell you, I'll never forget those good, kind people. That Roza Goldblatt and Pani Tierfman, and the Goldbergs from the Old Square in Lwów. Rachel Goldberg gave me a pot of pickled fish she made, and some cucumber pickles, and that's what we had to eat on the train for near on a month.

So we were all together on a train but we just kept on going and going because no place we got to would let us get off. So we kept on going and going. Weeks, weeks of going like that, from one place to another. Then I got off the train at one of those stops where they were taking water. I went to pick nettles and acorns in a wood so we could boil them in the train and eat. But I got sick. I fell, and couldn't get up, and the train went away. I know it didn't get to Kuibyshev because I was told that Kuibyshev is closed to us, no big city is open to us, so I don't know where that train will go. But they're alive, Pani Wlada and little Emil, they're with good people, and sooner or later they'll be let off somewhere from that train. And because there's this Polish army to be made somewhere, well, all of us will get there sooner or later, if we can.

—We'll do that, Kobza said.

Bronka had become very pale and now she leaned back and closed her eyes and began to sway.

—Well now, Kobza said. You, Kepi, why don't you take Panna Bronka to the women's hut? She needs to get dry, get some sleep, rest up a bit. And take whatever food we've got on the stove along with her, take what bread we've left.

—Perhaps I had better go along, Catherine said. Pani Mosinska . . . can be difficult.

—I'll do it, Kepi said. I know how to handle our old granite lady, specially if I bring the kasha and the bread. (And then to Bronka, suddenly so gentle and concerned that Catherine had to smile:) You come along with me now, little lady, come on with old Kepi. I'll see to it that you're taken care of. And one of these days, I swear it, we'll make those bastards pay for everything they've done. I swear it. Sooner or later, see, everybody pays for what they did wrong.

On their way out, they passed Professor Karolewski, who was coming in with the bucket he had filled at the well.

She watched him warily, never having trusted that curiously difficult and narrow man whose ponderous artifice had set her teeth on edge. He was an academic, a historian, a petty commentator on other men's greatness (as Abel had once described him) who bolstered his own stature in his eyes by denying the humanity of others. Not much, it appeared, had changed for him in Russia. She remembered what Cousin Wlada had said about this man's wholly human wife, a complete woman by any definition, who had fled from him as though he were the bearer of plagues, and had become the lover of a soldier. For that, she had been pilloried by society, along with her soldier, and he had been raised to the status of an afternoon saint.

Now, as she watched him, she heard another roll of thunder in the east. The rain would turn the clay tracks into quagmires. Kobza sat behind the table, watching the professor. The professor was putting the bucket on the stove so that roots, the odd plant, the providential small fish caught on a line in the lake, could be boiled for the morning's soup. He was searching behind Kobza's boxes for the twist of pepper that Kobza had bought from the village *lekpom* (pepper was said to be a cure for rheumatism) and for the last of their salt, and she was suddenly sure that he would find the body of the child and put it in the bucket. She watched in horror as he raised a long yellow bone and started to sniff it, then remembered: a horse had fallen at the mill and had provided meat earlier in the month, a bone or two were still on the stove to fortify the soup.

Her sudden fear subsided; the child, her last visible connection with the past, would never be found. The professor was stirring the soup with the long yellow bone. She began to listen.

—There is no doubt about that amnesty, then? Kobza said as she began to listen.

—None at all.

—Well? What do you think?

—I think it's an unfortunate, ill-considered word. It implies that we had all committed some sort of a crime. I don't know how our government in London could have agreed to such a libel of two million people. But that's what happens when you have a military man for a Prime Minister, I suppose.

—I think that it's a miracle, Catherine said.

—Oh, of course, a miracle, the professor said. Certainly, a miracle. And now a libel is going to be a part of our history.

—It's just a word, Professor, Kobza said. What counts is that our people can leave the camps and prisons. What counts is the army. It also means that we can't be arrested for what happened in the North, should anybody ever hear about it.

Professor Karolewski sniffed the yellow bone, weighed it in his hands, said over his shoulder: My dear Kobza, there are complexities to diplomacy, to history, to the creation of required international images, that simple and . . . ah . . . ordinary people can't possibly understand. For your own good, you ought to leave evaluations to persons whose . . . ah . . . minds are able to judge what is and what is not important. (He peered at the yellow bone, then flourished it.) This bone, now, do you think there's still anything in it?

Saddened, Kobza said quietly: Cook it, and we'll see.

—I think this bone has been cooked to death, the professor said. Are there any others?

—It wasn't much of a horse, Kobza said.

—You could have brought us the nourishing end of it.

Kobza sighed and said: Next time a horse dies somewhere I'll ask you to take care of it.

—Are we really going to spend this night talking about dead horses? Catherine said.

Irritated, the professor said: We're talking about the amnesty, not about dead horses.

—There is a treaty, then? Kobza asked. There is an agreement? There is no question that a Polish army is to be recruited in Russia? There is a Polish delegate in Kuibyshev now, and you did talk to him?

—*With* him, not *to* him, the professor said. One does not talk *to* a government delegate. Certainly I talked with him. It turns out that we know each other, we were at the university together, and it's quite possible that I shall be working with him soon.

—Oh, thank God, Catherine said. Thank God there's finally someone who can help us.

The professor laughed. —Help us? With what? Why? Don't you understand the meaning of priorities? If you're a soldier you can go to Kuibyshev and get a travel voucher and go to join the army. The government delegate can't do anything for anyone who isn't a soldier or who does not declare his intention of joining the army.

—You don't have to lecture her, Professor, Kobza said quietly, and added: Prrr-prrr.

—Then come the children, we must save all the children, the professor said. You understand the importance of saving the children?

—What comes next? asked Kobza.

—Women come next, the professor said. They have the next priority. After the soldiers and the children we're to save the women. I suppose that's some sort of chivalry, I don't know what it is, but women come next.

—Then what? Kobza said.

—Then, if there is anything left over for anybody else, perhaps something can be found for the rest of us. A few rubles, perhaps. A soup kitchen. Something. But it's going to be a very long wait. Don't count on any help from anyone. My friend the delegate just arrived from London, at the moment he doesn't even have a secretary. He doesn't even have a typewriter. He doesn't like the wording of the treaty any more than I do. Do you realize that there's not one word in it about the territories which the Bolsheviks stole from us in 1939?

—Perhaps it seemed more important to save the people and to form the army and to fight the Germans, Kobza said. Earth and old stones can wait, people can't.

Professor Karolewski threw the long yellow bone into the steaming bucket and came toward the table. —The time to negotiate with Russians is when their backs are to the wall, when they would give their grandmothers for room to take a breath, he said. There'll be nothing but trouble out of this agreement.

—But what about the army? Kobza said.

—Stalin has agreed to a Polish army of thirty thousand men to be formed in Russia. All Polish citizens are to be released from whatever hell they've been taken to, and the NKVD is to have no more jurisdiction over them.

—Such a small army? Kobza said.

—Stalin is not exactly a fool, the professor said. Did you expect him to agree to a bigger one?

—The bigger it is, the better for us, Kobza said.

—The bigger it is, the quicker it'll starve, and the less likely it is to do us any good, the professor said.

—I've been thinking something a little different, Kobza said to Catherine.

—Apparently the Bolsheviks also thought something a little different. They'd hardly have expected many of us to have survived the camps. Our people are coming down from the North at a rate of a thousand a week. More than sixty thousand men arrived to enlist in just the first month and, believe me, the NKVD didn't make it easy for them to get there. And there are twice that many civilians, old people, women, orphans, cripples of all kinds, who have attached themselves to this army as though it were salvation.

—Which it is, Catherine interrupted.

—Yes, yes, which it is, the professor said, irritated at the interruption. But for whom? Can you imagine the staggering problem of feeding these thousands? They're dying like flies. The Bolsheviks couldn't be less concerned about them, they send down rations for thirty thousand men and not a gram more. And since our army is still in training it gets the lowest ration category and no medical equipment whatsoever. The soldiers have voted quarter rations for themselves so that they can feed at least the women and the orphans. I don't believe that anyone has ever tried to organize an army under such conditions since the beginning of the world!

Catherine had ceased to listen to the words and figures.

She saw, more than heard described, the makeshift rafts flowing down the Volga with their loads of ragged, half-dead passengers . . . ; saw the long, bowed lines of men and women winding down from the Ural Mountains, through forests and uninhabited wilderness, walking hundreds of miles and marking each mile with their dead . . . ; heard

the fussy little man explain about ten thousand orphans found in Arctic settlements (and forty orphanages, supported by the army, could
take care of only a fraction of this number); . . . saw, on the brilliant
stage of her own mind, two million people on the march from every
corner of an icy continent, unaided, making their own way, riding on
open flatcars, sailing down the rivers, begging their way from village to
village among savage Asiatic tribes, and saw them not as people but as
one vast manifestation of the human spirit, as man's indomitable will
to live at all cost, and to be free in whatever way their freedom
presented itself to them. Life was more than merely the opposite of
death, she knew then, and to live was more than just to be alive. She
would live, she was suddenly sure, and so would everyone for whom she
felt love; for she and they had gone beyond death and the fear of dying.
Life, then, was possible if the will was there, and if fear was not.

—You can imagine how the NKVD feels about *that*, the professor
said.

—I feel so proud, she said.

—Proud of what? said Kobza.

—Proud of being Polish, I suppose, of our will to live. Proud that
after all our people have been through they can still make such an enormous effort. This Polish spirit that no one else seems able to understand . . . Oh, I don't know what it is.

—Proud? Well, why not? (The professor's voice was quivering with
anger.) But how many of these thousands will have to be abandoned so
that some may be saved?

—Nobody can be abandoned, Kobza said.

—Bravo, the professor cried. Spoken like a national monument, a
leader of the people! But it isn't only up to our authorities to decide
who can be saved and who must be abandoned, who can enlist in the
army and who must stay in some ice hole until the war is over. The
NKVD has its own rules about that. And treaty or no treaty, we're still
in Russia!

—I thought you said the NKVD had no more jurisdiction over Polish citizens in Russia, Catherine said.

—Yes, the professor said, as though instructing a particularly dull
and unresponsive student. But they're the ones who decide who is a *Soviet* citizen in Russia! They've excluded everyone from the amnesty
whose nationality of record is anything but Polish. That means no Jews,
because being Jewish is a nationality in Russia and most of our
deported Jews accepted Russian passports anyway! It means no Ruthe-
nians and no Ukrainians, no matter what they declare themselves to be,
because their language of record isn't Polish. These people are desper-

ate now, some of their families have lived in Poland for six hundred years, and there's absolutely nothing that we can do for them.

—So all these people will be kept out of our army? Kobza said.

—They'll never get near it. And the Russians will make sure that the world believes that we've abandoned them of our own will, and those poor wretches will do all they can to compound this libel because they'll be too bitter to know whom to hate.

His head down in his hands, Kobza sat in silence, then looked up and said: How big is this army of ours likely to get? Did the delegate say?

—His crystal ball hasn't been delivered, the professor said with heavy irony. How can I possibly answer a question like that? Think it out for yourself. Everyone who has heard about the amnesty and the army is on the move from one end of Russia to the other. The NKVD drove two million Poles to the camps and prisons in the twenty months that they held half of Poland. That's one out of every three men, women, and children who lived in an area almost as big as the British Isles. They carried off two hundred thousand soldiers as prisoners of war, most of whom they seized in their homes after the shooting ended. They forced another eighty thousand into their own armies. They re-settled about thirty thousand Polish Jews in Russia, most of whom came here voluntarily to escape the Germans. They just about depopulated the Ruthenian and Ukrainian villages in Poland and brought about forty-thousand of those poor wretches to colonize the tundra. If only half of all those people are still among the living, if they can be found in the tundra and the tiaga and in all those dreadful settlements, we could have a bigger army here than we had in Poland when the war began.

—And the bigger the army gets, the more anxious the Russians will be to get rid of it, Kobza muttered then, more to himself, Catherine thought, than to the professor.

—Ah. Congratulations. You are finally beginning to understand a part of the problem.

—But why wouldn't they want a big Polish army? Catherine said, then. If it's true that the Germans are beating them so badly . . .

—My dear young woman, the professor said contemptuously. The last thing that the Bolsheviks would want is a big Polish army in the middle of Russia. It wasn't their idea, anyway. They had to make themselves look a little better to the English, so they agreed to free us. But a Polish army in Russia scares the devil out of them. It's quite beyond their treacherous, Asiatic mentalities to imagine that our soldiers would be willing to fight a common enemy beside them. They think that we might do to them what they did to us in 1939, and the idea of a Polish army growing behind their backs, while the Germans are kicking them from one end of the Ukraine to the other, is the stuff that nightmares are made of in Moscow. There is nothing that they can do about it except let this army starve itself to death while it is trying to feed the rest of our people. And they won't be able to do anything else about it until the Germans give them time to breathe. I hate to wish the Germans any luck, but I hope they don't start losing the war for another year.

—They'll probably start losing it this winter, Kobza said. Everybody loses their Russian wars in winter.

—Well, well, the professor said as though a horse had spoken. Another historian? Let's hope they don't lose all of it this winter. I'd hate to think what would happen to us if Stalin no longer needed the goodwill of his western allies. I dread to think what *will* happen to us when *they* start needing *him!*

—But what I'm thinking, Kobza said. What I think may happen, is that this army won't stay in Russia very long.

—You can be sure of one thing, the professor said fiercely. Once the army is *armed* it won't allow anyone to disband it. None of us want to see the white bears again. Nor will it allow itself to be used piecemeal among the Bolsheviks. Once it is a real army, not a collection of ragged penitents, it's going to stay together for better or worse.

. . . Peace then, and silence with the others gone, a Nativity scene in the style of Russia in the fifth decade of the twentieth century. The child, born among beasts, is dead. The man is working quietly in the corner, fashioning a coffin. She sweeps the floor with a broom made of twigs and rushes. She sweeps in small circles. She has washed the table. She has banked the fire for the night, soon it will be ashes. She will put her boots and his into the ashes so that they may dry. She has spread dry canvas on the stove and covered it with straw and covered the straw with burlap. She has spread Kobza's dogskin coat over the canvas, the straw and the burlap. Her threadbare rags and his, when taken off, will become the pillows.

She was acutely conscious of herself as a woman's body, aware of that stained and soiled body's presence in the small, smoky one-room hut. Each of her tissues, cells, nerve ends, and follicles was clamoring for attention in a language that she has schooled herself not to understand. The unfamiliar body appeared to have narrowed, it has declared its neutrality in all her inner conflicts and now prepared to betray her again. It has, so far, refused to endorse her personal decisions.

Because her hands seemed to be wounds, and because she was angrily aware that she had consciously avoided looking into glass, into still surfaces of water, at anything which might have reflected her bruised and tarnished eyes (knowing that she could never again recognize herself as she had been), she thought of the framed photographs which had hung in her parents' home: herself as a child.

. . . Lost in the interlocking cellars of her parents' house (she could not imagine how or why she had wandered into that labyrinth of connecting junk rooms), she had listened fearfully to a distant locking of doors and receding footsteps. She had been sure that she'd be lost forever among packing cases, behind grumbling hills of coal, stacked yellow cliffs of newsprint which threatened her with an avalanche of slogans, in a surreal landscape of rotting trunks, ruptured hobby horses, headless dolls, and gutted teddy bears. Moving from one subterranean dusty chamber to another. (And where was she to sleep? Kobza, the janitor, she knew, slept in packing cases.) She had wondered what the years ahead would have been like, thinking that life was over. Would she have had children? (Little girls grow up, become ladies, and ladies have children.) She could not find the door to the cellar stairs. The doors, and there were many doors, all led to other cellars. Then she began to cry because there had been no one to witness her prayers and so they probably didn't count, and heard the gentle old voice (yes, she had thought it old, being a small child) muttering inside a packing case: Don't cry, little lady, you got to learn to look after yourself . . .

In this other world which she could remember now and then as the imaginary life to which she was heading, days had moved in measured cadence, making their somewhat stately progress between logical transitions, so that the end was always a predictable result of every beginning. Her father, who had instilled in her a respect for learning as a form of goodness, had taken comfort in logical progressions. Her own life had been designed with quite the same care. She knew that the large, quiet man in front of her, secure in his convictions and having nothing left to prove to anyone, having no personal crusades on which to lead children, was a man to whom she could entrust whatever portions of herself were of any value. But she was not sure that she was able to give as much as she had to take, either now or ever. In time, perhaps, in life. It was quite as possible that she would always hoard and guard whatever was most precious so that she would never be left without something in reserve. Russia had taught one dreadful lesson to them all: that human life could be seen as a trivial matter, an accident without individual meaning, and that nothing and no one could be fully trusted with everything at all times. In that respect, the logic of her life had been interrupted. She knew what it was like to have been left without nourishment or shelter in an internal wilderness, she was unlikely to allow herself to be rendered wholly destitute again. If he could take her on those terms, at least in the beginning, then she would give him whatever else she thought she could find.

. . . She sweeps and sweeps and knows that no matter how hard or how long one sweeps a dirt floor it will never be swept cleaner than it had been before the sweeping started; it will never be anything but hard-packed earth and dust unless one should sweep through it, through the core of the earth, across the molten heart of the globe, and out to the other side into a different daylight. There used to be pine planks on this floor but they had long since been pulled up and burned in the stove, not a trace of them had remained to mar the brown dust. The earth is hard and dry and trodden into the density and texture of marble, but it is still dust, the eternal dust which can never be transformed (by sweeping) into parquet flooring. Why is she sweeping, then, a floor which cannot be swept clean? For the same reason that she moves and breathes and hopes and believes and seeks the sense of her origins in an imaginary life. A reason which requires no further explanations. Her absolute attention is focused on the floor and on the small circular motions that her broom is making. Her mind, a graceful instrument, has folded itself in sleep. All her activity is, then, physical. She is not conscious of any other function.

She swept and she swept, her body neither closed nor open under her, neither clenched nor twitching. Poor Catherine, whose childhood fantasies were apt to fall upon parquet and run like quicksilver between cracks in flooring that smelled of oranges and lemons, heard the Fates knocking on her doors to drown the terror of thought.

There *was* a quiet knock then, on the door, and then there was another, and the door remained closed. Not a Russian, then, she thought, and played with the foolish vision of the horrid sisters waiting to rush in with their shears, looking for threads to snip. There are none left here, she told them formally, and wondered if it were true. Kobza went to the door, opened it, and stood there for a moment whispering to someone who had remained outside. She saw the extraordinarily pale face of the young Jew, the broken face which seemed so unaccountably familiar, which moonlight made silver. Briefly glimpsed, this imperial death mask was soon gone.

The door closed. Kobza was coming back toward her, shaking his shaggy head. In answer to her quiet questioning look he said: He wants to see me for a while.

—Are they coming with us?

—No. They have other plans. But there is something that they want to talk to me about.

She nodded, pleased, said: They trust you, then.

—They shouldn't, he said. I'm no different than anybody else. No one should trust anyone completely.

—Will you be long? she asked, and felt the sudden certainty of his return no matter how late on this night or on any other, savored the unexpected luxury of knowing that her aloneness had come to an end.

—I don't know, he said.

He looked longingly, his face sad with desire, at the bedding that she had spread on top of the stove.

—Well, she said, conscious of transformations. I'l be here when you come back.

He nodded. He put on his dogskin coat, apologizing for disturbing her careful arrangements. He left. She looked through the window until she lost sight of him. It had begun to rain once again.

Smiling to herself, making a tuneless and unmelodious sound, asking no further questions about anything, she swept the dirt floor.

Abel

THEN HE WAS BEING SHAKEN OUT OF UNCONSCIOUSNESS, dimly aware of a distant rattle, the booming drum-roll of nearby explosions. There must be a thousand guns firing, he thought. The flat dry crackling of anti-aircraft artillery drowned the drone of motors. The wall was trembling under icy sweat. The air was gray with dust. The blue-green robot's marble eyes were fractured with fear.

. . . Was this world, then, to end along with all the others?

The NKVD officer's arms were clasped about gray envelopes and brown-paper files; he clutched them to his chest and belly as though they were proof of virtue and a temporary armor, and Abel thought (absurdly) of schoolgirls awaiting the loss of innocence behind a barricade of textbooks in their sailor collars. He stared at the man's white knuckles as if mesmerized.

—Up, the officer said softly, and suddenly added: *Brother* . . . Get your things, you're leaving.

He stared about. The cell had become his sole reality, a divinely ordered universe fixed amid chaos. It had become impossible to imagine the moment of leaving.

. . . Deep booming sounds (*The Overture of 1941*, perhaps); a work for giant kettle drums and mallets and brass vats full of sullen air; for whirling chips of concrete, flakes of paint; for rattling iron shutters.

The light bulb trembled in its aureole of dust. (I can do nothing against superior objects.) The wall shook and sweated, the bucket gaped and chattered against a quaking floor.

(There was nothing personal in our attitude toward you, said the wall, the bucket, and the light bulb. We only tried to help you to become a socially useful object.)

—Thank you, he whispered, getting up, and the NKVD officer tried a difficult smile as he backed away. —Where am I to go?

—You're free now. You can go and fight the Germans. We're all brothers now, comrade.

He had forgotten all about the Germans and wondered, for a moment, why he was to fight them; they seemed to have no relation to the universe in which he had been living. Germans, he thought: an Indo-European people of great cultural merit. Brahms, Beethoven (or was he an Austrian?), Goethe, and Schiller . . . A nation of poets who formed military fours whenever they heard military music . . . There was that fellow Hegel, was there not? And that other fellow (or was he too an Austrian?). Can't seem to be able to remember the name of that fellow . . . Why should I remember? *He* hadn't created my reality, the world in which I have been living . . . And, anyway, hadn't he been some sort of a joke? I seem to remember . . .

. . . A giant cleared his throat remotely. Uhuuuu-uhuuuu. Hooomhum! Then there was wave upon wave of deep booming laughter.

(Ah, Abel thought. Yes. I remember. The cowlick and the mustache had not proved to be a joke, after all.)

Uhuuu-uhuuu. Hum!

—So, there is a war, he whispered cautiously. So they have come here too.

He sagged and would have fallen had not the NKVD officer supplied a shoulder on which he might lean. The officer stared at him surprised, opened his mouth, then closed it. Yes. Abel thought. He would have remembered to whom he was speaking. And where. And why it would be necessary to explain.

War, he thought. Germans. There had been a war. A short and terrible September. (Boots slide in sodden soil, the thin drawn hurrah . . .) He had thought then that his mind had fallen off a hillside. The war had been lost, but he had not felt responsible for losing something that he had never touched, never grasped firmly, never comprehended. It had been tossed to him with such unpremeditated carelessness that he had failed to catch it. It had slipped between his fingers along with all his hopes and fell (with a resounding military crash) and then was lost. Or perhaps it was he who had been dropped and lost. And now the war had come to find him again.

He wrapped his little bundle, followed the NKVD officer into a gray, darkened corridor full of men in motion.

—When did it start, this war? he asked, to position himself in a new reality.

—June twenty-first, said the NKVD officer in a voice that trembled with emotion. The bastards never gave us any warning, not one damn word . . . !

—No, no, Abel said. It was in September. I remember that much.

—No, it was June, said the officer. It was in June. September . . . that was another war.

—Ah. Then it's not the same one?

—Yes, yes, the officer said impatiently. It's the same one. It's the German war. The war against the Germans. It is now called the Great Patriotic War. The Germans are the hereditary enemy of the Slavic Peoples. You and we, we're Brother Slavs, and they are the Germans. And now (Uhuuuu-huuum!) you are free to go and fight the Germans.

—Are the Germans near?

—In Vyazma, they say . . . you can see Moscow from the hill at Vyazma . . . and this morning they cut the road to Leningrad. And in the south (again the booming laughter, the rolling thunder of nearing explosions) they're said to be in Tula . . .

—And am I really going to be set free at last?

Embarrassed, the officer muttered: The amnesty for the Poles was given in August . . . there were some complications . . . um. Yes, you're free now.

—Ah, Abel said. In August . . . I think something important happened to me in August . . . I can't remember what it was.

—I wasn't here in August, the officer said quickly.

—Was that when Avrum Mendeltort came here? Was that when there were showers? Something important happened then, but I can't remember what it was.

—I wasn't here, the officer said.

—And . . . what month is this?

(And then, suddenly, with a sense of urgency that seemed overwhelming:) What day is this? What year?

—October, the officer said as naturally as though he had been asked for the time of day. It's the sixteenth of October. And the year is nineteen forty-one.

—Twenty-three months exactly, Abel said. Could it have been only twenty-three months?

The officer shrugged.

—Well, Abel said. Well.

And now his own voice was booming, rolling, making echoes. The corridor had become the inside of a narrow drum and the floor was trembling. Ancient dust was boiling up around his knees, so that he could no longer see his shuffling boots, he could not see the white line painted on the flagstones, the line on which he was to walk. He could not see the line and wondered for a panicked moment how he was to walk, how motion was possible at all without the guiding and controlling line. A step to the left or a step to the right off the white-painted line . . . Aha, but, yes. (He suddenly remembered and could not believe:) he no longer needed to walk along the line. What was he to do now that he was free? He didn't have to watch his feet, watch his step, he could walk looking upward if he wished, he could turn around and walk backward if he felt so inclined. He could halt and stand still and not walk anywhere at all. I am free, he told himself. His knees collapsed under him and he sat down on the gouged and smoothly polished flagstones, on the corridor floor. His fingers, made invisible by dust, explored the cracks between the flagstones. He was free to do that.

—Stand up, the officer said, and then added through a twisted smile: Please . . .

—I am free, Abel said.

—Yes, said the officer.

—But what does it mean?

—Stand up, please, the officer said, and added, anxiously: It isn't allowed . . .

—What isn't allowed? Abel said. I am free.

—You are still . . . here, the officer said, and looked anxiously up and down the corridor. Please stand up.

(The officer was terribly afraid.)

—Oh, Abel said, nodding to himself. Yes, I see it now. Yes.

Then he said, cautiously, as if testing the temperature of a stream he was about to enter: I am not afraid.

No, he thought. I am not. Afraid. He thought that he'd never again *need* to feel afraid, as though fear were a placatory mask to be worn in the presence of a remotely contemptuous God and then stowed in mothballs. He was sure that he had gone beyond such ritual and that this was the liberation that the officer spoke of with such terror, as though the possibility of fearlessness anywhere in the world would rob him of his purpose. They were not so powerful then, after all, these gray-green robots with eyes like chips of concrete; they were not immune to the terror through which they existed . . . Was he, then, free of fear? And what was he to do with this godlike freedom?

At once fear was upon him, unreasoning and brutal; not so godlike, then. No.

Whites and grays revolved. White sheets of paint had cracked off the ceiling and sailed down majestically like gigantic snowflakes and fell on hurrying people. The corridor, and the other corridors and stairs and steps and anterooms and passages through and along which he walked beside the officer, were filled with hurrying people. Men and women in blue, green and gray and blue-green and grayish brown, with and without blue-banded caps, in and out of greatcoats, in concertina boots. Nervous, gloomy, looking at him with sudden new curiosity as if seeing him for the first time as a human being, asking mute questions as though he could answer. (And will you speak on our behalf when we're in the dock? Will you tell *them*, whoever *they* may be, that we had not tried to be particularly unkind?) . . . But someone has to answer, insisted all those curious and hastily averted eyes accidentally encountered in the corridors, someone must accept that responsibility! And if the myths of their orderly and secure existence had crumbled under German tank treads, someone new would have to tell them what to do. So, the eyes begged furtively, will you do that for us? Can you? Who can, then? What will happen to us? Yes, we are men and women, after all, not heartless machines. We can feel what you feel: doubt, uncertainty, fear are not your monopoly. No one can monopolize suffering, pain, and terror. Everything is cracking right across like a rotten canvas and all our certainties are gone. To call us less than human doesn't exalt your own humanity. So be forgiving. Understanding. Try to understand. It really wasn't anybody's fault. We . . . *they* . . . you, everyone, only follow orders. Regulations. We obey. We execute the orders. Order is order, it's so in any system, and every order is based upon orders. Try to see these matters from our point of view. We see only what is put in front of us, we do not question orders, we do what we are told for the common good. We don't attempt to understand more than we must in order to perform our function within the great machine. No. It would never do to see more than is absolutely necessary. No. It is that restricted and selective sense of vision which makes our lives internally secure within the machine. Do you blame cogs and gears in a guillotine for cutting off a head? Do you condemn the edge of a headsman's ax? Huh? No. But then something happens. There is an explosion. The machine falters, misses a beat or two. The continuity of your function is momentarily interrupted and the machine is no longer totally reliable. The mechanism staggers on but you can see the cracks in the armature; the myth of the infallible, irreversible machine is suddenly demolished and you . . . we . . . suddenly have new identities as fearful human beings. The machine no longer manufactures our necessary answers. Every component of the stalled machine must find his or her individual answers. What must we do to be safe as human beings bereft of our machine?

Then he knew, with a fatalistic sense of finality that bordered on euphoria, that he himself would never be truly beyond fear because he was human. I am a human being, he told himself, astonished, and free to feel fear along with all else, free to feel beyond thought, beyond calculation, beyond understanding. Convulsed in sudden silent laughter, he knew that he would never again need to be afraid of fear.

. . . Out of force of habit, the officer snapped his fingers and jingled his keys. There is an illusion of safety and reassurance in mindless routine. But the routines have lost their power to reassure, they have become their own mockery. The small triangular convoys of prisoner-and-guards run into each other. They impale each other and become entangled. The guards no longer try to keep the prisoners from seeing each other, there are too many little convoys in collision, too many prisoners to control. The prisoners call out to each other, stop to chat on corners, ignore the snapping-jingling guards. High-ranking NKVD officers run up and down the corridors shouting for order, silence, for instant obedience. Otherwise . . . Otherwise what, cocksucker? Eh? Um. Ah. (Uhuuuu-uhuuuu-HUM! in the near distance.) That's right, we're free. Who are you shouting at, you son of a bitch? The prisoners squat on the floor, lean against walls, talk and talk and talk. (I'm a lieutenant colonel of an allied army, you son of a bitch, so don't you tell me to shut up!)

Uhuuu-uhuuu-hum-hum . . .

—Please . . . ah . . . comrade. This way.

The guards stood at the corners of the corridors, arguing with each other about rights-of-way, while the cracked white paint drifted down in chaotic circles.

(Passing, Father Zenek said: Quite a day, Abel, isn't it? And Abel replied: Quite a day . . . And the priest said: Well, we'll see each other in the army? You know about our new Polish army? Well, we'll see each other.)

—What's all this about a Polish army? Abel said.

—Well, said the officer. Ah. I don't know anything about it. (Then muttered, uneasily:) On whose side would such an army fight?

—Yours, of course, Abel said.

—Why? asked the officer.

—Because the war began in September, not in June, Abel said.

The officer nodded, sighed, and pointed toward a door at the end of a descending flight of marble steps: This way, if you please.

Soldiers with rifles and fixed bayonets stood at each side of the narrow door and stared, bewildered, at the freed prisoners and their apologetic escorts. One by one, the prisoners were admitted into the room beyond the door. They did not come out.

The NKVD officer handed Abel a brown-paper file. Abel saw his name inscribed in purple letters on the coarse brown paper. The officer extended his right hand and Abel (automatically) held out his own crippled fingers. Hello there, fingers. If you had done your pointing at the proper time . . . The officer looked down at the ruined fingers, at the smashed knuckles, at thickened finger ends, at the splayed broad pads of what had been the ends of fingers without fingernails. His own hand hung in the air like a startled bird. He glanced away. He took

Abel's wrist in two of his own fingers. He shook Abel's wrist. He whispered so that the soldiers couldn't hear: I wasn't here until a month ago . . . And anyway . . .

But Abel wasn't listening.

—You're not a Jew or a Ukrainian or anything like that? said the officer.

—What? Abel said.

—You're a Pole? Your father's nationality was Polish? Your mother's nationality was Polish?

—Yes, Abel said.

—Well, said the officer. You'll be all right then, you'll be allowed to join this Polish army . . . A lot of those others are trying to turn themselves into Poles right now . . . But you'll be all right.

—Yes, Abel said.

—Yes, said the officer.

Then he looked up and down the corridor, and in a moment when the noise was loudest, whispered to Abel: But there are others here, Poles, who'll never come out, though they'll never know it . . .

—What is it that you're telling me? Abel said then. And why are you doing it?

—Nothing, the officer said. Forget it. I didn't say anything. Orders are orders and that's all there's to it. It's not for me to question my orders.

—Don't tell me anything, Abel said. I don't want to know.

—Yes. Well, goodbye.

—Goodbye, Abel said.

The NKVD officer hurried away. He clutched his files to his chest and belly. Abel closed his eyes.

The rolling waves of sound had become a continuous booming in his head.

Uhuu-uhuu—Hum-HUM!

Can a mirage be made purely out of sound?

Startled, an apparition peered at him from a mirror beyond the narrow door. A madly logical eye regarded him blankly. An elderly officer creased his parchment skin in a smile meant to be disarming. His soft womanly hands had polished fingernails, he clasped a pencil and rummaged among papers.

—Won't you come in, he whispered in a voice that rustled.

His mouth was purple, as though he had been eating berries. Abel stared at the purple mouth, at the glittering nails; he couldn't tear his eyes away from the pale pink symmetry of these undamaged hands; the long dry fingers were tapping military marches, pointing and com-

manding. The officer had draped a heavy sable fur coat across his narrow shoulders, and Abel wondered whether the furs served to keep the
damp chill of the narrow chamber out of the man's old bones, or
whether they were there to conceal his rank. Regal, barbaric, ancient . . .

And he was shivering for no reason at all.

The officer read papers in Abel's brown-paper file. He said nothing.
The point of an indelible pencil moved along the lines. He underlined
nothing. Occasionally he noted one fact or another on a flyleaf torn out
of a folio volume bound in cracked old leather. The book was a beautifully illustrated copy of *A Thousand and One Nights*, Abel saw, bewildered. The officer made his notations with the indelible pencil,
which he licked now and then. The pencil had stained his narrow
mouth and thin lips and tongue with imperial colors. His voice hovered
between a whisper and a distant creaking. His Russian was beautiful,
polished and unfunctional as his fingernails, redolent of times gone.

—You are a poet, my young friend?

—I . . . don't know what I am, Abel said, or whispered.

—You are a Christian?

—Yes . . .

—You forgive transgressions?

—Yes . . .

—You believe yourself washed clean of fault by the blood of the
Lamb?

—I don't know, Abel said.

—But Christ was sacrificed for you, was he not?

—Yes . . . among others . . . or so we are told.

—His sacrifice was necessary, then?

—Yes . . . I suppose it was.

With each *yes*, a piece of paper left the brown-paper file and arrived
face up but upside down on a little pile of documents growing beside
Abel. He looked at them as though each were an oracle in which his future might be read, he tried to recollect these topsy-turvy fragments of
his identity and he began to shake. His Polish army officer's identity
and service book, with its astonishing photograph of a boy who grinned
(although he had made such a brave attempt to appear humorlessly
martial) above the tight high silvery collar of a dress uniform borrowed
for the occasion; certificates of birth and baptism; the diplomas which
had ended his formal education; Catherine's old letters sent from
Lwów to America and carried back to Lwów; papers with seals, papers
with stamps and emblems and flowing signatures and spread-winged
eagles and rampant lions and Amazon shields . . . Piece by piece and
paper by paper, and also memory by memory and rediscovered thought

by thought, he was being reconstructed before his own eyes. Then he was looking into the other's eyes, all his faculties suspended.

—Do you pray? Are you religious?

—No, Abel said.

The officer nodded, said softly: I myself have great respect for God but none at all for prayer.

(Later, when it was so important to remember each tone and inflection of this rustling voice, when he was being asked to recall everything about this man, he could not even remember the color of his eyes.)

They were, he thought, the luminous eyes of loving women and of charlatans and prophets. He was suddenly cold and trembling, and his head was spinning.

—The only crime which can never be forgiven is to destroy a poet, the elderly officer said in his soft rustling voice. All other kinds of human beings can be replaced, all other sorts of men are interchangeable, like cogs in a machine. A doctor can learn to be a lawyer, a lawyer can become a university professor, a professor can be trained to lead armies, and all of them can be taught how to dig a ditch. They can be manufactured in whatever quantity is needed, then they can manufacture more of their own kind. The death of one of them or a thousand of them makes very little difference, more can be made at will. But an artist cannot be manufactured, you cannot learn in a school how to be a poet.

Abel watched and waited.

—That's why the world bows before the artist, even as it conspires to destroy him because he shows, by his very existence, the nonexistence of equality among men. That is why the artist is, necessarily, a lone and lonely man. I'm sure I'm not telling you anything new.

—Yes, Abel said. I used to think all that.

—And now? said the Russian.

—Now I don't know, said Abel. (The sound of the guns was muffled and unreal in the windowless chamber. Under the mad-lit messianic eyes the purple mouth looked bloodily engorged.)

—We know that one does not become such a man, the Russian went on. One is, or one is not. He has no equals, and never can have equals, and that is why he is always his society's victim.

—Always? Abel said.

—To be a Savior one has to be a victim, said the whispering Russian. Isn't that what we were talking about at the beginning? But there are limits to sacrifice, some sacrifice impoverishes all mankind.

The hooded eyes regarded him darkly and Abel was trembling; ideas clashed like cymbals in his head, thoughts came together and parted, the past and the future made their brief appearances and withdrew. A line, a phrase, a sound was running through his head (and did he really hear a bugle scattering crystal notes in cold cemetery air, were muffled drums beating out the well-remembered rhythms?). Catherine spoke to him remotely, coldly. He knew that he was hardly likely to keep himself from falling unless he gave the problem his entire attention. He was shaking but he didn't (couldn't) know whether this was an illness of the body, sickness of the spirit, a passionate hunger for light and for laughter, or madness . . . simple and definable as a military order.

> . . . Oh, drink the morning air
> In the dawn of the world . . .

(Abel was reciting.)

. . . And suddenly the officer who could no longer be called merely elderly, who seemed so ancient as to be antique, was reading from the brown-paper file which evidently contained Abel's entire life, reciting lines that Abel had forgotten and had never properly understood even as they (the lines) had appeared at the point of his pen: *The cat watches me warily / I say to him: You have nothing / to fear from me, Brother! / But the cat runs away . . .*

And Abel whispered, remembering: *Perhaps . . . Perhaps he knows my nature . . . my imperfect nature, better than I . . .*

The Russian sighed, rubbed his face, leaned back. The motion displaced his furs, which slid to the floor revealing a lieutenant general's shoulder boards edged with the light blue of the NKVD. He smiled. His eyes were suddenly candid in mockery.

—An ordinary person looks for a way to get through life without the need to end it, he whispered then. He clings to whatever he can understand, he pursues illusions, he keeps his eyes on the small print of his guarantees. How wonderful to be a poet, an artist who can create all the dreams that men can live by. Where would we all be without our little dreams?

Abel was clutching the edge of the desk to keep himself from falling.

—Well, said the Russian. You're free. I wish you luck. I'm sure we'll see each other again. And when you see your uncle again give him my regards.

—Who shall I say, sir? Abel said, and the Russian laughed.

—Oh, he'll know, he'll know.

He closed the brown-paper file and nodded toward Abel, who gathered his identity papers with hands over which he had no control and stuffed them inside his shirt.

He went through a tall narrow door at the end of the room, entered what seemed to be a small dressing room, then through another door into an empty, mirrored chamber which he immediately recognized as the room in which he had last seen his uncle and the threatening NKVD commander, where his connections to another lifetime had been restored despite his hopes and wishes. He hurried through the chamber, then through yet another door toward a staircase, then stumbled down several flights of polished marble steps. Marble, porphyry, gold-green-flecked malachite dazzled him with columns. A soldier waved him through yet another exit at the foot of the stairs and he was in the courtyard stumbling over cobbles. He was surprised to see that it was still daylight, and bright daylight at that; the rustling Russian in the narrow chamber had prepared him for night. The dark glazed rows of windows shuttered in black steel, dead as the eyes of corpses laid out in a mass grave, regarded him coldly out of another world. He took a breath, another. He would leave (he thought) with rue and a little grin, but it was not to be. Fear bit into his back with wolf's teeth, his own remaining teeth clattered against each other, and he lurched into a staggering gallop that took him to the ornamental iron gates and beyond.

A cold raw blizzard was driving speckled leaves across a crackling pavement; he breathed the city's fear with every icy breath. The street was full of people who hurtled toward each other, and at him, like planets on collision course, then spiraled aside. The prime luminary of this disintegrating universe smiles off a poster; the crimson galaxy of banners expands and contracts like a cosmic lung, and the motes of dust . . . the particles of fallen stars, asteroids, and moons . . . lurch into view, spin aside and vanish. So nimble, so afraid that they might touch each other. Each of these derailed planets had revolved around a multitude of suns, each had been convinced that it is . . . was . . . the sole valuable center of its universe, that it would always move along a fixed inviolable path through its particular heavens, held at precisely calculated distances from all other orbits . . .

He was weak and dizzy with the effort to stay on his feet, weightless and bodiless, detached and floating through chaos on no fixed course, pulled and repelled by bodies of greater density and speed, of deeper magnetism . . . looking about, with no idea of his purpose, for his own safe orbit. A world unto itself being born in chaos. Genesis, then. Worlds are born in chaos. But where was his Creator? Was he to create himself, to populate his planet with all the creatures that might inhabit it; was he to give them form and definition and assign their functions, and were six days really enough for that? Then he was trapped in plate glass and staring at himself across a cardboard wedding cake and crudely colored papier-mâché pears and a painted apple . . . but which was the image and which was the man, the reflected object?

. . . In the next window there were tables covered with newspapers, people bent over plates of soup. His own sunken eye regarded him intensely from the plateglass window. *Ecce Homo.* The loud passage of a gray-faced, weary, and unkempt company of soldiers (leaden boots scraping along the asphalt) cleaved a notched furrow in his consciousness and left him momentarily bewildered. He recoiled in horror from the soiled shoulders which brushed against him accidentally. His mouth was opening and closing in a tangle of gray-streaked beard, and he saw, in the flyspecked window of the restaurant, a creature which he had not yet named; it was surely a derelict carp rather than a man, it regarded him somberly with a disbelieving eye . . . And suddenly he was shaking in the grip of hatred, a craving for revenge had overwhelmed all his other hungers. He wished to kill. To mangle. To dismember. To violate obscenely. To corrupt and ruin. To inflict agony and to cause fear. To rip two eyes for one, to wrench a hundred fingernails from the hands of children. To impale upon pointed stakes, to hammer with nailed planks, to drip hot tar into empty sockets, to emasculate with shears, to crown with barbed wire, to suspend on meat hooks, to suffocate with hot sand and to drown with urine, to leave defiled and unburied on a dung heap, to hang from telephone wires, to crucify on barn doors.

Someone spoke to him and he looked into a concave face in which soft, wet, and hopeless eyes were begging; he saw the youthful beard, soft as down, the tremulous mouth, the pale cadaverous cheeks of the northern exile under the loose flapping prison cap . . . It, the creature, extended a hand and whispered of food, mercy, kindness, the love of a God . . .

—A kopek or two, brother . . . a crust of bread . . . anything . . . As you crave salvation . . .

. . . And then he was running among scarlet banners, cavorting gray puppets, the boom of explosions; running upon streets cobbled with fear, wholly beyond the bounds and restraints of reasons.

Loudspeakers, bellowing iron. The flash of blue fire overhead and the clanging of a signal bell.

> . . . *Ere Babylon was dust* (he whispered to himself)
> *The Magus Zoroaster, my dead child,*
> *Met his own image walking in the garden.*
> *That apparition sole of men he saw.*
> *For know there are two worlds of life and death:*
> *One that which thou beholdest; but the other*

Is underneath the grave, where do inhabit
The shadows of all forms that think and live
Till death unite them and they part no more!

Again blue fire and, again, the bell. A streetcar, then; on its shield the name of an eastern city. *To the Kazan Station.* Some words that he heard sounded like kettle drums and brasses in his head, some flowed into script, some stood before him in an orderly procession of hieroglyphics, others ran as pictures in blue and white and yellow and red. Whole phrases came to him in wordless color and sound, and the icy blizzard, with its whirling leaves, was uttering its command in every language he had ever heard.

. . . Who is right, who is wrong? What are my convictions? Everything has a goal, everything has a meaning greater than the total of the lessons it might teach. No experience is ever wasted on a journey of the mind and spirit, nothing is ever spurious, and we who crave vengeance, in whatever name, are merely hungering for forgiveness. (Oh, we, the Poles and the Jews, and the Ukrainians, the Germans and the Russians, the Turks and Armenians and Greeks, the Irish and the English, we, the Slavs and Teutons, the Caucasians and the Africans, the Mongols and the . . . the . . . other human beings who go about shouting to each other: Love me, love me, love me or I'll kill you!) Living in a kaleidoscope of multicolored words. Worshipping the heraldry of our own illusions. Seeing and hearing nothing that does not come out of ourselves, and able to hear it only in our privately-conceived-and-comprehended languages. It's just as possible that all of us are right, that is to say, that all of us are wrong.

(The streaked and spotted window of the streetcar is a moving frame, granted, and I am in it. I see myself in it. And through the streaked and spotted reflection of my face I see many people who are moving in and out of the frame of the streetcar window; their fragmentary passage through my frame may or may not be real, they may or may not have some bearing on my reality, but I am simply not concerned with that. Streets, buildings slide away; people appear and vanish. Which of them mean nothing and which provide those vital reference points needed on any journey? . . . How does one know when the journey has come to its end?)

Hunger and the nearly total collapse of his body, now identified as the enemy, were taking liberties with his nervous system; his mental wiring was being disconnected. A season in hell (who wrote that?), a season of isolation with a talking corpse (himself) had taught him much and nothing. Despite the penetrating cold, he was sweating. A real fever, then? Or what.

Then he was getting off the streetcar in the shadow of cupolas and walls made of alternating red and yellow bricks, shadows which had their own particular solidity under a pewter sky. Nothing penumbral or illusory under these shadows, comrade; no, this was not another existentialist nightmare, don't try to comprehend this reality merely by thinking. This isn't shadowed stone, bronze portals, a point of departure; this is a whole philosophy of life, beyond comprehension, by which man himself . . . is nothing. To cope with that you'd have to be living in another world, made secure by the arrogance and ignorance of distance.

The sound of the guns was then an angry growling, sullen and imperious in the northern suburbs.

Breath. Room to breathe. Room to move, for God's sake! He was cursed and struck, crushed in a mob of panicked Muscovites who walked upon a howling and protesting carpet. Several thousand people lay and sat, crouched and squatted on every level surface of the terminal; they clutched bags and bundles; they waited for room in trains that never came; they rushed the barriers and were beaten back with rifle butts; they slept and ate and defecated where they lay, they were crushed by boots. Double lines of stolid, gray-coated NKVD soldiers surrounded the platforms. They stood shoulder to shoulder with fixed bayonets like a bright fence before them. Inside the cordon, richly furred foreign diplomats and high government officials were taking the air. Conversations, with thoughtfully bowed and nodding heads, warm-gloved hands folded at the coccyx. Up and down the platform where bits of paper danced and whirled like tickets to a bankrupt circus. Up and down, somberly conferring. Their train was waiting for its dining car, its armored locomotives; their pyramids of baggage were being stowed aboard while a loudspeaker crackled military marches.

He fought his way through the milling mob, kicking and elbowing and gouging while being gouged and elbowed and kicked, and felt at one shocking point in this surrealistic progress a round hard object (a human head?) crack, buckle, and subside under his wooden bootheel. A *Broch!* a man said directly into his ear, making it sound like *aaar-broughkkk* on a stomach of stale sausage, sour black bread, and cabbage cooked in goose grease which he spooned from a jar, then showed him silver teeth.

—You just got here, Mr. Comrade, eh? I can tell. How can I tell? You're still on your feet. You'd better find a place to sit before curfew. They close the station then.

His rollicking drawl and lisp couldn't have identified him better than if he had been wearing a fox-fur hat with a city crest. In his best Lwów accent, Abel replied in Polish: A station like this they shouldn't even open.

—Did I know I was speaking to a landsman? the man said, grinned, proffered his reeking jar. *Zloty Panie! Nu.* What street are you from? You're not a Jew, I can tell, but what difference does that make? We are both from Lwów.

—Far from Lwów, Abel said, and reeled.

—What is *far*? said the Jew. So if it takes us another year to come home, maybe two, who's going to complain? We will *be* there! It's how far it is in your heart that counts.

—The bigger the heart, the smaller the distance, Abel said, remembering.

—So how far is that? the Jew said. We're as good as there. In winter, days in Russia are soon over.

Buffeted by the mob, struggling to stay near him, Abel cried: But are there any trains?

—There are and there aren't, said the Jew. For you and me there aren't.

—How long have you been waiting?

—All my life, the Jew said through the shouts and curses. But for what?

Then the mob swept Abel away among fists and elbows. To fall was to die. The feel of the crackling, shifting bones of the skull on which he had trodden seemed to have become a part of his leg. He turned his whole attention to the necessary process of staying on his feet. Already, with no train to board, he was feeling the advent of stupor, that hopeless lethargy peculiar to Russian train journeys in which no one knows how long the journey will last, what the next stop might be, or whether any food might be found there. Then, hardly knowing how he had got there, he was pressing against the glass doors of an ornate rococo saloon, saw gilded plaster angels, fat cherubs with lyres, a coffered ceiling dripping gold and scarlet, vast mirrors in which a vanished century conspired against time and trapped elegant men and women in foreign clothes who sat, bored and irritated, on expensive luggage. There the mob cast him for a moment and he was suddenly on his knees beside a man who hawked and spat and swigged from a bottle decorated with a picture of a prancing Negress. (An attaché? An embassy counselor? A consulate doorman?) He swigged, choked, shouted (to Abel): For cough! For cough, you nightmarish beggar! You hear me? For cough!

Sick with his own futility, Abel attempted a smile and agreed: Yes, for cough.

—You no tell me to for cough! the drunken diplomat (chauffeur? third assistant political secretary? ne'er-do-well brother-in-law of an ambassador?) shouted, hawked and spat. Got it, you miserable muzhik, you?

It was only then that Abel realized that both he and the man were speaking in English, a language so remote from his reality as to belong to dreams. Voice spiraling, shaking with relief and disbelief, assuming that he had once again become a part of his own fantasy, he said (in English): Oh God, are you an Englishman?

—He damn well is, or ought to be, or if he isn't you can be bloody sure he's not a bloody Russian. What are you, then? And what do you want? Are you some kind of an Intourist guide fallen upon hard times? Been writing dirty things on the Kremlin wall, have you? Going to take me on another tour of the bloody gasworks? On your way, quick, before I have you castigated for bothering an important foreign correspondent. Send you to bloody Siberia, I will, though it can't be any worse there than in bloody Moscow. And what are you looking so damned pleased about, all of a sudden, hmm?

—Do you believe in dreams, sir?

—Dreams, I don't even believe in reality.

—I used to dream about hearing English, Abel said. I used to hear my wall saying things like *Good show* and *That's the ticket.*

—Oh, for Chrissake, the Englishman said. Good show, my arse.

—I just never thought I'd ever hear that language again.

—You're not an Englishman yourself, are you? No, you're not. The accent's not bad but it's still too bloody continental. And what's all that about a bloody wall?

—At the . . . ah . . . Lubyanka.

The Englishman sat up, gave him a closer look. —You poor old sod, he said. You have had a bit of a time of it, haven't you? What are you, then? A dismantled grand duke? A former lover of Trotsky's secretary?

—I'm Polish, Abel said as though that simple label explained everything.

—Been in since 1939, then, have you?

—Yes.

—And what are you going to do now? You look a bit done in, old fellow.

Too much was happening too suddenly, too soon. His senses were not functioning correctly. Two plus two had not yet begun to equal four, sunlight did not mean daylight and night didn't mean sleep. He was stumbling on the edge of his particular chaos, looking for a word; illumination continued to elude him.

—The army, he said finally. There is a Polish army being formed somewhere. Do you know where it's being formed?

—Aren't you a bit too old for that sort of thing?

—I'm only twenty-six years old, Abel said.

The Englishman said nothing.

Then he said, quietly, soberly: Bloody hell.

Then he said: Oh, shit.

Then he said, getting up: Right, then. Sit down here on this fine American genuine imitation-buffalo-hide suitcase and watch the bloody handle, it can ruin you. I don't suppose you've had much to eat in the last year or so? Right. I'll see what I can scrounge up among my fellow correspondents and lesser diplomatic factoti. Have a drink, by the way.

Abel shook his head, whispered: The army. If I just knew where it was . . .

—Up the army, said the Englishman. First you, then the army. The bloody army can wait, and the war can wait; it isn't going anywhere anyway. Not much of a problem, finding out about your army, by the way. See that round little man over there? The smiling one, whose head is bobbing up and down. Always makes me think of one of those weighted ducks that people put on top of bars, the sort that dip their beaks in glasses of water.

—Yes, Abel said, understanding nothing.

—Well, that's Mr. Tak-Tak, whatever the hell *that* means. Nods his head like a bloody wooden duck and says *Tak-Tak* to everything. He's the new Polish ambassador to Moscow, although he's on his way out of Moscow at the moment, along with all the other ambassadors . . . He'll tell me anything that I want to know.

—Thank you, Abel said. The ambassador. I'll ask him.

—I rather think you won't, said the Englishman. Ambassadors only hear other ambassadors, they send poor sods like you to the tradesmen's entrance. So I'll just stroll over there and ask him, shall I? The one useful thing about all those governments-in-exile in London is that they're never rude to the native press.

—Thank you, Abel said.

—That's all right, then. Now be a good fellow, sit down on my suitcase and make sure no bloody Russian gets his paws on it. Never, in my entire misspent life, have I seen such thieving sods as our new gallant Soviet allies. Steal the fillings out of your back teeth, they would. Happened to a friend of mine, by the way, an American correspondent. He yawned at one of those Hotel Moskva press conferences of theirs and before he knew it . . . never mind, though. Be back in a minute.

Then he was gone.

Abel sat and thought about nothing.

He listened to the growling guns, the roar of the mob. He could distinctly hear the slow beating of his heart. He couldn't focus his eyes on anything.

For a moment measurable less in time than distance, he did not hear anything around him, didn't know where he was. Moscow . . . America . . . Lwów . . . Huge distances had become compressed and time had come full circle, and he was walking along a street among antiquated lampposts from which the glass had been shot out, walking uphill and slightly out of breath, coming home. He was no longer sure where he had been or why had had gone there; he only knew that he was returning; everything had become white and brown and blue; a gentle wind blew away the year's first snow. He was uplifted, soaring, joyful to be living, savoring his return. He was walking toward a glass-roofed railroad terminal but he knew that he would not be taking yet another journey; his family's home, such as it might have been, lay beyond the rails. It was still early in the day. Two ghostly streetcars slid through the morning fog, among the pockmarked walls of a captive city, among the caryatids which had not yet fallen . . . Then he was climbing a hill toward the dome of a baroque church, hearing behind him the endless dragging sound of boots, the passage of a huge and soiled army, the sound and breath of Asia itself, that seemed to be treading his own life into the freshly fallen disappearing snow. There was a sudden glare of sunlight behind the dome at which he was looking, and he was blinded; his ears filled with the malignant thud and clatter of those unkempt barbaric regiments that had turned his city into an echoing tomb. There were some cries, some shouts. The dreadful boots came closer . . .

And then his eyes were fixed and staring at a man who had appeared on the other side of the glass doors, shown to him for a moment by the milling mob: a tall man who raised both his arms toward him . . . And he recognized that familiar stiff-starched collar, the carefully knotted silk foulard . . . A tall, broad-shouldered man in his father's old and treasured cloak, wearing the broad-brimmed high-crowned hat that had been so much a part of Jozef Abramowski's private masquerade. The raised hands were spreading as though to embrace him or to prevent him from going somewhere, the apostolic finger lifted in a blessing or a curse. (He would wish him well, he had always wished him well, it was not his fault that he was unable to love anyone.) The long cupped hands hung suspended on air as though nails had been driven into them. They had begun to tremble with that familiar rage and Abel strained to hear the strangled, near-apoplectic voice which, he knew beyond all doubt, would (once again) issue a warning to which he would not listen and a command which he would not be able to obey. He listened, but no voice came. They had never had much to say to each other, the disappointed father and the disappointing son. There was no voice because there was no mouth. There was no face between the high starched shining edge of the collar and the black brim of the fake Parisian hat. Abel was looking into a void, an emptiness; he saw black distances unfolding, and he was seized by an unreasoning terror. Had he been able to run, he would have done so . . . Then the man (ghost, vision, residue of illness, the product of an unhinged mind, perhaps) was gone.

Then the Englishman was back, carrying a large cardboard box on which huge red tomatoes had been printed, muttering: A pound tin of caviar, Strasbourg pâté, a two-pound tin of Danish bacon. This awful horsecock is what Americans call Spam. And here's a pound tin of Australian butter. For God's sake, be careful how you eat all that. Your stomach's not used to it. Eat too much and it'll do you like a dose of arsenic.

Abel whispered thanks.

—Right then, the Englishman said, brusque because embarrassed. And about your army. It's forming up somewhere on the middle Volga, around a place that sounds like Boozy Look, although that's probably an association of ideas that exists only in my own gin-sodden mind. I've no idea how you'd get there. Best thing for you to do is to go to the Polish Embassy. It's closed now, of course, all the embassies are closed. But old Tak-Tak says that there's still someone there from the Polish Military Mission. You're to go there, make a declaration about joining up, and they'll give you travel vouchers and a routing. That doesn't mean a seat on a Pullman, but it'll give you carte blanche to travel about and it'll keep the bloody NKVD off your neck while you're doing it. Got all that?

—Yes, thank you, Abel said.

—Don't thank me, said the Englishman. I'm too bloody angry to appreciate anybody's gratitude.

—I hadn't thought about the embassy, Abel said. I had forgotten all about such things.

—I couldn't be less surprised, the Englishman said. The fellow at the Military Mission, by the way, is first-rate. I met him in London. He's named Prus, and he's a brigadier, a very tough bird indeed. Takes remarkably good care of his people, I'm told. He'll do right by you if anybody will.

—Thank you, Abel said.

—Look, you have simply got to stop thanking people for doing sweet bugger-all on your behalf. Now march your skinny arse to your embassy, knock twice, and don't say Charlie sent you. And good luck.

—Thank you, Abel said.

—Oh, for Chrissake, said the Englishman.

Evening. Streets empty long before curfew. The harsh tread of sentries. Long moments at the door of the shuttered embassy, an émigré merchant's villa in a cul-de-sac. There is a garden in which he could have waited had it not been so cold and barren and leafless and bereft of growth.

Once more he had fallen outside himself, repeating all his errors, and thought about Catherine; thought that it might be she who was then hurrying somewhere inside this abandoned building to answer the bell, to take him into her warmth, into the peace she had seemed to promise, once again into innocence, into goodness, into an illusion where he might float securely in a fantasy. But the footsteps he had begun to hear behind the door were heavy and slow. You ask too much, the footsteps told him wearily: Love and contentment are not for this century. Then the dark door opened.

—Yes?

(Of course, of course. He had idealized her beyond all bounds of reason. She was not as he had taught himself to remember her. She had never been as he remembered her, no woman could be that and still remain free in her own spirit. And what he did remember had never even happened; what she had said to him was not what he had heard, he had been listening only to his own loneliness in a wasteland. She had probably said something altogether different. Would there ever be a time when he could be free of dreams, beyond the need to hope, not at home when the sense of his own singular futility came calling? He longed for the impossible, that was the trouble with being a poet; he wished his life to flow in stanzas, in Homeric couplets.)

—Yes, the man said again, patiently.

(And would there never be anything for him beyond this permanent sense of loss, an emptiness that continents were unable to fill, a sterile loneliness that no one would ever want to seed with life? And would he always crave and always be denied; and, if so, could he go on with an exercise that must end as useless?)

Quietly, the man in the doorway asked: Do you have a tongue? And would you mind either coming in or going away? It's a damn cold evening.

Abel focused his eyes on the man, found himself examined with calm compassion, an acceptance beyond sentiment or its demonstration. The man would be used to broken and bedraggled callers at this embassy. His eyes were large and gray. The face was harsh, monastic and austere, reflecting a life of discipline, privations, and self-denials which would have helped to cement him in his certainties. A strong man, then, who had gone beyond his ultimate disasters and returned unbroken, who had perhaps learned, among all his lessons, that endless self-denial eventually denies the self and destroys the man. One sleeve of his darned khaki sweater had become unraveled; it was pinned up under a missing forearm.

Abel searched for words.

—I don't have to ask who you are because I can tell where you've come from, said the one-armed man. Faces such as yours are an autograph. The embassy is closed. There's nothing that anyone can do for you here. But come in and rest a little anyway.

He led the way into the empty, dusty littered entrance hall. Abel followed.

From one side, in what appeared to be a hastily emptied office, came the clatter of mess tins, the hot reek of a Primus stove, and assorted military curses hurled by a young voice.

—My staff sergeant, the one-armed man explained, leading the way to stairs. There are only the two of us left here now, the diplomatic staff have been evacuated. This building used to house a German military mission before their invasion, and might do so again in a week or two. However, we're still here. Are you hungry?

—Yes, Abel said, or whispered.

—Eat with us, then. My sergeant lays no claims to culinary skill, but at least it'll be something hot.

—Thank you, Abel said. It's . . . been a long time.

Dryly, the one-armed man said: I daresay. And now that you've found your tongue, what did you want done here?

—I came to join the army, Abel said. There must be something that I'd be able to do there.

—Were you in the army?

Yes, he had been, and said so, drawing himself up into a hopeless parody of military posture, struggling to halt the flowing chaos of his thoughts, to clip and trim his voice into the correct calm and precise intonation that had seemed so foreign on a distant road and in a forest in another lifetime. —Second lieutenant, Corps of Signals, reserve, Abel said, and added warily: Sir.

He groped in his pockets for his service book, his restored identification, and, perhaps, a clue to his identity as well (the thought of the youthfully grinning photograph made him feel a fraud), and began spilling tins. First the caviar slipped from inside his shirt and rattled down the stairs, then the Australian butter. The Danish bacon was the last to fall.

—Slowly, slowly, said the one-armed man. There'll be enough time later for the ritual poses. No, leave the tins alone, my sergeant will get them. Now, what's your name, son?

—Abel, Abel said, then corrected: Abramowski, sir. Last attached to the First Battalion, the Twenty-first Infantry, sir. I would like to report to General Prus.

—You're doing so, son.

—Oh, Abel said.

—Are you Jozef Abramowski's son? Zygmunt Dunin's grandson?

—Yes, sir, I am, Abel said, astonished.

—Don't look so worried, said the general. I am not omniscient. That's one horror that God has seen fit to spare me.

—You knew my father, sir? My grandfather?

—Your father was with me in the Ukraine in 1921. I danced at your parents' wedding in Pan Zygmunt's house. It was said to have been an incredible performance.

In ordinary times, whatever such times might have been (Abel thought), the general would have asked about them: Were they well? How were they? What were they doing, and where? If he had known them well enough to have danced at the wedding of one at the home of the other . . . But such times, if they had ever existed, were long gone. Within the context of their new reality, Abel said:

—They're both dead.

The general said nothing, continued to climb stairs. The final tin of food (Spam? Strasbourg pâté?) made its angular descent down his rib cage, clicked against fleshless bones, and rolled down the stairs. A very young soldier in British battle dress and frilly pink apron appeared, straightened up, clicked his heels, grinned upward. —Any more where that came from?

—This is Lieutenant Abramowski, the general said. He was kind enough to bring us some food. It'll be a change from your cooking, Antos.

—As the general knows, I can't cook worth a damn, the young soldier said. So this is like a gift from heaven.

—Another timely Polish miracle, said the general, ascending.

Once again rocketing through the near boundaries of silent hysteria, Abel followed. Making peace with himself was obviously not going to be as easy as all that; a sense of loss could not be covered by a uniform.

In a small office, barren of furniture and papers, he sat immobilized by gloom, anxiously attempting to discredit the evidence of all his senses. Here as in America, where he had come to be made over in another image, to shed the burdens of longing and loss (to come to terms with the *absurdity* of longing!), time settled on his shoulders like a nightmare and the memory of Catherine had become a torment.

The general was taking about loss (*I'm sorry about your father, he was a good hard-working officer, a patriotic man, a decent man although unfortunate, but the two often go together . . .*) and Abel had begun to listen to what he was hearing. (*Your grandfather's death is also a great loss.*)

—But if we were to grieve for all the persons we have ever loved who have been taken from us, said the general, we'd have no time for anything but mourning.

Calmly, Abel said: So it would seem, sir.

—Was there a young woman?

Abel nodded. He neither could (it was too soon for that) nor wanted to explain Catherine's former meanings in his private lexicon of symbols or her position in his discredited pantheon of illusions.

To nod, committed him to nothing.

—Listen, son, said the general. Tomorrow I'll be your commanding officer and my only interest in you will be the quality of your work. Tonight I'm an older man speaking to a young one, so take it for what it's worth. No amount of words is as good as experience but it *is* the simple things of life that teach us about ourselves, not the painful complexities of living.

—So I've begun to learn, sir, Abel said.

—Take love when you can, be grateful to get it, forget it when it's lost, said the general. It isn't supposed to be permanent.

—It isn't something I want to bury and mourn.

—Who's talking about mourning?

The general reached into a littered cabinet, found a vodka bottle and two metal cups, found and applied a corkscrew. He held the bottle firmly with the stub of his amputated arm against his side, pulled with his one hand.

—Ah, he said, and smiled. The corks come easier as the years thunder by. A lot of my days are measurable in corks and in women. In the long run, it doesn't seem to matter which was which. One or another may have been memorable, but none are worth a bullet in the head.

Again Abel nodded, knowing that to nod didn't imply agreement, it only showed that one had heard what was being said. Love and its permanence, he thought, could very well depend upon the lack of permanent arrangements. And did it really have to be conventionally defined? Did everything that happened between men and women have to reach some sort of a conclusion, as if an end was axiomatic to every beginning?

—Do I sound cynical? Unfeeling? said the general. Speak freely, I'm not yet your commanding officer.

—I don't know, said Abel. I suppose you sound the way you have to sound. You speak from your experience. I suppose that in time we all become our own experience. Time, that's the answer to everything, I suppose.

—I once lay in a ditch for three hours, the general said. Waiting for a young Cossack to turn his back so that I could kill him. At that time I thought that this was an incredible comment on mankind. Imagine, one young man waiting to kill another whom he doesn't know for a cause that didn't exist except in his imagination. Now I can't even remember what it was all about. Time doesn't answer anything, it only erases.

Abel nodded, waited, tried to understand.

—But we were talking about loss and women, said the general. And corks, and passing years. And bullets in the head. I had to learn to love and respect women as my human equals, it required an effort. It would shock you to know what an enormous effort it required. I made the effort, women became human beings for me, and I've never regretted it. As for loss, well, you can only lose something you try to possess.

Able drank and felt the vodka explode in his stomach, and a window rattled, and the long rumbling sigh of an artillery shell passed high outside the window.

—In that respect, too, I have some experience, the general said.

—Whoooo, Abel said, and struggled for air.

—If you've known love once, it's enough for a lifetime. Think yourself fortunate to know that such a thing exists. Label it, file it among your interesting memories, lock up the cabinet and throw the key away. Another drink?

—Thank you. Why should I forget it?

—Because it isn't here.

—Well, perhaps not *here*, Abel said. Not actually here. But somewhere, certainly, why not?

—Who do you think you are to expect double rations of something that the vast majority of people never even sees? You really must think a lot of yourself. Let me give you a piece of my precious widsom, never reach out for more than you're able to hold and defend. That's how I happen to have only one arm.

Abel drank, gagged, gasped, said: Perhaps my memories are . . . more recent than yours. Sir.

—Don't bet on it, the general said, and poured another drink. In fact, don't even think it.

—Yes, sir, Abel said.

More shells were passing overhead and more were exploding and now sirens began to wail their announcement of an air raid.

The room was overheated, stuffy; the air was stale and hot. The walls were moist again and he thought immediately: Is it spring? Moist walls had meant either late spring or early autumn in another context, and hard-learned habit was difficult to shed.

—And now back to what you were telling me, said the general. I'm sorry to hear about Tarski's death. He was with me in Warsaw in our terrible September . . . You are sure that he's been murdered along with your father?

. . . Someone had been murdered?

—I don't know, sir, said Abel. I don't seem able to remember.

—Then try to remember.

Yes. He would try. Yes, he remembered telling the general his entire story. No, he could not remember what his story had been all about. Tarski . . . his father . . . Langenfeld . . . the Mass in the Showers. He clicked off the reference points in his mind among the images of Catherine. Throw the key away, the general had said, but she could not be put away among memories as easily as that. She was alive, she had to be alive, she could not be dead. And she was whispering, smiling. A column of ice. There had been something about a grain of sand, an eternity measurable in hours . . . No, she was not for him, she was for no one, if she were still alive she would be for herself alone, and he would have to be for himself alone and so more for others, of his own wish and will, than if they owned a lease on his mind and body.

—The massacre, Lieutenant!

—Yes, sir. That's what this Major Langenfeld told me.

The general was on his feet, rummaging among papers, then leafing through a file. (*Damn papers,* he was saying. *I am beginning to feel like a damn historian. That's what I was doing just before the war, writing my damn memoirs . . .*)

. . . And he was listening to a long low fluttering hum as of a mass of birds' wings beating overhead, then a hollow booming.

—Two hundred and forty centimeters, the general muttered then. That means that they're within twenty miles now. Memoirs, for God's sake.

Abel said nothing. The images would recede, were receding. Nothing could be carried over from one life into another; a life must end entirely before another can begin, he knew, and waited for his contradictions to resolve themselves. Nothing had ever been particularly easy for him, so why should he expect, at such a critical moment, a sudden change in his destiny? Life itself would suggest solutions in its own good time.

(Outside there was a shout, a drumming of boots in flight and pursuit, some cries and then swift shooting.)

—The panic has begun, said the general. They've marched two hundred thousand people to dig trenches in the western suburbs but there are still enough people left in Moscow for a first-class panic. Well, we all have the right to panic once in a while. Did . . . ah . . . Langenfeld mention a place called Katyn?

—I . . . think so, Abel said. I believe he did.

—Did he mention someone named Zarubin? Someone named Szymanski?

—I can't remember, sir. It was a bad time in which to remember. But I seem to remember someone called Szymanski. It was in Lwów, I believe, some sort of a banquet . . .

—Can't be the same man, then, the general said.

He had sat back in his chair, sat in silence, the papers slipped from his fingers and flowed across the littered desk in the sweet, stale air.

—Well, he said. Yes. It's possible, I suppose. What isn't, in this nightmare country? But what we can do about it now is another matter.

—Sir? Abel said.

(There were more shots outside. He listened to the dry, flat rattling of machine-gun fire.)

—Is it the Germans? Abel asked, and added: Sir . . . shouldn't we do something?

—Good God no. It's just the NKVD controlling a panic. This *is* Russia, you know.

—Yes, sir, Abel said.

—How did he seem to you?

—Seem? Who? Sir.

—Langenfeld, Lieutenant! Did he seem ill? Did he look insane? Did he appear to be a raving madman? Was he frightened? Calm? Was he fat or thin?

—He looked like . . . a question mark, sir, Abel said. He was like me, like the rest of us. We all looked the same.

—And you haven't seen him since those showers in July or August?

—I've seen no one, sir.

—This is the damnedest thing, said the general, picking up some papers. You're sure he told you that your father was murdered by the Russians?

—Yes, sir. But . . . may I offer an opinion, sir?

—Offer an opinion.

—It would seem best to me, sir, to question the major.

—Yes, said the general. If we are ever privileged to see the good major. Which I think unlikely. We have already had one report from him.

—Ah well, sir, if you've already spoken with him . . .

—I have not spoken with him. He has not reported for duty with the army. You are the first to confirm that he actually exists. What we received from him, if it came from him, was a scrap of paper delivered last year to the French Embassy in Moscow and forwarded to us. Which, of course, means the Russians know we've got it. Which makes it unlikely that we shall ever see Major Langenfeld. We thought at first that his report was a provocation. It was certainly nothing that anyone was anxious to believe.

—Was it about that supposed massacre, sir?

—Yes. It was.

—Do you think, sir, that there could have been such a massacre?

—There could have, said the general. Anything is possible in Russia. It's also possible that this is some involved Soviet plot to undermine our position with our Western allies. What is *not* possible, however, is that ten thousand Polish officers would fail to report for duty with the army if they were alive to do so. Can you imagine men like Tarski or your father failing to report?

—No, sir.

—Neither can I.

He had got up and paced about the room, then stood before the window, peering out under the edge of a blackout curtain. Scattered rifle fire popped and crackled in the near distance, there was a roar of heavy motors. There were no more cries.

—I could imagine myself growing feathers and flying to the moon before I could imagine anything like that, said the general. Yet that's exactly what seems to have happened if we are to believe our new Soviet allies. Needless to say, it is nothing that we can mention to our other allies. We really have some remarkable allies in this war.

—What do the Russians say about it, sir?

The general made a contemptuous gesture, shrugged, looked away.

—The sorry tale changes every day. They'd have us believe in the impossible, some sort of mass dereliction of duty by men for whom duty is a synonym for breathing. Not one of the ten thousand officers known to have been at the camps of Kozielsk, Starobielsk, and Ostashkov in the spring of 1940 has been seen since that time. Not one has come to join the army in Buzuluk. They've simply vanished. The last letters received from them in Poland were dated March and April 1940. Since then, not a word. Some two hundred officers who had been in those camps, but who had been moved to a place called Pavelitchev Bor, reported for duty as soon as they were strong enough to walk to a train.

From them, from our own intelligence services, from our army records, and from the missing men's families in Poland, we know the names of all who are missing. We know where and when they were last seen. Thereafter, all the traces disappear. The only other officers to reach the army are those who were interned in Latvia and Lithuania after our defeat in Poland in 1939, and who didn't fall into the hands of the Soviets until after Stalin had annexed the three Baltic countries. But not one of the ten thousand taken out of Poland by the Soviets in 1939!

—But, sir, Abel said. If that is true, if the Soviets did murder all those men . . . well, sir, how can we be their allies now?

—Cautiously, said the general. With no illusions about the nature of this unnatural alliance. We would get no support from our Western allies if we pressed the matter, their experience with Russians is somewhat academic. And there is, after all, a war to be won.

—It's hard to remember, sir, who is a friend and who the enemy, Abel said. The lines are so blurred, the white and the black have run into each other . . .

—The Americans have even tried to make us believe that all these men escaped, and that the NKVD has not been able to find them! Does that sound remotely possible in a country where a bird doesn't fly without a movement permit? Where you must have a passport for travel between cities? Where every human being is on file from the moment of his birth? My respect for Americans stops at the neck.

—Are the Americans also in this war?

—So far they've let the British fight it for them. Very wise of them, I am sure. But when Roosevelt catches a cold Mr. Churchill sneezes. They'd be outraged by us if we demanded answers. After all, it wasn't forty per cent of *their* officer corps which was murdered by a gallant ally.

—I am afraid all this is a bit beyond me, sir, Abel said.

—Older heads than yours are losing their hair. It all makes sense in a terrible sort of way if you accept the possibility of the monstrous as being logical . . . However, logic or the lack of logic is a matter for the politicians.

—Major Langenfeld spoke of some sort of sacrifice, Abel said, trying to remember. He spoke about a Devil. He might have meant it metaphorically . . .

—Russia has made metaphor unnecessary, the general said dryly.

Then there was dinner. The young sergeant brought a tray on which a brown stew, army hardtack biscuits, sliced Spam and caviar, a tin of sardines, and a pot of coffee threatened to unnerve Abel altogether. The smell of the food made him immediately dizzy. His stomach clenched and leaped, then his entire body was shaking beyond control.

—Easy does it, Lieutenant, the young sergeant said. Just dip the hardtack in the gravy. Here, let me do it for you.

He began to soak the biscuits in the stew, then fed them to Abel gently as though he were a child. The general grunted, bowed over his food, kept his eyes averted.

—Can't say I'm a hell of a cook, the young sergeant said. But the cook has beat it, along with all them other civilians. So what can we do? Got to eat something, lousy though it is.

—It's . . . heaven, Abel said. Paradise.

—Heaven, is it? Hate to think what they'll feed us in hell, if that's the case. Easy does it, Lieutenant, don't swallow so fast. Chew it good. Take your time. Nobody's going to take it away from you here.

—You've got the makings of a good mother, Antos, said the general.

—Well, maybe that'll happen too before this war is over, Antos said. We've sure done some strange things and been to strange places since it started. And, like the general says, a soldier's got to be ready for everything. Now, goddammit, Lieutenant, I said to take it easy. Sir.

—You had better do what Antos Mocny tells you, said the general. I've learned never to argue with him about anything.

—Wouldn't . . . dream of it, Abel said.

—Now how can the general say something like that? the young sergeant said. I wouldn't hurt a fly, unless it was maybe giving me a hard time. Or maybe bothering somebody that's already got too much trouble on his hands. The way I see it, we all got to look after each other. There's none of them foreigners that'll give a shit whether we live or die. Begging the general's pardon, as they say.

—As ever, from the mouths of babes, said the general, smiling.

The young sergeant nodded, piled a metal plate with stew, and began to eat.

Despite himself, Abel stared, astonished. Could this be an army? Old rules and privileges of rank gibbered uneasily in his memory, the ghost of Tarski frowned. Hallowed traditions scampered in confusion, searching for a trustworthy ritual in which they might hide.

The general caught his glance, said: A great many things have changed for us. Many more will change. None of us are quite as we were before the war although the politicians are always the last to see it.

Abel choked then on food that he couldn't help pushing into his mouth as though each mouthful were to be the last. The young sergeant slapped his back, said: Now, goddammit, Lieutenant, there's more where that came from.

—A month ago our generals shared a Russian cell with privates, the general said. They ate out of the same bowls, swabbed the same latrine buckets, were starved and tortured side by side, nursed each other, kept up each other's spirits. In public, certainly, we go through all the military paces. Yes, sir, no, sir, by your order, sir. But among ourselves it would make little sense.

—It's just that the idea of a democratic army . . .

—Remains inconceivable, the general said dryly. But we're no less an army for a sense of brotherhood.

—I suppose there are too few of us for artificial barriers.

—Oh, we're not so few. We're the third-biggest Allied army in the West, but the only one without a deserter. We don't even have a military prison. I don't believe there's been such an army since the first Crusade.

—Somehow I can't imagine us as being anything else, sir, Abel said.

—Don't be in too big a hurry to applaud, the general said, and smiled without amusement. The performance isn't over yet. The historians haven't told us yet what we have been doing.

—Were you imprisoned, General?

—No, not this time. Sergeant Mocny and I left Poland together in 1939. We went to France, then England. We were in Norway, then in Africa. The army is a little different over there but, even so, it's based more on a sense of common purpose than salutes. You'll have no trouble getting used to it.

—I have this strange feeling, sir, of having come home, Abel said. But I no longer recognize myself in it. Everything's been turned around, everything is different, and nothing is as I expected it to be.

—We must all change, Lieutenant. People, countries, nations . . . If we don't change, we die. That's a law of nature. The old order passeth, and all that. If we grow while changing, then we live; change without growth simply means decay. But tell me, do you hate the Russians?

—No, sir. I find it hard to hate anyone now. Well, perhaps the Germans . . . But even that doesn't make much sense. Everyone seems to be obeying someone else's orders.

The general nodded, said: Well, that's history for you. No one will come out of this war with clean hands. Some hands will merely be dirtier than others, and perhaps that will finally show us all the stupidity and hypocrisy of war. I rather doubt it, though, knowing our historians.

—I note that you don't have much respect for history and historians, General, Abel said.

—History, yes. You can't really do without it as a human being. But historians are quite another matter. Tell me, what did you do before the war?

—I tried to be a poet, sir, Abel said.

—Were you a good one?

—I thought so. The critics didn't think so. It seems as if it all happened about a hundred years ago.

—Just think that critics are to literature as historians are to history. They never make it, they only write about it. They always praise the most what they understand least, and do their best to destroy everything that tells them something real about themselves as people. No one likes to see themselves as they really are. It's so much easier to smash a mirror than to do something about the image it reflects.

—I suppose so, sir, Abel said, feeling weariness return.

—Have you ever killed anyone? the general asked.

—I never even fired my pistol in the September war.

—Could you kill?

—I don't know, sir. I don't think so. I don't know. I don't suppose that promises much for my military future.

—It's surprising how easy it can be, the general said. That young Cossack I told you about never did turn his back, you know. I always thought that he knew all along that I was in that ditch but I could never imagine what he had been thinking. Perhaps it was the first opportunity to kill for both of us. Neither of us used it. But there are always other opportunities.

The young sergeant cleared his throat apologetically, said: I had a sergeant major once. Used to say to us: *When war starts, the Devil makes hell bigger.*

—For those who kill or for those who are killed? Abel said.

—Both, I expect, Lieutenant. Sooner or later everybody reports to the Devil. Is it all right to clear up these plates now, General?

—Thank you. Yes. We've finished.

—Thank you, sir, the young sergeant said.

Later, a cigarette. The violent night continued but he was at ease. He was tormented neither by love nor by hatred; he had declared a ceasefire with himself. The shuttered building had become yet another womb from which he would emerge into a new assessment of himself, defining his roles. No, he was not an author able to read his life before it was written; he had no goals, no rules, no walls, no other limitations —including the limitation of no change to any of that should the self-generating events of his life require that something be changed. He was again adrift, floating and content to be afloat, but (this time) he could sense a definite direction. This was a homecoming of a kind, he knew, and savored his peace. To be at peace, alone with his future which would confront him no matter where he turned; to be aware of motion while making no effort to get anywhere, to know that life was endless in its varieties of pleasure and pain and each of them was his. Innocence had returned, promising to restore him to passions and commitments. He knew himself to be finally independent, free to be himself as he was, not as he had rationalized himself into being. All love, as all life, seemed to him then a body of water of an unmeasured depth in which various jars of different shapes and sizes had been placed, each with its own flaws and manufacturers' trademarks, some holding more and some less of the fluid which filled them all according to their own capacities. The loss of one jar or another didn't reduce the quantity of the fluid, love as life was eternal, only its objects changed. A sense of loss was quite illogical under those circumstances. And had he finally relearned a child's capacity for unpremeditated loving, to love with no preconceived notions of what he wanted in return? (Because we all want something, because we are human and alive and only the dead are beyond both living and wanting . . .) Somewhere in all that lay the key for which he had been searching.

The lights dimmed then. The general muttered something. He was once more busy with his papers. He said: This dirty business is fit only for the politicians, but who can trust them with something as delicate as this? Clemenceau said that war was too important to leave to generals, why didn't he say something about politicians?

—Probably because he was a politician, sir, Abel said.

—That's probably it. Are you tired, Lieutenant?

—I was, sir. I don't feel tired any longer. And I'm sorry that I can't remember all that the major said.

—What major?

—Langenfeld, sir. Major Langenfeld.

—You probably remember a lot more than you realize. We'll go into all that in the next few days. But you had better try to get some sleep, we have a long train ride ahead of us, beginning tomorrow.

—Where are we going, sir?

—To hell eventually, according to Antos. But the first stop will be Kuibyshev, where the embassy and our civil authority have gone. You are our first living link with the Langenfeld Report, a lot of people will want to talk to you.

—I'll do what I can, sir.

—I'm sure that you will. What would you like to do once you're back in uniform? Your physical injuries won't keep you out of the line if that's what you want, but I'd like you to work with me.

—If you think, sir, that I can be useful.

—It's my job, you see, to find out what has happened to our missing people, to find them if they're still alive and to effect their rescue. I warn you that it isn't likely to be rewarding work.

—Not rewarding, sir?

—Not in the personal sense. Medals and promotions. There is little dash and glory in feeling your way through a snakepit in the dark.

—I've not had much experience of dash and glory, sir, Abel said. But I no longer need to be afraid of fear, I think I've learned that much.

—A good soldier is almost always afraid, the general said. A fearless man is too quickly dead to be very useful. And have you also learned to listen to yourself? Do you know how to think?

—I think so, sir. I've had two years' experience in listening to myself.

—Good, said the general. If you can think you have no military career to worry about. You'll do. Antos will give you a cot to sleep on. Borrow his extra battle dress, tell him to pull a couple of stars off my dress uniform for your own insignia. My spare boots ought to fit you. Report to me at oh-six-hundred hours.

—Yes, sir. And about everything else you said, sir, Abel said. I wanted to thank you.

—What are you talking about, Lieutenant?

—The conversation we had. About, well, personal things . . .

—Do I look like a priest? Is this a confessional?

—Sir? Abel said, astonished.

—I am not interested in your personal affairs, Lieutenant, the general said coldly. Good night.

—Good night, sir, Abel said.

He went down the long stairs in the hushed house, in the soft stale air. The guns no longer fired. The Russian night was silent now that it had begun to end.

Northern Lights

THIS NIGHT, LIKE SO MANY OTHERS WITHIN HIS MEMORY, was filled with unreason. Memory, of course, was not to be trusted. Reason had abdicated her responsibilities, giving way to instinct and to superstition, her last regal gesture was to declare a moratorium on all the rational workings of a civilized mind, and Major Langenfeld had made his peace with that. The Katyn Massacre, and all the other massacres that must still take place to conceal that crime, had confirmed the irrevocable departure of reason. Brought up in the traditional Jewish view of time, in which the present is only a purgatorial introduction to the future, he had no doubts about his own destiny. Year by year he had constructed his own determined world based upon reasonable alternatives, on service to his country, on recognition of himself as a contemporary man who could deny the miraculous and the accidental, on time as an eventual antidote to ignorance and prejudice, on the inevitability of justice, and now this logical construction gave way before visions.

He listened to the dull rhythmic clatter of the rails, felt the feverish tremors of the swaying boxcar, thought of the beating of great birds' wings overhead, as envisioned and proclaimed by Daniel. This was indeed the time of the beating of great wings, all the signs were clear. Even imagination was a fraud under such circumstances. He contemplated his own passing images as a man pitted against nature, as an improbable child. The image was improbable because it went against both nature and history and called upon a miracle for a resolution of its contradictions. Nature and history work against each other, he knew, conscious of a favorite paradox. Nature provides no explanation for the timely splitting of a rock, the seas that part exactly when required, the desert bush which explodes into flame at the precise moment needed to incinerate a doubt, while history casts about for reasonable explanations of nature's irrational behavior, confesses its own impotence, and mutters about God. But the miracle of this irrational behavior that so exasperates historians is that all these things happen, again and again, at the precise moment that history demands them. Signs, portents, visions (call them what you will), the twists and turns by which a people makes its way through its time on earth, come when no rational alternative will do. His own life (time on earth, journey to destiny, whatever) was now appearing to him as a similar exercise in logical unreason: part faith, part hope, and a considerable amount of charitable assumption that mankind, in the twentieth century, might begin to understand its history and transcend its nature. The various moments of his life were oddly vivid then, not imaginative in the ordinary sense (Major Langenfeld despised the instability and illogical nature of imagination); neither were they a hallucination brought on by his weakness, the depths of his hunger and exhaustion, and the penetrating dry cold of a new northern winter. The images offered no reasonable explanation for their appearances, nor could they, and Major Langenfeld suspended disbelief and his sense of logic and accepted them, as history accepts manna, with a curt biblical *and it came to pass*. Why, how, through what interplay of remote physical factors . . . It made little difference. It came to pass, for reasons that he was not obliged to seek at the moment, that he should see what he saw and hear what he heard. (What he would think about it later was another matter.) The various moments of his life appeared as tangible and solid as a train which might speed past the boxcar in which he happened to be carried, giving him sudden intimate glimpses into the flashing windows of a passing carriage, where he could see himself in another time. These were not memories, not ghosts. These were explanations of what he had done, his personal landmarks and turning points, the random sightings by which he had charted the course of his own evolution as a civilized contemporary man of his time and country: meaningless to anyone other than himself. The chronology of events was not historical, going neither backward from the present nor forward out of the first remembered moment, but a sense of order was quickly apparent. (A somber and intense young student cried out to him passionately in passing: *I shall always be a loving and devoted citizen of my country*, a momentarily embittered image of a patriotic young officer forced to accept his own involuntary resignation from the service, muttered irritably: *Always? Always is a long time*) and Major (no, not Major, no longer a major, but *Professor*) Langenfeld whispered to himself in the swaying boxcar: But Never is longer.

The sky, what he could see of it (no, not see, no longer see, but *imagine*) through the barbed wire wreathed icily about the frosted latticework of bars and iron plates bolted across the boxcar's ventilation hole, was a thick swirling gray, like a wintry sea; the pale blue-gray night had acquired the depth and weight of a brooding ocean. Her inner sense of vision and his hearing had been sensitized by months of solitude and hunger. It struck him then with sudden total certainty that time was an illusion, It was not an absolute state. What was real and unchanging was life itself in which time flowed as an endless stream carrying living flotsam past the reality on shore. If one could jump to the passing bank, and escape the illusion of time, one would find firm soil underfoot anywhere one landed. He saw his own past as something to which he might reach out and touch, as he could read a page from a book that he had put down yesterday, as he could hear a favorite symphony by playing the record. His pious practical dead mother was there exactly as she had been when she assured him that he was unique because he was a Jew and needed no additional distinction. She believed, as did so many others, that there exists a huge and dangerous chasm which separates Jews from all other kinds of men and women in the world; and since all things existed only through God's will, therefore the chasm was there by God's desire for it. It followed that all who would bridge the chasm were God's enemies. His scholarly practical dead father peered upward across books and ledgers, the Talmud and the rent-receipt book, parables and conundrums and brokerage investment reports, Judaica and the Annual National Economic Forecast, hagiography and compound-interest tables, to tell him that the excellence of a Jew was not measurable by extremes, that it was estimated neither by his piety nor by his wealth but by the perfection of the balance that he could strike between the one and the other. That, at least, had been the preordained theory of how he was to use his time on earth; it had little bearing on the life that Major Langenfeld had chosen for himself. The pride of a man lay in his imbalance, he declared, in the uniqueness of his flaw, not in his similarity to all of his kind. How could a true man, loyal to his view of the responsibilities of manhood, take pride and pleasure in being less than what he thought that he could become? he asked himself again. And yet that had been exactly what had been demanded of him by the community in which he had happened to be born. Now time and history, in the guise of the aimlessly wandering train in which he was carried, lofted him through a featureless infinity of nights without darkness and days without light— a crushing sameness, unrelieved by the illuminating contrast of extremes. The string of locomotives, with the long chain of boxcars and cattle cars and prison coaches attached, rolled slowly eastward, then north, stopping for days on end in empty windswept fields, on sidings hidden among trees outside towns and cities, and at each halt another sealed and padlocked cattle car was added to the train (each with its load of bearded, gaunt faces that peered through barbed wire and shouted for news), so that the slowly crawling serpent grew into a monster. Soon it had five locomotives pulling it, three pushing it, and two more in the middle to push and to pull. And all this at a time when railroad rolling stock was worth its weight in regiments because the Russians were clearly losing their Great Patriotic War! There was no way, including miracles, to reconcile the Russian contradictions.

. . . And it came to pass, Major Langenfeld muttered into the stench and gloom of the tiered shelf on which he was lying, into the stained boards that made the excremental bottom of another bunk six inches from his face, that we were brought to the dead gray hills east of Leningrad (the soldiers and the *komandir* of the NKVD convoy became more informative with each northward mile), past innumerable camps, black rows of triple barbed wire enclosing rectangles of silence, watchtowers straddling a wilderness of shale and wind, rolling north and east and then northeast through endless woods, past hills and huge lakes, past Petrozavodsk, where double-language signs welcomed us to the Karelo-Finnish Republic of the Soviet Union, north and east beyond the easternmost bays and inlets of Lake Ladoga thick with early ice. Winter caught up with us east of Byelomorsk, where a glimpse of vast gray water told us that we had come to the shores of yet another sea, this time Kara and not Red and unlikely to part for us or for anyone. On and on, speeding now at seventy kilometers an hour on a clear track not cluttered up by troop trains, hospital trains, evacuated factories, and entire republics on the move to new homes beyond the Ural Mountains, roaring and hooting and clattering into the NKVD's private continent through the marshy tundra dotted with dwarf trees. A dozen camps around each diminutive settlement of prisoners who had served their time but were forbidden to leave the North to keep the North's secrets, the camps so close to each other that the watchtowers of one were the only visible and believable signs of human habitation on the horizons of the others. All other worlds had ended for the men and women who were glimpsed and reported through the barbed-wired ventilation hole; the men and women who were always digging, burrowing, staggering under loads of logs and brushwood, constructing embankments with their bare hands, laying rails, pulling huge iron rollers through crushed rocks and swampland to make airfields, scratching from hilltops the foundations of future Soviet cities, industrial complexes, barracks, military bases. Long gray bowed columns wound interminably across the horizons, from one gaunt exclamation mark to another . . . Each night is colder than the one before and each defines us better to ourselves.

—Major? Major?

. . . And now it seemed that someone was attempting to define him further. Major? No longer, then, the barely courteous professor? Among these men, of course, yes; here he was a major. Here where each of them was a Jew who had an academic or professional title as well as a military rank that was so seldom used. He was a major by virtue of having been an improbably youthful and idealistic major in a time of crisis, a moment in his resurrected country's blood-spattered and bullet-pocked history which demanded that the laws of nature be briefly suspended; his coldly analytical mind had made his blood's fatal flaw appear unimportant when the Bolsheviks invaded newly independent Poland at the end of the Great War in Europe. Logic and intelligence were applied to military logistics and to the interrogation of captured Bolshevik commissars, who were, so often in those days of Trotsky's Red Army, themselves Polish Jews. (Mendeltort appeared briefly in his memory, acknowledged their first painful meeting and beginning of a lifelong friendship.) Then had come the Miracle of the Vistula, that divine intervention on behalf of civilized humanity, moral constants, decency, and God's law (as the Vatican announced it) whereby the Holy Mother herself had been seen soaring in the clouds above Warsaw, spreading her sky-blue cloak. The brilliantly maneuvering, ill-armed new Polish army of Jozef Pilsudski rolled up the northern flank of an overconfident Red Army and smashed it in a series of stunning encounters, and the Red tide withdrew sullenly into the Ukraine. *Europe Is Saved,* the headlines cried in Berlin and Paris; obviously God and not the Poles had done it. Under His supervision the laws of nature were quickly restored.

(. . . No such thing as a Pole with a heart and conscience, said the Jews of Poland, no Pole can be trusted to be anything but an anti-Semite, their bigotry is endemic; no such thing as a loyal Jew, a Jew who could be trusted to love the country in which he was born, said the honestly dedicated patriots who ran the Polish Army between the world wars, who had, indeed, won their country's independence. Look at our history with them, said the one and the other; to trust them, surely, is contrary to nature.)

Yet he still thought that he had never ceased to be anything but loyal to the legend that he had constructed, principle by principle, for himself. He had imposed service upon himself, sought his definitions within his own unique conception of his differentiating flaw despite the ordained chasms and the pleas for a reasonable balance between antipodal extremes.

Who had been right? Who had been wrong? And who could possibly care in the next millennium? Only I am obliged to live with myself, the major thought calmly; everyone else has a choice in the matter.

And now someone was peering into his face, tugging at his shoulder.

—Sir? Major Langenfeld? Will you please wake up?

—I'm quite awake, he said.

Impossibly, he was hearing music. His logical, precisely calibrated mind had always been cursed with the ability to understand a viewpoint other than this own; but now it seemed to have become a symphony orchestra where form and balance struggled to control an element of pure feeling, to harness and to channel a soaring emotional commitment and turn it outward for all men to hear. The glaring white lights of cells and inquisition cellars had destroyed his ability to distinguish colors; now he could see all forms in black and white, reduced to basic contrasts, flat as a mural daubed upon a wall.

He turned toward the bearded, middle-aged reservist, looked into luminous black eyes sunk deep within the skull. Elsner? Was it Elsner? And what did he want?

—What is it?

—It's the colonel. He wants you up front.

—How is he?

—He is dying. Since you're the next-highest-ranking officer among us . . .

—I know. An orderly transfer of command.

—It appears there must be an orderly transfer of command.

—No need to sneer, Elsner. Help me up. How do you know the colonel is dying? You are not a doctor.

—But he is, Elsner said.

He had become aware of change in the clattering rhythms of the wheels; the train was slowing down. Was this to be the end of the journey? The end was preordained and rigidly defined although the way in which it would come to them was still unknown. They had all decided how they would meet it, each had sworn to it, but Elsner was yet to make his wishes known. Shaped like a wooden tub, the fifty-year-old Lieutenant Elsner (journalist, former Bund deputy to the Polish Diet) was a man who had believed in nothing for so long that now there was no longer anything in which to believe. In this respect, as an unknown and undeclared quantity, he was a threat to them. Langenfeld peered closely at this man who held his arm and guided him solicitously among the moving, gesticulating shadows that had spilled from their triple shelves.

He asked: Have you decided yet? Have you made up your mind?

—Not yet.

—Sooner or later you'll have to decide. One of us breaking ranks will make all of us absurd.

—The only thing that matters is to live and to keep on living, said Lieutenant Elsner.

—That's the philosophy of a morally bankrupt man, Langenfeld said.

Elsner shrugged. —Better a live bankrupt, he began, but at that moment the train stopped abruptly, couplings clanged, and they were thrown against the cold iron stove. Above them was the ventilation hole and Langenfeld looked through it at a windswept field, saw a half dozen trains radiating to left and to right off the central switch points. Black silent trains on white snow, motionless and waiting. He was struck once again by man's inability to control his fate entirely: stasis, lack of motion, imposed upon him by forces beyond his influence. And yet he also knew that in this seeming suspension of progress from one point to another, from one state of being to another, time flowed to carry every unsuspecting traveler to a point far beyond his present awareness. Blinded he may have been in part, but his other senses had remained unimpaired. All his capacity for thought had focused into a light of its own that guided him through a variety of flat and colorless dimensions as certainly as if each of them were flashing its own coded recognition signals. The vast sweep of his ideas, his connection with a distant message center that signaled the twists and turns in his evolutionary progress, gave him the sensitivity of a crystal in a receiving set and translated messages before they were sent. To bridge the cultures, to reunify the continents, and to bring system to the miracles of nature! Surely, no sacrifice was too great for that.

Long rows of frosted white mounds paralleled each silent line of radiating boxcars, exposing naked blue-black flesh awaiting burial by fresh snow; they carried a message of their own, its meaning was clear even to a blind man.

. . . This is the Murmansk Railroad, the major told himself formally as though rehearsing an early lecture at the university (his restless students paying small attention to the incomprehensible truths of his specialty in Soviet economics): a single line driven through a thousand kilometers of shale and scree at the cost of three hundred thousand lives. Each roughhewn sleeper over which the train had thundered into the North could have been a dead woman or a man.

He was both moved and shaken, but this was a passion far beyond such naïve simplicities as hatred or love. It was acceptance of a fact that he was powerless to do anything about, and a determination to imbue the various moments of his life with a final meaning. Nothing and (he thought, glancing at the man who guided him through a variety of protruding shadows toward the dark corner where the colonel was dying) no one . . . *especially no one* . . . can be allowed to detract from that final meaning. There were seventy men, reservist officers one and all despite the laws of nature, sprawled about the boxcar. Five had died in the month-long journey between Moscow and the southernmost edge of the White Sea . . . At least, as far as he remembered, it had been five who had died. There was no question here of anyone's survival. No one could be allowed to destroy the dignity of their death. No one would. And yet, he thought, remembering that he was both a rational and a contemplative man, none of the so-called human absolutes can ever be finally defined. We, they (whoever), all of us . . . mankind . . . make a cardinal principle out of one solitary view of morality as though it were a rock which could split and divert the flow of time itself, as if all principles themselves were not momentary and passing, as if the meaning of any moment could survive that moment. Nothing is permanent, outside the endless totality of life, other than this continuing motion of mankind from one state of consciousness to another, from one expanding series of perceptions to another series. One lone and remote concept of what is right or wrong, with all its assigned artificial values, its hoary exhortations and gaunt prohibitions, and its unending call for human sacrifice for the principles of the moment, is the least permanent creation of all.

(A moment from the past. An Easter Sunday visit to the Modelskis' pleasant Lwów apartment, a ritual that combined courtesy with pleasure. Jozef Abramowski had called with his wife. Abel and Catherine were there. Tarski had been there. Old Jakob Mendeltort had come with his friend Zygmunt Dunin and Father Boguslawski to meet on this neutral ground with his apostate son, an annual Passover armistice which both men had been too proud to concede as such. Old Jakob Mendeltort explaining the ritual of Passover among the Samaritans, one of the loathed Peoples with whom an ancient Jew could have no dealings. Odd that he should have chosen the Samaritans rather than our own People, perhaps not so odd under the circumstances. The old man had pictured the people gathered on a hillock, and the sacrificial lambs, each a male without blemish, grazing peacefully at the feet of their slaughterers-to-be, and then as the sun of Passover eve touches the horizon in that great convocation of animals and people, the offerings and the ritual killers all dressed alike in the uniform white of robe and of fleece, the High Priest turns to this gathering of killers and their victims and begins to read the twelfth chapter of Exodus, so timing himself that the passage *and the whole of Israel shall kill it* is reached as the sun falls behind the hills. At the word *kill* each of the three official executioners cuts a victim's throat. The same knife must not be used twice on one victim, nor may the sacrificial offering utter a sound. The animal which cries out in its agony, or which is judged to be flawed in some other manner, may not be sacrificed; nor may such sacrifice be accepted. The death struggles of the victims are a signal for laughter and joy, the people are fulfilled and exalted, and the world's oldest rite, the aim of a whole People's existence, is brought to a close.)

The symbolism of white ritual robes and fleece was very clear to him as snow whipped across the wilderness and billowed suddenly into the stationary boxcar through the ventilation hole and upward through the excremental darkness of the narrow opening chopped into the floor.

. . . And have we come to this then, he whispered as he felt Elsner's hand tightening on his arm, that we'd now kill each other? If need be, yes.

—Did you say something, Major? Elsner said.

—I did not.

Then Colonel Feliks (seventy-two years old, psychiatrist, formerly a doctor in the Royal-Imperial Army of the Habsburgs, long retired but, even so, arrested by the NKVD in Lwów as socially unreliable) was looking up at him off the crude pallet of army coats and blankets in the darkest corner.

. . . Looking down, conscious of ritual and poses: —Major Langenfeld reporting by your order, sir.

. . . Looking up, conscious of the one inevitable ritual that goes beyond all poses: —Sit down, Maks. Nice of you to come.

The colonel tried to move to make room for Langenfeld on the pallet. He was too weak to do so. Langenfeld squatted on his heels, brought his face close to that of the old man. —How are you, sir?

—Just about done with the whole sorry business, the colonel said. And just about time too. Right now I'm supposed to be asking sadly *where have the years gone?* But to tell you the truth I don't give a damn.

—Were they such bad years?

—Good, bad, indifferent, they make no difference now. I lived a little and I loved a little and I tried to laugh as much as I could. And now I'm going to retire and spend eternity living on the accumulated interest of my emotional investments.

—Not a bad way of looking at it, Langenfeld said.

—Not a bad way to look at anything. And you, Maks? How are you going to spend your eternity?

—I think I'll start it off with a nice long rest. Then I'll see if God needs a good staff officer who knows something about Soviet economics.

Suddenly the old man giggled like a girl, said: Do you think He might have a question about your loyalty?

—Not after the demonstrations we are going to give Him, Langenfeld said, smiling.

Nodding, unsmiling, the colonel said: Yes. We are all going to prove something here that no one will ever entirely understand, but as long as we understand it that's all that should matter.

—There is, I suppose, no other solution, Langenfeld agreed. Are you sure there isn't one? Could there be something we've failed to consider?

—We've all agreed that there's no possibility of our survival in honorable circumstances, Colonel Feliks whispered with the violent and unreasoning stubbornness of the old. Honorable circumstances! That, Major, is the operative phrase.

—Yes, we've agreed on that. We've made our decision. Either way, whether by freezing in the boxcars or by forced marches through the winter tundra or by the slow attrition of entombment in yet another camp, death can't be avoided.

—Even death can have a living purpose in it, Colonel Feliks said.

—Yes, I suppose that's so. Still (and he nodded toward the others who had come off their shelves and moved about in little rhythmic dances to keep warm) I can't help thinking that their lives could still be before them rather than behind them, that there may yet be time to do everything . . .

—Not at the price of our honor, not at the price of loyalty to our country and ourselves. We're all agreed on that.

—Well, no, that's not entirely so, Langenfeld said, and looked about to see if Elsner was within hearing distance. There is Lieutenant Elsner . . .

—There is always a Lieutenant Elsner, said the old man. I am an expert in the paranoia of the insufficient, in empty little minds complaining that no one treats them as though they were great. They're born blind and deaf but unfortunately not dumb. And they're incapable of thinking of anyone but themselves.

—He may yet be able to look beyond his own narrow boundaries, Langenfeld suggested.

—With what? the colonel said. No, here you must make a surgical decision.

—If the eye offends thee, and all that?

—Certainly. Why not? Nobody here can qualify for sainthood. The Russians have not yet given up on the idea of converting us to treason. That's why they've separated us from all our other fellow officers who do not happen to be Jews. They'll come with their damned offers!

They're quite convinced that no Jew can be absolutely loyal to anything other than his profession of being a Jew.

—Not a uniquely Russian misconception, Langenfeld murmured then.

—Exactly. That's why no such thing can be allowed to happen. We owe at least that much to ourselves.

—It won't happen, Colonel, Langenfeld assured.

—There's a lot more at stake here than one man's wish to live at any price.

—I know it, sir. Try to relax a little. No one is going to disgrace us here.

But he knew that the old colonel wasn't listening to him and probably hadn't been for some time. Life had never seemed so sweet to the old man as it would at this moment of its end, his certainties had never been more clearly defined. Langenfeld thought of Mendeltort and wondered what he'd say if he were here to say it, and thought that surely Mendeltort's ideas weren't so very different from his own. Each of us, proudful in his imbalance, is the classic hero with the tragic differentiating flaw, each bears the weight of anguish as well as he can and never wonders about the origins of his pain. A man's anguish comes when accident hardens into habit, and what might have been only the passion of the moment finally defines the flaw.

The colonel was whispering, muttering, stating his own creed, and he bent to listen, thinking that these could well be the old man's dying words and so someone should hear them.

—No one can serve two masters at the same time, the old man was saying. For either you will love the one and learn to hate the other, or you will sustain the one and despise the other . . .

—You should get some rest, Langenfeld said. Why not try to sleep?

The old man was silent then; thinking, perhaps dreaming. Then he said suddenly, as though startled:

—What? Oh, it's you, Maks, is it? I must have dozed off. What are we talking about?

—The transfer of command, sir, Langenfeld said quietly. An orderly transfer of command.

—Yes. Of course. I won't last till morning.

—You can rely on me.

—But how is your eyesight? the colonel wished to know with sudden urgency. Can you see well enough?

—I can see what I have to, Langenfeld said. It isn't as if I were to be leading anyone into the unknown, is it? Or for long.

—Principles, Maks, principles, the colonel was whispering. It all must come to that in the end. Do you know the evils that flow from setting expediency above principle? There's just no end to them . . .

Langenfeld knew that, once again, the old man was addressing his own private visions. He loved the old man then, wished him well, wished him an easier death than the one that waited for himself, wanted to say the kaddish for him as a son might have done but there'd be no time for anything like that.

He looked about for someone who might take his arm and lead him to his bunk, listened to the brutal shouts outside, the baying of hounds, and heard the elderly captains and middle-aged lieutenants retelling their stories. Such unlikely heroes. Lawyers and dentists and university professors and journalists and mathematicians, an architect and a painter: Rabin and Gitler and Belcer and Dorman; Felderman, Rozenstal, Eisenfeld, Brandt. A certain rhythm in the measured cadence of their names to match the silenced rhythms of the wheels and rails; a certain madness in the logic of their retold tales, in their conformity to the laws of nature. Some gloom, some hangman's humor, introspection, manic self-derision, the contemptuous counterpoint of irony. Where, indeed, would we be without irony to put a clown's cap on the head of history?

(Never in Polish history has there been a moment as unnecessary as this one, Felderman was saying, and as ultimately useless. And Eisenfeld, a semanticist, queried scornfully: You find our history unnecessary and useless? And Dorman laughed and said: Find it? I'm not even looking for it. And Belcer said among lugubrious laughter, each of its decibels a measurement of pain: Oh God, has someone lost the damned thing again?)

Such unlikely military heroes.

—Perhaps (like himself) they were suddenly living in another time, running through the lost childhood hours of Purim eve, through the resounding streets in the old part of the city among the gongs and the rattles and the whistles and the whoops and the penny trumpets, their flushed excited faces carefully concealed behind the threatening masks of kings and Eastern potentates and biblical heroes, wearing the cotton beards of the minor prophets, faces of fools and pranksters and sages and commanders fashioned out of cardboard and fastened to their own with multicolored ribbons tied at the back of the head . . .

And then the colonel was whispering again: Maks? Did I say something about principles? About expediency?

—Yes, sir.

—Do you know how to tell the one from the other?

—I believe so. Yes.

—Lucky man, murmured Colonel Feliks. I never could tell. Thought I did . . . told people that I did. But now I don't know which was which. Still, I suppose that if I thought I was acting according to a principle . . . well, perhaps that is good enough?

—That's all one can do, Langenfeld said.

—We all make it so easy for ourselves to become confused. And, Maks, those people at Katyn you told us about . . . I don't suppose they had much of a choice, eh? Did they have a choice?

—Not much of one, I'd say.

—But we do, the old man whispered. Don't you see? That is the beauty of it . . .

Langenfeld could have said that the Katyn victims had also had a choice, that they could have joined the Red Corner at the monastery, as indeed Berling's men had done, and he opened his mouth to say it, then thought: Why bother? The dying old man is entitled to his moment of terrible joy.

He had apparently misjudged the old man who now looked at him steadily and whispered: Tell me again the names of the men at Kozielsk who were the first to join the Red Corner.

—Apfeld, Langenfeld said. Feldman. Grossman. Hirshner. And Berman, of course. But Berman was a Communist long before the war. Morawski was another.

—All Jews, of course, the colonel said.

—Berling is a Catholic.

—Yes. They'll forget that. They'll just remember all the others. Well. We'll give them a few more names to remember, eh? Langenfeld, Belcer, Rabin, Eisenfeld . . . Brandt . . .

—And Colonel Feliks.

—Well. Yes. Why not? Indeed, Colonel Feliks . . . and even if they never know about us, and never remember, we'll know. Yes?

—Yes, sir, Langenfeld said.

The colonel whispered on but he couldn't be heard above the thunder of sledgehammers that beat upon the thick layers of ice that had sealed the doors. And now someone was coming toward him (Elsner? Once again it was Elsner) to take him by the arm.

—We are unloading, I believe.

—So I see.

—You do? Have we had another Polish miracle?

—A figure of speech. You'll have to tell me what it is I'm seeing. Have you looked outside?

—I haven't. Rabin has. I'm too old to climb walls and, I might add, too civilized for the exercise. We seem to be near a coal ramp of some kind. It's full of women working with enormous shovels. That's one thing I'll say for the Communists, they do give their women equal opportunity.

The colonel was trying to say something, then. —Elsner, he began. Maks . . .

They both bent toward him, Langenfeld knelt beside him. The colonel struggled to speak, choked, closed his eyes and died. His eyelids sprung open and he regarded them with an ironic smile. Langenfeld closed the dead man's eyes.

Elsner sighed, said: Well, he at least is beyond the need to make a decision.

—We're all beyond that need.

—I wouldn't be too sure about that, Elsner said, looked toward the others. People have been known to change their minds when their backs are up against a wall. Reason may yet prevail.

—I hope so, for your sake, Langenfeld said. A coal ramp, you said?

—Rabin said it, not I.

—That means we're near a town. Murmansk, I imagine. I don't think they have any other large settlements up here.

—Lots of small houses, according to Rabin. Roofed with tar paper, corrugated iron. Scattered about capriciously, if you know what I mean.

—Please don't assign human attributes to inanimate objects.

—What?

—That *capriciously*.

—Well, really now, Elsner began (he had been both a journalist and a politician, after all), then sighed, shrugged, said: Oh well, if you wish. If you insist, Major. But must we be as military as all that? After all, we're all . . .

—Officers, Langenfeld interrupted, and wondered for a curiously detached and dispassionate moment whether all this clipped, unconscious arrogance was coming out of him. His habits of authority had been academic. Good God, he thought, all I need is Benedykt's monocle, Tarski's single-minded dedication to an unchanging and unquestionable principle, for arrogance to acquire that innocence that turns it into virtue. Yet he would do his best. —No matter what else we are or may have been, now we are officers. That's all there is to it.

—All? Elsner said uncertainly. Then we're impoverished indeed.

—That's enough, Lieutenant.

—Yes, sir, Elsner said.

Light, so much light with the doors pulled open. Or did he merely imagine, as so much now seemed to have become a matter of imagination, that the blue-gray Arctic dusk represented daylight? Was it night or day, and if it was day when did the night end? Night and day were indistinguishable in these latitudes at this time of year, the darkness contained the same veiled luminosity as though invisible flares were glowing within it to give it depth, dimension, and a definition it didn't possess. To Major Langenfeld the boxcar's open doors were a blurred pale square filled, he supposed, with the reflected glitter of the snow outside. But there were lanterns, torches, small imitation stars, and these provided the reference points toward which he moved. White and yellow fire ran along the edges of the bayonets and the dogs were baying on short chains.

—Outside! Form fives! And absolute silence!

. . . So had they shouted at the monastery as the columns formed; the formula was apparently unchanging.

(And would they all be waiting for him out there to join them at last? Jasio Poremba with his worried moon face; Tarski, who may have learned at least one law of nature [that, when in doubt, most men will do what is natural to them]; Jozef Abramowski, crippled in soul and body by an antique wound . . . Bereft of logic, we are doomed to the irrational, he told himself quietly; the formerly rational man takes his orders from forces beyond his control.)

Then he had jumped, was falling, landed on hard-packed snow. Ranks stretched to left and right, facing outward, their backs to the train. He looked about, could distinguish small structures scattered without order or delineation against the lighter darkness, saw weakly glowing windows in the near distance. Murmansk, or what? Had to be. Nothing else that size in these latitudes. So where do we go from here? Kola Peninsula, perhaps . . .

Beside him Elsner peered about, said excitedly: My God, there are thousands of us, thousands! They're unloading all the other trains. You don't suppose this has anything to do with this new Polish army we've been hearing about?

—I very much doubt it. Thousands, did you say?

—Six . . . seven thousand . . . maybe more. There is at least a thousand from our train alone. I can't see anywhere near the end of the column.

—Officers or what?

—Impossible to say. I see some blue police uniforms, some old cavalry cloaks. Lots of people bundled up like ragmen. Who can tell who or what they are? But if I were to guess, mostly judging by the speed with which the ranks are forming, then yes, I'd say most of these men would have to be officers, soldiers, anyway. You know, this *could* be some sort of an assembly point for the new Polish army.

—I wouldn't count on it.

—Why not? You don't suppose that all these men would know

about Katyn or some other dirty business the NKVD wants hidden? Hell, *we* know about it only because you told us.

—Believe what you want, Langenfeld said quietly. Just be sure that you remember who you are.

—I know who and what I am, Elsner said, and added unconvincingly: Sir.

—Whatever we do, we'll be doing it together.

—Whatever I do will depend entirely on the situation, Elsner said.

—You may be right at that . . .

Elsner laughed, said: Right? You may be sure of that.

. . . Right, turn to the right. Ri-i-i-ight turn! the command had traveled down the column, passed from rank to rank; they began to turn. Face right, face whatever seems to be right by your own definition; face whatever lies ahead calmly and with confidence; head toward a confrontation with your destiny, with a personal accounting, with each man's inevitable final evaluation of himself as a human being.

Almost everything in his life had been a matter of a chance seized or a chance denied, he had to admit, yet from all these providential encounters with nature and history a definite pattern had emerged. Life in the midst of death? Triumph through sacrifice? And nothing seemed so dreadful then to Major Langenfeld, not even death itself, than death to no purpose. To die as mindlessly and unnecessarily as Tarski must have died in the Katyn Forest . . . to accomplish nothing . . . would be to turn his lifelong obsession with living into an accidental joke.

Some low clouds had begun to form above the sea and promised a storm. They were in motion, then; they marched toward the dim lights of the sprawling town, past that haphazard collection of small shacks, sheds, dugouts, long barracks without windows, the blind walls of brick and concrete buildings protruding at odd angles into streets that were streets only in the sense that each was bordered by two open sewers (now mercifully frozen), into that chaotic ill-planned mass of buildings, alleys, refuse, piled stores, and rusted machinery that was Murmansk; they marched on snow, ice, cobblestones, broken pavement slabs, across frozen gutters where pale-faced children quarreled over unidentifiable objects, past low black wooden barracks surrounded by barbed wire, to a long wooden pier. No NKVD military band preceded them this time; a double line of soldiers with fixed bayonets paralled each side of the column and the other columns which flowed into it.

The column moved and stopped, moved and stopped, lurching from one hour-long hiatus to another as other columns from the other trains were fed into it, became a part of it: a dozen human rivers flowing into one. The low black clouds had finally begun to roll inland and spilled sleet and hail; a thick gray curtain hung before his eyes, horizons disappeared, and was this yet another prophecy that had to be deciphered? One by one the ancient prophets were stepping to the podium to collect their due. He stood bowed under the weight of the sudden darkness with his part of the column, that endless procession of sacrificial victims that stretched back through history into the origins of human superstitions, each man holding himself as far away from another's icy misery as he could, each shielding his own head with bundled possessions, sheets of corrugated iron and tar paper ripped by the wind off shack roofs; standing and waiting, he tried not to think but that (for him) was quite impossible. Thoughts leaped up in his mind like figures stepping off a roadside, out of the past, from the false darkness of an Arctic noon. Names, faces, accidental moments of perishable closeness. Fate or coincidence, it was all one to him. He had taken such pride in being a private person, self-sufficient in his own coldly reasoning universe, yet if anyone had ever given him a chance to be anything else he would have wept with joy. He was alone despite the sodden freezing thousands of men who stood in his darkness, cold in his own interior isolation as if the state of solitude were a hood drawn about his head, closing around him, as if this were his fate and nature and had always been. Yes, I must finally begin to believe in the immutability of nature, in men as predators who hunt and who kill. We can change form and alter behavior and control instinct but no one can change his nature, no one ever had. As you were, so you are, so you will be no matter what poses the changing customs of your own society oblige you to strike.

He had attempted to confirm his own humanity by believing in the possibility of permanent affections; he had sought unbreakable partnerships as though these were the inevitable rewards of patience and faith, treading with care through a confusing landscape of temporary nearnesses until he stood, once again, where he had begun, in the cold solitude of his interior air, listening to cries as hoarse as if he had shouted his defiance into too many winds. No one had heard him then, no one would hear him now; each of his warm and human moments had been an illusion. There was no one to hear anyone anywhere. His pleas for an end to loneliness had either died unuttered in his throat or one of the innumerable winds of his personal history had seized them and carried them away. Mercy had not been one of his qualities, he knew, neither for himself nor for anyone else; he had been reared in the awful shadow of an implacable and incorruptible God who held him personally accountable for anything he might do. (I'm from the old school, you might say, he muttered. I believe in doing the things that must be done, and in facing things, and in not running away from things that frighten me.) It had not been misunderstanding that he had always feared, he knew (he had learned early in his life how to live with that); but his unbearable loneliness had become a habit that he couldn't break. It was his lack of mercy for himself, his implacable sense of righteousness, that had allowed him to live dispassionately among principles and people and had created his individual conscience. A fundamentalist at heart, he knew that no one ever escaped from his own beginnings; (yes, I believe in right and wrong, in loyalty to those who have earned it and punishment for those who deserve it; rigid morality isn't foreign to my nature.) With his life's particular beginning, everything else should have been predictable, but at this point logic failed; because if no man can be a prophet to his own countrymen, how can a man prophesy for himself?

Sleet changed to snow. Out to sea, out toward the continent of eternal ice, blue and white and yellow lights were signaling a distant storm. Now nothing moved in the deserted street unless the wind moved it, no one seemed to live there, all windows were blind. Elsner was saying something and he turned to look into the self-indulgent face of a Grosz cartoon. The smile was rigid, fixed in place like a prehistoric fossil, long devoid of whatever meaning it might have had in life.

—Looks like we're going on an ocean voyage, Elsner was saying then, and then with some impatience: The ship, there, don't you see it?

What had seemed through the thick gray curtain of hail and sleet to be a tall, long building had acquired derricks, masts, a funnel belching smoke. Snow was already clinging to the cables.

—The *Klara Tsetkin*, Elsner was deciphering the name painted on the stern under the limp flag, then laughed. —Well, there's a good Jewish name for you. There's hope for us yet. About ten thousand tons, I would say.

—That's a lot of hope, Langenfeld said, and smiled.

—Eh? Oh, I see, a joke. I didn't know you had it in you, Major. Ten thousand tons of ship, not hope. The hope is something altogether different.

—You won't get an argument from me on that point.

Then they were moving, flowing into a vast enclosure bounded on three sides by a quadruple row of NKVD soldiers (there must have been at least twelve thousand soldiers, Langenfeld supposed: at least one thousand in each rank on each side of this three-sided living wall) with their bayonets and rifles pointed inward at the assembling mass, and they were bringing up their portable machine-gun towers to place at each corner. (And Langenfeld thought: Is this the final moment? Is this the vast execution squad that is going to kill us? In Katyn they had taken their victims away a hundred or three hundred at a time, but now time was another matter to them, they'd be in a hurry, for all they knew the Germans might be here in a week executing *them* . . . Then, no, he thought. No. That is not their way. They won't do this where anyone can see them. Not in the middle of one of their own towns . . . And then he asked himself, absurdly: But where in these latitudes will they find a forest? And, anyway, so many of us at one time . . . there's just no way to conceal such a massacre: the ground's too deeply frozen for burial without dynamite . . .) The massed men milled about, the column had broken, and other columns coming through other openings in the living wall collided with his own. And suddenly, immediately there were the inevitable questions: Where are you from? How long have you been here? And the answers came heavily through the falling snow, the leaden names which everyone understood without explanation: Five thousand men just in that morning from Franz Josef Land . . . three thousand from Vorkuta, been here a month, though, waiting . . . Mostly officers, it appeared, but also four thousand policemen taken off Polish streets (some jokes about that), about four thousand private soldiers, some gendarmerie . . . The officers' experienced eyes assessed these massed thousands at anything from fifteen to twenty thousand men (*about what you'd see if an infantry division was assembled for a field mass or something*). And then the other names which confirmed Langenfeld's certainty: Ostashkov, Starobielsk . . . transferred way back in 1940, March or April . . . oh, a long time ago . . . to Arkhangelsk and east . . . and now reassembled.

—Well, if they are forming a Polish army, Elsner said, right here is an entire division. And officers for five more. I think this *is* some sort of an assembly point, must be.

—Yes, I think it is, Langenfeld agreed. It is certainly an assembly point. But the Polish army that we've all heard about isn't the Polish army the Russians had in mind.

—Oh, you mean those Berling people? The Red Corner people?

—None of us here fit *that* definition, do we?

—No, I suppose not. Still, all these officers . . .

—Quite the wrong kind of officers for the new Polish army, from the Russians' viewpoint. And since they're really worried about this army anyway, what better way to stop it from becoming any kind of army than to make sure it has no officers?

Langenfeld looked about, peering into a blur of white gaunt bearded faces capped with snow, faces which seemed to have become narrowed with an intense concentration in which determination and the will to live and stubborn refusal to accept destruction and pride-beyond-reason and courage-beyond-logic reflected all that he had longed to be. Yes, I am one of them, he told himself quietly, nature's fatal flaws notwithstanding. He saw Belcer, Rabin, beckoned them toward him. Rabin, the youngest of his men and the only regular officer, reached him first.

—There's something happening at the far end of the pen, Langenfeld said. Over by the pier. There's a lot of movement. Go and see what it's all about.

Rabin nodded, pushed his way into the crowd, disappeared.

—Where are the rest of us? Langenfeld asked Belcer.

—We're all here. We've all kept our order. It's just that in all this mass . . .

—I know. We're invisible. Indistinguishable. Go back to your place and make sure that no one goes anywhere without everybody else.

—What do you think is happening here, sir?

—I don't know, Belcer. Rabin might tell us something.

Belcer nodded, turned, moved back among the ranks, disappeared.

. . . It was then one of those moments that he had often wondered about in anticipation, thinking what he might do when the cumulative weight of his disappointments became too much to bear, when everything that he had tried to do for himself and others met with one denial too many, one more failure on the part of someone else to understand his vision. No one can continue, indefinitely, to attempt to break through the walls of others' indifference. Plans, projects, vast ideas died at the hands of others, and would they now attempt to rob him of his last attempt to make his whole life entirely logical? He could not allow this, yet he was helpless to influence events any more than he had done already. Always, the world will be full of people too frightened to look beyond their immediate future and too dishonest to confront their own insufficient past. Old Jakob Mendeltort had had a way of talking about the ways of the world, a world which is ruled by men who love ideologies, not ideas and people, for whom expediency and compromise have replaced ideals, and perhaps that's the way that it ought to be. Perhaps Elsner is right; perhaps personal security and self-aggrandizement are more important than whatever service we might render to an idea greater than ourselves. Perhaps I've had it backward all along: an unimportant man trying to imbue his petty life with meaning . . . He had turned his life into a sacrifice for an abstract principle, an idea which promised to elevate him without denying the humanity of others, yet they (those innumerable others) had never failed to deny his own. Having no mercy for himself, he had expected far too much from others. Now he was sure that still he was expecting more than a mere human being was able to give: that faith that moves mountains, the trust in a future that none of them would see, that sense of mankind's inevitable progress toward dignity that is measured by horizons rather than in miles and, at the end, an intangible reward.

He heard a tinny groan, a whining metallic complaint coming through the thickening curtain of snow, and then a loudspeaker was crackling in his ears; it boomed and howled with unidentifiable Russian military music, the inevitable prelude to speeches and announcements.

. . . All officers who are of Jewish nationality to come forward now, the loudspeaker was saying . . .

He closed his eyes, he didn't want to see. His entire body had begun to tremble.

—Well, something's going to come out of this, after all, Elsner said.

—No, Langenfeld said. Stand fast.

He peered into the ranks behind him, fearing that, once more, he would find himself alone despite the decision to which all the others had agreed: to die on their own terms, in their own way, in a noble manner, as no Jew in Europe had been allowed to do in a thousand years. How could he expect anyone to stand by such decisions in the twentieth century! A Tarski or a Benedykt wouldn't have needed to make any decisions; they were soldiers, dying was their business. But we? God help us, we?

—But really, Major, Elsner said. Be reasonable, there may be some sort of opportunity . . .

—I said no. Stand fast. That's an order.

—That's idiotic nonsense!

He saw them then in their ranks: Belcer, Eisenfeldt, such unlikely heroes . . . Gitler and Dorman, Rozenstal and Brandt . . . Saw sunken eyes in bearded pale faces fixed on his, eyes which were mirrors of his own, asking the mute question. Soldiers? They weren't soldiers, they were dentists, lawyers, university professors, a painter, and an architect . . .

. . . All Jews to come forward now, the loudspeaker was saying, and he knew that all around him a thousand men had begun to look at each other and to smile grimly and to make contemptuous little nods. Of course, how else could it be? All officers of Jewish nationality, the loudspeaker was saying, please come forward now . . .

They watched him, waiting. He shook his head slowly. One by one they nodded, turned to pass his order to the ranks behind them. No, it was not an order, for they were not soldiers; it was a question as much as a plea. Oh, such unlikely military heroes!

Langenfeld closed his eyes, he was very tired. Elsner was cursing at the apogee of rage.

—Langenfeld, you're insane.

—Quite possibly.

—In the unlikely event that we come out of this alive, I want you to

know that I'm finished with you. With all of you. Staying with you
requires a degree of stupidity of which I'm incapable.

—Oh, Langenfeld said, and smiled. You're just being modest.

—I am behaving like an idiot, Elsner raged. Stupidity must be a communicable disease. This is quixotic. That's what makes it so utterly
inexcusable. It is . . . primitive!

—But . . . human, wouldn't you say? Perhaps even manly? Perhaps a
proof of something the world has forgotten?

—At least at Masada they cut their own throats, Elsner muttered
then.

—It hasn't come to that yet, has it?

—Hmm. No, Elsner said. But just tell me one thing. What had you
planned to do to stop me if I had gone forward to accept whatever it is
that they wanted to offer us? Had you planned to kill me? There'd be
no other way to stop me, you know.

—I hadn't planned anything, Langenfeld said.

—You mean you knew that in the end I'd prove to be as big a fool as
the rest of you?

—Oh, bigger, much bigger, Langenfeld said, and laughed. None of us
can escape from our own beginnings in the end.

The loudspeaker whined and boomed its orders and blandishments,
its promises and pleas, for another hour, then it fell silent. Snow continued falling. They stood in their ranks.

Then Rabin was back to report what he had seen and heard at the
far end of the huge enclosure where the pier began and where another
dark street led into yet another inland wilderness beyond the last sheds
and barracks of the town. He had seen watchtowers there, barbed wire,
black tar-paper barracks.

—What seems to be happening over there, sir, he said, is this.
They're forming up two columns, side by side. They have lists of
names, and they keep pulling people out of one column and shoving
them in the other. It's a typical Russian *burdel*, none of them seem to
know what the hell they're doing. But it all seems to make some sort of
sense to them.

Still angry with himself and pleased to shift his anger onto someone
else, Elsner muttered: That's the trouble with these Russian idiots,
whatever makes sense to them makes absolutely no sense to anyone
else.

—Two columns, Langenfeld said. Very well. We'll have to find a
way to stay together in one of them. And selection by names, did you
say?

—Names and ranks, it seems, Rabin said. All officers and whoever else they have on their lists are being marched down the pier and loaded aboard that ship and some metal barges. They have seven huge barges down there; you can't see them from here, the ice is piled too high along the shore. They're enormous barges. The other column is being marched to a camp.

—No officers in that column, hmm?

—No, sir. Anyone who's not an officer or isn't on their lists is marched to that camp. Their names aren't checked at the gate, they're just being counted.

—A holding camp, then, Langenfeld said. Now what about those barges?

—Well, sir, the way I have it from the men down there, about three thousand of our officers have gone aboard that ship . . .

—The *Klara Tsetkin*, Elsner said, still angry.

—Yes, the *Klara Tsetkin*. They're all belowdecks, battened down, no sign of life anywhere on board. And now the NKVD men are loading the barges. They're taking about a thousand officers on each barge. They're all jammed together there like upright sardines. There isn't even any room for anyone to sit.

—A short journey, then, Langenfeld remarked. Is there any escort?

—Not on the barges, sir. No need for one, I'd say. Anyone going overboard into that icy water would be dead in two minutes. But the Russians are handing out travel rations for three days.

—That's all that I needed, Elsner said. Three days in an open barge, in an Arctic winter. That is a lovely prospect. I simply can't wait.

—They're also giving everybody on the barges a new overcoat.

—Now that is unusual.

—Yes, sir, Rabin said, and started brushing snow off his chest and shoulders. I got one of them. Looks like gray blanket material, military cut, but I don't recognize the tabs and the buttons. Is it German, or what? That thing here looks like a damn swastika, doesn't it?

—It's Finnish, Langenfeld said. They must have taken them off some dead Finns in their 1940 Winter War. Well, a coat is a coat wherever it came from. They'll help on those open barges. What are the rations?

—Sugar for three days, eight hundred grams of black bread, and half a kilo of dried peas for every two men.

—Generous bastards, aren't they? Elsner said.

—A three-day journey, Langenfeld said. That's very familiar. I don't suppose they have a band down there playing Polish marches?

—A band sir? Rabin stared, astonished.

—Never mind. A joke. A sort of a joke. Three days in barges might mean the Kola Peninsula . . .

—Where the hell is that?

Thinking, yet knowing that the exercise was ultimately useless, that the time for thinking and considering and contemplating and other processes of logic and reason had just about run its course, Langenfeld waved his hand seaward, said: Oh, north . . . There is nothing there, as far as I know. The permanent ice shelf begins about a hundred miles beyond that . . .

—A lovely prospect, Elsner said, disgusted. But what else can a fool expect?

Suddenly Rabin laughed (with some charity, Langenfeld supposed, the cracked coughing sound could have been taken to represent laughter), said: Do you suppose, sir, that we might see an aurora borealis, those famous northern lights? I've heard it's something that can't be described . . .

—You'll certainly see something, Elsner said. And I doubt very much if you'll be able to describe it later.

Langenfeld paused at the point of giving an order, remembering how much younger than the rest of them Rabin was, still in his early thirties and anticipating a lifetime of events and discoveries, a brave young man who had been caught on the Rumanian border while leading men across the Carpathians toward the war in France. He had turned to delay the Russian border guards so that his men could get away to safety . . . A young man, with his whole life ahead of him and all its pains and pleasures to experience.

—Well, he said. I suppose we might. The Kara Sea is the place for it.

—That'll be something to talk about in the years to come, Rabin said, still smiling.

—Yes, Langenfeld said. Now go back to the ranks and tell the others what they can expect. Kola Peninsula is a possibility.

—And the aurora borealis, Rabin said.

—Perhaps even the aurora borealis.

They were once more in motion then, moving and halting and moving again toward the sorting area where a long row of NKVD women officers sat behind crude trestle tables behind a barricade of brown-paper files, where names were checked and the twin columns formed. A man stood there, swathed in furs; even with his own ruined eyes Langenfeld recognized that handsome Gypsy face whose eyes always moved. They were always swinging or lifting, he remembered, like the eyes of a cavalry commander pressing into new country. Sometimes

Szymanski looked so much like Mendeltort, he thought then. Was he commanding here too, as he had at the monastery? If so, there was no further room for doubt.

Their glances brushed each other's but neither man said anything. What was there to say? The decisions had been made a thousand miles away, for reasons that had nothing to do with either of them. Yet Langenfeld thought that in Szymanski's glance he could see distaste, almost a pained and vengeful irritation, as though the man had taken charge of things by necessity, simply because there was none other to do so. . . . At once his own distaste made him sick with anger.

Then there were pine planks which trembled under the boots of the marching men, and then the iced steel deck of the barge, and they were lined in ranks pressed against each other and facing the sea, that sea which was like no great body of water that might exist anywhere else on earth: gray viscous sludge thick with frozen bubbles in which soiled blocks of ice turned end over end. He looked at the sky while icebreaker tugs backed up toward the barges and lines were made fast, saw a pearl-gray dome reflecting something dark, of an unmeasured depth, something heavy that moved with hungry purpose behind a placid surface, then he bowed his head to shield it from the wind.

How to describe the texture of an Arctic night? That slight shift of minor halftones from twilight to dusk, the wind whose high-pitched howl never leaves the memory once it has been heard. . . . No, he thought, it isn't sinister, it is not malevolent; its awful weight lies in its absolute indifference.

He didn't look at any of the others, was unsure at first who stood beside him, knew that they all stood in the same position as his own: heads down, watching their beards freezing to their coats, numbed beyond thought. This was the moment for regrets if there were to be any, but he regretted nothing. Snow had dressed them all in white, each had been purified by his own suffering. A siren wailed on the *Klara Tsetkin* and the steel barge shuddered as it began to move. There was some movement, then, among the massed hundreds, some peering toward the receding land, the disappearing lights. *J'ai vécu,* he told himself quite suddenly, and thought that it might do for an epitaph: I have seen it all. But that final summing up of a life was his only by way of a book, the memoirs of a French *abbé* of the *ancien régime,* as rational as only a Frenchman could contrive to be, who had passed through the years of Robespierre and Napoleon unmarked by Dr. Guillotine's remarkable invention. He was quite sure, then, that his body had already died and only his mind, that beautifully functioning precision instrument, continued to function. He understood that mercy had finally come to him in the most unexpected manner, allowing him to step away from life with his qualities intact before age could harden him in his disappointments, turning his faith into bitterness, forgetfulness of past kindnesses and a nourishing of resentments. Thus young men become ancient monsters, but he would not.

When he looked up again, the land had disappeared. The thickening water surged around the barges. Towed toward the continent of eternal ice, and out of the world in which he had lived, he had no further questions.

What does a man think about when death is imminent and unavoidable? He didn't know. He had watched men dying, and listened to what they whispered in that final moment, but they had never told him what they thought. He had no personal precedent to follow. No hints came now from history or nature. Another man might have thought (done?) something else; he thought what he did, conscious of grace and mercy, grateful that his sense of irony had not abandoned him. For it was this, he knew, that would allow him to remain dispassionate.

The flat prow of the barge rose and fell with a metallic groan, the chest-high iron wall was thick with ice, there was no way to hide from the wind. He stood in the first rank of ten, a hundred ranks behind him, and he supposed that most of the men in this first rank, which was the most exposed to the murderous wind, were already dead. Elsner had died, he knew. He had seen the spurt of black blood that had burst from Elsner's nostrils as the brain fluids froze. Now Elsner stood at attention, frozen to the others, with twin black icicles protruding from his blackened face like a boar's tusks. Rabin was still alive at his other shoulder; he could see the young man's movements from the corner of an eye. Rabin was trying to hide his face in his arms, to protect himself from blindness in the wind. It was like looking through fogged glass, a mask of ice had formed between his face and the rags that he had wrapped around it; he knew that his eyes would be frozen soon and he would see nothing. Now he could still see the double V of Manila cables that stretched out before him toward the ocean-going tugs. He couldn't see the tugs, or the other barges; he knew that his was the last barge in the line of seven, each towed about a quarter of a mile before the next. While he had still been able to see, and while Elsner had been alive to tell him what he saw, he had composed an image of this iron column, the upright sails of ice floes cutting past like yachts in an annual regatta, the ancient torpedo boat wallowing astern. There had been some discussion about that escort ship before curiosity had been numbed with every other feeling, some talk of Finnish submarines lurking in these waters. Later the torpedo boat had sailed past the barges, belching smoke from its four antique funnels, and vanished up ahead. Now it had been hours since anyone aboard the barge had uttered a word. He heard the wind but he no longer felt it; his mask of ice grew thicker and his vision dimmed. Light, certainly, was coming from somewhere. The wind's keening howl and the clang of heavy ice against the sides of the barge were the only sounds. And yet they were not. No. There was something else carried on the wind. It had probably been there for some time, heard but unrecorded among the other sounds: the wind, the barge's strained complaint, the soiled cart-sized loads of ice banging against metal; a far-off booming sound as though waves were striking an invisible shore and echoing in ice caves. (Too measured, too precisely spaced to be thunder.) Surely weeks would have had to pass before they could have come to the southern reaches of the polar ice cap where waves might make such echoes among cliffs of ice . . . So it could not be that. He listened, suddenly intent, because this was important. The sound was flattened by the wind, of course; perhaps that's why it had a certain crack-and-snap quality as well as the booming. Perhaps so. Something familiar in that flat crack and the distant booming, that metronomic beat of a giant heart. Familiar but remote, it rose in memory in another context that he could not identify immediately. A very distant context: youth, an autumn day in the Ukraine (surely it had been autumn then? Or had it been spring? He, certainly, had been young, intense, committed, questioning a prisoner; the giant prisoner listening and responding, suddenly understanding something of Langenfeld's own commitment to a principle greater than a cause which, for all its promises of an international panacea, was only an extension of a historic tyranny . . . Red instead of White . . . *and what about the individual himself?* Langenfeld asked. *Who are you, Comrade Mendeltort? Why are you here, what's your reason for being alive? What will you use as a justification for your life when your last moment comes? For you too are a Jew, you too are personally accountable for all you might do . . .*) and all that time the nearby battery of French .75's was cracking and booming. This time, as in that distant moment, that sound was not attributable to nature; once more history was making itself heard.

So, he told himself reasonably and calmly. So that is how they're doing it this time. Very simple, really. Logical. No need to look for a pine forest in the tundra; no need to blast open a mass grave in soil that had turned to ice. And certainly no possibility that this grave will ever be found. Ingenious, really; quite brilliant, when you come to think of it . . . and so incredibly simple. Oh, you can trust the Russians to come up with something that ingeniously simple; in that respect you can always trust them . . .

He listened to the sharp and nearing sound of the torpedo boat's deck gun firing at the barges. They would have begun with the first barge in the line. They might need as many as half a dozen shells to sink each metal barge but they would be firing at point-blank range, probably from no more than a quarter of a mile away, taking their time as though in gunnery practice. They'd save their torpedoes for the *Klara Tsetkin.*

Then he heard nothing other than the wind, and the sudden swell of murmuring among the frozen men behind him, the shelling had stopped. They (the other officers, the regulars) would have identified the shelling much sooner than he. He doubted if all of them had already managed to identify the target. The shelling had stopped but it would begin again as the next towed barge came up to the gunners' marker, and the tugs would cast off their lines and roll away in the rising sea, and the deck gun would begin to crack and boom again.

The light had become sharper. Were he still able to distinguish objects, dimensions, and colors he'd see a burning barge, he knew. And then another sound came drifting on the wind, a thin collection of unmusical notes, scattered like bleached bones . . . and the gun was firing once again.

Rabin had ceased trying to protect his face from the icy wind; he peered ahead and, looking sideways, Langenfeld saw that the younger man was looking up toward him. A hand wrenched itself free of the ice to which it was frozen, clasped his own. Once I was someone in the country of my birth, Langenfeld thought of himself and the others there; soon we'll be only something in a foreign sea.

The shelling was loud, distinct. The explosions were unmistakable. The other sound was identified as singing. Of course, they would be singing now in the sinking barges. We shall all be singing. *Poland is not yet lost,* the anthem assured him, *while we yet live.* She cannot be lost, for she is an idea and a dream. And we, Poles of whatever faith, class, category, or any other of the artificial subdivisions that classify mankind, renew ourselves in every generation through that immortal dream.

He noted that the twin V's of the towing cables had fallen away, the barge veered suddenly broadside to the wind. The light ahead was very bright where a barge was burning. Rabin was saying something through white lips, he bent his head to listen. He knew what the young man would be saying then: the famous northern lights that can't be described had turned this Arctic night into his brightest day. He doubted if anyone had heard him as he began to sing, because everyone was singing. Rank upon rank, frozen to each other on the deck of the wildly swinging barge, the officers stood singing.

THE THIRD
INTERLUDE

In Memoriam

From a Report by Brig. Gen. Janusz Prus, Polish Military Mission in the U.S.S.R., to Gen. Wladyslaw Sikorski, Prime Minister of the Polish Government, London, and Commander in Chief of the Polish Armies in the West

Sir,

My dispatch No. 64 of the 12th December dwelt on the probability that approximately 14,000 Polish officers and an additional 6,000 enlisted men were murdered by the NKVD between April and May 1940 with what must be grave and dangerous consequences to the policies of Your government and, indeed, to the restoration of Polish independence upon the successful conclusion of the war against Germany.

2. To review known facts as they were established prior to the outbreak of the Russian-German conflict, the U.S.S.R., in alliance with Hitler's Germany, invaded Poland in September 1939 in contravention of existing non-aggression treaties, and occupied 51.6 percent of Polish territory. The seized territories were inhabited by 5,274,000 Poles, with the remainder of the population consisting of Ukrainians, Byelorussians, and a small percentage of other nationalities, in particular Jews.

3. Approximately 2,000,000 Poles and 200,000 Ukrainians, Byelorussians, and Jews were deported into the interior of the U.S.S.R., the Poles being directed to the heaviest labor in northern forests and mines. Due to a lack of warm clothing and medical attention, and disease born of malnutrition under extremely harsh working conditions, frequently the mortality rate among the Polish deportees exceeded 30 percent annually. In the gold mines of Kolyma and in the lead mines of Chukota the mortality rate was considerably higher due to the severity of labor in winter when temperatures reached —70 deg. F.

4. In addition, some 100,000 Polish citizens of Ukrainian and Byelorussian origin were illegally impressed into the Soviet armies. Among the

deportees were 380,000 children. An additional 20,000 political prisoners were shot in prisons on Polish territories.

5. The number of Polish military prisoners taken by the Russian armies was about 180,000, including police and gendarmerie and a certain number of attached civilian officials. The total number of army officers was approximately 15,000. At the beginning of 1940 there were in the three camps of Kozielsk, Starobielsk, and Ostashkov between 9,000 and 10,000 officers and 6,000 enlisted men, policemen, and civilian officials. It is against this general background that I respectfully submit this and subsequent dispatches and such comments as I may be moved to make within the limits of my competence.

6. Less public reference has been made to the 6,000 enlisted men than to the 10,000 officers, not because Army HQ in the U.S.S.R. is less concerned about their disappearance than about the disappearance of officers, or have been less insistent in inquiries for them, but because the need for officers to command the Polish troops in the U.S.S.R. is more urgent than the need to increase the total ration strength of the Polish army. There is no reason to suppose that these 6,000 enlisted men were treated by the Soviet Government differently than the officers and we believe that when we shall have established the whereabouts of the one group we shall also find the other. Of the 10,000 officers only some 3,000 to 4,000 were regular officers. The remainder were reserve officers who, in peacetime, earned their living, many with distinction, in the professions, in business and so forth.

7. In March of 1940 word went around the three camps named above that, under orders from NKVD deputy directors Reichman and Merkulov in Moscow (Reichman being then in charge of "Polish affairs"), the prisoners would be repatriated to Poland. All were cheered by the prospect of a change from the rigors which Soviet prisoners must endure to the hazards of relative freedom in Soviet- or German-controlled territory. Even their captors seemed to wish the prisoners well, who were now daily entrained in parties of 50 to 350 for the place at which, so it was told to them, the formalities of their discharge would be completed. Each prisoner was listed for transfer, all the usual particulars about him were rechecked and registered. Frequently fresh fingerprints were taken, and, in some instances, the prisoners were inoculated afresh and certificates of inoculation were furnished to them. Sometimes the prisoners' Polish documents were taken away but, in most cases, these were returned before departure. All were furnished with rations for the journey and, as a mark of special regard, the sandwiches furnished to

senior officers were wrapped in clean white paper—a commodity seldom seen anywhere in Russia. Anticipations of a better future were clouded only by the fact that 460 Poles had been listed for further detention, first at the camp of Pavelitchev Bor and eventually at Griazovetz. These were to be, as it has now turned out, the only known survivors of the lost contingent; but at the time, although no principle had been discovered on which they had been selected, they supposed that they had been condemned to a further period of captivity.

8. Our information about these events is derived for the most part from those survivors routed to Griazovetz, all of whom were released in August 1941 and have since joined the army, from the reports of other released civilian prisoners, and from the report of Maj. M. Langenfeld (please see my dispatch No. 18), which has since been confirmed as authentic by Capt. Abel Abramowski of my staff and the Rev. Zenobius Lenski, both of whom had spoken with Maj. Langenfeld during their confinement in the Lubyanka Prison in Moscow. Maj. Langenfeld has not been found in any of the Soviet prisons and detention camps in which we have searched for the remaining Polish prisoners.

9. Entrainment of the 10,000 officers from the three camps went on through April and the first half of May and that is the last that was ever seen of them alive by any witness to whom we have access. Apart from a few words let drop at the time by the prison guards, the enigmatic statement of NKVD Lt. Gen. V. M. Zarubin to the effect that the eventual fate of the entrained officers should be kept from them "lest they be driven mad," only the testimony of scribblings on the railway wagons in which they were transported affords any indication of their destination. The same five wagons seemed to have done a shuttle service between Kozielsk and the detraining station; and on these, some of the first detraining parties scratched the words: *Don't believe that we are going home,* and the news that they were being taken off the train at a small station near Smolensk. These messages were noticed when the carriages returned to the Smolensk station, and have been reported to us by prisoners at Kozielsk who were later sent to Griazovetz. The Germans overran Smolensk in July 1941, and there is no easy answer to the question why, if any of the 10,000 had been alive between the end of May 1940 and July 1941, none of them ever succeeded in getting any word through to their families in Poland.

10. But though at this moment there are no positive indications of what subsequently happened to the 10,000 officers, there is now available a good deal of negative evidence, the cumulative effect of which is

to throw serious doubt on Russian disclaimers of any knowledge as to what might have happened to the missing men.

11. In the first place, there is the evidence to be derived from the prisoners' correspondence, in respect to which information has been furnished by the officers' families in Poland through the communications channels of the Home Army Command, by officers now with the Polish army in the U.S.S.R., and by the Polish Red Cross Society. Up until the end of March 1940 large numbers of letters had been sent and received from the officers confined in the three camps; whereas no letters from any of them (except from the 460 moved to Griazovetz) had been received by anyone subsequent to that date.

12. In the second place, there is the correspondence between your government and that of the Soviet Union, which has been studied and analyzed by my staff. The first request for information about the 10,000 was made by our Ambassador Kot to Soviet Minister Vishinsky on the 6th October 1941. On the 3rd December 1941, You personally supported this inquiry with a list of 3,845 names of officers, among other missing persons. General Anders furnished the Soviet Government with a further list of 8,000 names. Additional inquiries were made of the Soviet Government again and again, verbally and in writing, by Yourself, Ambassador Kot, Ministers Romer and Raczynski, and General Anders. The Polish Red Cross, between August and October 1940, sent more than 500 questionnaires about individual officers to the Soviet Government. To none of all these inquiries was a single positive answer of any kind ever returned. The replies variously suggested that the officers had been released, or that "perhaps they are already with their families," or that "no information" of their whereabouts was available, or (as told to Ambassador Kot by Minister Molotov) that complete lists of Polish prisoners would soon be available and that they (i.e., the prisoners) would be delivered to the Polish authorities "dead or alive." But it is incredible that, if any of the 10,000 were released, not one of them has ever appeared again anywhere, and it is equally incredible, if they were not released, that not one of them should have escaped subsequent to the formation of the Polish army in the U.S.S.R. to report for duty. That the Soviet Government should have said of any Polish officer in Soviet jurisdiction that they had "no information" also provokes incredulity; for it is notorious that the NKVD collect and record the movements of individuals with the most meticulous care. Lastly, there is the remark of NKVD Second Deputy Director Merkulov, made to Ambassador Kot at a Kremlin reception where he (Merkulov) had become intoxicated, to the effect that the disposal of our missing officers was "a

tragic error." The cumulative effect of these confused and negative replies to our inquiries cannot be accepted as anything but presumption that the Soviet Government has something to hide, and that this government is well aware of what did, in fact, happen to the officers and other Polish citizens we seek in their territory.

13. Russian disclaimers of knowledge and responsibility are further diminished by reports from survivors reaching our army that some of the inmates of Kozielsk, Starobielsk, and Ostashkov were observed in transport to the Kara Sea as late as this month, as well as in the direction of Kolyma, Franz Josef Land, and Novaya Zemlya in the Arctic Circle, some or all of these being killed en route. As more evidence, of a concrete nature, becomes available, I shall submit it to You by hand of officer as soon as complete verification has been made.

14. There is no doubt in my own mind, or in the minds of General Anders and our staffs, that a "tragic error" in the form of murder has, indeed, accounted for the fate of the lost 10,000 but I respectfully suggest that, even if hard evidence of such a massacre be discovered, the matter be kept absolutely secret and that no representations be made to the Soviet Government about it. In its present climate of fear and hysteria, the Soviet Government would undoubtedly react in a violent manner toward our army and civilian population which we are trying to rescue from captivity. There is no doubt that further grave political consequences would follow.

II

From the Diary of Mme. Wlada Modelska, cousin of the late Prof. Dr. Modelski of Lwów University, as delivered to the Polish Army Documentation Center in the U.S.S.R. by Emil Modelski, aged 10, an orphan

30.V.41 — Today we were all unbelievably excited. Little Emil was offered the job of a shepherd, he will earn more than all the rest of us together! He is to get 150 rubles a month and 15 liters of goat's milk (which is worth another 45 rubles). Apparently he is also to get gifts and bonuses in eggs, butter, and cream from the individuals whose flocks he tends. He's in seventh heaven! He vows that now he will never be hungry again.

30.VI.41 — Emil didn't get the job. The child helps as much as he can, he carries wood for a well-established family of Jewish deportees, splits logs for firewood, carries water. Soon it will be a year since we have come here. But where is *here?* Somewhere in the Urals, that is all we know. I can't imagine any year in prison being worse than this. Bread and water, bread and water, on and on! Work becomes hell when one is so weak, so terribly hungry. Hunger is something awful. What horrible thoughts and ideas come to mind! If God's mercy ever permits me to return to the World, I will look for people who are hungry and take care of them.

1.VII.41 — My birthday. In other times we would have celebrated, but here? How does one celebrate survival? I thought, on getting up to work, how much I have changed. I felt no sorrow that this day, which should have been so special, will leave no special memories at all. But others remembered what I had forgotten. Ruchla Goldblatt, dearest Ruchla G., brought me a metal cupful of real coffee with milk! After we came back from work in the forest, everyone came to offer their best wishes. Poor Emil couldn't understand what "wishes" were, when I explained it to him he wished that none of us should ever be hungry again.

2.VII.41 — I am in constant pain. It's some sort of neuralgia. But the *lekpom* at the Timber Trust refused to give me a permit for absence from work. He gave me three twists of Veronal for the pain, to take at work, at the timber cutting, if I can't manage to overcome the pain. I spent most of the day in a daze, weeping, and in pain. It rained in torrents all day long. Emil tried to cheer me up by saying that we'd soon be on our way back to the barrack, but is the prospect of those five kilometers on foot, in pitch darkness, among fallen trees and ravines, something to raise one's spirits? Still, the child tried. I am grateful.

6.VII.41 — This night was simply beyond belief. The bedbugs and the fleas gave none of us a moment's rest. And the mosquitos were so thick in the barrack that they obscured the light of the lamp. At least in winter these terrible insects die. But so do we! Still, to have one night of sleep, in peace, undisturbed. It would be heaven, I think.

8.VII.41 — Today I tried to take Emil's mind off his awful hunger and asked him the old nursery conundrum: *What neither drinks nor eats nor has any fun, but always works and does it on the run?* The poor child, who has forgotten all about such things as watches and clocks, thought hard and then said: *An Uraltchik?* How well that describes us all!

14.VII.41 — Today we began our new 12-hour workdays . . . My little Emil will now have to take over the job of sharpening the axes so that I can get at least four hours' rest during what will be left of the night. When does a child become a man? Here, it is very soon. Will anyone ever restore him to the childhood which was stolen from him? Will any of us ever see the World again? I'm at the end of my strength. How much longer can I manage to get through these days? Bronka, God bless her, is a tower of strength . . .

16.VII.41 — Today Emil brought some kasha from the Goldblatts, he had also spent the day picking mushrooms and nettles and he had even caught five small fish on a line . . . and with all that he managed to sharpen 14 axes! A child becomes a man when he accepts responsibility for others. Yet we are like those little fish we ate, we live as best we may in a drop of water, but the end is clear.

18.VII.41 — Yesterday afternoon, while hauling logs to the river, I realized that we are coming close to our end. We are exhausted beyond hope of recovery and indescribably hungry. I worked until 11 at night and wept with despair. We have no money left, none of us are able to complete our *norm*, so none of us are paid. I prayed for a miracle and at night there was one. Emil was hired as a stableboy and Dubiakov (the kolkhoz supervisor) paid him 15 rubles in advance. Nine rubles went for bread and kasha. Bronka earned 4 rb. on mushrooms she had picked at work. Tomorrow we have our monthly day off, we plan to spend it searching for food in the forest.

III

From Supplementary Reports on the State of the Polish Army in the U.S.S.R., *by Col. W. W. Hudson, MC, o/c British Advisory and Coordinating Mission, to the Chief of the Imperial General Staff, London.*

Personal to Brig. Gen. H. J.-Wadsworth, DSO, o/c Allied Forces Coordinating Section. Classification: Confidential

My dear Hugh:

Permit me to remark that not in 20 yrs. service as a soldier in HM Forces, in the most godforsaken corners of the world, have I seen any-

thing resembling the cockup here in Buzuluk. Neither, I believe, have
you. These fellows have absolutely nothing which might help in the
creation of a militarily useful force, and our new Crimson Allies are
making sure that this state continues. We have spent one of the
severest winters known in this region of the Volga under *summer tents*,
on what amounts to quarter rations by HM Quartermaster's scale, and
the incidence of typhus, dysentery, and malaria, both among the officers
and other ranks, is such as to approach epidemic proportions. Medical
services can hardly be said to exist in terms of personnel and stores,
and, as of this date, 30% of average divisional strength require immediate evacuation to base hospital—a commodity quite unavailable to
them. Soviet Logistical Command supply training-scale rations for
30,000, or the approximate authorized strength of the two divisions envisioned in the Sikorski-Maiski Agreement of August 1941, while the actual strength of the forces now under Gen. Anders' command stands at
four divisions with a fifth in the process of organization. No weapons
have been issued to the Poles, who train with wooden rifles and such
few antiquated French Lebel's as the Russians have been prevailed
upon to supply from old Tsarist stores. The uniform situation, were it
not so heartrending, would be grotesque; everything from frog-braided
coats of the Lithuanian Gendarmerie to captured Finnish ski hoods,
and the scraps of Polish summer field uniforms which the wretched
Poles had been wearing through all the rigours of their imprisonments,
is seen on parade, so that one frequently has the bewildering experience
of passing from a Dostoevsky novel into a Straus operetta and back
again within an hour's walk through camp. There appears to be no way
in which Soviet LC can be prevailed upon to change these deplorable
conditions and provide adequate rations, clothing, quarters, and medical supplies which these troops require, nor will they permit supplementary supplies from HM Stores, Middle East, to be diverted to the
Poles from their own encampments. The civilian problem, described in
my last signal, also appears to be insoluble, since the Poles refuse to
divest themselves of their dependents; indeed, in all good conscience,
having witnessed the condition in which these wretched creatures arrive
in this area, I cannot blame them for doing so. An influx of Jews, who
have no wish to enter the ranks yet demand both feeding and protection, has increased the Army's supply problems to—or perhaps even
beyond—the limit. Since by Soviet ruling, these Jews, most of whom
have apparently become Soviet citizens while in captivity, may not be
permitted to join the Polish Army, their plight is truly desperate. Attempts to form them into paramilitary labor units, so that they may, at
least, qualify for military rations, have now been stopped by Soviet intervention as a contravention of the Amnesty Agreement. I shall have

more to say upon this matter. As to the Army's actual ration strength, it now stands at 115,800, with an estimated 100,000 civilian persons attached under the guise of Women's Nursing and Transport Column Services, orphanages maintained as pre-military training centers, and similar fictions. Gen. Anders' staff envisions transfer of all forces to the Tashkent region, where the climate may prove kinder, and where local purchases of fruits and vegetables may halt disease such as scurvy. Soviet HQ is yet to consent to the movement. I feel that perhaps the time has come to raise the question whether these five divisions of potentially excellent soldiers could not be transferred to British Command, Middle East, where not only would their rehabilitation and training be made easier for them, but where they might prove a valuable addition to available HM Forces. The Poles insist that they shall overcome all their difficulties and create a battleworthy army this year, but it appears likely that they will lose more men to disease than in battle, if the presently deplorable conditions are allowed to continue. As before, since such comment may not be sent through channels, I shall have Capt. D. Bellancourt of my staff deliver it to you by hand. He is a bright young fellow, with friends among the Poles, whom you might wish to question on various aspects of our difficulties here. And, of course, please accept my heartiest best wishes on your promotion. It always comes to him who serves, does it not? Yours, etc.

IV

From the Diary of Mme. Wlada Modelska

27.VII.41 — Sunday . . . Dear God, what a mockery that word has become. Yesterday, while trimming logs, I chopped off the tips of three fingers on my hand. My hands were incredibly dirty, gummy with resin and bark, but I just didn't have the courage to leave work and go to the *lekpom*. Today my whole hand is swollen to the elbow, and I am in fever. But I went with Bronka to pick mushrooms anyway, after work. We picked 3 rb. worth and Emil, again, caught two fish in the river. How much willpower it takes to go in search of food after 12 hours of backbreaking work! Yet, without that, we'd have no hope at all.

5.VIII.41 — Is it possible that God has abandoned us? I may not question God's will, for that proves loss of faith and lack of trust in His mercy, and I believe! I do believe! But I beg you, Merciful Lord, to shorten our suffering! We are merely human, we lack the strength to suffer as You've suffered! Show us Your goodness, God, and let us finish with this awful torment . . . Bronka is ill, she has sprained her back at work. Emil is ill. In the last three days we have eaten almost nothing . . . People are saying that they will all refuse to work, that we will all just go off into the forest to look for food . . . But that means that punitive troops would come here and we would all be separated and scattered through the prisons . . . yet what can we do? We must eat!

8.VIII.41 — Oh, God, You heard us! You have answered us! Today news reached us that a Polish army is to be formed in Russia! I am so happy. Emil will go to an orphanage and I shall become a nurse with the army. Bronka swears she will become a driver in a transport column if only someone will teach her how to drive a truck! And I shall be the kindest, most patient and gentle nurse that the world has seen. Now we are free of the NKVD, even those who have already been arrested for refusing to work without pay or food have been released . . . We shall soon be free! Only, where is this army? And how shall we reach it? Patience is needed. Patience and faith in God. We must believe that all will be well.

22.VIII.41 — We're at the end of our strength. Everyone is nervously exhausted. Once more we threaten to rebel and refuse to work and they give us each 5 rb. in advance on what is owed to us. It is enough for two meals of kasha, bread, and boiled nettles. I can't remember when I've had so much to eat.

24.VIII.41. — Finally we know something. Nikitin (the NKVD *nachalnik*) posted a notice that all Poles are free to leave if they want to join the army. And now we have another kind of conflict, this time among ourselves, because none of the Jewish families want to hear one word about any army! They were so kind and decent, we were all such friends in our adversity (I shall never forget lawyer Mintz, who shared his last piece of bread with us last summer, or dear Ruchla G., or Pela Blaszczyk, who looked after Bronka and Emil when they were both so ill, or Giza Kalbowa, who gave me a cup of milk when I was so weak), and now we are at odds! Because they say that if we go and leave them, they will not get the Polish papers issued to them. Yet how can we not go? They say that after all they've suffered they should be allowed to return to Poland with honors, no matter who frees our Land. So now much ill will has appeared and many friendships are ending.

27.VIII.41. — Nikitin has given new instructions. We will all get papers stating that we are Polish citizens (they are called White Papers, because they are printed on white paper ha ha ha) and we'll be free to go wherever we wish provided that we do not enter cities of the first and second category, nor the frontier regions, but how we get there is to be our business. As for our money, he said that few of us had met our work quotas (*norms*), so no one may be paid. We asked permission to telegraph the Polish Embassy in Moscow.

29.VIII.41. — Today we sent the telegram to Moscow but by nightfall we've received no answer, and Zolotov insists that all of us must be gone by morning! I spent an hour saying goodbye to Ruchla G., who did not get White Papers. She wept and begged me not to forget about her and her family, and to let the delegate in Kuibyshev know where they are. But will we ever get there? And what will we find there? We place ourselves in God's hands, His will is our way.

V

Excerpt from The Memoirs of a Soldier, *by Maj. Gen. Sir Hugh Joness-Wadsworth DSO, KCB (Rtd.), published by Cenotaph Press, London, 1949*

. . . It was at about this time that I received the strangest communication from my friend Wally Hudson, who was then chief of our liaison with the Poles in Russia, in which he said that the Poles were terribly upset about a supposed massacre of some of their officers in Russia not only *before* the Nazi invasion, which seemed bad enough, but, apparently, also *after* Russia had become our ally. They were, it seemed, convinced that some 15,000 of their officers were either killed off somewhere near Smolensk or drowned in the White Sea. Wally thought that most of the Poles' senior people were doing their best to keep a lid on the entire matter, at least for as long as they might remain in Soviet territory, but we were sure that such a story was bound to get out and that all sorts of trouble with the Russians would follow. I was inclined to treat the matter with curiosity but with scant attention, feeling that, sooner or later, the missing Poles were bound to turn up in one of the innumerable Russian prison camps; besides, from the viewpoint of HM Government, far more serious events appeared to be taking place among the Poles in Russia. It seemed quite certain, judging by reports, that despite Russian discouragement of Jewish enlistment (a discouragement to which some of the more conservative Poles did not particularly object), a large number of Polish Jews had managed to enter the Army, with no intention of staying with the colours once this Army were taken from Soviet jurisdiction. Since the Prime

Minister, at the urging of the Polish Government in London, had already induced Stalin to permit evacuation of this Army from its pestilential quarters in Tashkent to the Middle East, it appeared that we were about to import a large, well-trained force of illegal Jewish immigrants in contravention to HM Government's policy of the time. We had no way of knowing at the time (indeed, we were not to discover the deception until 2,000 armed Jews deserted from the Polish Army in Palestine in 1943) that we were witnessing the birth of the infamous Prus-Mendeltort Affair, nor that the well-known terrorist was connected with it; however, my suspicions were aroused and I immediately signalled Wally Hudson to get to the root of the matter. . . . In this regard, as later in Palestine, when the Poles refused to search for these deserters or to help us in identifying captured terrorists as their former soldiers, the Poles proved stubbornly uncooperative which, I must say, seemed like very odd behaviour for allies in wartime. . . . Still, we were reasonably sure that until the Polish Army could begin its evacuation to Persia and Iraq we would have quite enough time to discover what was going on. In this we were to be proven sadly at an error . . . Unwittingly (for who could have foreseen such an act of perfidy), while helping to bring those badly needed Polish divisions out of Russia, we were to saddle ourselves with the terrorist Hargan Organization which was to give us so much trouble later on.

VI

From letters to the author written by Jonathan J. Rash, M.D., Ph.D. (formerly Rashevsky), from New York and San Francisco, 1967–68

I wrote you last how we were set free from our *zsylka*, how we received our "White Papers" testifying that we were Poles, and how we set out for Tashkent. As you know, my parents had both died, but my sister Esterka took charge of us all, and having joined several other Jewish families on our way, we reached Tashkent sometime in the winter of 1941. Perhaps it wasn't winter, perhaps it was spring. I no longer remember. All I know is that it was warm there. But why go to Tashkent? Who brought up Tashkent? Who mentioned it first? Why? I don't know, I never heard of it before that day when we received our freedom. Perhaps it was Esterka's friend, Moishe Traurig, who mentioned it first. But this word *Tashkent* is a fateful word for me, for it was not the city of Tashkent to which we came, it was the region of it.

We could not go to the city because the ghost of my grandfather made it impossible.

No, I don't believe in ghosts. I am a scientist, a psychologist and philosopher (I do not like the word *psychiatrist!*), I have degrees from the Columbia University. They do not believe in ghosts at Columbia University. But my grandfather's ghost was always with us, it's with me today. He made it impossible for us to go to the city, because we had been forbidden to enter a First Class city, and my grandfather had been a fanatic about obedience to any kind of law. He was dead then, but he was still our symbol, the head of our family. Obedience to law was a biblical commandment to him and so to us. We chose a smaller place on the map I brought from the school. (Can you describe a Jewish-religious fanatic with allegiance to the Polish State and to our hero, the beloved Pilsudski? Can you describe a relatively wealthy man with ethical-religious convictions? Because Judaism is not a faith that relies upon miracles. It has no concept of Grace. It does not assume that an evil man may escape punishment because Christ died for him on the Cross. It demands every moment that the individual be responsible for his actions and that stern reckoning will be made, no matter what. My grandfather believed this: that no matter what, there could be no escape. And we, too, believed it. At least, I believed it. Esterka had begun to believe something else as well.)

The day of departure from the *uchastok* came. All I remember of it was that it was raining. Despite the warnings of Nachalnik Shestakov, an honest man in a corrupt society, that we didn't know how difficult and how dangerous travel was in Russia, we all ran to the trains provided for us on this rainy day. (We had a garden there and in that garden I used to eat the sweet green peas as they matured. I used to skip a day in eating them so that some would last longer than the others. The day we left had been an "eating-up day" and I missed it.) On that day I was in the freight train. It was dark pink in color. The color of the day was gray. On such days the mosquitoes buzzed and bit. We rode the train all day and, in the evening, we came to the Volga. The rails simply stopped on the banks of the Volga, and that was the end. What to do next? Someone said that a riverboat went up and down the Volga but that it left from a sand island in the middle of the river, and how were we to get there? Fortunately, private enterprise (or Greed) was not dead in the Soviet Union. Some fishermen came and, for a few rubles and some tobacco, they rowed us to the island. Then night came. It was terribly cold on the beach, in the wind, under the open sky. But, in the morning, the riverboat was there. Would it go upriver, or down? We wanted to go downriver, but if the boat was going upriver how could we wait for it on the beach until it came downriver again? How many weeks or months would that take? So we decided to board the boat no matter where it went. Everyone ran for the boat. Some walked to it on a narrow plank, others waded with their possessions held over their heads. They carried children, and old people in that manner too. Everyone wanted to get on that boat and most of them did. But I have a special memory of this moment because while I and Esterka and Kamila and Moishe Traurig and Ariz were on the plank, going toward the boat, a man stood up at the other end and told us we could not board. Why? He didn't say. I think that Kamila started screaming then. This man wanted us to perish on that island! And I went mad, I think. I was 10 yrs. old, and small. I attacked this man. I hit him with the basket that I was carrying and the basket broke, and everything that we had packed into the basket for the journey (jam, sweets, chocolate, sweet wine, bread, and pickles!) fell into the river. It was the most terrible moment of my life, I think. But the man threw up his hands and stepped away and we went aboard. Oh, you muddy waters of Volga, how I hate you now!

(Esterka sometimes tells a story that happened on the boat, which was named *Stalin*. It happened to a Jew we called the Millionaire. He had a hundred gold watches in a bag sewn inside the seat of his trousers, it was all he had. You could say it was his stability, his safety, his hope of a future. With a hundred gold watches in his pants a man can't starve in Russia. Well, he went to the toilet on the *Stalin*, the toilet was a hole at the back of the boat with nothing but the Volga under it. He went there, because he had to, and his bag of watches fell into the Volga. I cannot describe the terror of this man. With his possessions gone, his life seemed to go. You can describe this, my friend: describe the ultimate terror of this 50-year-old man who had belonged to the wealthy class of well-established Jews in Bielsko, and who, in one unspeakable and ridiculous moment, lost everything that could bring the temporal continuation of his life.)

From then on for the next two or three months we sailed up and down the Volga. Everywhere we came we asked: Is it good here? And there was always someone to tell us in Polish: No, it is not. So we went back aboard and sailed somewhere else. I remember Kamishin, Engels . . . I remember the empty kolkhoz settlements of the Volga Germans who had all been moved, an entire nation of them, somewhere to Siberia . . . No one has ever heard of the Volga Germans from the day they had been taken off in a hundred freight trains.

But finally we got to Kuibyshev, where, someone had told us, there was a Polish Government delegate who could help us, but when we got there the delegate was gone. A Polish army had been there too, and in a nearby place called Buzuluk, but it had gone away to the south. Where did it go? We were told: Tashkent. So we too would go to Tashkent, not to join the army but because we were Poles, we had our identity, and that was where all Poles were going that year; there was nowhere else for any of us to go. So, in Kuibyshev, we got on yet another train, and then another, and for another month it was first this train and then another, and no one knew where any train was going but, in the end, we got to Tashkent. The place in Tashkent Province where we got off the last of the trains was called Andizhan. That's how we got to Tashkent. What happened to us there is another story.

VII

From the Diary of Mme. Wlada Modelska, as published by the Polish Army Information and Education Department, Iran, 1943, under the title Lest We Forget, *ed. Teodor Haussner*

(Editor's Note: The notations between the 15th and 25th of January, 1942, which those of us who were there will always remember as a winter of particular severity, with the army barely managing to keep itself alive on the windswept plains about Buzuluk, contain descriptions of this indomitable woman's journey to a railway station and her days of waiting there for a train. She notes that no one seemed able to sleep night after night, that while they had been working in their captivity everyone would fall into sleep like the dead but, with liberation, sleep had become impossible because no one knew when a train might come. She also notes that waiting for the train meant that no one dared to leave the station, to search for food, in case a train arrived in their absence. TH.)

No date — Tonight we slept under a water tower. Someone had put up a screen of tarpaulins and corrugated iron to keep out the wind and the snow, but a *purga* was blowing down the railway tracks and, in the morning, two persons were found frozen to death. I thought I would die from the cold. My kidneys are hurting. We are terribly hungry. We have no money left and there is almost nothing left to sell. Besides, who would buy an embroidered summer blouse, made in Paris, in midwinter? I worry about Emil, who has not spoken one word for almost a week. He simply stares at the snow. He is very quiet. God, let him, at least, survive!

No date — Why is it that God always hears me when I speak to Him? Today we found a hut behind the railway embankment in which, in exchange for my Boul-Mich blouse, a peasant woman and her three sons allowed us to spend the night sitting on the floor. We were warmer then. But in the morning the man of the family came back from his work in logging on the river, and we had to leave.

2.II.42 — The cold, more than anything, has decided everyone to go south. We wait for a train that might be heading there. Supposedly, it is also easier to find food in the southern regions. But the waiting seems to go on and on . . .

7.II.42 — Since evening we've been standing on our heads with joy! It was then that we were notified that, this morning, there would be one wagon available for us. One for 60 persons! But I am praying that the wagon will be delayed because Emil had gone to Krasnoufimsk to sell a pair of brown stockings that Zula Ersbelsfeld had given him for the journey, and those people who had seen him there said that he planned to spend the night there and wait until the trading stalls opened in the morning.

8.II.42 — We have been waiting in the cattle car for 24 hours. No one has an idea when we might be attached to some train, no one knows anything. But at least Emil had a chance to come back and is here now. He couldn't sell the stockings. But he had stolen some bread from a stall. How is one to tell him that it is wrong to steal when one must kiss him and thank him for his courage instead? So today our stomachs are full of fresh bread and we can finally sleep.

1.III.42 — We are still here, in the cattle car, waiting to join a train. We are incredibly dirty, but at least we are protected from the snow and wind. There is even an iron stove in the car and we have been burning branches from the trees around the station in the stove. Outside others wait in the snow. Each day more people come with terrible news. At each station along the line, it seems, thousands of Polish people wait for trains. They wait for weeks at a time, sometimes months.

2.III.42 — We are moving! We are going somewhere! We have left Pyervouralsk at last! It is warmer now and everyone is smiling. Oh, those dirty, hungry smiling faces! How good it is to feel happy again.

5.III.42 — The train has stopped. It took us three days to go only 80 km. How is that possible? But that is what we're told. We are in

Khrompik, near Pyervouralsk, and the train has been backed into a siding because the locomotive is needed elsewhere. Emil has managed to sell his brown stockings and we get a permit to buy 10 dkg. of bread per person. (Editor's Note: In the U.S.S.R. it was impossible to buy anything, no matter how much money one had, without a permit based on productivity during working hours. Since the Polish travelers did not work they had, officially, no right to eat.)

6.III.42 — Many persons have become discouraged and talk about going back to Pyervouralsk, where there is work in the forest. But a *pud* of potatoes is said to cost 54 rubles there. In all of Pyervouralsk you can buy only two commodities now, and endless lines of people form right after work to wait until the stores are opened in the morning, otherwise they'd have no hope of getting anything. What they can get is horsemeat and honey! There is nothing else! The horsemeat costs 10 rb. per kilo, the honey sells for 30 rb. But they say the honey is already gone.

8.III.42 — We have been waiting here, on this railway siding, for 76 hours. The Turnheims have left for Pyervouralsk, and now Nathalie Blankenstein has decided to go back as well. The Honingbaums are still not sure. Before the Turnheims went, they gave me 50 rubles, said that I can pay them back when we see each other in Poland after the war! Have there ever been such kind people anywhere? Dear Nathalie B. did the same, and gave Emil a shawl because he was coughing. I shall never forget these dear, kind people. Never! Never! Should we go back too? Perhaps, in a day, we shall move again . . .

8.IV.42 — We are in Sverdlovsk. We have been here for a week, waiting at a siding. We were allowed to go into town, a large city, the famous Ekaterinburg before the Revolution, the first large Russian city that any of us had seen. We were stunned by the shop windows full of sausages, piles of white bread, Swiss cheeses . . . but when we tried to buy them everyone laughed at us. It was all made of cardboard and papier-mâché . . . an advertisement. No wonder there were no lines before those stores, no wonder . . . We looked for the Polish delegate in Sverdlovsk only to find out that he had been expelled. How do we go about joining the army? Where do we look for it?

(Editor's Note: The Diary then tells that the city authorities of Sverdlovsk protested the presence of the Polish exiles, as happened frequently in all such odysseys, so they were sent on to another town.)

No date — We've been sent toward Tashkent. We stop every 10 or 15 kilometers and wait for hours, or days, at sidings. Finally, when we had waited two nights near a little station without a chance to buy anything to eat, we sent a delegation to protest. It turned out that we were right to do so, they had simply forgotten all about us and failed to attach our car to the proper train. After that, still without an opportunity to buy food, we went off like an express!

No date — All that we have between 47 persons is 50 rubles and 40 grams of bread. What will happen if the trains does not stop anywhere? It has not stopped for eight days! What will we do then?

22.X.41— And still we are going. The first few days had been near tragic. We ate nothing for what must have been a week. Despair had seized us all. The train passed like lightning through the steppe and didn't even slow down at the stations. But for the last few weeks we have begun to stop again, and wait at countless sidings and little stations with no village near, and we have been buying goat cheese and camel meat. Yes, camel meat! Yesterday I bought a watermelon. I feel that I am terribly ill. I am in pain throughout my body. I have to put my kerchief in my mouth to stifle my own cries.

(Editor's Note: Tashkent did not accept them. They were sent on to Brevsk. Brevsk refused to admit them.)

No date — Where is our destination? Can't anyone tell us? We came to Samarkand but, even here, we were turned away. All our money is now gone. There are only 11 of us left from the 64 who had waited, so patiently, for this terrible journey to begin. Where will it end? And when? Is there to be an end to it or are we doomed, like the proverbial Flying Dutchman, to run through these brown steppes for ever and ever? But if so, Dear God, what sin have we committed? Why are we being punished in this way?

(Editor's Note: That was the last entry in the Diary of Mme. Modelska. Her journey ended in the train. Her little cousin, Emil, buried her in the steppe near, as best as he can remember, a small Uzbek village. He brought her Diary with him in December 1941 to Bokhara, where he arrived on foot.)

VIII

*From a Report by Brig. Gen. Janusz Prus to Gen.
Wladyslaw Anders, CO Polish Forces, Middle East and
U.S.S.R., entitled:* An Analysis of Supplementary Evidence concerning the Katyn Massacre. *Category: Most
Secret. One Copy Only. By hand of officer*

Sir,

In compliance with Your verbal order of 12 April, concerning German
broadcasts to the effect that mass graves containing bodies of Polish
officers had been uncovered in the Katyn Forest, I submit the following
analysis of all evidence available to date on this matter. It supplements
evidence already collected, analyzed, and submitted in dispatches to
Gen. Sikorski and Yourself.

2. Added to the above submitted evidence, there is now added the evidence of those who have visited the grave: first, a Polish commission including, among others, doctors, journalists, and members of the Polish
Assistance Committee, a former president of the Polish Academy of
Literature, and a representative of the Mayor of Warsaw; secondly, another Polish commission which included priests, doctors, and a representative of the Polish Red Cross Society; thirdly, an international commission of criminologists and pathologists, of which the personnel is
given in Annex I. The report of this commission forms Annex II to this
dispatch, and the reports of the two Polish commissions add little to it.
It is deposed by all that several hundred identifications have been established. All this evidence would normally be highly suspect since the
inspections took place under German auspices and the results reached
us through German broadcasts. There are, however, fair grounds for
presuming that the German broadcasts accurately represented the
findings of the commissions, that the commissions' findings were, in
most respects, well founded, and that the grounds were sound on which
the identifications, and conclusions of findings, were made.

3. There is also photographic and descriptive evidence collected by the
Special Intelligence Section of the Home Army, which penetrated the
Katyn Forest area *without German knowledge,* and whose medical specialists conducted a number of pathologic tests on several exhumed
bodies with no outside supervision of any kind.

4. Further, in the analysis of German broadcasts and reports, there is the fact that a mass execution of officer prisoners would be inconsistent with what we know of the German Army. The Wehrmacht has committed innumerable brutalities, but the murder by them of officer prisoners of war, even of Poles, is rare. Had the German authorities ever had the lost 10,000 Polish officers in their hands we can be sure that they would have placed some or all of them in the camps in Germany already allotted to Polish prisoners, while the 6,000 missing enlisted men, policemen, and civil officials would have been put to forced labor. In such case, the Polish authorities would, in the course of two years, certainly have got into touch with some of the prisoners, particularly if one bears in mind the extraordinary skill and efficiency of the Home Army's Intelligence Department, which operates even inside Nazi concentration and extermination camps. In fact, however, none of the men from Kozielsk, Starobielsk, or Ostashkov have ever been heard of from or in Germany.

5. Finally there is the evidence to be derived from the confusion which characterizes explanations elicited from or volunteered by the Soviet Government. Between August 1941 and the 12th April broadcast announcing the discovery of the graves, the Soviet Government had, among other excuses, maintained that all Polish officers taken prisoner in 1939 had been released. On the 16th April, four days after the German announcement, the Soviet Information Bureau in Moscow suggested that the Germans were misrepresenting as victims of Russian barbarity skeletons dug up by archaeologists at Gniazdovo, which lies next to Katyn. On the 26th April, Minister Molotov, in a note to the Polish Ambassador in Moscow, said that the bodies at Katyn were those of Poles who had, at one time, been prisoners of the Russians but had subsequently been captured by the Germans in July 1941, had been employed upon construction work in that area, and had only been murdered shortly before the German "discovery" was announced. The condition of the bodies, if nothing else, makes this last disclaimer quite incredible.

6. We must now add to the cumulative negative evidence the continuing reports from former prisoners in northern Soviet camps, particularly in the region of Archangel and Murmansk, that further thousands of officer prisoners had been destroyed by drowning in the Kara Sea; but whether the massacre occurred in one place or in several places naturally makes no difference to our sentiments and our conclusion must be that the Soviet Government is responsible for it. Comments found on bodies exhumed at Katyn—diaries, correspondence, newspapers—are

from the period of autumn 1939 to March and April 1940. The latest hitherto established date is that of a Russian newspaper of the 22nd April 1940. There were varying degrees of decomposition of the bodies, differing according to the position of the bodies in the grave and their juxtaposition to each other, but in most cases the sandy soil of the region acted as an insulating or mummifying agent retarding the process. Examination of the skulls showed, in most instances, the presence of changes which are not normally observed on bodies that had been interred for less than three years. These changes consist of various layers of calcareous tuft-like incrustation on the surface of the already loamy brain matter.

7. In strict compliance with Your direct order, I make no comment on recommendation which does not relate to evidence and its analysis, but I request that I may submit such recommendations through channels to the C.-in-C. and Prime Minister immediately. The matter is one of gravest urgency in the event of premature public disclosure.

IX

> *British Embassy to Poland*
> *45 Lowndes Road*
> *S.W.1*
> *May 24th*

No. 71
Most Secret
Sir,

With reference to my despatch No. 70 of today's date, I have the honour to transmit herewith a translation of a telegram dated May 15th and received by the Polish Government, through the Polish Military Mission in the Soviet Union, from the Polish underground organization in Warsaw.

2. I am inclined to think that the source from which I received this telegram had not been authorized to give it to me by the Prime Minister or the Deputy Prime Minister, and it may be that the text has not even been communicated to all members of the Polish Cabinet. Leakage to the enemy would of course at once put the Polish underground organization and the lives of certain identifiable members of it in jeopardy.

3. For these reasons I request that the text, and the fact that I have received it, and the substance of the message may be treated as particu-

larly secret; and that, if a copy of this dispatch is sent to any Government Department which works in close connection with any section of the Polish Government, the individuals in that Department should be warned not to refer to it to their Polish collaborators.

I have the honour to be with the highest respect,

Sir,

Your most obedient,

humble Servant

(   )

Robert Mallory

The Right Honorable
Anthony Eden, P.C., M.P.

X

*Enclosure in Mr. R. St. V. Mallory's despatch No. 71
Most Secret of May 24th*

Translation. Telegram from Poland dated May 15

1. At the foot of the hillock is an "L"-shaped mass grave which has been completely opened up. Its dimensions are: 16×26×6 metres. The bodies of the murdered men have been carefully arranged in from 9 to 12 layers, one on top of the other, each layer with the heads laid in the opposite directions. The uniforms, notes in the pockets, passports, and decorations are well preserved. The skin, hair, and tendons have remained in such good state that in order to carry out the trepanning it was necessary to cut under the skin and tendons. The faces were, however, unrecognizable.

2. While only two of the most recent graves have been opened, there are upwards of 40 similar burial mounds of similar dimensions in the near vicinity which, judging by the vegetation that covers them, were made at various times during the past 20 years.

3. At right angles to the first grave is a second mass grave which up to now has only been partially opened up. Its dimensions are 14×16 metres. All the bodies in this grave have the hands tied behind them with plaits of string: in some cases the mouths have been gagged with handkerchiefs or rags: in some the head has been wrapped round with the skirt of an overcoat.

4. Up to now 2,706 bodies have been extracted, 76 percent of which have been identified on the strength of passports, letters, etc., found on them. . . . In no way could those documents have been inserted into the murdered men's pockets after the time of their deaths . . . in many cases the documents are pierced with bayonets in the places where corresponding wounds are found in the bodies. . . .

5. It is presumed that in the two graves together there lie the bodies of from 3,500 to 4,000 officers: in only a few cases are they reserve officers in civilian dress.

6. A characteristic feature is that nothing except watches has been removed from the murdered men: note cases, money, and papers are still in their pockets: sometimes even rings are still on their fingers.

7. All the bodies have a bullet wound in the back of the skull. The representatives of the Polish Red Cross who were present at the exhumation took pains to collect the bullets extracted from the heads of the murdered men, the cartridge cases and ammunition lying in the mass graves, as well as the cords with which the hands of the murdered men had been tied. . . .

8. . . . . There was taken from the clothing of Major Solski a diary written up to April 21st. The writer of the diary stated that from Kozielsk they were taken in a prison train to Smolensk, where they spent the night: reveille was sounded at 4 A.M. and they were placed in prison motorcars. At a clearing in the forest they were turned out of the motorcars and at 6:30 taken to some buildings there, where they were told to give up their watches. At this point the diary ends.

9. . . . . All of the officers identified were from Kozielsk with the exception of one from Starobielsk.

10. Careful contact was made with the local civilian population without German knowledge. One person (name deleted) reported that he had been surprised by NKVD patrols in the forest sometime early in April 1940 and had hidden in a tree, from which he observed the execution of between 50 and 70 Polish officers in a manner consistent with the condition in which the bodies have been found. This person had not been shown the exhumed bodies, nor could have had prior knowledge of the way in which they had been tied, gagged, and executed unless he had seen the massacre take place. Other local inhabitants stated that in

March and April 1940 one transport of Polish officers, to the number of 200 or 300 men, used to arrive in the area every day.

11. The clearing in the forest at Katyn covers several square kilometres: on it there used to be NKVD rest houses. According to older local inhabitants, from about 1924 the entire forest was marked with signs: *Special Zone of the G.P.U.—Unauthorized persons forbidden to enter.* A large part of the forest was ringed with barbed wire in 1931 and ever since it has been constantly patrolled by NKVD guards with dogs. End of Message. (Code name deleted.)

XI

From a personal letter by Brig. Gen. H. J.-Wadsworth to Col. W. W. Hudson, British Liaison Group with the Polish Army in the Middle East

. . . Well, the Polish kettle has finally boiled over and all of us are being made to look extremely silly. The Katyn business is in all the papers and the Prime Minister, I am told, is furious about it. We all know, of course, who did the dirty, but it is hardly likely that anyone in Whitehall would say so in public. On the contrary, we are all supposed to shake our heads at this "irresponsible" Polish attitude to Jerry propaganda and condemn them, one and all, for undermining Allied unity. No one quite cares to wonder what the Poles are supposed to have done about it and all our press, particularly the pink-tinted journals, are having a field day. The Poles have been threatened with suppression of all their own newspapers if they breathe one more word of this unsavoury matter but the damage is done. But who among the Poles leaked that stuff to the Foreign Office and what did he have in mind? You say that it could not possibly be Prus himself and I'm inclined to agree. It simply wouldn't fit what we know of the man, but we think it's someone at your end of the line. Will you look into it? If there are to be any more surprises of this kind we'd rather like to know about them before they explode in the Prime Minister's face.

But what we really have to know about is this Jewish business. The Jewish Agency people are most unhappy to have this Mendeltort fellow anywhere near them, and there is no doubt that he is in Anders' Corps, stationed with the depot in Ribat, having been in the first lot of the Poles to be shipped over from Russia. As we get the story, M. must have made some sort of an agreement with the Poles to enlist his own people, unlikely though it seems. . . . Anders himself would hardly be a party to anything like that, but Prus' name has popped up in reports. Do try to find out from your informant what M. may be up to and in what manner Prus may be involved. Specifically, is there a *sub rosa* Jewish group in your Polish Corps and if so how large is it and who is its liaison with the Poles? I must say that I always thought Prus to be a damn good soldier, hardly given to sentimental meddling in political affairs, but it does begin to seem that the Jews had "sold him a bill of goods," as the Americans say. I understand that Mendeltort has a nephew on Prus' staff, perhaps that's the answer. . . .

I shall have to see if we might have Prus' group dissolved, particularly since the whole Katyn *gaffe* appears to have started with his search for his missing fellows (and they've been found, haven't they?), and have P. himself transferred over here where he might be less likely to fall into temptation. . . .

Do get onto this as quickly as you can, won't you? There may still be time to stop the rot before it spills all over us in Palestine. And, by the way, your Derek Bellancourt is a delightful young fellow. Should go quite far, I'd say. . . .

XII

From a Report by Brig. Gen. Janusz Prus, on detached service with HQ, II Polish Corps, Iran, to Gen. W. Anders, commander of the Polish Forces in the East

Sir,

With the dissolution of *Polish Military Mission in the U.S.S.R.*, as ordered by the C.-in-C. In London, I submit a final analysis of evidence in the matter of the Katyn Massacre, with special attention to terrain and the region's natural features which appear to be relevant.

1. Smolensk lies some 20 km. from the area where the common graves were discovered. It has two railroad stations and, in or near the town, the main lines from Moscow to Warsaw and from Riga to Orel cross and recross each other. Some 15 km. to the west of Smolensk stands the unimportant station of Gniazdovo, or Gnyezdovo, a mile from a place known locally as Kozlinaya Gora or "The Hill of Goats." The district of Katyn, in which this small hill stands, is covered with primeval forest, mostly coniferous, but the pine trees are interspersed here and there with hardwoods and scrub. The month of April normally brings spring to this country and by early May the trees are green; but the winter of 1939–1940 had been the hardest on record, and when the first parties

from Kozielsk arrived on 8th April there would still have been occasional patches of snow in deep shade, and much mud on the rough road from the station to the Hill of Goats.

2. What follows may appear to be unsupported speculation, yet the condition of the bodies, and the known features of the landscape, as well as the known execution methods of NKVD Special Liquidation Groups, suggest that at Gniazdovo the prisoners were transferred from their trains into trucks and buses and taken in small groups along the road to the Hill of Goats, and it must have been when they were unloaded from the motor vehicles that their hands were bound and that, indeed, they fought for their lives. If a man struggled, it seems the executioners threw his coat over his head according to established NKVD practice in such matters, tying it round his neck and leading him thus hooded to the edge of the pit, for in many cases the bodies were found to be thus hooded and the coat to have been pierced by a bullet where it covered the base of the skull. Most of the younger officers were heavily bayoneted with what were clearly the standard Soviet three- and four-edged bayonets before they were shot. Their bodies were methodically arranged in the pits, packed closely round the edge but in less order toward the middle of the graves. Subsequently, young conifers (Scotch pine) were transplanted into the covered graves.

3. The climate and the conifers are not without significance. The climate accounts for the fact that, although the Germans first heard reports of the massacre in the autumn of 1942, it was only in April 1943 that they could open the graves. Normally in winter the ground around Smolensk is frozen so hard that it would have been impossible to uncover corpses without dynamite or such other violent means as would have destroyed the possibility of identifying dead bodies. The winter of 1942–1943 was exceptionally mild and the Germans put some prisoners to work on the graves as soon as the ground was sufficiently soft. The little conifers also deserve more attention than they have received. In the first place, they are presumptive evidence of Russian guilt, for, considering the speed with which the German Army advanced through Smolensk in July 1941, in full expectation of early and complete victory, it is most unlikely, if the Polish officers had been murdered by them, that the Germans would have bothered to cover up their victims' graves with young trees. In the second place, these trees under examination by a competent botanist revealed beyond any possibility of doubt that they had been transplanted in the spring of 1940. Thirdly, the two open graves are by no means the only such graves in the area. Seven other graves appear to be of approximately the same date, to judge by

the vegetation upon them. Others date back to the times of the Cheka-GPU exterminations of the Civil War and the 1920's, yet others appear to have been made in the middle and late 1930's, the time of the Yezhov Purges. The Katyn Forest has a sinister history of which Polish Intelligence Services have been aware since the end of the Bolshevik Civil War.

4. The Soviet Government has now revised its various explanations into a single story which may be summarized as follows: Before the capture of Smolensk by the Germans, Polish prisoners were quartered in three labor camps 25 to 45 km. west of Smolensk. The camps were not evacuated in time and the Poles fell into the hands of the Germans. They were, if the Russian story is to be believed, seen working on the roads near Smolensk in August and September 1941, but not later. Access to the localities where executions took place had been barred but truckloads of Polish prisoners were often seen being driven there and many shots were heard. The Soviet report then passes to the time when the Germans are said to have been preparing for the announcement of the massacre's discovery and states that witnesses were tortured to give false evidence of Russian culpability; that 500 Russian prisoners (all subsequently shot) were employed to dig up the corpses and introduce forged documents into their pockets, and that loads of corpses were brought to Katyn in March 1943. In short, the Russians state that the inmates of the three Polish prisoner of war camps were moved in April and May 1940 to three Russian labor camps near Smolensk, captured by the advancing Germans, and shot at various times during the subsequent four months.

5. There is no way to reconcile this claim against the evidence of at least one indisputable set of facts and one essential assumption which is incredible. The Russian story assumes that about 10,000 Polish officers, employed on forced labor, lived around Smolensk from April 1940 until July 1941 and passed into German captivity without a single one of them having escaped or fallen again into Russian hands or reported to a Polish consul in Russia or to the Polish Underground Movement in Poland. This is quite incredible to anyone familiar with Russian prisoner of war and labor camps, or who pictures to himself the disorganization and confusion which must have been part of the German sweep and the Russian flight from the Smolensk area; but the essential assumption to the Russian case is actually destroyed in the Russians' own words. The revised Soviet report now states that many Polish prisoners did, in fact, escape after the district of Smolensk had been overrun by the Germans, and describes the frequent "roundups" of escapees

organized by the Germans. The Russian story gives no explanation of why, in these circumstances, given the forested features of the terrain, which would have been ideal for long-term fugitive concealment and travel, not a single one of the Poles allegedly transferred from the three prisoner camps has ever been seen or heard of alive again.

6. So much for the assumption essential to the credibility of the Russian story. The unexplainable set of facts is the same which has dominated our researches from the start, namely that from April 1940 onward not a single letter or message was ever received by anyone from the officers imprisoned up to that time in the three prison camps (except the 460 sent to Griazovetz); and that not a single inquiry about these men was ever answered, nor did such inquiries elicit a definite or consistent statement from the Soviet Government, until after the German announcement of the discovered graves.

7. In compliance with the orders of the C.-in-C., and subject to Your wishes, I hereby conclude the assignments of my special sections, and request new assignments for my officers, enlisted men, and myself. I particularly request that I may be allowed to make urgent personal recommendations to General Sikorski, in his capacity as our Nation's political leader, on a dangerous and potentially destructive situation which has now emerged in the Soviet Union as a result of this matter having become public knowledge.

XIII

From a letter to the author written by Dr. Jonathan J. Rash, from Tokyo, December 1969

I'm sorry that I have not continued my "autobiography" for such a long time, but what with some family difficulties and my new position as special instructor in the psychological conditioning of interrogated prisoners in Vietnam, I have had very little time to think about my past, or—as the great Carl Jung would have said it—my myth.

As I recall, I wrote to you last how we came to Andizhan: I and my sisters and the young men to whom they had become engaged, a good-natured and not too intelligent giant named Ariz (he was a blacksmith, I believe), who was later killed somehow in Palestine, and Moishe Traurig, who is now a general in the Israeli Army. I remember that when we arrived in the village, or town (it's hard to know what to call these Central Asian places), the day was sunny and warm. So, since winters in Uzbekistan and the Kirghiz Republic are unbearably cold, this must have been in spring 1942. A world of a Thousand and One Nights opened itself to me. We were all loaded on two-wheeled carts, each drawn by a horse, with the driver sitting on the horse and all of us in the high wooden cage of the cart, so far above the horse and the rider that they were quite invisible. We moved into a land from a fairy tale, among mud walls with small, secretive entrances, amid orchards hidden behind other walls where we could smell unseen fruit, in a cloud of dust among swarms of dogs, watched by mysterious women whose faces were hidden behind nets made of horsehair, and by brown men in multicolored coats with knives in their belts. Our driver started singing one of those monotonous Central Asian songs that go back to the times of the Khan Uzbeg, founder of the Uzbek race and heir to the great Genghis Khan.

An Uzbek home is made of unbaked, dried-mud bricks shaped like an American football, which are welded with more mud to scant wooden frames into a one-room house. There never is more than one room. The mud roof is smoothed and made to slope slightly forward so that, in winter, sleet and snow may be shoveled off it before it has a chance to melt, while in summer the Uzbeks sleep on it in the chilly nights.

Such a *kibitka*, to use a local word, was given to us at a collective cotton farm called Izvestia, where we were told that we could work and live. Paradise? Well, after where we came from and the way we had come it did look and may sound like paradise. I don't know. It turned out to be a lot less than that. Because the only work that we could have was in the cotton fields, and that was just too hard for us after what we'd been through. So how did we survive? The predominant movement in contemporary anthropology asks the question: *How does a given group or individual survive in the environment in which it finds itself?* If it can eat, it does; if it can't it doesn't, that's my answer to it.

My sister Kamila (who died later in Dzhalal-Abad, she had been left in Russia by the Polish army!) made an optimistic statement as soon as we had unpacked our bags in our windowless *kibitka*. She said that she had seen a child eating a peach, and that the dogs in the street were fat; this, she said, meant that we wouldn't starve. But she starved, and we almost starved, and many other Jewish families were starving. In his prologue to *Faust* Goethe speaks about *"die Vielfalt der Gestalten"* which submerged him. That's what I feel as I'm writing this. I recall the many people who were starving and who later died. I have studied Eastern philosophy (my Japanese girlfriend is a Shinto Buddhist) and I know that "to understand everything is to forgive everything," but I understand nothing of what happened to us then and I forgive nothing. We lived by selling our possessions but we could never get enough to eat. A pair of silk stockings would get us only one kilo of bread! Then the rains came. It rained as heavily inside our *kibitka* as it rained outside. To get out of bed was an act of heroism. We resigned ourselves to death. We were so hungry we began to suspect each other of getting more than a fair share of food. Esterka divided the food and we all watched her like hawks when she did it—at least I did. I think I hated her then for giving me so little, although she always took the smallest portion for herself. Esterka and Kamila worked somewhere in the kolkhoz. I don't remember what they did. Traurig and Ariz worked in the cotton fields. I used to dream about food, I made up stories about food the way children make up stories about enchanted castles. There was some Polish organization which gave out food at first (400 gms. a person) but then, one day, it stopped and we could get no more.

So how did we survive? We survived by making black-market deals. Yes, we the Rashevsky family from Zywiec, for whom a criminal act was beyond forgiveness, became black-marketeers. Do you remember what I wrote you about my grandfather and his fanatical obedience to law, any law? My grandfather's ghost was with us then, as it is with me now; we knew there could be no forgiveness for an immoral act, but we had to eat. First we sold our dollars to a Jewish woman by the name of Krieger, who was far from starving; in fact, she had so much food that she used to beg her children to eat! Esterka found out that the Krieger woman made black-market deals with the Uzbeks and the Polish soldiers who had one of their camps near Dzhalal-Abad; she used to buy milk from the Uzbek women to sell to the soldiers, then she bought tobacco and sold that as well. Soon everyone was doing the same. And we did it too. Not to have done so would have meant our deaths. We had to eat in order to survive.

(Today I am lying in an air-conditioned room in a Japanese luxury hotel, waiting for my girlfriend, and we shall shortly go out to an expensive restaurant, and it seems inconceivable to me that there was a time when I was a small boy who lived in a windowless, wet *kibitka* and cried because he was hungry. It is inconceivable but, yes, it is true: there was such a boy and he is always with me, just as my grandfather's ghost is always with me. I have never recovered from the terror of hunger and death and I never will.)

Then two events took place which were to have a marked effect on us all. First, the Polish army came to our district and a rumor started that the army would soon be leaving Russia and that we'd all go with it. So we lived on hope. Ariz and Traurig went to join the army but they were refused. Why were they refused? It seems the Polish army didn't think that Jews made good soldiers. The Polish army didn't care that we were human beings and that we were starving. They didn't want Jews. The second event was that, as soon as the Polish army came, signs appeared everywhere that black-marketeering was forbidden. I remember a meeting outside a building that was some sort of a Polish headquarters. Most of the families at the meeting were Jewish and had come to the district just as we had done, having gone through the same terrible experiences, thinking that we would get help from the Polish army. An elderly officer spoke to us (he was a *podpułkownik*), and he made anti-Semitic remarks. He said, if I remember my Polish: *Ja tutaj nie przyszedłem aby wam życie ułatwić, ale utrudnić.* Maybe the word was *uprzykrzyć* not *ułatwić*, I don't quite remember, but the gist of what he said was that all of us were to go back to wherever we had come from because the Polish army would do nothing for us. Why not? We had our "White Papers" that said we were Polish. Why would the Polish army do nothing for us? I couldn't understand this. I thought that we had misunderstood this *Pan Podpułkownik*. How could he say this to us, the Rashevsky family from Zywiec? What would my grandfather have said to that, he who had taught me to love our beloved Pilsudski? Was this justice? Was this even human? But I was soon to learn that I had not misunderstood that *Pan Podpułkownik*, he meant what he said. A wave of anti-Semitism started among the Uzbeks. Before the Polish army came, they called us *Urus*, or Russians, but after the army came we were called *Zhid*; we were no longer *Urus* to them and soon they would have nothing to do with us. I don't know how this was done, how it was arranged, but the Uzbeks wouldn't even sell us any food, and so hard times began again but they were only a beginning. A great many non-Jewish Polish families had come with the army and there were soon orphanages and Polish schools and there the anti-Semitism was really bad. It was directed mostly against those youngsters who spoke only Yiddish; the Polish children made jokes about them. So you see, on top of all the other crimes and plagues that had befallen us we now had anti-Semitism as well. It was then that I understood what it is to be a Polish Jew. I understand it, but I cannot forgive it, and I will never forget that elderly *podpułkownik* who had said that he had come to make our lives not easier but more difficult. The memory of that day is so very vivid that it seems as though it had happened only yesterday. I can't think of it without rage.

But there was more, much more. The Polish army embarked on a clear-cut campaign of anti-Semitism. I don't know how this was done, other than depriving us of our livelihood, but it turned the Uzbeks from our friends into enemies. Then a number of soldiers of Jewish descent were discharged from the Polish army. And finally we were told that when the army left Russia we would not be able to go with it! Can you describe the despair that seized us all then? Can you imagine how we felt? And why was this done to us? Why?

(Today I often wonder about those officers like that *podpułkownik*. What kind of men were they? I was with the United States Army in Korea and my American lieutenant colonel treated me with respect. Today I teach American officers who also respect me, and these are strong, victorious soldiers who did not surrender meekly to the Russians like that *podpułkownik*. If they can respect me, why couldn't he? Who was he? What made him as he was?)

You'll have to excuse me, but I can't continue this narrative any longer. I will have to write to you again on another day. Because, of course, we did get out of Russia in the end with the Polish army but we were among the lucky few. Thousands were left behind. My sister Kamila is one of those who stayed in a Russian grave.

XIV

From a personal letter by Col. W. W. Hudson, British Liaison Group with the Polish Army in the Middle East, to Brig. Gen. H. J.-Wadsworth.

My dear Hugh:

. . . Actually, I'm awfully glad that we do have this private means of supplementing my official bumph. . . . To send this sort of thing through Signals would be pure folly. Thanks to our journalists' enthusiasm, dear old Uncle Joe Stalin is such a favourite with our other ranks that one doesn't quite know who one's cypher clerks are working for. . . . Derek will place this in your hands next week when he's in London with my *Status Report on the Polish Forces in the Middle East* for CIGS.

First of all, let me assure you that no one in Whitehall needs to worry about the loyalty of the Anders men, no matter what new macabre revelations come to light in Russia, nor what the Soviet Government might do in the aftermath of the Katyn revelations. They're now in the process of transfer from the Tashkent-Samarkand-Bokhara region of the U.S.S.R., along the Krasnovodsk-Pahlevi route (the Russkies have provided the most dreadful old transports for the journey across the Caspian Sea) to British Command, Middle East, where the first Polish units have arrived in August. All should be there by the spring of 1943 unless Stalin's people have another fit of uncooperativeness and stop the whole thing. These are fine soldiers and all they want to do is to fight the Germans, win the war, and *then* mourn their murdered compatriots. Anders himself has told me that "the sooner the war against Germany is won, the sooner we may liberate all those of our people who have been left behind (in the U.S.S.R.)." Were the conditions better, and were the Russians more cooperative, at least another two Polish divisions could be formed. But, as matters stand, it is only a matter of time before Stalin orders the gates slammed shut on this evacuation, so we must speed the Poles along, even though more than a million of their people will be left behind. . . .

But to return, for a moment, to the Katyn business. Could HM Government not do something to restrain our journalists' attacks on these unfortunate survivors of our noble Soviet Ally's barbarity? The things the Americans are writing are particularly ignorant and inflammatory. I am less concerned by the effect of this clearly orchestrated campaign of defamation on the morale of the Poles, who are among the most determined and serious-minded soldiers I have ever seen, than I am by the effect that these jackals' jibes have upon our own other ranks (and the more simpleminded of the officers as well!). Just last week a crowd of our base wallahs (the RAF, thank God, not the Army) invaded one of the Poles' hospitals and pitched those wretched sufferers of Stalin's hospitality from their beds. You know best, although none of us may ever admit it, how far Whitehall has gone to limit Jewish enlistment in the Polish Forces, as indeed we must, so that the charges of anti-Semitism are particularly absurd. . . . but I shall return to that Jewish affair in a moment.

I fear that unless measures are taken to muzzle our own and the Americans' scribblers, the Poles will *not* be able to keep the lid on yet another piece of awful business that would make *further alliance with the Soviet Union morally impossible for us*. There is now incontrovertible evidence, based upon sworn eyewitness testimony, that the Russians murdered more than 7,000 Polish officers, by drowning them in the Kara Sea with artillery fire, *after* Hitler's invasion had turned them into our allies and that of the Poles! If the Prime Minister was furious when the Katyn cat got out of the bag, how would he react to that revelation? Surely the murderers can share a dark smile only with Pontius Pilate; can we afford to join them, and could we afford not to? I shudder to think of what might happen to the course of the war should that monstrous act become public knowledge as did the murders in the Katyn Forest. The Poles have exercised an iron-willed discipline in this matter, conscious as they are of their responsibility to their Western Allies, and to the hundreds of thousands of their countrymen who will have to be left in the Russians' hands if *any* are to be saved. They have said, and will say, nothing. Could we not exercise some semblance of similar restraint upon their behalf? Even an iron-souled commander like Gen. Anders, and the superbly motivated soldiers of his army, may find it difficult to contain such an awful truth when fed a daily diet of abuse and insult. . . .

The political background against which these (and God only knows how many other) terrible events must be viewed is a matter of undisputed history, including as it does all the long story of partitions, insurrections, and repressions, the Russo-Polish war of 1919–20, the mutual suspicions that this left behind it, the unannounced invasion of Poland by Russia in September 1939, the subsequent occupation of half of Poland by Russia and the carrying into captivity of some two million of its inhabitants. More recently comes the refusal of the Russian Government to recognise as Polish citizens all the inhabitants of the seized districts, particularly the Jews and other minorities who had been citizens of Poland, the suppression of relief organizations for Poles in Russia, the expulsion of Polish Government delegates from the larger cities, the difficulties placed in the way of continuing recruitment of the Poles in Russia, and the persecution of Poles refusing to change their nationality for a Russian one.

It is in this light that the Poles here see all these events, and many of them have naturally concluded (though I do not here give it as my own conclusion) that the discovered and reported massacres prove the Russian Government's intention to destroy the very foundations upon which an independent Poland could be rebuilt after the defeat of the Germans. This sinister political intention poisons the wound and enhances the suffering of a fighting nation which is already outraged and dismayed by the conduct of the Russian Government and, it must also be admitted, that of the governments of their Western Allies who appear to be deliberately condoning all that has been done. The Polish military here, as elsewhere, I am sure, will fight and die in silence in our common cause if fight and die they must. But how long may we depend upon the disciplined silence of the Polish civilian politicians in London unless some relief from this concerted campaign of denigration is given to them? I must say, my dear Hugh, that even with *our* sort of background I don't know what I would do were I in their place, in which (Heaven be praised) I am not. . . . However, in the matter of the Jews admitted to the Polish army in Russia, as in this highly questionable Mendeltort affair, the Poles continue to be uncooperative in a most uncharacteristic manner, as I shall shortly show. They have discharged 11 officers who are Jews, and who were members of Col. Berling's "Red Corner" (as these converts to Communism are known to their fellows), as well as some of the other ranks whom we have indicated as politically unacceptable, or whose return the Russians have demanded as self-declared Soviet citizens. But they are obstinate in refusing to place any other obstacles to Jewish recruitment, so that soon we shall have some 5,000 of them, and their families, in the Middle East. Should more of them wish to join the colours, I am afraid there is little we could do to stop them without revealing HM Government's interest in this matter. . . .

XV

From a letter written by Dr. Jonathan J. Rash, from New York, May 24, 1972

The last time that I wrote to you about my ordeal I told you about the terrible situation in which we found ourselves in Dzhalal-Abad (we had moved there sometime in the summer of 1942) after the Polish army came. I managed to become enrolled in one of the Polish schools which was attached to an army orphanage, and what I suffered there I have already told you. I was not a victim of any of the cruel gibes and jokes because I spoke Polish as well as any of the other children there (indeed, I thought I was Polish too!) but the treatment of the youngsters from the less emancipated Jewish families, who spoke only Yiddish, and who came to the school just to get the food, soon opened my eyes. There was, among their worst tormentors, a boy I knew from Lwów (his name is Poremba and he is now living here in Manhattan, where he is in the insurance business, and respected in the Polish community), who was an orphan, like myself, but whose sister was a whore. He made life unbearable for the Yiddish kids, and I began to hate him for it as I had begun to hate all those Polish officers who treated us so badly. You must know what it is like to hate, having been in prison, but do you know what it means to be filled with hatred for injustice, not for one's own suffering but for the oppression of others? That kind of hatred changes everything for you; it can even give you a new identity. So this is what I learned in that Polish school: to hate, and to look for a new identity that I wouldn't have to hate. But I must be honest with you, I have not yet found it. It is a terrible thing to hate what you are. . . .

But let me give you more examples of anti-Semitism that I began to see for the first time in my life. I don't know why I had never noticed it before, perhaps it was my grandfather's fanatical obedience to authority, or perhaps I simply hadn't wanted to see it before, but suddenly it was all around me like the air I was breathing.

There was another boy at the orphanage whom I had known from Lwów. His name was Emil (like you, he is a writer now but I don't know where he is). My family and I lived in his parents' house while we were in Lwów. We were always friends. We were taken to Russia at the same time, on the same train, and I used to share my tea with him when I could. Well, in that school he wouldn't look at me. He never spoke to me. He looked at me as if we had never met. I don't know what made him so cold and so indifferent, but to me that is a classic example of anti-Semitism; it's a disease that spreads through the air we breathe. And the woman who ran this orphanage, a Pani Mosinska, she just hated Jews. She said that Jews had welcomed the Russians with flowers when they came to Lwów, so that now they should be happy with the people they had welcomed to Poland. She once made a speech to the whole school about *ludzie cygańskiego pochodzenia*, and about how we (that is to say, the Polish youngsters) should never trust anyone of mongrel birth. *Cygańskiego pochodzenia* means "of Gypsy descent," if you still remember your Polish, but everyone knew she was talking about Jews. Poremba turned right around in his chair and looked at me when she was saying it. And there were other things, too many to mention, that I heard about. . . .

In the material sense, things did improve a little for us at about that time. My sister Esterka married Moishe Traurig (who, as I'm sure you know, is now a famous general in the Israeli Army) and both of them managed to join the Polish army in Dzhalal-Abad. He was made a private in the infantry and she became a nurse. My other sister's fiancé, Ariz, also got into the army but Kamila stayed out of it to look after me. She feared any kind of violence and was obsessively terrified of soldiers (I think she lived in terror of all men, even of Ariz) but if she had joined the army I would have had to be put in the Polish orphanage, and we didn't want that. Again the proud unbending ghost of my grandfather stood in the way of our accepting charity. . . . But if you think that what I've just written contradicts the truth of the Polish army's anti-Semitism then you would be wrong. The Poles had to take some Jews into the army or the World Opinion would have been against them; they would not have had the support from America and England that they needed to get their army out of Russia . . . and there was yet another matter that I didn't know about at the time. It seems that there was a Jewish secret organization in Russia, led by a Great Hero whose name I don't remember, who made a deal with the Poles to enlist some of his people so that they could, later, become Freedom Fighters for Israel. The Poles wouldn't have minded taking in those Jews if they knew they would be rid of them once they got their army out of Russia. . . . I don't know how this was done since it is still a great secret, but Esterka, Traurig, and Ariz were members of this secret Freedom Fighters' Army, and if you are ever in Israel you can ask my brother-in-law, General Traurig, about it. So you see, there was no great kindness in what the Poles did by allowing the enlistment of some Jews, they had no choice about it.

The Polish army had a theater group which toured all the camps and made fun of Jews. There was one sketch I remember in which a small man with a mustache played the role of a Jewish soldier. He was very good. Usually he came onto the stage alone, a caricature of the cowardly Jew, and he was always greeted with applause and laughter. He delivered a monologue in the Jewish-Polish accent: he had to march a lot and he had flat feet, the food was bad, and what was it all for? He'd much rather sleep, like an Uzbek, on the roof. Then the sergeant would come on, a fine-looking Polish soldier, straight like a ramrod, and he'd start yelling at the Jew: Rabinowicz, what are you doing here, why aren't you on guard? Where is your *karabin*? Then Rabinowicz would start to run around searching for his *karabin* and he'd hand it to the sergeant saying that he is a *rabin* and afraid of the *karabin*, and everyone would laugh and applaud. To make such jokes about another people is a cruel, wicked thing . . . it is immoral and it is unjust.

But hunger, that terrible hunger that no one who has been in Russia in that time will ever forget, was the most terrible of our sufferings. Many Jewish families were starving because the Polish army destroyed their livelihood, their means of survival, and gave them no food. Esterka, Moishe, and Ariz brought us food while they were still in Dzhalal-Abad, as did all other Jews who were in the army and shared their rations with their families, but the two men and Esterka were soon sent away and I and Kamila were alone. We survived on what Kamila could earn in the cotton fields but the work there was so hard that she became ill. The only food we had then was what I was given at the school and that wasn't enough even for me. I thought then that if I ever got out of that hell that was Russia I would spend all day, every day, in eating and eating. All I could think about was mountains of food. I fought for it in the school, I took it away from smaller kids, and then the bigger kids, like Poremba, would take it away from me. Sometimes I was so swollen from the beatings I got in that school defending my food that I had to stay at home to recover and that was the most terrible thing of all because than I knew that I would miss something edible that day.

In the autumn of 1942 the army started leaving, and Esterka and Moishe Traurig were among the first groups to go. Kamila was then so ill that she could not get up any more and, in December 1942, she died. Ariz came to see us then and he buried her in a field outside Dzhalal-Abad and then he took me to the Polish orphanage and went off with the rest of the Polish army.

I was alone in Russia then. I had no one. I cried for days. How

I got out of Russia and into Persia and then to Palestine is another
story and I will have to write to you about that on some other day.

XVI

*From a personal letter by Col. W. W. Hudson, British
Liaison Group with the Polish Army in the Middle East,
to Brig. Gen. H. J.-Wadsworth, as cited in part in* Memoirs of a Soldier

. . . As for the existence of a *sub rosa* Jewish organization among the
Poles who were recruited in Russia and who are now in the process of
evacuation to bases in Iran, Iraq, and Northern Palestine, we have little
to go upon except rumour and a few denunciations which have a
stronger flavor of personal hostility to Brig. Prus than of fact. There are
3,506 Jewish officers and other ranks in the two Polish infantry divisions, the armoured brigade, and the reconnaissance and support regiments and units now being reorganized under British Command, and
most of them appear to be genuine. More are to come in further transports with the remainder of the Poles now on their way from Russia,
but their numbers, including civilian members of their families, should
not exceed another 3,000 to 4,000 . . . None were among the 15,000
men already sent to reinforce the Polish naval and air force squadrons in
Britain, and there are fewer than 100 who serve in the Women's Transport Columns and in the Nursing Corps attached to the Army. If the
supposed Hargan organization does exist among them, the Poles appear
to know nothing about it.

I can't tell you how awfully sorry I am to hear that Prof. Karolewski
has seen fit to by-pass me and to turn to you directly with his allegation
of Prus' involvement in a conspiracy with the Jews, particularly since
there is no tangible evidence to support such an accusation, and I am
sure that you'll dismiss the allegations of bribery with the contempt
that such a slander upon the honour of a reputable soldier must deserve. . . . Still, the matter does bear further investigation and since
Prus has now been transferred to Polish advance HQ in Egypt, I would
suggest that you invite him to London for an honest chat.

What we did establish was that there had been a meeting between
Mendeltort and Prus during the winter of 1941 when the Polish Army
was organizing near Buzuluk in Russia, the meeting having been arranged by Mendeltort's nephew, Capt. A. Abramowski, who was then
Prus' ADC in the PMM/USSR. The subject of the meeting has been
reported as a matter of additional assistance to Polish Jews living in

Russia, but this may not be entirely true. Such assistance would have been a function of the Polish Assistance Committee and its relief organizations which operate under civilian control, and of such local Polish Government delegates as Prof. Karolewski. Apparently Capt. Abramowski was the only witness to this conversation and claims to have been present only during the first few minutes of the meeting but since he now commands a Signals company here, and may be watched closely, we may yet be able to track down the truth. Derek Bellancourt, by the way, is a particularly close friend of Abramowski (they knew each other as boys before the war) and I have put him on the scent. . . .

As for Mendeltort himself, who had been in the first transport of Poles to arrive in Iran, no further enquiries can be pursued in that quarter since he has, apparently, deserted from the training depot which the Poles have in the Syrian desert, and has not been found. The total number of Jewish deserters so far is about 70, and the Poles have been most unwilling to look for them. They have, in fact, consistently refused to join our searches of the Jewish settlements in Palestine under the pretext that we are not really searching for their 70 deserters but for illegal Jewish stores of arms. Since all these desertions took place in the first month of the Poles' arrival, and since none have been reported since that time, I feel it is too early to assume that a large-scale desertion by Hargan followers is planned as your Jewish Agency people have reported. Still, we shall persevere. . . .

You may be sure that I shall get to the bottom of the Mendeltort affair, which has now become my main occupation here.

XVII

Excerpt from The Memoirs of a Soldier, *by Maj. Gen. Sir Hugh Joness-Wadsworth*

. . . There then took place an act of such senseless and outrageous barbarism, that even hearts inured to the horrors of war, as all hearts had surely become in the fifth decade of the 20th Century, must have been moved to hatred and contempt for the perpetrators. . . . For it is one thing to inflict death upon an armed and resolute enemy, or even a hostile people capable of resistance, and quite another to slaughter hapless infants, women and old men, a community of inoffensive Christian Arabs which had never taken part in any of the innumerable Jewish-Arab conflicts. . . . Before the massacre, the population of Dair Yassir had been estimated at about 1,500 persons divided into approximately

74 families, but of these some 740 youths and men of military age were absent, most of them being subject to conscription in the Husseini Arab Legion, so that all male victims were either younger than fourteen years of age or older than forty-six. The body count, as such things were then becoming to be known, exceeded 500, but it was known that all the murdered infants and many of the younger children had been thrown into the village well which was then dynamited, and we had not the hearts to open this mass grave but merely had it sealed and ordered that Christian services be held over it. Many of the old and infirm men and women had been either dragged or driven into the waters of the sea and the river for drowning and few of them were found. No one present at Dair Yassir on that barbarous day is said to have escaped the slaughter although, later, some persons would claim to have survived the massacre as children and would, indeed, form an organization dedicated to vengeance against the Israelis and bearing the name of the month in which the massacre had taken place . . . thus murder breeds itself and perpetuates itself long after the event, and the senseless acts of terrorism of the Palestinian "Black December" movement have their roots in the Jewish Hargan's slaughter of the innocents at Dair Yassir. . . .

Of the attackers, only one was taken prisoner by a detachment of the King's Own Royal Dragoon Guards which, on patrol several miles away, noted the red glow of a conflagration across the brown domed hills and hurried to the rescue, but since the murderers had set fire to the village only after their dreadful work was done, all but a handful had managed to escape. Because of the wounded prisoner's age he was, at first, taken for one of the victims and treated with the most considerate care. Later, he was identified as a former employee of the Palestinian Railway, a Jew of about eighty years of age, who had once been a member of the Palestinian Police Force Reserve and had been sought in connection with several bombings upon the railway since the Jewish-Arab troubles in the early 30's. Unfortunately he did not survive his interrogation at the PPF barracks at Latrun and could give little coherent information about the perpetrators of the massacre. . . . Yet we were certain, even then, that this brutal act was a signal of Mendeltort's presence among us and subsequent events were to prove this assumption to have been correct. . . . In fairness, it must be said that the horrors of the massacre brought an immediate denunciation of the Hargan by the existing Jewish authorities in Tel Aviv and were to lead to the repudiation and exposure of the terrorist himself. As for the Hargan, it would continue on its course of bombings and assassinations throughout the British presence in the Palestine Mandate and, indeed, beyond it, under the leadership of yet another young deserter from the Polish

Army who, at that time, was known to us only by his code name of Shomayr (Heb.: *Guardian*). It may be an ironic footnote to a tragic story that the present Kibbutz Barzel-Shomayr stands upon the ruins of Dair Yassir.

XVIII

From a carbon copy of a personal letter to General Wladyslaw Sikorski, Polish Prime Minister and Commander-in-Chief, found among the private papers of the late Brig. Gen. Janusz Prus after his suicide in London in 1945. It is doubtful whether Gen. Sikorski ever received this letter since he was killed in an air accident near Gibraltar at about the time the letter was sent to him in London.

Drogi Wladyslawie:

I write to you this time as an old friend, not merely a dutiful subordinate, being encouraged by the warmth you showed me during our brief meeting in Alexandria this week, and moved only by that terrible concern for our Country's future which you share so fully. The specter of a new enslavement is already present in the formation of the Russians' *Committee of Polish Patriots* in Moscow, in the desertion from our army of Colonel Berling, and in the resumption of Polish recruitment in the Soviet Union into a so-called Polish People's Army to be led by Berling. It is so clear what the Russians have in mind for our Country's future, that they will seize any opportunity to sever their relations with Your government, prevail upon our allies to follow suit, and to invest their puppets with the powers of the Polish State. It is with this in mind that I have tried to reach you on numerous occasions to advise and to beg that no publicity be given to the Katyn tragedy, or to the horror which we have now uncovered in the Kara Sea, since it is now no longer a question of seeking justice on the murderers of our 10,000 friends and countrymen, but a question of preservation of Poland's freedom when the war is won.

The men who were slaughtered at Katyn and in the Kara Sea are dead; their deaths are a devastating loss to Poland but our just outrage will not bring them back to life again. As I have told you during our brief talk, I cannot say how my Most Secret dispatches found their way into the hands of hostile British and American journalists via the British Foreign Office; I may merely assume that there are placed in the Foreign Office some importantly positioned persons who are either in close sympathy with the Kremlin's policies or in its employ. They may have wished to render to Stalin this macabre service to provide the pretext for which he is looking. I must, of course, accept responsibility for this tragically untimely revelation since these materials were under my control. Should your Council of Ministers require my dismissal from the Service, as a partial means of appeasing British indignation and Soviet propaganda, I am at your disposal. I shall report to you next week in London as instructed.

I know you too well to fear that you will fail to understand the jeopardy in which we would be placing the future of our Nation by any further public notice of the massacres which we have discovered (indeed, for all I know it may already be too late!) but I beg you to restrain the partisan politicians of your civilian Cabinet to a greater discretion. We are closer here in the Middle East than they are in London to Russian reality; closer to the Russian cruelty and deviousness and possible intentions: and so I write to you as a friend from former, happier days—happier in the sense that they were victorious against the same brutal antagonist, and that they confirmed Poland's independence—to urge that you do *everything* to assure the return of Poland's legitimate government to Poland once the war is won. I urge you to sacrifice our pride, to suppress our grief, to close our eyes to murder, and to force upon us all the humiliation of accepting the murderers' lying claims of innocence. I know that this is a terrible decision that you will be making but I beg you to remember that unless you do so the Katyn victims will have died in vain and our Country, under whatever puppets the Russians install to rule it, will become yet aother republic of the Soviet Union. Since all matters relating to the Katyn tragedy, from the moment of the German discovery of the graves, have been handled personally by yourself and Count Raczynski with Churchill and Eden, then you know best how far along the road to possible disaster we have been brought by the Allies' need to appease the Russians. The violence of the American press has made *us* appear to have been the perpetrators, not the victims, of a monstrous crime. Would you consider me at least morally a traitor if I were to tell you that, in my view, the British attitude has been the correct one? In handling the public side of the tragedy, the British Government have been constrained, by the urgent need for cordial relations with the Kremlin, to appear to appraise the evidence with more hesitation and lenience than they would have done in normal times; they have been obliged to distort the normal operation of their intellectual and moral judgments; they have been obliged to give undue prominence to our supposed "tactlessness and impulsiveness" and to restrain us from putting our case clearly before the public. With the importance of their American and Russian alliances in mind, they have suppressed any attempt by the public to probe the ugly story to the bottom. Indeed, our Western Allies have used the good names of America and England, like the murderers used the little conifers, to cover up a massacre. Yet in view of the immense importance of an appearance of Allied unity, few historians will think that any other course would have been wise or right. I urge you that for the sake of a truly independent Poland, which may be assured *only* if your government returns to Warsaw on the day of victory, we too be forced into such dislocation between our public attitude and our private feelings. I do so knowing that this is a course which you, the Government, and the Polish people whom you represent, will find morally repugnant, yet the alternative is to place our entire Nation in unjustifiable jeopardy. Could we really be so blind that we would expend our energies in outraged mourning for 10,000 or even 100,000 victims of a massacre if, in that public mourning, we were to condemn 30 millions of our countrymen and their succeeding generations to enslavement by the murderers? May we not take the long view of our Country's future, defeat the devious processes of Soviet puppetry before they may be put into effect, and stifle for the moment the just voice of our horror and moral indignation? Our allies' need for the goodwill of the Katyn murderers obliges us, for the sake of Poland, to keep our anger inside our own hearts and minds. Here we can reaffirm our allegiance to truth and to future justice. Ten thousand and more of our brothers have been slaughtered; more than one million of our countrymen remain in Russian hands and will, most probably, never be found again. It is to them, as well as to the future generations of free-born Poles, that we owe this act of faith and allegiance.

My dear friend, I beg you in the name of everything that we've held dear in our lives as soldiers, to lead us beyond grief and anger and even beyond the reach of the fallible human intellect, beyond humiliation and a patriot's rage, into that cold assessment of reality where great decisions are made by great men. Lead us home to an independent Poland which we shall keep free.

XIX

From a taped interview by the author with former Brigadier Moishe Traurig, Member of the Knesset, made on Dec. 5, 1973, at Kibbutz Barzel-Shomayr

. . . Some mysteries are best left untouched. Some truths can hurt the living more than they can justify the dead. What good will it do to bring up . . . or to exhume, as seems more appropriate . . . that whole Mendeltort-Prus affair? Mendeltort is dead. Prus is dead. But there were other people . . . many other people . . . involved in that business. Poles, Englishmen, some Americans, some of our own People. (Long pause.) Some acted well and some acted badly, but who is to say after all these years who was right and who was wrong? My God, man, that was thirty years ago! Thirty years . . . Thirty years ago I was barely twenty, a young man full of fire and a young man's convictions . . . Mendeltort was a god to me, but I wonder how I would look at him today? We all change, you know. Age has its smoothing influence on us all, it's like our desert wind polishing a rock . . . (laughs) even my wife has stopped throwing grenades and throws plates instead (laughs) . . . No, that's not true, not true. Esterka is far too civilized for anything like that, but I am practicing to be a politician, do you see, so I make the jokes . . . Thirty years ago there was nothing to make jokes about. No, we were serious then, deadly serious . . . Serious as only young people can be, the kind of young people who had forgotten how to laugh . . . We were deadly then. We did some things, all of us, that are best not talked about today. I have a son who is in our diplomatic service and doing very well. I have a daughter who is doing things in a laboratory that I'd rather not even think about . . . How will it help them to know what their father did when he was their age? They, you see, are serious. We are all serious in Israel, we have to be serious. (Long pause, sounds of movement, the pouring of liquids.) Mendeltort is dead. He is a legend that no one really knows very much about, he is a myth . . . something like your Trumpeter of Cracow, eh? No one really knows if he was ever real, in the sense that you and I are real. He is a rock half buried in the desert . . . let's leave him alone. You lift up such a rock and you can see some very ugly things buried under it . . . things that don't help anyone to know about. It's all best forgotten. Some of the people involved in that business are still alive, they are useful people, they're doing good work, living decent lives . . . it wouldn't help them if we were to exhume their lives of thirty years ago . . . You talk about history, about getting to the bottom of a truth, but history is more than names and dates and places and the dimensions of a grave. That is all historical statistics, that isn't the truth . . . The truth is what was happening in the hearts and minds of living people, it is not historical statistics, it's more than facts and figures and asterisks and footnotes . . . The truth? My truth of thirty years ago was alive thirty years ago, now that truth is dead. When you begin to dig up all these dead truths you dig up a smell . . . no, you can't do it. Mendeltort believed in something and that's why he was killed but the people who killed him also believed in something and that's why they killed him . . .

Their truths were just as true to them as his was to him (pause) and to me . . . and some of them are still alive, and some of them are good and decent men who are doing good and decent things . . . things that are important to a lot of people . . . it would do them no good to dig up that business about Mendeltort and Prus . . . and all that other business . . . The man who betrayed him is alive and doing good things. Leave Mendeltort alone, forget him. He is best forgotten. His truth is the truth of thirty years ago. We live today's truths. The dead should not intrude upon the living. I am sorry you've come out all this way for nothing. Goodbye.

Second tape, made on Dec. 10, 1973

. . . I've thought about our last talk. I've read Jankele's letters that you left with me. That's why I asked you to come out here again. One has to be fair. There are some things that can be said without hurting anyone, I don't have to tell you everything. We'll talk a bit. I still get tired easily. I haven't quite got over that little present the Syrians sent my way two months ago on the Golan Heights. I'm told you were there? Well, then you know how it was; *a damned close-run thing,* as the Duke of Wellington is supposed to have said after Waterloo . . . It had better never be that close again. (Pause, sound of movement, the rustle of papers.) All right then, some things I can tell you. There's not much I can tell you about that meeting between Mendeltort and Prus. Oh, I was there all right. But I was in the anteroom most of the time with Abel Abramowski . . . He and I share a very strange, a very human story . . . We didn't hear much of what went on in the other room. Once in a while Prus would call for something and Abel would go in but they didn't say anything, I mean Mendeltort and Prus, while the door was open. They talked for about two hours. Then they both came out. You couldn't read anything in Mendeltort's face, you never could, the man was like a rock. But I remember that Prus looked very tired. Abel was looking from one to the other but Abel was being very military then, quite the perfect ADC, you know, so of course he wouldn't ask anything. But I remember the long look that passed between Mendeltort and Abel and the way they shook hands. It was a . . . sort of confirmation, a sort of welcoming and thanks at the same time . . . Mendeltort was capable of a great deal of warmth and this came through quite clearly then. He and Prus also shook hands but that was a lot more controlled, almost theatrically so, as if they didn't want to let any emotion show . . . Well, we left then. Mendeltort gave

me some orders. There was a certain plan, you see, and he told me that
the plan was operational now, to get going on it. That plan is something we won't talk about, it's quite irrelevant to what you want to
know and . . . I'll be frank about this . . . it would lead you into a line
of inquiry that I don't want you to pursue. Then Mendeltort went back
to Moscow and I went back to the *uchastok* where Esterka and the
others were, and then we started doing what had to be done. The
others in the settlement, Catherine and her Kobza . . . (Have you
talked with Catherine in America . . . ?) They were about to leave in
search of the army. They had no idea where to look for it, but they
were determined to find it if it killed them. Well, it killed some of
them. I could have told them exactly where to find the army, I had just
come from it, but that would have shown that I knew more than I
could be expected to know. Esterka and I talked it over and we decided
not to tell them. You understand, of course? We were already soldiers
then, in an army of Mendeltort's imagination, and this was one of
those command decisions that soldiers have to make. Imagine, two children aged nineteen making command decisions! But that's the way we
had to do things thirty years ago. I've sometimes thought that if we had
told them, perhaps poor old Kobza could have reached his beloved
army. Perhaps if we had told them it could have saved some lives. Perhaps not . . . Ah . . . you see the sort of wasteful speculation you
might fall into when you open up old graves? Not at all helpful to anyone, least of all yourself. It really is best to leave the past alone. I don't
think it would help Catherine now to know that I could have told
them exactly where to go. Although who can tell? In her American life,
after all this time, perhaps it wouldn't matter. Things have a way of
turning out in the end the way they were supposed to turn out all along.
Mendeltort used to call that sort of thing *anticipating history*. So I
didn't tell them and they left. I saw Catherine later in Palestine. She
had even found her little brother by then. So it all turned out for her
the way it was meant to. As for us, that is to say, for myself and Esterka, Jankele, Kamila, and Ariz, we set out for Tashkent when it was
time to do so. Jankele's letters tell a fairly accurate story of how we got
there and what happened to us but of course he didn't know the entire
story. It's not a story that is generally known. He wrote it for you as he
thought he knew it and so as far as he's concerned that's the entire
story. You've never met him? Russia stunted him, the way that Russia
stunted many people whom it robbed of childhood. Such people . . .
yours and mine . . . were forced to leap from childhood into middle
age with none of the necessary reflective transitions . . . That sort of
thing is bound to create a rather backward-looking attitude, a self-centered viewpoint, don't you think? They're not to blame. It isn't their

fault. There's nothing that they could have done about it at the time and there's certainly nothing that can be done for them now. Their myths, their legends as Jankele puts it, demand that they remember the story in a certain way. Jankele might have been more charitable in his memories if he had known the entire story of what happened thirty years ago in Russia, and later here, but he didn't know. The way he remembers that awful Russian odyssey is the way in which most of our people remember it. Just as your people have their own way of remembering it, in keeping with their legend. And charity toward another viewpoint is seldom the stuff from which history is made, in fact it often gets in the way of the myth. The myth, you see, is more important than what really happened . . . But I don't care to comment on that any further. I don't believe in legends. And it's no use talking to the survivors of a legend if you want that truth that people want from history. History is never there to explain itself. And neither legends nor statistics add up to any kind of truth. What is true is what happens in the present, right now, but even here we have two events taking place, not one. I am talking to you and you are listening to me, but perhaps I am saying one thing and you are hearing something else. It all depends on what I want to say and on what you want to hear. So, you see? Even this event isn't that one single truth that history is supposed to be. And tomorrow, after the event, when we are listening to this tape, we are going to have yet another interpretation of what happened here. And in memory each of us will create yet another truth.

. . . But to get back to Mendeltort and Prus. Yes, there was a meeting. There could have been other meetings later, there probably were. Mendeltort was not a man to leave much to chance. The only chance I ever knew him to take, I mean a real unpremeditated and uncalculated chance, a matter of trusting someone absolutely without checking out all other possible or available options . . . ah, but that's another of those things that we won't talk about. (Long pause, footsteps, the sounds of a radio being turned on, then some modern music.) Well, what do you think? Shall we take a rest? It's almost time to eat, anyway. I feel as if I've been talking for about thirty years. What do you think, eh? We can have another talk tomorrow.

Third tape, made on Dec. 12, 1973

. . . I'm sorry we couldn't get together yesterday. The doctors wanted to take another look at me, those Syrians had meant business. I've listened to your tapes this morning. Some of that stuff could come out but

we'll see how it goes, eh? I know what you're after and I think you're
getting it, at least enough of it to say what you want to say, but we'll
have to go a little slower from now on. Words have a way of coming
back to haunt a man in the least convenient moments (laughs). Don't
forget you're talking to a putative politician. Some of those personal
reflections and generalizations may be unnecessary.

. . . But what you're after is, in part at least, a matter of record. You
may find some of it in archives and most of our archives are accessible.
We're a young state, in the contemporary sense, so we've not had the
time to commit the crimes that other states lock up in bombproof
archives. Talk to Professor Oskar Bauer at the Department of Contemporary Jewish History at the University of Tel Aviv. What you're after
is his specialty. He knows all about it.

I think that there were . . . in fact, I know there were . . . other
meetings between Mendeltort and Prus, or between someone else and
Prus, and between that someone else and other Poles in Russia.
Erlich and Alter had talked to Anders much along the lines of what
we're talking about but, of course, they were quite the wrong sort of
people to talk to Anders about anything. But I think you'll find it a
matter of record that someone talked to someone and made an agreement of some kind, and that as a result of that agreement what happened later in Palestine was allowed to happen. Professor Bauer may
tell you that much and perhaps more. But for the sake of your tapes
let's assume that it was Mendeltort who did all the talking with Prus
and with the other Poles with whom he would have had to talk. Prus,
you see, had neither a command function nor political authority, and
an agreement such as we're supposing to have taken place would have
needed both. Later, of course, when the Hargan was operational in the
Palestine Mandate, it became necessary to cover many tracks . . . even
to find some scapegoats for what had become highly embarrassing for
very many people . . . and so you have the so-called Mendletort-Prus
affair. Mendeltort was killed in 1943, in the month of Nisan, which
may have a symbolic value . . . Prus was hidden away behind some
desk in London and two years later he had committed suicide, which
also may have some symbolic value . . . And that is how history has received that particular affair, and that's the way we'll leave it. But common sense is not a matter of historical statistics and it suggests that
Prus must have taken Mendeltort . . . or someone . . . higher up his
own chain of command to get the agreement which we are supposing
. . . you notice that I said merely supposing . . . to have taken place.
The facts and figures of Jewish enlistment in the Polish army in Russia
are all in the archives. You can find out how many men enlisted . . .
and don't forget that it was a volunteer army, there was no conscription

possible for the Poles in Russia . . . how many deserted in Palestine and how many stayed on to fight as loyal Poles in the Polish army in Italy and elsewhere until the war ended. You will find out that about two thousand deserted or were honorably discharged in Palestine in 1943, but you'd be wrong to assume that all of them were members of the Hargan, the Irgun, the Stern Organization, or any other group. Some people desert from armies simply because they don't want to serve in armies. Some do it for another purpose. I don't think it would help anyone to know how many of these two thousand men and women who parted from the Polish army in Palestine were members of this organization or another. It's fair to say that very many were. If they weren't a part of the conspiracy that the British had suggested at the time . . . a suggestion that resulted in that rather frantic covering up of tracks that we've mentioned . . . in other words, if they were not active members of the Hargan, or any other group, at the moment when they said *shalom* to the Polish army, many joined us later. Sooner or later you'll find that in archives. And I think that this is all that I would want to say about that. It all happened thirty years ago but for some people . . . good, decent, and important people in whom many other people have a great deal of faith, whom many people need . . . well, for them, for those necessary people, all this is still a sensitive matter. It's best if we leave it alone. As I said, once you start turning over buried rocks you find some things you'd be better off not to have known about.

. . . As for my part of this story, I'll say only this. Esterka and I arrived in Iran in August of 1942, as part of the Polish army evacuated from the Soviet Union. Ariz came over later in the year. Jankele was brought over with the civilians, the orphanages and the schools. Mendeltort came on the first transport with Esterka and myself. We were in different units. Mine went to southern Persia. His went to Iraq. I won't say that this was the last time that I saw him. After all, it is the truth that we're supposed to be dealing with here, isn't that correct? But it's the last time that I spoke to him.

. . . What kind of man was he? You won't find a consensus on that point here or anywhere. Perhaps if he had lived to lead the Hargan he would have been a historical figure like Begin rather than a legend but that didn't happen. What happened was something altogether different. Perhaps he came here forty years too early or thirty years too late . . . What may have been logical in the Diaspora, especially in Russia, was no longer logical here. The time was wrong. An imperial dream didn't fit that point of Jewish history, don't you see? And so he acted in spite of logic, time, history, the needs of the moment . . . Why? I don't believe he could admit that even to himself or that he

understood it . . . I'm talking about that Arab village and the massacre
. . . Shouldn't the bringing of us all out of Russia have been enough?
Why that bloody village? We don't ask such questions in Israel now,
too many of us have memories we'd rather not have . . . At what
points does the adventurer reform, the terrorist become respectable? Is
it true that we never feel secure until we too have persecuted someone,
and that then our persecution turns to patronage? Had Mendeltort
lived we might have had the answer. No, we don't love that period of
our lives, and you won't get from me another recital of that interminable tissue of combat and misery, cunning and bloodshed to which our
circumstances compelled us . . . ah, enough of that . . . Still, there is
something that can be said about Mendeltort, he deserves *that* much.

. . . He towered above his contemporaries, he was biblical and also
an extremely modern man, a breaker of traditions, and perhaps that
was the attraction that he had for us . . . Youth needs a violent commitment and we were very young and that is why so many of us followed him and believed in him but I don't think anyone ever loved
him . . . and that, perhaps, is what he wanted most. We don't like to
see ourselves now in the context of his legend but the legend continues
to haunt many of us, as, I believe, it finally haunted him . . . It was a
murderous and reckless world in which we lived thirty years ago and
Mendeltort was murderous without being reckless until that business
with the Arab village. If he had not existed we would have had to invent him for our own convenience. However, in a wonderfully precarious and unpredictable way, he did exist in a period when, free from all
restraint, he could arouse us from the sleep of ages . . . Yet it was his
dream that we were following rather than the man himself, we were
caught up in his dream until we saw it as a nightmare from which we
had to wake . . . ah, but again we come close to something I'd rather
not talk to you about.

. . . I think of him now as fiction, as a sort of blend of Muhammad
Ali—no, not that boxing fellow but the real one, the one who tyrannized the Egyptians out of the Middle Ages—and the mad Emperor
Theodore of Ethiopia, yet even there a touch of nobility intervenes because . . . until that Arab village . . . his every action was motivated by
a public conscience. He was a thoughtful, devious, courteous man and
no one has ever contested the fact that he had that sort of unthinking
courage that comes to some people as naturally as the air they breathe.
I am sure that he believed right up to the moment of his death that he
was destined to restore the glories of Solomon's empire and in that
cause his personal and moral daring were boundless.

. . . That may have been the trouble. His judgment became impaired by his dream. You can't be the heir of Solomon without

Solomonic wisdom . . . But then, perhaps, he thought that he was running out of time. Certainly, he was ill, none of us knew how ill he really was, how little time he knew he had to drive us out of what *he* thought were our own spiritual Middle Ages . . . He had no time and so he was impatient with people who could not understand his urgency, who thought of him as the dangerously dreaming megalomaniac, the raging reformer who finds his reforms rejected and wants to pull down the whole world in ruins to appease himself for his failure . . . I think he must have known that none of us would follow him into such things as that Arab village, to senseless butchery . . . I think that by that time he was like a child who knows that he is doing wrong, yearns for forgiveness, looks for some way out, and finding none, gives way entirely to his anger, hoping that it will create its own justification. Had he anyone to help him to adjust himself to the terribly difficult business of living and working in a modern world without loss of dignity, it might have been a different story. But we're not here to speculate . . . The truth is that he was a man who had outlived the imperatives of his time and who had to find a way to destroy himself. But then you have to look at all of this in the context of his time, of thirty years ago, of the conditions as they were then in the Palestine Mandate. History provides bad vantage points from which to study legends.

. . . So (laughs) do you have any more tapes that you want to waste? I think I'd better save my voice for the Knesset (laughs). That's what I think is so good about being an Israeli, you know; we get to do so many different things. We can be so many different kinds of people in only one lifetime. Today you are a soldier, tomorrow you're debating in the Knesset, day after tomorrow you're an ambassador somewhere or you are teaching in a rural school, and the day after that you're a farmer and you drive a tractor and you watch things grow. And thirty years ago you were something altogether different. (Laughs, then a pause, sound of movement, another voice speaking in another language, then BBC-style introductory music.) You can tell Jankele if you write to him that I've become addicted to television in my middle age. But for God's sake, don't tell him that the only television that's worth watching in Israel comes from Amman. Too much truth isn't good for anybody's legends.

PART SEVEN

AS AN ARMY
WITH BANNERS

Catherine

ONCE MORE SHE WAS ADRIFT, her mind transported to the cloudless copper sky, as she herself had been transported in yet another train (aimlessly, and against her will, in an unknown direction), coming from one point of the compass to another, from one set of diminishing circumstances to another, refusing to surrender. Someday, she thought, someday I will think of trains as a mode of transport, as a link between distant places, as a means of bringing people together rather than as the rending of families and peoples, as something that can bridge distances and cultures and *not* (as in this endlessly repeated series of journeys into the unknown) as mass graves on wheels.

The rust-brown reeking string of cattle cars was lost in the haze behind her, in a dull brown landscape dotted with strange plants like clumps of saw-edged bayonets; yellow and red-veined leaves hung limp in the midmorning air and defied her dim memory of botany texts. One more vast land in a continent of spaces, a stop on the journey. It didn't need a name.

There had been so many places, people, since she and Kobza and Kepi and Bronka and a dozen others had left the settlement in the country of Samara in search of the army. Vast crowds of faceless people stirred in her memory, a gray human ocean with no name; the tides flowed, retreated, left debris . . . Professor Karolewski and the granite lady had all but disappeared from her memory, Esterka had vanished. She was alone, momentarily separated by a fold of land from the hundreds of others who had spilled from the train in search of food and water, hidden from them and from her own reality, searching for another. Hunger had sent her mind reeling among visions. She glimpsed odd moments of remembered joy and could no longer identify herself in them; happiness and the thought of happiness were as incomprehensible in her reality as the unknown plants which she tested absentmindedly for texture and water content. Could they be eaten, would they poison her? The only way to tell was to chew the leaves and to suck the sweetly pungent blades of the unidentifiable grasses that resembled bayonets and sabers. She did so without thought.

. . . Where am I, she thought, and why have I come here? Where am I going and why? Where did this journey start? Life begins as an accident, ends in an indifferent moment. Somewhere between these two points in the journey there are stops for food, for nourishment, for testing unknown substances . . . There are (there *must* be!) joyous moments, memory can't be totally indifferent! She searched her memory for such moments as an antidote for the sudden weakness that brought her to her knees. Kobza, dear Kobza. Yes, he was a constant: a fixed point in a revolving universe of chaos; but could *anyone* afford to find her constants among objects as perishable as people? The fragility and impermanence of people and affections had been more than adequately demonstrated. She loved him. No, she told herself formally, she thought that she *could* love him and this seemed as good as the act of loving, but that meant an investment of herself in him, and was she still able to make such investments? She thought not. That way lay commitment. She did not think that she would be able to survive another disaster, there had been quite enough. He represented loving kindness and perhaps that was enough to reconstruct a faith in goodness, to deny the terrible indifference in which she was living. But her need for him was a danger to her; she felt herself threatened by her own inability to give him more than a body and one half her mind. To give him (anyone!) more than that which didn't matter to her would rob her of what she had to have in order to survive.

We have been trained to love, she thought, searching among bits and pieces of vanished memories and lost moments and buried illusions: to come to love as though this were destiny, both promise and fulfillment. But there is something desperately dangerous about this. It no longer works as an amulet against the evil eye of loss, of emptiness, of the awful deprivation that comes with aloneness . . . it does not cure the fatal illness of living in a world where hatred and pain and cruelty are the only constants on which one may depend. To give is to be robbed. To take is to remain alive in whatever manner, to defer the moment of an indifferent end . . .

And she would live, she would not give way to promises and illusions. There are, she told herself, to be no more illusions of any kind.

Impatient, she returned to the tangible reality of dry soil, strange cacti, the search for water and food. The cloudless sky hung above her like a copper lid. She stooped among strange growth, digging with her fingers among roots.

They had been spilled out of their train on flat parched soil near a huge brown river, in a vast crowd of exiles from the North; a thousand men, two or three thousand women and children, the old and the infirm, lay all day long in the scorching heat under black clouds of flies, shook in an icy paroxysm at night. Each day the trains brought others. No one brought any food. The river crawled like a monstrous reptile between sandy banks, mottled in browns and greens, thick with reeking slime, in which the wasted human refuse sought some relief from thirst and the noon's molten heat.

Coming back, her pockets and her hands full of strange roots and berries, she topped the small rise which had kept her hidden from the riverbank. This was the Amu Darya River, the Oxus of antiquity, flowing north from the Pamirs where ice never leaves the towering peaks; but here, in this endless space, it barely moved in a broad sluggish stream. Downriver was the Aral Sea and the cotton fields and that was, perhaps, their destination, although no one knew anything for certain. The army (if, indeed, there was any kind of army to which they could go) had become a vaguely recalled dream.

They had been brought here weeks earlier, unloaded and left to their own devices. Many of them were already dead. Lice lay in a thick yellow blanket over most of them. Typhus and dysentery had reappeared among them and, in a terrible irony that threatened her reason, she could hear the dying among whom she walked as they whispered about the good old days when they were prisoners, not amnestied allies of the Soviet Union, when the NKVD was their directing force, when they were given their pitiful rations of gray bread. Their trains (their wandering homes) still stood on their sidings bereft of locomotives and going nowhere a mile or so away from where she observed them and she thought for a dull, uncharacteristic moment why none of these parched skeletons looked for shelter in them, then remembered: the trains contained the dead, their stench had begun to reach the banks of the river.

She took a deep breath of the hot dusty air. Slowly, so as not to waste precious energy, Catherine walked down the gentle incline that sloped toward the sandy riverbank, noting that in the middle of a small crowd of Uzbek camel drivers, wandering local shepherds, curious old men from an inland village, and a few Mongol soldiers, Kobza had already started his day's performance. It would mean a few rubles or a gourd of goat's milk or a few flat cakes baked among the Uzbeks out of flour milled from cottonseeds. Kobza was ill, he had been in fever only the night before and his dysentery had become a nightmare, but no one would know that to look at him now. He caught her eye and a brief smile passed across his ruined gaunt face; quickly, she looked away, seeking her defenses.

She had sewn his costume: a long black robe made of a Jewish caftan (its dead owner had had a mouthful of silver teeth, she remembered with passing indifference, teeth that Kepi had knocked out after the man died to use as currency for temporary survival), a costume sewn all over with crescents and moons and triangles and stars; the three-cornered eye of Osiris stared at her with vacant idiocy from the middle of his chest. His unkempt gray-streaked beard straggled in all directions like an upended old broom; his eyes fixed on her for a sadly knowing moment. Once ill with the bloody flux, a man's life became measurable in days.

—Here! he croaked, and pointed at Bronka, brown-skinned and darkly wrinkled and of an age that couldn't be determined (a crone whom Catherine knew to be little older than herself): the Comrade Mother Demetria who sees all and knows all! Just look into those dark eyes fixed on visions that only a true muezzin may see, a servant of the One True God, prrr-prrr. True, she's a woman and so unworthy to know Truth. Who is a woman to be shown a vision? A woman has no soul, the Koran has made that clear. Would anyone here question the Koran? But what have those eyes not seen! What mysteries have they not fathomed! And her dark smile, note that dark smile, all you younger comrades, and you older men who remember other times, oh, those times of peaceful evenings in the *ulus* when comradeship had another meaning. Look at her, listen to me and forgive me that I speak in Russian, but I am not of your great race (and now his voice fell, trembled) . . . and (it was genuine, this trembling, Catherine thought) so perhaps unworthy . . . still . . .

Kobza paused, drew a breath, leaned on Bronka's shoulder, then went on: Still, that smile, comrades, isn't that the smile of the Egyptian Sphinx? But she's no *arap*, this seeress, she's from your own soil even though she dare not speak your language in your presence, which, as you know, would defile the language . . . after all, a woman . . . hmm . . . But she has the gift of looking into the future and sees into your heart and knows what is to be. Ten rubles open her secrets. Ten rubles. What is that to men such as you? Or if ten is too much then she will see something for five, or even for three, although it wouldn't be as much as she'd see for ten . . . Have you not heard for some time from someone you love? Has a son or a brother or a friend been taken from you? And for fifteen rubles, what is fifteen rubles, I myself will look into your hands. I would read there such mysteries as would awe the civilized world!

A voice laughed among other laughing voices and shouted in Russian: What language is it written in, this mystery in my hand?

—A hand is a hand, said a voice. And there's nothing in it.

—What? Kobza said. Did I hear you right? Are you calling the Great Stalin a liar?

—What? What? said other voices.

—What does the Great Stalin have to do with this! I never said . . . I only said . . .

—Didn't the Great Stalin tell us all that the fate of the word lies in the hands of the proletariat? Didn't he say that the history of mankind is written in the hands of Russian workers, peasants, soldiers, sailors, and policemen? So who was it who said there is nothing written in our hands? Prrr-prrr. Ooof. I never thought I'd hear anything like that under this sky.

—I never said, the young voice began to argue, but the others laughed. Stalin never said anything of the kind, he said no such thing . . .

—Oh, Kobza said. Now he tells us what Stalin *didn't* say! How much he knows, this educated young man from the North, this red-haired man! Are you saying you know as much as Stalin? Don't you know that only Stalin is great enough to know what he's talking about? But there are mysteries that can be talked about and that's what I, who know the secrets of the stars, and the Great Comrade Mother Demetria over here, can tell you about. So step right up, comrade, that's it, be the first as befits a Russian. Now what do I see in this great honest hand of an educated worker? I see a long journey . . .

—Hey, none of that! the man said, pulling back his hand, but Kobza held on to it, said soothingly: No, no, not that kind of journey . . . this is a hand full of happiness!

—Well, the man said. Happiness?

—Happiness.

—Well, it's all right, then. So what else is there?

—I'll tell you. And while I'm reading the good fortune waiting for this fine young comrade, who will look into the dark eyes of the Great Mother who knows everything? Only ten rubles, maybe five.

Once more she looked across the heads of the squatting Asiatic plainsmen who had become the herdsmen of her terrible indifference, her neuter state suspended between faith and fear. Their dark cruel faces were all but invisible under shaggy fur, and slitted eyes had fixed upon her own. She saw him sway, thought that he would fall, but

Bronka moved her shoulder against his hip so that he leaned upon her and, at once, Catherine felt the promise of her loss. Only last night she had clung to him for warmth in the cold hours just before the dawn and found herself chilled instead; death, she could see, had brushed his face with pallor under the grime of journeys, his eyes had had an opaque luminosity in the firelight as though a candle had been lighted behind a wall of ice. He was too ill to sleep (so ill, in fact, that she had misread his silence for the final one and pushed away from him in fear and revulsion) and so they had talked, and she had told him that she loved him and then that she couldn't, that to love anyone was surely to become eventually diminished, she thought that he would understand. Love no one and no one will be taken from you, he had asked, is that it? Something like that, she had said. His silence was so long that she peered into his eyes expecting to find them glazed and upturned, but then he sighed and said: A sad prospect for you, I'm glad I won't see it; but only you can make decisions for yourself. I . . . well, why should I lie about it, we've not done much of that . . . I won't be much help to you or anyone in a few more days. Oh, it's not that, she had whispered, and wondered if she lied, it's nothing to do with you, it's true for everybody; I just don't ever want to belong to anyone but myself, there's nothing that I want to give to anyone, don't you see? It's . . . (and he mocked her gently:) too diminishing? Well, she had said, you're not yet a saint. I am particularly unsuitable for sainthood, Kobza had replied, but I fear for you . . . your future as a woman and a human being; you might find that you had given away too much with that decision. I'm only trying to be truthful with you, she had said, I've a right to that, I don't want to make you suffer but I don't want to lie; I'd love you if I could but I can't. I know that you've tried, he had said. Yes, I've tried, she said, but it's as you've said to me yourself, that there's no authority for any kind of truth but our own individual conscience, that even if we are not the sole creators of our circumstances we are responsible for our reactions to them, for our future condition and final destiny, that since we must all suffer the consequences of our acts we might as well be allowed to make all our decisions. I seem to have said that once before, he said. She said: Then you don't feel badly about what I've said? I need your friendship, I still want to be a part of your life in some way. Oh, he said, no, what you really mean is that you want me to remain a part of *your* life as long as necessary, but I don't feel badly about that; no, not at all, I believe in friendship, I have a passionate belief in humanity. Now you sound bitter, she had said. I never thought I'd hear bitterness from you. Bitter? Not bitter, disappointed; I am convinced that any kind of animosity is a mental illness, that there does exist some sort of brotherhood between all living things

. . . Yes, I know you think that, she had said, but I can't believe it (and, seeing the pain in his face she had gone on quickly:) We have been taught to think that love is calm and even and lasting and that its price is a dedicated lifetime but it seems to have become something else in this century: hypnotic absorption in oneself, perhaps, or mutual intoxication in unconnected moments; bodies move and posture, faces change, and disappointment follows each encounter. Oh (she said), I've tried, you know I have, but I'm not like you, I don't believe that there can be love and peace in the world, I've no reason to suppose that the entire system would change just for me, and I can't relive over and over the mockery of something that has never properly existed. I'm sorry to hurt you but I have no choice. Oh, of course, he had said, and once again there was a long silence in which she watched the tears rolling from the caverns gouged into his face by anxiety and hunger; the shrewdness and the hard lines had melted into weariness. Tears, he had said, at my age? Well, prrr-prrr, I suppose it's some kind of relief since I've no sense of sorrow. Sorrow, you see (he went on, now invisible as the firelight dimmed), is the result of all the effort we make to keep ourselves separate from another, and I've been living quite differently in our recent months. She noted his air of the long-distance runner exhausted at the end of the marathon and said: I can't explain my indifference except that it is safe. Really, she said, I'd love you if I could but I can't love anyone who'd want something from me, and it applies to everyone, not just you. To buy security at the expense of one's humanity, he had whispered then, seems somehow . . . inhuman. And she said quickly: Please don't argue with me; this isn't something to argue about. And he said: There is no argument, I must accept whatever you decide for yourself because no one has the right to interfere with another's journey to their destiny, nor will advice prevent an event from following its cause. And then he added: Oh yes, I should know that much. (It was her turn for silence.) After a long moment Kobza spoke again but (she was sure) more to himself than to her, saying: The soul is a living thing, it can't be excised but it can be eaten away. Indifference, though? That's the grandfather of all the evils that have ever happened. I'd warn you against that, if I could . . . She shook her head then, pulled away from him, turned away knowing that he was watching her, and went sick inside.

Watching him now across the heads of his grinning audience, seeing him stripped of his dignity and playing the fool, she saw an old ghost in motley and a dirty caftan whose face she would fight to forget. Their frigid parting of the night before had been the decisive moment; until then she had not been sure that she could go through with it. Now she was cold and, in a surge of self-protective bitterness, determined. He was already dead, she knew; he had died in the night, and it was only an accusing ghost which had sprung up now to confront her in this place that was too full of horrors anyhow. Bitterness fogged her eyesight and she turned and moved away as he began his harangue again, walked carefully down the muddy riverbank toward the small enclosure of sand, mud, and stones, roofed with rags that Kepi had constructed for their communal home and where he lay beside their bundled belongings. Fifteen rubles, she heard Kobza say in a voice from which all life had ebbed. Ten rubles? Five? Three? A gourd of milk? A handful of seeds?

Yes, she thought, loving kindness is an active force, capable of working like a force among human forces, but it is not enough. It is not an antidote to fear, it does not excise a permanent emptiness. They had been living in a dream both magic and mythical, with dream plans for a future which had never happened, and she couldn't go back to make it happen. Maybe I don't like the present very well, she said to herself, but I'm in it, and I can only change it in little ways. I can't make it the past again, and I won't try. I want to stay sane.

But she was waiting for him after his performance—if, indeed, such a degrading show could be called performance; it was humiliating to her to see him so reduced in his own eyes. For months she had been amused by the farce, the cheap mounteback tricks, the cheating and conniving, without ever thinking how much it cost him in terms of his own dignity, in his rising contempt for himself, to keep her fed with all her hopes intact; it was so easy and convenient to concentrate on the farcical, as though her physical survival had not been the issue and he had become a performing bear of his own choice and will. She lay against the sand wall of their dugout wondering why he couldn't hate her. She listened to the wailing of sick women and despised their weakness, thinking it her own, and to the screams of hungry children and to the grunting blasphemies of men driven into hopelessness beyond their limits of endurance. *He* had endured, she knew, and also knew that it was in this inability of his to compromise his essential promise that her survival had been founded. He came in pale and shaking, sweat soaking the back of his robe, the hem of the caftan wet with excrement and blood. He fell beside her and stared at her bleakly. She couldn't talk. She took his arm in both hands and kneaded it while she rested her forehead on his shoulder; his bones were hard as sticks, naked he was a skeleton. He gazed down at her in dismay, his eyes disarrayed. She had stopped feeling bitter, stopped thinking about herself; she could feel none of that while she thought of him posturing, begging, wheedling, and cajoling before the savages outside. Give us this day our providential bread, she whispered into his shoulder, no matter what the cost, and felt him shuddering with self-disgust and illness. His stench was appalling, she thought him old beyond reckoning, she wished for nausea and revulsion so that she would be able to lift her face from his chest; instead, she pitied him, knew that he'd not be able to bear pity and kept her face hidden.

—Twelve rubles, he said finally. And a cottonseed cake. And camel shit, of course.

—They threw things at you, then?

—Ah, there's no pleasing everyone . . .

—But even that's useful, Bronka said. It's dry. It'll burn. We'll have a fire later when it's cold.

—It's good to be useful.

She peered into his desolate old face, said: Don't talk now, just rest.

—There's news about the army.

—Later, she said. There's time for talking later. Now rest a bit. (And then because he looked startled at her lack of interest in news about the army:) It's fine about the army.

—Just fine, is that all? It's our salvation. Or yours, anyway.

—*Ours*, she said. It always has been ours, all of us. If there's a way to get you there in time . . .

But he only grunted, sighed, and leaned back with his eyelids twitching.

—Where is it? Bronka said. Is it far?

—It's near Samarkand and Bokhara and around Tashkent. About two or three hundred kilometers, from what the Uzbeks tell me. Not that they figure distances in kilometers, they talk about "rides." A day's riding is a ride, I expect. But you will be walking.

—Don't talk now, she said. Rest. We'll talk about all that after you have rested.

—I'll have a long rest soon.

Above her head she heard his long shuddering sigh and his gaunt body subsided under hers. Calmly, she told herself: Is he now dead? Has he finally died? Has my last moment of a human closeness ebbed away at last? But he drew a short breath and said to Kepi: If you get one of those Uzbek carts . . . We have the money for a few days' hire . . .

—Two or three hundred kilometers, Kepi said. Not far by our reckoning, seeing how far we've come. But without a *cart* we'd not get halfway there in under two months.

—Somehow you'll have to get one, then. So get one. How you keep it is your business, do I have to tell you?

—Not about that kind of business, you don't have to tell me, Kepi said, and spat into the sand. I'll get a cart and I'll keep it too and we'll all get to this Samarkand or that Bokhara or wherever the hell the army's at. Don't worry about that.

I'm not worried, prrr-prrr. Just go get that cart. As soon as the others around here hear about the army, I mean that it's so near, you won't get an Uzbek to part with a cart for a hundred rubles. The village, as I hear it, is about ten kilometers downstream.

—Well then, I'll see you later, Kepi said.

He got up, stretched, peered about. Bronka rose beside him, took his arm. They left.

—It's hard to believe, isn't it, that it'll soon be over, Kobza said. Just a few more weeks, maybe a month, no more. And then you'll be among your own kind, safe.

—Don't you want to rest?

—Wouldn't you rather talk while we still can? he said. It's what I'd like best.

She shook her head quickly, then paused and nodded it. —A part of me would, dear, the weak part. But there's a strong part too. I have to believe in my own strength, that's also something that I learned from you. I do believe in it. And I don't want you out of my life, not really, and I don't want to be dependent on you (she turned her face away from his shoulder and spoke into his chest). You don't know what it's like watching you out there . . . in the middle of all that . . . that . . . (she shook herself slightly). It's a mockery of everything that I care about, you don't belong out there.

—It's hard to say where a man belongs, Kobza said. Until he's in it or he's out of it. I'm in it now, soon I'll be out of it and that's all there's to it. Hardly worth a moment of your thoughts.

—It . . . you . . . are worth a moment of my thoughts. There is so much about you that should be loved, that must be admired. Not merely used or mocked. But . . . it's such a precarious thing, don't you see?

—What is? That love business?

—This love business, yes.

His mouth had fallen open and he seemed unable to breathe for a moment. He shook his head. His voice trembled. —It's not true, he said.

—It is for me.

He shook his head. —No.

Bitterness came back in a flood, along with pleasure, gratitude, a sense of exultation which she immediately seized upon and questioned. Was this what she had hoped for and wanted all along? An argument at the end? Anger? Disagreement? So that things could become finally disagreeable and she could feel justified in her determination, using him to the end. She saw his distressed eyes and felt for his hand. —Don't hate me for telling you, she drove the point home. But I no longer need anyone, least of all a man.

—Not this one, anyway.

—Not anyone.

—Well . . .

—That's how it has to be for me, she said finally. I must work out my own life in my own way, dependent on no one. I don't want to hurt anyone while I'm doing it, least of all you, but if that's how it has to be, then that's how it will be.

—How did it all get turned around like this? he asked finally, speaking (she thought) to himself rather than to her. I don't seem to understand anything any more. Perhaps it's just as well, perhaps I really don't belong in this . . . Do you know who I feel like now? That damned professor fellow who talks about history repeating herself.

—Karolewski? she said contemptuously. You could never be anything remotely like him. That musty, evil little man . . . so full of hatred for anything that lives.

—Perhaps that's something he learned over the years.

—Nothing has happened to make you feel that way. We have been telling each other the truth, *his* life has always been a total lie.

—I wonder if he thinks so. What was his wife's name? Didn't you say she was a friend of yours?

—No, I never even met her, but my cousin Wlada was very close to her before their marriages. Her name was Lala, a wonderful woman, but not strong enough in the end, perhaps.

—That's hardly a sin. Didn't you tell me once that she went off with some general?

—Yes. His name was Prus. Karolewski has always envied him and hated him too . . . that's who he talks about whenever he raves about National Monuments and cripples. But why are we suddenly talking about all that?

—I don't know, he said.

—Then let's stop talking. You should rest, anyhow, try to sleep a little. I'll go outside and build a fire for the night. When Bronka and Kepi come back we should eat something hot.

—What? he said.

—I don't know, she said. Perhaps I'll find something before nightfall.

She couldn't stand the banality of this marital discussion with a dying man, a man who would be buried before long, forgotten in a year with all his wisdom and his kindliness. She was sick with anger at this degrading exchange of trivialities. Nor did she want to quarrel, after all. Her thrust for independence was not aimed fatally at him; it was a denial of her history. She was, in effect, saying no to everything that had happened to her, small victories along with the disasters, as though with this negation of the past she might attempt to step into the future. Before he could say anything else she scrambled clumsily from the dugout and made her crablike progress among prostrate people away from the riverbank and toward the sheltering sand dune where she had hidden earlier in the day. She had become addicted to death and wanted to break the habit. But apparently the time for brutal ironies had not yet gone.

. . . A man was pulling up his trousers, each leg sewn from a skirt of a different color; his sticklike legs, like her own, were branded with deep black craters: the apogee of scurvy known as *Soviet visas*. An old woman twisted toward her knees in some internal spasm and wiped rheumy eyes with dirty brown paper. A child was uttering rhythmic cries to which no one listened. Eyes like shrill curses followed her when she trod and stumbled over living bundles of rags tied with twine.

The dune seemed mountainous but she persevered. A strong wind was blowing from the distant Pamirs, sand danced before her eyes. The dead brown land lay coiled underfoot; it narrowed her horizons into earth, water, sky, holding her a prisoner in herself: parched soil cracked into a desert, infertile and useless, a home for the demented wind. The sun had dipped into the afternoon, the light was going unwillingly, she thought; far to the north and east the cotton fields had acquired half-tones of Prussian blue and turquoise. In childhood her internal imagery had been musical, poetic; in the North she had constructed her thoughts exclusively in pictures so as to understand and cope with her reality; was she now to return to adjectives and adverbs? Night, she knew, would come like the blow of an ax.

And then what? she asked herself, placing her mottled swollen feet carefully in the sand that had acquired the jagged solidity of granite. Something would happen, something always happened, there either would or would not be a miracle; light came to her in waves that boomed in her interior caverns and splintered on doubt.

In childhood she had crouched in the ambush of her cot waiting for the blue-gray light of dawn to illuminate her morning challenge, the dangerous passage among swamps and serpents that hid in her carpet. She had to make her way from her white cot to the white-painted door precariously balanced on her toes, a ballerina poised upon a tightrope, along the sun-bleached yellow swirls of her Persian rugs; red-brown swamps and blue-green jungly depths filled with yawning monsters awaited her unbalanced fall. Each morning she forced herself into that desperate winding journey among snapping jaws and sluggish brown masses where huge bodies rose toward her with reptilian patience; her narrow path of safety tempted her with detours and perilous leaps. In the false light before sunrise the colors moved and shifted; she learned that light could be a liar, that an abyss could open where, she was sure, only yesterday the road had been safe. Each of her small footsteps had been an exercise in terror; but once launched upon her course she couldn't turn back and so went on, treading among disasters on a course as devious as it was uncertain, willing her own safety, on and on despite rising panic, to the refuge of the white-painted door. Behind that door her parents' ordered world began and there were no more terrors.

Hidden behind the dune she had not been aware of time's passage but the chill of the approaching night and a shrill screeching call, as of massed cranes flying overhead, brought her to her senses; a long line of Uzbek carts, perched high on their huge wooden wheels (spokeless and rimless and solid as tabletops and studded with nails), creaked across her immediate horizon. Lean dogs with spiny backs ran among the carts, snapping at the horses. Crouched in herself and suddenly in tears, feeling a need for a warm furred creature full of trust and love, an undemanding friend on whom she could depend, she followed their progress hungrily, willing them to turn. She searched her pockets for something with which she might tempt an animal toward her and found the cottonseed cake that Kobza had begged; unthinking, she broke a piece off it, threw it toward a small bitch which had begun to trot confidently to her; unthinking (for had she thought about what she was doing then she would have been appalled), she threw another piece of bread, then another, each falling closer to herself, and the dog came on in small bounds with her tail waving. She was full of warmth then, her compassion reached toward the animal in magnetic waves, and she began to call out in soft small-girl sounds, offering innocent enticements, forgotten endearments, thinking (if, indeed, she thought anything at all) of goodness and pity and kindliness and love, and her left hand quivered, went out toward the dog with her last piece of bread, and the enormity of this gesture confused her for a moment; was she about to *give?* The last things learned are the first things forgotten, she whispered to herself full of pride in her gentleness and humanity, and her right hand closed upon a stone. The brindled bitch was performing a complicated ballet for her benefit, with little sideways skips and circlings and nearings and retreats, brown eyes alight with the joy of the game, the burred tail an enthusiastic banner. There, my precious, there, my little friend, Catherine crooned and whispered, come to me, you and I have

nothing to fear from each other, we shall be friends forever, we'll protect each other, you'll sleep at the foot of a lovely bed when we're with
the army and I'll get lovely little things for you to eat from the officers'
mess, don't worry, I know how to do it, I learned it in the North. There
now, there now, come to me, there. The dog crawled toward her as she
began a slow and patient duck walk toward the dog. Oh, let me love
you, Catherine whispered as the animal finally bounded forward to take
the offered bread. Eat, my dear, there, eat; an offering, a communion
between kindred souls perhaps. There now. Eat this in memory of Me,
Catherine said with joy to consecrate the moment, and be grateful, and
her right hand flew up from the ground and struck the animal terribly
in the head, then struck again while one shocked glaring eye leaped out
of a head and another skewed, then again into the bloodied tangle of
hair and splintered bone, again and again among scattering teeth, in
blinding red tears and the deafening echoes of her own crazed howl.
There and there and there! The light, which seemed so loath to leave
the copper sky, vanished in the west, night overtook her and sped toward the red-brown horizon. The bloody stone fell out of her hand
while the dead dog still twitched and trembled between her sprawled
knees.

In darkness, she unfastened her skirt to shroud the carcass, slung it
across her shoulders. All the way up the dune and then down the other
side and into the dugout, she whispered her endearments and thought
about the sticks she would have to seek and find and gather for the
cooking fire in the dark.

Later that night, while she slept without dreams, Kobza died. He had
said nothing while she rolled the carcass of the dog into the dugout,
nothing while she skinned and gutted the dog with the sharpened end
of her prison-camp spoon, nothing when she dismembered the victim of
her enticements and wrapped the crazily mangled head and the shabby
tail and the swollen entrails in the victim's skin, nothing when she
began the fire and skewered meat on sticks, nothing when Kepi and
Bronka came back with their tale of triumph, nothing when they ate.
He leaned against the wall of mud and sand saying nothing, looking
at her with remote uncommunicative eyes, and she was careful to keep
her own eyes off his parchment face. Kepi whooped and laughed as he
told about the cart he had managed to hire for a week (sonovabitch
Uzbek wanted all we had, wanted Bronka too as likely as not, but settled for a day's pay and a promise!) and Bronka laughed, and wiped her
mouth and licked her fingers so that none of the dog's fat should be
lost to her, and said: Honest to God, you should've seen us there, you
should have seen those heathen Uzbeks in their striped caftans and

those little embroidered caps they wear, and those mud houses they live in with all their fleas and dogs. First the kids wanted to set the dogs on us, the way they always do, and old Kepi here must've kicked a dozen of them across the road, and all the time the Uzbeks sat outside their houses like a lot of Turks, chewing dates and playing with their beads, and everybody watched us like a couple of lost souls. I thought we'd never get to say a word to anybody, honest to God. Ah, but then, Kepi said, but then the goddamnedest thing happened. This one old fart comes up with a skinny kid that understood Russian and then we have this talk. Yes, we say, we're from Lehistan, which is what they call Poland around here; no, we're not fucking Russians, and we've an army around here somewhere, and how's about renting us a cart so we could get to it? And the old fart starts something going, he shouts and waves his arms and all the goddam kids get their fucking dogs the hell out of the way, and then all you hear is *Lehistan, Lehistan,* going from mouth to mouth, and all of a sudden everybody's smiling, and bowing, and we get asked to sit down under this big tree and before you know they're bringing us tea! And then they tell us this story, honest to God, you wouldn't believe it, Bronka said. What story? Catherine said without interest. About our trumpeters, Kepi said, about the *Hejnal Mariacki,* you wouldn't believe it! How can she believe it if you don't tell it to her? Bronka said.

. So Bronka sucked the marrow bones and chewed the dog meat and told the story about the Trumpeter of Cracow and the Trumpeters of Samarkand as well, an event that happened on December 2, 1941, when the first troops of the Polish army came to the ancient city; they were a sorry-looking lot by most armies' standards, food was scarce and most of them were still weak with dysentery, scurvy, and malaria. Their uniforms were bits and pieces of everything the Russians couldn't use: old French helmets from the Great War, and Latvian and Estonian and Lithuanian tunics, and Finnish greatcoats and prison-camp boots, but they were free and they were soldiers and they had drums and trumpets and eagles and banners. The trumpeters from Lehistan created a sensation. A delegation of old men went to meet with the Polish garrison commander, bringing a Russian interpreter, and the old men asked if the Trumpeters from Lehistan couldn't possibly play for them on Friday evening, any Friday evening, outside their Great Mosque of the Bibi Khanum, the golden mosque founded in 1388 by the favorite wife of their own Timur the Lame, known in the West as Tamerlane, to fulfill a prophecy. Ah, a prophecy, hmmm, said the Polish commander, and grinned in his beard; well, why not? We'll play them something to remember us, something wailing and Asiatic, and then perhaps a little *Oberek* for a change of mood . . . But the old men asked most respectfully for a particular piece of music, a very special performance if it could be arranged without too much trouble . . . That only one soldier should play, and that he should play that music which his ancestor had been playing when they, the Uzbeks, had been in Lehistan and shot an arrow through the throat of a trumpeter on a tower, that he should finish the music that had been played then . . .

(And the Polish commander was no longer grinning, and his officers lost some of their superiority before these ancient natives, and each stared at the other with bulging eyes, and eyes full of tears, because every Polish child has known for seven hundred years, and every Pole throughout the world has known, that each day a trumpeter plays a strange soaring melody on the highest tower of the Mariacki Church in Cracow [first to the east, then westward, then to the north, and then to the south] and that this hourly ritual ends on the melody's highest note and is never finished, the music dying on its highest note just as it died, unfinished, when a Tartar arrow pierced a trumpeter's throat during an invasion in the thirteenth century . . . Was it all truth or fantasy, a legend or history? One tends to flow into the other and becomes the other and legends create the history as likely as not, but for seven hundred years this has been the story each Polish child had been told. And so these Polish soldiers who had come to Samarkand with trumpets and banners, whose own children were lost or dead and buried in the tundra, stared at each other and listened to the gentle pleading of the old Uzbeks and couldn't believe it. These white-bearded, sparsely bearded old men in their striped caftans and embroidered caps also had a legend connected with that fact-or-fiction event in the thirteenth century, this piece of fanciful fantasy or history, a legend born during their long retreat and twilight as a people, in their disasters of the thirteenth century and all the horrors and disasters that had befallen the people of the Amu Darya since that time to this one . . . Their holy men had been explaining to them for seven hundred years that their defeats and tragedies and their disappearance as a mighty nation, their plagues and their famines and enslavements, had come to them as retributive justice, as punishment by Allah because they had killed the muezzin in Lehistan while he was calling to his God from his temple tower, that God's justice is one for all and it is terrible to bear, that it must be borne with patience until the debt is paid, and that there would be neither peace nor plenty nor freedom nor contentment for the people of the Amu Darya, nor any happiness or greatness for the Uzbek nation, until the banners of Lehistan had come to Samarkand and the Trumpeter from Lehistan played, once again, the holy music they had interrupted.)

—And that's just what happened, Bronka said. That's what the old men told us. Our trumpeters played the *Hejnal* at the mosque. They couldn't finish it, of course, because nobody knows how it's supposed to finish, but they played it last December at the mosque and all the old men from the village had gone there to hear it.

—Did it really happen? Catherine said, and looked finally at Kobza, saw the half-ajar eyelids twitching, saw the pale smile in the ravaged face.

—I wasn't there, Kepi said. So I don't know. But that's what they said.

—And that's why we got the tea and honey and the dates and the little cakes, Bronka said.

—And the cart, said Kepi. They're going to bring a cart here for us tomorrow morning. They didn't even haggle much about it, gave it to us for ten rubles. Now if that's not a miracle I don't know what is.

—Shows you that good things can happen, said Bronka. We think we know it all, we make plans, we try to figure this and that, we think it's up to us to make good things happen. But the really good things come from somewhere else that we don't even know anything about. Honest to God, it makes you think a bit.

And she was looking up at Catherine with a confident birdlike air as though she had proved something that no one would be able to dispute, a woman's look given to another woman who could be presumed to accept mythology in the place of reason. Eat this in memory of Me, Catherine thought while Bronka sucked the marrow from the dead dog's bones, and be grateful. For no experience is wholly wasted, as Kobza has said. He had said nothing during Bronka's story, nothing while Kepi explained about the cart; he had eaten nothing. He was looking at her as a man might look as he tops the last rise in the road and sees the way ahead, straight and clear of obstructions all the way to his destination. She wondered whether he was seeing her at all, whether he wasn't contemplating the end of a vision of who and what she might have been or could be, whether he could truly see through her and beyond her into those areas of her being where she had no access. If only he'd attempt to reach her once again, perhaps she'd understand why she could feel nothing for anyone but herself. Bronka's raptures over the miraculous nature of coincidence offended her deeply.

Kobza said nothing; his face had grayed and narrowed. She looked at him and Bronka and Kepi and saw them, for the first time, as persons not related to herself, as separate and individual creatures whose ways were individual and mysterious, and she saw herself as a private person of particular purpose not related to the purposes of anyone else; their common image had fractured and was gone. She watched herself in her

new reality and watched her hand as it stabbed the sand, time and time
again, with the bone of the dog.

Kobza got up, swayed. Slowly, with infinite care, he turned and
walked out of the reach of light, heading toward the river. He walked as
though he were following a winding narrow path among a variety of in-
imical darknesses, treading his way toward his own conception of safety
and peace. He left behind him a cold emptiness and a void which darkness rushed to fill.

Kepi sighed, spat, lay back on the sand. Bronka leaned over him and
began to whisper. They were replete, glistening with the greases of their
meal, conscious of their hopes. She, Catherine, had none for anyone,
least of all herself. She would survive, endure, go on to whatever end
seemed necessary to her, seeking nothing that could be taken from her,
offering no illusions. The firelight dimmed as she stared into it and, before she knew it, she was sleeping. She did not dream, no thoughts troubled her; she thought herself only half asleep and conscious of someone
standing near her, looking down at her: a gentle presence, perhaps a
ghost of childhood, a memory of an abandoned innocence. The light
was very bright on the devious sun-bleached path that she would have
to travel in the morning; and then it was morning and she was awake.

She awoke in the cold hour before dawn, near the dead fire. Kobza's
empty boots were standing by her head. Kobza had not returned, Kepi
was gone, Bronka was silhouetted on the riverbank beside a stooped old
Uzbek in a striped caftan, sheepskins, and a huge fur hat. On top of the
sand dune stood a high-wheeled cart, a horse, a boy and a dog. Another
dog was howling mournfully behind the dune. There was a creak of
wheels, the soft lapping of the malodorous river among its spilled
debris.

She was awake and waiting. Soon the sun would rise. She rose,
looked about, saw Kepi coming from a distance carrying a burden of
old rags. She knew without the need to be told that this shabby bundle
was a dead man and that it was Kobza. She didn't need to hear Kepi's
explanation of where and how he had found the dead man to know
that he had killed himself rather than become an impediment to their
journey: a dying old man, a sick man, a useless mouth to feed for no
purpose other than the fiction of affection; he had drowned himself by
lying face-down in a shallow pool.

—Sonovabitch, Kepi was saying then. Sonovafuckingbitch. I warned
the poor bastard, I told him, everybody's got to look after hisself.
That's what he used to say hisself, and then he forgot it. I told him,
didn't I? I told him, what d'you want to saddle yourself for with a fucking woman and a kid? The poor old bastard didn't know how good he

had it. But what do you want? An old capon thinks he's a young rooster, so what can you do? Well, he's a dead chicken now.

She wanted to say nothing, so she said nothing. Let everyone mourn
in his own way. If love were not to be gentleness and kindness then let
it be anger. Tears were pouring down Kepi's concave cheeks as he
cursed and looked at her with hatred. She would weep for no one, least
of all herself.

—Never yet met a fucking woman, I didn't, that didn't walk away
with meat in her teeth. Take all they can. Watch a man kill himself for
nothing.

—He had to look after his people, Catherine said then, quietly.

—He had to look after his people, Kepi mocked her. He'd have done
better, a whole lot better, looking after hisself. Well, shit. What the
hell. Let's bury the poor bastard.

—Bury him? How can you just bury him? Bronka said. Honest to
God, don't you men know how to do anything right?

—What do you want me to do with him then? Kepi shouted. Eat
him like a dog?

—Here, Catherine said, and pointed to an old weathered cabin door
from some riverboat, some old craft that had run aground long ago
somewhere; the cabin door had washed up on the riverbank and had
served as the flooring of the dugout.

—What d'you mean *here*? Kepi said. We can't bury him here. The
dogs would have him out of there an hour after we've gone.

—I mean we'll carry him on that, Catherine said, and pointed. Up
the dune.

The old Uzbek had come up to join them, and Catherine, Bronka,
Kepi, and the Uzbek carried the weightless dead man up the dune; his
thin legs dangled over the edge, his one blue-gray foot trailed in the
sand. It scraped a narrow furrow. They dug a shallow hole in the sand
on top of the dune, from which Catherine could see the bluing white
of the cotton fields to the north and east, brown hills in the southern
distance, and placed the dead man in the shallow hole. The upturned
dead old face was gray, the eyes red with his final vision. Kepi closed
the eyes. They filled the hole with sand. They piled stones into a small
cairn over the grave to keep the wild dogs of the Uzbek steppe from
digging up the bones, and (she thought, conscious of the vast emptiness within her, the huge internal distances she had crossed) to serve as
a marker of a kind, a milestone in her journey. Kepi sighed and spat.
He was no longer cursing. Bronka kneeled and prayed. The old Uzbek
and the Uzbek boy went down on their hands and knees before the
new day's sun. Catherine walked back down the dune toward the
dugout and the ashes of the cooking fire where Kobza's boots were wait-

ing. She had slit one open in another lifetime, had sewed it up again in yet another lifetime and had filled its foot with soft rags in which a stump could rest with some comfort. She unwrapped her own rotting footcloths from her puffed feet mottled with *Soviet visas* and wrapped her feet in the soft rags taken from Kobza's boot and put on his boots. Being so much bigger than her own, they'd be comfortable, she thought. Then she shouldered all the bundles that lay in the dugout and carried them up the dune.

—Well, that's it, Kepi said. Let's get started, then.

They piled their bundles into the two-wheeled cart. The old Uzbek mounted the horse. The boy took hold of the plaited horsehair bridle at the horse's mouth. The dog ran down the dune and into the steppe.

—*Ut!* said the old Uzbek. *Ut!*

The horse started down the far side of the dune.

She looked back then, toward the cairn, which the wind had begun to heap with fresh sand. It was, she supposed, an obligatory gesture, taking leave of the past. She settled down to walking. The boots on her feet were well worn and soft with use over many miles. By midmorning they were deep in the red-brown country moving eastward, away from the river and toward the sun, marching under the cloudless copper sky.

Mendeltort

THE WIND CAME IN GUSTS off the water, bending the wild grass on the domed brown hills. The sun kept breaking through the fast-moving clouds, intensely bright in those accidental moments but carrying no warmth. It was the early afternoon of the twenty-fourth day of Kislev, the day before Chanukah could begin, and he stood on the inhospitable northern shore of the Sea of Galilee, among the rocky spurs that tumbled down toward the narrows of the Jordan, and watched the old man. If once again he comes alone, he thought, if he brings no young men, then I will know that there is no one to be trusted here, that I am not the hunter but the hunted or soon-to-be-hunted, that I have outlived the imperatives of my time. For there is always a choice, is there not? You hunt or you are hunted, you take no risk at all or you take them all.

It was early, but light and sound played strange tricks in this barren wilderness, creating their own impossible realities out of shadow, so that he thought he heard a bronze bell on the wind and saw a blue twilight gathering in folds among the brown boulders, the diseased-looking trees . . . He was a specialist, the coldest thing on earth, he would give no substance to illusions, yet having come so far and so long toward this appointment in the land of his most lasting and magnificent obsession, he suddenly saw himself as a man from another planet who owed no allegiance to anyone on earth. I will do it for them, with them or without them, he told himself. Against their will, if that is necessary. Or nothing will change here as nothing had changed. The lies and fears of twenty years ago were the same, the illusions were the only constant. He would not accept them as true today when he had rejected them twenty years ago; this brown barren home of superstition and of revolutions cradled in barbed wire, of strangled utopias and of stillborn dreams, would not destroy his hope. They could not be blind forever to his vision, these transplanted peddlers; they could continue to proclaim the fullness of their hope for liberation by peaceful acquisition, but he knew that when people say that they are full of hope it usually meant that their despair was so sharp that they could no longer feel its edge cutting into them.

The old man came on, it was time for Mendeltort to make himself invisible. He went down on his knees and watched the frail figure inch its way toward the small brown house that seemed to crouch in uneasy ambush among the twisted flat-topped trees.

He lowered himself carefully behind the barricade of innocuous debris (a broken wheel, some boxes, some unraveled baskets, some lengths of old frayed rope). Behind him the waves lapped against the pilings on the little dock where the moored fishing dhow was lifting and falling and creaking on its ropes. He had made sure that the light felucca was safe in the shadow of the dismasted dhow's lofty prow, and that he could see all the possible approaches to the house. When making a contact, position was everything; the lesson had been taught to him so long ago that he had forgotten the occasion as well as the teachers. Protect yourself by being able to observe all the paths by which you might be reached, keep rapid undetectable escape available . . . and do not wait where you are expected to be. It worked with objects, it was less reliable with people, hence there would always be the element of the unexpected; every operation was foolproof on paper until you added the human element, that unresolvable contest of passion and reason steeped in vice and virtue that was always present wherever human nature could be found.

He kept still behind his barricade and watched the path behind the old man, then scanned the rim of the domed hills and the deep blue shadows trapped behind the house. Would there be others? And, if so: what others? He willed the shadows to transform themselves into eager young men . . . it made no difference to him in that moment whether they would be coming to join him or to kill him. There must be times when life and death are not the issue, he muttered to himself; the issue is weariness, the soul shredded by too many contrary winds, the old hull battered by too many hostile shoals and craving resolution. He was worn, tired. He had not slept in several nights of scouting the brown hills, mapping his routes of approach to what would be the target if he got the men: observing the daily life in the shabby doldrums of the Arab village: the black tents and the crumbling hutments and the dusty barefooted children, the lean dogs and goats, the dirt and refuse piled behind the dwellings, the squalid indolence of the old men in their jellabas and old British greatcoats, the tumbled Coptic church tower (for these, he had been told, were Christian Arabs, settled for a century among the piled debris of other people's lives); watching the dipping headlights of British armored cars and timing the sequence of the permanent patrols; then writing the letters and dispatching the old man in the hour before dawn. The small bronze bell in the Coptic tower was part of the madness ringing in his head; time had been standing still among those mud-and-wattle huts, centuries had receded like a frame set around a picture, yet there was always movement of a lethargic ambulatory kind: the donkeys on the riverbank and the feluccas gliding by, and the buffalo released from his wheel and sliding into the blessed coolness of the mud. It was a stage rather than a place where men and women lived; the occasional, artificial whiff of humanity that came to him in traces of the smoke of the cooking fires, of dry cow dung and of Turkish coffee, of some sweet and heavy scent, jasmine perhaps, and of water sprinkled in the dust, made it no more real. A Roman soldier would have seen his own People in much the same setting, in much the same way, before the plunge of the huge red sun obliterated squalor. It was a story of decline and of disintegration, of the enthronement of mediocrity and of indolence, and it was justly doomed. For what had these people done to command respect or deserve compassion? Three centuries of barbaric squalor had had their effect.

The sun didn't warm him, the wind did nothing to refresh and invigorate him. His nostrils were full of the dry rotting smell of sun-bleached tarry rope and, once again he felt the vise begin to tighten in his chest, his upper arm awakened to the pain, and icy sweat moved down his forehead like a blindfold . . . Oh God, not yet. He waited to see how bad it would be this time, numbing his mind to make thought impossible so that he need not reflect on his own sudden panic. The vise would tighten further and he'd begin to drown, and the pain would stream down his hand to fingers that clutched and tore at whatever lay within their reach, and he would close his mind to pain and wait until he could float upward out of it, knowing that if he failed to do so the commitment of an entire lifetime would have been suddenly, awesomely revoked, for there would be nothing to be done to save it . . . In his detached and drifting mind he would engage his recent history in a dialogue, with the shock of pain working in him like a truth drug, knowing himself to be a fatherless and self-conceived creature who wanted to create a patrimony with a gun. He was the last of the historical voyagers into the unknown, soon to approach the passage of the clashing rocks, the Scylla and Charybdis of conscience and duty, for there was nothing that was worth the loss of a lifetime's commitment. The issue, then, was not one of success and failure as such things are reckoned by the deceivers and the temporizers; the issue was fear. And so you still insist, he said to the discredited memories of the men among whom he had lived, that every problem has a negotiable solution? It isn't true, it just isn't true. There are certain kinds of problems that cannot be resolved unless . . . unless, mind you . . . the reality that you want to possess is only living death. Why do I need your help now, before my men are ready? Because reasonable people in this most unreasonable of professions have to help each other . . . Because we need to create the chaos in which our new world may be born . . . Because the world understands only fear, reacts to coercion, bows before the gun . . . Because faith itself creates reality and an unswerving devotion to principle will pay off in time . . . Because the world does not pity the slaughtered. It only respects those who fight and kill. For better or for worse, that is the truth . . . Flexibility is a sign of weakness.

. . . Outraged and cursing the timidity of others, the people whose sense of vision failed to encompass the truths of his own, he felt himself to be the last man in the world who stubbornly refused to contemplate the imminent dissolution of the universe, then forced himself to calmness. (Outrage is not a substitute for reason, the hated leonine-looking compromiser croaked in his memory; no, he said, neither is it a substitute for armed men.)

The vise had loosened. He could breathe again. The pain would remain in his upper arm and in his leg for a while longer but his fingers were no longer ripping through the dust and shingle. Sooner or later someone would come to him . . . This month the first of the Hargan would be arriving in the Mandate, all should be there by the month of Nisan . . . But he would have to let his presence be known, his purpose declared, the first great blow struck so that the Hereditary Enemy would become reacquainted with the sick taste of fear. And time had suddenly become his worst enemy. Once more a short spasm; the vise cracked his chest, his mouth was full of ashes of old dreams; he could not wait for his own men to come to light the first beacon.

Then the vise loosened, he could feel the steel jaws releasing his heart. The Heart of the Zealot is the repository of his Nation's future, Lopatsky's ancient voice assured him, and begged him (so please take care of it, eh?), coming up out of their heroic past, a past which may have been discredited by the pragmatists and the sentimentalists but which was, for all that, glorious. For glory is something to be pursued for its own sake alone . . . His breath was restored to him for the moment, his eyes had cleared and he could see again. Old Ben came on, much older at close quarters than he had appeared in the distance, walking with steady tread among the thorns and the arthritic trees. No one had come with him, no one walked behind him; in the heatless rays of the sun held captive by clouds his narrow body seemed to struggle to keep itself erect. Old Ben, or perhaps only a memory of a murdered father, Mendeltort muttered to himself. There was no irony in his voice, only the tragic irony of the circumstances.

. . . What's needed for my People is the resurrection of their human spirit and the liberation of the mind, the point beyond infinity which is another state of being altogether, in which an act provides its own morality, in which life and death, the real and the imaginary, the past and the future, the communicable and that which may not be expressed are no longer perceived contradictorily . . . Otherwise (oh, but that was unthinkable) the commitment of a lifetime will have become its own awful mockery.

Mendeltort looked away from the old man, looked toward the house in which Old Ben would expect to find him: a small brown house of dried mud roofed with corrugated iron held in place by a pile of stones. Like the tormented trees and the bleak hills around it, this temporary refuge had the air of having been there a long time. He had begun to feel indigenous himself in his three weeks there: a shunned and feared wild animal that foraged in the hills. He was a stranger in the land to which he had come as though it were his home, like a lover who hurries to a certainty of welcome only to find himself mistrusted and resented, and where he had to be more on his guard than ever before. Here he could have neither anonymity nor that inaccessibility that safety demanded: the small brown house was a compromise, which is why he felt uncomfortable in it.

Old Ben had vanished in the small black doorway. Mendeltort scanned the path again, watched for the telltale shift of shadow among the brown boulders. But no one else had come, neither prospective follower nor assassin. He got up and went swiftly toward the house only to meet old Ben coming out again. Puzzled surprise was threatening to become the old man's permanent expression.

—No one would come?

The old man shook his head.

—Can't any of them realize that in order to keep what you have you have to risk it? That to get what you want you must fight for it?

—They have life, Old Ben said with the septuagenarian's bittersweet lack of expectations. Isn't it enough to have life?

—No, by God, it isn't!

The old man raised his hands in a gesture at odds with his unkempt frailty: the freeing of an imaginary bird.

—What did you tell them, then? Did you tell them anything? Did you see Asher himself and what did you tell him? Did you even go into

the kibbutz? Or did you go to sleep for the morning and come back
with lies?

He didn't intend to be rude and violent to his only ally but he was
suspicious; fear of betrayal, fear of what the old man might finally tell
him (what his own reason had been telling him for days), fear of the
loss which would become inevitable with his ulimate rejection by these
People whom he had come so far to love, made him stiff and stupid.

—To keep what you have, he repeated mindlessly as though reciting
a catechism learned in a lost and forgotten childhood, and knew that
he was talking like a man in a dream, feeling the pain as a presence in
his upper arm. There was no real menace in his voice; it was alarming
in its emptiness.

—Oh, well. Forgive me. I'm tired, that's all.

—Are you ill again?

—I've never felt better.

—Now who is lying? the old man said softly. I've something here to
make you feel better. One thing I'll say about the English, when they
divide to conquer they supply good whiskey.

—Is that all the message Asher sent?

—No. There is more. But we can talk inside. Don't worry, no one followed me, no one knows that you're here. Come inside now and rest
and have a drink with me.

Smiling and nodding, making welcoming motions, Old Ben backed
into the little brown house and Mendeltort followed him into the dark
and dusty structure.

Had, in fact, never left it; or so it seemed. It was all too common in
its familiarity, it fueled his impatience and contempt. The interior
resembled the nest of a giant magpie choked with objects lifted from
the context of other people's lives: an iron bedstead piled to the ceiling
with old mattresses, a stack of folded army cots, holed blankets and
goatskins, burlap sacks stuffed full of clothes and angular objects,
trunks and footlockers in a pyramid that had toppled in a parody of
overthrown greatness across a barrel that reeked of naphtha, coils of
wire, coils of rope, coils of stripped leather, a wooden birdcage tied with
fowler's knots, oars and boat hooks and tangled mounds of netting, flat
loaves of cracked and crumbling cork, a cask of oil and one of yellow
powder that reeked of raw sulphur, a plaited reed chair with the bottom gone and an old cane-backed Victorian rocking chair with three ornate initials woven into its back, an old-fashioned black iron safe without a door, a huge desk piled to the ceiling with yellow newspapers, a
gramophone with a curving trumpet and a pile of records, a mound of
padlocks in an orange crate, a crystal receiving set from which no good

news could ever be expected, axes and hoes and rakes and shovels (all with broken handles), a roll of wire netting beside an open trapdoor with the top of a ladder sticking up out of it (the scene to be repeated in the cellar for any visitor descending), the wreckage and debris of uncounted lifetimes, the atmosphere of lonely waiting time.

The old man busied himself with a Primus stove, lighted the wick of an old kerosene lamp. He wore an Indian Army officer's gray flannel shirt and wool riding breeches, a pair of freshly oiled jackboots laced to the knee with rawhide thongs, a belt with *Gott mit Uns* stamped into the buckle and, on his gaunt head, a flat frayed straw hat. In the lamp's sudden light he looked like a nightmare that was about to end. He was obviously very old but his eyes were clear and sharp.

—Would you like some music?

Without waiting for Mendeltort's answer he picked up a record, blew a small dust storm off it, put it on the moth-eaten old turntable, and cranked the metal skeleton of the handle. A woman sang a sad German song in a metallic voice. *Das Lied ist aus . . . Frag' nicht warum ich gehe.* There was a play of emotions on the old man's face, a sentimental mixture of pleasure and pain.

—The song is over, eh? he said. Don't ask me why I'm going. That's what you do when the song is over.

He turned his head with an apologetic smile and used his fingers for a handkerchief. —You go when the comedy is over, he said. That's why you go away.

Suddenly he cackled, said: People always said I would go far but did they think I'd go as far as this?

He spoke in Yiddish with a peculiar lilting accent and Mendeltort said: You're from Vilno, aren't you?

—From Vilno, yes, the old man said, and lit the Primus stove. There she goes, listen to her hiss. Soon have some food ready, we will. And where are you from?

Mendeltort shrugged, thought for a moment, said: I don't really know. I know where I was born but that means nothing to me. Does Vilno mean anything to you?

The old man smiled not only with his eyes but with his mouth as well; his brown lips parted to show brilliantly white false teeth.

—I never think about it, he said.

—When did you come here?

—When? Oh, after the war.

—Which war?

—Which war? The old man seemed perplexed, then said: Oh yes, of course, there have been so many since my war. Well then, which one was it? It was the one in which the Japanese sank our fleet.

—You mean the Russo-Japanese War in 1904? Mendeltort said, astonished. The battle of Tsushima Strait? The siege of Port Arthur?

—Was it that long ago? Yes, I suppose it was. The Japanese took me at Port Arthur . . . They put some of us to work in another country and then I came here.

—What did you do in Vilno?

Old Ben smiled, nodded, said: I lived there with my wife. Only, you see, I wasn't home for months, sometimes many months. I was a locomotive driver, I traveled a lot . . . you know what it's like on the railways in Russia?

Mendeltort nodded.

—Well then, you know how it was. You're away from home a lot when you're a locomotive driver. I know, I know, it's no good for a young woman to be left alone, but what could I do? A man has to make a living when he has a wife.

Like all old men, Mendeltort knew, Old Ben was grateful for an opportunity to talk about the past, feeding on his memory of the world's most unremarkable creature: a young woman who had not yet begun to grow up; she'd never know the meaning of happiness because she'd always confuse happiness with excitement and excitement with a mindless frenzy, a creature of no particular merit made memorable like Dante's Beatrice by the mind of a lonely man who still hungered in his solitude. He'd need to love no one as long as he could be sure that no one had loved him.

—My wife was very beautiful, Old Ben said. Unfortunately she was much younger than I was. When I came home from a long trip one day, she was gone. She left me a letter.

He handed Mendeltort a bottle of whiskey labeled FOR USE OF H.M. FORCES ONLY—EXPORT LICENSE NOT REQUIRED and from the folds of his shirt he drew a tin of American corned beef, which he split in two with one blow of a hatchet. He found a cracked white teacup among the piled newspapers on the desk, blew dust out of it, wiped it with his fingers, and passed it to his guest. It bore the initials N.A.A.F.I. He threw the corned beef into a metal skillet, put the skillet on the Primus stove. In the stove's bluish light his white teeth and eyes were brilliant in his lean brown face.

Outside the sky had begun to clear. The small glassless window framed the clouds as they passed across the face of the sun and cast the shadows of great violent birds on the calming water. It would be a bright, starlit night.

—I knew him, Old Ben said. He was a tailor, even older than I was, but a good-looking man. In the letter she wrote that he could do for her what I couldn't. She never said what that was. And that she had remorse. I ask you, what can you do with someone's remorse? She should choke on it.

—You never forgave her?

—What does forgiveness have to do with a man like me?

The old man stirred the meat in the skillet with a curved Bedouin dagger, himself hawklike and weathered by the hot desert winds, reached for the whiskey bottle and poured a full measure into a cracked cup. He drank, spat, said: Ah, you mean I should have forgiven her?

—You should have forgotten her by now. She is probably dead.

—So all right, I never did forgive her and I never will. I hate her.

—If you hated her you'd have forgotten her long ago.

—You're right, of course. I never could hate her. I wanted her dead but I couldn't hate her. But that makes no difference, does it?

—None. Don't drink so much, we have to go out again tonight.

—I can drink and go out too. That's when I started drinking, you see, after she went. And then I had an accident. They said I was drunk on the job, didn't see the signal, some people got killed. So then I had a choice, do you see? Ten years in prison or twenty in the Army. So I took the Army. It's a lot easier to escape out of an Army than out of a prison, eh?

—I've found it so.

The old man cackled, coughed, stared into his hands: Yes, you have, Mr. Barzel (using the name that Mendeltort was using). Yes, so have many others as I hear. But I didn't even have to do that much. We were taken by the Japanese, all of us. Thirty thousand of us were sent down to another country to build railways, so you see I was soon at my old trade again, driving a locomotive. I don't remember the name of that other country, it seemed to have a lot of names and one of them was the Land of the Morning Calm but it should have been called something else. The people there, you see, use human shit to fertilize the rice fields, they carry it out in buckets every morning, on their heads, and they've been doing it for a thousand years, so that everything there smells like shit. I was there, in the Land of the Morning Shitpile, for five or six years and then I came here. Oh, not right here, to this house, oh no. But to this country. Here. That must be almost forty years ago. And will you believe it that I still can't get the smell of shit out of my nose?

—You must have been one of the original pioneers.

—Not me, the old man said. I never owned a pair of khaki shorts. You've got to wear khaki shorts and a white shirt to be a pioneer. And you've got to be able to smell only oranges. If you can smell the shit you're not a pioneer.

—Why choose this country, then? Why not some other, if it made no difference?

—Did I say it didn't make a difference? You want me to say that I came here because this is the Homeland of the Jews? Well, all right, I'll say it for you Mr. Barzel, only right here it's Transjordan and over there is Palestine and it's an English colony in an Arab country. I came to the Homeland of the Jews, Mr. Barzel, but I'm still looking for it.

He sat down in the Victorian rocking chair that had been picked up from a pile of discarded furniture outside some hotel, or stolen from the veranda of an officers' mess, and drank his whiskey and rocked back and forth and looked into his big cracked hands. He made a bowl of them on his knees and stared into them like a diviner looking for the future in the deep black creases, but the small repetitive shaking of his head denied the presence of a future there.

—Why did I come here? he said. Why not? What did I have waiting for me in Vilno? I came here because it was here, not there, and that's all there's to it. Only when I think of Sarah and that tailor . . . ah . . .

—You came here for a new beginning as all of us do, Mendeltort said.

—You think so? Well, at first it seemed to be a new beginning, but perhaps it was only an old ending even then. Do you remember what it's like to be innocent, Mr. Barzel? They say that as you get older you understand more but that isn't true. Maybe what they mean is that you have a chance to understand more if you are willing to understand it when the moment comes, but when my moment came I didn't know that there was anything more for me to understand than I already knew. So for about thirty years I was like a child, putting my truths together piece by piece and understanding nothing. I must have been living with my eyes shut because I didn't see what was happening in the world around me. All I could see was myself and I thought that maybe I had learned everything that I had to know, the way it's taught in Russia, which is that you eat your anger for breakfast and drink your bitterness for supper, and you keep your eyes on the road ahead of you and you never tell anybody what you think. I knew that there was something different here but I couldn't tell what made it different or new. For many years life here seemed like everything else that I had learned about. Let me tell you, Mr. Barzel, I was never a religious man in Russia; I did what I had to do to keep the neighbors off my neck, but I didn't think about religion one way or another. I drove a locomotive, I wasn't some superstitious peasant living in a *shtetl*. So when I got here I didn't have much to do with the few Jews I met. When I first got here I worked on the docks, where all the other stevedores were Arabs, then I got work as a switchman in the railyards, but it didn't take me long to see that there were no Jews working on the trains. That was in Haifa, but it was called Jaffa then. It was an Arab town, there weren't many Jews living there then. Tel Aviv, Mr. Barzel, was an Arab village in those days! That was the Jewish Homeland to which I had come, a country where the policemen were Sikhs, the soldiers were Irishmen and Hindus, every official was an Englishman, and there were two hundred Arabs for every Jew you'd be likely to see. It may have been the Jewish Homeland to anyone who was living somewhere else, but you couldn't drive a locomotive on the Palestinian Railway if you were a Jew. For that you had to be a Scotsman or an Englishman or an Anglo-Indian. That was the country to which I had come and it didn't seem all that different than the one I'd come from . . . but there was *something* here, something . . . I didn't know what . . . But maybe I'm boring you, Mr. Barzel? An old man talks too much, everybody knows that.

—No, Mendeltort said, feeling his pain creep down into his lower arm. Go on. Unless you want to tell me first what Asher had to say?

The old man sighed, drank whiskey, said: It's nothing you've not heard from the others. Maybe you better hear it on a full stomach, eh? As for the rest of it, it took me thirty years to understand it and you want me to tell it in one minute? Have another drink, the food is ready, by the smell of it.

He got up and turned off the Primus stove under the burned corned beef, ladled the stringy meat into envelopes fashioned from Arab bread, passed one to Mendeltort, and returned to his rocking chair with the other.

—Besides, he said. After I told you what I want to tell you maybe you won't have to talk to Asher and the others. Eat. It tastes better if you drink some whiskey.

—Not to me, it doesn't.

—Are you in pain again?

—No.

—The whiskey helps, eh?

—It helps. Now tell me what Asher had to say.

—Is he married, that Asher? Do you know?

—He's married.

—He shouldn't be away from home so much if he has a young wife.

—She's twice as old as he is and she's got a mustache twice as big as his, Mendeltort said. Asher doesn't have anything to lose. Now tell me what he said.

—You said it yourself, Mr. Barzel, Asher has nothing to lose, so he will risk nothing. He has an ugly wife and he's away from home a lot and he has a nice crease in his khaki shorts. Also he has nice hand-writing.

Old Ben fished in the breast pockets of his shirt and produced a piece of paper, a sheet torn from a receipt book, on which Asher had written with a fountain pen: *Shall I give more of my children to the glory of a God named Barzel?* Whatever name he used at a given moment, Asher could be counted upon to parody a classical allusion.

—This is a friend of yours? Old Ben asked.

—No better than any others I have had. I like him even less for man-gling *Medea*.

—He'll go far, said the old man. His wife does a nice job on his shirts.

—And that's all he gave you?

—That's all he gave on paper. But he talked a lot. The American was with him, that Mr. Salaman, you know the one I mean? The one that looks as if a pyramid had fallen on him when he was learning how to walk. The one with a voice like a rusty foghorn, and a breath like an ashtray.

—You should be more respectful of American money, Mendeltort said, and tasted the sour bitterness that rose from his stomach. It seems we wouldn't last a week in our Homeland without it.

—So I'm told. But just because I have to eat from the gutter, does it mean that I have to wag my tail like a dog? Anyway, what Asher said to tell you was that he had nothing for you, that his people will do noth-ing for you, that everyone's agreed that you should go back to wherever you came from because nobody wants you here or needs you here. He talked a lot about his people and your people and other people's people, and I kept thinking aren't we all one People? But apparently not. He said more. Do you want to hear it? It's all the same thing.

—You might as well say it since that's what you went for.

—He said that when your own people join you, his people and every-body else's people will do everything they can to stop you. He said you've already caused too much trouble with the British turning Pales-tine upside down to find you, and finding a lot of things they're not supposed to know about while they're looking for you, and that this has to stop. And then he wished you luck.

—You must have misheard him.

—He laughed when he said it. He said that if you tried to do what you want to do then you'd need all the luck that anyone could wish you because everybody would be against you then, not only the British. He told me to remind you about Stern.

—He needn't have bothered.

—Stern, the old man said. That's the man who got hanged?

—Yes. For a murder he didn't commit. The Agency, that means Asher, hired two Arab killers to murder one of their own doubtful men, then blamed Stern for it, denounced him to the British, and the British hanged him.

—Nice friends you've got, Mr. Barzel. So will there be any more messages to carry?

—No. Asher was the last. You've been to all the others.

—So are we still going out tonight? It'll be full moon.

—All the better to see the Arabs with, my dear, Mendeltort said, bowing to his pain.

—But what's the point of it if you have no men?

—Maybe that's the point. And I have you, don't I?

—Nobody has me, the old man said. That's one of the things I learned in those thirty years that I talked about. But when you've heard the rest of my story then you'll know what you really have.

—Right now, Mendeltort said. I have a need for air.

Outside the clouds were gone and the sky was clear. The sun had dipped toward the west but in the east new black clouds were beginning to gather, so that the sun's brief reign couldn't be counted upon to resume next morning. He climbed the path down which Old Ben had come earlier in the afternoon and looked about at this most ancient and artificially divided of all lands, Samaria and Judea ruled by an Arab kinglet, a palimpsest (as a literary English lady had written in another context) in which the Old Testament is written over Herodotus, and the Koran over that. How could he have been so foolish as to hope that this could ever be one country of one people when there was no such thing as One People in it. The Arab compromised, schemed and bargained and occasionally killed, always threatened; the Jew made rash hysterical gestures to satisfy his pride; and both races when aroused were absolutely ruthless. Yet his faith in his People (who were not just his own Hargan, nor Asher's political operators, nor the hopelessly confused Irgun, nor Stern's dazed and embittered remnants, nor Ben Gurion's well-oiled mechanized steamroller, but One People for all their jealous and quarrelsome subdivisions) continued. If they had compromised their sense of biblical destiny it would be only for a moment, a few brief and unimportant decades in their vast continuity; and as long as they could love their independence more than luxury they could be brought together when the choice before them was finally stated as unity or death.

Freedom is all, they had cried through their millennia, having no freedom in their choice of dying; they longed for life and went out in search of death as a moth would seek the coincidence of a flame. His body told him clearly that his own time was measurable in months at most; each time the vise was tighter, the pain thrust deeper and, in a lesser form, it had become a permanent condition in one arm and leg. Time had shrunk for him into the inevitable event of his approaching end, and he had to use whatever time was left, playing out the gloomy and inhuman role that had been destined for him, and pass into the artificial world peopled by phantoms of unreal greatness where no one else would ever want to follow. An execution would be arranged for him, that had been made clear, but first a legend had to be induced to commit suicide.

Somewhere in these bleak domed hills crumbling into the parched wilderness of ancient Judea, the past ran its courses, each yesterday ascending the spiral that men would call history. In this place, more than in any other, the future showed itself to be no more than an endless repetition of the past, each circle closing upon its own beginning at a higher level and sweeping round again into the next comprehension of reality, lifting mankind in its patient vortex from the cave to whatever stars were its destiny. A Jew whom Greeks called Christos was said to have come here to make his choice between mysticism and revolution, to contemplate and to reject temporal temptation and to select the legend that would commemorate him throughout mankind's ascent; Judas, the man who loved him more than all his followers (loving him for that freedom that he represented) and saw the promise of his People's freedom betrayed by the revolutionary who became a mystic, had to destroy the man whom he had loved in order to preserve the vision of the freedom in which he believed; the Pharisees computed all their possibilities, Caiphas contemplated the probabilities, and later the imperial viceroy washed his hands. It made no sense to speculate on what would have happened had the Galilean chosen revolution, yet the thought was tempting. Would there have been a liberation then? But from what, to do what? Drive a herd from one paddock to another and how have you changed its condition? To be free from one form of bondage was not to be free from them all, Mendeltort knew, and an ascent is merely an upward movement unless it spans the contradictions. Time was now making his decisions for him. The only choice that was still his to make was the quality of the legend that he would become; history was not that country of his imagination in which he wished to live.

The wind, hot with the breath of the desert, brought the maddening irregularity of the bronze bell into his shuttered skull; he heard it as the booming of cannon in a Russian dawn, looked into the reflection of his destiny in Szymanski's eyes, heard Zarubin's antique voice rustling with information about the procedures for destroying legends. (First we destroy the legend, then the man.) And if the legend had always been greater than the man, then the legend must be made to destroy itself. Otherwise the dead man might continue to live as a guiding myth, the legend might be misread as a prophetic set of blueprints for an unwritten history, and the new spiral toward the next predictable reality would become warped; the patient upward vortex would become a whirlpool in which the ascent would be reversed.

He went down the path toward the coolness of the beach and the dark and dusty house where the old man waited with yet another story.

Yet history would not let him make his exit as easily as all that. A weight had seemed to shift more comfortably on his shoulders and his pain had ebbed, and lines from Mark Antony's funeral oration were passing through his mind (shortly the alarums and the trumpets would subside as well), and then he, who had never been able to accept coincidence as containing any kind of truth, saw the crude letters carved into the rock. The sun had angled just right to send a sharp beam into a granite surface as smooth as a shield, a flat abutment polished by the wind where a bored patrol would have rested.

The years had stamped their own LEG X FRET upon him (and not all the carving would show on his surfaces, as did these initials hammered into cliffside in so many places of his captive homeland), the mark of the Tenth Roman Legion of Fretensis whose iron-studded shoes had clattered on Samarian and Judaean goat tracks for hundreds of years. He bent to examine the symbols of the fish and the galleon carved under the mark of the legion and saw them in the context of their times, as Old Ben's prosaically cracked N.A.A.F.I. tea mug had to be considered, as would the regimental symbols woven into the back of the Victorian rocker. These were the captors and oppressors who had crushed the Jews and had been fierce in their defense against the depredations of all other Romans, taking an inward pride in the difficulties they encountered as they tried, time and time again, to put some substance behind Vespasian's optimistic boast that (finally? finally) JUDEA CAPTA ET DEVICTA EST. So had the subjugated Jews taken ambivalent pride in the exploits of *their* LEG X FRET, the victors of Jerusalem and conquerors of Masada, who had stood unmoved and unarmed under the flashing knives of Zealot dagger men, chanting in chorus: *The oath! The covenant!* until their last man fell. Such victims and such executioners could understand each other.

He had been born in February, which, as his occult-minded countrymen insisted, cursed him with the ability to see every possible side of an argument simultaneously, but signs and portents and omens (in short: coincidence) had never played any kind of role in his calculations. Yet this sunlit carving was the second coincidence of the day. Old Ben's tale of the unfaithful young wife and the Vilno tailor was very familiar to the son of Jakob Mendeltort.

In the small house, the old man smiled inquiringly toward him as he ascended from the cellar with a box and a bundle balanced on his head.

—You look better, the old man said. You've made a peace with yourself?

—What can one man do? Mendeltort replied.

The old man's bright blue eyes disappeared in their nests of wrinkles.

—Ah, you say that? What can one man do? We escape from an evil but we bring it with us. And why not, if it's in us?

Tenderly, he lifted the box and the burlap bag off his head and placed them on the first conveniently empty space he could find on the littered floor.

—So we leave the evil that we know about and go to the evil we don't know. In later years we look wise and heroic, bigger than our times because we went to look for bright new lands. But do you know something, Mr. Barzel? Nobody leaves where he is and goes to look for a new beginning in a distant place unless he is, in some respect, a failure. Still, having become a fugitive from failure, a man may become wiser next time . . . don't you think?

—After a time there is no next time, Mendeltort said.

Old Ben laughed happily: Well, that's God's joke on us. He is entitled to His joke. And a man is entitled to his own. Be patient, Mr. Barzel, an old man is entitled to talk in riddles because most of the time he talks only to himself, there's nobody to misunderstand him. It becomes a habit. But you ask, what can one man do? He has to see what is happening in the world around him.

He was stroking the burlap bag he had brought from the cellar, he patted the box.

—I will tell you something that I did before I left Vilno. I couldn't do anything to her, do you see? Not to Sarah. That would be like doing something to my own life. But somebody had to pay, somebody had to suffer. Why should I be the only one that lost something important? So I denounced the tailor to the Okhrana as an anarchist.

Rocking rapidly in the Victorian regimental chair, he shook with silent laughter. —That man an anarchist? All he ever talked about was making lots of sons for himself and being a rich man. But he took something that was important to me and made it unimportant and nobody can be allowed to do that. It's like you said, Mr. Barzel, to keep what you have is very important even if it's only a dream. I don't know what happened to this man but something had to happen.

—He went to Warsaw, Mendeltort said. He became rich enough to buy himself his own Russian prince. He and Sarah had four sons and two daughters. But don't worry about that, he lost everything, he and your Sarah and all their children are dead.

—Eh? What is this? You know him then?

—No, Mendeltort said. I never knew him at all. But it's a good way to finish your story.

—So Sarah is dead? Old Ben said.

—What would you expect after all these years?

—In me she is not dead. I've tried to kill her in me like she killed something in me but I could never do it. It's a good thing I never think about her, eh? It's a good thing to be an old man who no longer thinks about everything that's been taken from him.

—It's even better not to believe that there can ever be any truth in a coincidence, Mendeltort said.

—Now you talk in riddles.

—Perhaps it's catching. Perhaps that's what happens when a man is too much alone.

—Maybe so.

The old man picked up the little burlap bag and put it on his lap and stroked it as though it were a small companionable animal to which he had become attached. He stroked it in the abstracted tender way in which lonely persons, who have not yet learned how to feed upon their solitude, transfer their anguish to writing letters, listening to the radio, the feeding and the care of pets. He rocked back and forth in the intricately woven depths of the Victorian rocker, kneading the small contents of the bag.

—One man alone, he said, smiling into his collection of shadows and objects. What can one man do? That's what people used to say in Vilno, that's what they said for centuries in the Pale. One man alone before God and waiting for a sign, what can he do if God will do nothing? But then something happens, the man begins to see what is happening in the world around him and what is happening in him . . . Ah, but tell me Mr. Barzel, have you been to Jerusalem yet?

—Not yet.

—You must go there soon. Go to Jerusalem before the English leave it and then you'll know what it is that we've all come here for. No, I don't think it's a new beginning, Mr. Barzel; it's more like the beginning of an end of waiting for something to happen. But for what? I don't know what it would be for you, for me it was what I thought that life ought to be. I stood there while the day got hotter and the sky got wider, listening to the old *bekishes* droning by the Wall, and then something was happening outside me and inside me too, and then I understood something.

—You're trying to tell me that each man is his own Messiah? Mendeltort said.

—Is that what I'm trying to tell you? You're an educated man, Mr. Barzel, you'd know better than me what I'm trying to tell you. Something happens on the outside and on the inside too, and until you understand that these two things are one, you will keep on waiting, you will never know what you've come here for. Can you believe that I was thirty years in this country before I went to Jerusalem? Can such a thing be imagined? But as I said, I wasn't religious, I wasn't a *shtetl* peasant, I was a locomotive driver living in a country where no Jew could be a locomotive driver. So to work on the trains I had to pretend I wasn't a Jew. And although I never even thought about the Temple, Mr. Barzel, one day I went to see the Wall. I stood well back among the tourists, looking. There were about a hundred men praying at the Wall and at first, you know, I felt embarrassed because it's like something out of the Middle Ages, and I thought what does all this have to do with me? It's what kept the people in the *shtetls*, it's something from a ghetto, what's this got to do with diesel engines and with electricity and with the world as it is? And then I heard this tourist Englishwoman talking to a man. Every word she said is carved in my head. Terribly emotional people, aren't they, she said. And the man she was with, a tall bored-looking Englishman, said: Terribly. And then she said: I mean, really, I don't quite see why they should make such a fuss, do you? I mean, it was all such a frightfully long time ago, after all. It's really a classic case of a storm in a teacup, wouldn't you say? And he said: Oh quite classic. Then they laughed. That's when I knew that something was going to happen, I could feel it happening. It was the fall of the Temple she was talking about, Mr. Barzel, and to her it was a storm in a teacup, something that happened a frightfully long time ago. I couldn't breathe. I knew I was weeping. I hadn't shed a tear since that time in Vilno when I found Sarah's letter. Those had been tears of rage and these were the kind that come from the soul when it's torn apart. And the Englishman said: Oh, they're a frightfully neurotic lot. Just like their hand grenades, you know. And she said: Oh, really?

Hand grenades? And he said: Frightfully neurotic. Go off in your hand. And I was listening to the old *bekishes* wailing at the Wall . . . Ah, it's good to be old, Mr. Barzel. When you're an old man you don't have to think about things like that.

—Just as you never think about Sarah and the Vilno tailor.

The old man laughed. —That's just how it is, a storm in a teacup. She wrote me a letter, that she had remorse. How can you blame someone who writes she has remorse? How can you blame someone who is stupid, so stupid she can only see a wall and not what's *in* the wall? No, I can't blame the woman. I remember how hot it was, and the droning of the old *bekishes* whom I saw as she must have seen them, as ugly black insects who'd always keep droning no matter how many of them you stepped on. A storm in a teacup! And I remember how a bomb went off in my head. My tears were the tears of outrage, Mr. Barzel. But outrage at what? At the stupidity of the woman? One should expect stupidity from a woman. Outrage at myself because I couldn't do anything about what was happening to me? But, like you said, Mr. Barzel, to keep what one has is very important. I knew then what was happening inside me and outside me, and I knew that it was all the same thing, and I knew what had been taken from me and what it was that I had given away. It was what Sarah and her tailor took from me in Vilno, what the Russians took away from me in their army, what the English took away from a locomotive driver who could get to be a brakeman on the Palestinian Railway only by pretending that he wasn't a Jew. My self-respect, my feeling that I was a man. But if there's nothing that a man can do then what is this man? What can he be and where does he belong? Can you tell me that, Mr. Barzel? No, you don't have to tell me. Because, you see, there is always something that a man . . . one man alone . . . can do, if he is a man.

Thick clumsy fingers fondled the leather thong that held the small burlap sack closed on the old man's lap, pried loose the fowler's knots and opened the bag. Gently, with loving care, the old man extracted a small black cylinder with a bright copper cap; the bag was full of such small cylinders, and Mendeltort began to smile and to shake his head unbelievingly.

—You know what these are, I can see, Old Ben said.

—What are you doing with dangerous things like that?

Tentatively, as though the small metallic objects he was touching were blackened memories and nerve ends, and perhaps something that called for reverence, the old man said: They used these on the Palestinian Railway as emergency fog signals. You put it on the rail, you see . . .

He replaced the guncotton detonator in the bag and picked up another. —Ten years ago, he began, then stopped, then forced himself to go on: That's when our troubles with the Arabs were beginning . . . And I thought this was something that one man could do . . .

He stopped and tried again, and Mendeltort fixed a ghastly smile on his face because he felt the beginning of the nausea in the cold pit of his stomach and the first icy clutch of the vise closing upon his chest. The sunlight was blinding through the glassless window, and the old man's watery blue eyes were alight with rapture and ferocity, and he threw the blasting cap against a wall, where it went off with a sharp crack and a swift yellow flash.

—I was a brakeman then on the Taggart line, Old Ben said. I was a brakeman because I made sure that everyone I knew had forgotten that I was a Jew. I even joined the Palestine Police Force Reserve and did my turn on the roadblocks, and learned to say all the things that Englishmen said. About how the Jews were trying to buy themselves a country, how they were always pushing themselves where they weren't wanted, and how it was small wonder that the Arabs had had enough of it . . . The Taggart line, do you know about that, Mr. Barzel?

Slowly, with infinite care, Mendeltort managed to shake his head, sinking within the whirlpool of his pain.

—That was a single track that ran from Haifa to all the Taggart Forts that the British built to keep us away from the Arabs. They weren't real forts in the proper sense, more like barracks with towers and a courtyard . . . Like the police barrack at Latrun, that's the last of them . . . Well, when the troubles started, the British put Sikhs and Arab Legion soldiers in the Taggart Forts, and once a week they sent this special train along the Taggart line. It had a sandbagged platform car in front with a field gun on it, and then there was the locomotive and the tender, then there was a boxcar with the doors opened on both sides and machine guns pointing from the doors, and then there was a passenger wagon and another boxcar for supplies, and then another boxcar with machine guns and then another platform with a gun. Because I was in the Police Reserve I got to be a brakeman on the Taggart line. That's how I happened to go to Jerusalem that time I told you about. And after that, well, what could one man do? I knew the line, I knew where a man could wait in ambush for the train. It took me two months to learn about dynamite . . . ah, it was easier with the inkwells and the six-inch nails.

He smiled into the bright slanting air, into the reeks of guncotton and that suddenly resurrected world of fanatical heroism and determination and unspeakable treachery: the vibrating blue flame of his outrage and his hatred and his memory of vengeance. His old eyes were alight with a mystic fury, and the thin veined wrist repeated over and over the whip-and-snap which had propelled the detonator with such ecstatic rage into the littered shadows, but the voice had become apologetic and shamefaced.

—It never came to much but I'm glad I did it. I'd be glad to do it again, now, with you Mr. Barzel. Of course, I know . . . well, I was a bit younger then, but I still remember a thing or two, so . . . And if you don't get any of your young men in time for what you want, if nobody else comes . . .

—No one else will come.

—Well then, we can do something with these, eh? All you do is crimp a slow-burning fuse in this end of the cylinder and then you tape the cylinder into the neck of a bottle that you've packed with powder . . . just ordinary black blasting powder from a quarry or from a tunnel works . . . Or you can use a quick-burning fuse and then you throw the bottle. Inkwells (he said suddenly), inkwells are particularly good. And if you tape a dozen six-inch nails to the inkwell . . . well . . .

Then, in a voice gone sour with the certainty of rejection: Well, Mr. Barzel, what do you think?

—I am not thinking anything.

In a voice which pleaded: I know, you're thinking: What can I do with just one old man, bottles, and blasting powder? . . . But if that's all you've got, Mr. Barzel? If that's all there is?

—What?

Mendeltort couldn't hear. His eyes had become unfocused with the pain. He was willing himself once more into silence so that he might drift upward toward consciousness. He opened his mouth and said again: What?

—I know! the old man cried. We can get Druses! The Dair Yassir people are of Syrian stock and Druses hate Syrians! You can't do better than the Druses for what you want done. They are descended from the Kurds and the Kurds will kill anything if you pay them for it. The Druses don't think of themselves as Arabs, they look down on Arabs. We can get Druses and some other people that I know about. There are such people all along the border and no no one knows or cares who and what they are . . . Bedouin outcasts, English deserters, criminals . . . and some of them are Jews, if that's what they must be. They're like the Cossacks used to be in Russia four hundred years ago . . . I can get them for you! What difference does it make what they are if they do what you want done?

—It makes no difference.

He could breathe easier, then. His eyes could focus on the old man's eager smile but he thought of nothing. When he had told the old man that he wasn't thinking anything, that was the truth.

Always before he had been able to believe in words like *honor* and *the public good* and in a glorious end as justifying the most appalling means, but there was no way to justify a public act whose true motives have become personal. His legend had become a burden to the very people whom he had tried to serve, and he knew (beyond the need for thought) that it had been the legend which had done the service, not the man.

And he could hear the old man:

—Well, Mr. Barzel? You don't think I'm telling you the truth?

—I am not thinking anything.

And, paradoxically, he thought that he would never have to think again.

Not then and not later that night, lying alone and watchful above the rim of the Arab village that he had marked for the death of a legend; nor seven nights later.

Six days passed while Old Ben had been away, collecting his cutthroats; six days of lighting the Chanukah candles and drinking Old Ben's whiskey and packing bottles with black blasting powder and trimming the fuses, and an ebullience that might be made to testify to an unquenchable spirit or, at least, to the momentarily joyous anticipation of absolute peace. He knew that he would never cherish another idea, for the only idea that is worth pursuing is one charged with passion, the one that tears life open at the gut, and if a man can no longer conceive of such an idea then it is best to have none at all.

The German woman sang to him metallically *Das Lied ist aus*, the comedy was over. Each night the condemned man ate a hearty meal and joined the German woman with *Frag' nicht warum ich lebe*, for life without the crystal airs of total dedication to a principle was only penal servitude and he no longer needed to lie to himself.

Six days passed and on the seventh day, between the hour just before the sunrise and the hour that followed upon a sunset made lurid by fire, the village of Dair Yassir was destroyed and all its inhabitants given to the knife, to the hatchet, to the sea and the river, to the village well, to the few bullets of Lee-Enfield rifles and of Mauser carbines and the solitary Sten gun (he had given orders to limit gunfire), to the strangling wires and the bell rope in the Coptic tower, to pitchforks and to clubs and to fishing nets in which the older women and the more infirm and helpless among the old men were bundled and drowned.

Old Ben had proved himself as good as his word; his two score and ten border outcasts went about their antique trade with professional dedication from sunrise to sunset. A more villainous crew couldn't have existed since the days of Herod's infanticides. They crushed their victims with the sportive care accorded to flies, and Mendeltort walked about the stacks of the massacred dead sipping Old Ben's whiskey.

Passing between the village's only shade tree, the traditional tree of idleness, and the barricaded door of the little Coptic church where several dozen of the women had run to save themselves, he saw Old Ben murdering another. The old man had stunned her with a stone and now sat astride her chest and sawed at her throat. His eyes were closed, the dust in the hollows of his caved-in cheeks was streaked with blood and tears, and he was making small whinnying sounds. His blunt Bedouin dagger kept slipping from his hands. Mendeltort wondered which of his women it was that Old Ben was murdering: the faithless Sarah who had robbed him of his self-respect and ran off with the tailor, the Englishwoman whose stupidity had shown him how he had been robbed, or some other personification of pain and betrayal at the careless hands of another woman; for every act of mindless cruelty creates future victims and it is seldom the person who is murdered that is being killed. Either way, Old Ben was an honest man who paid his debts in full.

Noon came and passed and still the killers worked in ecstatic frenzy, as if the reek of blood were an intoxicant and each victim a sacrifice that called for another, but now the carnage had shifted to the roofs and cellars where those who hadn't tried to escape from the village had crawled to hide themselves; they were found and killed invisibly, the parched square resembled a silent battlefield (but no, not a battlefield, since no weapons lay there) where a few looters stalked among the corpses. The sun was high and hot, several squads of killers disposed themselves under the tree of idleness to rest and to eat. Some were already drunk, some in the process of becoming drunk; the Moslem laws against spirituous liquors were not observed in a Christian village, the village store stocked barrels of Cyprus brandy.

A dozen men were making halfhearted attempts to batter down the door of the Coptic church and get at the last of the women, then started to pile bottles full of Old Ben's explosives around the walls and the doors, and it was then that the old man was shot.

A blue-eyed man with long sun-streaked hair had tripped over his rifle, fell and broke the bottle in his hand, eyed in drunken rage the blood that spurted from his severed wrist while the others laughed. The injured man picked up the offending weapon and hurled it butt-first

against the tree. The rifle fired. The bullet struck Old Ben in the spine.
Mendeltort walked over to the old man and squatted beside him. He
passed him the bottle of whiskey; there was enough in it to rinse out
the mouth.

—Are you in pain?

—Your turn to ask, eh? Old Ben whispered. No, I feel nothing. Is it
the spine?

—He couldn't have hit you better if he aimed.

—If he had aimed, the blind camelfucker, he wouldn't have hit me.
But what luck I have, eh, Mr. Barzel? Then, on the other hand, why
should it start changing now? As it is, I've lived forty years longer than
I should have and how long can a man live without his heart?

—No longer than he can.

—Do one thing for me, though, Mr. Barzel, let me light the fuses.
My hands still work all right.

—They're not long enough, Mendeltort said about the fuses. And
you're too close to the building, it'll bury you.

—Maybe it won't. And does it make a difference? The song is over,
eh, Mr. Barzel? Please let me light the fuses. They're my fuses . . . !

Mendeltort shrugged, said: All right. But wait until everything is
over. I don't want any smoke in the sky until it's all done here.

—You're worried about those drunken camelfuckers, Mr. Barzel?
They're getting bored already, they'll be gone as soon as all the brandy's
gone and all the women are dead and after they've found everything
that's worth stealing. And in a place like this one there's never very
much.

—I'm not worried about them, they're not my men.

—They're not even their mothers'. Let the British catch them. Except they won't catch them. I remember how it was in the PPF. Search
the hell out of every vegetable truck going to a kibbutz, strip the
women in the sentry boxes, but turn your back and work on your shoelaces when a camel train went through. You should've seen those PPF
people.

—I've seen them.

—Here, you've seen them? You've seen people like them? You know
who they are, those PPF people? They're what the Irishmen called the
Black an' Tans, moved over here from Ireland when that job was done.
You just make sure they never get their hands on you, Mr. Barzel.

—Sooner or later, Mendeltort began, but the old man interrupted
him: You just watch yourself, Mr. Barzel; you're still a young man.
Will you get the fuses over here then, and put the matches in my
hand?

Mendeltort motioned to a group of men to lead the fuses toward the old man, gave him the matches, and looked at the sky.

Justice, injustice? Such words had no meaning when there was neither love nor hatred but only indifference. There was no right and no wrong and nothing was different than what it had always been. The burned-out idealism behind this operation would reach the next necessary spiral as what such things had always been, as they always will be: obsessive but marginal and as full justification for slaughters-to-be. Some politician would apologize, another would build a hospital and a school . . . those for whom it is convenient to remember massacres would have a massacre to remember, everyone else would forget it just as soon as the next thought presented itself. He knew that he would never be forgiven this massive assault upon his own legend but (he grinned, remembering Ben's fuses) it was his legend to destroy. In the end it would prove more useful in its fall than in its construction.

Having toppled the legend, he had made it easier for the executioners to get at the man; he didn't think that it would take them long. Only three persons knew the place in which he was to wait until the month of Nisan. One of them could be trusted to confront his conscience in the name of that imperishable idea of freedom that still waited to be won. A young man, true, but used to terrible decisions, he thought with affection. I've trained him well: he won't turn his back on his duty in the name of his own love for me.

He left the village then, and climbed the first of the small brown hills he would have to cross to reach the house in which he was to wait. He felt no pain and he didn't think about anything. But now as he walked in the about-to-happen twilight of his world he saw the land of his People for the first time . . . its many pasts and something of its future . . . as men sometimes perceive the soil from which they have sprung. He wanted to continue the longing for that which cannot be because it is gone as soon as one realizes what it is: one's self, justified.

In that last moment of clarity, with the sun poised to plunge into the piled brown hills, and motes of dust revolving brilliantly like light itself, so that life did seem more important than death, he thought of a friend, once a man, about whom he hadn't thought in years: Bukharin confessing to the crimes he hadn't committed. Bukharin, innocent of any wrongdoing other than his faith, crying his *mea culpa* before the Great Red God of duplicity and blood: an act of repentance for a life of service to an impossible ideal.

For in the end all must come down to faith in an idea greater than oneself, vaster than one man's life even if that life happens to be his own . . . and if you lack that faith in the final moment you must create it in yourself, otherwise you will have lived for nothing.

His eyes had blurred and the pain was vivid in his arm and shoulder. The sun had turned bloodred in the western sky and the air was remarkably still; the hills were hushed and waiting, poised on their rocky pediments for flight into the night, when he began to hear the muted flat thunderclaps of Old Ben's homemade bombs exploding in the wreckage of his past.

Catherine

LOOKING DOWN AT THE CERULEAN SEA of Nineveh and Tyre, the hot white sand. The wind had died down. The afternoon clouds had scudded inland leaving wispy traces. The soldiers' singing was muffled by the dunes. The soldiers marching inland in rank upon rank of cocked Australian hats, sunburned knees under the rims of vast khaki shorts, hobnailed boots pounding out the rhythm.

> *. . . Za-po-lem-sto-iii gajina!*
> *Raz! Dwa!*

A meaningless song of cadence for the pounding boots, the beat of the pulse. Laughing red blistered faces. Huge hopes and an enormous faith. Eyes wrinkled against the sun. She let the sand drift across her bare feet, leaned against the palm tree. Emil didn't speak.

Only a few months ago, she thought, we were the living dead and how different everything seems to have become. Even the air smelled of life, the sun warmed, the sea breeze was cooling.

Life and the processes of living had become so simple. And yet . . . not. Not entirely. Because she knew that this simplicity was as deceptive and as temporary as all the earlier rituals of living that had to be abandoned. The future was no longer a matter of getting through a day alive. The future included more. Her future, and that of all these other men and women in the miraculous army, contained a question that no one could answer. Her present was the army and the war. Peace would conclude the war and dissolve the army, and with that moment the future of them all would assume the shape of a giant question mark. Peace would return them all to a world in which no home awaited them, a life in which there were no precedents for such young women as she had become. What to be and where to be now that a lifetime of wandering about the earth had become a certainty. And how to *be* that which she had become.

Yet no such thoughts would trouble her at the beginning of a day.

. . . The day begins with trumpets, reveille. She stands among the ranks of clean, fresh-smelling young women, listening to the morning trumpets in other parts of the vast encampment, seeing the companies and battalions marching out to training in the desert: the regiments formed out of ghosts, the miraculous army. For they are all the children of a miracle, of that they are sure, and they are all deeply and unbelievingly grateful for this miracle of life in the present, even though the future promises a lifetime of exile. *Raz! Dwa!* The marching songs begin. The regiments disappear in the desert, and Catherine goes about her daily task with wrench and spanner and oil can and lubricating grease, polishing and petting her ungainly Bedford truck as though it were her own most treasured possession. In some other world and in another lifetime there had been another kind of Catherine for whom the truck would have been an incomprehensible mystery but that Catherine no longer exists. The reconstructed Catherine, the one whose days begin with trumpets in a desert camp and end with evening trumpets, moves through her predictable military days in restored spirit and warm flesh, wearing her rebuilt and polished body like a uniform; she bullies the huge mechanical monster that had become a part of her identity across desert roads and if the beast should break down she'll know how to fix it. Nothing seems impossible for this re-created Catherine except thought of that predictable procession of days in her own home and country that is the basis of all civilization, for that idea has been doomed by distant politicians . . . And there is one other thing which is no longer possible. And that is everything that had been the basis of her former lifetimes, that wholly vanished past in which her beasts and monsters had not been mechanical and could not be bullied . . .

(*Never again* is a phrase with a special meaning for women like Esterka, and a particular meaning for these renewed young Polish women of whom Catherine is one: the sunburned, resurrected women who wrestle with trucks and lorries across the Syrian and Iranian deserts, who drill and qualify with the Lee-Enfield .303 rifle and the A-6 grenade, for whom the processes of living had lost all mystery. *Never again* . . . yet who can be sure when the future is a question mark? The world had not grown for her; it had shrunk into coincidences, providential meetings, into paths that crossed and recrossed and converged and spun off into deserts as if accident were an antidote for human loneliness and doubt.)

One! Two!

The soldiers' singing cadence echoed among the dunes.

She looked at Emil, searched among her thoughts for something that she might say to him that would mean as much to him as it might mean to her, found no such thoughts or phrases. And, anyway, Emil didn't speak.

In the beginning there had been a hope that the boy would return to normal (Pani Mosinska, resplendent in her military rank and terminology, insisted that he was *malingering*) but as the months had passed and he continued to maintain his unnatural silence it had become rather obvious, even to the General's Lady who ruled the orphanage, that he didn't speak because he couldn't. The boy lived in silence from which he peered in ambush at the world: it was his refuge and he would not leave it for any inducement. His quiet intelligent eyes were open to everything around him, his tranquil questioning smile seemed never to have been obscured by any kind of sadness, but he said nothing to anyone. Watchful as a small animal crouched in its subterranean sanctuary, the boy communicated nothing. He did not speak and had, apparently, not uttered one word from the moment when he had come to Bokhara with Cousin Wlada's diary: a little traveler who would never be able to tell the story of his private journeys.

Now he was looking at the blue ruffled surface of the sea, at the diminutive waves that came to the shore. With his right foot he drew V-shaped sea gulls in the sand.

—I wish you'd speak to me, she said suddenly, but he shrugged and grinned; his eyes peered upward from his round brown face like intelligent almonds. He grinned and scrawled a message in the sand.

Why? said the message.

—So that I can hear what a nice voice you have.

Not nice, Emil wrote in sand. Then he erased the words.

—Well, you don't have to sing to me, she said. I don't expect an aria. But it would be nice to hear a friendly voice.

You have friends.

—I can't think of one. There are a lot of people who try to seem friendly and some of them, perhaps, are. But accepting friendships is a dangerous business, most of these so-called friends take far more than they give. In fact . . . well, never mind. Do you have friends here?

No, Emil scribbled swiftly. And added the word *need.* Then he squinted sideways toward Catherine, grinned, and wrote: *How's Abel?*

How indeed? she thought, and said: Little brother, the contents of your head scare me to death. But at least you're no longer saying things in triplicate.

Grinning, Emil wrote: *HA.* Then added two more *HA's.* Then added *Ludicrous. Remember?*

—I also remember *insufferable,* she said. And you are certainly growing up to be just that.

Ergo, he scribbled.

—Ergo nothing, she said. No. These are all things I'd rather not
remember.

Why?

—Because it's all a part of a world that we've put away. Our childhood. Faith in people. Dependence on others. I understand that on the
Island of Bali, in the Pacific Ocean, parents purposely frustrate their
children so that they learn to look for their fulfillment in art rather
than in people. But I suppose you know about that.

Yes, Emil wrote, then erased.

—I keep forgetting that you're not an ordinary child.

Not I, Emil wrote, then shook in laughter without sound.

—I wish we had been brought up like that.

Emil looked up at her, then pointed to what he had written and then
erased it quickly.

—Why not?

The boy smiled, poked at the sand with the bayonet-shaped blade of
the palm frond with which he had been scribbling his messages and
comments. He looked at the sea, at the softly rolling waves, and threw
the stripped palm frond toward the blue water. He smoothed out the
sand.

—No more to say? How are you doing on your diary?

He wrote no reply. He stared at the sea. Some seabirds flew close to
the water and, occasionally, one of them would dive.

Had it not been for Cousin Wlada's diary he might not have been
able to identify himself in Bokhara, she knew; if there were real miracles in which to believe then finding him had been one of them. He
had come alone the last two hundred miles of his journey and he could
not speak. But he had pointed to his name in the diary he carried and
then to himself, then he collapsed and was unconscious for some days,
and then he drifted in and out of fevers (typhus and malaria and a
touch of pneumonia at the end), into and out of an orphanage and
a school and sometime during these months he acquired a pencil
and a copybook and in it he wrote an account of his family and himself,
a child's brief history of a journey that didn't belong in anybody's childhood. This had identified him to Pani Mosinska at the orphanage she
directed in Bokhara and so, eventually, Catherine had found him.

She said: I never did see your diary. Will you show it to me? No, I
don't mean now, but *someday.*

Emil shook his head.

—Author's pride? she said. Or is it the idea of *someday?* That does sound like a fairly tale, doesn't it, and we're all done with that. But is it true that Teodor Haussner took your diary to publish, as he published Cousin Wlada's?

Emil grinned and nodded.

—I hope he sends you an autographed copy, but I doubt if he'll think it worth his while.

Emil clutched his stomach, pretended to vomit, opened his mouth in another soundless parody of laughter.

She said: Yes. Well. That's my view exactly. I hope that you are never driven to become a writer. Our family has kept itself respectable for several hundred years and it would be such a pity to spoil it all now. Still, it's a good thing that you kept your diary, isn't it, and that Pani Mosinska published your name in the circulating lists, and that I finally discovered where you were. Do you realize that until last month I still believed you were dead?

Emil crossed his arms on his chest, rolled his eyes upward, and put out his tongue.

—Yes, she said. That's just about how I imagined you. Bronka kept saying that the age of miracles was not past, that if she could learn to drive and repair a Bedford then surely such minor miracles as finding one small boy in the vastness of Russia and Iran were at least *equally* possible . . . But I didn't want to hear about any more miracles. I didn't think I'd be able to bear another disappointment, particularly if it involved someone I cared about. And even though I had convinced myself that I would never care about anyone again, because that's just an invitation to pain and disappointment, I couldn't help caring about you. You see, we are all that is left of our family and we must have someone . . .

Emil shrugged.

—You don't think so? Well, I suppose that too is an idea from the past. An antique notion of belonging. Should we all be totally self-reliant, then? Thinking only about ourselves, never giving anything to anyone? It sounds like a safe and sensible idea, but can it work in a world in which we are strangers? Because, you see, it's most unlikely that we shall ever go home. Shouldn't we help each other in some way?

Emil turned his face to the sky. I don't know what to say to him, Catherine thought. I'm talking to him as though he were a child but we have gone far beyond anything like that. Childhood and its varieties of innocence had become an impossible idea. A sudden fear for her own existence was making her weak. How much more bleakness can I stand in my life, and when does being a tragic figure turn into a pose? She had sworn to herself that she would turn her back on every commitment, but it was obviously not going to be as easy as all that.

She watched a shirtless soldier as he made his way carefully up the dune toward her and Emil; despite herself, she found that she was thinking about Kobza and then about Abel, and then she thought: No. I don't want to feel anything for anyone other than myself; it's the most economical way to be a human being.

Emil was watching her with an inward smile and she saw, with a sudden sense of shock, that he was not seeing her at all. She meant nothing to him. He did not need her: she saw herself unaccountably diminished. Look at me, she thought with quick anger, see me as I am! Who are you to make me feel unnecessary? . . .

Then the boy was smiling directly into her eyes.

—I don't quite know what to say to you, she said. You're the first miracle I have ever talked to. But I wish, my dear insufferable miracle, that you'd scribble one of your replies. I'm getting rather bored with doing all the talking.

Emil was yawning and she felt desperately alone.

She said: You're just pretending to be bored, aren't you? I hope you're just pretending. I'd hate to think that I was boring you and wasting your time as well as my own . . . But couldn't we treat each other as civilized human beings, if not as people who might mean something to each other? I hate to be trite, but . . . ah, but I've already said that, haven't I . . . about you and me being all that is left of our family.

Emil nodded, smiling.

—Do you realize how many strings I had to pull to be assigned to this supply run for the orphanages? The army has seven of them, you know, and every driver in the Transport Service would like to take a daily trip to the seaside and to spend a little time among children. It's such a change for us from our usual fare of men and machines . . . I actually had to blackmail my dispatcher sergeant!

Emil had spread his hands in a rounded gesture of contemptuous amusement and she realized, with a shocking sense of déjà vu, what it was about him that had disturbed her from the start. He was making a gesture calculated to throw her off stride and he must have known whose favorite gesture this had been: he had spied on Abel and herself often enough to know all of Abel's gestures. She looked at him and saw Abel and knew that the gesture was too cruel to be innocent, and wondered why he would wish to be cruel to her. The small man-child was quite as imperturbable as the curved cloudless sky, to all appearances no deeper than the eye could see but filled with distances and darknesses beyond imagination. Now both the boy and the man whom he was imitating had become strangers to her, and she was totally alone; or perhaps it was she who had become so surprisingly a threat to her own contented and assured image of herself. Apparently her new reality had to be approached one step at a time. An earlier Catherine would have damned all caution to the winds.

Cautiously, in Abel's words (which, she remembered irritably, often belonged to someone else), which, in this instance, were really St. Augustine's timeless definition of growth, she could feel herself begin to move *out of that future which is not yet, into the present that is just beginning* . . . and then how did that go? *Back to the past that no longer is,* which seemed to be the unavoidable destination.

Endlessly, with the finality of judgment, the sand danced and shifted; the desolate wind swelled in the desert and subsided behind the dunes. And would this day be yet another dull lost witness to the cycle of the sun, of which she would have neither memory nor regret?

Carefully, like a surprised animal testing the air outside an unfamiliar lair, she said to the boy: I've quite forgotten what a dangerous child you had been.

The sun had shifted, the sea was dark blue. The boy had rolled over on his bare brown stomach and began to draw another picture in the sand. He drew a building that might have been a castle or a church, under an arch that could have been a rainbow or a bridge. He drew a huge bomb falling on it all. He sat up and watched the picture crumble and disintegrate in the swift wind slanting from the desert.

His eyes had taken on the peculiar aspect of the desert dweller, the constant stare of pupils that seemed darker, rounder, more absolute.

She smoked desperately and stared into his indifferent eyes as though to find, restore, and reaffirm her own indifference. I don't know who he is, she thought. I don't want to be trapped into caring for anyone again, or expecting that life could be zoned for safety and order, or that we might be governed by decency and reason once again, or that faith could have value; because if one keeps getting disappointed over and over again, then we begin to expect less and settle for indignity and humiliation. But if I don't care for someone, she thought, how will someone be able to care for me? Loneliness is a communicable disease, and it is terminal.

And, in the meantime, the hot sun was pressing on her forehead; Emil's eyes seemed to have become as yellow as a dog's. She watched her clenched fist jerking in her lap. Her inner void had become a desert that oceans could not fill.

Then she was looking at the shirtless soldier who had climbed the dune, a small middle-aged man with a difficult smile, seeing him as he had been in Russia: eyes sunken in sockets round with ancient hatred, unfleshed face a thing of bone and sinew stretched over quivering nerve. His quality of an ancient parchment manuscript, on which many men had written their versions of history, had crumbled away, yet the skin around his eyes remained drawn tight with strain and with shock.

Surely, this can't be yet another accident, she thought. There had to come a point beyond which coincidences ceased to be ironic.

—Hello there, said the shirtless soldier as if he and she had seen each other only the day before, or perhaps earlier in this day. Ooof. What a climb.

Wondering about coincidences, and suddenly remembering what she had felt for and about this man in Russia, what he knew about her, she agreed that it was indeed a difficult climb to the top of the dune.

—Especially in this sun, she said.

—We could have used a sun like this in Russia, eh? he said.

Smiling, she agreed.

—But when do you ever get what you want when you need it, eh? Itzek Fogel said. It's always too much of one thing, not enough of another. But maybe it all evens out in the end?

—One ought to think so, she agreed.

—A beautiful day, isn't it? Itzek Fogel said.

—Yes, she said. Beautiful.

—But very hot, Itzek Fogel said, and sliced the sweat off his chest with the edge of his hand; his lips had parted in a diffident smile that exposed a set of metal military dentures.

—Yes, she said, then went on urgently, responding to his mild friendliness and wondering what had become of the hard-edged inner flame which had made him seem unextinguishable in a frozen wasteland: You're the last man I would have expected to see . . .

—Here? he said.

—Anywhere. The last time that I saw you . . .

—We were cutting off your friend's foot, Itzek Fogel said. He died, didn't he?

She nodded, suddenly unable to speak. Were memories engraved so deeply, after all? And would the other Catherine never leave her alone in her blessed indifference? Then she said quickly: There were other times.

—Yes, I expect there were, Itzek Fogel said. But that's the one that I remember best. He was a real *mensch*, that Kobza, eh? Do you know what that means?

She nodded, thinking suddenly of Abel's grandfathers, of her own dead father, then of Kobza, and then, for no apparent reason, of Abel. She said No.

—But a leader is only as good as the place to which he leads the people, eh? Itzek Fogel said. I know about such leaders. Do you want me to say I'm sorry he's dead? But will that make him alive again?

—No, she said.

—So I won't say it, Itzek Fogel said. Besides, what is one dead man among so many?

—Nothing, she said, meaning *everything*, and suddenly she hated the small shirtless soldier for reminding her about kindliness and kindness and gentleness and generosity and affection which she had gone to such pains to destroy. To turn aside her own anguish, she said: I used to see you at the *uchastok*, before we started to look for the army.

—Yes, Itzek Fogel said, then added surprisingly: Those were good days.

—Good? she said, astonished. You thought they were good?

—We were all going somewhere together then, Itzek Fogel said. We followed an idea. But now we know that we were going nowhere all along, we were just trying to get away from where we were. Does that seem to you like a real journey?

—Poland, she said. Our country . . .

But he smiled ironically.

—I won't see it again, neither will you. Do you want to live in a country ruled by *them*?

—No, she said.

—So that's that, Itzek Fogel said. So where will you go after the war is over?

—I don't know, she said.

—Neither do I, Itzek Fogel said. I'm too old to be a pioneer in another country. I want to go home.

—Home? Or to the sentimental, unreal memory of what might have been home?

—When you're my age you'll know that memory is more real than what your eyes can see.

—You're lucky to have such good memories.

—Who says they're so good? Itzek Fogel said, convulsed in ancient fury. But they're mine! I made them! They belong to me! And I'm entitled to live with them, good or bad, because they are mine. I'm entitled!

Then he was making vague apologetic gestures, said: Well. I just came up here to tell you that we're almost finished with your truck. Five or six loads and that'll be that for this week.

—I'll be down in a minute, she said.

—Take your time. We are taking ours. We know that you want to talk to your little brother. My grandson would've been just about his age had he lived.

—Don't call a slowdown on my account, she said harshly, because harshness was a repellent and she didn't wish to attract anyone.

—Why not? None of us ever qualified as Stakhanovites in Russia, there's no need to set any records here. The war will be going on tomorrow, like it is today, and what will we have day after tomorrow? So take your time, little lady.

—Don't call me little lady, she said. I don't want to hear that stupid, patronizing phrase again. I am a soldier, just like you.

—I don't doubt it, Itzek Fogel said, and began to pick a blister on his narrow belly, a watery sunspot among the small black craters that had been red-and-white rosettes of pain in Russia: But shouldn't we help each other while we can?

She shrugged, averted her face, thought indifferently: What would this unexpectedly mild and inoffensive little man, this foolish middle-aged man who had lost an idea and a destination, think if I were to write him a reply in the sand? *Never again* . . . But he would probably think that I was talking about something else . . .

—Yes, Itzek Fogel said. We ought to help each other. A clean hand needs no washing, eh? But whose hands are entirely clean? And a squirrel gathers nuts for the winter one at a time.

—Spare me your country wisdom, soldier, she said.

—As you wish, soldier, he said. Five minutes, then. But if you want more, you can have it.

She didn't look at him as he made his way down the dune. She looked at Emil, who was watching her with a smile that took all the warmth out of the sun.

She said: I may not be able to come here next week. I'm assigned to a long-distance convoy in the morning, it's possible I won't be back in time to come here next Sunday.

Emil saluted her with a mocking smile.

—Don't do that, she said. Sit down again. Please? We still have five minutes.

Four, Emil showed her on the fingers of one hand.

—I see what it is that you're doing, she said. I understand this now. You've become a clown. That's very good, very safe. A mute clown is about the safest thing to be. You can get away with just about anything when you're a mute clown.

He nodded, undisturbed.

—I'll come to see you every week as long as we're still stationed here, she said. But the army is moving to Palestine soon, perhaps as far as Egypt. Eventually the schools and the orphanages will follow the army but that may take some time.

She said: I think that you're quite right to keep your thoughts to yourself. Most people talk too much, they make too many promises. People talk only so that they may have an excuse not to listen. They'd rather listen to their own voices telling them only that which they want to hear . . . Yes, I suppose that I am no exception.

She said: At least I have no illusions about who and what I am. I want you to believe that. Most people will go out of their way to make you believe the worst of yourself because only in humiliating and degrading you can they make some sort of sense out of their own lives. But you must believe that you're a fine human being no matter what happens. Can you do that?

Emil placed his left hand behind his back, his right hand on his chest, advanced his right foot, and raised his chin skyward.

—No, she said. Please. No more Napoleons either. We've had quite enough of that. Now what are you doing?

(Because the boy had put one hand against an ear and began to snap his head from side to side like a metronome. When he extended three dusty-brown fingers she understood his performance.)

—Three minutes, very well, she said, and thought: What does he think of me? Why doesn't he say something? She said: Why can't we be friends?

Smiling toward the sea and concealing his own eyes from her, Emil stretched a thin brown leg, dotted with the same black indentations which pitted her own flesh, and, with his heel, slowly spelled out: *Why?*

. . . Ah, she thought: there it is again: one of the most frequent questions that life has asked, and the one that no one seems able to answer for anyone else. Emil was grinning, holding out two fingers. Two minutes? Very well, two minutes. Then he had formed his thumb and forefinger into a circle, as cold as the absolute zero, into which he blew, and stood back as if to watch an invisible dandelion blowing away in the wind.

—Ah, she said. Is that what you think? All right, then. Do you want to go back to the others now?

But he had already plunged his arms up to the elbows in the deep pockets of his huge khaki shorts, his round face vanished under the rim of the bulbous white pith helmet, and he began to trot by himself toward the orphanage enclosure. There, among tents and Nissen huts, miniature soldiers marched about, and elderly men and women taught classes in the open air, and the smoke rose cheerfully from the cookhouse chimney and nobody was laughing.

She passed a small boy who stared at her with bright hostility out of his private shadows, wanted to move toward him with a friendly gesture. But he backed away, turned and fled. At least I'll be able to tell Esterka that I saw him and that he looked all right, she thought: Little Jankele had few friends, wanted none, it seemed.

Near the administration Quonset, she saw Pani Mosinska pacing back and forth. Professor Karolewski was walking beside her. Teodor Haussner, as ubiquitous as ever, was making animated gestures . . . And she felt a sudden need to hide from them, to sever all connections with that part of her past which they represented . . . And wondered if that severance would ever be entirely possible.

(Then she was making her awkward, surreptitious way past Wiesio Poremba's watchful calculating eyes—awkward and surreptitious because she didn't want to be seen and stopped to talk to anyone there— noted the cynical old-man eyes in the small boy's face and tried to make her own calculations of the murderous price of his survival . . . saw Ziuta, glazed in virtue, leading small children to the infirmary tent, where each would receive American orange juice and cod-liver oil . . . heard Zygfryd Bunt declaiming behind a blackboard, noted Professor Kukla's white birdlike hands darting about his head as he spoke of History . . . And the hot sun seemed to lurch overhead, and time came full circle to another afternoon which had contained not sun but sleet and snow, a day in which she had hurried to a transformation.)

Emil had disappeared.

She looked about, wanting to wave to him as she got aboard the Bedford, but he was nowhere to be seen.

Correction, she instructed herself silently: he is to be seen somewhere. But not here, not by me.

The soldiers had unloaded the supplies that she had brought to the orphanage and now lounged about, talking in low voices: lean and bronzed men, none of them young; their new flesh clung closely to their bones. Now their training days were ending: endless marching days and uncomplaining days that ran into each other like the mindless ten-day weeks of French Revolution, life-giving days to the skeletons that had come from Russia. Now other days were coming. *Dies Irae*: their return to the waste and spillage of a war. Now each of their days had become rare and precious to them. Now they resented the end of each day.

She looked about for Itzek Fogel, wanting to say something to him; she didn't know what she wished to say. He had provided a rare human moment, brought back to mind a permanent memory.

. . . Well, you're all set, little lady, someone said, and this time she merely smiled and nodded and did not object. Thank you, she said. See you next week, little lady, said another soldier. Well, God keep you all, she said. And you, they replied. May you have a wide road.

She put the truck into gear and drove past the white-and-red painted gate, past the crowned white eagle spread in a vast mosaic under the flagstaff of the small parade ground. The eagle and its shield had been pieced together from chipped bricks and smooth white pebbles carried by the children from the sea. She drove past the limp white-and-crimson banner, past the striped road signs that pointed into an endless distance: into the past which was always near. Lwów, said the road signs; Wilno, Warszawa . . . as such road signs had pointed the directions to other armies marching toward Poland across exiled centuries . . . and then came sets of figures, astronomical to her imagination, each a kilometer that each of them had crossed . . .

The road ahead lay hidden under dust. The desert unfolded in arid vistas of stillness and silence; her horizons had no limits then.

She brought the Bedford to a halt, climbed out of the cab. In three or four hours she would be back among soldiers and their tents, back in the life of others; this was a moment of solitude to be savored, as her freedom from the hopes and fears and from too much love of living was to be savored; this was her gift from the deceptively empty desert.

She walked around the Bedford and automatically inspected its eight enormous tires, passed a loving brown hand over the cleats and fastenings of the rear canvas. On the truck's shaded side, she perched under the door of the cab, her back against hot metal. She lit a cigarette. Long shadows had begun to run into the desert. They slid away from her into shallow pools of darkness: the blue and purpling stains that crept eastward among the boulders and the crumbling dust of lost civilizations . . . For here, she knew, there had once been cities, and men and women lived among their dreams and watched their lives collide with the vast sweep of armies, illusions and fears . . . Smiling and humming to herself, a tuneless little ditty redolent of childhood, she made an attempt to comb the sand out of her short-cropped hair, kicked off her heavy shoes and peeled off her socks. She was herself, alone, returned to her beginnings. There were no eyes to look at her within a hundred miles. The road before her was like the road behind her: a barely discernible track trodden into a wilderness in which a hidden and mysterious life offered sudden detours and unexpected turnings and strange confrontations. And these coincidental meetings and separations that she thought providential showed her a sense of order in a world where nothing else appeared to make sense.

Surely, that was a sign that she could not ignore.

She thought about her brother, the mute clown. And, because of Emil's cruelly calculated gesture, about Abel. He was alive, she knew. She hadn't wondered about what he looked like, what he thought; what

anyone thought about anything had made no difference to her. Professor Karolewski had made sure that she knew Abel's whereabouts; each
time that they met at the orphanage, where this warped pedant came
to visit with his granite lady, he would manufacture cumbersome sets of
oblique comments about the once-upon-a-time father of her dead child.
She hadn't even wondered whether Abel knew that they had had a
child; he, like his child, had been buried in the debris of another lifetime and she was not yet sure that she wished to have him resurrected.
Yet, for one reason or another, people kept resurrecting him for her! Esterka had been the first to tell her about his survival; Esterka's strange
young unsmiling husband had been a clerk in Abel's company before he
deserted. Kepi was Abel's driver, and Bronka's permanent-sporadic
lover, and Bronka shared Catherine's tent, so that although Abel would
have had no idea of Catherine's existence she was very well informed
about him. She supposed that sooner or later they would meet, because
few human paths ever crossed without recrossing in some manner, but
she had been in no hurry to bring that about.

(What would there be to say? What was there to do? There had
been too many transformations. Her life was in herself, she could think
of nothing that she wished to share. He had been what he did. Joyful,
irresponsible perhaps [she was to be beyond judgments, she remem-
bered], complicated, simple as a line marching across a page, a fragment of his time and moment, of his own suicidal kind, no more substantial than a straw in the wind. He had longed for life free of the
incomprehensible restrictions of an irrational destiny, and sought proof
of his own life wherever he could find it. With her as much as in any
other mirror. Never more than that. Life would appear to him in a variety of disguises and if these apparitions proved to be illusory, being less
life than death masquerading under enemy colors, then that, she supposed, was his destiny. He had become a shadow among other shadows:
a ghost, a memory, a mythical beast. The lone sane humorous illogical
self-proclaimed madman mocking an utterly unmad humorless but logical society which had created the insane civilization to which he ob-
jected. And it had given both of them a strange exultant sense of power
and contempt for people who were failures or who spent their lives
wanting things, to tease his destiny. She had never been able to blame
anyone for anything, did not suppose that she could do so now. But he
could find it in himself to blame innumerable kinds and categories of
people, nations, this class or another, this or another heritage, his huge
dwarfed father, the ruin of a woman who had been his mother . . . all
wrecked on the reefs of their own distant past . . . and injured everyone who came close to him because, having the value of love, they
offered him proof of the life he sought as fervently as he feared it. He

struck them down so that they wouldn't dazzle him with the promise of a controllable fate and a destiny which was not irrevocable. Let him play Diogenes, if he wished, scowling from his barrel; she had no illusions about anyone's honesty, for she knew that it was easier in this century to find an assassin than an honest man.)

Peace of a kind had been part and parcel of her terrible detachment, but now it seemed as false as the deceptive stillness of the desert.

Then she was shivering. The great night chill of the desert would soon be upon her, nature's ironic paradox whereby lost travelers had been known to die of the cold in what was, in daylight, an arid bowl hot as molten metal. But she was not lost, nor could ever be. In this moment of heightened sensibility, she was aware only of new beginnings, conscious of the future like a liquid before it is tasted: a formless substance which we know is there because we can see the goblet that holds it. She was convinced that just as night was about to happen to the world so was a new morning, and that she and all the others were in it before it happened. She was in the light and in the darkness and the particular music of each was flowing through her.

If she could live like this (she thought), moved by a sense of purpose that she need not question, without swapping false dollhouse seductions for bits of flattery, she knew that she would reach her destination, whatever it was, when it was time to do so. The desert, as the army itself for that matter, were only stages in a vaster journey which was nowhere marked as having an end. She had come far from her starting point, so far that neither memory nor imagination could provide trustworthy landmarks. Could she believe that nothing that had happened to her had been accidental? For in that sense of order that seemed to lie in each coincidence, in that apparent supervision of mankind's affairs (no matter how unpredictable and capricious it might seem at times), there lay a denial of human aloneness and an affirmation of purpose to a life that was not wholly a matter of chance.

Perched on the high step under the Bedford's door, she had an immense view of the darkening desert. In that light, it was like a frozen ocean, silent and unrevealing but filled with hidden life and clearly defined by its dark horizons; it was a geometrical assertion of life's mysterious continuity, the endless process of invisible renewal, a demonstration of the proposition that unless life were contained it could not be.

She pulled on her socks and shoes, then rummaged in her new American valpac bag for the green-gray sweater with its leather patches and military insignia. The motor turned over at first try. She slid the Bedford into the first of its many gears, released the brake, and drove.

Two hours and a half later, with the sun falling behind her back, she drove into camp.

—Honest to God, Bronka said. What will they have us carry next?

—What's the matter?

—Twenty lorries for tomorrow morning, Bronka said. Ammunition, signals stuff, and hospital equipment. At least thirty hours on the road and no escort.

—Why not?

Bronka nodded toward Esterka Traurig, who had come into the tent.

—Because we have to carry the nurses along with their equipment. So there's no room for the escort trooper in the cab.

Catherine shrugged, said: We all know how to shoot.

—Still, with ammunition on the man-eee-fest, Bronka said with a cold glance at Esterka, there ought to be an escort.

Unbending and aloof, Esterka said: I'm told that Palestine is well policed these days.

—Well, don't blame us for that too, Bronka said, and laughed. We don't wear table napkins on our heads, and anyway it isn't the Arabs I'm worried about.

—No reason for you to worry about them, Esterka said.

—I don't want to worry about anything, Bronka said. Honest to God, it's time to start living, you know? It's really time for that!

—Well, eating, anyway, Catherine said, and Bronka laughed again.

The girl's round face was crimson as a sunrise. She had become spherical, Catherine noted fondly; she was always eating. None of them would ever be without food close to hand, she supposed; an indigestible memory of hunger will always see to that. Now Bronka took a loaf of fresh white bread from her footlocker, unwrapped a half-pound package of Australian butter, spread the butter on a slice of bread as thickly as though it were cheese, and began to hack open a tin of sardines. She eyed the food with fierce concentration, humming a village song about cows and geese and other rustic creatures which, perhaps by coincidence, were all edible.

—Anybody want some? Bronka said.

—Not just now, Catherine said, then turned to Esterka: How many of you are coming with us tomorrow?

—How many of us? Esterka said.

—Nurses, Catherine said.

—Five nurses, Esterka said. Only five of the trucks are ours.

—And it is Palestine that we're going to this time?

Esterka nodded, glanced away.

—Well, Catherine said. At least you'll be going home.

—I still say it's a rotten deal to carry ammunition without escort, Bronka said. That's asking for trouble.

A quick light appeared in Esterka's eyes and she turned her head away, then shook her head and said in a carefully controlled, expressionless voice: Mendeltort has been caught.

—There are others like him, Bronka said.

—No, Esterka said. There are not.

—Where have they got him, then? Catherine said. Do you know?

—Somewhere near Lydda, I believe, Esterka said quietly. Why do you ask? Are you thinking about Abel now?

—Yes, I did for a moment, Catherine said. An odd sort of thought . . . Have you heard from your husband since he went away?

—You mean since he deserted, Esterka said. No, I haven't heard.

—And if you had you'd never admit it, Bronka said, and Catherine watched as the darkly handsome young woman inclined her head briefly, then she said gently to Esterka: It doesn't matter to me, you know, to any of us. None of us will be able to go home, so why should we interfere with your dreams?

—Would you help? Esterka said.

—You're here, aren't you? Bronka said. You've been helped.

—What do you mean by help? Catherine said.

—Nothing, Esterka said. I mean . . . *meant* . . . nothing.

—Because it really doesn't matter to us, you know, Catherine said. Whatever war you're fighting now is against the British, it has nothing to do with us.

—They are your allies, Esterka said.

—Yes, aren't they? Catherine said. And that's why they will win *their* war and we will lose *ours*. It was supposed to be the same war at the start, and perhaps it was, just as *your* war and *ours* were supposed to be one war . . . But, really, do we have to talk about wars? How did we get on that subject, anyway?

—This is insane, Esterka said. Does anything matter to you any longer?

—Some things do, yes, Catherine said. I'm just discovering what they are.

—Lots of things, said Bronka. But if I keep Kepi waiting much longer, that won't matter either.

—Is he here again, then? Catherine said.

Bronka flushed and giggled. —Honest to God, that man. Can't get enough of it, he's here every weekend. I don't know how he gets so many passes. (Then, with a sly peasant sideways glance, she said:) He says that Abel is a real easygoing company commander . . .

—Good for him, Catherine said. And good for you too. (And then to Esterka:) So if you want to trust me, go ahead.

Esterka shook her head. —It's too late for that.

—No one is searching for your husband, are they? Catherine said. It's not as if he had anything to do with that Arab village.

—He had nothing to do with it, Esterka said quickly. We can't be held responsible for the act of a madman.

—It doesn't matter to us, Catherine said.

—This is insane, Esterka said, and rose and turned her back, and Catherine could see how expressive of emotion a turned back could be.

. . . Yet there was something here that called for attention, an unexplained quality of falsehood just under the surface: a dark and dangerous purpose that she didn't understand. Death had been so commonplace in everyone's memory as to arouse little curiosity . . . Why then this uncharacteristic nervousness concealed behind anger? But Catherine was aware of a faint icy prickling in her own scalp and along her spine, noted the familiar dryness in the throat. She couldn't pinpoint the source of her uneasiness.

—I ran into Itzek Fogel at the orphanage, she said. Do you remember him?

—What is this? Esterka said. An interrogation?

—What? No. I'm just trying to understand something. He started talking to me about the need for all of us to help each other. He said that no one's hands were clean. He said something about leaders who mislead their people . . . at least I think that this is what he said.

Esterka shrugged: Perhaps he was trying to philosophize.

—I didn't know what he meant, Catherine said. I didn't give him a chance to say much of anything. Now I have a feeling that it was something to do with your Mendeltort.

—He's not our Mendeltort, Esterka said quickly.

—Itzek Fogel was devoted to him. So were you and your husband.

—History is full of false prophets, Esterka said.

—Can you dismiss him as easily as that?

—He has dismissed himself!

—There's something wrong here, Catherine said. This doesn't ring true. You wouldn't be that upset about an Arab village.

—I'm not concerned about an Arab village, Esterka said coldly. I am concerned about a Nation and the world's opinion. Mendeltort has never been as dangerous to anyone as he is to us now, and every minute that he lives in a British prison keeps alive the memory of what he has done.

—Well, Bronka said. They'll hang him soon enough, I expect.

—Oh no, Esterka said bitterly. They'll keep him alive forever if they can. He is a prize exhibit of our *intractability*, our inability to listen to reason! There's nothing quite so useful when you are trying to destroy a People than to be able to prove that they are inflexible, myopic, concerned only with their own problems . . . hasn't your own Katyn disaster taught you about that? Hang him? They'll never hang him. I wish they would hang him. But why should you concern yourselves with that? It is not your problem.

Catherine shrugged, said: You don't have to explain anything to me.

—I'm not explaining anything, Esterka said harshly. Nor am I apologizing for anything. This is our business, not yours, and we shall take care of all our own affairs.

—When the time comes? Catherine said.

—What?

—Nothing. It's just a phrase I suddenly remembered from another time.

—Yes, when the time has come! And in the meantime . . . Ah, as someone said, we are at war and killing is a part of that.

—And traitors must be shot, Catherine said quietly.

—What? What did you say?

—Once more, a phrase from another time. Nothing to do with your Mendeltort, I am sure.

—I told you not to call him that, Esterka said.

—Has he become inconvenient?

—Incon . . . (Esterka had begun indignantly, then opted for patience and mild irony:) We want a country of our own, not a new religion. When you allow a mystic to define your national aspirations . . . ah, but here we're getting into your mythology, aren't we? Poland, the Christ of the Nations, and all that.

—Honest to God, Bronka said. You two really have a circus when you get together.

Night came soon after.

Then bugles were playing and the clear high notes slanted across the desert floor and the high-vaulted night. First at divisional headquarters, and then at each brigade, regiment, company, battery, and troop, the trumpeters of Kraków, Lwów, Wilno, and Warszawa stepped to the edge of darkness and soothed the fearful disappointments of the cold new night. The notes soared and hung crystal-clear among stars and fell and promised rest and made yet another implied promise to an army which was, once again, thinking itself invincible . . . For hadn't these men and women already proven that they were indestructible? Such confidence isn't learned, it is earned. Yet it was all ending for them, even then.

She stepped to the open tent flap, looked out and listened to the music of three hundred trumpets calling to each other in a foreign night and, once again, time grinned ironically; time moved, inscribed a circle, named this night another: a night in that other country where locomotives cried mournfully to each other across a city gripped in the jaws of a Siberian winter . . . Then she was listening to yet another sound, a pervasive rustling as of a wind gathering among dense foliage and swaying green crowns: the sound of absent trees, of nature's persistent continuity . . . The sound of memory which was both cruel and unforgettable in the way that the most oppressive memories are also the most precious. Here, in the desert night, removed by so many astronomical miles from the cities whose names the exiled armies painted on all the road signs of their history, it was the sound of soldiers in hundreds and thousands tramping back to quarters for the night. Good night she thought, good night. One by one the bugles and the trumpets finished the night's music. She watched blue-shielded flashlights swinging in the freshly populated darkness, watched their hooded beams darting about like fireflies among the somber acres of tents; her true historical beasts crouched for the night under canopies of cloth that simulated forests. She listened to guffaws, calls, bits and pieces of marching songs, to muffled cries. Good night.

Bronka brushed past her, going out. —You'll cover me if the section leader comes to check the tent?

—Don't I always?

—There's always the first time.

(And then the spherical young woman was saying, not unkindly:) Why don't you let Abel know where you are?

—I'll think about it.

. . . Thinking of other times, of friendships made impossible by centuries which had nothing to do with the individuals concerned, by wars and public gulfs that even genuine affection couldn't bridge, she said to Esterka: Will you ride in my truck tomorrow?

—If you like. Good night.

. . . Thinking, and then not thinking. Listening to herself. She was alone then, and the green walls of her tent seemed particularly confining. She turned down the flame of the lantern that hung from a hook in the center pole of the pyramidal tent. These were the final minutes of precious solitude before the six other women, with whom she and Bronka shared the tent, came back to their cots for the night.

They would talk, giggle, gossip, complain, and confide. She did not want to think, fearing dreams.

Night fell like death, abruptly. It was a darkness without time. All about her, crouched in the corners of her eyes, were the terrible things of her memory and imagination. She could not see them because there was no light. She did not dare to open her eyes for fear that the terrible moving things would acquire an identity. She could hear the moving things gathering behind her. Her heart clenched like a fist. She lay quivering under an icy sheet, while the darkness gathered to fall upon her with a savage cry, and she prepared her own triumphant wail of terror and pain, and all creation plotted against her survival.

. . . In sleeplessness, dark thoughts launched their assault and mocked her loneliness, that pit that yawned beneath all their yearnings: their constant reproach to the world and to themselves. In a greater sense, this was not a personal anguish but a bewildered query directed at the times, and the times' allies who traded off small loyalties against justification of a greater treason. Each night was a gibbering assembly of derisive ghosts wrenched out a history filled with similar betrayals. Beyond the myriad dark things moving in the night, there were living beings for whom this huge political rejection of their country and their own humanity was a personal loss.

Oblivion was something to long for, sleep was a fearful horror to resist, awakening was a slow nightmare of blindness and perplexity. She was smothered by darkness. The darkness was an icy stone roof against which she arched her back until it seemed ready to break. The darkness was a thick obscenity forced down her throat by faceless tormentors. She heard creaking voices that babbled meaningless endearments, and names that had become alien symbols. She was adrift in a suffocating memory that enveloped her like the stench of a charnel house: the white nights in the heart of darkness in which she had lived, in which something essential to her humanity had seeped out of her.

Then, mercifully, she had died and moved toward the daily resurrection. Out of death toward life, toward light. She was warm, not cold. Under a white sheet on an army cot, not impaled under ice. Daylight came so quickly that she had no time to remember how she had overcome her tormentors to fall asleep. Dawn came with trumpets: She returned to Herself. She could see the pale outlines of the other women to her left and right, and she marveled to see how tame her world could be, how unthreatening were the shadows that had vanished.

(The trumpeter blows reveille. The bright-faced women run from their conical tents, form ranks, face the morning . . . brightly. In rows of cocked berets, in neat pale khaki dresses cinched with huge military belts. In filled-out bodies and reconstructed spirits. In the golden brightness of a Mediterranean morning, in the land of milk and honey and plum jam and all the white bread and margarine that God could manufacture. Then roll call: Present, present, present! Companies report! All present or accounted for. One does not think of those who are permanently absent, those whose names belong to the night, those for whom no one will ever be able to account, for they had fallen by the wayside, they've stayed behind in another lifetime which dies with each morning for the length of the day. The companies will come to the position of attention. Atten-SHUN! Face the morning music. The anthem. The ancient invocation. Bow the head for prayer. About-face, dismiss to breakfast, brightly begin a predictable military day.)

If she could live like this, in the predictable and ordained, without night! But she could not. For night, like day, is a matter of spirit. A new day could contain both beauty and life, she knew, if only she could recall where to look for them. They could be found where they had always been: in the heart and spirit. Having lived close to death, she wasn't tempted to assume that the sun rises and sets only in the world outside. The day burns and the night falls endlessly within each separate and lonely human being, she knew, and all of them, in their infinite variety of goodness and evil, were needed to provide the world's light and darkness, and all the passions of life and death that lie between the start and finish of the journey may be designed just to that end of final recognition of what we've always known within ourselves without understanding what we knew.

Then again the dust, a road: brown vistas unfolding under an aloof sky innocent of cloud. Through the dust cloud hung above the road, the sun was a red stain in a yellow sky. Let future critics argue (she thought) that the sun is never red in daytime in these latitudes, that it is white or yellow and that the sky is blue, like the Mediterranean in which it is reflected, then let them drive a Bedford truck in a column of Bedfords through the thick powdery yellow dust that billows a quarter of a mile up into the sky. She eased the Bedford into lower gear as the grade increased toward the foothills where the pass began, leaned out of the window to peer through the dust. The huge brown snowcapped mountains whose name she had forgotten lay across her horizon like a barrier to all her definitions.

—What's the name of those mountains? she said.

—The Heights of Golan, Esterka informed her.

—It's the border, then?

—For some people it's a border, Esterka said.

—But for you it isn't?

—No more than the Vistula would ever be your border. Everything here is historically ours from the Nile to the Euphrates, no matter what borders have been penciled into maps.

—It may take you a few hundred years to get it.

—What's a few hundred years after thousands? Esterka said. We have the time. And please don't tell me about the need to recognize the historic rights of the Arabs.

—I envy you this single-minded certainty, Catherine said.

—Everything is possible if you are totally committed to a principle.

Then they were silent, peering through the dust cloud; they would begin the winding ascent into the pass in less than an hour. Somewhere behind them nineteen other lorries had disappeared in the dust, yet she knew that they were safer on this road than she; she drove the first truck in the column. Were there to be an ambush, her Bedford would be the first to be exposed. But this meant remarkably little to her then, for nothing seemed impossible for the re-created Catherine, and she exulted in this discovery.

Rocking and swaying through the dust among gray-brown rocks glittering with mica, she passed caravans of camels and of goats and women, the women swathed in black and staring up at her with palable curiosity through their oiled leather masks; and fierce-eyed men in green and yellow turbans who paced beside their docile flocks of animals and women with shining bandoliers crisscrossed on their chests. The men's eyes fixed on her like talons, they held their long cruel ornamented rifles cradled with infinite care in their arms. To them she was unclean, an abomination: a woman who held her face naked for the world to see.

Heading toward the mountains and the windswept passes, she drove into the desert: raw brown escarpments streaked with the green-moss stain of turquoise and yellow with jasper, under which mud-walled villages and vast black pavilions of the nomads' tents crouched like sleeping beasts out of the times before history. Suddenly she was overjoyed to be out and away from the coastal regions that were overrun by regiments and soldiers: the army with its convoys, requisitioning detachments, depots and training camps, its cities of tents and marching companies, its hospitals and orphanages and artillery parks and rumbling tanks and motor pools and workshops. When she could see no more soldiers, trucks, fluttering multicolored pennants, the trampled white parade grounds, the smoke of cookhouse chimneys, but saw instead only the vast expanse of deserts dotted with their infrequent caravans and villages, when she could see only grazing herds of goats and of oxen, and the occasional lone horseman galloping along the horizon, she looked at them as though she were seeing all of this, and all that this implied, for the first time. What moved her and pleased her the most were the young women she passed near the village wells: barefooted and bangled and looking shyly at the apparition she must have presented, and laughing among themselves and chattering in shrill birdlike voices; young and healthy women without dozens of officers hanging about every one of them.

. . . Which brought Abel to mind once again, for a moment. And she was finally thinking about him as better than he seemed, as a man who could express more than most men can feel because he felt more than most men were capable of expressing. Such men were bound to do some damage wherever they went; she thought that she could afford to be tolerant. It would do small harm to see him once again. One word to Bronka and Kepi would report her whereabouts to him . . . and Catherine shrugged and smiled because Kepi's hatred for her had become proverbial; poised at the point when hatred comes full circle and becomes self-love, it had become so intense and impersonal as to be meaningless. She would make this yet another entry in her lexicon of hatreds: hatred in the name of a love and a loyalty to a past that had never been more than imagination, yet it was something that she and Kepi had shared with a dead old man. It had seemed to her that all life was composed of an unending variety of hatreds, some old and recently disinterred and some so new as to appear as original inventions, and all of them were rooted in the memory of someone loved and dead.

Now the wind was raw and she remembered that this was still winter. January had just about ended and in two more weeks (if she recalled correctly) Abel would have a birthday. This was the first month in the first year that Catherine had not been part of the life of a man. It was Year One of her personal revolution and concern solely with herself, yet perhaps life could be made considerably richer. Really, she told herself, what kind of barbaric centuries have we passed through to come to this point; a woman can't measure her years by the men in whom she had believed or those who had constructed their own fantasies around her: sooner or later such years could end only in bitterness and complaint. But a wholly self-centered life was not the answer, the present must always be a compromise between the future and the past. The stained-glass Madonnas had been cracked in Russia, the fogs of the tundra had obliterated the placid smile and the gently-folded hands and that traditionally unquestioning tranquillity on which men depended, and yet she knew that no one could ever belong entirely to oneself.

Miracles did exist, after all.

There was the miracle of finding Emil; the miracle of survival and of growth despite a plethora of diminishing circumstances, of faith in herself and all her possibilities . . . these were not to be discounted by any means.

The road was twisting violently among precipitous gullies; she slammed the Bedford into lower gear. Caution was the password for this day. She would set about the reconstruction of her miracles once this day was over.

—Tell me about your future, she said to Esterka.

—Why? Are you thinking about yours?

—I have been.

—Does it depend entirely on yourself?

—Not entirely. But how do you see yourself next year? The year after that?

—That doesn't depend entirely on myself.

—I really thought that I could live independently of everyone else, Catherine said. But that doesn't really work very well, does it?

—No, said Esterka. It doesn't.

—But what would you like?

—Oh, what we'd all like. Peace, stability, a home, work that is useful . . . self-respect.

—Affection?

—Oh, certainly, affection.

—Will you have children?

—That's almost a duty.

—Where will you live?

—In the country. That's where I'd like to live. But that's something else that doesn't depend entirely on myself.

—Wherever you live and whatever you do will be entirely new.

—Do you really think so? For you, yes, the end of the war will mean the end of everything. Whatever you create for yourselves will have to be new. But for us there'll be only the oldest idea in the world, a fight for our lives.

—You chose it.

—Was there really a choice?

—This sounds like something I've heard all my life.

—I told you, there's no such thing as a wholly new idea, just new people discovering something they must have, something that other people have forgotten. We can use our discoveries in new ways, perhaps, but the idea is always the same.

—You've changed so much in the last two years.

—So have you.

—Most of it seems to be only on the surface. Your changes seem to be somehow permanent.

—They only seem that way.

—Do you remember the talk we had, in that first village where we came with Kobza after the camp uprising?

—Yes, I do.

—I didn't think we'd ever talk to each other again, after that.

—Are we really talking?

—Perhaps we're even listening to each other now.

—It's best to part as friends, Esterka said quietly.

In her mind she was writing her letter to Abel. She wrote: I have changed, have you? Could we meet? No, it won't be under the rampant billy goat on Dominikanska, and nothing important is going to happen between us, it's too late for that; too much has happened to us separately, we have been severed from each other by our experiences not united by them; but could we be friends? Could we act as each other's allies in a world populated entirely by strangers? Is it too late for kindness? Surely there is more to our lives than mute cruelty, indifference, the betrayal of a friend's trust, the looting of another's pride, the abuse of devotion, the inability to give without expecting at least as much in return, the rationalization and justification of our own selfishness and greed, the cowardice in the face of responsibility whereby we are so swift to forgive ourselves for the injuries that we inflict on others . . . If nothing that happens to us is an accident, then shouldn't we believe, again, in the coincidence of affection? And if so, then (surely!) simple friendship is still possible . . .

Later, at the mouth of the pass, where she brought the Bedford to a halt so that the column might close up, so that the twenty trucks could make the difficult ascent together among the precipitous ravines, Catherine said: To part as friends? That's still possible, then?

—I don't see why not, Esterka said.

—But what if it's not?

—Some respect for each other's viewpoint is as good as friendship.

—That's not quite the same thing. And anyway, can anyone ever truly respect another's viewpoint?

—No, I suppose not, Esterka said, and laughed suddenly. Imagine what would happen to us all if we could do that! How would we manage to have hostility and bitterness and anger and contempt? What would we do for hatred? We'd have no choice but to love each other, and isn't *that* an outlandish idea? Imagine what would happen to us all if we ever tried *that*.

—I'd like to be able to imagine it, Catherine said.

—But isn't there always some kind of martyrdom involved in that kind of thing?

—I haven't thought much about martyrs lately, Catherine said. If Father Boguslawski were alive he'd tell us about it.

—Or if Poremba were alive, Esterka said quietly. There was a man who had no respect for anybody's viewpoint, not even his own. That is the best kind of martyr.

—Is Mendeltort also a sort of martyr, then? Catherine said, and Esterka laughed.

—Oh, certainly. Every idea must have its saints and martyrs. Otherwise how could anyone believe in it? And when a man decides that he is an idea . . . well, that's practically a godhead! But one God is quite enough for us, so Mendeltort has turned out to be *not* such a good idea.

—I feel sorry for him, Catherine said.

—Why? Have you ever met him?

—No.

—I never have either. But I did believe in him. I suppose when you believe in someone that gives that person a reality. And when you can no longer believe in a person that makes them unreal.

—And if that person is no longer real then he or she becomes an illusion, is that it?

—Sooner or later, that's how it seems to be, Esterka said. And who but an utter fool would follow an illusion?

—What will you do about Mendeltort, then? Can't you get him away from the British?

—Oh, I suppose we could. But what would we do with him once we'd got him? No one would follow him. No one needs him now. His usefulness is over even to himself. If he is still useful to anyone it is to the British.

—I keep thinking about what you said last night, Catherine said. I keep remembering what Itzek Fogel said. I suppose that you are going to have Mendeltort killed?

—I? Esterka said. How can I have anybody killed?

—Your husband, then? Your organization? Because there was something very odd about our talk last night . . .

—I have no idea of what you're talking about, Esterka said.

. . . We have not seen or spoken to each other for such a long time, Catherine would write to Abel, our lives have not touched each other's through so many events, that I don't know if real human contact is still possible for us. The coincidence of affection is a perishable matter. It tends to wither, like any other living plant, if it is neglected.

. . . I've had some disillusioning moments lately, some involvements which invariably turn out to be exhausting and depleting, proving once again the folly of expecting honesty where none can possibly exist. But there have been some good moments too, so I don't write from a sense of bitterness. I am alive and so are you and the material problems of survival seem to be nearing their own solution, and how long has it been since either of us could have been sure of that? Yet I find that the light which, traditionally, is supposed to appear at the end of this sort of tunnel, is another illusion. Material things have become totally immaterial to me while my so-called human connections show themselves to be wholly materialistic despite their claim on humanity and the like . . . It's really an amusing situation.

. . . This makes me skeptical of all suddenly resurrected claims on my affection, or even on my interest. I am sure that you can understand how I can feel that way since, I suspect, the same must be true for you . . . But in the cause of nourishing our own particular affection, there are some things that ought to be made clear. I wouldn't want either of us to follow an illusion.

. . . Always before (before what? Perhaps before Russia. Or before the growing process into maturity could begin) I sought real human contact as proof of my own humanity. No, not those mindless gymnastics with a procession of boring opportunists, disloyal husbands, or confused adolescents seeking reassurance, but those providential comings-together of people, that sense of instant recognition which has been so terribly spoiled by the pragmatists as well as the romantics. That's what I thought you were. And if, indeed, you had been that for me then you were the last. I am starting a long journey back to my beginnings, if you have any idea what that means, now that our greater journey is coming to its end. Certainly, I want to continue to care for you and to help you whenever no one else can give you what you need, but our common past is dead, whatever happens between us from now on will have to be new and none of our connections can have anything to do with whatever I had felt about you before—or you about me. Yes, I am still capable of feeling that depth of commitment, but I can no longer deprive myself of anything for anyone's sake. I am sure that, eventually, the day will return when I shall be able to give more than I receive from another person but, at this moment, I can give only what I get, and I don't want anything important. I don't think that any of this is at all unfeeling. (I have no quarrels with anyone's private choices.) It is only a matter of confronting one's reality and saying a final No to abuse and to exploitation—and that includes the abuse of hope that we all foist upon our expectations—and to that peculiar mechanism that constructs our private romantic illusions.

. . . I know that no man can ever accept the idea that he can become no more important than any other man to the woman who had loved him, who had wanted him, who had made him the center of her life. His need to be the unique experience in the life of a woman, his need to think himself unforgettable, can't tolerate equality with all other men. That too is a paradox in a life of paradoxes, don't you think? But that is beside the point I am making.

. . . The point is that Yes, you *had* been all these things to me, but you are no longer. I had wanted you to be the man around whom an entirely new life could be built, but such ideas died in Russia with all our other dreams. Both of us must exist independently of each other's lives. I offer you my friendship and affection, nothing more than that is possible for me at this point. It's possible that this is all that I shall ever be able to offer.

. . . Why have I written all this? (Indeed, Catherine thought: shall I even write it?) Not to hurt you, but to reassure you. Because the subject was with us, unspoken because it wasn't understood, but present nonetheless, at No. 3 Dominikanska Street, in the *fin de siècle* rooms where we had begun to construct a beautiful illusion, and it should no longer be a part of either your consciousness or mine.

. . . If what may happen between us now, dear Abel (Catherine knew that she would write when the day was over), is really as good as it might prove to be, being based in honesty and mutual affection and on living our lives as they *are* rather than as they might be lived in someone else's dream, then let us meet again. Kepi, who'll bring this letter to you, will tell you where I am . . .

And then she was braking the Bedford to a sudden halt.

—What is it? she cried, although she knew that the boulders piled across the road in terrible symmetry were not an accidental landslide.

(No, not this orderly construction which was suddenly erupting in smoke and the crashing roars of automatic weapons!) The dust that soared high above the ridges obscured the assault.

Shock made her dizzy, her movements were mechanical. Terror would come in moments, as soon as the imagination could break free of ice . . . Ice closed upon her heart again, a howling wilderness opened in her brain. Dear God, she cried within herself: Why now?

—Ambush, she screamed above the crashing roars, and the Bedford slewed across the road, broadside to the barricade. But whose? Why? To what end? Dear God, she thought: to die like this, for nothing, when it was all over . . . when it was no longer necessary for anyone to die . . . Dear God, would there never be anything but this unending demonstration of Your huge contempt?

The Bedford tilted, running up the side of the mountain. It groaned with rent metal, hissed with steam as the radiator burst. My poor dear beast, she thought, as another truck ran into her own.

—No! she heard Esterka say as she reached for the rifle clipped between the seats. No! Don't do anything and no one will be hurt!

—But why! Catherine cried.

—We need your trucks, Esterka was saying. Don't do *anything!* We don't want to hurt anyone . . .

—Oh, God *damn* you all! Catherine cried . . .

. . . All.

(No matter who you are, and where you have come from, and where you are going; without concern for your hopes and dreams and ideologies, your slogans and symbols, your sufferings and your needs; with no regard for your claims and their justifications, and for your rights and for the nobility of your motives; all of you for whom such words as *Freedom, Mercy, Justice* are understood in only one language and apply only to yourselves . . . for whom pride-in-self has become love-of-self, and pride in separateness from all other people has replaced a consciousness of indivisible humanity; you pietists who use another for your sacrifices, who trifle with another's self-respect and inflict indignity, for whom the precious objects of another's caring are to be used for a moment's mindless pleasure).

—Damn you!

—No! cried Esterka. Sit still!

But Catherine was already half out of the Bedford, her rifle in her hands.

. . . From the rear of the invisible column, invisible because shrouded in dust and in smoke, came the crunch and crump of grenades exploding, the tympany of bullets pinging off the boulders; showers of stone were rolling down the mountainside and, in a moment, an acrid chemical fog was drifting toward her and curling upward into the narrow neck of the pass before the barricade. Someone was shouting behind this stone barrier, and waving a white cloth, and the firing dwindled, and she thought with a vast shudder of relief: Well, at least no one *has* been hurt . . . they've just been shooting to make sound! And then a Sten gun spluttered tinnily in the dust-and-phosphorus cloud, and a white line of bullets ripped across the boulders, and she thought: Oh God . . . Someone is firing back at them . . . And, immediately, rifles were snapping and crackling all around the column, and the tearing sound of machine-pistol bursts slanted through the dust cloud.

. . . A truck was burning: black smoke billowed hugely.

Someone ran past, with shrill cries.

Esterka was on her knees beside her, tugging at her rifle. The man with the white cloth had dived down behind the barricade of boulders.

—Don't shoot! Esterka cried. Don't shoot!

And, at once, Catherine's hand tightened upon her rifle and a bullet crashed out and winged into the side of the mountain, and another white-phosphorus grenade crumped among the trucks, and a fresh wave of chemical miasma ascended her nostrils.

—Stop it! Esterka cried. Don't shoot! If only you'd stop shooting . . . ! We don't want to hurt anyone!

—But why are you doing this at all?

—We need two Bedfords!

—What? Why?

—Bedfords! Esterka cried. Army lorries! Oh, why don't you people ever understand? We need them to get into Latrun . . .

—What?

—The Latrun Barracks, the fort near Lydda . . . to get Mendeltort.

In tears now, Catherine was convulsed with hysterical laughter.

A spray of bullets stitched the dust beside her, kicked up a row of flowers and shrubs and bushes fashioned out of soil in which nothing had grown for centuries of arid stillness . . . Oh, but, she knew, such stillness is always deceptive . . .

She ducked, hugged the earth, then looked up.

. . . Saw a woman running.

Saw the ungraceful round body leap as though someone had pushed her hard between the shoulder blades.

—Honest to God, she heard herself muttering, and felt her throat tightening upon fear, and prayed chaotically as the ungainly running woman stopped and doubled over and went down upon her knees with arms outstretched as if to pick the sudden flowers of dust . . .

—Honest to God, she said while she saw and heard nothing, while the fallen woman folded herself quietly in the dust.

Catherine felt nothing then. Catherine was running. Her rifle lay discarded, her mind was awry with pity and with shock and with bitterness and anger. She was wholly conscious of futility. She was aware of Esterka running beside her, behind a white mask into which black eyeholes and a twisted mouth had been burned by grief.

. . . Only a moment ago, she thought as she looked at Bronka, in the morning hours . . . among the trumpet calls. Hope. Life. A future. Illusions. Expectations.

And others were running

A man had climbed onto the barricade of boulders and shouted and waved his arms, and the firing stopped, and lean, bronzed men were sliding down the sides of the mountains, and they were leaping across the barricade, and she saw Traurig coming at a run.

Bronka's entire back was bubbling with blood. Kepi had turned her face-down across his knees so that the blood wouldn't flood back into her throat and choke her; her purpling mouth opened around a word but only a thin whistling sound was coming out of it. Esterka held her hands and splashed her with tears.

The women drivers were huddled in a dusty group.

—If only you hadn't fired back at us, Esterka was saying, and Traurig, who was no longer pale but bronzed, drew her upward against his chest and stroked her dusty hair.

. . . And would he now put his booted foot upon the carcass, Catherine thought without bitterness or anger, and have his photograph taken with the trophy? His dark face had closed about his scars but his eyes were full of sorrow and pity and pain.

Kepi mourned.

He had torn open the back of Bronka's uniform to stop the bleeding but the young woman's plump white back had been too cruelly butchered; she had been torn open from shoulder to shoulder, and now she flexed her knees, and then her shoulders moved once, commandingly, as if to shrug off this last indignity of naked dying before strangers, and she sighed an acceptance of her role.

Dead flesh, Catherine thought. Alive a moment earlier, going to love only the night before. Now only another corpse on a pile of offal that never stopped growing. The jaws of agony were closing on her throat;

when would it end, this immemorial ritual of appeasement of temporary Gods . . . this killing for causes in which only the innocent and the unimportant were thrown upon the altars? Oh, let it all end, finally and forever. Let there be no more sacrifices, no more Gods. Let men kill their Gods, for a change, so that life on earth may acquire value.

Her clenched fists twitched and jumped and she looked at them, and raised them as though to beat upon a grave, and looked upward into a mild blue sky.

PART EIGHT

IN THE MONTH OF NISAN

Abel

IN THE DARK, THERE SEEMED TO BE NO SKY but only galaxies spread out beyond imaginable spaces. With sunrise, the particles of the world would acquire identity, now they displayed no labels. Yet there was a small passing whiteness sliding silently between the sky and the air above the arid plain below the escarpment: the barely audible hum of trucks inching toward the checkpoint under the balcony.

Behind his back, behind the blackout curtains, the party to which no one had wanted to come went on, the smiles awry and frozen into lines of weary resignation. He listened to the harsh grating American voices of the guests of honor, to the polished and uncertain phrases of his own dispirited countrymen, and heard in them a foretaste of their lives to come. He drank from his bottle. His embarkation orders seemed to have acquired the weight of Sinaic tablets in his left breast pocket.

He thought about Italy, where war awaited him, then thought beyond the muddy limitations of a war into a time of peace, a time of no killing. Below the balcony, the convoy of kibbutz trucks was inching past the checkpoint which, on this night, was occupied by officers of the Palestine Police Force and Arab Legion soldiers. The trucks were winding past the shuttered hostile faces like a routed army; the hatred flowed back and forth between the searchers and the searched like an electric current powerful enough to illuminate all the nights to come. His own contempt was focused upon the visiting Polish-American delegation: upon the Millionaire whose crude self-satisfaction seeped through the blackout curtains, upon the Politician and the Fat Priest and the Small-town Lawyer and upon the Drunken Dentist whom everyone was trying to avoid.

The balcony had provided him with a temporary refuge from the party behind the blackout curtains; the curtains, so unnecessary in the warm, safe Palestinian night, so many air miles distant from German bomber bases, allowed the conversation to reach him as filtered particles. It was a party that had gone on too long, and they were all tired of each other and of themselves, and of this contrived celebration of an anniversary which no one honored in the country from which they had come. Five colonels, ten lieutenant colonels, and twenty-odd majors, each carefully chosen for the number of multicolored ribbons he could pin above his left breast pocket, were the humiliating proof of how desperately the Polish Government in London was trying to win some influential friends in these final hours of its recognized existence. The Katyn story had made them seem a party to a Nazi slander of a gallant ally, the Russians had already broken off diplomatic relations with the Polish Government, and the Western Allies were sure not to be far behind. A Polish National Committee of Liberation was functioning in Moscow, complete with its own new generals, of whom few Poles had ever heard, and all the poor wretches who had not managed to reach the army before it sailed from Russia—and this included all the Jews and the Byelorussians and the Ukrainians whom the NKVD had barred from the army—were being conscripted into this committee's Polish People's Army, whose eagles had their crowns shorn away. Berling was now a Russian general in Polish uniform, and there was also a General Szymanski in this Polish army (along with several hundred other Russians who had Polish names), and Meyer was a colonel in charge of political education, and that was quite enough to tell what kind of Polish army this would be and what kind of state machinery it would impose on Poland once the war was over.

Because such thoughts brought to mind the bad faith of allies, treasons and betrayals, he thought of Mendeltort, as he had seen him only hours earlier, then as the man he had known in boyhood and youth: the kind of man who laughs out loud when he reads Aristophanes in Greek, the kind who knows that factual truth was not important in a Polish story, or a Jewish one, where only spiritual truths had ever counted.

In the hot dry night below the balcony, beyond the officers' cars and the Americans' borrowed limousines parked in their own shadows against the hotel wall, the kibbutz trucks were halted at the barbed wire of the checkpoint, and Abel thought, ironically, in keeping with the conversation behind the blackout curtains, that nowhere did these people (whichever of my Peoples I'm talking about) show a greater spirit of compromise than in straddling a traffic lane. His mild cynicism, he knew, was his own compromise in a century which no longer tolerated neutrality. This century, this civilization of which he had thought himself a part, whose distinctive contribution to the art of government has been the concentration camp, were hardly in position to look down upon and to condemn a man who could kill.

(Driving back to the town, and to the party for the Millionaire and the Politician and the Fat Priest and the Small-town Lawyer and the Drunken Dentist, an artificial celebration of a "Hero's Birthday"—a *Hero of Two Continents* who would have been appalled were he there to be honored—he had begun to explain Mendeltort to the British colonel and, he supposed, to himself. But one can't explain an elemental force without a complete system of equations, for here the mathematics of existence had come into play. Courage plus Endurance may . equal Survival, but to say such things to Colonel Hudson would have done little good. Instead he had explained, feeling the hot anger that comes from humiliation at the need to explain: No, never a monster . . . Driven beyond the bounds of reason, perhaps, and who are you to judge him? No, you don't know this man; you judge him by those of his acts which are convenient to your private legend. For all his monstrous acts—and Dair Yassir will always be monstrous, beyond justification—this man is more than a mere military psychopath. The public man is not the private man I've known. Under the ruthless man of war, the remorseless soldier who fought and killed again and again until his enemies had learned to think of him as murder incarnate, there is another man: the son of a Vilno tailor who had walked to Warsaw with a stolen young bride and with one steel needle hidden in the lapel of his black alpaca coat, and with a vast dynastic dream surging in his head . . . This man is the product of an old man's dream, he is feared by empires because he wishes to make an empire, a Russian princeling who had helped to make a revolution that abolished princes; this is a man beset by an infinite loneliness, the true solitude of greatness, who knows that greatness is everything that men have to do to cope with their smallness, yet longing always for the opposite of what he has to be; a legend shouldered unwillingly by a man who needed no more than the warm healing understanding intimacy that overcomes shyness . . . a contradiction built out of a certainty . . . *Oh, come now, come now, Abel,* said Derek Bellancourt, *the man is not a God. He is not even a justifiable idea* . . . There was a flame in him, Abel said, a fire kindled millennia ago that had never been allowed to flicker out and which burned in him stronger than in others, and there were times when he couldn't keep the wind from the outer darkness from blowing in on him and fanning this fire into a conflagration . . . but that's what happens to a man like that when he's so much alone . . . But Colonel Hudson had looked merely embarrassed.)

Thinking of Mendeltort as he had seen him last, bowed brokenly in

shackles in a white-painted cell designed by Pavlovian experts to give
the eye no reference point, to convince a prisoner of his helplessness, he
was convulsed with nausea, remembering his own Russian cell. He listened to the boom and snap of thunder threading out surprisingly
through the whine of motors on the Latrun Road, carried by the warm
wind from the dark massif of the escarpment that lay below the town.
The sky was clear, the stars were abundant, the thunder was surely an
anomaly: a storm in a clear sky . . . Yet such things were possible in
this ancient land where a darkness could come at noon in the month of
Nisan to end one civilization and to begin another.

He waited for this night to end, for all his own endless nights to pass
into light, for the unhurried dawn, and for a resolution of his contradictions which seemed to span the spaces behind the stars.

Below the balcony, Kepi said: Well, so we're going tomorrow?

And Itzek Fogel said: We're going, but what for?

And another soldier said: What do they have in that Italy, anyway?

And Kepi said: They've got olives and mules and mountains and mud
and a million Germans.

—And spaghetti, Itzek Fogel said.

—What's spaghetti? said the other soldier.

—It's something you can eat, Itzek Fogel said.

—I've got something you can eat, Kepi said.

—Ah, Kepi, Itzek Fogel said. Will you ever change?

—How do I know? Kepi said, then went on in a voice gone dark with
bitterness and hatred: Change . . . change . . . there's never anything
new. Just when you think that something good's going to happen to
you, when you start to believe that maybe there's something fine for
you somewhere . . . ah, that's when God starts laughing.

—You'll get over it, Itzek Fogel said. Nobody mourns forever.

—I'll get over it when I'm dead, Kepi said.

—So she's dead, Itzek Fogel said. So are you the only man who lost
somebody? Among all these thousands of us, you're the only one?

—I can't tell about thousands, Kepi said. I only know about me. And
I'm telling you a man's a fool if he thinks anything can change.

—Nothing is ever the same, Itzek Fogel said.

—Ah, what the hell do you know, you crazy little Yid?

—Well, Itzek Fogel said, *some* things stay the same, ha ha . . .

—That's what I'm telling you, Kepi said, you crazy old bastard.
What're you doing in our army anyway? Why aren't you deserting with
all them other bastards? That's what you all came here for, isn't it?

—Must be some other bastards, Itzek Fogel said.

—Someday I'll find that Traurig. Then I'll kill the bastard.

—There's always somebody for a man to hate, if that's what he wants.

And Kepi said: I don't want to hate anybody, but what else can a man do? A man's a fool to think it can ever be different . . .

And Itzek Fogel said: I know. It's a choice a man makes, I think.

In his own Russian cell, now brought back to mind so vividly, where he had been the only sentient object between the wall, the bucket, and the electric light bulb, Abel had known that he was going to die and then he had not died and nothing would ever be quite so bad again. Hanged by his thumbs with Pavlovian logic before the featureless white-painted wall, he had been shown the step-by-step procedures of his own inevitable destruction, the natural and never-to-be-questioned fate and condition of the prisoner, yet this fate had been deferred, put aside: he had been reprieved. Since boyhood he had been unable to tolerate mediocrity or to accept the possibility that he was merely one individual among many, one straw among thousands hung upon the wind, and this forced gathering of officers who had too much to do to waste their time here, and of scurrying civilians who seemed designed by an ironic-minded Providence to bow and scrape before such imitation dignitaries as the visitors from America, turned his anger inward. Yet he had found, just as Mendeltort had told him that he would, that the valley of hopelessness and fear does not keep descending forever; somewhere there is a bottom, eventually bedrock can be found, then a man can start to climb again. He had sat in the Police Superintendent's office in the Latrun Barracks with Derek Bellancourt and Colonel Hudson, who had brought him there, and sipped liqueurs in stale air and waited for his uncle to be brought to him, and shut his mind against the memory of their meeting in the Lubyanka (when their roles had been so ironically reversed) and swore to himself that he would not identify him to the British . . . But Mendeltort had had his own ideas about that.

Something had crystallized in that agonized head, Abel knew: one ice-cold thought, reduced to diamond clarity and hardness refining the experience of millennia, had led this man far, so far as to make him seem wholly unrelated to his own beginnings. A thought had led him far enough to reject the entire mental system of the world in which he had been born and in which he lived; it carried him to the peaks of the most isolated loneliness, where rulers of empires had begun to fear him, while to many others, perhaps millions of helpless and uncertain others, he had become that new thing: the Light from the Pit. Looking at Mendeltort in the Latrun interrogation cage, Abel had suddenly known what heretofore he had been able to suspect, even to assume, without comprehension: that a single event in a single mind may sometimes change the world. For generations, more so in his than in any others, the world had been awash with movements and theories of history that discounted individuals as makers of history; but history was as unpredictable as the human mind in which ideas were born. That sudden opening and the sudden dawning of something in the mind of this unaccountably aged and broken man in the Latrun cage—a man who would make no apologies for anyone's barbarism, not even his own— found an immediate echo in Abel's shocked brain.

No, he had begun to say, I don't know this fellow, and Mendeltort was smiling with his broken mouth, beyond acknowledgment of pain and of feeling, and saying: But I want you to identify me, I've been counting on it . . . But I don't want to be the one that betrays you, Abel whispered back. ·

. . . And Mendeltort was no longer smiling, saying softly: Oh, that has been done, someone else did that, and there'll be something else that he'll have to do . . . because we Jews believe that our souls live on in memory, and in the remembrance of our friends, and in our influence on their lives, and it's time to bring this legend to an end. Of course, if I'd had children I'd live in them too. But we've been spared that complication.

(Then he was winking broadly.)

. . . If I may interrupt this sentimental journey into the Jewish soul, said Colonel Hudson. Is this the man you know as Avrum Mendeltort? He is an ordinary monster who thinks of murder in metaphysical terms, you should have no qualms about identifying him; now be a good chap . . . Actually, old man, said Derek Bellancourt, it's quite immaterial whether you identify Mendeltort for us or not; we know who he is, don't you see, but it's nice to keep everything tidy, wouldn't you agree? Of course, in the end, I shouldn't think it would make a terrible lot of difference . . .

(Abel had nodded, said: No, I shouldn't think so.)

Ah, but a monster? That wasn't how Abel remembered the ironic man who had given him his first edition of Mickiewicz bound in blue leather and embossed with gold. This was a man beyond ordinary comprehension, who thought in quite impersonal terms of terror and killing, and Abel could see suddenly beyond the terror into the millennia of resistance and rebellions and acts of desperation and of the unaccountable follies of his People (whichever of my Peoples I'm thinking about), and he could see in this testament of reasoned violence a People who refused to be only victims.

(Really, old man, Derek Bellancourt had said. Why do you chaps always make things so terribly difficult for yourselves? Why do you refuse to help us in searching for your deserters? They are *your* deserters, you brought them here, you know . . . Why don't you feel a sense of responsibility for what such people do, or will do if they're given the slightest chance to do it? We don't enjoy our role as Roman proconsuls who must keep assorted barbarians from murdering each other, but can you imagine what will happen here once we've gone? They'll be murdering each other forever in the name of freedom . . . Fellows like this one, or that fellow Begin to whom you gave an honorable discharge . . . What do you have in common with people like that? Why do you protect them? It's hardly what one would expect from a loyal ally.)

Hardly, Abel said.

(After all, old man, it's not as though you had been so terribly kind to them in your own country, is it? said Colonel Hudson.)

To hell with all the legends, Abel said.

(So why don't you chaps be a little more cooperative? It's in your best interest . . . After all, your own position isn't so frightfully good, you know . . . It isn't very likely that you'll be going back to your own country, is it? . . . Oh, it's all terribly unfortunate, of course, and we're all terribly upset about it, but one does have to be realistic about that sort of thing . . .)

Indeed one does, Abel said.

. . . For something had begun to happen in Abel's own mind: an idea had flared, had hung momentarily suspended in a lurid glow, had begun to narrow to a pinpoint focus; a thought had begun to form, and he needed time for this thought to crystallize and harden and to acquire texture and a definition and all its dimensions: time for him to come to terms with this realization of who and what he was and what he could become, and neither the interrogation cage in the Latrun Barracks, nor the artificial celebration in this very good hotel, nor the balcony to which he had escaped from the celebration, was the place in which one could come to terms with anything. He needed time to understand what he had begun to feel. And it was not a matter of ideals or ideologies. It was the thought of an individual as a creator of events outside the laws of cause and effect, the rule that asserted that history —the endless story of the evolution of mankind—was governed by inevitability in which ideas were merely phantoms of the human brain . . .

And there was more, if a man could go beyond all his labels and his personal definitions.

So: Yes, he had said. This is Mendeltort. But a monster? No.

. . . And he was looking, then, through a gap in the blackout curtains, at the British colonel who wore a magnificent mane of white hair and a clipped white mustache, and who looked out at a precisely delineated world with clear blue and particularly penetrating eyes. Here, you would say instinctively, is the True Commander whom you'd be able to trust implicitly, but your instincts would be wrong: because those piercing eyes had not lighted on a battlefield since the opening days of a war two wars and three generations ago . . . And if you were to put your life in his hands you'd never get it back.

(Prison . . . God, prison! There were so many kinds of prisons that people constructed for themselves, and the smallness of their spirit wasn't the least of them, yet no man who had ever spent any appreciable time in a real prison, who could remember the emasculating sense of his own entrapment, the stench of his terror, the certainty of his own unavoidable destruction, ever could come near a chained and captive man without feeling himself imprisoned once again. If he could have denied the picture of Mendeltort in the British prison, as he had denied his longing for a life lived with dignity and reason in the country of his birth as well as of his choice, he would have done so, for he knew that anger was no substitute for fulfillments made impossible by events. He knew that he had only himself to blame for his varieties of anger no matter what he'd think about it afterward, in bed, beside whatever body he would have obtained behind the blackout curtains to help him into sleep. The accidental body, like the life upon which he would be embarking once the war was over, would be only a pale memory of a dream, an illusion of worth and valued affection, unless he could create whole new sets of definitions for life and for himself.)

. . . An image of a freckled knee swung across his head, a moment brought forward out of a vanished past and swiftly discarded . . .

In the deep shadows below the balcony, the soldiers were talking. He heard their soft voices, watched the glow of their cigarettes. The kibbutz trucks had vanished in the blackness under the escarpment where the passes wound toward Jerusalem among dark orange groves.

—They say the Americans told General Anders they'd put up a monument to him in New York if he'd just get us to fight for them in that Italy, Itzek Fogel said.

And Kepi said: Stupid sons of bitches.

And another soldier said: Why shouldn't the general get a monument?

And Kepi said: Because he don't need one. We're his fucking monument.

—And where do we go from that Italy? Itzek Fogel said. *Z ziemi włoskiej, do Polski?* Is it going to be like that again?

—That don't seem likely, said another soldier. We don't have a country any more. They gave the whole goddam thing to the fucking Russians.

—So what are we going to do when the war is over?

—If you're lucky, you won't live that long, Kepi said.

And Itzek Fogel said: I've lived long enough . . .

And another soldier said: I'd like to live longer. Maybe in America . . .

And Kepi said: You can be the general's monument in New York.

—And what about you, Kepi? Itzek Fogel said.

—Me? I don't know, Kepi said. They've killed my woman, they gave my country to the fucking Russians . . .

—There're other women, other countries, Itzek Fogel said.

—Not for a man like me, Kepi said.

—I don't even know how to talk American, said the other soldier.

—It's just like English, Itzek Fogel said. All you got to do is put a handful of walnuts in your mouth.

On the balcony, Abel closed his eyes and pretended that this was part of one continuous nightmare from which he'd soon awake, that he would wake beside Catherine and watch her smiling in her sleep, that the light in which he would see her would not be lying to him, that he would plan a day that would not be distressing, a day that would not end bleakly. He had so often felt numb at the thought of losing Catherine, unable to believe the good fortune of his conditional possession, that the reality of his loss left him comparatively calm, but it was the calmness of a desert, as though the passions that had moved him had all been spent and only the mystery remained, still unsolved. He could not pray. He could not contemplate the silent spaces of his mind as he had done in prison. There was nothing on earth to praise and nothing to ask for; faith itself seemed to have become no more than a deferment of ultimate disaster. Love? It had been his last handhold before the fall from grace into chaos, but he could no longer remember what it was about or how one went about it. The memory of Catherine had been the safety spike driven into the rock-face of his hopes on which his sanity had been hung . . . Yet she had worn her beauty so casually that he hadn't been properly aware of it until it lived only in his imagination, remembering detail of texture and dimension and color and sound (the freckled knee, a long tawny body turning in his hands, a lazy luxury of contour, a face that was wholly lenient moving down upon him) but oblivious of her totality.

In prison, he had begun to discover her as entirely human, not a character in his personal fictions, and now his sense of life was ready to expand correspondingly, but none of the contemptuously collected substitutes for Catherine seemed to do the trick. Much that had sometimes annoyed him about her (her forthright directness, her determination, her trust in the goodwill of charlatans and opportunists and her apparent inability to harbor contempt) had become something to long for and admire in a world in which nothing else was admirable. The fact that she lived life to the full within her self-imposed limits aroused a fierce delight and a sort of unbelieving tenderness, as well as terror that he would never be able to reach her through vulnerable innocence again. Because if she were still alive, or even somewhere here in the Middle East among the civilians or the army women, rescued from whatever camp or prison had been her personal Golgotha, how could innocence have remained a part of her reality? Yet, in some ways, she would have remained vulnerable, he knew, and wanted to warn her about people like himself.

Then he was listening to the conversations behind the blackout curtains, where the officers and their accidental women had frozen into poses like a Greek chorus preparing for the tragedy and farce of exile, like statues in an Italian garden with the night fallen upon the landscapes in which they belonged. Doomed as centaurs amid social smiles from which the light had fled several hours earlier, they were exchanging the glittering phrases that were so much a part of such vocabularies as his. We are as dazzling and original as Polish thought itself, he wanted to tell her, that thought which flows so swiftly into cast-iron molds and hardens into deadening concepts . . . He wanted to protect his unreal memory of Catherine against that witty meretricious Polish charm that could evaporate so quickly into injured vanity and hatred.

Yet he knew that he had idealized the invisible Catherine beyond any woman's capabilities; stripped of the hunger of his longing for perfection, the poet's vision unrolling in measured couplets of color and sound, she was only another woman, one of the indifferent procession of his many women, a mechanism for inducing sleep. We get our greatest pleasure from retroactive contempt, not the act of loving, he wanted to tell her, and even jealousy is no longer a strong human passion.

Behind the blackout curtains soomeone said ringingly: *Statistics are people with the tears wiped off*, and he began to laugh. As women lost their value to themselves, and became statistics, so men could only love them less, loving themselves more.

Now he could stare dry-eyed in his anger at the barren escarpment which gave its name to the road below the balcony, and to the orangy liqueurs that he had drunk on those heights in the afternoon. The Latrun Heights lay on the horizon to the west and south; against their large darkness and the larger darkness of the sky, the lights of the town flung out their own meretricious challenge. The wind was warm, thick with antique stenches, and Abel thought that he could smell his anger like a faint, sour fermentation in the air, but perhaps it was only the odor of the prison on the heights from which he had hurried to this celebration. The balcony had been as much a refuge from his memory of Catherine as from the other distressing events of the day.

(And he was listening to the talking soldiers, and measuring their vision of the futures and their essential selves against his own prospects and possibilities, and heard a small song that one of them began to hum: *Wojenko, wojenko* . . . Little Lady War . . . so necessarily feminine in gender.)

The wind, he noted, was becoming colder.

Then he became aware that someone had come out to join him on the balcony, turned and looked into Teodor Haussner's restless eyes; their glances darted back and forth like sparrows in search of a providential meal.

—Why are you out here all alone, Abel? Haussner said. Or could it be that our American half-brothers aren't quite to your taste?

—I don't know, Teo, Abel said.

—It's all good solid peasant fare, you know. Salt of the earth and all that. Their names speak for themselves, wouldn't you say? Mr. Rybka, who has made a fortune stuffing sausages, the Reverend Marchewka . . . oh, and the eminent Dr. Kapusta, so thoroughly pickled . . . all of it edible and dull as potatoes. . . . Don't they have anything in America except transplanted peasants?

—I can't remember, Teo.

—It's going to be quite awful living among people like that.

—Why must you live among them, Teo?

—Do I have a choice? Don't tell me *you* are thinking of going back to Poland when the war is over? I wouldn't believe such a thing if anyone had told me. . . .

—Whatever happened to your *Ascent from the Abyss?* Abel said.

—Eh? Oh, I'm working on it. It'll be quite splendid! What an indict-ment of the Bolshevist Tyranny. . . .

—As I recall your original intention . . .

—What do you mean, *my original intention?* How would you know my original intention? Of course, I had to *mask* my original intention . . . how else could it be? But now that we are free to decide for our-selves . . .

—I don't feel free to decide anything, Teo, Abel said.

—Dear Abel, you simply fret too much. Think of it all as progress.

—Ah, progress, Abel said. So that's what it is.

—That's how to look at it, Haussner said.

—Someone once told me that progress is when people trample over something beautiful that they no longer understand.

—Or need? Think about need, said Haussner. Even a tragedy should provide some new opportunities. I never understood our national mania for denouncing people who are able to seize an opportunity. Our Amer-ican half-brothers have something to teach us there.

—They probably do, Abel said.

Haussner shrugged, laughed briefly. —And to think that I had always thought you a contemporary man! Poland is an emotional booby trap filled with bits and pieces of broken lives and dreams . . . dear to us in memory, certainly, but gone! Gone, Abel! Our ruins are not just histori-cal monuments, you know. Good God, man, would you spend the rest of your life among debris?

—If that is all that I can remember.

—All that you must remember now is that not every man has a chance to be born twice.

—It seems you've always managed that well enough.

—Certainly. Why not? There is a far larger life to be lived outside ro-mantic little limitations. And why should it be unpatriotic to be com-fortable? Our American half-brothers have really managed it all much better than we have.

—But do they have a war to remember?

—I'm sure they would if it was useful to them. But, my dear fellow, war should be more than a memory. It is an event from which some-thing should be learned.

—But what, Teo? What?

—Whatever is useful! And that's for everyone to decide for himself. Some of those glittering gentlemen of ours are planning lives of gloomy exile, as a sort of walking reproach to the conscience of the world, and I assure you that's the last thing that the world will ever want to notice. Perhaps that way they might be able to delude themselves that their lives have some sort of importance. But will that be useful to anyone but themselves?

—I wouldn't know, Teo.

—You should think about it.

—Later, perhaps.

—This could all be an excellent opportunity. Our American half-brothers may be a crude and graceless lot but they've certainly done quite well for themselves. And here they are, to bestow their patronage, and we're all very glad to take it, aren't we?

—It's too soon for that.

—Too soon for what? And why is it too soon?

—There is still a war.

—Oh that, Haussner said.

—Yes, there is that.

—Brrr, Haussner said. It's getting cold out here.

—It's not long to dawn.

(A man's a fool if he believes in anybody but himself, Kepi was saying under the balcony. A man's a fool if he thinks a woman can make his life for him, women don't last long . . . A man's a fool either way, Itzek Fogel said, so why shouldn't he fool himself a little from time to time? It's what makes life worth living . . .)

. . . And he was listening to the glittering phrases behind the black-out curtains.

(War, someone said brilliantly, quoting someone else, brings people together and opens their eyes. Honor, country, duty, someone else was saying to the Millionaire, who went about the room pinching the gilded frames of mediocre paintings: these are the building blocks of civilization . . . If you don't kill the beast there'll be no meat for supper, said the Politician. And yet another someone said: Did you know that this year we shall celebrate the Seventy-fifth Anniversary of the Invention of Barbed Wire?)

The night had begun to grow pale on the balcony, the circle of time and history was becoming closed.

. . . The Millionaire stared about with suspicious eyes, the Politician held embarrassed colonels by their tunic buttons while he regaled them with scatological jokes, the Fat Priest had become irritated because no one paid him as much attention as he wished, the Small-town Lawyer wanted to be photographed with a real general, the Dentist, who had drunk too much, but not yet enough, had begun to giggle . . .

Rigid with self-contempt, the officers made heroic efforts not to look at watches; the round mouths of the women had the dried evaporated look of rings left on the piano by drained cocktail glasses.

Then Abel was staring at them all, he was laughing at them (a soundless laughter that streaked his face with tears) through the blackout curtains which had been hung to remind the visitors that a desperate war was being fought somewhere (oh, to be sure not here where anyone could be hurt), that a Nation from which their ancestors had gone to their American comforts needed their intercession and support, and (perhaps) to suggest, with a dramatic sense of historicity, that this was the traditional Ball before the Battle, the Last Mazurka before Dawn, from which the Gallant Officers would make their polite exits at Midnight, with wounded but brave smiles, like Wellington's young men before Waterloo, to ride to Death or Glory.

(Derek Bellancourt was sitting at the piano, and Colonel Hudson had placed his palms before his face as though in search of a prayer he might say, and rubbed, again and again, the flesh beside his nose; and Pani Mosinska, glittering in certainties and decorations, was making angrily dramatic gestures above the bridge table; and Professor Kukla was whispering to Professor Karolewski).

. . . The Millionaire was explaining nasally about the Golden Rule by which life, as he understood it, was lived in America . . . a life to which Abel and his kind would have to become accustomed, a rule which they had either forgotten or never knew about, which was why, according to the Millionaire, their lives had lost coherence and why they had lost control of their own lives. Puzzled but polite to the end, Professor Karolewski offered an opinion on Primitive Christianity. The Millionaire said no, because Christianity had nothing to do with it, because the Golden Rule, as every child knew in America, merely meant that the man with the gold made the rules, ha-ha. Ha-ha, said the Politician, come to see us in America when all this is over. All this, he said, and waved his arm to include the rooms and all the men and women in them and the blackout curtains and everything that lay beyond the curtains in this and all the other nights through which they had come . . . Your generosity is . . . ah . . . overwhelming, Professor Karolewski managed to reply . . .

(But really, Abel thought, now doubled over with laughter, why is he so surprised? Midnight is long past, as is our gallant youth, and our guests are too concerned with their own importance to note such subtleties as the blackout curtains, and Glory never came to parties such as this . . . although, as someone had just said behind the blackout curtains, Death, our eternal mistress, is sure to be near.)

Then he was thinking about Tarski and of his own dead father, and of his two grandfathers murdered behind the manor, and of Father Boguslawski's message of human unity and love, and of all that they had represented. For this too was part of the road along which he had come to this resolution. He thought about General Prus, who had been dismissed into forced retirement, and Major Langenfeld and Dr. Poremba, and he remembered Catherine's destroyed family who had lived by an unwritten rule that had seemed both golden and imprisoning . . . and saw himself, finally Cyclopean, in the glass of the french doors that led onto the balcony, and everything that lay beyond the balcony and the ending night. A one-eyed Cyclops, deprived of sustenance by a clever throw; Circe had been his neighbor in the myths . . .

—Well, then I'll see you later, Haussner said and went back inside.

—But what I want to know, Itzek Fogel said under the balcony. Are you going to give the captain that letter, or not?

—What letter? Kepi said.

—The one the little lady gave you.

—Oh. That letter.

—How many do you have?

—She can mail her own letters. Goddam woman. I wouldn't take her if she was wrapped in rainbows.

—So now you're going to hate women too? Itzek Fogel said.

—You know what she did to that poor old Kobza?

—You sure about what she did to Kobza?

—I know what I know.

—Well, if you know that much, Itzek Fogel said, you ought to know something.

—Goddam you anyway, you crazy little bastard, Kepi said. What do *you* know about anything?

—Never enough, Itzek Fogel said.

Abel shaded his eyes against the operatic rising of the sun, an incredible fireball hung in a flame-streaked haze; thunder rolled and rattled under the blue-black ridge where the night was making its last stand. What he was facing now was not so much the twilight of his Gods as the immolation of his interest in them.

Tarski, his own dead father, the memory of Catherine . . . these burned among the pale disappearing stars in deep space; for all their awesome distance they would always be no farther from him than his heart and spirit. But surely there was more, there had to be more. In this respect he couldn't fault Teo: no one could build a future on mourning.

The new day, this third day of spring, four days after Palm Sunday, which was a day of triumph that led to Golgotha and then, inevitably, to a resurrection, was the time when the sun crossed the equator and made night and day of equal length in all parts of the world. The vernal equinox, redolent of promises that had to be kept. The day could promise nothing new for him, nothing better than the promises made by all the days that stretched from the times of Grandfather Zygmunt's *Journal* to this day and beyond. Yet, Abel knew, everything would have to be altogether different for him from this day on. The war would be won and lost in the very same moment, this miraculous army of which he was a part was becoming an army-in-exile even now: soldiers without banners and without a country to which they might return, young men and women marching into an embittered old age, each of their days a commemoration of a fallen hope, their entrenched and barricaded lives a permanent retreat. This, too, was part of the age-long Polish ethic that turned each generation into gallant debris that aged and withered on a foreign pavement, among memories of defeats transformed by legend into moral victories, in longing for their own dead youth, in waiting for something that could never happen, the impossible return. He thought of the impassioned, immemorial dream contained in Grandfather Zygmunt's *Journal*: the imperishable idea that flowed, like arterial blood, across the generations; and knew that it was the idea which had always mattered and not the men and women that had died for it.

. . . And what of Abel?

(Because some practical provision had to be made for Abel.)

. . . Well, he thought. Well. Hmmm. You can go to America and learn to live by the Golden Rule; you will swear by the worms of your ancestors to honor and obey each rule and proscription; you can buy a glass eye through which to view the angers and the fears and disappointments and crushed hopes of persons other than yourself, a painted manufactured pebble that might mirror the true condition of your soul; you can buy a pair of kid gloves to wear on your wrecked hands and no one will ever guess your several mutilations . . .

(Oh, it was time to bring this awful celebration to an end.)

. . . For there were always other countries, other women.

(Last night, there had been a red-haired woman, with haunches like a mare, who had plunged down upon him like a vacuum pump, but for a moment he had been able to see something beyond her savage concentration on her own performance. It was the way that accidental moonlight had slanted on her cheekbones and softened her features and made her wide eyes seem gray-green rather than merely blue, the hair less red than yellow . . . It was a fragment lifted from the context of another time, the kernel of a memory buried under incrustations of contempt.)

Down, memory, he said, and hurled his empty bottle into the new exploding day. Let the romantic love be left to the unrequited poets who had invented it, for after Catherine there can be no affection.

And then he was laughing.

For this was surely the most romantic phrase of all the self-deluding and glittering phrases of his disappearing kind . . . for who but a man enthralled with a memory could make such a statement? It was the tragedy that was farcical, unreal; the comedy had to be seen as the truth of it all.

. . . And he was listening to the thunder that didn't sound like thunder but, with the war reduced to an anticipated memory, he didn't know what else these strangely flattened rolling sounds could be. Once, he had defined a battle in terms of a single visual and emotional image, that of boots sliding in red mud and of a mind tumbling off a hillside. Now, listening to the thunder on the Latrun Heights, he thought in terms of a musical performance, wondering why he found the tympany of musicians more satisfying than the imagery of philosophers and poets. Perhaps because killing, like the act of love, was a wordless business. Here was no orchestration, no symphony of death, as the professional nonparticipants are fond of describing it. Here was cacophony, an absence of rhythm, the loss of form. Behind the blackout curtains, the voices came and went; measured, metronomic. A green flare arced momentarily above the escarpment, and Abel knew, beyond the possibility of doubt, that this had something to do with Mendeltort, who was imprisoned there. Perhaps an attempt to free him. Or to kill him. Some such thing could be read into his oblique remarks of the afternoon. The conversation behind the blackout curtains had dwindled into silence and the air had suddenly acquired the nervous sultriness of the khamsin wind. Shadows retreated through the amaranthine plain, night fell back in disorder into the caves under the escarpment.

He wondered why he had come out onto the balcony, from what he had been trying to escape. He had not come alone. Crowding behind him were familiar shadows, classic in the simplicity of the lessons they had taught. They marched in pairs, each revealing to him something of his vanished substance: the drama through which he had passed as seen through the dead eyes of parents, friends, and lovers whose names he would never be able to recall unless he turned them all into a scholar's, or a poet's, safe classical allegory. For allegory, he knew, is memory made respectable. It is history with the love and the hatred excised and all pain removed.

Thus he would think of them by other names if he had to think of them at all. Abraham & Isaac, Joseph & Potiphar's wife, Odysseus & Penelope, Pygmalion & Galatea, Zeus & Prometheus, Clytemnestra & Aegisthus, Daedalus & Icarus: the woman who had turned in fury on the youth who had scorned her; the disobedient one and the punisher; the man, long thought dead, who returned to his woman; the son who didn't measure up to his father; the father prepared to sacrifice his son at his God's command; the man who effected a woman's transformation; and the woman who encompassed the destruction of her man. It had all been told before in Homeric couplets and would be again, time and time again, in whatever form and language were needed for the telling, in whatever time it needed to be told.

There was no further need for the blackout curtains. Abel pushed them aside, went into the room.

. . . The Small-town Lawyer was no longer asking that a genuine general be produced so that he might be photographed with one for his hometown newspaper, the Fat Priest had subsided into a muttering litany of complaint, the Drunken Dentist had fallen asleep. The Millionaire and the Politician were demanding breakfast. Fixed cruelly in this moment of time's passage through clean morning light, they had become a burnished copperplate engraving.

A young Duty Officer from a Highland regiment had run into the room and had begun to whisper loudly into the ear of Colonel Hudson, who bit down on the ends of his military mustache. The senior Polish colonel offered him a drink with an ironic smile. From outside, below the balcony which Abel had abandoned, came the blaring klaxons of army ambulances driven at high speed, the coughing roars of a motorcycle escort, and the threatening rumble of an armored car. Latrun! Hargan! and something about Mendeltort: the words fell like stones. Abel and Derek Bellancourt stood very still and looked at each other.

Abel marched through the room, down the long curving staircase and outside.

The end of his journey was very near then. A sense of valediction heightened his awareness of beauty in the drama through which he was traveling and through which he would continue to move as long as he lived. Never had life seemed so stark and simple, never more beautiful in that simplicity; and since the precious cycle of partings and reunions, conclusions and beginnings, departures and returns forms our deepest pattern, we never recognize it more clearly than at the end of our long and lonely marches.

Kepi stood at attention beside the Hillman halftruck, Itzek Fogel was opening the door.

—Where to, sir? Kepi said.

—Back to camp. We've a lot to do before tomorrow morning.

—Seems like they're shooting up a storm, back there at Latrun.

—None of our business. And drive carefully, will you?

—Yes sir, Kepi said. And . . . ah . . . Captain?

—What is it?

—There's this here letter . . .

The huge new sun was burning in his eyes. The desert road unfolded, straight as a warrior's spear lifting from the dust. Abel weighed the soiled and crumpled brown army envelope absentmindedly in his hands, shielding his eyes with it from the sun's white glare. He buttoned up the letter in his left breast pocket beside his embarkation orders and the photograph which he had taken off his father's desk so long ago, and which he had carried with him about the world; the photograph, whose antique flavor had once seemed incredible to him, did not seem at all remarkable now.

ACKNOWLEDGMENTS

The March is a work of fiction, yet to say that it is all invented, that no such things ever happened, or that every thought and image it contains is wholly mine would be quite misleading.

The hegira upon which this novel is based is history, as are all the major events that occur in it. But the needs of the novel take precedence over historical statistics, and to attempt a sterile academic separation of factual detail from the fictional whole is, in my view, useless. In the end, the real and the unreal are equal parts of the same human experience, each containing a fragment of whatever passes for historical truth.

The March is rooted in history but, as a novel, it is free to range beyond historical events into whatever may have been possible, on whatever level, for the people of its time and places. There has been some rearrangement of chronology so that certain events, important to the evolution of invented lives, might fit into the time-span of the novel. One such leap in time is the destruction of Dair Yassir, which happened later than *The March* suggests, and for quite different reasons. The documents relating to the Katyn Massacre have been compressed into a shorter period than the years that passed between the search for the missing victims, the discovery of the murder site, and the final evaluation of responsibility and results. The massacre in the Kara Sea may have taken place in other Arctic waters and at an earlier date. Testimony on this subject is contradictory and vague. As with the fully documented Katyn Massacre, there are no living eyewitnesses to this second and parallel tragedy, but since the first was possible for its perpetrators, so, certainly, was the second. In any case, my purpose in re-creating these events isn't to expose, once again, man's inability to live with himself, or to feed the cancer of historic hatreds, which, to my mind, are mankind's most unreal and enduring fictions. History has neither heroes nor victims; it contains only people who suffer and who inflict suffering on others. As a novel, *The March* employs historical events. It isn't supposed to serve any causes other than its own.

As with events, so with the novel's people. Most are invented. The viewpoints and experiences of others are based upon fact. Their letters and diaries, as used in the Third Interlude (*In Memoriam*) are, for the most part, factual, and have been rephrased only insofar as this was necessary to fit invented persons. The Katyn documents, used in *The March* as a series of fictional reports, exist as official correspondence in British government archives, and have been used by other writers dealing with this matter. Neither did I invent all of "Cousin Wlada's Diary," which was published by the Polish Army in Iran, in 1943, as a supposedly authentic record of one family's destruction. These materials, as well as several hundred interviews and letters, provide the documentable historic content of *The March*. The rest must come from life itself, and since there is no way to account for those innumerable influences, evil along with good, there is no way to acknowledge my full indebtedness.

Yet I can name and thank some of the generous men and women who have helped to make this book possible. It is dedicated to my mother, whose personal act of bravery in September 1939 saved me from experiencing the events which the book describes. Many years later, Edward J. Piszek set in motion a series of events that brought about my release from a foreign prison. An Israeli diplomat, named Mordechai Palzur, to whom I am indebted for much valuable material, saved my life during the Turkish invasion of Cyprus in 1974, and the Kościuszko Foundation offered shelter and continuous assistance in a difficult period.

Help came at various times from the Authors' League, and from the American P.E.N. Center under the presidency of Jerzy Kosinski. Old friends like Walter Kozloski and Witold Kawecki provided much of the means whereby this book, ten years in the making, could be finished, and Don MacNeil, of Middletown, Connecticut, offered me his home in the final months. Throughout that time, the faith and patience of Betty A. Prashker, editorial director of Doubleday & Company, supplied stability.

Some special means must be found to thank Walter Golaski, who came to my assistance, time and time again, on this and other projects, and to Eugene and Krystyna Kusielewicz, whose personal kindness toward me appears to have no limits.

Finally, if it is possible to close this list of dedicated friends, there is the care and affection given by Max Gartenberg, Yana and Nat Brandt, James and Betty Stein, Mary van Starrex, Ed and Ewa Parmele and Don Robertson. Perhaps by thanking them I may be able to thank everyone.

W.S.K.

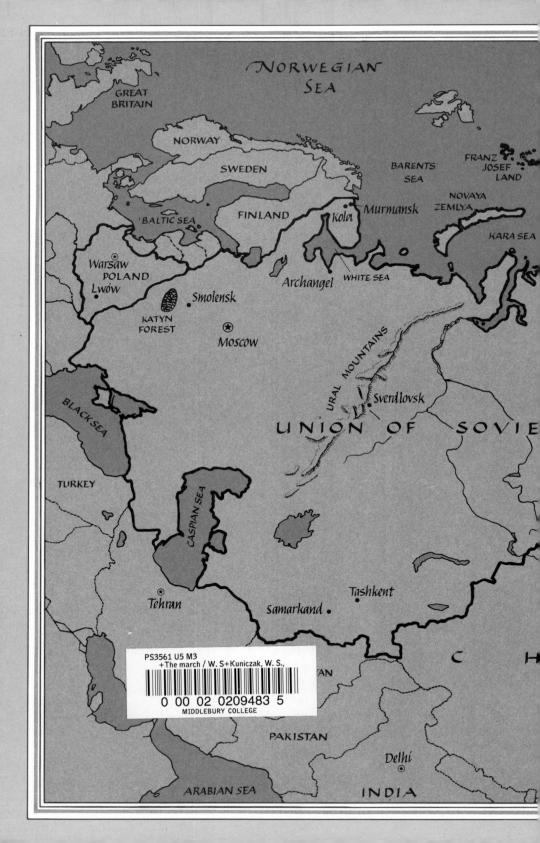

PS3561 U5 M3
+The march / W. S+Kuniczak, W. S.,

0 00 02 0209483 5
MIDDLEBURY COLLEGE